Crown of Caphedra

Interior illustrations by the author.
Front cover design by BetiBup33 Design Studio.

ISBN: 978-1-7779710-0-7

Published by the author.

Ottawa, Canada.

www.ianrobertross.com

Crown
of
Caphedra

Ian Robert Ross

To Stephen,
until we meet again on
criss-crossed trails.

Acknowledgements

Before leaping into the actual story, it's customary to preface things with a bit of exposition and tributes.

The opening scene of this novel was written in the spring of 2018, after my full time profession brought me to Ottawa. It was in the middle of the school year, and my family wasn't joining me right away, so I found it to be a rare opportunity where I could concentrate and stretch my imagination in a house that was empty of furniture and most other distractions.

Afterward, my most productive hours started before my household woke up, when I'd sneak downstairs at five in the morning with only the cat for company. I kept at it, and by the end of 2019, I had finished the first draft.

That's when I first shared it with others. I was naively pleased, and had no inkling of an idea that I would spend the next two years in rewrites, editing, and proofreading.

In the end, much of this book was done in consultation, and I wish to express gratitude to those who had a helping hand in seeing its completion.

A thank you goes out to Ania Swiatoniowski, who provided proofreading for much of the later drafts of this text. She cleaned up the verbal clutter in no shortage of sentences and provided thoughtful reflection to influence the final crafting of several key scenes.

My deepest gratitude is for Tracy Hughes and the absolutely invaluable efforts she went through to analyze and scrutinize this book, chapter by chapter, leading me to hone many of the crucial elements underlying the story. Her critical eye as a developmental editor helped put a fine point on my writing and rippled out to cast its influence upon my world.

I also wish to comment on how much I appreciated the long time friendship of Stephen Hughes, who shared this dream of writing with me ever since those first days we spent together in the coffee shops of Halifax, communing over the craft. I will miss him.

To undertake the publishing of a novel independently, by the very nature of the word, is to embark on an endeavour by which one anticipates a generous measure of solitude. I have been fortunate not to have been alone in this pursuit, and now, I am very pleased to share my work with you.

Ottawa, 2021

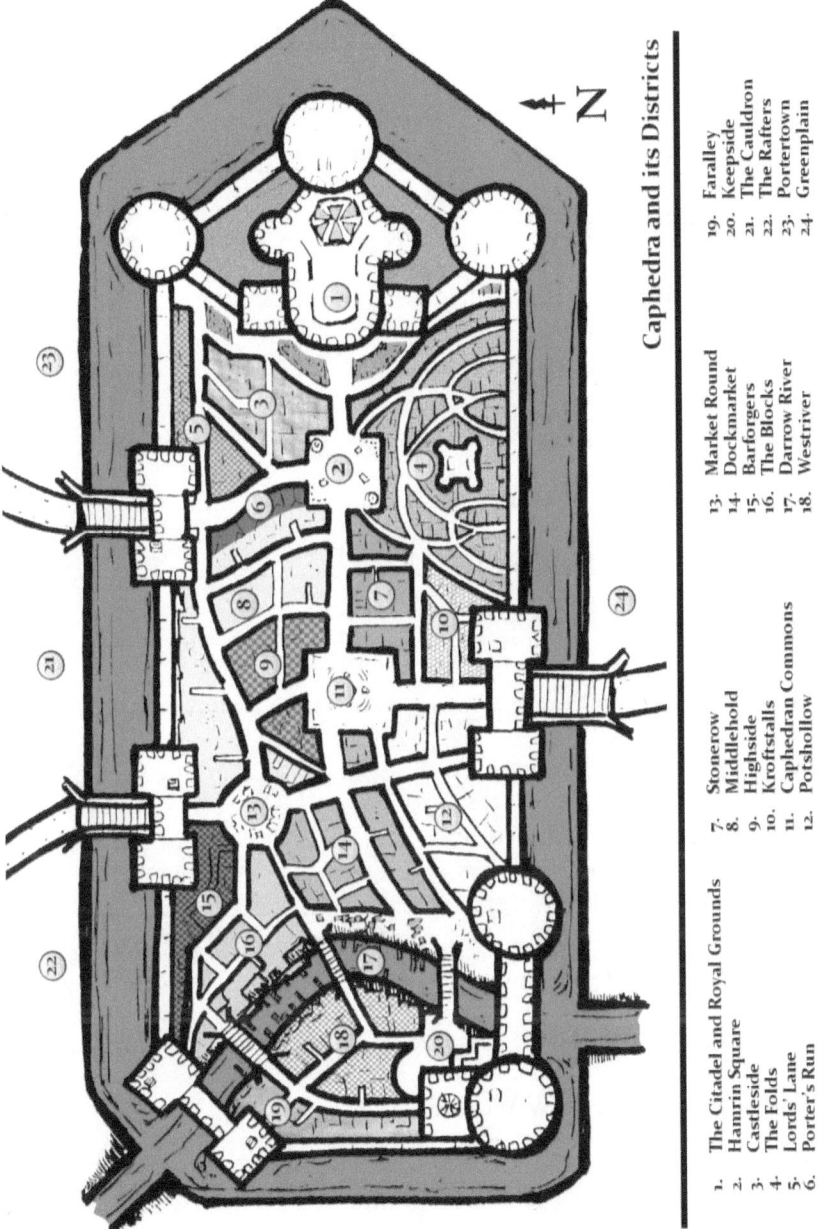

Caphedra and its Districts

N

1. The Citadel and Royal Grounds
2. Hamrin Square
3. Castleside
4. The Folds
5. Lords' Lane
6. Porter's Run

7. Stonerow
8. Middlehold
9. Highside
10. Kroftstalls
11. Caphedran Commons
12. Potshollow

13. Market Round
14. Dockmarket
15. Barforgers
16. The Blocks
17. Darrow River
18. Westriver

19. Faralley
20. Keepside
21. The Cauldron
22. The Rafters
23. Portertown
24. Greenplain

TABLE OF CONTENTS

CHAPTER 1

Visitors to Fal Ghreeg

O len clenched his body tightly within his thick broadcloth cloak, warding away as much of the damp and cold as he could. The flattened grass on the hilltop offered a rare, dry nest upon which to sit, hunched with his arms wrapped around his knees, and observing the approaches to the empty marshlands of the Fal Ghreeg until nightfall would come and rob him of his sightlines. He had held this pose for hours—and he had held this unenviable post for years.

Beyond the murky clouds that occluded the sun, dusk was lazily settling in like a curtain being slowly drawn. The frogs' croaking increased as the light dwindled. Wildflowers closed their petals for the night. Pockets of smouldering peat fires pervaded the landscape with earthy smoke and a soft glow between the ridges that, in daylight, provided for slightly drier and safer crossings, from one moor to the next.

The marsh was cold, wet, and familiar, but Olen ever assured himself that after showing such undying dedication, his future might take him elsewhere. He once expected that the Lord Marshal's staff in Caphedra would recall him, as there were no longer any substantial fears of rebellion coming from this soppy demesne. But he remained anchored to the bog more than a decade after the conquest of the southeast, twenty years after he had turned his back on the bloody back alleys and gutter-bred cutthroats that infested the place where he grew up. Knife fights were a wasted life when one could aspire to sword fights.

Olen focused his eyes on the key landmarks of terrain—

depressions, mounds, and the hard-to-spot pathways that would let one pass through without having to wade through waist-deep swamp. There were a few flickering lights from fireflies, swamp gas, and the handful of peasant hovels within the extent of his view. One tiny, well-lit cottage, in particular, sent forth the welcoming aroma of what he figured would be a big pot of marsh otter stew. That was Ayren Freigh's cottage, and Olen's billet, so long as he was posted out here on the bog. The temptation to head in early for supper infected his belly through his nose.

"Curse the old man and his cooking pot," Olen said.

These days it was quiet. At times when he was alone like this, he missed the hard-pressed days of horizon-wide encampments and cluttered battlefields. He lamented that in spreading the king's dominion, his energy all went to realize the very passivity he had come to resent. In the two decades that King Ramis ruled from his citadel in Caphedra, he had won all four of the great capitals of the land. Through his many garrisons, he pressed them firmly into the earth with the weight of edicts he imposed and threats to raise a bigger army should they protest.

But everything changed last year when the king traded his velvety imperial throne for a cold crypt of a royal mausoleum. The news of his death—like all news—was slow to reach Olen out here on the marsh. Even now, many months later, the announcement of the king's successor was still forthcoming and a cause of considerable speculation and anxiety.

Twilight had almost slipped beneath the mantle of night. The evening's rain was picking up, shedding bigger drops, and an accompanying wind blew through the reeds, making a sound not unlike ocean waves.

He had just decided it was time to retire—at least for the evening—when he stopped still and steadied his breath. There was an out-of-place noise ringing from out across the marsh. Metal scraping on metal. Peering at where the sound came from, he saw shadows that began to take the form of men on horseback, cutting across the grasses.

They'll be heading toward the cottage, Olen thought.

The men were difficult to see in the light, and they were not intentionally making *much* noise, but they did not seem to be hiding or trying to sneak up either. This far from the main road to Lanstad, and likely being armed, there was enough reason to be suspicious of them, nonetheless. Olen gathered himself and started down the slope, hoping to intercept them before they arrived.

The cottage owner was a widower named Ayren, who had just passed his sixtieth year. He had come south after losing both his sons on a frigid field called Icemeadows, where they fought and failed to repel King Ramis's encroachment. In despair over their deaths, he had left his home then spent much of his subsequent life selling himself as a mercenary on a path that eventually carried him to the Fals, where he peculiarly opted to settle along the soggy marshlands at Fal Ghreeg. He claimed there was a treasure he had heard about and intended to find before age finally overcame him. Sometimes over a good drink, however, he admitted that this was the only place he had travelled where nobody ever asked him to raise his sword and fight, and that had value all on its own. He was an affable sort, a capable cook, and tended hives of honeybees amidst the marsh flowers. The mead he produced from their honey was openly shared, giving him a reputation of having a good, generous heart.

But it was not always that way with Olen. When he was first assigned to be billeted at Ayren's house, it brought a great deal of displeasure to the old cottager. Ayren would refer to him as 'that Caphedran,' and his ire over the disaster at Icemeadows would often reignite. If this had been up north, a soldier of Ramis's would never have made it through his door.

Things improved a few years ago when at the risk of crowding his little hovel, he took in a demure and dark-haired young lodger named Livet. The young girl had escaped a horrible past, having been cast out onto the streets of her hometown of Lanstad. Begging and thieving for her sustenance and targeted by the city's armsmen, she struck out into the Fals and found sanctuary with the good-hearted Ayren. Livet helped fill the gap left by the loss of his two brave sons. She took care of him as much as he would let her, and despite her own distrust of the king's troops, proved to be a pleasant intermediary within the four walls of the cottage. She helped Ayren and Olen bridge their distance and even to become reasonable friends.

Inevitably, her shy sweetness also attracted a well-bred and well-educated young cavalryman named Denn Wellum. His job was to suppress rebellion, but these days there was a dearth of uprisings. He spent more of his time observing the compliance of the locals of the cottage–especially that of Ayren's infatuated lodger. When he visited, he stabled his great chestnut charger in one of Ayren's outbuildings and often stayed for days. Ayren and Olen shared some misgivings but shuffled aside to also give Denn a seat at the table since it pleased Livet.

Despite enjoying Ayren's hospitality himself, Olen often derided Ayren for being generous to a fault. He knew that his host would undoubtedly welcome these men that rode up tonight, even though they were strangers. It would be up to Olen to vet their intent.

So, he studied the men, their demeanour and disposition, as he slipped down the moor and dashed to the cottage on foot. There were four men, their steeds carrying them at an unhurried walk despite the damp and drizzle. Olen noted that the horses were slender, well-kept animals, fit for riding, standing about 14 or 15 hands in height. They slowed their gait naturally and respectfully as they came to the cottage.

The horsemen grouped their mounts in a dry spot under the overhanging roof, next to where Denn kept his broad, strong-backed charger, Naobe, during the times he paid his amorous visits to Livet. That she was here now meant Denn must have come calling, too.

Naobe stood tall, chestnut in colour, with a star on her forehead and markings that appeared like two linked diamonds on her right side. One horseman broke off to the side and circled the warhorse, taking note of her presence and sizing her up. She snorted and stomped with her hooves, warily suggesting he keep his distance.

The lead horseman dismounted. He was not as tall as Olen nor as heavy-footed when he walked, but he had the gait of a soldier. The rider left his sword in its scabbard, strapped to the rigging on his saddle. He pulled aside the hood of his cloak, displaying a dark brown beard. His hair was closely cut, save for at the top of his head where strands fell longer and limp from the dampness and sweat. Raising a worn leather glove, he knocked three times on the thick wooden door to announce himself and his party. "Friend!" he called to those on the other side, "May we poor, wet travellers engage your kindness and warm ourselves up by your fire?"

Olen chose this moment to respond to them and, purposely in a loud voice that could be heard inside the cottage, called out, "What brings you men here tonight?"

The leader turned and quickly took stock of the hefty-looking observer descending the slope. The man's eyes paused on Olen's burnished black cloak pin, which was in the likeness of a pair of twisting black eels, then calmly his gaze ascended to Olen's face. He smiled politely. "We are on our way to Lanstad. We thought we'd look here for some place for us to come off the road. There's no dry ground for a camp anywhere to be seen in this country, nor any good, dry wood for a fire. None that we can find, at least."

"No," Olen said. "Not this far away from the main road, certainly I wouldn't expect so."

The window shutter of the cottage cracked open slightly, and Olen saw the shadow of a face looking out and watching.

"Foul night," the leader said as rain dripped off his forehead. "Yours was the only light we saw from out there, so we considered the matter and agreed amongst ourselves to cross the swamp and make an introduction. My name is Balix. This gentleman here is Temis," he said, pointing to the rider who'd inspected Denn's horse. "Behind us ride Romwin, and lastly Colden. We mean no bother but would gladly accept any hospitality on a night like this."

The other horsemen bowed their heads slightly and pulled open their hoods to show their faces clearly. The last two had a clear resemblance that made them appear to be brothers, although one had a more crooked nose that suggested he'd had a harder go of life.

The one introduced as Temis also caught sight of Olen's cloak pin. He had a shrewd look to him with a tuft of dark whiskers for a beard, and the hair on his head was drawn tight to his scalp in braided rows. He addressed Olen in a clever-sounding voice. "Pleased to be acquainted, Sergeant. I have a cousin in Westriver," he said and nodded at the cloak pin. Then referencing Denn's great chestnut charger, he said, "I suppose that's not your horse, then? She must be from the cavalry. I particularly like the markings."

Westriver was the namesake home to his native infantry company, and as such, Olen did not ride; he marched. His company did not keep any horses themselves, save for those that pulled their quartermaster's wagons. Westriver was a rough district in Caphedra and a good source of men who like to fight, so a company had been raised there early in the king's grand campaigns. Being close to the banks of the Darrow River, where eel fishing was common, the unit took up the symbol of two twisting black eels for its standard. Olen had been with the company since it was first stood up.

"Very well," Olen muttered, and with resignation, he formally announced himself. "I am Olen Kierk, sergeant of Westriver Company, 5ᵗʰ Brigade. This is my watch but not my cottage, so it's not my decision to let you in."

With that, the person in the window disappeared. The cottage door opened, and Denn stood against the backdrop of light. He was fair-headed and lanky, and despite several years soldiering in the saddle, he'd not lost all the brightness of his youthful visage nor the courtesies of his more privileged upbringing. Denn addressed the rain-soaked wanderers from the doorway. "Gentle sirs, the master of the house has informed me that he would like to invite you inside. You may sup with us tonight."

If Olen was to put a stop to this, he had to decide now. He considered ordering Denn to get back inside and lock the doors while he deterred the men, but it was too late. Ayren had granted his welcome blessing.

"We gladly and graciously accept," Balix said with a wide smile. He tied the reins of his horse to a hitching post under the lip of the roof. Romwin and Colden likewise dismounted and secured their rides. Lastly, Temis, with a stretch and crack of his sore legs as he got down from his horse, led his steed to a free hitch near Naobe before also accepting Denn's invitation.

Olen stood aside and let them enter the cottage.

The cottage swelled to accommodate the guests around a great central hearth that smouldered with shimmering red coals. While far warmer than the outdoors had been, the room's atmosphere soon became even more humid as wet woollen cloaks were hung up to dry, and the heat from so many crowded occupants began to stifle the air.

While divvying up the coat hooks, Olen could not help noticing that one of the men also wore a cloak with an even rarer brooch in the shape of a golden castle tower, signifying a member of the Lord's Guard. He tried to remember which horseman it belonged to and settled on it being the one named Romwin. The Guardsmen were the personal heavy mounted soldiers of Lord Marshal Incis Myrhic, master of the king's army, yet oddly, these men were on simple rounceys, and the well-worn cloak itself wouldn't pass muster by the Lord Marshal. What reason they might have for travelling this far out of the capital was another matter for suspicion.

He could have stolen it, Olen thought and fixed himself to stay on his guard.

Supper was almost ready. The irresistible aroma of a hot meal of meaty stew upon the thick air enticed them to bunch up even closer to the simmering cooking pot. Ayren rested his hand on a counter and reached up with the other to bring down more bowls and cutlery. Well into his later years, with a lifetime of battles and soldiering, he was slower and more careful with his movements. However, nothing showed his age more than the thick, mammoth white beard that clung unkempt to his face and the long-hanging bedraggled hair, like a glacier melting down his stooped back.

Turning to the newcomers, the old man asked, "You've eaten venison before?"

Colden licked his lips, and Romwin leaned in toward their host. "Yes, of course," he said eagerly.

"Well, this tastes almost the same," Ayren said, giving another stir to the stew pot and setting it a bit farther away from the heat.

For the first time, they noticed the young, unassuming girl with soft cheeks, and hair like sable, who slipped in to help Ayren place the table settings. Livet was waifish and fragile. She wore a thin, grey linen gown that showed a multitude of mends. Quietly, she moved around the room, appearing to totter slightly as she did so. Her darting eyes, with their big black pupils, flitted from stranger to stranger, while her face remained expressionless.

Temis watched her curiously. "Are you hurt? Maybe I can help with those?" he said.

"She's fine. There's nothing to mention," Denn chimed in

protectively before rising to offer his height to aid her insufficient reach and help with drawing down the serving bowls.

"Please, stay seated," Livet said to Temis, emptying a jar of thick biscuits onto a plate. "It's nothing new." She smiled placidly at him and carried on, trying to disguise her hobble.

Olen remembered her telling him that she'd had the deformation since she was a young girl, running with some rabble on the streets of Lanstad. It was done *to* her, in a sadder and darker lifetime, and the leg had never correctly healed. She could still walk on it—not always too fast or so straight—but well enough to make her way from Lanstad and settle down here in the Fals at Ayren's cottage.

Whatever the cause, it had left her wary and somewhat timid by nature, so Olen could sense she entertained these guests only by summoning staunch reserves of her own courage. Livet put a hand on Denn's shoulder as she passed, then disappeared again to mix up a bowl of batter with which to pan-fry more biscuits.

Across the hearth, there was a smacking from Ayren's lips, signalling the readiness of the stew. He wielded a large ladle and portioned out thick brown gravy with meaty chunks, bright carrots, earthy turnips, and spicy chopped onions broaching the bubbling surface. He passed bowls along to Balix, who divided them between his men and sent others along to Denn and Olen. It smelled hearty and luxurious, and as the heat cast from the fire eventually started to cut through the thick moist air, the room's occupants began feeling like they were drying out at last.

After a time, Balix went out to check on the horses. When he returned, he brought a bulky leather saddlebag full of coloured glass bottles, each full of dark, ambrosial Caphedran wines that he boasted had been infused with the richest of Hasen spices. Temis immediately wrested the bottles from him as he returned and started filling glasses around the room.

"As superior as your mead is, Ayren, it can't last the whole evening. Let us share our bounty with you. I was lucky to make a highly prosperous deal with some Caphedran vintners and secured some of their fine product," Balix bragged.

The room chorused its praise, which was not unearned. With generous pours of drink, and with their bellies sated, the spiced wine began loosening conversation. Leaning back from the table, Temis said nostalgically to Denn, "I had a horse like yours, once."

"You're a cavalryman?" Denn asked, somewhat excited.

Olen listened carefully for a mention of the Lord's Guard but was disappointed.

"In between misfortunes, I spent some time travelling in the mountains beyond Bren Hills," he answered. "Coalfire was my steed's name. She was pitch black, tall at the shoulder, broad and strong. I remember I had a tough time getting her up Spire Peak, though I suppose she had a tougher time getting me down." He smiled briefly, close-mouthed, then leant forward and obscured his face in his mug.

"Hard country for a horse," Denn muttered.

"Drier ground than here," countered Temis. "Easier on the hooves."

"Yourself, Denn, where did you serve?" Romwin asked.

"I am assigned to the Twelfth, out of Falbeth. Keeping public order," Denn said simply, then awkwardly failed to expand his statement further.

Olen knew that Denn's lack of fighting experience put him at a disadvantage speaking with seasoned soldiers. He'd spent years studying without putting his learning into use. He virtually skipped tenure as a squire, assuming the duties of a cavalier right away on account of his wealth, which had permitted him to outfit with gear superior to any others in his training cohort. But his rank progression stopped there. Denn often confided to Olen that his constable despised him and resented such a quick ascension. The constable promised Denn would never see sergeant, much less rise to captain a company of his own.

"That's sure a beast of a horse to squander on unruly bog dwellers," said Romwin.

"Do they even let you carry a sword?" teased Colden.

Denn turned red in the face and took a deep breath as if preparing a verbal rebuke in retaliation but, finding restraint, defended himself simply. "I am well acquainted in matters of arms, and I hold my post with pride," he stated, and Ayren nodded at him approvingly.

But it was a lie. Olen knew that Denn had a lot more ambition. The expectations in his family were high, sometimes too high. The boy just needed to test his mettle, but it was almost impossible now that so much of the land was pacified.

"Your cup is too empty, Denn. Let me help you," said Balix. He reached over and topped up the mug with a fresh bottle of wine that had been left warming by the fire—a technique that brought out the piquancy of the infused spice.

"We're all brothers in the king's army. Let's toast to King Ramis!" Romwin said, holding his glass aloft. "Son of our forebears, brother to our land, father to the army. May his will be restored, and calamity befall his transgressors and pretenders."

Six cups ascended above the old wooden table, meeting to seal a bond of comradery under the fellowship of a common crown, but not all in the room joined the ceremonious pledge. Ayren gave no indication he would share the toast, and Livet also coyly refused at first until Colden challenged her reservation.

"Are you not fond of the wine, Miss?" he asked.

She shifted awkwardly in her seat under his attention and forced herself to take a tepid sip.

"It's warming," she said. "A good wine, I s'ppose."

"It *is* a good wine, Livet!" Denn declared, sounding almost precocious with his enthusiasm. "The spice inside is brought all the way up the Darrow River from Hasen, where it gets selected for fragrance and flavour by the master vintners in Caphedra. A lot of swindlers try to fake it with locally grown herbs, but I can tell that this is truly authentic. I haven't had any since I was in Caphedra. It's almost enough to make me want to go back—though not quite."

Livet and Denn shared a short gaze, and her face lit up in response. Grasping her cup in two hands, she sniffed the bouquet of the wine and then let the elixir pass her lips, swallowing deeply. Temis grinned and observed the two with a cat-like fascination.

Abruptly, a fist slammed down upon the table.

"We should toast the king's heir," said Romwin heartily. "You seem like a rather dutiful and devoted servant of the crown—which one do you prefer, Olen?" he asked.

Olen knew the question was both prying and dangerous.

King Ramis, the patriarch of the Wolstett line, had left three children, each on the cusp of coming of age. The eldest, Ravon, was favoured among the clergy of the Faith of the Pillars. She grew up cloistered away, receiving her childhood education in the Grand Temple of Caphedra under the tutelage of the Precept himself. The middle child, also a girl, was Ramisa, and she was being raised somewhere outside the city with her maternal cousins, the influential Farathemuns. The last was a boy, Ramid, and although he was the youngest, a large contingent of the army was keen to see him take the crown to maintain the power of the lords and commanders who now served under arms. Since his youth, he had been mentored by the potent Incis Myrhic, his father's indomitable Lord Marshal.

However, there was an impasse. The Caphedran Council had yet to decide on recognizing a new monarch, despite the established rules of succession. Rather than immediately supporting the coronation of the eldest, Ravon, the discussion had become protracted. Councillors appeared to be enjoying their period of unchallenged power and prolonging the formalities of the affair. Some councillors were even accused of biding time for the younger siblings to consolidate support and return to the city with the necessary backing to force their own case for the crown.

Olen was too far away from politics now. He had a chain of command, and whoever directed his captain would be the one from whom he took his orders. Still, he sized up the visitors and tried to gauge their loyalties to avoid provoking the situation.

"I imagine that it would be more suitable to raise a toast toward a simple, peaceful succession. I would like to see the issue of the crown resolved for the good of us all," he said finally.

Romwin turned in his seat to better face Olen and menacingly suggested, "If you still have some fight in you, it might be a good time to go back to Caphedra and push the right cause. You're a soldier, aren't you? Swords have a way of making decisions when councils can't."

"I am a soldier, yes, and so long as I am, I'll serve the holder of the crown. I'm grateful to have my post here. I do not miss the filth of the capital—its politics included. I grew up watching my brothers pick fights in the alleys of Caphedra. Fighting, yes, but that was no life to be proud of. Know that I am happier keeping watch over this bog than trying to find my way in the sewers back there. The army gave me a better life than I would ever have had in Westriver."

"I am sure there are drier places to be posted," said Balix helpfully.

"Maybe I'll be assigned to one after they name the heir," Olen responded unenthused.

Colden grunted. "The army wasn't such a godsend for me. I would have been happier staying in the alleys of Caphedra than watching my company mates dangling from the trees at Fallen Oaks."

Romwin placed a hand on Colden's shoulder while his brother clenched and unclenched his fist, head bowed. Ayren's ears perked up at the mention of the northern forest.

An uprising among the woodsmen, Olen had heard about the massacre at Fallen Oaks years ago. The place became known as Bloody Oaks throughout the ranks, and following the ambush, the Lord Marshal's retribution upon the locals became infamous. If Colden was a survivor, he could only imagine how life may have changed for him after that.

"Tell us of the march on Lanstad," Romwin prompted, and his chair scraped as he shifted his vantage to listen.

Olen put his speculations aside and complied. His purpose in Fal Ghreeg was not founded on holding any such secrets of his own, so he began.

"It was the summer of Ramis's fifth year. We'd been raised in the 2nd Brigade and had been training two years at Keepside before we were ordered to join Lord Vlass's troops and start our march—just a couple of miles away from here—to attack the old keep in Fal Ghreeg."

Livet turned her face with obvious displeasure when he mentioned the name of Vlass. Olen was aware of her dislike for the present Lord Mayor of Lanstad.

"Vlass was still just a middling little landlord in those days, without much in the way of his own holdings, so even a small keep was like a palace to him. Ramis liked him because he was loyal. Lord Farn Rhowan was master of Fal Ghreeg, but the fort was so tiny and unprosperous that he probably thought we'd pass him by. I don't know how Vlass arranged it, but he got them to open up the gate in the middle of the night."

Softly, Temis lowered his glass to the table and was listening intently now. "He sounds like a cunning fellow," he said, and Olen grunted in agreement.

"As soon as we got inside the walls, they—we—slit Rhowan's

throat then did the same for the men that were holding on to the place."

Livet looked at Denn and shuddered when he responded with a silent, confirmatory nod.

"Now they say the fort's full of ghosts. I hate it there and prefer to be billeted here. I figure it happened so fast that those things that used to be men still haven't realized they're dead. It's one of the least enviable posts to this day."

A round of murmurings emanated from Olen's audience, including Temis who mumbled something about feeling a chill before he poked at the coals of the hearth fire and rejuvenated it with a stick of wood.

Olen continued, "Then came the surrender at Fal Margoon. Rhowan's remaining men laid down arms and either joined Vlass or disbanded and headed home to their hovels in the bog. Our biggest losses came afterward when we marched on Lord Stern. We got rained on with arrows at Floral Marsh. A pretty place, but now I expect there's a lot of ghosts there too. The bodies just sank into the muck, and they never found most of the dead."

"I never much liked Vlass," Ayren said, hovering beside the table collecting empty dishes. "Hated Rhowan more, though. He was a greedy jack. I imagine his spirit is still floatin' about the blockhouse trying to draw blood from the mosquitoes."

"Maybe so," Olen said. "But except for Rhowan, let's say a toast to the hope that we all find our own peace in the end."

"None for Vlass, neither," Denn added, to Livet's apparent appreciation. She rewarded him with a caring smile and affectionately moved a few inches closer.

They all tipped back their mugs deeply.

"I'll be back in shortly," Ayren said, still holding the stack of bowls. "The rain's slowed down, so I'm going to take care of these dirty dishes."

Romwin stood up. "I'll help you draw the water," he said.

Ayren appreciated the offer and uttered a quick, "Thank you, lad," as the two went outside to take care of the chore.

"Time for some cheer!" Temis announced. He nudged Colden before putting Balix on the spot. "What's that one about the man from Northport that always gets a rise out of your brother, here?"

Balix took the cue and in a surprisingly loud voice, sang:

In Northport, she found him
  At the dockside one day,
Spent all her time 'round him,
  And begged him to stay,
He said, 'No!' so she bound him,
  And had him buried in clay,
'Til the tide came and drowned him,
  At the mouth of the bay.

Colden didn't join in. When the song was done, he brayed in disapproval and opined, "That's not cheery at all!"

"Good for drinking to though," Balix answered. He poured more wine and, finding the bottle empty, opened yet another to top off Denn and Olen's cups. "Drink up," he said. "I'm happy to find someone that appreciates good vintages."

The wind caught the door as it opened and slammed shut again. Romwin returned and took up his place next to Colden.

"Ayren still out there?" Denn asked. "We were just about to ask his opinion of Northport girls," he laughed, causing Livet to roll her eyes.

"He'll be in after a moment, I expect. That stew was pretty rich. The old man's stinking up the outhouse now. He's gone from cleaning his bowls to cleaning his bowels!"

More wine flowed around the room. Denn took a deep draught and sat back. "Speaking of rich, I am very impressed with your taste in wine. I didn't think to have something like this brought way out here. The last time I had Hasen-spiced wine was a few years ago in Caphedra. This is exquisite."

"Your taste in wine is quite respectable as well, not like what you'd expect from a lowly horseman out here in the swamp. What brought you to the capital? Army business?" Romwin asked.

"Nothing so pleasant," Denn said. The firelight was glinting through the red-coloured glass of the bottle as he held it up in front of himself. He somberly rolled the bottle in his hand, making the reflection twirl and sparkle. "I buried my brother."

"Very sorry to hear," Colden said, glancing at Romwin sympathetically.

"Older? Younger?" Romwin asked.

"He was my older brother," Denn said. "Heir to the family and all that. A lot of pressure that he didn't need to deal with but had put upon him, you know? It wasn't fair for him the way he grew up. After we put him in the ground, I never wanted to go back."

Denn's eyes drifted then he mimicked a toast. "To never going back to Caphedra," he said and took a great swig of wine.

In shared contempt of the capital, Olen announced, "I'll drink to that," then also imbibed a deep draught of wine.

But Romwin rudely scoffed and mouthed something under his breath. Olen took notice and saw red.

"And why would I want to go back?" he challenged his detractor. "Ain't none of us Kierks walking the land except myself, and I don't need any reminders of why that is!"

"But you've served the king for all of—what? Almost twenty years? That's a long time to remain loyal. Why not stay so now?" Romwin's words were provocative for the old sergeant who was bordering on inebriation.

"What are you saying? Did you just call me a traitor to my face?!" Olen was feeling the effects of the alcohol in the wine and pushed the table back, ready to rise and quell the slander.

Balix instead got up, raising his hands, trying to calm the pair.

"I'm sure that's not what Romwin meant, is it?" he asked, turning to the accuser.

Romwin continued. "You, and all of us, at one time or another, took an oath to King Ramis. Only one person remains able to carry out the king's will, and that's Lord Marshal Myrhic. Any man of arms ought, by rights, to stand with the prince's army and follow the Marshal."

Colden raised his glass in concurrence.

"Don't you have that backwards? I will follow my orders, and they will be brought down by whomever the Council of Caphedra names," said Olen angrily, doubtful that the council would be easily cowed into supporting the Marshal. Myrhic might have carried out the king's will throughout Ramis's reign of conquests, but he did so in a manner that was well outside of reasonable bounds, spawning legends that gave him a reputation for cruelty and intemperate violence. Not all was done for the king, either, for the Lord Marshal was known to be driven by self-interest.

"That useless council is running out of time to settle this," Romwin said and leaned forward conspiratorially. "The Marshal's collecting his men at Wodwarden. They'll march on Caphedra by the end of the month—that's Midsummer's Eve, at the latest. When they do, Prince Ramid's supporters will be the ones to take over. Those damned Pillarmen won't stand any chance against a trained and experienced army. You should march with us if you want to be counted among the heroes."

"Midsummer, eh?" Olen echoed.

"Before Midsummer," Colden menaced.

Denn sat back with his foot up, cup in hand. "My father will no doubt support both sides if it means more wealth. He deals in ores out of Palinor and supplies the smithies in Barforgers. I expect he's doing well with all this talk."

"It's not talk," Colden sharply rebutted.

There was silence until Olen pointed to Balix's shoulder. Like the other visitors this night, Balix was dressed in leathers, with tall boots, arm braces, and a lamellar tunic, but one thing that made him stand out was the leather pauldron that arched over his right shoulder with a distinctive jagged red stripe incorporated into its design.

"I'm guessing that you didn't get your attire in Caphedra," said Olen.

"What suggests that?" asked Balix, quizzing him.

"That's a Hasenite marking. I studied them a bit," Denn boasted.

Balix corrected him, "It's Jerozian."

"What's the meaning?" Olen inquired.

"We all picked it as a bit of a company sigil. I was with Kroftstalls Company in Hasen. We captured the Greatcamp but were robbed of the Highgrounds, so we crossed the Darrow and eventually garrisoned in the ruins at Jerozi."

Denn sat forward. "My uncle told me that story. He was a cavalryman in the same brigade."

Balix grunted to the others as if signalling approval of Denn. "A pleasing coincidence. Perhaps you know that they recalled our commander, but not the companies. Some of the old fighters trickled away after that, but those fellows that stayed made the old ruins into a rather decent home. But when Ramis died and they stopped paying us, it was too much. I left the sand and dust to the other boys and headed back upriver to the capital to make an honest living there. Of course, I brought lots of Hasen spice with me, and the vintners in Caphedra were quite pleased to compensate me for my efforts."

"Not paying you?" Olen asked, returning to the small pertinent piece of information. "Because you lost the head chief? Rough punishment."

Balix smirked. "Because Chancellor Havel is a miser. They might not be paying you either. You should look into it."

"My pay gets locked away safely at the garrison. No one will touch it," Olen said.

"You should *really* look into it," Balix repeated. "And how well do you trust Vlass's men not to touch it? Do you think the ghosts will scare them off?"

Such an implication sat uneasily with Olen. Lord Vlass's troops were undisciplined and not nearly as reliable or professional as those that came from Caphedra proper, like Olen's unit—even if one considered that the Westriver Company presented from one of the worst of the capital's districts.

"Hang on." Olen pressed him with what he saw as a fair question. "If no one's getting paid, then who's providing for the Marshal's invasion?"

"We'll be paid when we take Caphedra. The Pillarmen have squeezed every gold dame and sire ever minted, and we'll be emptying out their vaults soon enough," Romwin answered.

Temis, who'd been quiet throughout most of this discussion, was looking tired, but he slid even more wine across the table and topped up Denn and Olen's glasses. "Still enjoying the wine, friend?" he asked Denn.

"I must say," said Denn, "I've known Hasen-spiced wines since I was a young lad, and this is one I can't trace. Reminds me of an old medicinal my wetnurse gave me as a boy." Denn puzzled as he savoured it on his tongue.

"Did she have any Jerozi war stripes on her?" asked Colden sarcastically.

"What do you think, Olen?" Temis asked, ignoring the brother's jest.

"I don't think a wet nurse should be giving wine to a boy. As for the wine, I just drink it and am thankful for it," said Olen bluntly and took a huge gulp to emphasize his point.

"Drink deep, and you'll figure out what it is eventually," Temis promised.

Denn pushed himself away from the table, wobbling a bit as he stood. "Excuse me. I'm going to go see if Ayren is ready to make room in the outhouse."

"That's a brilliant idea," Balix said.

"Aye, it's time to contribute to the bog," laughed Temis. "We'll go together," he said.

The trio chuckled and rose from their spots. Balix reached up to pull their cloaks off the pegs on the wall and distributed them to Temis and Denn, who opened the door. Outside, the rain had abated, but it was dark, and the cold marsh breeze intruded briskly into the smoky wood-fired air of the cottage. With a shudder, they stepped out in a procession into the night.

Livet closed the door behind them. The unevenness in her walk was a bit more pronounced with the effects of the wine. She had a concerned look on her face and muttered something about the lateness of the hour.

"That damp sends the chill right through you," Olen commented. "I'm going to stoke the fire. Livet, is there more wood?"

"I'll get some," she offered and turned to take up a bundle of sticks from the firewood box in the corner.

Olen rose from the bench on which he sat, but he faltered and staggered forward a bit as he stood, feeling unsteady.

Romwin got up quickly and held on to him. "Let me help you, brother."

But Olen had to struggle in order to regain his stance. He realized late that Romwin was holding his arms tight and not letting him find his balance.

"Too much to drink?" sneered Colden.

With every effort he could manage, Olen tried to wrest free of Romwin, but his mind was swimming. In a fury, he applied his sizeable mass toward a great lunge forward and away from the elder brother's grip but could not regain his footing when he broke away. From beside him, the younger brother was moving upon him with something in his hand. Olen tried to duck but ended up just spinning on one foot, overcompensating out of dizziness, and collapsing onto one knee. Instantly, the crooked-nosed Colden brought down a heavy cast iron pan against the back of Olen's head in a crippling blow.

Olen's skull felt like it was splitting in two. His eyes spun. Everything blurred. He heard Livet cry out and Colden's voice shouting, "Come here, you!" as Romwin let Olen's body crumple to the rough floorboards.

Colden turned toward the panicking girl, grabbed her by the throat and picked her up. From his view lying on the floor, Olen could only see Livet's legs hanging as she was held aloft. Her toes on one foot scraped against the wooden floor as she tried to find the ground. Her other foot, dangling at the end of the shorter of her two legs, could not reach so far; it flailed in the air before she used it to kick herself free.

Livet landed with a thud on the floor but sprang up quickly as Olen lost sight of her within a shadowy, cloudy haze. The hot flow of rushing blood overwhelmed him, and popping and twinkling stars overtook his fading vision. For Olen, everything that happened that night ended at that terrifying moment.

The last sound he heard was an interruption from the doorway as one of the other men ordered the rest to stand down and withdraw.

"Romwin, grab your brother!" said Temis. "We have what we came for."

CHAPTER 2

The Empty Keep

"**S**top moving! You're bleedin' again," Livet commanded the old soldier with the shattered head. She reached above the hearth fire and snatched down a strip of linen that had been laundered and left there to dry.

Olen mumbled something as his caretaker surveyed the state of his injury.

"Of course, it hurts," she said dismissively, and drew the ends of the cloth tighter around his head to keep everything held in and staunch the flow of blood.

"Curse the Lord's Oath," Olen growled fiercely.

Olen had been bleeding off-and-on for three days since he'd taken the blow to his skull. Once their attackers had gone, she had rushed to him to verify that he was still alive and then did everything she could to keep it that way. Even now, she would lean in and press against him whenever he tried to sit up too quickly, and slap his hands away when his bandages were loosened by his fussing with them.

Ayren survived too. Livet searched and found him bound with rope, not far from the cottage. The last thing the old man heard was the racket of singing coming from inside before he was set upon. Then the stranger named Romwin clubbed him with something weighty and left him tied and gagged in an old shed, away from the house. When Ayren woke up, he began crawling up to the door of the cottage, which is where Livet found him and freed him in the early morning. The old cottager was shivering cold and sporting a big lump on his scalp, but not so severe nor endangering as Olen's head wound.

Livet had spent the night in the wet grass. As Colden grabbed her, she frantically kicked out, dropped to the ground and was able to scamper under the table. As the beast began to hunt for her, the man named Temis suddenly re-entered the cottage and grabbed him, saying they had what they came for and were finished.

The distraction allowed her to scurry between some chests and barrels then slip through a crack in a side door, out of the cottage, and away. All night, she sheltered herself among the tall reeds outside to hide.

The four men took no money so far as Livet could tell; there was little to take, anyway.

What they had come for—or at least left with—was Denn. They captured and slung him across the back of Naobe, then tied the charger at the bridle, to follow behind one of their riding ponies. The giant mare complied, placated only by the nearby scent of her master prone across her back. Livet watched the five horses ride off over the marsh, heading northwest—not to Lanstad. She was too terrified to leave her grassy refuge until she had lost sight of all five shapes as they disappeared into the obscuring fog.

Livet's arms and neck were bruised, but the discolouration was beginning to fade, and she was otherwise unhurt. Her main concern was to figure out how to best help Olen so that he could help her to save Denn. She needed him to regain his strength and senses. Only he could go and find help.

The afternoon following, Livet walked to the end of the path leading away from the moor where Ayren's cottage stood. The small dwelling had offered her safety when she fled her home, but now it was also marred with a frightening memory, in testament to the growing violence of these times.

There was an etching, low to the ground on Ayren's signpost. It was a kind of mark—Scrawl, it was called—that she had been taught to leave from the time she was young. Livet soberly marked the transgression by scraping, with an old carving knife. The older symbol had resembled a triangle with spiral horns, like a ram's head, before she defaced it with a crude zig-zag pattern. If there had been any of her friends left alive to read it, this recent edition transfigured the sign from a glyph of safety into one of warning. Here, an attack was now recorded; the place was no longer safe.

❖   ❖   ❖

Ayren took a knife and sliced off a piece of cheese, which he handed to Olen. With Livet's permission, the stout fighter was now sitting up more regularly and his appetite was returning.

"Could have been worse, lad," Ayren said. "I remember lots of knocks like that back up north. They love their hammers up there."

"I'm pleased to be alive, I'll admit," Olen said, keeping it in perspective.

"That pan was pretty flat. Probably cracked your skull but didn't crush it," Ayren said. "You'll recover, except maybe for the rattling your brain got. That's been known to mess a few people up."

"Maybe 't'll do this one some good," Livet chided but instantly could tell it bothered Olen. He clenched his teeth and she heard him take a deep intake of breath. Something personal had bothered him—knowing him, he probably felt guilty somehow. She was not good enough with words to absolve him, so she just held his hand to calm his feelings.

Olen took turns closing one eye and then the other. He stared at his hands and then fixed his gaze across the room. He tried rubbing his eyes. "I'm having some trouble, Ayren. Everything I see is in double."

"Take yer time. It'll sort itself out."

Livet got up and stared out the window, as she had taken to doing out of habit. But with nothing to look at, she returned to Ayren and Olen, and with a dour expression said, "We 'ave to talk 'bout what we can do to get started huntin' for Denn."

"Yes," Ayren said. "Seems your wee cavalier is in a mite of trouble."

Olen straightened up. "We need to alert his superiors. They will have the men to get out and search for Denn and to bring these outlaws down. They won't see their man harmed at the hands of any deserters."

"You're hurt. Maybe I should go and talk to his commander at the garrison," Livet offered.

"No. It has to be me. But we will go together," Olen said. "I have to see the state of things for myself... and they'll want me to present a report. Denn is under the command of Constable

Hannellin at Falbeth, but there should be someone quartered at the old keep that I can speak with quicker."

Ayren got up and began rummaging around the larder like a badger after grubs. "Pack food. You'll need it for strength. I have a couple of waterskins you can fill."

Olen agreed but said, "It's just my sight is spinning a bit. My body's not in a bad state. I have energy but just need to watch my step." But while still sitting on the bed, he appeared to teeter.

Olen and Livet travelled on foot. Neither owned a horse, nor were they used to such animals. Going on horseback was precarious anyway, on account of the soft earth. The keep was only a couple of miles away, but the actual path stretched a bit farther as they had to navigate along the tops of ridges that crossed the marsh. These crests of drier ground kept them from sinking into the peaty morass, where they would get stuck with each footfall.

"This is the approach we took the first time," said Olen, reminiscing as they stomped through patches of sour deerberries, which the people of the Fals used to make tart wine, and past cattails, which they would grind up into a kind of flour.

There was precious little high ground here save for the one high moor upon which the keep was built. It was manned to project control over some of the fabled Fal forges, which Ayren had told Livet about once while exchanging tales around the hearth fire. Unlike the wood or coal-fired forges in most smithies, the Fal forges burned the flammable gases that emanated from jets in the bog. Their fires burned so hot and regular that objects crafted in them could be made from nearly any metal, and to almost any specification. Even Olen's prized sapphire-encrusted sword, Coldswept, was forged in one, so Ayren figured. Olen claimed to have seized it from the armouries of Fal Ghreeg years ago, and the sword was indeed unique, for whenever it took a life or got close to doing so, Olen was convinced that a ghastly shudder rippled along the shining blade.

Besides the tale of how he came to own his broadsword, the old soldier had told her more stories of the Fal Ghreeg raid often, though he'd neglected the details about slitting throats. He only provided that enhanced telling on the night the riders came. Showing off, Livet imagined. That time in his life was important to Olen, who often confided that it was the closest he had been to nobility, marching along with Lord Vlass through the conquest of the Fals. It was years later now, and Vlass lived comfortably in the Lord Mayor's villa in Lanstad. He was master of a duchy, conquered in King Ramis's name, and probably commanded at least as great a number of men as Lord Marshal Myrhic, and maybe greater. But besides a fancy sword, Olen only went on to win a dank post where he would spend more than a decade on uninspiring guard duty.

"Quite the commander," Olen commented about Vlass, after telling the story to Livet.

"I don't think so," Livet said after listening through the whole tale, quietly and patiently.

"Oh?" Olen said, raising his eyebrows as Livet broke her silence and disagreed.

"He was a brute," she said.

Olen slowed his stride and waited for her to continue, but when she failed to, he prompted, "What do you mean?"

"He is a source o' the reason I left Lanstad."

"He was the cause of your trouble there?" Olen asked. "Did you run afoul of the local Commandery. The reeve's not still looking for you, is he?"

"I don't think they know that I still exist," she said. "They came for my people—our Kindred, we called ourselves—and for my protector. He was the one that ended up raisin' me when my parents run off, after leaving me on a doorstep like a cast-off. That was Kell, and he was the father to us all until they took him."

She had told Denn these things, but never Olen. He had always respected her privacy and she didn't want to discourage their friendship by unloading a library of recollected woes. But Olen now took a softer tone and probed again. "What was Kell's crime?"

"Apostate. Unfaithful to the tenets o' the Pillars. Precept Golmarra in Caphedra sent the orders t' Lord Vlass. His soldiers in the city rounded up everyone they was told to."

"So, they took you into the dungeons?" Olen asked.

"Yes. Beaten and broken, twisted, and some even torn up— the evil tools they 'ad."

Livet stopped walking for a moment. She had upset herself

by allowing the memory to come back. That place had been horrible. It was dismal, rat- and lice-infested, and heartless. The darkness itself did not bother her back then, for she lived in the crypts and catacombs of the city, from where they usually only came out at night. They kept themselves alive with petty thievery or selling slivers of information. A few would come back in the morning with their pockets jangling and blood on their hands.

She never had any schooling other than what he gave her. Kell taught her to read his Scrawl and she memorized the symbols. She learned to see things differently through his eyes and developed the talent to remain unseen in the eyes of others.

But they were not invincible. And when Precept Golmarra brought adepts and curates from Caphedra to help Vlass's men hunt them, they were captured, one by one. Eventually, Golmarra himself arrived. Livet saw the bodies of her Kindred strung up and helpless. She remembered the sounds of the agonized screams and the smell of piled dung, burning oil lamps, and septic filth leftover on the floor. She remembered the pain and the cracking sound of the bone in her leg, as she was punished for trying to look out a window, and then left to crawl while the appendage grew discoloured and infected, without any dressing or splint. Perhaps the sight of the wound on a child was horrendous enough that it awoke a glimmer of mercy in one of her gaolers; that came when she was freed.

Yet even so long after the ordeal, she still lived with the fear that they would seek her out again. Always, she felt like someone out there, somewhere, was hunting her and the thought dogged her with fearful imaginings.

"I was still very young, but close t' dying there, so one of the adepts took pity and let me out after a while. I 'ad to beg on the streets, even for water, as I could barely lift meself up to reach a dog trough. I 'ad to take what food I could find, whether it was rolling in the dirt or was something already spoken for that might risk me getting' thrown back in. The cuts and bruises went away, and 'spite all the blows about me head, the singin' in m' ears stopped after a time. I had to beg while I waited for my leg to heal enough that I could walk away from Lanstad and not come back. It never did heal right, but I manage now anyway. I'm used to working around it now, and I'm as quick as before."

"Vlass usually kept a good leash on his soldiers and kept

them in line, but I never really liked them."

"Maybe they was Vlass's soldiers that came to Ayren's house? That put that crack in yer head? That stole Denn?"

Olen grimaced and appeared embarrassed.

"I don't think they were. Someone else," Olen sighed. "I am sorry. I should have been more careful not to let them come trespassing. That was my duty."

Livet let the breeze wash over her. She had never spoken this much to Olen before. Only Denn was able to coax so many words out of her. She sensed that Olen was now feeling ashamed for once having been allied with her tormentors, in addition to his failure to sound the alarm the other night.

"I don't blame you," Livet said bluntly, though a little dishonestly, as she fought back the desire to scowl at the infantryman and hold him as a surrogate for her resentfulness. But Olen was a trustworthy, honest man. He was helping now, after all, and the look in his eye told her that he would not give up until Denn had been returned to them.

❖   ❖   ❖

Over the next rise, at the top of the moor, the old stone keep hung over the wetlands like a hunched sentry who had fallen asleep while on guard. The bricks of the tower were misshapen, and considerable crevices in the mortar demonstrated how unsafe it had become. But for all its dilapidation, the walls were surprisingly intact.

"Open the gate!" Olen shouted to whoever held the watch along the walls, but there was no reply. The keep was quiet. There was no smoke from fires and no sounds of habitation. He scouted along the wall then approached the hulking timber door that stood in the entrance arch. Olen tried tugging on the handle, which gave way and pulled out instantly. Nothing but rotting wood surrounded the bolts that held it in place. He dug his hand into the decaying wood and gripped the shredding fibres of the door instead. The door swung on its hinges, revealing the empty courtyard inside.

Livet climbed up the slope and surveyed the structure with Olen. He had his sword drawn and was entering with great care, but there were no signs of any bodies, nor any recent battle scarring, either. The collapsing fortress was abandoned.

"I can't believe they all left," Olen said, and concern flowed over his face. He began to appear anxious. "Wait here!" he instructed Livet, but she immediately, and disobediently, pursued him as he dashed across the yard.

Rushing over to the base of the tower, he kicked and cleared away a small pile of bricks and debris to open a door and slip past, with Livet next in tow.

Inside was an office coated in dust and cobwebs. An old desk sat to one side covered in shards of glass from an inkwell that had been crushed by falling stones from above. Sconces on the walls showed the drippings of wax from left-behind candles that were never replaced. The most prominent piece of furniture was a flung-open iron cage containing wooden chests and crates. The crates were smashed, and all the chests appeared to be pried open.

"Thieves," Olen muttered. He ran his hand down the shelves from top to bottom, resting on a bulky, compromised strongbox that hung halfway out from the bottom of the armoire—one of a dozen that looked the same. Burnt into the wooden top, in scripted letters, it carried the name 'Olen Kierk' with 'Sergeant' painted in above that. Olen knelt over it. The lock appeared to have held, but the iron bandings that kept the box together had been wrenched apart to force it open, and the wood splintered, spilling its contents.

"This was mine!" Olen snarled to Livet, who was standing behind him.

"Yours?" she said, awaiting more explanation.

"My pay. My money. Everything I earned by standing knee-deep in the muck of this swamp for twelve years. More than half of my career."

"And these were the men you thought would help us save Denn?"

Olen pushed himself back up. He wobbled from the rush of blood to his injured head but in his anger, he recovered quickly. "Look around. Take what you can. We'll journey on to Falbeth. If we hurry, we'll make it back to Ayren's by nightfall, inform the old man, then get kitted up better for the trip. We can leave again tomorrow morning."

Their exploration shifted to salvage, though everything of value appeared to have been stripped from the fort. What food was left behind was now stale or rotten. The wine had all been drunk and bottles smashed.

The whole of the keep was in as poor a state as the tower, except for the walls, it seemed–though Olen's explanation of why was wanting. He told Livet of how there was a story of how at night the ghosts of Lord Rhowan's soldiers would busy themselves repairing breaks, placing rock upon rock, and sealing them with some unearthly mortar. Even now Olen acted uneasy, like he was under the gaze of those dead men who he had helped dispatch ages before. On the wind, he said he could swear they were laughing at him from somewhere unseen.

They combed the ruins further and made their way to what had been the quartermaster's stores, according to the sign above the compromised wooden door. There, Olen found a useable shield, but it was painted with the sable boar's head of Vlass's garrison troops, so he cursed at the animal, left it in place, and kept rummaging. Suspended from one wall was a crossbow. He pulled it down and scavenged for a leather case and a fistful of bolts with which to make it useable. Lastly, propped up against a wall, he came upon an old wooden carrying frame, with some handy pouches affixed to it, which he could load up and strap onto his back.

"Who belongs to this stuff?" Livet asked.

"We do now," Olen said. "This is a down payment for what they took from me. I'll be sure to collect the rest."

Still scavenging, he packed a few lengths of rope, a small whetstone, and a piece of oiled canvas to round out the pouches of the frame, which he said would unfold and make a good tent for when they travelled. The remaining space in the pack would hold food once they could find something edible.

Livet managed to locate a leather satchel, which she filled with a collection of small tools and items she thought would come in handy. With the situation more dire, she was convinced that a weapon would be needed, so she contented herself to pocket a twisting rondel stiletto made of black steel. She frightened Olen when she appeared holding the dagger in front of him.

Newly provisioned, they left through the gate of the keep. As the pair proceeded back across the wetlands, Livet now felt the eyes from Olen's ghost stories upon her, watching them depart. It seemed her companion's uneasiness was spreading.

❖　❖　❖

The crossbow turned out to be a gift for Ayren. Even though they did not expect Denn's kidnappers would return, Olen felt a bit more relieved about the thought of leaving the old man, knowing he had a little something extra to surprise any future undesirable visitors.

"What happens after you talk to his constable?" Ayren asked that night over supper.

"I will offer to accompany them," Olen said. "I don't know how many men the garrison will be able to commit to retrieving Denn, but I should be a part of whatever rescue is planned. It was my fault, after all. I should have had better sense to turn those men away."

"It was hard to say no to that wine," Ayren consoled, causing Livet to shoot him a sharp, scolding look.

"It was uncommonly potent, whatever it was mixed with," Olen said, his hands instinctively rubbing his temples.

"Eat, ev'ryone," Livet encouraged, refilling Ayren's cup.

The trio of remaining comrades passed around a steaming bowl of stewed roots and began filling their plates; perhaps it would be the last home-cooked meal they would enjoy for a while. Livet was much hungrier than usual, which Ayren attributed to her day's journey.

"It's my cottage and I permitted them," Ayren said, "It's not all on your shoulders, Olen. I'm the gullible old fool that opened the door to them."

"What we need t' decide is not who t' blame, but where we can find help," said Livet.

"They claimed they were on their way to Lanstad," Olen said. "But I don't know what good it would be. Denn has no clout there, no knowledge of city defences. The city is garrisoned by Lord Vlass's troops, not Caphedran cavalrymen tethered to the Fals. I don't know what would inspire them to take him there."

"I'm not so keen on goin' back to Lanstad, even if that were the case, but they left by travelling the other way—northwest t'ward Caphedra," Livet said. She swallowed a mouthful and washed it down with a mug of mead.

"If they just wanted to nab a soldier, there are hundreds they could have taken before travelling all the way here," Ayren pointed out. "Why not take you, Olen?"

"I probably looked like I'd be a bit more trouble than I'm worth," Olen said. He then observed, "They brought that wine as if it were some kind of bait. Part of their plan."

"If you already had a taste for it," Ayren said. "Showing off around the wine would tip them off that he had come from wealth. Still, awfully particular of a destination for them to come straight away if they were just on a fishing trip to kidnap some rich young man."

"Most men have a taste for wine. But I agree he was their target, either because they thought he had money back in Caphedra or..."

"...or he was worth money t' someone back in Caphedra," Livet interrupted Olen.

"So then, it's a ransoming," Olen declared after their joint deduction. "That's not bound to go well. I'll need to inform his family in Caphedra after we notify his commander at Falbeth."

"The way Denn got along with his family, do you think they would pay?" asked Livet.

Ayren stuck his fork into a turnip and answered, "Don't know. Just because Denn hated his father, doesn't mean his father hated him the same," he pointed out. "But it's no matter. Olen, you should hurry."

"We go together," Livet said. There was no way she could abandon Denn now.

Olen grunted audibly and gazed toward the old man.

"Ayren's fine. He looks after me as much as I look after him. He could use the peace an' quiet," Livet argued before Olen could protest.

"And she can be with you to hold yer head together if it starts coming apart again," Ayren offered.

"I know you want to see Denn safe, Livet," Olen said hesitatingly, but then agreed. "Very well, let's take our leave from Ayren at first light."

Setting out at daybreak, the trip took two days on foot. They made a habit of greeting each of the travellers they met on the road and quizzing them as to whether they had spotted riders matching the descriptions of Denn's captors. On the second day, they spoke with a merchant returning from Caphedra. He said that he'd passed by several men that fit the strangers' appearances, as well as a sizeable horse that sounded like Naobe, based on a description of double-diamond markings upon her right flank. It was enough to confirm to Olen and Livet that those they sought were heading back to the capital.

Falbeth was a small village, but it offered several taverns and other amenities befitting a garrison town. In olden times, the vast swamps had extended out this far, but over generations, a sprawling web of drainage ditches had given the earth time to dry out. The fertile soil left behind was worked extensively to provide food for the capital. As it gentrified, they had even evolved the place name into the one-word moniker people used today, a name that developed a reputation for loyalty to the crown. Lord Capel Holl had been unfailingly faithful to the decrees of Ramis in his administration of the hamlet, but it was uncertain what allegiance he held now.

The garrison, Olen explained, had started out as just a scattering of tents, surrounded by a palisade of sharpened timber walls, which were reinforced by stones pulled out of the marsh and the surrounding hills. The builders stopped halfway up, so its walls were not nearly as high as you would see in bigger towns. Even Fal Ghreeg's walls were higher. Permanent buildings were later additions.

As they stood, Olen became quiet and rubbed his jaw. He scrutinized Livet and then shook his head and frowned. "They won't allow you inside the gate."

Livet had expected as much. The whole garrison must be full of soldiers, and she would only stand out or be outright identified as an undesirable if caught alone on the premises. But Livet knew how to remain out of sight. It was a practice she had learned well—exceptionally well—back in the underside of Lanstad.

"Would ya prefer that I slip inside anyway?" she offered quaintly.

"Of course not. We don't need to be breaking any rules. They'll be upset enough that we lost their man. If his commander is not too busy—or too furious—I'll be back soon and will let you know what he says."

"Yes, *Sergeant*," Livet said, mocking him slightly, then she watched him disappear inside the fortress.

Livet did not feel like standing around, but neither did she wish to venture off too far. Her back was aching from the time spent journeying here on foot. Her uneven gait always led to a painful, twisting strain in her back when she spent too much time walking.

Taking a deep breath, she was at once also reminded of how she did not like being on her own in unfamiliar places. She looked around and decided to find a place to stay out of sight. She had no money on her to enjoy any of the drinking or eating establishments, as attractive the aromas of their victuals were, so she scanned the street and the uneven flow of passersby. Quickly she spotted an unattended wagon. Her old habits sent her mind to wondering if it might hold something of value, or at least some curiosities to entertain herself with, but exercising some control, she remained satisfied to use it as just a temporary refuge from being observed.

The wagon was loaded and hitched to two cart horses. At first, there was little to distinguish it from any other, but as she approached, she stopped and stared. Two circles were etched into the side, one larger than the other. Parallel arrows were carved into them, emanating from each. The sigil was something Livet immediately recognized. But why was this wagon displaying the Scrawl for the word 'friend'? Livet had searched for a sign like this since her first day of freedom from the Lanstad dungeon but approached the intriguing mark with caution.

Then, as she pondered the sigil and wondered if it was just a coincidence, Livet felt a slight, gloved hand perch upon her shoulder. Livet withdrew quickly and spun around. Her fingers fumbled to find where she had stashed the rondel amongst her many cloak pockets.

"Can I help you?" asked the matronly woman who had chanced the interception. She was smiling, despite the appearance that Livet may have been about to rob her wagon.

"I am waiting for a friend," Livet said abruptly. "I just wanted to get out of the people's path and wait 'ere by this cart." She was worried that she sounded defensive and nervous. In hindsight, it sounded like a poor excuse.

"I'm glad," said the woman. "My name is Portia. I was

waiting for a friend also."

"So..." Livet began awkwardly. "Should we wait together, then... or... something?"

"Okay," Portia said, accepting the improvised invitation with a chuckle. "I think that I am nearly finished with waiting, though."

Livet shut her mouth to keep from saying anything until she could get a better sense of the woman's intent, although nothing malevolent or harmful could be gleaned from Portia's expression. On the contrary, the cart's owner seemed rather charming and disarmingly amiable.

"This is your wagon?" Livet asked.

"Yes."

"Did you..." she could think of no other way to find out than to point to the etching on the side and ask directly, "carve this into it?"

"I did," Portia admitted. That made Livet very nervous, but not the least bit astounded to find the clandestine glyph materialize here in Falbeth. Portia's acknowledgment only solidified her unsettling confusion until she explained, "I saw it in a dream, and I liked it, so I was encouraged to carve it on my wagon for luck. You recognize it, do you?"

"Why would I?" Livet shot back, trying to avoid giving up anything that might carelessly tie her to her roguish past. A moment later, Livet bit her lip nervously and persevered with another line of inquiry. "You aren't happenin' to be travellin' to Caphedra, are ya?"

Portia cocked her head and asked, "Seeking to make a journey? I have room in the wagon if you like. Your friend too, yes?"

"He takes up a bit more space than I do, I'm afraid," said Livet.

"That's fine. I'll charge him extra, then," Portia said with a sly smirk.

CHAPTER 3

To the Garrison

S eldom having had any reason to fraternize with the cavalry overall, Olen had never been inside the headquarters of Constable Tray Hannellin. His office was housed in an unimpressive stone building located to the rear of the military stables, across a narrow, empty parade ground. A red brick chimney rose out of the roof, sending smoke aloft to lap at the dangling pennant of the 12th Mounted Infantry, proclaiming that the unit's constable was present in the garrison. The standard displayed a pair of argent wolves passant on an azure background, denoting the strength of unity that the cavalry promoted when they rode, sixty-strong, into war.

Hannellin was a sharp-eyed man with unkempt locks of black hair and an inch-long beard bordering his face. He dressed in leathers and kept his sword strapped on as if his time in the office was only a brief and most unendurable administrative burden from which he could depart at any moment. However, his reclined state—with his chair against the stone wall and feet in riding boots propped up along the edge of his desktop—betrayed an overwhelming vice of slothful lethargy. The wood along the top of his desk was deeply pitted and scratched from all the times he had uncaringly let his spurs strike and gouge at the trim.

Approaching the office cautiously, Olen was mindful to present himself with the utmost officiality. He walked in, standing tall and rigid, his body pursuing textbook posture and timing as he reported at the doorway and was gruffly beckoned inside the office.

The cavalry maintained a fancily furnished headquarters, but despite the unexpected lavishness of the room's décor, the smell of stale beer and horses assaulted him. Overcoming the protests of his senses, Olen endeavoured to present Denn's case as quickly as he could, doing his best to gauge the constable's mood. So informed, Hannellin would undoubtedly leap to the aid of his man, order the saddling of their horses, and engage the whole of the Twelfth in exacting raging vengeance.

But it turned out that Hannellin was not furious at all. He listened attentively to everything that happened the night the strangers came, but when the report concluded, the constable started to laugh.

Olen frowned, and his nostrils began to flare, but he held to a rigid reporting stance and awaited Hannellin's verdict.

"So, he got himself captured?!" the constable chuckled. "I wonder if they taught him how to get out of a situation like *that* at school. I'm sure he's got some great strategy to escape. Why should I be concerned?"

"He's your man, sir!" Olen said.

"If he'd spent as much time learning how to throw an actual punch growing up, as he did brushing shoulders and memorizing toasts in the tactician's school, he could have had this sorted out himself that very night, I would bet. Did you see them carry him off, Sergeant?"

"Sir, the mistress of the house witnessed them take him away. I can bring her to you if you like." Olen felt odd calling Livet the 'mistress' of Ayren's cottage, but he wanted her testimony to have gravity if it was accepted.

"You didn't see them leave personally? Without your clear observation of the manner in which he left, naturally, I am forced to admit the possibility that he did so willingly. That settles the matter. Desertion, it is!"

"He did no such thing!" Olen reacted incredulously.

"He wouldn't be the first. I'm down to fewer than twenty men still under arms, according to my roll." Hannellin sat up in his chair, reaching for a quill and thumbing through some parchment. "Our best have stayed on but a lot of the weaker, aimless men have deserted–forfeiting what they're owed in pay, of course."

"Are you going to send any men after him?"

"Hardly! He's not my concern any longer. I'm taking him off the muster."

"Sir?" Olen queried.

"He won't be missed by me," Hannellin said with a final grunt. "You said your part and did your duty. I'll have your captain commend you for your diligence. Now let me get to my work. I'll advise Caphedra of this malingerer."

"He is a good man!" the sergeant countered.

"Then, I'm sure his tormentors will let him go peacefully, and he'll have no trouble finding new employment or landing a plump inheritance from his family vault on Stonerow, to see him get by on."

Olen's eyes opened wide, choking as he spoke, "At least give me a couple of men on horses to track them. He's in danger!"

"I'll give you permission to leave," Hannellin said. "That's the best you'll get out of me in regard to the likes of a spoiled whelp like him!"

❖ ❖ ❖

Clenching his fist around the top rung of his travelling kit, Olen left the cavalry office and struck out across the courtyard to where a pair of twisting eels were burnt into the boards of a rigidly reinforced door. He came to an abrupt stop, then reached up to slam the knocker down.

"Enter!" came a voice from inside, followed by a cough.

The room Olen burst into was a less formal office than what the cavalry maintained. The Westriver Company's home at the garrison held a long oaken table that could accommodate scores of men when needed. A motley assembly of padded armchairs, originating from many random sources, were scattered around a fireplace that burned with belaboured cinders and gave off far more smoke than flame. A hapless attendant was trying to mitigate the problem, but it was clear that the dry firewood must have been used up, and he was burning green branches to keep it going.

Watching the attendant fuss, Olen's captain—a man by the name of Redwyn Ersmine, whom they called 'Red'—sighed and chuckled in between coughs. "Fan it up the pipe or something," he said to the desperate stoker. Turning, he greeted Olen as he entered. "You're usually more cheerful, Sergeant. Problems on the Fals? How have you been faring?"

"What's happened to this place?" Olen brushed wood shavings from the back of an armchair but changed his mind before availing himself of it.

"Well, we found more furniture!" Red said with mock pride.

"They're trimming down the cavalry rolls next door. Hannellin says he's down to twenty."

"Well, I'm still at twenty-six, so that's a bright spot, I suppose. What brought you over to the Glorious Twelfth, anyway? Looking to mount up and change jobs?"

"We were set upon by mercenaries the other night at my billet. I was with Denn Wellum, a cavalryman from their company. After giving me a good knock on the head, the culprits rode off with him as a captive. I came here to report it as a crime against a King's soldier, and gain help in tracking down the offenders, but his constable has refused. He just wrote him out of the regiment and left it at that."

"He doesn't have the money or men to do anything about it," Red said. "Ever since the Caphedran Council gave the administration of the army over to Lord Chancellor Havel, he's ordered a halt on funds to three-quarters of the troops—most of those outside the capital. He is saying the coffers are empty."

"What happened to Lord Marshal Myrhic?"

Red groaned ominously, "He left Caphedra with all troops who swore loyalty to him and is encamped in Wodwarden with Prince Ramid."

"The army is split? What's happened with the succession?"

Seizing a poker, Red stabbed at the coals of the fire and exhaled enthusiastically to rejuvenate the flames.

"Myrhic supports Ramid, of course, and has provided him with an army, with which he can return and take the crown. He's not paying them, but Myrhic commands a lot of respect, and you'll find that's gone a long way to keeping them under arms. Ramid is the youngest heir, but quite suitable considering his upbringing."

Prodding the fire some more, he sent sparks hopping inside the hearth.

"Who opposed him?" Olen asked.

"The Lord Chancellor supports Princess Ravon and has released just enough money from the treasury to keep his own force on retainer. The elders in the Faith of the Pillars have also begun recruiting for their own private regiments, partly to protect their direct interests but also to support Ravon's bid as successor. The council is split, but they haven't taken any steps toward removing Havel from power the way they ousted Myrhic."

"And the younger princess?"

"She is with her cousins, the Farathemuns. But without any backing of force, they may have to give her up and choose a side along with the other lords who have yet to come out officially. I expect she'll support her brother."

"And Lord Vlass in Lanstad?" Olen asked. "What is he up to?"

"I don't know," Red said. "Have his men said anything at Fal Ghreeg?"

Olen scowled. "They're gone," he said. "The fort has been ransacked. I assume they did it right after you pulled your men back with our things."

"You were my last man in Fal Ghreeg, Olen. If you didn't fetch your things, then I'd assume they did. They've likely been recalled to Lanstad by now, or at least Buchan, or the Meadows."

"So, you don't have my money?"

Red brushed his hair back and pursed his lips, exhaling in concern. "I'll assign some men to track our possessions down, but for now..." he retrieved a small copper chest from beside the fireplace and opened it with a key slung around his neck. "This is what you're owed. Just be warned that I don't have any more for you."

He handed over a jingling leather pouch but looked away as he did. Olen paused, then gingerly plucked it from his captain's hand. "This will hold me over until next season's pay," he said and thanked him.

"No," Red corrected him. "I don't have any more now, and I won't have more next season either. I'm saying I can't keep you on here with the company. This is your severance, Sergeant. It has been an honour, but... well, you understand."

Olen stood silently, staring down at the unimpressive pouch of coins.

Setting down the poker, Red reached out and rested his hand upon Olen's shoulder and advised him, "Blame Syr Havel—and if it galls you enough, you should consider joining up with Myrhic and the prince. That might help you get back on your feet and find some justice when the time comes. Otherwise, see if there's a reward out for your friend. I presume that if he's a Wellum, then he must be related to *Phon Wellum*, the merchant in Castleside, right?"

"Yes. I suppose I will be off to see his family next." Olen closed his fingers over the meagre pouch in his palm. "Goodbye, Sir."

"We'll meet again, old friend," replied the captain.

Olen kept his composure until the high timber gate of the garrison was shut and barred behind him, then he gritted his teeth, drew his blade, and swung it powerfully, hacking a great furrow into the portal. Wood chips splintered in all directions.

A passing soldier, showing concern, appealed to Olen with a meek, "Sergeant?"

Olen snarled and spun around, his eyes stabbing the poor trooper with their wrath.

"Um... you could get charged for that," he proffered with hesitation.

Feeling more than prickly, Olen wanted to redress the man for omitting rank, but the rank was no longer his to protect. With a rumbling growl, he clenched onto his purse of coins and looked for a tavern where he could gather his thoughts.

Just across the road from the garrison was a tiny, button-down alehouse called the Ploughman. Being that it was the nearest public house, Olen selected it with rapid expediency. Ayren's mead may be an excellent drink but having good ale around the cottage had been a rare luxury; the old man always insisted on using his available grains for baking biscuits. A strong ale might settle his temper, he thought, and mellow him in advance of what would inarguably be the next leg of his travels.

The inside of the tavern felt immediately refreshing to Olen. It was dark and cool. The townsfolk of Falbeth were arrayed up and down long drinking tables like oxen in barn stalls. A sizeable woman server was coming out to bus the tables, taking orders as she passed, and Olen marvelled at how such a huge woman could stay on her feet for such a long time. Somehow, within a moment of his sitting down, she was upon him, and he appealed to her for his deeply sought libation, which she procured for him just as lightning quick.

Over and over, he counted the coins his captain had issued

him. If he tightened his belt, he could make it stretch, but inevitably he was forced to accept that his only other source of wealth was buried under the floorboards of a place he desperately had avoided ever returning to. He detested the idea of going back home.

As he sat and brooded, consuming his ale preciously, he wondered what Livet would think of Caphedra. It was a forgone conclusion that she would see the matter of Denn's salvation through to the end, as far as she could, and that meant taking her to the capital too.

Olen was aware of Livet's disdain for the city of Lanstad, but she might take an interest in seeing the grandiose spectacle that was Caphedra, and especially the pristine and affluent district of Castleside where Denn's family lived. But he was disinclined to bring her on any visits to his own neighbourhood. If he took her to Westriver or Faralley, it was likely to send her reeling back into nightmarish memories of begging in the Lanstad sewers. Similarly, he would do well to keep her away from the Temple of Caphedra. She would not be comfortable to see the parade of adepts crowding the streets there.

The serving woman shuffled between the tables like a barge floating in a canal. As she passed, she picked up empty mugs and replaced them with full ones, all in one motion. The hefty hostess transited like a celestial body, an event of its own, and Olen couldn't help but be mesmerized. She slapped mug after mug down in front of him before he could even pretend to protest.

Olen hoped they would find Denn, as much for Livet's sake as any. If Denn stayed true to her, he could set her up pretty well in the capital, although it was nigh unimaginable that a family as high-status as the Wellum household would accept such a union. But Denn was at odds with his family and had bitterly rebuked his father the last time he was there, he told Olen. It was quite well possible that he would do so again. Free of the constraints of filial piety, perhaps Livet held a real chance of keeping him. Olen reflected on the situation while staring at his half-empty mug, conscious that the ale was beginning to have its prescribed effect.

His temper now eased by the effects of the drink, Olen couldn't abandon Livet any longer. He produced a few coins from his purse, paid off the serving woman generously, and edged toward the door, leaving her satisfied and happy behind him.

That was when he noticed two long-haired men in travelling clothes camped out next to the Ploughman's window. Rather than look at each other, they were observing the garrison across the road, and Olen saw one whittling notches onto a staff periodically, two or three at a time.

Olen reversed himself inconspicuously and returned to the hostess. He pretended to be concerned with some matter related to his already-settled account but was intent on pressing an inquiry concerning the men.

"What do you know of that pair? They seem to have an interest in the garrison. They're keeping track of something."

"No, not the garrison," she whispered to Olen, correcting him. "They're watching the road traffic. There's been wagons and soldiers coming through here from Lanstad, quite on the regular."

"You're certain?"

"Oh, yes, dear. They've come and gone from this tavern a few times, now, only to be replaced by others once the first ones ride off."

Scratching at the beard on his chin, Olen quizzed, "Where do they ride off to?"

"I reckon Kramwen, judging by their speech. Lord Larsen has little love for Lord Vlass, and with so many Lanstad men on the highway going north these days, I'm not surprised the Larsen's got men watching out to see what's on the go."

He nodded, accepting her explanation, and reached back into his purse for a few more coins which she skillfully palmed. With a slight clearing of her throat, she crooked her neck and pointed to her blossoming cheek.

Olen smiled, leant in to give her a coy peck, and left the alehouse merry and renewed.

It was difficult to spy where Livet might be skulking about, but that was normal. The girl had an unnatural knack for staying out of sight or making you think that your eyes were lying to you when she could be right in front of you.

The garrison door was close by, but the road was busy, so Olen moved aside to where there was a gap, hoping she would see him waiting.

It only took an instant before she accosted him, and he was startled by her voice beside him.

"If we're going to Caphedra, I'm not walking anymore! My body is aching too much." Livet laid her small fingers across Olen's forearm and looked up sternly.

"Might be expensive to pay for a carriage," Olen said, his face melting into a frown. "I don't have much money."

She rolled her eyes then cast sight upon the tavern door dismissively.

"There should be enough in here to hire a wagon," Olen said, producing his sad fortune for her inspection. "When we get to the city, I can find more stashed away, I think."

Livet pointed to a horse-drawn cart outside a small crafter's hovel with a sign that marked it as a glazier's workshop. Sitting atop the driver's bench was a woman. Long curls of brown and intermittently silver hair flowed out from under the hood of her spruce-green cloak. She made no attempt to hide her face, which boasted strong contours and warm brown eyes.

"She's a merchant," Livet explained, "She's takin' glassware and clay pots to some of the taverns in the city. She told me 'er name is Portia."

"You've already hired her, I suppose," Olen said.

Livet nodded. "It might be a slow ride as she can't risk the glass being smashed along the way. I told her we need t' hurry, but the pace should be better to finish healin' yer head."

"My head's feeling alright, now," Olen said, conscious that his breath reeked of ale.

"Wait 'til you're sober, the pain'll be back," she advised, then dragging Olen along with both hands, she took him over to the wagon and forced him to present himself for an introduction.

"Good afternoon, madame," Olen said politely.

"And to you, sir!" greeted the woman on the cart. She turned to Livet and said, "I'd like to get started before the daylight stretches much further. Why don't you send this fellow to the back to sleep off his midday constitutional, then you can sit up with here me, dear. If you're hungry, I have some food that we can eat along the way."

Olen handed Livet his pouch of coins, and she counted out what she needed, returning the remainder to him.

"This is what we agreed on," Livet said.

Olen hiccoughed.

Portia took the money and looked him up and down skeptically. "On second thought, there's room up here," she said. "I wouldn't want him to get sick all over my deliveries."

Olen blushed but eagerly took her up on the offer.

Once they had both climbed up, Portia picked up the reins and pulled them until taut. She clucked to the horses harnessed in front. Picking up their feet, they pulled together, and the pair of drays led the cart down the cobbled street and onto the high road that led to Caphedra.

As they clopped along, more soldiers passed them. Several greeted Olen with a cheerful, "Hullo, Sergeant!" and "Peaceful travels, Westriver!" For as long as the ale kept him jovial, Olen waved back and returned their pleasantries.

The only ones who said nothing, Olen noticed, were on wagons journeying northward. These men had shields that bore the boar's head, identifying them as being Lord Vlass's men. It conflicted with Captain Ersmine's suspicion that Vlass was recalling his men to the south, closer to Lanstad. No wonder he knew nothing of Fal Ghreeg. Clearly, the captain was not even keeping a close watch on what was passing right under his nose.

"Why do you think they are this far north?" Livet asked him.

Olen considered the mystery but had no ready answer. Vlass was known to adhere unfailingly to the Faith of the Pillars. Were these troops congregating under the standard of their religion? Could they be in some arrangement with the Marshal? More importantly, did any of these boorish itinerants know what happened to Olen's money?

CHAPTER 4

Bound for Caphedra

J agged sticks of straw poked and scratched at Denn's cheeks, as he lay in the back of a hay wagon. Crammed in between weighty grain sacks, he struggled to shift even a little. He was tied with his hands behind his back and a gamey-tasting strap of leather gagging his mouth. There was a ratty blindfold covering his eyes too, but from time to time, it would loosen sufficiently for him to brush his head against the sides of the wagon and permit a narrow view. An archaic moth-eaten blanket provided one more layer to conceal him from outside eyes as they travelled. The many gaps and tears in its weave permitted tiny glints of sunlight during the day, but those same holes also let the dewy air seep in at night, leaving him to freeze under the dampening fabric.

He was granted barely more than a splash of water whenever they paused on the road, and the four riders who directed the cart stopped infrequently, so he was continuously parched with thirst. Each halt was more of an opportunity to reacquaint him with violence to match that which had led him to his present miserable confinement.

The one named Romwin conducted beatings regularly as if he were performing the duty on a schedule and his patterns of onslaught became easy for Denn to trace and predict. First, he would drag Denn out of the wagon the clobber him about the head. Next would come crippling kicks to each of his legs and then a punch to his guts. It would always be up to Balix or Temis to haul Romwin off or limit his brutality.

Worst among his captors was Romwin's brother, Colden, as he was entirely erratic in his dispensing of thuggery, and no amount of reasoning from the others could elicit mercy from him. Each instance ranged from a brutal trouncing to downright sadistic torment that would last until another in the party—usually Temis—would deflect the bully's attention. This might be a tease or insult, which would spur a demand for redress or the announcement that someone had prepared food and Colden's greedy stomach did the job of distracting him. From time to time, he would even force the cart to stop so that he could dismount and make his way back silently, unexpectedly jumping into the cart and landing with his full weight, crushing his captive. For this reason, Denn braced himself every time he felt the wheels stop turning.

It all led to growing despair and a regret that he had not been more suspicious the night the strangers came. If only he were a better fighter and could have put up a struggle long enough for someone in the cottage to be alerted. If only he were strong enough at this very moment to break his bonds or sufficiently nimble to work his fingers through the knots and get free. But for all these wishes, he had only demonstrated that he was as utterly incapable as he had so often been accused of being throughout his twenty-five years of life.

He feared that any retaliation would be for nought, anyway. He had no knowledge of what violence befell his friends or of how that evening had ultimately ended for them. He worried they might not have been spared at all if the purpose had been to capture him. But if they were still alive, most assuredly, they would be on his trail. That is, as long as they recognized that the strangers had been lying when they announced Lanstad as their destination.

Denn had noted the change in their route quickly. The road to the north had a distinctive sound when hooves fell upon it, like a drier, sandier grinding. It was intimately familiar to his ears after so many years of riding the Fal's soggy slopes and traversable isthmuses with Naobe. By morning, the one side of the cart grew warmer and steamier much faster in the early sun's rays, confirming the cart's east side. With this information, Denn deduced that their path was taking them north to Caphedra.

He also knew that Naobe was travelling with him. He could hear her footfalls on the path and her breath as she snorted derisively at the carthorse, and at the quartet of culpable equines led by his oppressors. He feared, however, that he would lose her at

Greenplain where any number of traders would offer a tremendous purse of coin for a charger of her splendour. Alternatively, that jealous shrew Temis might choose to keep her for himself. Denn gave equal odds that would be the outcome, and maybe it was the more infuriating of the two possibilities.

From time to time, he could hear people travelling in the other direction passing by them, but he could never tell their number. If he cried out for help, he would likely just commit those innocents to a fate as unlucky witnesses. Instead, he waited, calculating that he would have better odds of soliciting help when they passed through Falbeth, where the garrison was.

But that turned out to be a poor plan. As the noise of the village first faintly reached his ears, the cart stopped. Denn closed his eyes and tensed up. The oilcloth stretched out above him was pulled back, and Colden was upon him in an instant.

"Ungh!" Denn exclaimed in pain as his ribs crumpled along his side.

"This is comfort!" Colden exclaimed, lifting up his foot then driving his heel back into Denn's leg protruding from underneath. "Stinks, though. You wet yourself back here?"

Colden laughed and checked the tightness of his prisoner's blindfold then he leaned in despicably close. Denn could hear his breathing and feel it on his neck, putrid like the smell of slop in a pigsty. The brute pressed a cold metal blade along his jawbone and into the soft part under Denn's right ear. "We'll ride together for a bit, now. You keep quiet and you'll likely be alive by the time we reach Caphedra," he said menacingly. "But pipe up one note for anyone to notice you, and I'll slit your throat in a heartbeat!"

The carthorse pulled again, and the motion of the wagon continued. Noises from people on the road filtered into the cart as they passed. Idle talk from roadside merchants shilling their wares or farmers complaining of pests and weather trickled past his ears. The smell of stews and roasting vegetables wafted from cottages along the way, frustrating Denn's empty belly.

Yet, he complied and made no sound. He even heard horses—heavy destriers that were most likely from his own company, the Twelfth. Their riders' voices had a familiarity to Denn, but he dared not call to them for fear of the knife being thrust into his neck and severing his windpipe.

The loudness of Falbeth diminished as they passed the village square and continued through. The ground was becoming drier on this side of the village and once they'd achieved an appreciable distance, his kidnappers moved off the road to encamp. Romwin dragged him out from the straw and pushed him to the ground. Denn's knee banged bloodily into a tree root, but he was left there without further harassment. The beatings had become fewer, owing to his captors becoming tired of the journey and bored of tormenting him. He felt the warmth of the fire as it started crackling nearby, then sensed hands on the back of his head undoing his blindfold. Temis removed it, then his mouth gag, and then his wrist straps.

"Be good and eat," he said, allowing Denn to seize a bladder of water and gobble up a dry biscuit for food. With a full mouth, he started to feebly thank Temis, but it was returned with a sudden glare of warning that made him hold his tongue so as not to attract attention. Why Temis treated him differently than the others gave him reason to wonder what the relationship really was between the men.

Naobe was hitched to an old ash tree not far away. She scraped at the dirt with her hoof and bent low to graze on the grass growing at the base of the tree. She kept an eye on Denn as she nibbled. At least, Denn thought, his horse was okay. His concern for Olen, Ayren, and especially Livet was not yet alleviated, however.

When Romwin spotted the contraband biscuit, he walked over closer to Denn and Temis. "We'll have to add the cost of that to our ransom, boy," he sneered.

Denn snorted skeptically. "I'm just a cavalryman. My company won't pay to get me back, although they'd be happy to hunt you down and run a sabre through your gut."

"Why would we come this far just to grab some soldier?" Romwin posed the question to him, but Denn stayed silent. "Phon Wellum's a wealthy and proud man, Balix tells me." He rubbed his hands together and cracked his knuckles. "Maybe he'll be less wealthy and proud once we get to the capital with his boy all bound and beaten up, and the old man is forced to pay up."

Starting to seethe with anger, Denn said, "It's been two years. We don't miss each other at all. He's got more attachment to his gold than to me. You'll see."

"Then we'll find out what value he places on pride. We might have to make this situation all the more embarrassing for him before we kill you. When the end comes, you won't get the privilege of choosing your own time to go, like your brother did. We'll keep you guessing!" he sneered.

That ignited Denn's anger, and he sprang upwards to lunge at Romwin, but he couldn't do it fast enough, and in his weakened state, it was quickly countered. Romwin grabbed him with both hands and pressed downward, aggressively crumpling him against the base of the tree. Before he could regain his breath, he had been bound again, and the gag replaced in his mouth.

"Not yet," Romwin said.

The following day, Denn knew they were getting close to Caphedra from the smell of manure that rose around him. Unlike the excrement from the cattle that pastured further south, this had the distinctively less sour and more clinging scent of horse. They were finally coming upon Greenplain and its endless grazing meadows, expansive stables, and horse markets. He could see nothing through the blindfold now but had visited the area so often as a child—and later as a cavalryman—that he could paint it in his mind's eye and knew they were well along toward reaching the city.

The cart wheeled and rocked ever onward, yet at each moment Denn remained on edge. Now, he didn't fear the random beatings so much as he did the inevitable farewell to Naobe. This was the heartland where horses were bred and raised for the whole of the land. The largest auctions were held here and a horse like Naobe, gently obedient, yet fearless and broken in for war, would command a considerable sum. Truth be told, they might get more coin for his horse in Greenplain than they would receive for him from his father in Castleside.

But the cart did not stop. Time dragged on and by nightfall, the sounds and bumpy undulations of the dirt road changed into a grinding under the wheels and the heavy clopping of hooves on cobbled roadways.

One of the riders, possibly Balix, could be heard directing the others, "Steady now and straight on in. No stopping or wandering off until we're safe and settled."

There was a jolt to the cart and the cadence of hooves altered slightly, letting Denn know that they were now crossing the bridge into the city through the Southgate. It was still early enough in the evening that the portcullis and gate were open, and no guards stopped them. From the straw pile in the back, it was hard to judge which way they turned, but they did not venture too deeply into the city before they stopped, and he heard his kidnappers dismount.

Denn attempted to narrow down the possibilities of where they were. They had not travelled as far as Stonerow or Middlehold but were undoubtedly in one of the crafters' districts just inside the wall. From the main road through the southern gate, a visitor to the city could turn west to Potshollow, where pottery shops, brickworks, and kilns were clustered, or they could go east into Kroftstalls, which was full of artisanal studios, tapestry makers, weavers, and markets.

Now, someone outside was manipulating a heavy iron lock or pin. It scraped noisily and thumped against wood a handful of times, rhythmically as if swinging on a rope.

With a sharp bump, they moved again. The carthorse whinnied, and the noise from the wheels sounded to Denn as if they were on wooden boards. Abruptly, the oilcloth was pulled back, and he saw that they were in a small carriage house. Balix and Romwin each grabbed a leg, and they pulled him out roughly, forcing him to stand. His joints and muscles ached. The older brother ripped off his blindfold, which Denn had already worked to displace.

It was a tiny room, and the other horses had to be hitched outside. He couldn't see Naobe. Temis was nowhere to be seen either, likely tending to the horses as he seemed to have the most experience with that. The floor was littered with sawdust and straw. The roof was low, with an old swallow's nest affixed under one of the trusses. Colden had managed to spark an oil lantern to provide a bit of light. It flickered against his face, illuminating his foul grin and crooked nose while shadows settled around his deep-set eyes.

"Move!" Balix commanded, his countenance ever serious. From behind, Romwin kicked at Denn's heels to get him moving. A very steep set of stairs like a ladder was suspended from a trapdoor above. They made him climb up while his hands were still bound so that he could not pull up or save himself should his knee buckle and he were to fall, but his gag prevented any vocal protest.

Peering over the lip of the trapdoor then pushing himself up higher, he ascended into a cramped hayloft. Through the dark, he could see it was mostly empty. The floor had hayseed and sticks of straw scattered about, mixed with piles of tiny, elongated pellets of rat dung. That made up most of what he saw. Clearly, the owner was not utilizing the place frequently, if at all. Denn ducked his head and moved over to where he could faintly make out a small bale of hay in the dark. He nudged it a few times with his foot to scare out any rodents, then when satisfied it was uninhabited, he dropped down on his uninjured knee and fell over onto the bale, head resting against a roughhewn wooden board on the wall beside. Amid the dust and staleness, he allowed himself to breathe heavily.

Balix and the two brothers were whispering downstairs. They mentioned something about ransom, and one could be heard demanding paper and ink.

With only the light from the trapdoor visible, Denn tried to scan the room for anything that could help him escape and, looking up, he saw something that caught his eye.

On one of the rafters, there was an old, rusted pitchfork that nobody had thought to remove. In the low light, he could make out the prongs, and from the way it was balanced, the shaft must be intact. If he could just free his hands, he would easily be able to wield it to surprise and dispatch the first assailant up that ladder. Then it would be far better odds. But how could he cut his bindings? He had to hope that they would free him to eat as they had done before. It was still a very perilous prospect that he could move fast enough to both procure the pitchfork and press it into service.

There was a rattling of wood and iron below as someone opened the door to leave. It was Balix who instructed, "Keep this door barred. I'm going to take this note to Wellum. I expect to be back in an hour. Then we can sup and have a drink. Watch our boy while I'm gone." With that, the door below slammed shut. The loft shook and rat droppings fell down onto Denn's head.

Colden and Romwin were left together to guard the wagon house and, through a crack in the floor, Denn could hear them talking. Alone, they spoke more like brothers. Their voices sounded so similar, but Denn was getting used to Romwin's clearer intonation and stricter manner of speaking, in contrast to Colden's detestable snickering and habit of grunting acknowledgements when spoken to. But their conversation was taking on the air of an older brother scolding his junior, and their voices got louder.

"I don't want to be doing this again!" Romwin stated to his brother. "This is not the kind of business we should be in, and you should have known that before taking the oath. You should not have offered to do this job when Balix came knocking."

"Did you tell the captain where we were going?"

"I told him we were off to spy on Vlass. We'll explain this other diversion when we bring back a share of the money."

"He'll approve of it then," Colden sniggered.

"This sort of scheme smacks more of thieving than soldiering. Even if Alamm permits it, I would not be so quick to think the Lord Marshal would likewise approve. He left us here with a job to do and this is not it."

"I seem to recall—before they dunked me into that bathwater—that the oath I took was to the king," Colden said, "and he's dead."

A chair leg scraped the floor, and their shadows crept upward and fanned out as someone stood in front of the lamplight. "Make no mistake," he said to educate his brother. "Your oath was to the Lord Marshal. He represents the king on this earth until the prince is ready."

"No mistake," Colden repeated. "I understand, brother."

Denn heard more movement, then the ladder shifted as a boot was placed on a rung below. He looked up at the pitchfork. He made fists with his hands and rocked them together, trying to break or stretch the straps on his wrist, but it was useless.

Colden's greasy, clumpy hair rose out of the trap door hole, followed by his ugly, misshapen face. Having to swallow his brother's chastising with humility, it would not be unexpected for the brute to expend his frustrations on Denn instead.

"Well," Colden said, hauling himself up. "You must be happy. All back home now. Probably not the same part of Caphedra *you* grew up in, is it, Wellum? This part of town's a bit *rougher*."

Instinctively, Denn curled up and braced himself.

Colden continued, "That's right, make a little ball."

Denn groaned in pain as a fist came down to smash into his back. A thought flashed coldly through his mind: there'd be a chance he could end it by breaking his neck if he rolled and fell through the trap door in just the right way. No, he had to endure. His hair was pulled, and his head raised up so that Colden could view the anguish on his face. His tormenter poked a finger lightly into his cheek, then one upon the bridge of his nose. Each time, he cackled and said, "Poke!" Then he jabbed a tight, closed fist abruptly into Denn's nose, causing him to see stars. Had he not been so parched, his eyes would have watered. His nose bled, though.

"I should keep that up, so your nose'll look like mine," Colden chuckled menacingly. "That's how I got to be so handsome!" Denn tried to spit at him in response, but his mouth came up as dry as his tears.

Just then, the big wooden door downstairs creaked open and was slammed shut again quickly.

"Colden!" cried Romwin from the first floor. "Temis has returned!"

"Did you sell the horse?!" Colden shouted down through the trapdoor.

Temis made a cautiously affirming sound, followed by some vague murmuring. Colden slid across the floor and dropped down through the hole, out of sight. Denn lay still, listening, and feeling the pain in his back, and in the bones of his face. *Where was Naobe now?*

"My man will have the money for the horse tomorrow," Temis could be heard saying.

There was a pair of approving cheers.

"Balix is off to deliver the news to Wellum," Temis said, then added, "And I have brought you both some bread, cheese and ale."

"Thank the stars," said one of the brothers audibly enough.

Denn rolled over, pangs of hunger at the thought of the enviable victuals were coupled with the aching of his bruises. The brothers were saying something, but it was now indecipherable as their mouths were full. They were gorging themselves. While they did, Denn caught sight of Temis's braided scalp ascending into the loft for a quick look around. He noted Denn's condition then sunk back down again without a word.

"News then?" inquired a voice sounding like Romwin's.

Temis, in his characteristically light-timbred voice, answered, "As we expected. The chancellor still holds the strings of the royal purse. Myrhic is known to be in Wodwarden with the prince, and the sister sits in the Temple of the Four Pillars waiting to act upon her queenly aspirations." He concluded, "The news is that she is likely to move within days, to take possession of the castle and the citadel."

"Does she have enough people? Not monks, but soldiers, I mean?"

"The troops garrisoned in the city will likely stand neither for, nor against her, for now. They are busy with their own thieving," Temis answered. "Chancellor Havel is paying them a fraction of what they're used to, and they make up the rest any way they can, raiding the markets or plundering the brothels and alehouses. Food is short. I wouldn't be surprised if the livery I went to gets robbed, and our horses cooked into stew for the local commandery."

"A king needs to be restored to set things right. Not a priestess," said one.

"Whoever it is will need an army," said Temis. "They won't always work for free when they can take what they want unchallenged."

Someone belched. "I want to sleep. Temis, take the first watch, will you?"

"Aye," said the other brother. "Let me rest too. I will relieve you in a couple of hours. Wake us if Balix returns from delivering the ransom."

"I will," Temis said.

Again, the ladder creaked as it was pressed down, and the brothers, one at a time, climbed up into the loft. Colden scuffed along the wooden boards with his feet to sweep away the sawdust, before securing his own spot to rest. As he did, he kicked up a storm into Denn's face, causing dirt to get into the prisoner's eyes. Helpless and tearless, Denn had no means to remedy the stinging it caused.

Colden picked a spot from where he could see Denn and monitor their prize. Romwin laid down closer to the trapdoor. They said little but revealed their profound fatigue. Temis stayed down below.

After some fidgeting and fussing, the two appeared to be sleeping. Denn quietly lay in his spot on the hay bale, propped up so he could rest, but also so that it would be easier to rise should his situation change. He wondered if he could somehow twist and slip his legs through his bound arms to at least get his hands in front of himself. Then, sneaking past Romwin, he could hang off the lip of the trapdoor and drop down to the bottom storey. That still left Temis to deal with, however.

Suddenly, he heard a noise below. The bar on the gate was being lifted. Balix must have returned and would no doubt be both empty-handed and angry with disappointment. Denn prepared himself for the real possibility that his time in captivity would soon be ended by either a knife blade or at the end of a length of rope slung over the rafters above him.

Romwin, who often displayed keener instincts, opened his eyes wide. He appeared temporarily in a fog. Scanning what was around him with a distressed look, he reached for his sword, rose with a clatter, and rapidly dropped down through the trapdoor. The commotion disturbed Colden too, who scampered over to the edge and peered down to see what was happening.

The gate swung, wildly unhinged now. The noises from the street and colder evening air penetrated the carriage house. Someone, maybe Romwin, shouted loudly, and a scuffling broke out. Colden followed down the hatch as a spate of violent, moist, puncturing sounds subsumed his brother's cry. Then two loud crashes resounded as both brothers hit the ground floor simultaneously. One landed on his feet. The other sounded less likely to have done so.

Denn could sense there were several men downstairs now. The new intruders thrashed around the lower room and could be heard swiftly circling the parked wagon to all corners. There was an alarming sound of metal ringing against metal as two blades connected. He heard Colden howl in pain or fear. A body thumped hard into the flailing wooden gate, swinging it on its hinge. Heavy footsteps on the ground clattered outside, their thunderous stomping fading amid a rapid departure.

The tumult ebbed with the light from a lantern now dancing around wildly. Someone was climbing up the ladder to search the upper floor of the carriage house.

Only Denn was left there in the loft. Whoever held the lantern seemed to take comfort in this and drew a small hood over the light to dim the glare. As he did, Denn thought that he recognized the man's stern, craggy face. His name was Yael Larkin and he was the capable hand who carried out every task or command issued by the father whom Denn had repudiated for so long.

"Are you hurt? Can you walk? Do you need to be carried?" Yael tossed out questions like crossbow bolts. Denn guessed he was too slow to answer, so Yael began shouting down to the bottom floor. "Help me get him moving!" He sliced off the gag and cut through the leather wrist bindings.

Instantly, Denn placed his hands around his head and over his face, taking a further moment to recognize his captivity was over. With the gag off, he feebly informed his rescuer, "I can move."

His voice must have sounded tremendously dry as Yael reached down to hand him a leather water bladder to drink from. Once he gorged himself on the water and handed it back, Yael poured some of the rest into a small linen rag and reached up like a clumsy mother to wipe Denn's face of its grime and blood. Seeing Denn flinch, Yael paused momentarily, but since he presumably still looked unacceptable for the son of a high merchant, Yael gave him a couple of additional passes for good measure, dislodging more of the dirt but having no effect on the bruises and cuts.

He was helped down the ladder by two more men. They each wore dark, woollen cloaks but had pulled the hoods back to show faces that were more youthful than Denn's.

"Lean on me, sir," offered one.

With their help, Denn stood straighter and that gave him a better vantage to survey the room below. All those audible items now were unveiled: the chair, the broken loaves of bread, and the unlatched bar on the gate. Also, he saw a pair of brown leather riding boots stretched out in a puddle of pooled blood. Out of them protruded a pair of legs which proceeded to a perforated torso and finally to the grim face of Romwin, dead on the floor.

"The others?" Denn asked aloud.

"We killed their messenger man, earlier," Yael said, now firmly back to the ground and standing beside Denn. "The one that was below is gone and the other one that was upstairs with you took a few cuts but also managed to get away, I am sorry to say." Something grabbed his attention, and he knelt beside the warm corpse. Denn heard him curse under his breath as he fingered an embossed clasp, which was fastened to Romwin's sword scabbard and compared it to a matching cloak brooch he picked up off the floor.

"Caphedra Castle," he said examining the image. "The Lord's Guard can't be so hard up as to resort to kidnappings for money." He undid the straps around the piece and hid it away in a pouch on his belt, then concluded, "Must be stolen."

The men did a quick sweep of the room and finding nothing else worth dwelling on, they helped Denn out onto the street to where a dappled, grey horse stood hitched to a cinder-black, two-wheeled gig. Yael got up onto the seat and grabbed the reins, issuing the command to his underlings to search hard for the one that got away.

"*Two* escaped," Denn corrected him.

Yael nodded.

"Will you take me to a lodging house?" Denn struggled to sit up straighter to feign vitality.

"Home. Your father wants to know you are safe," Yael said. Then, with his hands upon the reins, he made a couple of clucking noises from his cheek. The horse and the gig set off on the street, away from Kroftstalls.

CHAPTER 5

Hidden Talents

Their driver proved to be an amiable and uninhibited travelling companion on the ride north. The wagon moved at a lumbering pace that frustrated Olen, but Portia was very adept at filling gaps in conversation. She even coaxed some discussion from Livet, who was otherwise entranced with seeing the lush forest and blossoming orchards beyond the Fal marshes for the first time.

Based on her accent, Olen guessed that Portia was from further north than Caphedra. She had the same harsh pronunciations and drawn-out vowels as Ayren did–whenever the old man got drunk or excited, anyway.

"Not so far north," she admitted when asked. "I came down from Greyforest many years ago, from a very small camp where I was born. Most of my business is in the capital now." With that, she probed back, "You look like you've been in the army for a long time, Olen. You must be from Caphedra somewhere. All the old ones are."

Olen nodded again. "I am," he said, hoping this answer was sufficient.

It had taken several years for King Ramis to begin recruiting from outside the capital, so most of the longest-serving veterans were natural-born Caphedrans. It was only after the construction and maturation of the main garrisons at Falbeth, Darrow River, Bren Hills, and Northwood that the army felt they could impose their need for men upon the locals of those areas. Typically, the recruits would be formed up, trained as spearmen, and then sent off to Keepside in the capital to be taught the sword and siege arts. Some, with greater means, might be sent to Greenplain to learn horsemanship and serve as cavalry. Archers were raised cheaply, wherever unattached men needed steady work.

"I expect you must be from west of the Darrow River. I've seen that eel brooch on your cloak before."

Her thrusts were becoming more accurate. She was trying to find her mark.

"I *was* from Westriver," Olen said, feeling rather sullen to speak of it as a thing in the past. "I suppose I'll be going back there now, though I haven't been—not for a long time."

"I know that place well," Portia said. "You must have family who will be interested in hearing of your adventures?"

"No. There's no one now," he said, his eyes shunting away from her and staying locked on the unruly scrub brush they passed along the roadside. Portia also appeared to grow more reluctant to press Olen. She backed away from pursuing the topic any further and instead recruited Livet to liven up the conversation.

"How about you, my little blackbird? Ever been to the capital?"

Livet broke from her trance-like watching of the passing greenery and looked up at Portia to say, "No. Is it like Lanstad?"

"Oh? That's where you're from, is it?" Portia said inquisitively. "You have that look. A bit, anyway. The dark black hair." She smiled jubilantly as if celebrating a victory for having coaxed words from her tiny, reserved guest. "It's very different. Caphedra is much larger than Lanstad. It's not all baked brick cottages and crafters' hovels. The stonework dates back hundreds of years or more, although I must admit, it's definitely showing its age."

"It must have beautiful buildings," Livet said. Olen noticed she was slowing her speech to pronounce her words more carefully in front of Portia.

"Yes. Great halls, temples, the palace with its great rose-violet starlights. There used to be a lot of money flowing through there. The trade and goods from Palinor, Northport, Hasen, and Lanstad, all went through the merchants in Caphedra, who then lined the king's pockets with their taxes. That's how Ramis was able to afford such a large army when he became king. But when he finally put his wealth to use and conquered the other cities, he stifled the merchants. No more trade and no more money. The city's quite empty-pocketed now."

"Good for them," Livet said scornfully. "It was them that ruined Lanstad."

"It's still the seat of power in this land," warned Olen. "Don't you doubt it."

There was a short spell of silence as the three paused their discussion, but Portia eventually added, "I'm glad to have you two for company. Since Ramis died, it's become less safe to travel alone, especially when riding a wagon full of wares. I certainly don't remember it being so bad as now and I've travelled this road quite a few times over the years."

"I've actually noticed more soldiers," said Olen. "More soldiers. Fewer merchants."

Throughout the trip, Olen had been taking a keen appraisal of each passing party and often commented to Portia, who would add perceptive detail to his observations, and Livet, who quietly took it all in.

Mostly, they noticed small bands of men protecting heavily laden carts and wagons which were journeying steadily southbound in the direction of Lanstad, or lightly outfitted men of arms marching north alone. He noted that these errant men, while not travelling with any units, were still moving in substantial numbers and bore many mismatched unit crests or insignia. He especially kept a careful note of those with the boar's head shields, not entirely forgetting his lost savings and their likely culpability in the theft.

"I wonder what they're carrying," Olen said.

"They're highwaymen, out to rob and pillage," Portia said.

"The capital won't be looted! There's not an enemy left in the land that could overtake the city," Olen countered.

Portia shook her head. "The army's largely been disbanded, as you know. These men are collecting upon owed wages, and there's only one way to do that. Under the king, all the wealth flowed to the capital, so that's where they go to retrieve it. You'll see more of their shameful behaviour when we get to Caphedra."

As she spoke, another heavy, covered wagon trundled toward them, this time from the south. Portia drove her wagon slowly, so as not to damage her load of glass and pottery which allowed them to be overtaken easily, to Olen's dismay. The approaching wagon was bulky and, despite the road becoming broader beyond Falbeth,

Portia was nonetheless forced to pull over to the side to allow it to pass. As it did, they heard belligerent voices coming from the back and could make out that this one was a military transport. Shields displaying Lord Vlass's black boar were slung over its side. They took no particular interest in Portia, Olen, and Livet, but continued onwards, scattering stones, and kicking up a cloud of dust as they went.

"It's not just simple looting. They're mustering. More soldiers are going north than returning," Olen said, but also noting that the wagons travelling south, if driven by Lord Vlass's soldiers, often had passengers. These passengers were dressed in travelling cloaks, but underneath, they wore blue doublets. That meant they were not troops, but curates of the Faith of the Pillars. Every time one passed by Livet huddled in a little closer to Olen and pointed them out for the tally.

Only Olen was not too troubled by the curates' presence, having yet to acquire any reason to fear them, but Livet fidgeted, and her discomfort was mirrored by Portia, who would tense up and grow quiet when they passed anyone in blue. Though he knew more of Livet's history, he could only speculate as to why Portia so oddly mimicked Livet's fearful uneasiness.

When they had made the best possible use of the daylight in progressing toward Greenplain, Olen reluctantly suggested they stop for the night. Portia clucked to the two horses and called, "Haw! Haw!" guiding them to pull off the road and into a small grove of birch and alder. It was far enough into the thick of the woods to avoid the notice of any nighttime travellers passing on the highway and would give them privacy to light a small fire for supper.

Olen set about gathering armloads of firewood, breaking branches over his knee and chopping at stubborn pieces with his sword. Livet busied herself by collecting moss and kindling. Her rondel was not well-suited to the task, so she used a smaller blade borrowed from Olen's pack to get at the insides of drier branches and whittle out small pieces from which to start the first flames.

Stooping over the fire once it was ablaze, Olen poked at a stick, letting loose a rush of sparks. He sighed and grumbled to himself, then when Portia was tending to the horses, he whispered to Livet. "We are travelling too slowly."

Livet looked up at him and curled her lip in a look that both sympathized and implied helplessness. "There weren't many wagons goin' north that weren't full of soldiers," she answered. "I had to choose the one I did. I'm fast enough when I've need to be, but when I'm walkin' a long ways, it's too hard on my leg and my back hurts. 'Sides, all the other folks going north looked like robbers."

Olen put his hand on Livet's shoulder and nodded. "She's nice. Pretty, even," he said of Portia. "It is faster than walking, but I'm just worried it's going to take too long to find Denn."

Livet frowned. "'Ow much farther from 'ere?"

"At this speed, we'll arrive in Greenplain tomorrow but maybe have to camp or take lodgings for another night. Two more days to Caphedra for us, at the least, but I suspect the ones that took Denn are there already."

Livet swallowed hard against a lump in her throat and turned her gaze back to the wood peelings. The slip of a tear trailed down her cheek. "In the mornin', I'll ask Portia t' hurry faster," she said sadly.

"Perhaps," Olen said, "We should part with her and try to purchase a fast horse when we reach Greenplain tomorrow."

"But neither of us are good riders," Livet pointed out, but Olen chose not to acknowledge.

At that moment, Portia re-emerged.

"I'm afraid I have less food to share than I thought," she said returning from the horses and wagon. "I found an apple tree back there, and we have a bit of dried biscuit, but I'm afraid there's no meat, my dears."

"I'm sure it'll see us through the night," Olen said, smiling placidly.

Livet was silent. Her gaze was toward the edge of their campsite, to where a brown rabbit had zig-zagged out of the brush and stopped, nose twitching, at the edge of the bushes. Livet tracked its gentle movements with her eyes, then, with a lick of her lips and a quick look toward Portia, she smiled and disappeared out of sight into the dark undergrowth.

The rabbit remained still, sniffing, and testing the air. It was looking at something that triggered its instinct to freeze in place. Olen waited for a tell-tale rustling or a flash of movement that might give away Livet's position. He could tell that Portia was mesmerized by the game too, both from curiosity and the thought of what might lead to a soon-to-be vanquished hunger. Olen kept vigilant.

What might it be looking at? Was there something else?

The rabbit's focus was to the fore, while Livet was sneaking up from behind. Whatever the rabbit saw was assuredly *not* the tiny huntress. Portia gently put a hand on Olen's arm, and she took his cue to be quiet and keep her wits sharp. If something—or *someone*—were there to startle the rabbit, it could be dangerous to them as well.

The rabbit continued its motionless vigil, staring at the far bushes. Then all of a sudden, and soundlessly, a pair of petite hands closed around its throat. Livet appeared from behind, where she had been imperceptible all this time. She seized the bunny and wrung its neck.

"Incredible," whispered Portia.

"Livet's got a few tricks," he commented. "She can be a sneaky one when she needs to be." Olen could tell she was impressed with Livet's uncanny ability to best even the wariest of nature's furry denizens.

At its core, the hiding and sneaking he had grown used to. He knew of the girl's talent to disappear in a heartbeat or move silently like a beam of moonlight when she wanted to, despite the limp. When Olen first met Livet, it took some getting used to. How the sudden emergence of her big, dark eyes and sallow face could startle you, appearing from nowhere—it was sometimes as if she wasn't living in Ayren's cottage, so much as haunting it. For a soldier tasked with upholding the king's laws, it was an unsettling reminder of how a young Livet must have managed to transgress them, relying on such skulking and cunning to survive the alleys of Lanstad. He begrudgingly granted her absolution, of course. His own childhood was spent picking pockets and snatching coins under threat in the slums of Faralley and could be recollected no more honourably.

"It was more than a trick," Portia said, taking exception. "The rabbit thought it *saw* something. Nothing was there, but somehow it was convinced there was something in the bush—and that almost convinced us too."

That was too ridiculous for Olen to speculate on, but this *was* an exceptional demonstration. Olen was left scratching his head over how she pulled it off. He had seen an entertainer casting his voice around a room once, and maybe Livet had done the same, audible to the rabbit, but not to them. Regardless, this feat was of a higher order. Portia was acting as if Livet had cast some kind of spell, and the thought was making Olen's head pain him again. He pushed it from his mind and filled the aching cavern of his head with visions of only rabbit and rest.

Returning to a spot next to the fire, Livet brought her prey back and retrieved the small blade again from Olen's pack with which to skin and clean it for supper. "You like rabbit?" she asked.

"Superb," Portia said. "Tell me, what did you do to befuddle that poor beast?"

Livet smirked. "They're easy to fool."

"You wouldn't do that to me, would you?" Portia poked in jest, her cheeriness returning to overcome her wide-eyed curiosity.

"Just rabbits," Livet said.

Then, at that very moment, another rabbit appeared close to where the first had emerged from its trail.

Olen's eyes widened. "Luck is ours tonight," he whispered, his mouth watering at the sight.

Portia glanced over to where the second one sat, cottony tail in the air and exploring the grass of the clearing. The fading light certainly made it harder to see, but it was more observable when they stared intently.

"There's nothing there," Livet said, giggling smugly.

"What?" Olen asked, letting go of his brief excitement and settling back onto the log. The soreness of his head was now throbbing. He supposed that was the reason he was seeing things.

Portia's face soured. "A phantom," she said. "Likely the very ghost of our poor dinner!"

"Just a trick," Livet said, humbly.

"It's magic. You should call it what it is," Portia said, and with that, her merry countenance remained but she paid much more careful notice of Livet for the rest of the night.

Morning brought another brilliant, sunlit day for travel. Dew steamed upward off the wagon's canopy and cicadas resumed their buzzing, brashly encouraging them to get moving. Olen scattered the remnant bones of the roasted rabbit into the forest for the scavengers to feast on and circled round their site to ensure everything they brought was accounted for before leaving. The horses were now watered, fed, and rested. Livet returned from scouting the road and reported it clear. It was too early for wayfarers to have made it this far outside the towns and the early rising farmers would already be behind them, setting out southward to Falbeth's markets.

Portia was bent over, tightening a rope around her bedroll when she called out to Livet to come over. While she pulled at the knot, she wanted to draw Livet's attention to something she had been keeping tucked away. Olen listened in from the other side of the wagon.

"Tell me, Livet," she said, drawing out a piece of folded parchment. "Can you read this?"

Livet took the paper in her hand and unfolded it. It was a letter, but the script was arranged in an odd melange with other symbols squeezed in. She stood up and walked over to where the sunlight shone down more brightly, her eyes scanning the lines of text. She spent a long moment studying it.

"No," she said, sadly.

"You've not seen anything like this?" Portia reconfirmed. "You seemed to take a long time just to determine that you've never encountered it before."

"I am very sure it can be read by the person it was sent to," Livet said sharply. Then she walked over to where Olen was hoisting his pack onto the wagon and hovered near him until they were ready to depart. Portia said nothing further but continued to cast concerned glances toward the young girl who was now shielded in a sombre reticence.

As the day established itself, the dew of the morning gave way to more dust and the hoofbeats of the horses clopped more noisily again. Green pastures of clover and ryegrass undulated as the woodland flora retreated. Soon only the odd shady tree remained, standing here and there in the fields like emissaries playfully advocating for a return to the wild.

Olen struggled to bring up the subject of going separate ways but wished to inform Portia before they reached Greenplain. With Livet resting in the back, tired from an early morning watch shift at the campsite, Olen engaged their driver directly.

"I fear that we may have failed our friend, Portia."

She tried to console him. "I am sure the young man is resilient. I am confident that you will see him again."

"Nonetheless," Olen said, "I think Livet and I should look to procure a faster steed once we get to Greenplain. I am sure we could find a swift pony at the garrison there, or at the markets."

She remained silent and didn't overtly acknowledge what he had said.

"I appreciate—*we* appreciate you bringing us this far."

With a smile, she finally responded. "I've enjoyed and benefitted from your company also. I'd like you to take back your money and if you wish. Use it toward your own mount. I'll take you to the stables when we get there."

"Thank you," Olen said appreciatively, albeit regretfully.

"But Olen," Portia added, "Your friend—when you see him— do advise him to be cautious. I foresee that he is a part of a plan that is not his own. He is soon to confront one who will condemn him, and by whose actions your friend will know death."

She waited for Olen's reaction, her hand rising to her chest as she breathed. Her eyes closed thoughtfully.

Olen paused to ponder. "What would ever give you reason to say such things?"

"Livet's not the only one with gifts. I have a habit of seeing more than others," she iterated.

Olen's mouth twisted in both skepticism and amusement. "Is that so? Some kind of fortune teller, are you?"

"I wouldn't say that out loud," she said. "But my intuition keeps me out of trouble, most of the time. It led me to the two of you after all. I'd planned to leave Falbeth a lot earlier that day, but happenstance encouraged me to stay a bit longer... and it's a good thing that we met, I think." Portia cast a look over her shoulder to the back of the wagon where Livet rested. Her face was brighter when she faced forward again.

"I am a devout believer in luck, Portia, but I do not put much of my faith into thinking that the design of a man's life can be prescribed such certainty. My destiny was to find death on the streets of Faralley. That was the curse that befell my brother, my father, and the whole of my kin, but I took it upon myself to leave that place and find a new future. So, while they are mouldering in the dirt, I stand here now. I am the last of the Kierks of Westriver and a survivor of my own making."

❖   ❖   ❖

At midday, as they reached the edge of Greenplain, horses in herds of chestnuts and greys, rusty reds and midnight blacks, roamed the verdant hills, all galloping, grazing, and greeting each other with springtime flair. The traffic picked up on the roads as well, with horses neighing as they were led along the roadside. Riders urged their steeds to shift sidelong and allow the jangling, clinking wagon to pass. Their loud commands and complaints woke Livet from her rest. Olen saw her emerge from under the canvas cover and pull herself up onto the bench between him and Portia.

"Olen tells me you'll be leaving me soon," Portia said to Livet.

With a deep breath, she sighed and said, "Yes, we must hurry. I'm sorry to say goodbye."

"That's alright. I am confident we'll meet again. Just promise me something?" She placed her hand on the girl's shoulder and Livet cocked her head attentively. "Don't be so quick to show off," she warned.

Livet's face grew serious, but she appeared to heed the advice and pledged her compliance with a soft nodding.

Portia reiterated. "In Caphedra, like in Lanstad, the curates are always watching—even more so now, on account of how the king is said to have died."

"What do you mean?" Livet asked.

Olen also perked up his attention and interrupted, declaring hesitantly, "He was stabbed—stabbed in a bathhouse."

"Yes," said Portia. "But they're not sure in Caphedra if it happened before or after he was boiled in his own bathwater. They suspect an unnatural power at play."

"Absurd! They're spreading rumours. No doubt to pardon the failure of his guards," Olen said. "Simple folks, like us, have too much slack in our imaginings in days like these. I was a boy when the king's brother, King Hamrin, was crushed under a stone the temple builders let slip. The same kinds of rumours spread around back then too."

"Nevertheless, they have begun an official hunt for those who demonstrate an ability to twist nature beyond that of the norm. The Faith of the Pillars is searching out anyone they can discover to accuse of the act. The king's guards, too, in fear of the same, have flocked to declare their loyalty to the Lord Marshal and they're upending the stones on the streets to seek out culprits themselves. It's not a time to flaunt any marvellous witchcraft or enchantments."

Livet replied to Portia's cautioning directly. "I know how to hide," she confided. "I had time to learn that much."

Greenplain was blessed with some of the most fertile soil in the land and its produce is what primarily sustained the capital. In its south, independent landowners held much of the land, each with legions of indentured labourers to work the fields.

However, it was horses that Greenplain was most famous for. In its central vales, King Ramis's surveyors marked the land for pasture so that the king could raise and outfit a cavalry force during the early years of his reign, with which to spread his power farther and faster into the outlying cities he coveted. Greenplain Garrison became the provider for all equestrian requirements, and it was here that the cavalry schools took uncommonly skilled or well-connected soldiers and spun them into expert riders, like those of Falbeth's 12th, with whom Denn had ridden.

Stationed here to guard the garrison, its stables and grassy ranges, were the cavaliers of the 6th Mounted Infantry. The horsemen's swallow-tailed guidon of a golden lance on azure flapped from above the gates, high above those men who carried the simple green shield of Greenplain's own company of infanteers. Status was reserved for those who rode on four legs, not those who walked on two.

The garrison was busy today. The great portcullis was raised, and hostlers were leading mounts of all breeds and bearing along the dusty road leading inside. Olen pointed at one of the stablemen along the road, signalling for Portia to guide her carthorses nearer. Once they had gotten close, he forced a friendly smile then called out, "Good day, sir!"

The man was dressed in faded blue with heavy boots caked in dry muck. He kept trudging forward with his hand on his horse's lead, but replied with a gruff, "Hullo."

"You plan to sell that horse to the garrison?" Olen asked. "I'm looking for one myself. You've got a price you're asking?"

"He's already sold."

"Shame. Are all these horses spoken for then?" Olen said, pointing to all the other animals that were congesting the road to the garrison. Sitting high up in the wagon, they could see dozens being herded toward the fortification.

The man absentmindedly spit into the grass at the side of the road. "Aye," he said. "Some were even sold twice," he laughed.

"What do you mean?" Olen asked.

"Well, the commander usually buys for the garrison each month, but this time he was late. We had a visit from Lord Larsen's son, out of Kramwen, a week before, and he offered to buy the lot!"

"So, these horses belong to him?"

"Nope. The commander ordered all the horses into the garrison, under the threat that he'd sooner drive a lance through them than let any of them go to the Larsens."

Olen looked skeptical. "He can't keep them all locked up in there. Where are they all going that he can't spare horses?"

"I'm sure they have their plans," said the man.

"Taking them to Lord Marshal Myrhic then? The Faith?"

"To High Constable Durrow, at least. He'll decide who gets 'em, if and when he decides to stop sitting side-saddle and throws his own spurs into the fight." The old horse trader hacked and forcefully spit again. "You might see them back on the market again one day though. Some are saying Durrow's too old to fight anymore." With a lopsided smirk, he added, "and I think the old constable agrees with them."

Olen's mind raced to calculate the balance of forces between the growing Faith and the splintering army. "How soon do you think war will come?" he asked.

"Any day," was the ominous answer.

Having spent last night camped out, there was less of a wish to do the same now that they had reached the town and evening was falling. Fated to remain together longer, Portia found a stable in which they could quarter their horses for a fee, while next door lay a small tavern with rooms to let. For safety and economy, they decided to share a room, but only Portia and Livet were quick to take advantage of the rest it offered. Olen begged for a temporary leave of absence, having a desire to spend a bit more time to himself downstairs.

The Trough and Barrel was the alehouse's name. It was mostly catering to travellers and a few farmers, who brought the smell of the barn inside with them to compete with the stench of stale, spilled beer, and Applewood smoke. It was not a large establishment by any stretch, but long communal wooden tables spanned its length and allowed for a good number of patrons should they be in attendance. Fewer than a dozen people were there at the height of this night, however, and they dwindled away over the several hours that Olen remained in place, emptying repeated glasses, and washing down strips of salted beef, served up by a stout, old bartender. While he drank quickly, he chewed slowly, so that he could eavesdrop on the conversations around the room.

Of particular interest to Olen was a table where three men sat. There were two soldiers supping with another companion. The soldiers belonged to Lord Vlass and, although their telltale shields were not in easy view nearby, they wore the same studded leather tunics and blue-grey cloaks that Olen was used to seeing on his visits to Fal Ghreeg garrison. Indeed, one of the men, who sported the trappings of a captain, was painfully recognizable but Olen had forgotten his name.

The captain sat at the centre of the table. He had deep-set eyes under a thick cleft brow that gave him an angry, almost subhuman countenance. On his right cheek was a distinguishing dark mole while scars scored his left. He had the look of having been less recruited off the street than having been snagged by a rusty hook and drug out of the bog itself.

His mates leaned in close and were whispering. The accompanying soldier, a young, simple-faced man, seemed only half there, leaning forward on both forearms with a look of fatigue. The other man, however, was more relaxed. He would raise his hand to his face when he spoke, half cupping his mouth to veil his lips. As he did, however, his cloak would slip apart slightly and allow Olen a view of the man's fancy blue doublet. He was a curate of the Faith of the Pillars, and the elaborateness of the garment implied he held elevated status.

Olen now remembered the man's name was Pryst—Captain Edil Pryst—and that he'd been there as a raw and untested soldier the night they stormed the keep at Fal Ghreeg and dispatched Lord Farn Rhowan, seventeen years ago. Even then, despite his inexperience at the time, he had that unforgettable mean and beastly look to him.

Out of the blue, there was a hand on Olen's shoulder. It was familiar and warm, but relentlessly firm.

"I know what you are going to do," said Portia. "It woke me up, so I came here to stop you from doing it."

"Stop me from what?" Olen interrogated her, not hiding his confusion.

"Let those men pass undisturbed," she commanded. "You won't get your money back from them and it will only cause problems later on." Portia kept her eyes on Olen and stared him down. He had given no indication of his interest in Pryst or that this unhandsome man might be tied to his lost wages, but somehow Portia was aware.

Olen gave a sound between a grunt and a growl. "How do you know I won't get my money back? I should be owed at least this one last chance to force them to make good. That ugly lout knows who took my money—if it weren't him in the first place."

Just then he heard Pryst's brutish voice chiding him from across the room.

"Look, boys! That old fella's being called home, it seems. S'ppose she'll have him by the ear next!" The other soldier sat up straighter to look over at Olen and Portia, then laughed at the captain's joke.

Pryst sneered, "Not bad looking I'd say, although, she's a little old. You should offer to go with her, Bairn, and let that sad bastard finish his drink," he said to the other soldier. Then he sat back proud of his jibe.

Olen stood up and removed Portia's hand from his shoulder. She continued to glare at him, but Olen dismissed her, turning to the far table.

"Tell me," he began. "Was it you who stole from King Ramis's soldiers at Fal Ghreeg, or did you order your men to do it?" Purposefully invoking the king's name buoyed his authority and drew a line that most retainer troops like Lord Vlass's were instinctively fearful to cross. Any hint of insubordination from a man serving a vassal—or worse, outright criminality on their part—would see that soldier's entire company bloodily wiped out by the king's men within a fortnight, and the lord most likely removed and forced to indignantly try and claw his way back into favour.

That was in the old days, of course. Now, the accusation of thievery brought the men to their feet. At the corners of the tavern, several thick-handed horse farmers also took notice and braced for trouble, in case they were called on to eject an instigator. But while appearing capable of easily manhandling Percherons, none of them looked eager to tangle with professional soldiers. The conversations in the room halted, capped off by the sound of scraping chair legs and thuds from tankards being lowered.

Captain Pryst stood up and pushed the curate out of the way into a darker corner of the back wall. The other soldier, Bairn, was now wide awake and backing up his superior officer.

"I think," Pryst began, "that it's time all of you toe-kissers had better run off and hide behind the walls of Caphedra. You should either leave this soil for good or find yourself lying in facedown in it!"

Olen was immediately out of his chair and closing upon them. His jaw was clenched, and he hardened his stare, making Pryst step back from the sheer menace of his advance. But then, like a crooked-faced badger, the captain caught himself and stamped his foot down to dig in and square off.

Despite there being no room to draw swords without risking a slice into one of the sidelined patrons, Bairn reached into his cloak and produced a dirk. He stepped forward to meet Olen's rush ahead of his captain. In an instant, however, Olen overpowered him, wrenching the aggressor's arm violently so that the man instinctively dropped his blade.

Now raging, Olen had almost come within reach of Pryst, but Portia advanced more quickly and dangerously. She had Pryst in firm grip around his bicep, surprising the Lanstader, who turned his head to face her. Their eyes locked.

"She's a little old, a little old..." Portia whispered at him, mocking his earlier insult but in an almost rhythmic way that rippled over the man's face as if it penetrated his thoughts. "She's a little old. I see what is...what always is and forever becomes. What is old? Maybe you are a little old?"

"What are you saying?" Captain Pryst said in a voice that sounded even more of a whisper, somewhat raspy and tinged with unnerving anxiety. His fist unclenched partly, but his fingers remained curled, talon-like, and shaking in the air. With each inhale, his chest took in less breath and lost its bold puffery. He stooped and strained his neck to keep staring at her, then sat back down. He swallowed and looked at his hands. Slowly, perhaps painfully, he opened them and closed them.

"A little old, a little old," Portia continued saying to him, almost inaudibly to the others were it not for the silence that now overcame the tavern.

"Enchantment! You're the Chieftain's Daughter!" said the curate, who stepped in with his eyes on Portia and his hand clutching Pryst's other arm to haul him away from the table. In a pleading voice, he said, "Stand up, Captain, please. Come with me."

Pryst, Bairn, and the curate spoke no more, but they exited the tavern slowly and without further disturbance. Olen's ire was extinguished, replaced with confounded awe over what Portia had done.

When they were alone again, Portia leaned toward Olen with regret and quietly told him, "I'm sorry. I should've killed that priest."

CHAPTER 6

A Concern of the Family

D enn awoke in his own bed. His eyes opened and he groggily recognized the scrolled mouldings, the iron-framed glass window, the cherry bed frame, and the sturdy oaken desk where he had completed his lessons as a boy. The light was coming in through the glazed windowpanes and its familiar southwest facing told him it was mid-afternoon. He did not know if it had been hours or days since the tormenting events transpired that brought him back to his childhood world. The bedsheets were crisp and tight, but during his slumber, he had managed to stain them red with the seepage of blood.

On his right, near the door, someone had placed a red candle which stood burning as a prayer to the Pillar of Resiliency. The devout professed that it conferred the energy of the flame to the strengthening of a loved one's constitution and fed the inner will amidst recovery. In appearance, it was richly coloured and moulded to resemble its namesake, a colossal column which thrust grandly into the sky in the northwest corner of Caphedra's central temple, balanced by its three peers. It was identical to those his brother Lehn used to make when he had first entered the curacy and was tasked as a chandler.

Denn tried to shift in the bed, but his frail ribs threatened to collapse and the bruises over his body complicated every motion. Half-sitting, he found a pose in which it did not hurt to breathe, so he inhaled deeply and steadily, the fresh intake helping to clear his head. Tensing, he held his breath against the pain and made an effort to extend his arm toward a silver platter of food on a table at his bedside. Someone had brought him breakfast—or supper.

There was a tiny golden bell there too. Denn remembered how, when he was growing up, his mother would place it beside his bed during times of sickness to summon one of the chambermaids to his assistance.

He tried taking bites from a slab of pork, but his jaw was sore and tender. Swiping his tongue side-to-side in his mouth, he reassured himself that his teeth were–thankfully–all still there. The bread was a chore too, but he could break parts off to soak in water and then, with effort, swallow them. That subdued the pangs coming from the void in his stomach and he felt much better.

A housefly buzzed past him then found the open window. Of all the comforts of his convalescence, this struck him with the true realization of where he was, and that this was the first time in countless ages that he could sleep without mosquitoes tormenting him.

But he wouldn't let that, nor any reacquainting with contentment and luxuries, soften him. As soon as he could stand to ride, he needed to get back to his post. Constable Hannellin would be spitting mad, and no doubt accuse him of loafing if he knew where Denn was right now—regardless of the circumstances. He would probably lament that Denn's ordeal hadn't gone on longer to really toughen him up. That man had never liked him and Denn seethed with resentment every time the man reminded him of his inherent failings.

If it meant getting upright sooner, he might as well try the little bell. His boots were by the door, and a fresh shirt and tunic hung over a bed pole. He would call the chambermaid to help him rouse and clothe himself, then try out his feet to see if they could transport him out into the hall and down the stairs.

He picked it up in two fingers and it made it jingle. He felt guilty for having to ask for help, but the deed was done, and footsteps were already coming up the hallway. The latch on his bedroom door sank down with a clunk and the portal was pushed inward, opening softly.

"Brother?" inquired a tender, hopeful voice as a pair of ocean-blue eyes gazed in at him from above the thin smiling lips of Denn's cherished sister.

"Serenn?"

"I heard you awaken and wanted to be the first to steal your attention!"

"Where's the maid?" Denn asked.

"Not working today," she said, moving forward gracefully to the bedside. With a sweep and tuck of her satiny dress, she alighted beside him on the bed. Delicate muscles drew her face tight in sympathy.

From a spot near Denn's bedside she produced a moist sponge and softly gave his cheek a wipe. "Those bruises won't wash off, I'm afraid."

"Yael and his boys saved me," Denn said in his first attempt toward remembering it all.

"Yes," Serenn said. "A man came to the door looking for money. He said that they'd taken you and threatened dreadful things if we didn't pay him. But as soon as he made his demands, Yael seized upon him. I turned away, so I didn't see what happened next, but I've been trying to clean the mess in the hall for days."

"But... the maid?"

Serenn abruptly shook her head and continued, "Your horse is here too. Yael saw to that. I've heard her neighing outside."

"Naobe is safe?" Denn excitedly confirmed.

She nodded, "Yes. The groom is checking her over."

Now it was even more critical to see his health restored, at least enough so that he could get downstairs and out to the stable. Naobe was more than just a steed. Until he met Livet, Olen, and Ayren, she had been his closest companion during the months of contemplation and emotional solitude that followed his brother's death.

"They found me so quickly," Denn observed.

"You know that Yael has eyes and ears all over this city," said Serenn, looking out the window as she spoke.

"Indeed," said Denn, again appreciative of the man who had ruthlessly dispatched his abductors. Yael had been recruited by Denn's father from a position as a senior armsman and reeve under Feryl Morea, Master Prefect of the Caphedran Commandery. A considerable sum lured him into Wellum family service, but it paid off time and time again. Yael's insight and connections generated heaps of gold for the Wellum family in the years since and—more importantly—kept it safe and accounted for. Denn and his brothers had always held him in a bit of awe.

"I've missed you so much. Mother is so cold, and Father is preoccupied. Lehn doesn't come around hardly at all, and when he does, it's on Faith business."

"That's too bad," Denn said. He lowered his eyes and thought of his younger brother, whom he had irresponsibly left behind when he headed off to rejoin the cavalry. From letters Serenn sent him, Denn heard how Lehn came to redouble his commitment to his studies and immerse himself into the Faith of the Pillars. It helped to suffocate the pain of losing Hann, he had said. Not long after, he had mostly stopped coming by the manor. Perhaps this filled the space Denn left behind, as Lehn came to reside full time in the temple and Serenn boasted that their brother's fervent dedication was being rewarded with the attentions of no lesser than the High Precept, Averin Golmarra.

Serenn set the sponge back in its wooden bowl and moved it to the side. "You will eat more?" she asked.

Denn grunted and pulled himself up. "No. Let me up. I wish to see to my horse."

"Oh, Denn!" Serenn began to try reasoning with him to stay at rest, but he'd been in bed long enough. "Can I at least call Trin to help you down the stairs?"

"No. Just have the maid clean up a bit and I'll see you shortly."

Serenn looked at the dishevelled bed and accumulation of uneaten dishes in the room and sighed. She rose and tugged on the draperies to expose more light into the room.

Everything hurt. Denn grasped the bed rails and pulled himself up. Once on his feet, he paused while the dizziness in his head abated, then stuffed his feet one by one into the leather boots by the door. Lastly, he pocketed a couple of firm, round apples from a serving tray that lay upon a small trestle desk along the wall near the door.

"Is father home now?" he ventured to ask.

"Events in the city have kept him away most every day and night," Serenn said with a tone of lament. "You don't have to worry."

Denn had never realized how narrow the hallways of his family manor were. Maybe it was the skewed recollection of childhood perspective, for which everything eventually grew to seem smaller, but part of it was, no doubt, his professional acclimation to the broad, stone passages of garrisons where several outfitted troops could march abreast.

As he pulled himself along and ambled forward, he sought support by running his fingers along the piece of trim that divided the plastered upper wall from the stained panel wood below. While the quietness of the house was altogether typical, Denn noticed his fingers were picking up a layer of dust, which was very much out of the normal state of things. He drew his hand back uncomfortably when it bumped into the next door frame in the corridor. The door was closed. Beyond it was the room that had belonged to his brother Hann. He stared reverently for a moment, remembering the devastation that followed from the last time he had turned the knob and entered uninvited.

It had been springtime—a little earlier in the year than now—and Denn had finally managed to be granted leave to visit his family. Having written often, Hann's letters had begun alluding to an explosion of troubles that had been brewing between him and their parents. Denn had wanted to travel home to show love, gratitude, and support for his brother who, unfairly by birth, bore the weight of being the eldest son of a notoriously demanding lineage.

Denn had hoped to surprise Hann by bursting open that door as soon as he'd arrived, but when he did, it was the sight of his brother's ultimate, irrevocable act that caused him to recoil in shock. In his memory, Denn almost floated across the floor in that moment. He grabbed Hann's swaying form tightly against his shoulder with one hand, then with the other drew and arced his steel sabre overhead to slice the rope. It wasn't a clean cut, but Hann's weight strained the fibres, and they gave way nonetheless. Denn had miscalculated again. He couldn't hold up his brother, and he crumpled under the mass of the falling body, outwardly and inwardly.

Hann must have been there for hours, without anyone bothering to look in. Denn's bawling shook the household to awareness, however. Lehn pulled Serenn, the youngest of the siblings, back from witnessing the scene. Their mother screamed and wept. Her ceaseless anguish then and in the weeks to follow helped absolve her of some complicity, but not all.

It was the unaffected, frigid proclamations of guiltlessness from their father, however, that hardened Denn's soul against that man who cared so little for his offspring. This was the man who lashed his own sons with leather straps when they displeased him, until they were too sore to be scared; the man who meticulously appraised them based on their every shortcoming and demanded better should they wish to carry his name. He bragged he would slice off any hint of weakness, like an orchardist prunes peach trees, but each cut eroded his sons by just a little more each time, his efforts more akin to clipping coins. Denn angrily shook off his father's attempt to immediately saddle him with his brother's burden. There was no doubting his father's anger, but this time Denn showed how determined he could be and responded with an even greater wrath, unprecedented in this house. They parted in irredeemable hatred.

Yet now, his father cared enough to send Yael out in Denn's defence. There was no telling if the close-fisted old merchant would have paid the ransom, but he did send help immediately as if something had finally engaged a paternal sense of obligation to one of his sons. Had his father had some change of heart that led him to act to protect his errant brood? Maybe the events of the kingdom had unsettled him. Perhaps it was old age. Regardless of his motive, Denn had to recognize something he detested. He now owed a debt to his father.

He wondered, *what would Hann have done?*

Still standing in the corridor, devoured by memory, Denn began reaching out to try the knob and open the door. But as his fingers began to extend, his throat contracted. A lump formed, against which he swallowed hard, and he withdrew his hand. The time to visit his brother's chamber would be later.

Throughout the manor, Denn saw signs of neglect. The ashes in the fireplace overflowed and soot darkened the surrounding walls. The expensive glass windows of the parlour, brought in from Lanstad, were smudged and dirty in places, diffusing the warm sunlight, while along their bottoms were the husks of dead houseflies left to their mortal slumber. In a final condemnation, tracks of mud could be seen along the edges of the room in all the places not deceptively hidden by the thick varicoloured rugs which were spread across the centre of the floor.

"I'm sorry," said a voice escaping from a dark alcove. "We sent the maid away."

A slender and pale feminine figure rose and approached him. Denn stiffened, and bracing against the inescapable pains in his ribs and chest, attempted to stand straight to receive her anticipated embrace.

"Mother," he said.

Gently, with arms around him, Esta Wellum kissed his cheek and said, "I am so happy you are home."

As she walked into the light, he saw the shadows from creases on her face that had not been so noticeable before. He observed that her hair was a bit longer, its curls tied back and held up under an ancestrally-gifted golden circlet bejewelled with topaz. While the gem reflected the parlour light softly, the naturally vivid red tone of her locks was now less pronounced, bleaching perceptibly toward a ruddy ochre hue.

"We've put out a notice for a new girl to tend the house, but your father has been very particular. He sent the last one away, thinking that she was spying for Neraine Toloss."

"Was she?" Denn interrogated.

"Well, it's something Neraine *would* do if she had the chance. The girl was far too pretty for it to be believable that she was forced to make her way in life as a *house servant.*"

"So, Serenn has been cleaning?"

"Yes. I think she's a bit overwhelmed, to be truthful. Thankfully, your father has kept the scullery maid on. Supper should be served shortly if you feel like eating. I would imagine you are famished."

Denn nodded. "Yes. But I'm off to the stables first. Serenn says Yael retrieved my horse."

"Indeed," Esta said. "One of his men brought it by just before they left here looking for you."

"I thought Yael had brought her here himself. He's the one that knows her markings."

"I'm pretty sure it was that shifty young fellow with the knotted hair who arrived with her," Esta maintained. "Your horse is out with Trin now. He's quite good with animals but says she's been quite antsy not having you around. I expect that seeing you up and about will calm her restlessness."

Denn nodded. "Yael examined her, at least, yes?"

"Rest certain. It's definitely your horse, dear... and she's fine," Esta reassured. "You needn't worry."

Stepping out into the courtyard, Denn's eyes laboured to adjust to the bright sunlight of mid-afternoon. Steadier on his feet now, he walked back the dusty path to the stables and carriage house on the other side of the property. The whole area was walled off from the city and only the peaks of the surrounding Castleside homes and the spires of the citadel were visible. At the back of the barn, an old man in tattered rags was shovelling manure from the stables into a wheelbarrow. Beside him, swinging a pitchfork into a stack of fresh hay from atop a wagon, was the servant-come-swordsman, Trin, whom Denn recognized from the night he'd been rescued.

Trin was younger than Denn. He had fair hair and thin features set atop a disproportionately solid chin. He wasn't overly muscular, but the way he stood atop the wagon suggested he had excellent agility. He stopped working the haystack when he saw Denn approaching, plunged the tool down deep into the wagonload, planting it firmly, and wiped sweat from his forehead.

"Good to see you fit and well, sir," he smiled.

"And it's good to see you here, that I may convey my thanks, Trin." Denn reached into his pocket to assure himself that the apples were still there. "Naobe's inside?"

"Yes, sir. I just brought her in a short while ago. Sun was getting high, and I didn't want to tease her appetite with all this hay too soon," he laughed. "She'll be happy to see you!"

Entering the stable, his eyes now had to adapt to the dark. The sweet smell of fresh hay caught his nose and a fly zipped past. As he pushed the door open further, a wiry grey cat leapt from behind, fleeing out of the way as Denn intruded rudely upon its nap.

An excited thumping against the old wooden boards alerted Denn to the stall where his steed was stabled.

"Naobe!" Denn exclaimed.

The great charger stomped her solid hooves against the floorboards. She snuffed and snorted enough to knock clumps of dirt from the walls and eject sawdust across the barn floor.

He ran his hand along her neck then produced the apples, which she heartily enjoyed.

"It's good to see you, girl," he said more softly. "I'm alright, too." He rummaged the next stall to find a brush with which to work her coat. "We'll both be out of here and back to our post very soon. I promise." He stroked her and laughed, "Don't get too used to the city. The mosquitoes in the swamp miss us terribly, I bet."

It took a little time for Naobe to calm down. When Denn's hand and arm tired, he sat down on a barrel within Naobe's view and continued to soothe her with conversation until at long last content that he had his partner back and she was healthy and happy. He rose, gave a quick inspection of the bridle hanging beside her and made a promise to look in on her again in a few hours.

Naobe whinnied as he rose. He stroked her mane one last time, then stooped and patted the grey cat who'd since returned. He securely latched the stable door with a thick board and made his way back across the walled yard to the manor house. With luck, a tack shop might be open where he could acquire a new saddle and the two of them would be able to embark in the morning, back to the Fals.

He was a few steps short of the entrance when Serenn's voice called out from one of the windows.

"Denn! Come in. We have company. Lehn is here. He had no idea you were home!"

Denn mused at the good fortune that his brother had saved him the effort of visiting the temple. With Lehn coming to the manor instead, Denn could satisfy the familial obligations that much quicker and more comfortably.

Both sister and mother had invited Lehn in, and they each took up their own places in the parlour to observe. Serenn was reclined on a settee, acting witness to the two brothers' reunion. But Esta appeared more concerned. As Denn made his way to the parlour, he heard her mutter something about 'such matters' being their father's interest and not a subject for her to be involved in. She turned as Denn entered, again embracing the older son sweetly and forcing a smile. "Supper will be soon." Turning to Lehn, she advised,

"You should toast your brother's fortunate return."

With that, she excused herself.

Lehn had grown since Denn saw him last. He'd always been tall, but now his face had matured. His chest had expanded more solidly to fill out the vibrant blue doublet he wore as a trained curate to the Faith of the Pillars, and now the garment was flecked and threaded with gold embroidery to make it even more lavish.

He had only ever partially resembled Denn and Hann, in that he had the same light blonde hair, inherited from their father, Phon. More atypically to the lineage, his eyes were small, yet nonetheless striking. They sat back under a brow line that suggested a severe and humourless personality. People said he got that too from his father's side, and the odd portrait in the mezzanine of Phon's study displayed ancestors who grimly matched that visage. But now those tiny eyes widened in surprise to see his remaining older brother standing before him.

Lehn glanced over Denn's wounds and bruises, commenting, "I didn't think they had much trouble in the southeast. Should I assume Falbeth is a rougher town than they've let on?"

"I was ambushed," Denn said, minimizing the details of how he actually came to Caphedra. But honesty got the best of him, and he confided, "They said I was to be ransomed, but my persecutors failed, and I am here now, ready to return to my post."

"You don't look ready," Lehn commented. "I'm surprised to see you. I thought father had disowned you—or was it the other way around?"

Serenn interjected with a disapproving cough. "Lehn is here on business."

"Seeking donations for the temple again?" Denn asked.

"Yes, as a matter of fact, since Father's not been paying them."

"Really?" Denn asked with feigned bewilderment. "I thought our father was one of the strongest backers of the Faith in Caphedra." The Wellums had always made a show of pledging their payments to the Faith, as acts of outward devotion, though in private Phon cursed them as extortive.

"He kept up his respects until the king was gone," said Lehn, who then raised and displayed a rolled piece of parchment in his hand. "Now he is delinquent, and I've been asked directly by Precept

Golmarra to appeal to him one last time. Elsewise, I am to issue his Due, which would serve to wipe out his business dealings with all the faithful in this city."

"Differences with our father aside, I can't believe you would let the temple extort from your family at such a time! Think of the money—Wellum money—that's fed that beast of an order for generations."

Surely Lehn must be picking up on the neglect and austerity of the family manor. Denn could not confirm his own suspicions about Wellum affairs but seeing the manner in which his brother made such unconditional demands awakened this realization. Although Lehn had remained behind in Caphedra when Denn left— or abandoned him—he too had turned his back on the family and their agonizing past. The Faith of the Pillars, hungry for wealth, must have eagerly offered him admittance. Now through the years, as evidenced by the luxuriousness of the attire he sported and the confidence with which he spoke, they had granted him greater respectability also.

Lehn lowered the parchment and with the soft tone of offering counsel, rebutted. "It's more important than ever before that Father prove his dedication to the Pillars. When Queen Ravon takes the throne, there will be an accounting for from amongst those that refused to support her... or the Faith. She is the eldest child of King Ramis. Of his heirs, she is the most greatly educated in the learnings of sages and the wisdom of our Paragons, and she has powerful supporters inside and outside of Caphedra. Her ascension is a certainty."

"You sound so secure in your religion's might, but Prince Ramid has Lord Marshal Myrhic, doesn't he? And the Marshal has the army."

This brought a stern look back to Lehn's face as he scoffed, "Myrhic has only stragglers, criminals, and deserters. The heart of the military remains in Caphedra, under our own lords and captains. More importantly, they are under Lord Chancellor Havel's expert provision. Their loyalty is assured because, unlike Myrhic's men, Havel's are supplied, fed, and paid regularly. Who do you think keeps the last vestiges of order in this city? Never mind weapons and steeds, Myrhic's men only ever eat if they sneak into the city to steal bread."

"But—," Denn began, then stopped. What if Yael was wrong and that his kidnappers had not stolen the golden tower clasp but were *actually* soldiers aligned with the Marshal. Loyalty to the army aside, was it wise to preach the virtues of men of such unmitigated violence and implied desperation?

"You're not being paid," Lehn stated bluntly. "I know where all the coin in the southeast is going, and it's not to any of the king's units. Not even to the honoured cavalry."

"Then to where? Mercenaries?" Denn asked.

"To allies we can count on to further the legitimate coronation of Ravon. There will be fighting, bloodshed, yes. You can guarantee it, and afterward, the Faith of the Pillars will see the most deserving sovereign take her father's throne."

Temporarily silenced while he deduced who those allies could be, Denn heard footsteps in the hall. Serenn appeared with a bottle of wine and two crystal goblets. In the height of conversation, Denn had not even noticed her slipping out of the room.

"Brought this from the cellar," she said, "Pour the wine yourselves. I'll be in the dining hall setting the places."

Denn sighed and gestured to Lehn to sit down beside him. He uncorked the bottle and poured the swirling, burgundy liquid into both glasses.

Lehn amiably accepted and raised his to toast. "To your wellbeing."

Somehow Denn questioned his brother's sincerity but responded in kind. "To the wellbeing of us all," he said.

The brothers each took their glass in hand and tipped back to drink. Denn was now cognizant of how perilously close the stability of the realm was to an inevitable clash. He still pondered over the identity of the lords who were coming out in support of the Pillars.

"You always wanted to be a leader of armed men," Lehn said. "Show leadership now. The Faith of the Pillars would embrace you and elevate you immediately."

"Why would they do that for me? Because I'm your brother?"

"You reflect all four of the virtues—the Pillars upon which all existence is built."

"Go on," Denn said indulgently, and Lehn obliged.

"You've demonstrated *Resiliency* in your recent adversity, but also in the rugged nature of your years under arms. Your descent from a long-honoured household and your contribution to renewing its martial traditions demonstrates the virtue of the *Heritage* pillar about you. *Wisdom* is a pillar that I have always attributed to you in admiration, my older brother, and it is one that you should rely upon now to realize the value in supporting Ravon as Queen. That leaves but one pillar which you may aspire to in time, I am sure."

The idle praise felt hollow. If any of them present here were wise, it was Serenn, who had managed to mellow the conversation with wine. Lehn was now speaking more conciliatorily, though still unmoved in his position. At least Denn was finally able to converse with the brother he had left behind and who had also moved on without him, or the family.

There was something else Denn observed. When Lehn spoke of the eldest princess by name, Denn could detect his brother's cultivated countenance soften, and it hinted at a familiarity beyond the devotion of duty. Lehn's voice lilted and lingered minutely but perceptibly on each syllable.

"I remember my studies. The last pillar is *Progeny,* and you are correct that I have none. But let me ask, has the Faith found you a wife yet?" Denn was cordial but careful.

Lehn's elusive eyes narrowed. "I have voiced my intention, but it is not yet endorsed."

It was subtle, but the query had reinserted a wedge of discomfort between them.

"There must be lots of suitably faithful women serving the Pillars," Denn prodded.

"I serve the Queen only," Lehn declared. "Besides, while Father lives, we have the duty afforded to us as offspring. We sons must compensate for our father's shortcomings by showing that his obstinacy is inarguably asymptomatic of our respectable family, and not to be passed to the next in our lines."

"The Faith demands gold from its congregation. I don't have my own wealth, Lehn. No more than you do."

"The dedicated are only expected to contribute from what they have. Father controls the family wealth, so the expectation is for him to grace the temple with a suitable portion from his obvious surplus. You could publicly forfeit your claim to the family wealth and dedicate your sword. It could be repaid with the honour of commanding a multitude—not to mention the resources to feed them, arm them, and train them as you would know best. We welcome talented leaders."

"I only have a horse, Lehn. I don't even have a sword right now," Denn sighed, and reminded of his own fitful feelings of uselessness, grew dark and vulnerable. "Besides," he said, "my constable hates me. I have been awarded no merit nor given any rank. My name would carry no weight at the temple were it not for the influence of *your* position, and the *promise* of accessing our father's wealth."

"All the better. There is a benefit to having been a field soldier these past few months, and one who is not too tied to the politics of higher echelons. Incis Myrhic has been active in manipulating the loyalties of the troops garrisoned here in Caphedra, so now they lack reliability. We've had to direct the chancellor to stand most of them down or exile them and we've had to be wary with our hires. Even now, agents of Myrhic calling themselves 'Marshal's Men' are actively attempting to usurp the crown for that runt of a prince and undo the lawful order of the succession. It's set up a grand game for the Council of Caphedrans to amuse themselves with, such that around the temple it is called the *'Carnival of Caphedrans'* these days."

"I remember my captors praising the Marshal quite highly–venerating him almost. The two brothers, they specifically spoke of an oath to the Marshal."

Lehn grunted dismissively.

"They would be his agents then. Rogues and cutthroats all! The bunch of them gather at the Azure Bathhouse and make their pledge in the very pool in which the king took his last bath. Once Ravon is on the throne, we will move to seal off their sanctuary. The Marshal's Men erroneously believe sharing the remnants of the water will harden their souls, like quenched daggers in a smithy, or blood-tempered blades in a heathen sacrifice. Myrhic sees himself as the mortal hand of King Ramis but supports the prince only so far as he can manipulate the boy into acting the way he wants him to. If he truly believes he can heed his master's call from beyond the grave—well, I can assure you, he does not have that talent."

"Does anyone?" Denn responded, allowing himself a measured laugh. "Who did murder the king? Does anyone know?"

Lehn took a deep breath. "What rumours have reached you

in the countryside?"

"Very few," Denn said. "Tell me about what happened, if you know."

"Sorcerers outside of the sanction of the Faith," Lehn declared. "And all those accountable, when uncovered, shall be seen for the threat they represent, and we will expunge them."

"Are there many people capable of such feats?"

"No," Lehn said. "It is a lost art that is now mostly promulgated fraudulently by pretenders. However, there are potentially a few who deserve to be apprehended. They surface now and again. Our curates are always on the hunt and educated in the means to uncover them."

Denn saw his brother's gaze shift to look out the window at the city and he felt his brother's eyes burn with intensity as if he were watching for the culprits even now.

"Tell me, what did these sorcerers do to the king? Was it as terrible as they say?" Denn asked as if their ages had reversed, and he was seeking a bedtime story. In answer, his brother turned to look at him again and deigned to detail the specifics of the crime.

"The king had enemies. He sat on the throne squandering the wealth of the city on quests and conquests for years. He courted his demise through stubbornness, and it was not a simple death, though it was fitting. He perished in his bath. The water transfigured itself at the time that the old man died. One might say it boiled in aqueous rage, and that the water itself was the murder weapon."

"I am confused. The king drowned, then?" Denn asked.

Lehn leaned forward and spoke slowly and clearly, like a tutor to an ignorant student.

"An incantation turned the water itself against him—it boiled him until grotesquely blistered and red, and cooked the king in his bath like a shank of mutton before he could escape."

"Did these sorcerers bring down a bolt of lightning to heat it up or something? Swap his bath for a witch's cauldron, maybe?"

Lehn continued portioning out his knowledge in a tone of superiority that hinted at boastfulness. Beneath his thick brow, his eyes became sharp, and he spoke ominously.

"One with a strong will can encourage things to exaggerate their natural state or manifest ideas already in mind. What one wills can be made to be. Maybe the hot spring water actually became hotter and boiled... or perhaps the king's body was coerced to *convince itself* that the already hot water was scalding him, and his heart stopped from the shock. There is more than one way to do it. The potential for power is immense, and now the Faith of the Pillars has become very vigilant at the possibility of such powers being employed by apostates."

Denn swallowed hard and listened with concern as his brother, with alarming simplicity, described acts which Denn would have relegated to fairy tales or frightening campfire stories. Were these ideas part of the dogma of the Faith's elite? What world did Lehn now live in, that superstition and magic were commonplace perils of his vocation? The Faith had seemingly twisted his brother away from the fabric of reason and, more worryingly, deposited him into some manufactured panic that underpinned the Faith's policies of harassment and imprisonment for their enemies and detractors— or apostates, as they called them. For a moment he thought of men like Lehn torturing prisoners like Livet and he became repulsed. If she had suffered so terribly for her mundane trespasses on the streets, he shuddered at what cruelty they might inflict on those who waged war on the Faith's very beliefs or challenged them on a plane beyond this one.

"This is the work you do for the temple now?" Denn observed. "It is a change from melting beeswax for candles."

Lehn's face grew long and ominous. "We all must perform the duties prescribed to us. Today I act as Summoner and am tasked to ensure that you understand how important it is for you and me— and our father—to be on the right side of the divide by whatever time Myrhic brings Prince Ramid to the gates. Ergo, today my obligations have brought me to our family's manor with this final appeal."

With that, a bell rang from beyond the hallway.

"It seems Serenn is calling us to eat," said Denn. "You must at least have a duty to stay fed. Challenging apostates is best done on a full stomach, I would venture. Please come and sit in. It could be the last chance we have to dine together for some time, for I am to depart in the morning." Denn inhaled the odour from the dining room. "Smells like they've killed a chicken."

"Given the nature of my visit, it would be unseemly to dine here tonight on my father's food," Lehn said. "I've been far too social already."

"I'm sorry I left you behind when I ran off," Denn declared, fearing perhaps, that this would be his last chance to say so. "Hann would have been ashamed of me to abandon you and Serenn."

"In the end, it led to more auspicious consequences. You see, I am favoured by Centurra, the Paragon of good outcomes and possibility. I no longer grieve what was but seek only to guide what must be."

Then rising stoically, the curate announced, "I am assembling tonight's cohort to assist in a matter at Hamrin Square. You should join. Find a sword to bring from the armouries. The apostates promise to be out in numbers tonight. They must be driven out—or under—before the prince shows up at the gates. Ensure that you pass along my message to our father and tell him how urgent it is that he not likewise find himself in opposition to the Pillars. His time is already short."

"And what do I do if I run into a sorcerer?" Denn chanced to quip.

Lehn used his hands to press down wrinkles in his doublet, then he carefully wrapped his fingers around a small item hanging from his neck. At first, it looked like just a pendant, but then Denn saw it was a locket, with hinges on one side.

"If it were me, I'd kill them where they stand, then report the body to the temple for collection. Like all apostates, they pose a danger in their ambition to challenge the crown and the Pillars. They aim to poison this land."

Denn followed his brother out of the parlour, still noticeably weak on his feet but strengthening. With a creak from the great oak front door, Lehn slipped out of the house and down the great stone steps to the cobblestone avenue below. When he had wholly disappeared, Denn shut the door tight and turned the lock. With his limp still lingering, he began the trek to the dining hall.

He had not fully understood the zealousness of those who had once punished Livet, but now he felt intimately aware, and it both saddened and angered him that his own brother could be an accomplice to such vileness—even to the point of threatening his own family. But Denn had also sworn his loyalty to King Ramis, and Lehn's account of the frightening potency of the king's killer was a worrying revelation.

CHAPTER 7

The Chieftain's Daughter

"**I** admit that I have trouble following my own advice," Portia bemoaned to Livet.

Livet's companions had returned to their room above the tavern. They regretfully roused the sleeping girl to relay their dismay over the outcome of the night's altercation with the two Lanstad soldiers and the Pillars curate.

Sitting quietly, Olen's head slumped as Portia absorbed the fullness of blame. But when he tried to tell his account of the story to Livet, it was clear he hadn't fully realized the significance of making an enemy in the curacy. On the other hand, Livet sensed the severity right away, but said only, "I know Olen 'as a temper. It's probably good that you stopped 'im."

Portia elaborated further on the night's events from her perspective.

"When we first bedded down, I fell asleep so quickly. I think I was unused to the softness of a good bed," Portia recalled. "I slept almost immediately, and when I did, I slipped into a rather vivid dream, of the type that I often have."

With that, her eyes scanned Olen and Livet, as if pleading that they would not take her for mad, but Livet was one of the rare few who were predisposed to believe in odd talents.

"I dreamt of the men downstairs... and Olen. There was danger in the dream. I rushed there, right away, to try and stave off their meeting, but I was too late."

Olen frowned and, with a twinge of aggravation at Portia's over-protectiveness, dismissed the premonition. "It was just a dream. Had you done nothing and left me to my own handling of them, all would be well." He hiccoughed.

Portia shook her head, "No, you would have been dead."

Olen continued grumbling. He was fighting off exhaustion, having not yet slept, and Livet could see his eyes crossing and drifting as he tried to stay awake for the conversation.

Portia spoke directly to Livet now, continuing to embrace the young girl in confidence.

"My dreams are sculpted to show the future and the past, from a source that stems from far beyond just me. In my dream, it was the same man as in the tavern below, which is how I recognized him immediately when I entered."

"But now ya've gone and changed things, right?" Livet asked.

"The tellings of the dream still bode poorly," Portia said. "Olen's alive—as are we both—but when we reach Caphedra this man will have allies waiting."

"And then?" asked Livet.

"When we get to the city I will be sure to reach out to my people. They will protect me. In the meantime, this is not the first report of my travels to be sent to Averin Golmarra, but when he hears that I am not in the city it might mislead him of my whereabouts, for a short time. At least, I can hope."

"Wait," said Olen tiredly. "He called you a chieftain's daughter—and I know you are from the north, as you mentioned Porter's Run before. Whose daughter does that make you then?"

"My father is Barr Hart, Chieftain of Berryboughs. I am his daughter, Baressa."

"But—," Olen stammered, questioningly.

"I've travelled under the name Portia for more than a dozen years."

Olen pressed, "Your father is—*was* loyal to King Ramis, wasn't he?"

"He pledged fealty very early in the conquests when the king's men threatened to burn down our orchards and to run us through on their swords. Father sent me away for safety and then bowed his head to the crown. But Lord Kullen of Wodwarden continued up the Greyforest Road toward Nor'port. I was in Starpond and still a young girl—around your age, Livet—when the soldiers marched through and killed Chief Rudd Joran. Roderin, his son, took the surviving men and joined Earl Lorram in defending

Nor'port. They failed, but Roderin got his men out. I was old enough to join them—and *him*. We married that summer, just before I was captured by the Faith."

This part kept Livet's attention, not just in remembrance of her own incarceration by the king's men, but in the stories that Ayren told of Northport, around the hearth.

"The man I lived with, in the Fals, who took me in after Kell, 'e told me about Chief Lorram. Ayren fought with 'im at the Icemeadows."

"Yarr Lorram was a hard fighter and good man, and he lived many good years," Baressa said.

Livet had always enjoyed Ayren's tales, and she was just as intrigued to be in the presence of another of his people, who had carried the same fight. However, she could not ignore the concluding act from Baressa's account. Self-consciously, she laid her hand along the thigh of her damaged leg. "Tell me, what did they do to you when you were captured?"

"Not as much as they wished. I suppose they wanted me as a hostage, but as soon as we were admitted past the northeast gate of Caphedra, I slipped away."

"So simply?" Olen asked, disbelievingly.

"In no way unlike the fashion by which our dear Livet can slink away unseen when she wishes," Portia, now Baressa, said and smiled coyly at Livet. "I recognized some of your tricks."

The warmth in the way she said it convinced Livet to chance opening up. This woman, Baressa, was proving to be an apt bearer of the sort of knowledge Livet craved. Kell had taught her quite a few things, but there was always more he had left unsaid. He would disappear for weeks on end at times and often return with coinage from across the land, and whenever Livet had thought she would surprise him, he would find a way to outdo her. He always knew more than he passed on and was ever hinting toward a more widely dispersed circle of compatriots than just the Kindred in Lanstad. Livet's curiosity was exploding.

"Who is Gardia? How did she know Kell?"

Olen's head jerked as if he had fallen asleep and missed the jump ahead into a conversation. He belched then nodded off again.

"Gardia?" Baressa drew a breath, tsk-tsking. "I knew Kell would have taught you more than just a few letters of that script if he trusted you," she said smugly. "So, after all, you do know what the letter I showed you said."

Livet shrugged, then nodded.

Baressa straightened her skirt and turned squarely to explain to Livet. "Gardia entrusted the letter to me, to travel to Lanstad in the hopes that we might find some of Kell's companions—or if not, perhaps some of his belongings could at least be retrieved. We'd been on the quest quite a few times but never successful."

"Kell owned nothin'," Livet said. "We lived poorly. He took me in when my parents abandoned me and taught me my tricks to make a livin'. Then the Faith took us all. They let me and some of the youngest go, but Kell and the rest were murdered. Nothing of him remains, livin' or lurkin', except for me."

"He feared that was going to happen, so he wrote to Gardia."

Long ago, Livet lost hope of discovering any other members of the Kindred, but it was a calming comfort that she faced the promise of allies, if Kell did have other confidants. That better explained the sigil carved into the cart.

"It seems he taught you to be a court magician. Suggestions and sleight of hand to add to your roguery. Parlour tricks. Did he ever take you to his workshop?" Baressa asked.

Livet shook her head negatively. Their accommodations had never been much more elaborate than one-night stays in empty houses and subterranean hideouts scattered throughout the city's catacombs.

"Kell learned a great many trades, but most importantly, he was the custodian of disciplines practiced by the more ancient, fabled crafters of Lanstad. He knew their art and he was a good thief because he could appraise the most eclectic of artifacts. Those that were mundane, he could transform into highly potent items himself. It wasn't always just simple weavers and potters in that city. Lanstad was the source of great creations, and for such a peaceful town, it also produced great weapons. We didn't want those skills to fall to the Faith."

"If he 'ad such skills, why did he live so poor, then?"

Baressa took on a consolatory tone, "Maybe he couldn't risk the attention, nor trust any would-be customers. Vlass invited the Faith into the city, and they immediately began to root out their adversaries. We all had to keep to ourselves, else the Faith would seize us, and what was ours." She clenched her teeth at the thought but conjectured to say, "That, or he ran out of materials. Ramis's rule choked off most of the caravans that would bring the purest metals from Palinor, the richest oils from Hasen and the rarest woods from Greyforest. Kell would take such prizes and work them all together in a Fal forge, where the gases from the swamp burn with an unbelievable flame. When put to use, a skilled smith can use the forge to melt any metal, natural or unnatural. But their exact whereabouts are mostly rumours. The Fals are easy places to lose things in. I had supposed that's why you fled there for hiding."

"I knew Kell would disappear into the marshes from time to time. One day, I thought of doin' the same. Then I came upon Ayren, and 'e took me in and helped me t' get my strength back. But all this you say Kell had and done, would have ended when the Faith murdered him in their prison. They wanted it to be like he never walked the earth. Anything of his they took, and they'd 'ave burned it to cinders, for sure," Livet said. "No one ever even saw his body, but I knew he was gone because I was there to see him die, then they tossed me out and I crawled away as fast I could. I begged for food. I begged for money. One day I begged a man for a walkin' stick and used it t' get out of there for good."

Tears were softly streaming down Livet's face. She clutched her knees and pulled herself into a ball. Baressa placed her hand on Livet's shoulder to sooth her.

"The Faith wouldn't destroy anything," Baressa countered. "If he had the knowledge written down or recorded, they'd study and use it. They have a very keen interest in these things but will not suffer anyone else to share such learning. That is why they convinced the king to seize my sisters at Starpond and why they hunted the streets of Lanstad for your found family. What they manage to grab, they take back to the Temple of the Pillars in Caphedra."

"Were you ever able to free your sisters?" Livet asked.

Baressa brushed back her locks of hair and her brown eyes glistened with her own nascent tears.

"Many took to the forests. Roderin helped them evade the hunting parties." She choked back her emotion and had to stop to clear her throat. "We lost some in the raid, of course. They killed them. Of the captives, besides myself, we worked to find them and free them, but it has been an ongoing trouble. If they catch any of us returning too close to the waters at Starpond, we are hunted again."

"They hold your people now?" Livet asked.

"Continuously," Baressa lamented. "Which is why you must understand that I am also in a hurry to return to Caphedra. Then I must make my way to find my husband and travel back to Starpond to renew myself, and my resources, to resist anew."

A snort from the corner of the room caused Baressa and Livet to look over. Olen had succumbed to the combination of fatigue and spirits and was snoring harshly.

"Poor thing," Baressa said through a soft smile as she surveyed the slumbering heap of a man across from them.

"Will the priest come after us, d'you think?" Livet queried.

"Not alone, he won't... nor will he with only two soldiers," Baressa answered. "Which is good since Olen's had no chance to sleep and those dear old nags pulling my wagon can't hit the road without some rest either. I think we need to risk the night here as we planned. We'll be in Caphedra by midday and when we arrive, I'll take precautions and find protection."

Livet's brow wrinkled pessimistically, "We need to set up a lookout or somethin'."

"Then I'd ask you to take care of that, Livet," Baressa said. "If I sleep now, there may be more to my dream, and it could help me see what is in store for tomorrow. It wasn't that long ago that I dreamt of you, Livet."

Baressa reached into her pocket and withdrew Kell's letter. "Just in case," she began, then handed the letter to Livet. "If anything should happen to me, you can mention my name to most folk in Porter's Run and they'll look after you. But, if something *does* happen to me, I need you to make your way to the place they call Faralley, inside the city, and way to the west of the Darrow. Go to a tavern called the Peahen and tell the owner how you got this letter. Tell not a single soul otherwise until you get the all-clear from Gardia herself. She'll have questions for you, but you best be honest with her from the start. She's less forgiving than I am if she thinks you're holding back."

"I understand," Livet said. "I'm going to have a look in on these soldiers and the priest."

"Be careful and don't be seen," Baressa warned, then laid

down upon a bed to rest.

Livet took in all that she heard, nodded, and stood up. She walked to the window where the breeze tousled her dark hair. She ran one hand along the stone sill, examining the construction of the building and the width of the ledge. She panned her head around outside to assess the irregularities of the stonework and the proximity of the eaves and trusses. Then, in a blink of an eye, she obscured herself behind the hanging draperies as they billowed in the breeze and disappeared.

Livet pulled herself along the shadow of the inn's gables. She found the men's window and with one ear cupped, Livet tried eavesdropping upon within.

Silence. She heard some activity, but the men were quiet and solemn. Livet wanted to try and get closer—to look inside—and do so without being seen.

So, she relaxed her breathing and let the scenery change before her. In her mind, she was used to focusing on seeing things in more than one way—almost as if she were listening to her vision or smelling with her eyes. Sometimes, she could taste a hot, bubbling stew by looking at it. With concentration, she employed every sense toward harnessing the shade being cast under the gable and along the roof.

As she did, the shadows drew close to her. Hungrily, like the form of a wild animal anticipating a scrap of meat, the darkness stretched. It encapsulated her, until she was submerged into it—and into a brightness that only she saw.

This was the moment Livet knew she was imperceptible. She felt safe. It was what Kell, in his teachings, had called an *umbrage*— an intentional oasis of shadow cast by her own determination. The glow she experienced around her was constructed from the very light now being snatched from the eyes of the men. She sat in illumination, while those who gazed in her direction saw blackness, as though nothing was present.

The upset and timid men recovering from Baressa's bewitchment earlier in the night did not wish to encounter another threat so soon, and this is what fuelled Livet's deception.

Kell's teachings to Livet had always presupposed two things.

To convince another of something illusory, or to conceal something that was really there—including yourself—could only be done when you willed it to be replaced by something they already either expected to see, or desired to see. Such a trick could gratify their sense of reality with whatever they longed for, or with something already anticipated. "Fool them, by letting them fool themselves," he would say.

Livet gently interfered in the men's minds. They sought the secrecy and privacy to regroup and strategize without outside contact and she willed them to believe such was true. So long as the shadows embraced Livet, she was but nothingness at that moment. She was just a myth or a distant worry.

Within the umbrage's cloak, Livet peered over the sill, into the men's lodging and observed. A scarred and cleft-browed fighter with a mole on his cheek sat on the edge of a bed, motionless save for a percussive rasping from his chest as he took laboured breaths. His young companion-in-arms stood by the door, while the curate brandished a quill and scratched lines of ink across parchment paper by the candlelight. A blue doublet hung from the back of his chair.

None of the men showed any sign of preparing a counterattack. They seemed just as nervous as Livet's own companions had been back in the room.

The curate was sure to be informing his order of what and whom he'd discovered here. Livet was uncertain how he would manage to send the letter off to his superiors. If she could intercept its journey, it would help secure their safety as they arrived in the city, but the room was just too small to sneak safely into without coming nearly face-to-face with one of the three men.

Livet reversed herself and the light she saw around her faded as she dispelled the envelope of darkness. This was the dangerous part, for her own eyes had to overcome a temporary blindness and readjust to only seeing moonlight. It took a moment.

Bereft of any other immediate solution, she navigated back, stepping where the stonework jutted out slightly. Despite her old injury, she'd had years to adjust her sense of balance and relearn how to use her leg. She had to habituate to her own asymmetry with every step she took on solid ground, but it made no difference to traverse with uneven footing here. If anything was unfamiliar, it was the height. There were no tall buildings in Fal Ghreeg, and she felt a sense of excitement to be so high above the ground, even if it was only a couple of storeys.

As she returned to the room with Olen and Baressa (both now fast asleep) she elected to extend her hours of watch, and sentry from outside the window overnight. She braced herself against the frame, pressed her back into the side jamb, and gazed out over the pasturelands to the darkened farm homes of Greenplain. Perhaps she'd be able to share a moment like this with Denn someday, if he could be recovered safely. When they would arrive in the city tomorrow, she calculated ten days would have passed since he'd been taken by the strangers. Livet had no idea how long it would have taken the men to drag Denn back to the capital, but they were most certainly there now, well ahead of her and Olen. She grappled with anxiousness until the first rays of dawn began trickling above the horizon when she pulled herself back inside and began gathering their things so they could depart as soon as possible.

"It's a good time to set off," said a freshly awakened Olen. "It's going to be a hot day. First real hot one of the season, I suspect!"

The three travellers had quietly crawled out of bed in the pre-dawn hours so they could lead their horses without disruption to the tavern's carriage house, where their wagon had been stored. Now, as twilight arose, their preparations were almost complete.

Baressa pulled down hard on an old stiff rope, whitened and sun-bleached with age, and secured the covering over the wagon. She ran her hand along the trace to check the hame and pole straps of each horse, giving the proud pair of hard-working creatures an affectionate scratch along their long necks and withers as she went.

"You should 'ide in the back," Livet suggested to Baressa.

"And which of you two are good at steering a wagon?"

Olen shrugged. He was peering through a gap in the great wooden stable door. The pink-lit dawn was now flooding the cracks with morning sunbeams and dust motes floated in the brightness.

"Anyone out there yet?" Baressa asked.

"No one now," he answered. "We should move quickly though."

Livet paused at Olen's side, and he knelt slightly to hear her. "It's already been so many days, Olen," she whispered. "Do you think us chasin' 'em down will make a speck of difference now?"

Olen smiled, though Livet could tell he was hiding some uncertainty himself. "We *must* go to Caphedra, Livet. What else would you have us do?"

At that moment, he looked helpless. It was at times like these, she would recall him professing that *stubbornness can be a virtue.* That self-construed axiom appeared to be driving him on, but it did not go quite far enough toward reassuring her. What if something terrible had already happened to Denn?

"Perhaps you should go back to Ayren... but then again, I don't have enough money to hire you a coach and it's not safe anyway. I'd much rather you stay with me, so I can watch over you."

"Oh? So far, I think you've gotten into more trouble than me," Livet said, pestering him.

"No matter what..." Olen said, "We will only find out what has happened to Denn once we get to the city."

Livet felt herself grow dizzy for a moment, as Olen's words kindled her most cynical speculations. He was right; they had to know, one way or the other. She nodded to her towering sympathizer and slinked back into place.

Baressa shot a coarse whisper across the stable. "Are we ready?"

Under her travelling cloak, Livet spread her fingers over the handle of her rondel dagger. Olen stepped back to the side of the door and got ready to release the latch. His blade, Coldswept, was strapped to his back. Baressa did not seem to possess any weapon but remained alert.

"I'll sneak a better look. Those men still don't know my face to recognize me." With that, Livet hopped to the top of the wagon, reached toward the rafters of the stable and hauled herself up to the open bay window of the hayloft. She scanned the yard and then turned her eyes to the upper floor of the tavern, where the soldiers' window was now shuttered.

"Go!" she called down.

Olen spread open the doors and Baressa commanded the horses to propel the wagon through them. The heavy conveyance groaned. Its wooden wheels pressed furrows in the sawdust of the stable floor, before *clop-clomping* over the threshold and down into the ruts of dried earth on the other side. Livet emerged through the hayloft window and dropped neatly onto the back of the wagon as it passed below. Shutting the doors behind them, Olen sprinted to catch up and swung himself up onto the back of the cart, rather nimbly for a man of his determinate solidness.

As they rode away, Livet pointed to a large, black carriage with bronze fittings that poked out from under a copse of trees behind the stable. On its side was a familiar boar's head etched onto its dark surface. There were no horses hitched to it, which could mean that their adversaries were not yet underway. But Olen pointed out that it could also suggest the soldiers had left on just horses alone.

"I think they're still here unless you are so important that they'd leave that carriage behind unattended." Livet reasoned to Baressa.

Their driver shrugged off the question. "Keep your eyes open on the road today," she said.

Their wagon made steady progress as they trundled along the road, and the day began to accumulate its anticipated warmth under the rays of the sun. It felt summery and humid, which led Livet and Baressa to doff their cloaks and greet the sunlight enthusiastically, its brightness elevating their moods. Olen sat beside them, moving only periodically to wipe sweat from his brow or brush flies from his cheek.

Their wariness of being followed remained with them a long while past Greenplain, but as they progressed toward the capital, the tension of keeping one eye over their shoulder and glancing back for pursuers, began competing with the compulsion to take in the growing signs of the imperious city ahead. Most of the approaches to Caphedra were built up with quaint and curious crafters' hovels or cottage farms that promised all manner of produce and fare for consumption or exhibited some dedication or another toward handiwork or artistry with which to supply the Caphedran markets and shops beyond.

But Livet struggled to see signs of the inhabitants.

Olen likewise observed, "Quiet here, these days. Where are

the people?"

Indeed, nothing was lined up for sale. Signboards hung from homes, but they were perched over secured and unwelcoming doors. Smoke from cooking fires floated above a smattering of chimneys, but the windows were blocked with heavy shutters and the gates to villas rested firmly in place, braced by heavy bars.

"When I was young, the road was lined with sellers. Now, there's not a single cart or a barrow," said Olen.

Baressa nodded her own confirmation but explained, "It's not safe now."

"So quiet," Olen said again, with a hint of disappointment. "Though that's much better for us, I would think."

As they rolled along, Baressa eyed something on the side of the road. She pointed it out to her companions who saw that it was the carcass of a dead horse lying still and putrefying in the ditch. Ominously, someone appeared to have pierced its heart, for a stain of crimson blood caked the animal's now-collapsed rib cage.

"Too many robbers and ruffians on the road these days. People need to be careful," Baressa said.

"This always used to be the safest road," Olen said with concern. "You'd run into robbers from the caves along the road to Palinor or in the thickets alongside the Greyforest Road to Northport, but there's not a lot of places for hideouts here."

"Greyforest Road's always been safe for me," Baressa bragged. "And I'm no stranger to the cave-dwellers either. I have a few friends in Harthal Vale."

"You keep some desperate company!" Olen snorted.

"Desperate is a bit of a harsh brand to put on them, although I suppose Taringer can be a bit crabby at times," said Baressa. "I miss him, though—and the rest."

Just then, something else attracted her notice. She sat up straight, then jabbed Livet with her elbow, not so sharply, but amicably enough to get her attention.

"What is it?" Livet responded, looking ahead down the road. "Robbers?"

"We're approaching a rise. From the top, you'll want to keep your eyes open!" Baressa said to Livet, venturing a grin. She clucked to the two horses, prodding them to speed up a little.

Livet overlooked the smirk and took her words as a warning

of danger at first. But as the wagon advanced, a ridge of grey, crenellated stonework became visible through the hot, rippling waves of afternoon haze. As they crested the hill, she learned that very little road was remaining. Livet gasped and gawked at Caphedra's walls. They stretched to the east, from where eddies of a late-day breeze flitted by them, to the far west, where the sun had descended into far-away foothills. Its rays reflected on the battlements.

It was only a short distance to the southern wall of the great capital. Their route led toward a large, humped bridge, upon which the road arched into an immense fortified gate of iron and timber. The bridge provided the means to traverse a wide moat of lazily circulating water, which Livet surmised was fed by the frothy river she could barely make out, flowing from its own passage through the wall farther west.

Olen leaned into her, following her gaze and pointing, "That's the Darrow River. It passes through the city." With a soft look of perturbance added, "My home was on the other side."

Livet murmured in comprehension, then reached out and squeezed him in both arms, offering physical affection to comfort and reassure him. Olen smiled simply and purely, returning the gesture by resting his sizeable hand on her delicate shoulder and sighing tiredly.

But the hill had obscured their view of what else lay in store for them. At that moment, one of the horses pulled on the harness and attempted to rear back into the cart. There was a glint of red sunlight upon metal—either a blade or speartip off to the side. Baressa had to pull hard on the reins to keep the horses together, now that one had been spooked.

Men had been lying in wait opposite the crest of the hill and converged on their wagon as soon as they broached it, distracted by the nearness of their destination. From out of nowhere, another man approached from the front, blocking the road. He was armed.

"Hullo there!" came a grimy voice beside them as a tall, ribbony thin man emerged. He gripped a long, barbed polearm that matched his physique. "Easy now, girl," he said to the nearest horse. "Just come to collect the toll!"

Olen wasted neither words nor a moment in hopping off the wagon. Landing on his feet, he charged into the highwayman, nearly knocking him over with his broad chest. "Under whose authority?" demanded Olen.

"M- m- me, uh... and my friends," the man sputtered.

"Thought so," said Olen, who immediately wrenched the spear from the man's hands. He struck out powerfully with his other hand, landing a punch like a thunderclap studded with knuckles and crushing the man's nose into his face. Globs of blood sputtered and erupted. The man keeled over in muffled screaming.

Baressa wrestled to keep hold of the reins and prevent the horses from panicking. From behind the wagon, two more figures rushed forward, trying to clamour up quickly toward Livet and Baressa, who bunched close together and desperately tried to dodge the assault.

Then the wagon rocked. A cry arose from one of the men who shrank back away from the women with his face full and white with terror. Olen, sword drawn, had nearly cleaved off his leg, using the wagon like a cutting board.

The third man struggled to pull himself up and over the sideboards of the wagon, forfeiting his lunge toward Livet's seat and using his momentum to tumble over the other side instead. Livet, however, had leapt forward, toward the horses, to somehow calm the beasts or at least keep them in place. She stayed there, ducked down, and balanced on the cart shaft between the animals with as tight a grip on their harnesses as she could manage.

Heavy footsteps dashed past the rear of the cart as Olen emerged from behind one of the wheels. The last robber had already taken to his feet to escape, and Olen let him go. He turned back to the first—the skinny highwayman who was now choking on his own blood as he tried to cry out for help. The geyser from his nose blinded him, obscuring from him the knowledge that his remaining compatriot was sprawled out in the gutter, draining of blood and life.

The thin man moaned in obliviousness, but Olen roused him to listen.

"We don't answer to you, or your friends," Olen proclaimed, coldly. "Now, get out of our way!"

He grabbed him by the collar, spun the man around, and wiped off his blade across the back of the robber's tunic, which was the only unbloodied patch of meagre clothing the man still had.

Satisfied, Olen pushed him to the ground where the man collapsed and passed out.

Unapologetic when he returned to their wagon, Olen chanced to look up at Baressa then over to Livet. "Thanks for letting me handle that one, madame," he said proudly to Baressa.

Slightly aghast, she replied, "By the stars, Olen, we're not even through the gate, yet!" She chuckled heartily.

Livet jumped back up from amidst the horses to sit in the middle of the trestle, and informed Baressa, "That's the temper I told you 'bout!"

"Simple cutthroats," Olen said, sounding like a connoisseur, then as if salivating he added, "There's bound to be more!"

Livet settled back into her place and redoubled her vigilance toward the roadside. Looking up, she knew Olen's role as a protector had been re-established. He rode along sitting high and she detected reinvigorated confidence in his eyes, his shoulders, and in the set of his jaw.

Baressa turned wordlessly to Livet, then with a shake of her head and a gratified smile of unmistakable admiration for their valorous champion, she slacked the reins and urged the horses forward. With a clopping of hooves on the cobblestones of the bridge, she proceeded to drive them toward Caphedra's portentous gate.

CHAPTER 8

One Last Thing

The enticing aroma of spit-roasted capon beckoned Denn toward the dining hall, where his cheer was restored by the arrangement of savoury victuals that Serenn had laid out. The roast fowl was at the centre of an assortment of steaming turnips, plump pies, and fresh-cut greens.

Three places had been set intimately together at one end of the table. The drapes had been pulled to let in the last of the afternoon sunlight, but candles were already in place should the meal persist into darker hours. The Wellum dining room was long but narrow and corridor-like with artful tapestries on the walls that had been collected over centuries. Denn had seen enough of them growing up; his hungry eyes rested on the food.

"Sit in," Serenn directed as she entered, carrying another bottle of wine.

From outside the room, his mother Esta added, "Have Denn sit at the head of the table, Serenn. I don't expect your father to come until later tonight."

Assuming the head place setting conflicted Denn. It was his father's seat at the table and not one he'd ever sat in before. Somehow, he felt hesitant to sit in the same spot in case his father's pretentious and unforgiving bearing might somehow transfer to him. That was ridiculous, though. In his father's absence—and without Hann—Denn was the senior member of the Wellum family, so he stood behind the head chair and waited for his sister and mother to join.

Serenn slid in beside him, stood in her position, and made a rude coughing noise toward the entranceway next to the back hallway. Gracefully, Esta entered. She stepped lightly, her face now more composed than before with cosmetic touches to add colour to her cheeks and enhance the depth of her grateful gaze. Still wearing her golden circlet, she had changed into a lavish, velvety gown with wide, bombard sleeves. Once she took her place at the table, all three sat down in unison.

"You have set a lovely table, my darling," Esta complimented Serenn. "Did you manage to do this all by yourself?"

"Of course not, mother," she responded. "It was Nelissa. But I helped."

"Summon her then," Esta said.

Serenn took a deep breath as if she were about to call out for the girl but then reconsidered and seized a small, shiny bell that resembled the one that had been in Denn's bedchamber. She gently held it between her fingers and jingled it.

"Yes, Ma'am," came a voice instantly from behind them. The kitchen maid—a slight, dark-haired girl—emerged from a dark corner of the room. For more than a moment, Denn almost convinced himself that it was Livet that had manifested there silently, so plain and pretty.

Esta seemed satisfied by the maid's promptness and declared, "Nelissa, we need more bread."

"Right away, ma'am," Nelissa answered, pivoted smartly, then exited like a leaf taken by a breeze.

Serenn poured wine for the table as Esta opened the conversation.

"I trust your horse was as fit as you had hoped. Serenn tells me that you plan to depart tomorrow."

"Yes, to both parts," Denn said.

"Will you not wait for your father? Do you still refuse to speak with him?"

"No," said Denn. "I wish to thank him for my release." He sliced into the meat on his plate and forced a quick mouthful to avoid saying more than he needed to.

"With all the troubles in the city, we'd feel a lot safer if you stayed around," Serenn said.

Denn swallowed his bite and waited for it to reach his stomach. "If I were as useful as you suggest, I wouldn't have ended up..." his mind raced through the experience of capture, "...*as I did.*"

"But you got through it, despite everything done to you," she said. "I couldn't—nor could I even imagine it!"

Too late. Denn's mind was spiralling back to thoughts of his ordeal. He rotated the shaft of his fork slowly in his fingers.

"If I see that brute Colden again—or that horse thief Temis..." Denn said, quivering slightly. He scraped his knife against the dinner plate dissecting his capon with projected forcefulness.

"Horse thief?" Serenn questioned, alarmed at Denn's rising anger.

"Not the kind of talk appropriate for the table," Esta decreed, then turned to watch Nelissa approach with a wooden platter hosting a loaf of crusty bread.

Denn also turned, this time satisfying his mind by noting all the differences between the unfamiliar maid and Livet. He thought upon all the beautiful and delicate qualities he missed. Livet's nose was smaller and her hair darker, he remembered. She was just as quiet, but if she had something to say, Livet didn't wait to be spoken to. How he missed her.

"What did your brother tell you this afternoon? Did you have a good talk?" Esta asked.

"It seems he's making his way upward in the Faith," Denn said, shrugging. "All his hard work has paid off."

Esta feigned gagging. "Golmarra singled him out the first moment he arrived upon the temple doorstep. Saw him as a walking key that would get him into the Wellum family vaults. That old monk has only ever coveted gold and power."

"Lehn has done well," Serenn interjected calmingly. "He took his lessons with all the other novices, boys and girls from the best families of Caphedra. He even studied with the princess, Ravon. He used to go on and on about her like they were regular chums."

"He mentioned her today. He is quite dedicated to her, I gather," Denn said.

"Dedicated," Serenn repeated. "Yes, that's a word for it."

Something about her tone intrigued Denn. He raised his eyebrow and queried her, "What word would you use?"

"I suspect from some things he told me that he has quite the affection for her. But the king would never have allowed it. Lehn is not in line for either wealth or title. He's not a suitable match."

"The king is not alive. Would not the elders in the Faith of the Pillars have a say in it now?" Denn asked.

"He'll still need to bring more to the courtship than good intentions," Serenn said.

Esta coughed loudly and interrupted the siblings' conjecture. "I'm sure there is plenty else to catch up on," she suggested.

"Yes, indeed. How is business, then?" Denn asked his mother as if moving on to another agenda item from some prescribed list.

With a measure of habit, Esta responded, "Steady." That word was always her noncommittal response that neither bragged nor griped but gave up little. However, Denn felt it was coldly delivered and reinforced the distance that stemmed from their parting two years ago. At that time, though to a lesser degree, he'd also spoken out against his mother over her silent endorsement of the mistreatment that forever had characterized their years of uneven homelife. The lifestyle that Phon provided her with had purchased her passivity through its lavishness. She ignored the strife between father and sons and placated her daily frustrations by abusing servants instead.

Esta ventured no more information, so Serenn bridged the gap. "All is well, but the king died while leaving us numerous amounts owing. We have no certainty of seeing those monies until things settle. Chancellor Havel has stopped all payments during the interim."

"How have you managed?" Denn inquired more deeply.

"Father's taken precautions, so we're not in danger of any dire calamity," Serenn replied. "He tried doing business in other commodities, but it's been hard to import trade goods on the highways due to the increase in banditry. We can't rely on all our old customers either. The smiths in Barforgers still owe us for much of the iron that Father brought down from Palinor. With so many soldiers being disbanded, the market is flooded with weapons. Prices have dropped to next to nothing, but no one has money to buy them. I hear they are melting down swords to make horseshoe nails. Father's also spent more on wages as we've hired more hands than just Yael—like Trin and Brae, who went out after you the other night. I'm sorry that I don't know all their names yet. They are mostly disbanded from the army and hired on Yael's approval. With so many desperate men congregating in Caphedra these days, most of those in the Merchants' Guild have done the same."

"Which was the one looking after Naobe?"

"Trin Curraw," answered Serenn. "He's been with us a while. He was a squire with one of the horse companies here in the city before he came to us. He's quick with a harness and takes wonderful care of the stock in the armoury."

Denn raised an eyebrow, "He must be older than he looks. I didn't think him more than seventeen or eighteen years old when I saw him."

"I know. I tease him a bit," Serenn said, smiling, which earned an eye narrowing from her mother. Serenn blushed and took a deep swallow of wine to wash down the giggling that threatened to overcome her, giving her mother a brief moment for an acerbic aside.

"I don't think he'd know what to do with a woman unless he found one who needed a good brushing and had a fondness for oats," Esta quipped, causing Serenn to lose control of her wine in a fit of coughing and choking.

Denn laughed too and felt admiration for his sister. Serenn's good nature washed across her face with such sweetness. He marvelled that somehow, despite everything, she had preserved her tenderness and her cheerful humour. "I'm surprised that our father hasn't tried to marry you off yet," he said.

"Before I turn into an old hag, you mean?" she joked.

"Perhaps she should spend less time around the hired hands," Esta snapped in reply, but Serenn did her best to avoid acknowledging it.

"I would think it might be *you* who's first in line for his matchmaking," she prophesized to her brother.

"Well, he best be quick about it. He has until tomorrow morning. Once I've expressed my thanks, I wish to depart for my post."

That caused dismal looks upon the faces of both his sister and mother, but they didn't pursue it other than for Serenn to say, "I'd like to go over Father's ledgers with you before you go. Since you've been gone, he's made me privy to much of his business dealings, but it will all fall to you someday. You should spend less time in the saddle of that horse and more time sat down at a desk, acquainting yourself with the family books."

"I would argue that I belong more so on the back of a horse,"

Denn said.

Serenn smirked, "If you're calling yourself a horse's backside, I won't disagree."

Esta rolled her eyes, saying, "Eat up, children!" but she finally appeared content to bask in their banter, no doubt finding it sadly unfamiliar over these recent years. Perhaps the tension and strain of their recent trials had exhausted her. After that, she interrupted no further but appeared to enjoy the meal awash in a peaceful, motherly glow.

Once sated by the supper, and with his strength restored, Denn made his way, alone, to the centre of the manor where the family armoury was housed. He withdrew a lit candle from out of a candelabrum and used it to light his way, spreading the flame to the wicks of whatever other candles he found inside.

The room was laid out hexagonally. Mammoth iron racks crammed with vicious weapons spanned the walls to his immediate left and right. Across the room, other artifacts were displayed more reverently. These were the favoured antiques of those in his family line who, like Denn, had taken up arms instead of commerce. The opposite wall hosted a workman's bench complete with whetstones and leatherworker's tools. Flanking it were two heavy trunks brimming with a soldier's wardrobe of girdles, gauntlets, straps, and harnesses.

The chamber was designed to offer some structural security. Its walls were supported by a series of buttresses. The doors were edged and reinforced with iron fittings and heavy metal bars were within easy reach to immobilize them, should there be a need to seal off the room from a threat.

Denn walked to the centre of the chamber and stood on an ornate but frayed patterned rug. A square outline of threadbare ridges across the surface betrayed the contours of an age-old trap door underneath. He and Hann had opened it once when they were younger. It led to a passage through ancestral catacombs—and it was a private way out in the event their safety was ever jeopardized. Denn remembered that they had ventured almost all the way down the ladder before Hann shone a candle on the first tangle of bones below, and the two boys nearly sprouted wings to fly back up in a panic.

Before his return journey tomorrow, Denn had to reoutfit himself. He sized up the inventory of the room. Many different weapons, from flails to falchions, hung from the racks. In more prominent places rested those arms that had been personally used by the Wellums of yore, while flaunted even more ostentatiously, were the ones used by their enemies, which were captured in battle, or some cases, through guile.

The profoundly historic Wellums were further honoured by their collection of shields, mounted on each buttress, and displaying centuries of iterations of the family arms: a honeybee, or on gules, banded by an engrailed line below and a wedged, indented line chief across the top. The bee represented apian-like productivity while the bars called out to wealth drawn from the deep fires and ores of the soil. It was a modern symbol, aggregated and selected to supplant the old Wellum salamander, which likewise celebrated the family riches drawn out of the infernos of the earth, but which became considered more fanciful and aggressive in time. The whole chamber was a shrine to a martial legacy that Denn alone carried forward into this generation.

Lifting open one of the trunks, he began pulling out any pieces he thought would be of use to him. First, there was a pair of laced, leather bracers and heavy cowhide gauntlets. For his legs, he found a couple of greaves to match the bracers, and cuisse guards for his thighs, which had leather backings wide enough to prevent chaffing while in the saddle. In the morning, he decided he would visit one of the cobblers in Stonerow for a sturdy pair of new riding boots.

The last piece of armour he wished to procure was a breastplate. He seized a couple but was displeased to discover that he had yet to develop the robust pectorals of his predecessors. The pieces were all too wide and they obstructed the movement of his arms. So instead, in a final plundering of the armour trunk, he took up a brigandine vest of leather, housing small metal plates for extra measure.

Thus, being reminded that he came up lacking in size and strength, it was now a matter of finding a sword that would match the shortfalls of his physique. His weapon had to be strong but light because his lack of power meant he counted on swiftness and agility to be on his side. It had to be effective on the field of battle, both when dismounted and when employed from horseback on the charge. He ran his eyes along the racks until they fell upon an ideal blade that was long but tapered and fullered to make it light and lethal.

The weapon had a name carved into it: *Longlimb*. He recognized it as having been once owned by his uncle, Phar Wellum. Born after Denn's father, he too, was a second son that took up arms to find his fortune and rode with a mounted infantry company sent to Hasen. The sword still had the etching of a seven-petalled jasmine flower near the hilt. Phar came home to Caphedra severely injured from a skirmish near the Glass Plateau and died after a short-term convalescing. Denn remembered some of his stories, however, and dearly cherished the memory of his uncle's warm, sociable manner.

Holding the sword proudly, Denn made sure it was seated tight in its scabbard, then stood rubbing his thumb along the smooth, polished leather. A sharp horn-hilted dagger caught his eye and he snatched it up too. The removal of these weapons from their places in the armoury carried a private, personal obligation that their use would be in service of the family name. To Denn, it felt almost like he was provisioning a loan from a moneylender, but with honour as its currency. His feud, after all, was singularly with his father, not his forebears. The Wellums of history had been good people.

But raising his head to the collection of shields above him, they hung like relics. The bearing of these arms was symbolic of a past age when the Wellums maintained a hereditary lordship of their own. It had caused a scandal when Denn's father refused to assume the title upon the death of his own father, as would have been his right. The old man's reasoning was that it made simple economic sense. The titular lordship included no taxable lands from which to generate wealth, yet it still carried an obligation to provide men and resources to the reigning monarch. As such, Phon Wellum had shrugged it off as an unprofitable whim of vanity. Now, should he subsequently die without ever taking on the title, it would pass into obscurity rather than to Denn. If that were the case, perhaps the argent wolves of the Twelfth would be the only emblem of arms he would ever lawfully carry, and he couldn't help but feel a pang of disappointment. Perhaps he had inherited some vanity after all, and not just from his mother's side, he thought.

Gathering all the things together, Denn blew out the candles and made his way back to his room to prepare for tomorrow's leaving. But as he did, he spied candlelight leaking into the hall from the direction of the study. Immediately, he held onto his breath to quiet himself and began walking softly on the balls of his feet, like he did as a child, until he caught himself and stopped. Ashamed of his own temerity, he stood upright and vowed assertiveness.

His father had returned home.

Denn stood in the corridor, unmoving and silent, while he pondered the moment. He had already decided that his rescue was a cause to suspend his imposed hermitage—his determined avoidance—and he expected to adhere to that decision. Now, before the evening ended, he would commit himself to this last task.

The door to the study was open. The flickering of the candlelight was punctuated by the shadow caused by Phon Wellum's movements in front of it. Denn did not enter but knocked with a burst of three short, truncated raps.

The whispering motion ceased inside and after a brief pause there came the clearing of a throat and a stern response. "What is it?"

Denn pushed the door, widening the crack, then walked through. After two years, he couldn't predict if his entrance would be met with stony silence or spiteful interrogation, but he was determined to adhere to politeness if only to assert his own dignity in the confrontation.

"Father," he said, choosing to get the most challenging word out of the way first. "I have come to thank you for securing my release from my captors."

Instantly, Phon laid down the roll of parchment he'd been reviewing and turned toward his visitor. He took a step forward and Denn could see him more clearly. The past two years had not changed the ever-present wrinkles of skepticism or acute wariness on his face, but his complexion was different. It was paler and he'd lost some of the fleshiness in his cheeks, so that they could almost be called sallow. His hair had grown out too. It was perceptibly oily and unkempt. Most oddly of all, he was smiling.

"You've recovered!" he said with unexpected joy. "I am pleased."

Denn faltered, having not devised a strategy of anything further to say. Phon maintained an inviting look but also hesitated, waiting for his son to lead the direction of the long-evaded conversation.

While Denn searched his mind for something to say, he eyed the room. This was a place he had seldom been in growing up. Phon's study was comprised of a preeminent library of texts stacked upon layers of shelves ascending to a second floor. Candles in sconces around the room burned away, but atop the desk, a bright oil lamp gave off a steady, reliable luminance. The tools of a learned man—telescopes, compasses, a reading stone—were strewn in various alcoves and on ledges, as were the heads of trophy animals long dead. Prominent to the room were two enormous ivory tusks that jutted out from the upper storey. Like tree trunks at their base, they were each the weight and length of several men, and they curled gloriously outward from a towering portrait of the myth-inspiring beast that had surrendered them.

In the centre of the study was the immense oak desk upon which Phon updated his ledgers and composed his contracts and correspondence. The mayhem across its surface led Denn to conclude his father was still an excessively busy man—and not without an irony in comparison. Denn was a trained soldier, but he had yet to take a life. How many lives, on the other hand, had his father ended by cutting off payments or refusing credit, evidenced on these very ledgers? How many poor tradesman or merchant customers were left to exercise the same option that Hann did? His father was ruthless in business. He rejected any victory that did not include seeing desperation in the eyes of a rival—and to him, everyone from beggar to potentate was a rival.

"I am told that you showed great resilience, young man," Phon said, finally breaking the silence. "I don't think I afforded you the proper credit all of these years. Though I provided you with opportunity, I negligently did not appreciate your dedication to realizing your own outcome." He took a few more measured steps, his eyes still fixed on Denn. "You have carried our name well."

He did not need to compliment Denn. It would have been more natural had he chastised him for being stupid enough to be caught in the first place. His father praised his 'resilience' without commentary on his mental lapse and physical shortcomings—the endemic weakness—that prevented him from overcoming his aggressors.

After all, that's how he had badgered Hann right up until the end.

"Why do you say this?" Denn asked, seeking a purpose rather than meaning.

Phon's lips curled into a more evident smile.

"My son," he said, then paused on those words.

Denn waited a moment for him to continue, but the filial salutation only reminded him of Lehn and the afternoon's meeting.

"Lehn visited the house today. We spoke. He had a paper for you, from the temple," Denn informed.

Phon turned and reached toward a stack of parchment on his desktop. Denn saw that he had been presented the paper already and had opened and read it.

"No doubt he explained that the Faith feels that I have not expressed my piety enough, financially, and they seek more. The Marshal has them frightened, so they're purchasing a great number of outcasts and mercenaries to carry the banner of the Lady Ravon. All so expensive."

"Will you pay it?" Denn asked.

"I have yet to declare my intentions. In normal times, their black mark would be a threat to my livelihood. Still, I daresay now I could be well-compensated by simply doing business solely with the horde of merchants that they are likewise threatening." He tossed the Due down onto the floor and coughed dryly. "It loses a bit of the effect, you see, when everyone is supplied with one."

"Lehn said that it was urgent you comply," Denn warned.

Phon's smile levelled off, the corners of his mouth dropping down. "I've turned down more serious demands before, as he should know. Such is the price of siring an overly ambitious son. What is urgent for them is that something be resolved in terms of the crown. My money is just one way for them to help expedite their scheme."

"And your money is..."

The smile returned to Phon's lips. "Safe," he said brightly. "I've stepped back from my spending habits for appearances' sake. It is true, I have several debts to collect upon once business improves but should the situation in the capital require that family funds be made available in the near future, I assure you they most certainly will be."

Denn stepped into the circle of brighter light shining from the desk and stood closer to his father. "I recognize that I too owe you a debt for ending my ordeal."

Phon raised an eyebrow and cast his attention back to his desk. His hand reached out and grabbed a clay pipe from among the stacks of papers.

"Please, you make a father's compassion sound like a form of usury!"

Leaning toward a candle, he puckered and drew air to relight the pipe. Smoke drifted out of the bowl. Then he stopped and faced Denn abruptly. "That's the wrong word," he said.

Attentively, Denn tried to follow his father's face to get a sense of where he was going.

"Duty, not compassion," Phon said. "I recognize that I have a *duty* to you as your father, which the last two years in which you exiled yourself have come to impress upon me. Compassion is not the reason I sent Yael to secure your liberty. Compassion is what I offer you now."

"Compassion? Where did you learn compassion?" Denn prodded him spitefully.

Then he heard something for the first time, quite unexpectedly. It was something that had never been said to him in all his twenty-five years.

"I am sorry," Phon told him. He gave his pipe a puff which obscured his face momentarily while Denn pondered the significance of that statement.

"Sorry?" Denn repeated, flatly and quietly.

"Yes," came the confirmation. "In my heart, over the years you were growing up, I dwelt on you and your brothers' failings as if I were losing an investment. Had I taken time to nurture you boys, I may have seen Hann turn himself into the man I wanted him to be, much like the man you became on your own—away from my demands and expectations."

"You're flattering me to get me to stay home," Denn accused him.

"No. Your future is bigger than this house alone could

contain."

With that, Phon walked back behind his desk and began sorting papers. Feeling the conversation had ended, Denn turned to walk to the door.

"Serenn informed me you plan to leave in the morning. Is that correct?" Phon called out questioningly.

"Yes," Denn said, "Unless there is something that I can do to satisfy my debt of appreciation before returning to my post." It felt like a mistake to say that, and Denn regretted pushing the offer further but wanted to close the loop cleanly on this reunion before departing.

This time, Phon seized on it.

"There is *one matter* that is important—and you are the best suited for it."

Denn felt uneasy. The old conniving and self-interested businessman was resurfacing now. "A task?" he inquired cautiously.

Phon held up a piece of parchment that showed a map. In the centre was a sketch of Caphedra, but Phon's finger began tracing a line going west.

"Do you remember my friend, Lord Brevin Farathemun?"

"Yes, the late queen's brother," Denn answered.

"This is something he's asked of me, and I couldn't trust it to just any hired armsman. You see, it's not a favour for me, personally, but something of great importance nonetheless, I believe."

Returning to the desk and the centre of the room, Denn peered over his father's shoulder at the map. He was examining an ancient road that bisected the deserts of Hasen and the foothills approaching Palinor. It extended faintly, all the way to the coast and a small town marked as *Fallowsea*.

"Here," Phon pointed to the town. "This little fishing town was granted a few years ago to Brevin's son, Kentin. He occupied a tiny, forgotten fortress there among the shanties and now plays host to a rather important cousin of his."

Fallowsea was not a well-known town, to Denn's knowledge. Very little was thought to dwell in the area. The landscape was rugged, and it was not well-regarded. The waters off its coast were eternally calm, with natural reefs far out into the sea taming the waves, and the winds seldom blew there. Inshore fishermen could row out a short distance and gain sustenance, but the town was inaccessible to any ships from farther out, for if one were to chance the trip from ocean to shore or vice versa, they were impeded by an enduring windlessness, and ultimately left drifting back and forth against the reefs until their ship failed.

"You see," explained Phon further, "I am not alone among the citizens of this city in questioning the wisdom of choosing between a cult of religious zealots or a return to an unbridled regime of conquest, requiring endless consumption and lives."

"Doesn't that provide you with more business and profit though?" Denn asked.

Phon replied, "I allow that I've made a good fortune on the metals and ore that fed the weapons of war, but there is no money left in the coffers of the castle to pay me or anyone else. The merchants of this city acknowledge that Lord Ramid's army would continue to bleed our resources without compensation. In the same manner, the minions of the Lady Ravon and that pompous priest, Golmarra, would seize—*not purchase*—anything they wanted from us. They would choose to extort our wealth directly, as you see they've already begun to do."

"So," Denn confirmed, "This is why the Council of Caphedrans has dragged out the succession. They lose either way."

"Rules of Succession are not clear in this case. They favour sons, but also the eldest child. In his laxness to administrate responsibility, Ramis never declared an heir. Now it's up to the council to adjudicate."

Denn nodded, understanding the predicament, and transposed it as a cause for Lehn's threats and semi-hostility. If anything happened to Phon, Lehn would be showing up on Denn's doorstep next.

"Some on the council have identified a third way. A way by which they could win," Phon said. "The Lady Ramisa is neither a militant nor tainted by duty to the Pillars, and she lies in waiting to be called back from her fosterage in Fallowsea. The merchants and many nobles are of the mind that she may be *our* champion and, fortune willing, our *queen*."

"What would you have me do?" Denn asked skeptically. "I am just a cavalryman."

"Then you can ride a horse. Lord Farathemun requires an escort for his niece's return to Caphedra. I have confidently recommended you if you are willing to undertake this task," he said, "as a *favour*, in return, to me."

The old man paused, the price of Denn's deliverance having now passed his lips. Here was the task he would be required to do to satisfy his honourable compulsion to clear the slate. Denn was content to remain bitter, but not beholden. Yet his father was asking him to take a side in the coming conflict and it gave him misgivings.

He looked carefully upon his father and, though the harshness was now absent, there was still the inescapable, foreboding shrewdness in his eyes that Denn hesitated in trusting. How providential it was, in fact, that Denn's long-awaited return home would occur just as his father required him.

"I don't think that I can," Denn said. "I must return to my post. I have a duty to my company, even if there is no sovereign to command it."

Phon patiently nodded his head. "Please consider it overnight, before you commit to your journey."

Nodding his acquiescence, Denn began to pull away and made toward the doorway leading out. Phon halted him, however.

"I'm not sure if Lehn has tried to sink a barb into you to side with the Faith, but I urge you with great necessity to avoid contact or association with your brother, for your own good."

He spoke with a more deeply conspiratorial undertone. That was no surprise. Denn had anticipated at least one more wagered shot before he departed, but as the old man voiced this last statement, Denn detected some other, underlying concern that seemed to lay behind his father's mask.

"Why not?" he chanced to ask.

"I shall only give voice to what you likely already suspect," he said. "Your brother's ascent in the Faith has come with irredeemably dirty hands, and my money can't cleanse them. The price would quickly become bottomless."

Something seized Phon's thoughts and Denn could see him calculating.

"But with today's visit, I am shocked at his audacity to return to the trough so soon. Perhaps my answer had not been communicated."

Regret again washed over Denn for having left Lehn behind when he rode out to join the cavalry in the field. While he had little stomach to imagine any further transgressions his father was guilty of, he burned to know what his brother's crimes were, and how unforgivable they may be. Denn cursed inwardly. He could not stave off the feeling that everything he left behind in Caphedra was horribly full of rot. It was now just a question of to what degree his family had been involved while he'd been away.

"And let me also add that if, as a man of warfare, you are considering the Marshal's camp, pay heed to your recent ordeal."

Denn turned his head, but his body remained squared toward the exit. "Why?" he asked.

"Upon your return the other night, Yael reported back to me that two of your captors were from the group of loyalists they call the Marshal's Men. If they are indeed such a desperate bunch as to engage in ransom schemes to replace their lost wages, I can assure you that dark times will befall this city should they make it back through the gates as an army numbering in the thousands, all seeking vengeance and bloody compensation. Certainly, you would not wish to be a part of that."

With such dire warnings, neither option presented a cause for Denn to wish to stay in Caphedra any longer. He moved to the doorway leading out of the room and placed his hand on the cold latch.

"Thank you again, Father."

Then, with measured steps, Denn quietly walked out.

CHAPTER 9

Porters and Priests

S outhgate was open and unguarded. No one stood to obstruct their entrance. Nowhere along the multitude of limestone arches and crenelations of the monumental approach to the capital were there any guards stationed to challenge entrants or deny passage. Arrow slits that pockmarked the rocky grey walls on all sides betrayed no movements, nor did any unblinking eyes stare back from places of concealment. Only a grim aggregation of blackbirds in the battlements high above remarked on their arrival, with their caws and scratchy croaks.

Baressa drove the wagon under the shadow of the gate. Light squeezed out from between buildings. As they emerged into the heart of the capital, they finally found people hustling about on afternoon errands. The deeper they ventured, the busier the city became but still no one paid them much notice.

"I honestly thought they'd be watching for us," admitted Baressa. She shrugged and encouraged the horses onward. Passersby moved to the side and let them pass without a word of objection. A man, hauling a two-wheeled cart full of amphorae, angled around them, and continued on his way without concern. A hawker peddling wooden carvings did try out his pitch on them as they rolled through, but Olen refused him right away.

"This neighbourhood is Kroftstalls. It's where the artists do business." Olen waved his arm around, pointing out all the crafters' shops and studios to Livet. "Potshollow is to the west, between here and the river—which is where they bring up the clay. Most of your pots, bowls, and jugs are made there. Bricks too. North is Stonerow, where the banks and the guildhalls are. There are some fancy shops there, and schools for those so inclined."

With huge eyes, Livet absorbed the entirety of the view, up and down the streets. Further along, the crowds on the roadside began to bunch up, with vendors and hagglers paired off among errand runners and craftsmen labouring on the peripheries.

"It's so much bigger than Lanstad! How are we going to find Denn's family?"

Olen frowned. "With as much money as I suspect they have; they'll live somewhere in Castleside. The King's Avenue runs through Stonerow. It will take us there."

"Then what?" Livet asked, concerned for the lack of a definite plan.

Baressa bent down closer toward Livet and told her, "Don't worry. One of my fellows will likely know the house. Porter's Run is very near Castleside and some of those who live there are the type to take keen interest in the particulars of the more-monied folks." A devilish curve overtook her smile, and she chuckled.

The atmosphere of the city was a drastic change from the rural roads of Falbeth. Other wagons crunched over gravel on the ground around them. Through open windows, they heard weavers slamming their looms down in the production of their cloth. Across the road, a burly man was arguing prices with a pair of gaudily dressed merchants who'd propped up a display of brooches, feathered caps, and ornamented walking sticks. All these sounds magnified against the sides of buildings and generated a constant din throughout the street as their wagon drove onward.

To their credit, Baressa's pair of cart horses re-adapted to the city quickly. Their hooves clopped and the wagon rocked slightly. Its wheels settled in along the ruts in the road that must have been formed over many years.

Kroftstalls was colourful. Its buildings displayed beautiful decorations to attract buyers. Adorning each were images advertising the talents of whoever dwelled within. Many of the homes and cottages were also made of brick and Livet noticed how much lighter was the shade of clay the local brick makers used, compared to that which builders sourced back in Lanstad.

After rolling through this neighbourhood, they came to an arterial road beyond which the building facades lost their aesthetic diversity. Across the way, the architecture shifted to austere and monumental granite stones and dull, grey masonry. The traffic on the streets increased also, and Livet worried that soon they would not be able to easily maneuver the cart. She addressed her concerns to Baressa, who responded with a solution.

"We'll go through Stonerow. That is the last place they'd permit any mobs to cause trouble," Baressa declared.

Olen turned to Livet and added his agreement. "She's right. Even if the army is stood down, Stonerow is flush with gold and those people have their own little armies to protect them."

Livet craned her neck. Stonerow's skyline of buildings loomed over them like unassailable cliffs. Sharply cut, squared windows lined upper storeys, but even though they looked out from high off the ground, they sported protective iron bars that alluded to a distrust of all those outside. Balconies protruded, but appeared more like cages, except for those at the very top levels. On those highest floors of the buildings, the walls were whiter and the balconies more expansive, with parapets hinting at a luxury unavailable to those consigned to walk on the ground—those who would never ascend from the mundane earth and dust below.

Livet stiffened in her seat and pointed, "What are those?"

"Where?" Olen asked.

"Those parchments on the doors. They have the Four Pillars on them."

Tacked onto wooden doors or impaled through metal spikes and poles in front of many of the buildings, pieces of paper fluttered in the breeze, marked with the iconography of the Faith.

"Oh," said Baressa. "There are quite a few, aren't there!" She twisted over in her seat and leaned out to examine one as they rode past. "Those are notices of Dues. It seems the curates have been around to collect from the bankers—and in force, judging by the number of notices."

"So, they owe money to the Faith?" Livet asked.

"Recommended *donations*," answered Olen, rolling his eyes.

"A kind of business fee," said Baressa. "They extort it from those with money, under threat of ordering their followers to withdraw all commerce from those who refuse to pay."

"A loyalty test to measure support for Princess Ravon, too," Olen added.

The ever-ascending towers began to part and a much larger

road, running east and west, lay just ahead.

"More people!" Olen complained as the chaos returned again. "You two steer from up here. I'm going to ride on the back and make sure no greedy hands start creeping up under the tarp to pilfer anything."

He grabbed onto a handrail and reversed along the running board to take up watch at the back but sitting high enough to have an all-around view. The road they approached was a broad avenue, but despite the extra width, it was packed solid. Merchant stalls and sellers' tables choked the way forward, consuming as much space as they could hold dominion over, and all around them, a legion of filchers and petty thieves orbited. Whenever one eyed their wagon, Livet saw Olen stare them down menacingly.

Baressa pointed out Middlehold to the north, which served as home for those comfortable in life, but who were neither wealthy enough for Castleside nor well-enough connected to procure estates in the hilled villas of Highside to the west.

Ahead and to the left, Livet observed a noticeable change in construction as stone houses gave way to simpler timbered abodes covered with heavy wooden siding set upon frames of log work. Some of the foundations were of post-style construction, without cellars or stone footings. Livet breathed deeply, for the air here was sweet with the scent of pitch and sawdust.

Baressa also seemed more at ease as they approached. "This is the edge of what's called Porter's Run. It's mostly made up of Nor'porters and errant folks from Greyforest who've come to the city. They've left the trouble up north and took root here—like clippings from a big old tree."

Suddenly, Livet was startled by a low, growling roar and a powerful snort that cut through the noise of the street. A dark brown beast with long, coarse hair stood in front of them, biting at the air and licking its lips. Two big black eyes, bordered in yellowy amber, were hungrily following the hand of a bare-chested man who held up a sizeable shank of meat. With a cheerful shout, he surrendered it to the creature, which dropped down greedily on all fours and began devouring it. Livet could see its black claws were each as long as her whole hand.

"That's the Chief," Baressa said to Livet in explanation.

"That man with the creature?"

She laughed and corrected her, "No, the bear! We call the bear, Chief."

The animal's ears perked up when it heard Baressa's voice. For a moment, it raised its head and appeared to acknowledge her, before dropping back down onto the meat and powerfully crushing the bone with one awful crunch of its jaw.

"We named him that after Earl Lorram died. We figured that if they were still coming after our chiefs here, no one really wanted the title. We gave it to the bear instead and he did well to discourage any challengers."

"The earl died trying to defend Northport, didn't he? That must be an old bear!" Livet said.

Baressa shook her head, "No, the earl didn't," she said. "And no, the bear's not *that* old. When Nor'port fell, the earl was taken to Northwood Garrison and made to kneel to the king. Then, stripped of title, he found his way here to the city where we all looked after him for a while. But then a few years later, the old earl got into a fight in a tavern, and someone knifed him, poor man. They kept his chair empty at the Travellin' Trapper ever since." She shook her head, sighed, then cleared her throat. "But I suppose that makes The Chief around eight or nine years old."

Livet listened reverently and said nothing. Everywhere, she supposed, could testify to at least a few brutal moments of history.

At that instant, Olen shouted from behind, "Oy!" and the wagon lurched as a gargantuan figure in a ratty green cloak spryly vaulted up and over to just behind the driver's seat. Before Olen could reach him, the man's arms shot forward in unison and embraced Baressa tightly and enthusiastically.

"Astir, boy, you'll collapse my cart!" Baressa cried, struggling for breath.

"Don't be angry," the man said, releasing his bearhug and scratching the back of his sweaty neck nervously.

"Why?" Baressa demanded.

"You missed Roderin. He just left for Ashcamp."

"Damn. I never seem to catch him," she sighed. "That's quite far south. Any reason?"

"Army's been pulling troops out of the forest to march them down here—and I think he's fixing to have a go at Stonebriar Garrison once it empties."

"East of the Greyforest Road, he must be with Roy's Boys, then?"

"Yeah," Astir answered. "They sound like they're getting along just fine." He laughed.

Olen, whose eyes drifted between Astir and the minding of the cart, called up to them at the front. "Baressa, you're all good with this pile of a man, then?"

Baressa beamed, "Of course I am. He's like a big, little brother to me."

Astir leaned back and with caution advised, "Friend, you might not want to say that name outside of Porter's Run."

Olen stared at him for a moment, then wordlessly returned to his watch.

Seeming reminded of her neglected pleasantries, Baressa made the introductions. "Astir, these two are my friends, Livet and Olen. I approve of them, so keep them well and looked after as they travel through here." Then she gave Livet a quick squeeze of the arm. "Especially this one," she smiled.

"Aye," Astir acknowledged.

"Livet and Olen, I present you with Chief Astir Flamran, eldest son of our famed Chief Grint Flamran of Greyforest. His family presided over the same woodlands upon which the garrison at Greyforest was built."

Astir's cheeks went pink. "We don't own it now, so you can do away with the 'Chief' part, m'lady."

"I told you no one *wanted* the title," she said aside to Livet. Then, with a light laugh, she contradicted Astir. "You looked after the old Earl for years, and it was him that made you so. So that is what you are," she countered, and her countrymen surrendered helplessly.

As with the districts before, Porter's Run was soon behind them, too. Baressa began slowing the cart as they came to the end of the wooden-walled district. A large central plaza became visible where the road opened up just ahead.

"My friends are looking for the home of the Wellum family," Baressa said.

"You mean the merchant, Phon Wellum?" Astir asked.

"If he's the richest one of them, then yes," said Olen.

At that, the big man whistled loudly through his fingers and temporarily pierced the racket of the crowds. Livet recoiled and Baressa ducked her head, hiding her face to avoid the instant attention.

"Kirt!" he called, waving over a hunched, leather-clad man with dark, but greying hair. He approached the cart, leaning gingerly on a long, wooden walking staff. Seeing Baressa, the lines in his face eased. He closed his eyes for a moment and contentedly nodded. When he did speak, he said, "Are these the ones you dreamt about?"

Baressa nodded. "They need someone to help them find the home of their friend. Can you be of aid?"

"Friends of the Wellums seldom need help from the likes of us," he said, "But yes, I can you show the way."

"I'd like Astir to take the wagon and store it behind the Trapper. It's too big a hassle to navigate any farther and they're expecting these goods at the tavern. We four can go on foot from here if nobody minds."

"I can walk it," Kirt said tiredly but committedly.

Baressa turned to Livet and softly informed her, "Kirt spent time in the king's gaol at Northwood Garrison," she hesitated, "for *agitations* at Veldon Grove."

"Fifteen years," he said bitterly.

Livet's face went pale. "Such a long time. I am surprised they didn't just kill you."

"I was surprised too, for a while. But eventually, they found a reason." He reached up to help Baressa down off the wagon while she handed the reins to Astir. Olen hopped off too, one hand grabbing his wooden-framed backpack. Livet jumped down with Baressa's assistance.

"We need to cross Hamrin Square but be warned. Some holy men have set up a protest there and the Pillarmen are taking notice and assembling their armsmen. If it's too bad, we'll need to go around. Evening is falling, and that could spell trouble."

Tapping along with his staff as he walked, Kirt led them on a path that wound around the north of the plaza. The square was overflowing with people and their shouts and calls to each other saturated the cooler air of the evening. The sun had gone down, and great braziers were being lit to provide light for the patrons of local establishments. The smell of delicious foods wafted about. The sellers here favoured fatty meats and pastries far more than the hawkers they had passed to the west. Elegant and enviable public houses bordered the square, which was regally and appropriately named for the king who had ruled before Ramis.

King Hamrin Wolstett had been the brother of Ramis and an avowed miser. Like those of his line before him, he built upon generations of trade wealth for Caphedra. What money he spent during his reign went to realize his personal dedication to the Faith of the Pillars—which unexpectedly proved to be his undoing. While inspecting a magnificent addition to the central temple, a winch collapsed; a ton of hewn stone plummeted down from above and crushed the pavilion he was attending from.

Subsequently, Ramis was recalled from the field. As a second son, he had undergone military training since boyhood and this rather dissimilar rearing dictated how he would choose to administrate. Without his brother's reservation—or any temperance in the least—he opened wide the royal coffers to fund a campaign of conquest. He satisfied his fraternal obligations by redirecting a small pittance to this pre-existing square and the notion of commemoration was satisfied by naming it in his late brother's honour.

Hamrin Square provided a nexus between Stonerow, Castleside, and the Folds—the latter taking its name from the likening of its winding alleys to the wrapped robes and gowns of its priests and curates. The original Temple of the Four Pillars was housed in this place and officiants emanated outward from its centre to enforce the Faith's tenets and ensure collection of resources and wealth.

Livet was especially attuned to watching their blue-vested stooges slithering through the crowds. Attention fixed, they moved in organized patterns. They watched and listened while the disenfranchised called out for things like relief for the impoverished, or that the armies stand down now that the king no longer influenced the ambitions of the city.

Passing alongside a shambling beggar—a poor, small man with failing eyesight—Kirt stooped over as if asking for advice or directions. The blind man nodded in answer to several questions, which made Kirt's expression grow more profoundly sour. The two clasped hands in a brotherly manner and the beggar shuffled off.

A handful of the curates were interacting with the crowd. Olen, Baressa, and Kirt ignored them as they passed, but Livet couldn't help but be stirred to disgust at hearing their oft-taught philosophies, if only in remembrance of how they were once forced on her while she lay crumpled, in the dark of her Lanstad cell.

Ahead of them, one prominent curate lectured loudly to the masses. She wore a blue dress that was the same colour as the tunic sported by the regular clergy. In an uplifted voice, to an unwavering audience, she began educating on the Pillar of Progeny, which lay, she explained, to the left of the temple entrance.

"The only guarantee of ultimate victory in life is to pass along the struggle to the next generation that they, or their offspring, shall receive our glory and achieve greater things. All failures in this life can be erased and losses restored by the efforts of those yet to come."

The crowd vocalized their agreement, but Livet cared not. Her struggles were not inherited from her mother; they were precipitated by her loss. The only father figured she'd ever known was Kell.

"The Pillar of Resiliency, to the right, is the first bulwark against intrusion and outside threat," the preacher continued. "Persuasion may motivate, and planning may circumvent, but physical strength is ultimately what causes the mundane to move and manifest. And greater than sheer strength is resiliency—to dedicate one's physical effort continually. This is why even the gentle forces of streams and breezes can wear down the mountains and carve out canyons."

Again, her listeners buoyed her statements with murmurings of concordance. This time, Livet found less to argue against.

"Standing behind us all is the Pillar of Wisdom. Actions require purpose and that purpose is guided by wisdom. But the wise path is often hard to see, which is why this pillar is always located behind the temple, diagonal to the pillar of Progeny for new generations often have the farthest to go to reach its attainment."

Livet was disturbed to see that the woman commanded such a flock. She was a mature figure, though younger than Baressa, with curled auburn hair and a relentless manner to engage those surrounding her.

"All that exists, on and under the soil below us, is a result of what has transpired in the past and shaped by the efforts of our forebears to be a fountainhead for all the other pillars. Their continued teachings provide wisdom, their seed generates the descendants who will one day lead, and their struggle has sustained and tempered the community with resiliency. Their lineage stretches back through the ages and is symbolized by the deep-rooted Pillar of Heritage. This is the instruction you receive today."

Several voices together then said, "The Pillars support the people. We support the Pillars." Coins clinked into metal collection bowls at the woman's feet. Among the handfuls of bronze and silver coins, Livet's keen eye picked out golden Caphedran dames and sires being tossed in, the currency of Ramis, along with golden points and silver sheaves of the type minted by Duke Murgan, the former sovereign of Lanstad. There were others that she didn't recognize as well. A long-submerged and covetous part of her old self began to well up inside. It hearkened back to her days in the street when her tiny hands would have nimbly snatched up as many of the treasures as they could then sneak away to stash her plunder.

A hand on Livet's shoulder nudged her back to her senses. "You're falling behind us, Livet," said Baressa.

"I'm sorry," she said, then set her jaw angrily and concluded, "I don't need to hear any more o' that rubbish."

Just as Livet spoke, the speaker's demagoguery was interrupted by an old man with a trim white beard and close-cropped hair who called out just as spitefully, but significantly louder, bellowing over the lectures of all the nearby curates.

"Do not speak of these things and ignore true power! Thieves! Murderers! It is you and your temple that are a blight on this city!" He shouted fearlessly at the blue-clad curates who fast began congealing into a mob that advanced on his spot to snuff out the dissidence.

The man continued, "It is you and your temple that drove sweet Queen Tressa to insanity!"

Several mismatched peasants flanked the man and began beating staves on the ground around him for emphasis and, perhaps, intimidation to dissuade any suppression of the agitator's continued rebuke.

"And it is you and your temple that basks in pride over the

murder of a king and whose crown you seek to abuse! You, who revel in the vile bewitchment and murder of a queen!"

Around Hamrin Square, a tide of raised voices rolled through the crowd with incredulity that someone would so blatantly brand the Faith with culpability in the monarchs' murders.

But staves were smashing on the ground now, swelling with the fury of all those whom they could rally to their cause. Kirt had lowered his own staff, forcing open a path before him as he walked, and distinguishing his from those of the crowd lest it be picked out from the throng and he implicated along with these radicals.

Ahead, Olen rammed through the crowd, keeping close to Baressa and Livet to better shield their escape. His face looked fierce, and he pointed east to the high stone statue of Queen Tressa, Ramis's consort, on the outer edge of the plaza. "Make your way to behind the statue if we get separated!" he ordered.

Above their heads, torches, bludgeons, and cudgels were now out and swinging. Kirt disappeared into the crowd while Livet felt like she was being submerged under Olen's protective bulk. He held onto her with one hand and dragged her along underneath him, determinedly trying to crest the crowd and crash through it.

"Baressa!" Livet called out, no longer able to see her.

"There!" Olen announced, nodding with his head to a space in the mob just ahead. His height afforded him a better view and he indicated he could see their companion squeezing her way through, farther on.

The severity of the clash amplified and shouts and stomps from before were now full-out screams and cries of panic. The square was filling with young men and women dressed in the garments of Pillar clergy, but the worst were those who wore grey instead of blue. They exuded a youthful brashness that suggested they were new initiates. The veteran curates could be heard ordering them to advance, exploiting this fresh tenacity. Rebellious dissidents were not the only ones to fall afoul of them, however. Crying out curses to the "Apostates!" they were tearing around the entirety of the crowd in a frenzy of arm-wrenching and head-smashing, indiscriminately.

Whether the detractors had managed to gain supporters was difficult to tell. Still, they did succeed in fanning the anger of many in the crowd. In response, dozens were beaten, smashed, and bound in chains, then dragged by their necks—or hair—to menacing iron cages on the backs of a row of boxed wagons that had emerged tumultuously into the square. The lording curates and the fearsome acolytes shepherded the offenders up ramps of planks and behind the bars, where they stabbed at them between the rungs with the protestors' own confiscated staves.

As one carriage was crammed full, the next was wheeled forward, and demonstrators were marched into it, screaming, and lashing out if they could manage to do so.

Olen stopped, and for a moment Livet felt his grip loosen. His eyes fell upon the men driving the wagons and the troops now flooding the square supporting the curates. They bore the boar's head shields of Lord Vlass.

"He's pimped his soldiers to these bastards," growled Olen.

It was too much for Livet. Even more infuriated than Olen, she pulled away from his hand and plunged into the crowd.

Fearful of being trampled, she slinked and shimmied through the people until she was up against one of the cages. Faces were being pressed into the bars, trying to mouth pleas for help against the crushing force behind them. Arms dangled out between the rungs, some obviously broken and hanging down at grotesque angles.

Then she saw the face of the man who had been speaking, and he saw her. His wise and wondering eyes followed her, and for a second, Livet could feel his desperation depart. Her hands reached out and found a large, iron padlock that was suspended from chains, securing the bars of the enormous trap. She had no key to open it, but she was sure that her minute hands were tiny enough that she could reach inside and, with a bit of help, spring the locking bar directly.

The cage was swaying and heaving with the weight of those inside. From a fold in her waistcoat, Livet procured a slip of metal. She plunged the small crook into the lock and worked its insides over. This was one of the more practical skills that Kell had taught her, besides those that Baressa called 'parlour tricks.' The shackle spread open like a winged iron bird and the chains fell to the ground with heavy thuds.

The bars of the cage sprung open, and a torrent of bodies flooded out to regain their freedom. The old man was tussled in the fray, but his eyes were still transfixed on Livet. She grabbed his hand and pulled him off the wagon, saying, "Run!" then slipped herself between the wagon's axles and out the other side. Another caged coach was only a few arms' lengths away.

Once they saw the ongoing mass escape, the curates tried to form up their soldiers to block the prisoners' flight, but it was mayhem. People were fleeing by any route available, and the soldiers were too busy running down too many disparate targets to be reined in for a collective response.

As Livet handled the last lock, she felt a hand on her shoulder again.

"Olen?" she said, turning, but the face looking back was not her friend. It was a furious Pillar soldier wearing a nasal helm, and a tell-tale blue demi-cape over a scored leather cuirass.

Wordlessly, he wrenched her away and pushed Livet violently into the side of the wagon. She struggled, but he pinned her against the boards with one strong hand while reaching to draw his short sword.

Livet twisted and squirmed but was helpless. She was gasping now from the weight of the giant mitt pressing upon her chest.

But before he could thrust the sword into her, one of the prisoners in the wagon was able to reach out from the cage and grip onto the soldier's arm, pulling it back while another helped hold it in place against the bars. Another hand reached out from above Livet, and tipped the soldier's helmet off his head.

Distracted and riled, he drew back and tried to wrench his arm free, loosening his hold on Livet. She kicked him, her foot impacting into his groin, and his grip relaxed instantly. Livet dropped to the ground and rolled under the wagon, out of view.

Bracing herself against the axles, she focused her concentration on the darkness of the wagon's underbelly and the glow of an umbrage overtook her.

"You're dead!" he cursed loudly. "Let Dagremahr have you all!"

She heard screams above her as the soldier's feet came back into view and with motions like ominous dance steps, made moves toward the wagon. Then he dropped to his knees, his snarling face peering underneath to see where she had gone.

She stayed still and let the shadow charm cloak her.

The soldier growled with frustration but did not see her.

Ample sweat rolled down Livet's forehead. She dared not move until the soldier withdrew and stomped off to search for her elsewhere. When she was certain he had departed, Livet touched down onto the dirt, and with relief, crawled carefully out from under the wagon. She wiped her damp forehead and saw that it was not sweat, but blood.

She didn't think she had been injured—and she wasn't. She quickly realized that the blood had seeped through the floorboards of the wagon. The soldier had rewarded the prisoners' aid to Livet, with retribution from his blade.

Crying, Livet returned to the last lock. She looked up and saw the anguished faces of the prisoners urging her on desperately. One more moment and the lock popped.

Strong hands inside lifted the bars of the cage and most of the prisoners fell out, save for a small group huddling near a lifeless body lying prone on the floor of the cage.

"Go! We'll carry him!" urged a voice from behind Livet, and with tears welling up, she regretfully took to her heels and darted off.

❖   ❖   ❖

At the foot of the statue of the late Queen Tressa Farathemun, Livet's companions reassembled in the night. Kirt was resting, propped up by his staff. Baressa faced the square, watching sadly out over the field of violence. Olen had turned his back to the crowd and gazed up at the demure, gentle face of the queen. The statue bore no evidence of the torment that was said to have haunted the dear lady's final days. It merely stood unmoving and hollow-eyed, facing southwest toward the Temple of the Four Pillars.

The outpouring of the mob grew less frenetic as fresh compatriots of the riot's instigators came to assist those in flight from the evening's orgy of imprisonments, even pushing back in places. But while the square mostly purged itself of people, none among the displaced fled uphill toward Castleside's opulent approaches. None of the night's participants were of the privileged classes. Once she reached the edge of the plaza, Livet's path to her friends at the statue was clear and open.

The soft-sounding footfall of her leather boots upon the cobblestones remained unheard, until she appeared out of nowhere, and announced herself, safe and alive.

"Had your adventure with the Pillies and Hogheads?" Kirt asked her sarcastically.

Baressa hugged her and then looked over to Olen, with a smile that conveyed her relief, but as she caringly brushed back Livet's hair, she shrieked and exclaimed, "Is that blood?"

"Not mine," Livet said. "I'm okay."

"Kirt says the house you're looking for is at the top of the street behind us. That's Phon Wellum's place. You'll find help for your friend there, I hope. It's a good idea to get off the streets, anyway." She reached for a flask of water from Kirt and dabbed the blood from Livet's forehead.

"Thank you," said Livet.

Olen approached but was tongue-tied. He made a few sounds and then gave up, nodded to Livet, and took a deep breath of night air to reset himself. Finally, he managed to return a smile to Baressa.

"I suppose our trip together is concluded. Thank you, Portia."

Baressa laughed. "Just remember to come look for me if you have any trouble."

Olen nodded obediently.

She crouched down and took Livet's hand. "Come find me as soon as you can, once you've helped your friend."

"I will," Livet said.

"And keep the letter," Baressa said. "If you can't find me for some reason, or if you decide you don't have any patience," she sniggered, "look for Gardia where I told you. She and Kell were good friends, and she will help you also."

"At the Peahen in Faralley," Livet repeated, remembering their conversation the previous night.

Olen raised an eyebrow. "The where?!"

Baressa turned to him to say by way of exposition, "My friend's tavern."

"I know the establishment," Olen said, then informed Livet, "You'd be better off drinking at the place with the bear."

Livet prodded Olen, "We should go. Denn needs us."

Baressa waved and Kirt, too, nodded his farewell.

As Olen and Livet started the trek up the street to a walled manor at the summit, they could see a light burning in one room, which gave them hope to find at least somebody still up at this hour.

When they arrived, they ascended impressive stone steps and stood side-by-side before a thick wooden door. Olen reached up to grab the doorknocker and smashed it thrice, in quick succession. A moment later, they heard a latch open from the other side, then the creak and groan of the door as it rotated slowly on its hinge. A young woman with honey-coloured hair, thin lips, and calming blue eyes stood cautiously in the entrance. Behind her, Olen saw another pair of eyes as a man with short, wedged hair, and a patchy and pointed beard watched suspiciously.

"It's late. Can I help you?" the woman asked.

Livet nudged Olen and stayed mute.

"We have come from your brother's post in Fal Ghreeg," Olen told the woman. Then he paused, a bit uncertain, and asked, "This is the family house of Denn Wellum, isn't it?"

The girl gave a short laugh as if a bit surprised to have to explain that this was indeed the Wellum family home. "Yes, it is, and I am his sister, Serenn. Have you come to see Denn?"

"Well," Olen said, "Unfortunately, we bring news that he was taken captive by criminals ten days ago, m'lady."

Livet coughed and corrected him with some shame and sadness, "Eleven days ago."

Olen's head bowed and his eyes shifted downward, betraying his discomfort. The girl did not seem distraught at the pronouncement, but perhaps was still trying to fathom the terrible news. Perhaps Denn's feud with his family ran deep and she didn't care.

"I'm sorry. We've come because we thought that you could help. We were trying to save your brother," Olen said.

"Can you 'elp him?" Livet asked bluntly. "'Ave you 'eard anything?"

Serenn looked them both over. Her smooth brow pinched with a deepening wrinkle as if perplexed. "Denn's been home for the past three days," she said. "Do you want me to fetch him?"

Olen and Livet stood dumbfounded on the steps, mouths agape in surprise.

CHAPTER 10

More Unexpected Guests

D enn wanted to check on Naobe one more time before turning in for the night, as well as retrieve some saddlebags he had seen in the stable, that he could bring in and pack with supplies for the next morning's journey back to the Fals. But as he reached the door to the courtyard, Denn heard his sister approach and call his name.

"What is it?" he asked.

"You have visitors," she replied. "They look like travellers."

Denn twisted his face, looking confused. "Who knows that I am here?"

Serenn shrugged. "A big man. A little woman."

Following her back to the front hall, he clutched the scabbard of his newly adopted longsword. He did not know how many people knew that he was back in the capital—his vow of exile temporarily rescinded. His suspicions were elevated, as were Brae's. The young ex-soldier with the pointed beard stood watch beside the entrance, positioned next to a finely etched chestnut side table, where he concealed a loaded crossbow, ready to employ it within an instant's notice.

Since Denn's father was in residence, Denn presumed that Yael Larkin, his father's guardian, and his own previous saviour, was also nearby. He would undoubtedly be attentive enough to respond if there was any new trouble. Less certain to appear was Trin, the other hired guard, who was likely at rest in the coach house, his duties done for the day.

"You summoned me? Who is there?" Denn called to the visitors outside on the doorstep.

Hearing his voice, Olen replied, "Denn, my boy! It's us!"

Rushing into the room and startling the greeters, Livet shot toward Denn. Brae raised the crossbow and tried to track her bounding into the room, but her tiny stature was unexpected and before he could aim it, she was wrapped solidly around Denn in a wild embrace, making any shot impossible. So instead—seeing the girl's obvious affection for his employer's son—he smirked, blushed, and lowered the weapon.

Denn squeezed Livet tightly in return. Still holding on to her, he lifted his head toward Olen and asked, "How did you know I was here?"

Olen stammered and shook his head embarrassedly. "We didn't," he admitted. "We came here for help after we couldn't find any elsewhere."

"Huh?" Denn asked, finally loosening his hold on Livet. "You came all this way? You should have checked with Constable Hannellin. He could have dispatched some horses."

"He wouldn't," Livet explained. "He accused you of runnin' away."

Olen twisted his mouth and gritted his teeth. "He refused to help. Then the rat removed you from your muster roll as a deserter."

Denn looked shocked. "A deserter? Did you tell him we were attacked?"

"Told him everything," Olen said. "He's a dirty, useless prat, and didn't seem to care much for, or about you at all."

"No, he never did," Denn said begrudgingly. With that, he moved back from Livet and sat down in a nearby armchair with a defeated look on his face. "Any use even riding back to sort things out, you think?"

Olen shook his head. "They're dropping men as fast as they can. The Lord Chancellor has taken over the purse of the army, and he's closed it up tight. For Hannellin, it was any excuse he could find to be rid of one more man that he wouldn't have to pay for." Olen added, "Not just your unit. I've been dismissed from mine, too."

Denn's stomach convulsed in a knot at hearing the news. He closed his eyes and lowered his head, cursing. "I'm sorry," he consoled. Then in a soft voice, changed the topic to ask, "How is Ayren?"

"He survived fine," said Livet. "Those men just tied him up

and left him 'side the outhouse. I found 'im the next mornin'.'"

Nodding, Denn ventured a more contented expression. "Good. We're all accounted for then. You both must be starving!"

Relieved at seeing her brother's joy at reuniting with his friends, Serenn chimed in. "I'll go fetch Nelissa and have her assemble some bread and meat to fill up your friends' bellies." Smiling politely, she slipped out of the hall toward a tiny side stair that led to the servants' quarters.

Olen bowed slightly as Serenn left, seeming to improvise his manners as he went. Denn could tell that he was not accustomed to homes like the Wellum manor. Olen's jaw was hanging as his attention bounced from tapestry to painting, and from velvet settee to marble bust.

"You grew up here?" Olen asked.

Denn nodded.

Livet also looked to be mesmerized by the wealth in the room, so Denn tried to overcome their distraction and keep the conversation going. "Come and tell me about your travels," he said.

Olen grunted, "I doubt it'll match the story of how you were freed so quickly!"

"I'll tell you all about that too," Denn promised, placing a hand amiably on Olen's arm and guiding him along a corridor to the dining hall. His other hand warmly grasped Livet's and he led her along as well, tugging amusedly only a few times, to prompt a quicker pace and postpone her gawking about until after they had time to eat and rest.

They sat together at the same table Denn had dined at with his mother and sister earlier. Nelissa brought them food and jugs of cool water up from the cellar. Esta kept to the background, coming and going from the room, as did Serenn until Denn invited her to join the conversation. She happily sat down, and introductions were made.

"You must be very fond of Denn to have come all this way on account of his safety," she said.

Livet smiled in her shy way, but it was Olen who answered. "Aye. He's been excellent company to us, out in the Fals. You've got a fine a brother, m'lady."

"I still find it hard to picture him as a soldier," she said. "I have too many memories of him when he was a small, scrawny boy."

Olen chuckled and nudged Denn's shoulder, saying, "I assure you that he's grown into quite the small, scrawny man!"

Denn pushed back, "I'm taller than you are!"

Olen accepted the rebuttal but retorted, "We've tried to fatten him up, but it just won't take." Olen broke apart a crusty loaf of bread and dipped it into his water to soften it.

As they talked, Serenn's eyes darted between Denn and Livet. Her mind appeared to be twisting itself with curiosity, but she held her tongue. Denn didn't say much to confirm his sister's apparent imaginings, but his hands regularly reached out to caress Livet's, and that betrayed his affection with doubtless clarity.

Esta, on the other hand, had her eyes fixed on Olen's greasy hands and the gravy that was pooling at the edges of his mouth. He noticed her and sheepishly wiped his face off on the back of his arm, slowing his consumption and exercising more care after that.

"Your rooms will be waiting for you when you are ready," Esta said, then whispered something to Serenn, whose face turned noticeably grey for a moment.

"You must be tired. I can guide you upstairs when you wish to sleep," Serenn offered. That earned a satisfied nod from Esta, but then Denn's mother took one last quick, dismissive look at Olen and followed it by a more critical scan of Livet, before bidding them a good night and withdrawing from the dining room.

Now more relieved to continue the discussion, Olen had another question. "What have you heard of the army Myrhic is assembling for the prince?"

Denn's expression grew cloudy. "Nothing other than the word that they are assembling north of here—likely around Wodwarden. He still has supporters in the city, however. They're called the Marshal's Men, and they made up at least a couple of the ones who kidnapped me."

"I've heard of them," Olen said.

"Why did they come for you?" Livet asked.

Denn shrugged. "I don't know. Serenn tells me they showed up seeking a ransom. If so, that means they are either desperately short of finances or they're just common ruffians now, without any honour or discipline whatsoever. Of course, both could be true, though I find it hard to believe that the Lord Marshal would condone this brigandry."

"Left on their own, without a leader close at hand, it doesn't take long for some men to drift into such dishonourable pursuits," opined Olen. "Besides, there are lots of ex-soldiers inside and outside of this city, all without any respectable prospects ahead of them and harbouring some dreadfully empty bellies right now." He swallowed the last fingers-full of torn-apart bread. "But not my belly. It's full, and my next path is clear once your thoughtful sister shows us the way to our beds."

Flattered by the complimentary summons, Serenn used her most charming voice to respond. "You seem well-deserved of your rest. Denn is fortunate to have loyal friends such as you. Please follow me and I will escort you to your rooms." Her gaze shifted to Livet to await her response as well.

Livet looked to Denn, then back at Serenn to respond. "Thank you. I'm fully exhausted," she said, yawning to compound the statement.

Holding high a flaming candelabrum, Serenn led the way up the staircase to the second floor. When she stopped on the first landing, she pointed to the closed door beside her and announced, "Olen, you can sleep in this room, here."

The look on Denn's face projected his uncertainty. "That room?" he asked Serenn.

"Yes," she confirmed. Then quietly, she nodded and said, "I know, Denn."

He watched as his sister pressed down on the latch and pushed open the stiffly swinging door leading to Hann's room. As she did, Denn saw that it was no longer kept as he had remembered it. For all the days he had spent back home, he had still lacked the courage to enter, so the changes to its décor and furnishings were wholly unknown and unexpected.

"It's a guest room now," she said to Denn, softly brushing her hand along his shoulder and patting him on the back.

"Thank you. It looks very comfortable," said Olen.

Denn forced himself to peer inside. Any trace of what he remembered had been erased. He took a breath and brought himself to accept what he must. "I am in the next room if you need anything," he said.

"And Livet will sleep in my room, *with me*," Serenn added haughtily.

She didn't give Denn time to counter her. But perhaps, he surmised, it would be wise to not act brashly until Livet had a chance to settle in.

"As I said, Livet, I am next door if you need anything," Denn said.

"She'll be fine," said Serenn, obviously ensuring there would be no mingling this night. Denn wasn't sure whom she was more concerned about protecting—her brother or the seemingly innocent young lady guest she had just met.

"Then good night, all," Denn said. He gave Serenn a kiss on the cheek as he started back down the stairs. To Livet, he turned with a sharp smile. She glowered at him for a moment, then cracked a smirk as she continued up the staircase alongside Serenn to her host's elegant bower, a half flight of steps higher.

Denn slipped into his bedroom and settled on the bed. From the room next to his, he heard the thumping of Olen's boots as they hit the floor and a creak as the old rope bed stretched beneath the soldier's weight. Less than an instant later, there was snoring.

From up the stairs, however, he could hear muffled voices as the two girls had set themselves to their own private discourse. They carried on well beyond the time he began drifting off. Denn did not doubt that his sister would be interrogating poor Livet until the girl could stay awake no more.

It was a bit odd that Denn's father hadn't made an appearance. He wondered if the old man was even still in the house. His business and the affairs of the city had kept him constantly engaged and away from home so much since Denn had returned.

And likewise, as Denn lay on the bed, his mind swam with his own preoccupations. His journey back to the Fals was now uncertain. He was no longer counted within the ranks of the Twelfth and, even worse, he now had the burden of clearing his name should he ever seek another appointment with the army. Only, he didn't know whose army he'd join. Maybe his brother's offer to command men for the Faith really was an option, although Livet would never tolerate it, nor did he think *he* could stomach the deeds they expected of their hirelings. Perhaps he could find his way with Olen since both of them were in the same straits—or maybe he should consider the journey to Fallowsea. He didn't have to do it for his father's sake. The trip itself held merit if it provided a more moderate answer to the matter of succession that might better benefit the ordinary people of Caphedra. To serve the good of the city would be a noble task.

All these possibilities drove a wedge of tension into his brow as he lay in his bed. But his mental meanderings ultimately slowed. A breeze blowing through the window cooled his head and the distant noises of the city at night floated in. Before long, he too began to snooze peacefully.

With a start, Denn awoke to the sounds of shouting in the courtyard. It was still dark in the room and night outside, but an orange glow was visible beyond the open window and the breeze carried through the frightening smell of smoke.

Fire, Denn thought, then yelled out loud, "Fire!"

He couldn't tell right away if it was the house on fire or the stables down below, but he had to rush and help. From the sounds of voices, it had already been discovered and Yael must have roused his men to begin fighting it.

If it was the stables, Denn hoped that they'd gotten there in time to rescue Naobe and the two carthorses.

Pulling his boots on quickly, he jumped up and made his way swiftly to the door and into the hallway. Olen was awakened by his shout of alarm—as were Livet and Serenn—who had grabbed cloaks and were hurrying down the stairs in case it was some part of the house that was burning. Though much of the exterior of the manor was brick, the inside was framed by timber in most places.

Olen grabbed Denn by the arm before he could follow the girls down the steps.

"Grab your sword!" he said. "Someone might have set this."

Comprehending the danger immediately, Denn said nothing but turned on his heels, ascending back toward his room. His sword was hanging in a scabbard on a chair by the bed. As he re-entered his bedchamber, the light from the fire outside appeared much more intense, and he could see spirals of sparks rising into the sky through the wide-open window.

But he hadn't opened the window so widely when he settled down for sleep. Was it the force from the rising winds of the fire? The oddness struck him unsettlingly, then as he reached for his sword, the weapon was forcefully kicked from his grasp.

Denn swung around and came face-to-face with an intruder in his room. The glow from outside lit the ridges on the man's crooked, ugly nose and immediately he recognized the silhouette of Colden, his former captor.

"Feelin' up for a fight, are we?" Colden sneered, darting across the room, then sliding in between Denn and the entrance. He spun around and backed up against the door, blocking escape, and pushing it closed.

"H-how?" Denn stuttered in fear and shock.

"Climbed the trellis," Colden said smugly. "Lookin' for that murderer, Larkin. My luck to find you first!" He lunged at Denn, who was forced to duck and retreat further back into his bedchamber.

The room was prohibitively dark and Denn was no longer familiar with its layout and all its furnishings. The flames behind him lit up Colden's form each time he advanced, but Denn was unable to see anything that he could use to help him in the fight. They circled the room. Colden had a nasty rapier which flashed as he probed out sharply and caught the light reflected from outside. The brute laughed at his helpless quarry, then thrust and stabbed again.

Now remembering the trellis outside, if Colden could climb up so easily, surely Denn could climb down just the same.

The only thing he found within reach was a jug of water that had been beside the bed. He seized it and threw it at Colden's head. With a smash of clay shards, Colden jolted back and collapsed down to one knee. After letting out a wounded grunt, he staggered back up to his feet—but Denn had already gotten to the window. He grabbed the curtain as he propelled himself outward and hung from it momentarily until his feet swung around and found a rung on the outside trellis. His hand then connected with a firm hold. He quickly planted his other foot, scaled down the wall and was away.

As he dropped to the ground, he fell onto his backside in the dust. Surrounding him were swirling eddies of smoke, the whinnying of horses, and the heavy, hurried footfalls of the water-laden fire fighters. Above him, Colden's fearsome face looked down from the window, then ducked back inside without a word.

"Grab some water from the cistern!" he heard Olen yell at him.

He answered clumsily, uttering his words in staccato, "Intruders! In the house! Marshal's Men!"

That instantly drew Yael Larkin beside him. "Keep fighting the fire!" he called out to Olen. Then he turned to Trin, the fair-haired hand from the stable. Slapping the young man on his shoulder, Yael bade him follow into the house to flush out the invaders.

"The horses?" Denn asked Olen as the big man hustled buckets of water to douse licks of flame on the stable roof.

"They're safe!" Olen answered loudly over the noise, breathing hard as he did so. He redirected himself back to procuring another bucket of water from the rain trough in the courtyard, but the bucket clunked and scraped against the bottom as Olen drew water, and Denn saw the trough was almost empty now.

Across the yard, Brae had managed to pull the cart of hay from the side of the stable, cutting down on available fuel for the fire. The two carthorses and Naobe were also freed from the structure and herded across the yard, tied to a hitch near the closed gate. Naobe made a high-pitched whine when she saw Denn. Walking up to her, he stroked her and calmed her, noticing that the fire had singed some of her coat along the back of her neck. Her height had placed her closest to the burning roof.

"Easy," Denn soothed her. "It's okay now."

His voice helped, and she quieted down as he reassured her.

Then Denn felt a tap on his back. It was Olen, who pointed along the top of the back wall. Something was different. Something stood out. "Do you see the top of the ladder?" Olen asked. "That's how they got in."

Just then, there was hollering heard from the street outside the wall. "Burn Wellum! We'll be back!" someone shouted. "The Marshal will see my brother avenged!" More footsteps were heard flooding out of the house and there were sounds of the infiltrators being chased away.

Denn turned to Olen, shaking to say, "I saw Colden. He was in my room when I went back in."

"The same man that took you?"

Denn nodded.

Yael's return was welcomed as he approached from the manor. His deeply etched face was crisscrossed with black streaks of soot and his hand was still upon the hilt of the wavy flamberge which he carried, pointed to the earth. He did not look happy, but neither did he appear distraught.

"Your father is safe," he said to Denn. "Your mother too." He coughed up dark phlegm and spit it on the ground. "Your parents made it to the strong room. They're safe, but I've told them to sit tight until we have another look around the property. Trin is with them."

"Serenn and Livet?"

He snorted more ash from out of his nose and pointed a finger across the way. "Over there somewhere, also safe," he said.

"How many men did you see?" Olen asked.

"At least three came in over the wall with a ladder," Yael stated. "One got the fire going in the stable as a distraction. The ugly one climbed the wall to sneak into Denn's window upstairs and look for easy quarry. Another one must have got past us when we ran out to fight the fire. He was about to open the main door at the front when we caught him."

"Escape through the front door?" Denn asked.

"He did, but they had men waiting out there. Had we not advanced on him, he was about to open it wide for a pack of the bastards to come in. Certainly, more than we could have handled."

"Did you get any of them?"

Yael coughed and snorted more.

"Took a slice out of the one by the door before he made it out and Brae, I believe, may have grazed one with a bolt from his crossbow. The one from upstairs got clean away. He climbed out another window and we don't know which way he went. Just to stay safe, we'll take a run through the house to make sure that's the end of them for tonight."

The fire was still smouldering in the stable, but it was contained and no longer a threat to the house proper. The stone walls of the carriage house and the brick walls of manor, with its tiled roof, meant that the main danger had been to the roof of the stable, which was thatch. It had collapsed in and was still crackling and wheezing as the last remnants of moisture were drawn out of it into a pall of steam.

But the smoke was still thick in places and clung to the ground like fog. Several forms could be seen stepping through it and walking toward them. Ignoring Yael's suggestion to stay in the strong room, Denn's mother had joined Serenn. Livet, in turn, left the ladies to reunite with Denn and Olen.

They could make out the form of a stooped, long-haired man also arriving through the rising smoke—that of Phon Wellum. He was surveying the damage to his stable and carriage house.

"Father!" Denn shouted.

He didn't acknowledge the greeting, but commented dourly, "This is madness! How are these men so impudent as to dare attack me in my very home?!" Fury burned in his face like the embers of the stable blaze. "I will want this brought up in council immediately!"

"I will notify Lords Farathemun and Triyne to convene the council for you, sir," said Yael.

"Also, ensure that Chandly Stedness at the Merchants Guild is made aware of this escalation!"

"I will, sir," Yael promised.

Phon was seething as he glared at the mess of burnt straw and collapsed rafters sticking out of his ruined outbuilding. "I want Lord Wryn there also. He may have no love for the Marshal, but he is still Ramid's man in the city. He will need to explain this."

"I am certain he will be compelled to do so, sir," said Yael.

As the elder Wellum gave out his orders, Denn felt a small hand grasp his. Livet was standing beside him and looking up at him. She'd heard the commotion around Colden's reappearance and could sense Denn was newly disturbed. She embraced him and he clung to her in return. Olen blushed at the display and stepped back, but Phon remained in place. He stared at Livet and looked her over carefully, in a stern and serious manner.

"It's not safe for *that one*, here," he said to Denn. "I'd find her a place to stay away from any further danger. A lodging house. Keep her out of sight, too."

Denn hesitated.

"At least until we sort this matter out with Myrhic's supporters in the prince's camp," Phon said, relenting slightly. "I'll be hiring on additional men. It will be better for her here once those arrangements are in place."

Denn did not answer vocally but nodded. He didn't question the matter but stayed silent as Phon dismissed himself from their company.

A moment later, still standing together, Olen stepped up to where he could speak more directly. "Your father's men are quite a capable crew, don't you think?"

"I owe a lot to Yael, for sure," agreed Denn.

"I think you're in good hands with him," said Olen, then added, "and Livet's in good hands with you."

At the mention of her name, Livet imposed a handspan of modest separation between her and Denn. Olen appeared to want to give them some room to reacquaint though Denn wasn't so quick to accept it. He studied Olen. His friend's voice was wavering, his head hung a little lower, and he seemed troubled.

"Eh? Everything okay?" Denn said. "What are you getting at?"

"I think I've done what I can, and I don't know if I've been much help. I'm sorry." He sighed and looked to the ground with humility. "I didn't manage to be of much use at the cottage that night, nor could I even find help after you were taken."

Livet spoke up, "We did what we could, Olen."

"Yes, but again tonight, I wasn't much use to you, either. I shouldn't have left you to go back upstairs alone."

Denn stared back at him, saying, "Olen, there's not another man in the world I can trust as a friend so much as you."

Heavy-hearted, Olen declared, "Be that as it may, I think I might take my leave of you, at least for a while."

Livet frowned. "What you plan on doin'?"

"Now that we're in Caphedra—and now that I'm no longer employed as a soldier—I think I'll find my way back home to see what's become of the place. Why don't the two of you take some time to spend together. Just you two, alone. Go somewhere safe, as your father suggests."

They considered Olen's suggestion and Denn knew his friend had made up his mind.

"Where can we find you when we come looking?" Denn asked him.

"Ask for me in Westriver." Olen scratched his chin wistfully. "There used to be a place us fighting men called the Black Eel Tavern. Some fellas from my old infantry company used to keep the place in business, you might say. I'll be there."

Livet let go of Denn to hug Olen. "What about the Peahen that Baressa mentioned? I thought we might go and see it together."

"If you insist on going there, meet me at the Eel, and I will take you," Olen promised.

"I will," Livet said.

Denn put an arm around Olen's shoulder. "Come rest up a bit more. In the morning, we can all have a meal before you go."

Olen smiled. "The sun will be up soon," he cautioned.

"We must sleep," Denn said. "Let's go back in. The trouble here is over for now."

Olen sighed but accompanied them as they returned to the manor house.

CHAPTER 11

At the Council of Caphedrans

"**I** want to see the castle."

"Do you?" said Denn as his shovel scraped at the carpet of charred straw on the floor of Naobe's blackened stall. The young hand, Trin, had strung up canvas to replace the stable roof after the fire, to block the hot summer sun. Olen had lent a hand, then after one last congenial embrace with his friends, he departed for Westriver.

When they had first woke, late in the morning, Olen had confided in Livet that he felt out of place among the luxury of Denn's manor. He said he would be more comfortable somewhere less ostentatious, and in terms of Esta, somewhere less judgemental. Livet accepted him at his word but was sure there was more to it. She sensed he wanted to exclude himself to leave room for Denn and her, to let them focus on each other and enjoy their reunion. They granted him his leave but promised that if they did not hear from him in a few days, they'd come looking.

But for now, Livet was full of questions about the capital and was ecstatic to have Denn all to herself to ask them to. The great construct known as Caphedra Castle was high on her list.

"I want to see what the fuss is all about," she declared, holding on to Naobe's reins and struggling to reach high enough to stroke her flank and shoulder. The tall chestnut charger snorted, then buried her nose deeper into the morning's bucket of oats. She was none the worse for wear. The two carthorses were lucky to have survived, however, and one was nastily singed on its side and rump. A load of lumber was due later that morning to begin work on a new roof.

"I think a walk past the royal rounds can be arranged," Denn said, stopping for a moment to straighten his back and stretch. He laid the shovel down and reached for a pitchfork to begin reconstituting a new floor of fresh straw.

"I heard it 'as a purple roof."

"Yeah, it does—over the atrium, at least," acknowledged Denn, "It's all glass. Very delicate."

"What makes it purple?" Livet inquired, curiously.

"Well, it's got two panes of glass, red and blue. Put together they give it a purple colour," Denn explained and to placate his attentive audience, he continued. "The glaziers would add a little bit of gold to the hot glass to make the red and a little bit of copper to make it blue. Then they layered the two panes together to make it look purple when the sun shines through from above. At night, when the atrium is lit up, polished mirrors below bounce rays of light up through it from within, and from high points in Castleside you can see it radiating. We used to sit near the royal fountain in the evenings—my brothers and I—and we'd watch the glow it made against the night sky. We'd imagine some kind of powerful magic going on in there that would cause it to light up so."

Livet smiled brightly. "Maybe we can see it tonight, then."

"Not tonight," answered Denn. "I must go with my father to the Council meeting. We need answers as to why we've been targeted by the Marshal's Men."

"We'll both go, then," she said. "Your father won't mind, will he?"

"No. That's not possible. The floor is closed to most citizens. My father has the right to attend due to family prerogative, although he doesn't have a vote. I am only allowed to go because he put my name forward as a petitioner on account of the kidnapping. I'm to speak on the matter."

Denn frowned at what Livet presumed was the thought of retelling his ordeal, but she knew it was essential both to see the kidnappers held to account in the forum of the city and for Denn to make a record which would later help fight the charge of desertion.

"All done, Naobe," Denn announced. "Bring her here, Livet."

Livet looked up into the horse's massive brown eyes and pulled hopefully on the bridle. Naobe brought her heavy hooves down to step forward and gently complied.

"Beautiful girl," Livet said, praising her as she had often heard Denn do.

"I'm not surprised she likes you," Denn said fondly.

"Who can blame her? Spending all the rest of her time with the likes of you!" Livet ran her fingers along the horse's mane, then affectionately turned to tug at Denn's collar, pulling him closer. Risking the jealousy of Naobe, she kissed him.

When they left the stable in the afternoon, their glee turned to disappointment as clouds were gathering, and it was beginning to look like rain was soon going to fall on the city. The dark sky hung heavy, and the air grew close and thick.

"How far is it to the Council meeting?" Livet asked. "Is it held near the castle? I'm still worn out from all the walking I did to get here yesterday."

"No. The chambers are in Middlehold, which is pretty much the centre of the city." Denn reached down and collected some of his things, his sword included. "I'll show you the castle another day," he said.

Livet frowned. "You'll be off without me then? Is it even safe for me to stay here?"

Denn hesitated, then reach out and brushed Livet's dark hair back and away from the edges of her face. "We'll go together," he relented. "Then I think we will see about changing our accommodations. You're right. I can't guarantee we are safe here, and I don't want to see anything happen to you."

Livet looked more cheerful. "Good," she said. "I'm not so keen as to be apart from you, either now that I finally got you back to meself."

"Yeah," Denn said, but his eyes drifted off for a moment, and she could tell he was mulling over something troublesome in his head.

Livet presumed it was the council meeting that quieted him so she reacted out of support. "Whatever you say to them, I'm a witness to as well." With some trepidation, she added, "I can speak, if it helps."

He didn't press her on the offer, which was a relief. She knew it would take all her willpower to overcome her natural shyness in a strange room of civic officiants and judgemental aristocrats. Instead, Denn simply instructed her, "Get your cloak. It's going to rain."

Again today, it was impossible to ignore the tension on the streets. The crowds were disharmonious with renewed volatility throughout Hamrin Square and beyond, while dark clouds, in sympathy, threatened their own catastrophic cascade.

Along the King's Avenue, demagogues elevated themselves wherever there was room, appealing to the throngs. Sermonizers for the Faith of the Pillars attempted to drive the collecting of coins at a pressured pace. Here and there, bold apostates called them out and challenged the people to rebuke their growing domination, but circling around them, were the Faith's blue-doubleted adepts and scowling initiates in grey. They were waiting for any trigger that would commence their next purge.

Livet saw that Denn unwaveringly kept one hand on his sword hilt under his cloak while holding onto her outstretched hand with his other. At times, it felt like he was pulling on her. Livet's uneven gait made it a challenge to keep up with his naturally long strides, but they had to push on.

Even the side roads offered little in the way of ease for traversing. They were filled with just as many people appearing even more intent on causing disturbance. After several hard-fought city blocks, they began to see the brick and stone houses of Middlehold around them, and amongst those were several civic buildings with pennants and statues to herald their officiality.

Finally, Denn proclaimed to Livet, "We're here," and hauled her up a set of steps. Great grey columns rose high in front of the entrance to the building, evolving into grand spires. The doors were sentried and two well-muscled armsmen, the sanctioned cadre of protectors in Caphedra, stepped in front of their advance. They levelled their razor-sharp halberds at Denn, mostly ignoring Livet.

"Name and purpose," demanded one. His jaw was set so squarely and solidly that it pulled at the chainmail beneath his pot helmet, and Livet wondered if it didn't require a great effort for him to speak.

"Denn Wellum, to address the Council."

What he lacked in comparative brawn, Denn made up for in

the weight of his name. The guards stood aside unquestioningly.

As Denn and Livet passed, however, one spoke out to advise, "Servants must sit in the upper gallery." He was obviously indicating to Livet, and that caused Denn to stop abruptly and angrily spin on his heels toward the guard.

Livet had never known Denn to flaunt his highborn clout, but in this case, perhaps encouraged by the ease at which his name gained him admittance, he bristled and spat back the words of a high-born patrician, turning the slight around, saying, "Know your place!"

The armsman raised his head, obscuring his eyes under his pot helm, and humbly said, "Apologies, sir."

It was far less crowded inside. Along the outer vestibule, torches lined the walls and laboured to dispel shadows caused by the angled, cut-stone walls. Corridors led to a central chamber where busy custodians lit more luminous oil lanterns and positioned chairs appropriately for the soon-to-arrive lawmakers and lords.

Denn pointed out a nearby face he recognized at once, and it helped settle their nervousness. Livet looked where he indicated and saw Yael Larkin, whose presence here meant that Denn's father must be close by. As soon as Yael saw them, he approached.

"Good evening, sir," he said to Denn. "Your father is speaking with Lord Farathemun. You are welcome to join them." He gestured to a group of men in a corner of the room. "As for your guest," he said, turning to Livet, "best to remain with me."

Pointing across the vast, circular chamber, Denn said, "I'll be right over there. You'll be fine with Yael."

Livet could see the long white hair of the old man who, that morning at dawn, had been cursing in his smouldering courtyard. Denn bowed his head slightly and politely to Livet, then strode off to join his father for the coming session.

More people were now filing into the chamber as the commencement time drew near. Livet studied Yael's face, having not had much time to be introduced to the man that rescued Denn. Across his pitted complexion, she noticed several scars and folds that gave him his distinctively stern expression and aged him prematurely. This close, she could determine he was younger than he let on, though still quite senior to Denn. Perhaps, she thought, he was about Olen's age.

"Not many people here, compared to a usual session," he said, surprising her with conversation.

"I wouldn't know," Livet replied.

"A lot of people have stopped coming," Yael said, eyes on the arrivals as they appeared in the entrance corridors. "Every night, it's the same. If one faction proposes recognition for their chosen heir, the others vote them down. It's been months of deadlock."

"So 'ow does the city run itself, then?" Livet asked.

"City keeps running. It's the Kingdom that has stopped."

Livet pondered Yael's statements. He sensed her interest and perhaps spurred by the chance to pontificate on the intrigue of politics, he offered to educate her.

"You see, kings don't usually bother with the day-to-day business, anyway. These people pretty much ran the city already, and some feel that they can do a better job without anyone on the throne at all. So, they choose to prolong their power and vote down every motion to recognize an heir who might interfere or add to their workload."

Yael pointed to a middle-aged man in a feathered, black velvet cap and brown topcoat. "Like that one," he said. The man was walking quickly up to Phon with a demonstrable sense of importance. "That's Chandly Stedness. He is chief Guildsmaster for the Merchants' Guild and is usually the man that tables Mr. Wellum's business to the Council. He's the one, on account of last night's affair, that called for this session to sit—at Mr. Wellum's bidding, of course."

"Could you tell me about some of the others?" Livet asked. "Do you know who they all are?"

Yael guided her to a seat on a long wooden bench. He leaned back against it and considered the crowd. "Sure. I know everyone in this city," he stated. "Mr. Wellum pays me for that knowledge, but for you, I'll offer up some of it for free."

Livet was uncertain if he was being arrogant or speaking honestly, but Yael surveyed the room and began pointing at individuals of obvious importance. She sat up as straight as she could to see the heads and faces moving past.

"Lord Kalabraith Simms, Lord Scribe and Chronicler," he

said, gesturing to a snowy-bearded man with sagging eyes, perched upon a stool next to a high-legged desk and a voluminous library of parchment. Next to his station were quills, and a personal oil lamp that glowed brightly. "He records everything and archives it. Get him started, and he can spin ten centuries' worth of tales that have nothing to do with anything that anyone ever asks him. He is most irregular with his vote. He sometimes abstains, but usually he votes just to be contrary and switches support from session to session too, the old troublemaker. Nobody really likes him, but that seems to just encourage him to keep agitating for the fun of it."

He continued, "The other courtier of note is Lord Merix Drohen, who is Master of the Courts. He's that dark, curly-haired fellow with the neat little beard. Those two will soon be joined by Lord Alum Triyne, the City Magistrate who presides over the council. When he arrives, we'll need to be quiet."

Livet nodded in understanding.

A pair of bearded men were joking with each other. One had a long nose and wavy hair, while the other was young, with copper-coloured hair that was receding to expose a broad forehead. They laughed loudly enough to be overheard above the clatter and noise, drawing Livet's attention.

"Those are two well-known supporters of Prince Ramid. Fernwood Drosst is Head Guildsman of the trade guilds and represents many of the weaponsmiths who are hoping to see the army return to strength. Though it's trickier for him, as he also counts some of the stoneworkers and architects amongst his cabal, and they'd prefer him to switch sides and support Ravon so the Faith can get their hooks into the throne. That would mean more temples for them to build. The other is Olster Marck, and he's less conflicted. He represents Keepside, the army's main training garrison across the Darrow—a firm supporter of the prince."

"Near Westriver?" Livet asked, picking up on the mention of the river's name.

"Just south of there," Yael clarified but allowed some praise. "Good to see you're learning the map."

"Do any these men know about the ones that raided Denn's home?" Livet asked.

"We'll find out, here in council," he smiled calmly, evaluating the men. "Or, if not, we'll find out through other ways."

A prim and proper, clean-faced man in a black velvet doublet with elaborate embroidery approached Prince Ramid's men. Yael followed him with his gaze as he walked swiftly across the floor. Yael seemed even more interested to monitor this man's entrance.

"Another for the Prince?" Livet asked.

"Lord Khaem Wryn—Prince Ramid's tutor when he was a boy. Schooled the younger princess as well, for that matter. Now he's the eyes and ears of the prince, here in Council. He doesn't vote, though. He's only an observer."

"Who is supporting Ravon?" Livet asked.

"They're arriving as we speak. All are high up in the Faith of the Pillars. There's Wex Sulford, of Middlehold. He's that smug-looking fellow coming in now." Yael pointed to a man entering through a side doorway. "Behind him, that airy, long-haired woman that looks like she's still dressed in her nightgown, is Kabra Zimmin. She represents the Folds itself, so you know she's high up, even though doesn't look it. Behind her is Postella Aroon, from Highside, and she pretty much rules the roost with these three."

The last woman Yael identified was familiar to Livet. She was the one who was stoking the mob in Hamrin Square, just as the initiates were launching upon the crowds.

"I've seen her," Livet confided to Yael.

"Well, keep your eye on her. She's one to watch out for. Ruthless."

The three entered, followed by a round-faced, bald man, with deep, expressive lines around his cheeks, who also especially aroused Yael's attention.

"It is uncommon to see him these days," he said. "That's the man that pays the wages."

"Who?" Livet asked.

"Lord Chancellor Syr Havel. He doesn't normally attend. He keeps himself hidden in his tower at the castle, dreaming of new taxes and tariffs for the masses. When he does come by, it's usually alone, and not with those three. I expect this is not a good sign."

Finally, a large man rolled into the chamber, and Yael sat up straighter. The man's hat was of deep burgundy with hair that hung long, dirty, and grey beneath it, but sporting no beard or moustache over his jiggling jowls. Ornaments of office hung about his neck, and he carried a hammer-like mace.

"The magistrate," Yael announced quietly to Livet and pressed a finger to his lips.

Presiding over the assembly of appellants and adjudicators, Chief Magistrate Lord Alum Triyne sat at a place along a central bureau. He swept his hand over his desk to flatten a piece of parchment lying before him, and with a glance over its contents, he looked back up to the crowd, smashed the mace down onto a metallic brick with a *clang*, and bellowed through an amplifying brass cone. "For the 12th day of Perspica, in the 301st year of the noble and honoured Wolstett reign, this is the first session of the day—and the *session is commenced!*"

All babbling and murmuring stopped. Each faction around the circular court turned toward the centre and assumed positions at long, curved desks which ringed the chamber. The magistrate, Triyne, stared sharply ahead toward the man Yael had identified as Master of the Courts.

"Lord Drohen to begin," he directed, causing the man to stand up, scratching the borders of his smartly shaved beard and clearing his voice to speak.

"As is customary, I will apprise the council of all present concerns and findings related to the King's murder," Lord Drohen said

"Anything?" Triyne said.

Livet was surprised by how immediately they were thrust into such a severe and ominous subject, but around the council tables there was little shock. None seemed to be expecting much to be said that they did not already know.

"As you are aware, the king's death had a most unnatural aspect to it, which my men and those of the Commanderies under Master Prefect Morea, have regarded with particular interest. As a result, we take particular note of those who demonstrate such propensities, if and when they are found. I'd ask for the Council member from Middlehold to stand, address the Council, and repeat what he has recently related to me."

Yael nudged Livet to listen.

With an agreeable nod from Triyne and great interest upon the faces of those around the room, the smug man who sat amongst the Faith followers rose. Seriousness crept into his countenance as he related the incident.

"Within the past week, a respected curate, on business for the Pillars, Waldrin Rahm, was accosted by a pair of travellers, a man and woman, while at an inn in Greenplain. He claims to have been threatened first verbally by a man, of the late king's employ, and then, shockingly, by a woman who seized onto one of his companions. She did not physically strike him, but rather performed some manner of enchantment upon him, such that for that evening and well into the next day the companion was convinced he had become aged, and his actions were incurably those of a feeble, elderly man, despite him being young and robust, in the healthiest of his years."

Lord Simms, the Lord Scribe and Chronicler, was hurriedly writing out notes to record the report. As he did, he called out, "Appearance? What did this woman look like?"

Sulford continued, "Brown hair, with a bit of grey. Neither a maid nor an old woman, says he, but somewhere in the middle. Curate Rahm says she did not deny when he called out to her directly, identifying her as the fugitive Baressa Hart of Berryboughs, witch and rebel of Starpond, and already suspect in the murder of their royal highnesses, I add."

Livet gasped loud enough that Yael was taken off guard. He raised an eyebrow and leaned in toward her. Livet instantly froze her expressions and held her breath, trying to appear unmoved.

"You went through Greenplain, didn't you? Did you see this woman?" Yael quietly asked, so that no one else in the gallery could hear. Livet shook her head and gave up nothing more.

"No bother," Yael said. "They're desperate. They don't know—or won't *admit* they don't know the king's killer if they even suspect. But it wasn't her."

Relieved, Livet's heartbeat steadied enough that she decided to gamble a few words of her own.

"Do you know who did it?" she asked.

Yael broke eye contact with her. He bitterly muttered, "It's a matter we want no part in. Someday, an accused will be named, and that person will be brought before the axe when the time arises."

Below, the speakers continued, lobbing challenges and retorts, back-and-forth. "So where is Baressa Hart now?" called someone from the council table.

"We're investigating," answered Drohen. "I am not prepared

to state our speculations for the record—not for the time being."

"Comments?" Triyne invited the councillors.

An old man, with brushed back hair, an unkempt beard, and thick grey eyebrows stood, with some effort. Yael had not singled him out during his accounting of personalities.

"The chair recognizes the councillor from Westriver, Parachs Ghil."

The man carried a disparaging tone as he said, "Certainly, Hart's daughter has been a fugitive for longer than you've held your post, Lord Drohen. That you inherited this is probably one of the few things which give you some absolution, though I fear you'll be my age before you catch her. But in my observation, it seems you limit your investigation by ever-concentrating upon this one particular person, who has little or no clear connection to either the death of the king or the queen's unfortunate malady—other than these reputed peculiar occurrences reported by those who chance to meet her."

"Do you have a question, Parachs?" said Olster Marck irritably, from a seat nearby.

"Well," Ghil continued, "I'm just wondering why we only hear of this one woman? Are there not others that could be made suspect for holding similar capabilities? How about in the Faith of the Pillars itself?" He waved his hand nonchalantly toward Sulford, Aroon, and Zimmin. "You three, can you speak to whether the Faith of the Pillars, in all its omnipotence and learnedness, harbours any persons who share such incredible skills?"

Postella Aroon did not stand when she answered, and she rolled her eyes in disdain before shouting back. "What skills, Parachs? Regicide?" It caused some rumblings around the table. "I think not," she added. "I am insulted that you would accuse our people of carrying out such a reprehensible crime. We are the foundation of society. We do not undermine it!"

She was joined by Kabra Zimmin, whose voice sounded very calming to Livet. "The abilities taught by the Pillars are many, but this particular instance of ill-intended malice toward our peer has elicited our full attention," she said.

Aroon leaned forward. "Chief Hart's daughter escaped the king's custody—what, fifteen years ago now, Parachs? In addition to her own vindictiveness, she is known to be the consort of the rebel

Roderin Jorann which attests to her disposition to seek revenge upon our rightful monarchs. It is imperative that we focus on her in the matter of these severe crimes, or we risk their repeat."

Parachs Ghil remained silent but in the gallery, a dour-faced onlooker grunted disapprovingly.

"But Parachs," Sulford added, "if you know of others who can pervert the natural order as she does, we encourage you to name them so that any future threats can be thus annulled before the Queen—"

Olster Marck coughed.

"Before the next *ruler* takes the throne," Sulford finished.

"Consider the matter recorded and discussed. Moving on," Triyne directed, "We have been petitioned to hear another matter of criminality. Chandly, your most respectable guest is welcome to take the floor."

The Guildsmaster stood and turned to invite Phon Wellum to speak. Lord Brevin Farathemun shifted in his seat, to allow his passage. Together Phon and Denn moved forward into the circle. Denn appeared stern but prepared.

Citing care toward accuracy, Lord Simms, the chronicler, prefaced Phon's speech to ask, "Who is this with you, Phon? Am I to take that it this is one of your sons? Denn, I suppose?"

"As usual, you are correct, Kalabraith," Phon confirmed.

Guildsmaster Stedness turned to Phon. "Mr. Wellum, please relate your business to the Council."

Phon sized up the chamber but turned to Denn to recount the initial events of the preceding days.

"My son," he said, acknowledging the grown man next to him.

Denn looked at each of the dozen councillors' faces then began his tale. "I was serving at my post, housed at a billet in Fal Ghreeg, when twelve days ago, my companions and I were beguiled and set upon by a group of travellers. These men took me hostage, intending to demand a ransom from my father."

He stopped as if recollecting the most traumatic in-between events silently to himself before continuing. From the gallery, Livet wished she could have stood beside him. The reflection of candlelight on his brow showed he was sweating.

"The men were ultimately unsuccessful," he continued. "Two

were dealt with by my father's agents. The remaining pair fled. It was in their flight that our aid, Mr. Yael Larkin, noticed the unmistakable decorations that marked them as former members of the Lord's Guard. These men, I am told, now band together under the moniker of *Marshal's Men* and apply their brutishness toward ill-gotten pursuits and self-enterprise against the citizens of this capital city. Ostensibly, they claim to honour the King. Pragmatically, they pronounce their support for the prince. I say they are a mob of unchecked criminal ruffians who seek only to enrich themselves."

Phon placed his hand on Denn's shoulder and nodded approvingly.

"My son, amongst those of our household, was only the first to suffer. These men revisited us last night. They were identified to include the same culprit who had escaped my armsman on the night these abductors arrived in Caphedra with my son. They sought to harm my family, to gain entry to my home for others in their savage company, and they set my stable alight, risking the loss of three animals, including a rather expensive charger—which, like my son, has served in the army of the king and deserves the respect due its station."

With that, Simms looked up from his pen and corrected him. "I have a note from your son's company constable to state he is no longer on the company muster roll."

"That is also a matter to be amended for this incident is the source of that error and injury to his honour. I assure you he has acted in good faith of service. My son deserves to be lauded." Phon shot a look to Simms to indicate he would entertain no further word on that matter, and Simms dropped the case.

"We will consider that for his record, Phon," said Lord Triyne, who then absentmindedly began inflating and deflating his loose cheeks as he ruminated over the charge. He then asked, "To whom do you wish to address here, either for record or recompense?"

"Magistrate, I would like a response from Lord Khaem Wryn, who is here as an observer," said Phon.

"Very well," came the answer, "I will allow it. Lord Wryn?"

"Firstly, Mr. Wellum, let me express my heartfelt joy that your son has returned to you sound and healthy, especially considering..." he let that statement drift in the air and chose not to finish it. Instead, he mounted a defence.

"As you know, I am well familiar with the very *respectable and honourable* Lord Marshal, Incis Myrhic. I am steadfast in my assertion that he would not tolerate such dishonour to fester in any soldier under the prince's command. Therefore, I must state my certainty that these men have acted alone in their transgressions against you and your son."

Phon turned to face Wryn directly. "So, these men are not acting in the Marshal's service? You imply he would condemn them and their actions? Publicly, he would disassociate from them?"

"I reiterate, he would never associate with the likes of such men in the first place, nor do anything to tarnish the prince's esteem. If these men are acting in his name, it is at their own volition and not at the behest of a man of such shining repute as the Lord Marshal."

Another voice called out from the sidelines of the council. It was the bald, round-faced man who acted as the primary administrator for the city, if not the whole of the fractured kingdom.

"Lord Wryn," said Lord Chancellor Syr Havel, "I must insist that you stop referring to Incis Myrhic as Lord Marshal. He was stripped of that title when he abdicated his duties and left the city."

Lord Wryn smiled and, with some flare, stepped out into the circle at the centre of the chamber to dramatically draw attention to the Lord Chancellor.

"This man," he said, turning to Phon but gesturing at Havel, "Mr. Wellum, you should ask him about your issue with your harassers. Lord Chancellor Havel is now responsible for maintaining order within Caphedra's walls, so far as he has chosen to continue paying for the remnants of the army and holding them to the task."

Councillors Drosst and Marck both grunted derisively. It was a good deflection and caught the attention of many in the room.

"Tell me, Chancellor Havel, are there still soldiers enough to defend Castleside?" Wryn asked but answered rhetorically. "I would think so, yes? I think it's Lord Braydun Anders who enforces order in Castleside. I'm sure he, or any of his men who are still on the payroll, would be glad to mount additional security for the respected Mr. Wellum."

Havel stared at him in silence, appearing to genuinely

despise the prince's man. He continued to say nothing.

"Come to think of it, I haven't seen them around lately," Wryn commented innocently, then reinforced his attack by asking directly, "What is the current disposition of Lord Anders's 2nd Brigade? Are they in the city, or are they on the march?"

Lord Wryn was spinning the whole matter into an opportunity to flush out the location of forces hostile to the prince, but no answer was forthcoming from the chancellor.

Instead, Magistrate Triyne smashed his mace down to end the hijacking of Phon's petition. "These days are difficult on all of us, Phon—and Denn." His tone was conciliatory as he offered a solution to adjudicate the young man's ordeal. "Lord Drohen, will you assure Mr. Wellum that you will do everything you can to apprehend these men?"

Lord Drohen responded affirmatively. "Of course, Magistrate. It presses on all of us our duty to see order returned to Caphedra. This instance, as well as these other challenges to our security, serve to remind us that there are costs to this Council's half-hearted husbandry of this city."

Then with this, the Master of the Courts turned his head and looked toward the three members of the Faith across from him. He nodded, and Postella Aroon broke into a smile and stood.

"Lord Triyne—Magistrate—I would like to put forth a motion to help resolve this," she said sweetly.

"You only ever seem to put forward the same motion, Postella," Triyne said. "But go ahead."

"I motion," she declared in a confident tone, "That the princess, Lady Ravon Wolstett, eldest daughter of the honoured King Ramis and dear sister to the Faith of the Pillars, be recognized as the rightful monarch of this realm and be acknowledged as sovereign majesty to rule over Caphedra, its kingdom, and its holdings to the furthest reaches of ancient Almahria, from where we stand to where the water becomes salt, in all directions, as has always been tradition under the justly preserved laws of succession."

"It is her birthright as eldest," added Zimmin, "and it's criminal that this court so arrogantly ignores law and custom."

The chief magistrate hesitated, punctuating the importance of the moment. Finally, he asked those in favour to indicate their agreement.

Sulford and Zimmin, flanking Aroon, each raised their hands immediately to little surprise. A moment later, Lord Drohen stood and announced his vote in favour of the motion.

"This situation has made me realize," he said, "that we must resolve the inaction of this council and do so by affirming the succession of the crown."

His vote caused a shudder among the spectators. Yael leaned over to Livet. "He's not done that before. Something's about to happen," he said.

Livet grew paler. Inside she began to panic at the thought of the Faith being able to pull the strings of the queen as they had done with Lord Vlass back in Lanstad.

Lord Chancellor Syr Havel spoke up, staring toxically at Lord Wryn as he announced, "I am in favour, Magistrate. Let us finally resolve this impasse."

Lord Farathemun, quiet until now, expressed himself loudly to break their momentum and lead the dissent. "I vote against!"

"As do I!" Guildsmaster Stedness quickly echoed.

Fernwood Drosst and Olster Marck each shouted, "Against!" in succession.

"I also oppose," said Parachs Ghil.

"Five for and an equal number against." Moving around in his seat to better look at the court's scribe, Triyne asked, "What say you Kalabraith? I suppose you're going to abstain again?"

The old man smiled, "Am I so predictable, Alum?"

The magistrate's deep sigh sounded amplified.

"It reminds me," said Lord Simms, "of the story of the fisherman who wouldn't toss the tie line, as he kept trying to get out of his boat and step onto the dock to tie it himself. Each time he tried to get out of the vessel, it just floated farther from shore..."

"If you're looking for a rope, Kalabraith, might I make a suggestion?" said Postella Aroon, causing a few in the council to laugh.

When the jeers died down, Lord Drohen addressed the uncommitted chronicler with a very straight face and a burning stare. "What stories does the Lord Magistrate have in his archives about criminals running unchecked from keep to citadel? Mercenaries so numerous in the streets that they are only outnumbered by prostitutes? So much reduced cargo sailing on the

Darrow River that you can see the high-water mark from where the waters used to reach? Does his arithmetic help calculate, given the dimensions of the northern gates, how long it would take a thousand marauding men to pile through?"

Simms answered him, "I appreciate that as Master of the Courts, you feel challenged by lawlessness, but rushing the process of succession only threatens to debase those laws and functions that we still maintain under our control."

"Indeed, I am Master of the Courts, and all the commanderies fall under me as well. Perhaps I could repay you with a story from *their* archives? One about an old scribe who traffics in information about the private financial holdings of our citizens. Or perhaps the story of the same scribe who makes frequent intentional errors transcribing family lineages?"

"Enough," Simms said, trying to quiet him.

"You hold the deciding vote, Kalabraith," said Triyne.

"Well, Merix made some exceptional points earlier. I'll concede that there has not been such a degree of lawlessness for at least a couple of centuries. Furthermore, despite our fortifications and deterrents, no army of the size we now confront has ever gotten so far toward marching on the capital—not since King Venir, three hundred years ago. Though the intentions of Prince Ramid be simple and Myrhic's goals be professed to be honourable—by his own reckoning—it is highly likely that once unloosed upon the city this swollen rabble of deserters will not be any more lawfully dispossessed than those who have been named as having victimized the Wellum family."

Looking across the room, Livet could see Phon Wellum prodding Stedness angrily. Beside them, Lord Farathemun was fixated on the Lord Scribe and Chronicler, his lower jaw clenched. Similarly, there was an urgent whispering being conducted between Marck and Drosst in the Ramid camp, while the three councillors aligned with the Faith were almost salivating in expectation.

"I recognize Queen Ravon," declared the old scribe, causing the council to explode in shouts and catcalls.

It was Postella Aroon whose voice overcame the furor and demanded they quiet and permit the magistrate to formalize the verdict, but instead of Triyne, it was Phon Wellum who seized the moment.

"Magistrate, I am invoking my prerogative!"

Incensed, Aroon shouted back, "You cannot change the vote!"

Phon answered defiantly, "The vote is not completed, and I have full right as the head of the Wellum family to declare, at any time, the reclamation of our lordship—and with that, my council right!" He continued, "And I place my vote *against* this motion!"

Yael instantly sat forward in his seat. She noticed how instinctively his hand moved toward his sword hilt as his appraisal of the situation roused his utmost attention, though he only touched the handle with his fingertips and did not close his hand around it.

"Alum!" Aroon pleaded, her fingernails digging into the desk.

"Well, indeed, Lord Wellum's vote stands. I trust you are prepared to take on the responsibilities of your title?" asked Triyne.

"When a successor is declared by the majority, we will act as honour demands," Phon said.

"Very well. I hope you are not disappointed, however," replied the magistrate, forebodingly. "In this case of a hung vote, I am also exercising my right as City Magistrate to break the tie. This indecisiveness has gone on long enough. I cast my vote, and in doing so, the decision of this council is in favour of the motion to recognize Lady Ravon Wolstett as Queen of Caphedra, with all its lands and holdings."

The council chambers burst into a boisterous uproar. Onlookers in the gallery also ceased their silence and were shouting and gesturing in both celebration and rage. The dour man beside Yael and Livet got up quickly and raced down a nearby flight of steps to where the council was starting to exit.

"Does the prince's man not 'ave a vote, too?" Livet asked Yael.

"He's a lord but stands as proxy to the prince—so no vote on the council. He'll quickly relay this news back to their army up north, though, and I expect it's the last we'll see of him."

Yael placed a hand under Livet's elbow to indicate that they also needed to get up and move. Phon and Denn were speaking with Lord Farathemun and appeared to be strategizing. On the other side of the council, Wex Sulford was roughly pushing through the other councillors to get to the gallery, where he latched onto three young initiates sitting near the back. Livet saw them nod quickly and flee out the door.

Still empowered by her victory, Aroon called out to Phon, "I'll have the temple bursar sent 'round your house tomorrow morning, shall I, Phon?" Phon turned on the spot to make sure his back was toward her and resumed speaking with Lord Farathemun.

People were leaving the council hurriedly to be first to spread the news of the naming of the queen. In the commotion, Yael grabbed onto Livet, both to steer her through the crowd but also to force her attention.

"I recommend you find your own lodgings soon."

"What do you mean?" Livet asked, confused. "I go where Denn goes."

"Don't be so certain. Find a safe place for yourself and tell no one but Denn!"

"Aren't you sworn to protect us?"

"I work for Phon. I follow his orders," he said coldly. "But I suggest that you follow mine in this case. Now c'mon!"

He dragged her closer to where Phon and Denn were standing. Seeing Yael arrive, Phon quickly said goodbye to his friend and motioned to Denn that it was time to go. Together they fought through the stampede of spectators. Yael led the way, followed by Phon, then Livet. Denn guarded their rear and kept Livet close to keep her protected—a caution that was not unwarranted.

"Nothing has been resolved here tonight," Yael commented as they broke through to the outer foyer to the main entrance. "The Marshal will not be so quickly dissuaded."

As they stood upon the outer steps, fights were breaking out. The councillor, Parachs Ghil, was bleeding from a cut on his cheek, and the dour-faced man from earlier in the gallery was ushering him away, stopping to swing several heavy punches at the harassers on their heels.

Above them, the sky had begun to open up with weighty drops of rain, but people ignored how they were getting wet. Anger and shock were driving confrontations as resentments and rivalries erupted everywhere.

Quickly, Phon locked his bony fingers upon Denn's shoulder and pulled himself closer toward his son. Mustering enough breath to shout above the crowd, he levelled a grand pledge toward Denn.

"Farathemun is building an army in the south!" he panted.

"Undertake what I've asked, and I'll see that you command two hundred men when you return to Caphedra!"

Denn stood dumbfounded and had not yet answered when Yael pulled Phon back and moved squarely between father and son.

"We're going to split up," Yael directed Denn. He turned and looked at Livet but said nothing further. A fraction of a moment later, he prompted his master with an urgent, "Sir!"

Phon reached for Denn's arm one last time and said, "Keep safe." Then, forming up closer to Yael, he allowed himself to be escorted out of the danger surrounding them, and the two of them plunged into the madness

Denn stooped to speak into Livet's ear. "Do you see a good way out of here?"

Always attentive to an escape path, Livet nodded, then dragged Denn between two stone mansions, down an alley, and away from the Avenue.

CHAPTER 12

Home in West River

O len took long strides as he ventured alone and unhindered across the city. He hoped to reach Westriver before the rain started. Returning along the King's Avenue through Stonerow, he passed by the modest townhouses of Middlehold and lofty villas of Highside. He kept to the rows of sundry men and fishmongers in Dockmarket and skirted the seedy and worn clapboard warehouses of the Blocks. His path led him to the Midbridge, the central crossing over the Darrow River, into Westriver.

The impending rainstorm caused a frenzy on the streets as the sellers covered up their merchandise or lugged their goods indoors, but Olen was keenly aware of an undertow of information passing under the breath of the crowds as well. Just before he arrived at the bridge, it reached his ears. A young man, racing from shop to shop, cried uproariously, "They've announced it! They're naming the Queen! It's to be Lady Ravon!"

Olen processed the news quickly and imagined the same violence as witnessed in Hamrin Square now spreading to the whole of the city should the Faith be loosed, unquestioned and devoid of restraint, upon Caphedra.

As the rain began falling, he hastened his flight to the other side of the Darrow, wanting to find a warm, dry roof as quickly as possible. Maybe very little remained to draw him back there, save that he was *from there*, but that was enough for Olen to call it home now that he found himself in need of one.

Passersby were dwindling now, driven toward shelter by the rain. Olen stepped onto the big stone arch of the bridge and heard muffled voices from those who sought solace underneath. Above the bridge, however, he crossed unimpeded but was dogged by the swelling rain, as if he were the one responsible for bringing the storm to the western boroughs. The rushing river below gave him comfort as he looked out over the deep middle of the Darrow. Its waters were a cleansing and protective barrier between the corrupt, inwardly conflicted east and the shabby but familiar west.

Trudging heavily on the downgrade, he arrived at the bridge's Westriver end. There were the familiar signboards and voices that spoke in the particular tones and manner he grew up with. But reminiscences aside, it resurrected his restlessness and he set his mind to be more alert. Twenty years ago, this was not always a safe place for him, and there was no guarantee it would be different now.

Only one place could be counted on with certainty to be hospitable and welcoming. Over Olen's head, a freshly repainted wooden sign showed a pair of long, dark forms, twisting and writhing together. The lacquer repelled the raindrops, which formed trails down the sign's face before dripping weightily to the ground. As a young man, on his way out of town, he remembered the sign as only having one eel. Some unknown painter had since improved their number to two, matching the count on Olen's Westriver Company cloak pin.

Olen tugged on the edges of his hood to obscure his face and reached down to the hilt of his sword, ensuring it could be drawn free of the scabbard should he be walking into a mistake. In his pouch, he had enough remaining money for a meal but hoped to find the means to get more now that he was home. That would be the first task, he thought.

He pushed the door open to discover a busy room. A crowd of men were drinking, singing, and playing dice. By a radiant hearth fire, some children were sitting in dry warmth, petting a shaggy, wiry-haired dog that snoozed undisturbed. The fire crackled and punctuated the jovial laughter in the room. It was welcoming in here. Olen chose an empty chair at a spot along the bar, near the kitchen door and beside a couple of other patrons who also had their backs turned to the door. From his purse, he spread a few silver Caphedran squires and bronze jacks on the glistening, polished counter.

"Ale and sup," he said to the barkeep who was hanging freshly washed tankards onto hooks along the top of the bar.

With darkly-lined eyes and a dangerous grin, the host turned around and gave a shove to the man who sat beside Olen, a thin, deeply wrinkled man with a beard and an expansive forehead.

"Well now, do I detect some epic trickery on the part of the divine?" the barkeep said boisterously. "Watch out, Eysman! Three sergeants together. The men will begin to think something's up!"

Instinctively, several of the heads around the room lifted and looked toward the trio at the bar. Olen immediately recognized the barkeep as Sergeant Baygern "Bull" Draemun, who had been Olen's dearest, unfaltering companion in the Westriver Company. Beside him, was their sombre and ever-serious fellow sergeant, Eysman Rowl. All three had stood side-by-side on their first day of training when the Westriver Company was stood up. They had walked through the doors of the Keepside Garrison together to report for a job and a future under arms, serving the King. That was, of course, after meeting and committing to the scheme together, at this very bar, where a few glasses had helped seal their confidence and burgeoning friendship.

"Lord's Oath!" proclaimed Olen.

Olen remembered that Bull had been released from his post a few years ago with a small severance as compensation for maladies attributable to his years of austere soldiering. The sogginess of the Fals had gotten into his wounds and left him shaky and numb in some of his extremities. He appeared to have mostly recovered, but Olen still detected an awkwardness in his movements and an idle shimmy when his hand rested on the countertop. He chewed placidly on a licorice root that protruded from his mouth.

When Olen had last seen Eysman, the haggard old soldier was on his way to Falbeth to work as company quartermaster. He was well known to be an honest man, and this quality led to Captain Ersmine doing him the kindness of recalling him to the keep where he enjoyed warmth, food, and a muchly coveted roof over his head while he worked.

Eysman, whose wrinkles and furrows made him look perpetually worried, cocked his head upwards and agreed with the barkeep's pronouncement. "You're right, Bull, it can't be good. How'd you end up back here, Olen? We figured you were still out on the Fals, stuck in the mud somewhere."

"I just made it into town yesterday," Olen said.

"Where'd you spend the night?" asked Bull as he resumed hoisting up the clean tankards. The licorice dangled from his mouth like an old man's pipe.

"Castleside," Olen said.

Bull choked on a laugh, "Oh well, then! I'm glad one of us is doing well for himself!"

Olen started to contradict him, defensively denouncing the unfamiliar luxury he'd fallen into–and rejected–back at the Wellum house, when Bull reached under the bar for something.

"I suppose you won't be needing your key, then? It was brought here and has been hanging on a chain under the bar waiting for your triumphal return."

He handed Olen an ancient, pitted iron mortice key. "As the last, living true-blooded son of the Kierk dynasty, I graciously present to you the key to your castle, m'lord. Last I heard it's missing a roof, but the walls are still standing—of course, they belong to the neighbours."

Olen accepted the key sheepishly, palming it and hiding it from sight.

"Hope you brought a tarp," said Eysman.

"You might want something for the rats, too," added Bull. "For a few more of those squires, I could sell you a crossbow."

"I'd hoped someone had left the key here. I wasn't looking forward to having to bust down the door," said Olen.

Bull shrugged. "It's not like such occurrences aren't among the realm of normalcy for a neighbourhood such as ours. In five minutes, you'd probably have ten people offering to help you, in exchange for a cut of whatever you told them they could burgle once they were inside."

"Sounds like it's as I remember it." Olen tucked the key away into a pocket in his vest. He gestured to the pot hanging over the fire. "Anything good in there?"

Eysman turned up his nose and shuddered, which caused Bull to raise a disapproving eyebrow at him in return.

"House specialty," Bull said, responding more congenially to Olen. "Some carrots, cabbage, a bit of other stuff. Been simmering all day, just waiting for you. Try some." He ladled out a portion into a wooden bowl and passed it over the counter to Olen, scooping up the coins lying on the table as he drew back and added, "Let me get you some ale."

Before the dutiful barkeep was able to pour him a mug, Olen had already swallowed the full contents of the bowl. A second ladling of nourishment was quickly provided by Bull, who was sizing up Olen's fatigue and hunger, concernedly.

"Long time travelling, I suppose?" he asked.

Wiping the sides of his mouth with the back of his hand, Olen squeezed the handle on the ale mug and forcefully brought it up for a deep draught.

"Aye. Maybe I'm not done yet, either."

"I'm glad you like the stew," said the barkeep, presenting a thoughtful look.

"Some folks say the quality of the food's gone down since Bull took over," the other sergeant added.

"Probably more of a reflection on your ignorant palate," said Bull with a dismissive glance at Eysman who, in turn, kept staring forward with his deadpan grimace.

"I expect it's going to be trouble–me coming back, that is" said Olen flatly.

"That, my friend, was settled a long time ago," said Bull, lowering his voice and leaning in more privately, the spicy odour of licorice about him. To Olen, the cautious manner in which he provided his dismissal suggested otherwise.

"What of the Karavals? Is Domin still running his rackets?" Olen asked, seeking news of his perennial rivals.

Eysman grunted and shook his head. "He died not long after they put your folk into the ground."

"So, his bunch are no more?" inquired Olen.

Bull intercepted Eysman's reply and explained, "They're still around, and up to the same business they've always been up to. Domin's brother, Dance, is running the family these days. He took over the Half Moon and he's the boss now."

"Who's Dance?" Olen asked.

"That's the name they call Dirlen. I don't know why. It's just a name that they use, probably on account of him being a bit light and airy. He was always the skinny brother and not the meaty type like Domin."

"Don't turn your back on him, though," Eysman warned. "He still has enough men to do the fighting for him, and he's got just as much of a temper and desire to bring the blades out."

Taking a rag in hand, Bull began mopping crumbs and spills off the bar top. "I truly hate to say it, but the Karavals did well for themselves in the past twenty years. Once your family was out of the way, nobody else would lock horns with them. They pretty much came to run the borough, while the rest of us went off to fight for King Ramis."

Olen took another swig of ale then stared at Bull. "They give you trouble here?"

"No," said Bull. "Not yet anyway."

Eysman interrupted, "But they send men around to sneak about. Likely, they're sizing us up now that more fellas have been returning home."

"Coincidences," said Bull. "We're on the corner of a major thoroughfare here. Lots of people pass by." He continued to polish the countertop in front of Eysman. "Why? Who'd you see?

"I've seen those two long-haired boys that work for Dogfish," he said. "The other day, I saw that one with the moustache, too."

"Sasser Goll," Bull said sourly. "He reports to that old knifeman, Jensir Udal."

"I remember him and my brother Tolen at each other's throats once," said Olen, who swallowed and breathed deeply, suppressing a growl.

"Was he the one that did you brother in?" asked Bull.

"I don't know. That whole Karaval family is to blame for the killing, as much as my family was for keeping the fight going until they ran out of bodies. It would have been me, too, had I not sworn my oath to the king and marched out of the city with the lot of you."

"Well, no better company could you have kept, brother," said Bull, and Eysman agreed.

In the corner of the room, voices got louder and rose to a boisterous cheer.

"Damn you, that's eight!" A voice wailed out, "I'm out. Fortune has fled me, lads."

"And has come to me with your money," cried another jubilantly, echoed by a choir of buoyant laughter. "Next round's on me! One pull for each, except for Sergeant Kierk, who looks like he needs two!"

Hearing his name, Olen scanned the crowd of faces and recognized many of his men among them. He saw the strapping old form of Vyr Ocklso, with a wiry grey beard and a dense and coarse-knit blue sweater, hunkered down on a worn oak chair, looking quite sedate and peaceful.

The loser of the match was a rather sullen-faced Talton Terrod, who Olen had seen gambling almost every night since he'd known him, or at least since the raid on Fal Ghreeg, and appearing to be that much poorer for his vice after all these years.

The generous winner, to Olen's delight, was Nyrim Henser, who was a young, fast-acting, and quick-learning soldier when he first joined the company. Now the first traces of grey were just starting to surface in Nyrim's beard. He was a veteran companion of Olen's through the battles of Buchan Village and the Lanstad Commons but somehow had been able to conserve his energetic enthusiasm and vivacity. Nyrim held his tankard aloft in victory and flashed a grin toward Olen back at the bar.

Olen gladly returned the smile.

As the ales were poured, a small crowd formed around them, comprised of some of the same men who had been in the Fals just a few months before. There were a few new faces, but they were friendly enough. The presence of young people and those Olen assumed to be wives also lent the space a merry and hospitable air. The curly, brown-haired dog was even there, snoozing on the floor next to Vyr and the fireplace.

With effort, Vyr pushed himself out of his chair, sidestepped the comfortable cur and walked over to the remaining empty stool on Olen's left.

"Do you bring us news, old man?" he asked Olen, with the usual geriatric jibe. They were quite close in age, in fact. If you asked many, the money would be on Vyr being the older of the two. Even Talton wouldn't bet against that.

And there *was* news. Happy to take the subject off his travels, Olen passed along the proclamation he had heard as he trekked through Dockmarket.

"It was spreading on the other side of the Darrow as I left, that the council has named Ravon as Queen." He paused throughout the statement to make it clear and to emphasize its poignant profundity.

"Well, I guess I should hang the blue curtains up on the windows, then," said Bull.

"It'll probably help their recruitment," pointed out Eysman. "They've been putting out offers to hire soldiers for weeks now, though nobody was rushing toward them. This now takes some of the legitimacy away from Myrhic's camp, as to who is the true, recognized army of the realm."

"The Pillars already had legitimacy," said Bull. "They're the only ones still paying wages. Myrhic's men are in it for promises and plundering rights only. They figure they'll rob the temple when they get here and pay their troops with the loot."

Olen added another consideration, "Then there's Lord Vlass."

"What's that old ghoul up to?" Bull asked.

"He's got troops all over the eastern half of the city, supporting the Faith of the Pillars. I saw them muscling in on a bunch of holy men yesterday evening, smashing them up under the orders of some Pillarmen."

Bull nodded knowingly. "There's a few of those cultists around these days. The fear and the uncertainty draws 'em into the light, and they're pretty popular with those can't afford the Faith's regimen of alms."

"Or folks with so little left to lose that threatening them makes no bit of difference," added Eysman.

They continued to speculate, and Olen downed the gifted ales. He wished he could reciprocate and show his happiness for reuniting with so many of his comrades, but the jingle in his money purse was alarmingly muted. Instead, he pushed himself away from the bar.

"I'm going to see where I live," he said.

"This town's like a nest of vipers. I'm going to send a couple of the boys with you," said Bull.

Talton and Vyr got up from their seats.

"Don't worry about me, I'm fine to take care of myself," said Olen.

Bull deflected, "We look out for each other here. It's less safe these days than when we were at war." With that, he reached behind the counter and pulled out a blackened dirk and a weighty club, studded with metal nails. "Take these, boys."

"Where are your swords?" Olen asked, confused.

"Sold 'em," said Talton, "We're all in the same straits in that we've not been granted our severance. A good broadsword will pay for a man and a wife to eat for months—and after all, some of us are family men now."

"But if the city is still so dangerous, why?"

"Yeah. That's a tough one," said Bull.

Vyr elaborated, "We try to keep out of trouble. Most of the problems we do see can be fixed with one good punch. No need to go around murdering if we can help it. Captain Alamm would send his boys over from Keepside to tear the place down if he thought we were organizing."

"Karavals and all the other common criminals go after easy marks," Talton said reprovingly. "They won't pick on a bunch of us together, but if they were to catch one of us on our own at this hour of the night, that'd tempt them. Let alone if they learned you were a Kierk, then they'd be right quick to stick you with the sharp end of something."

Eysman handed Vyr and Olen a pair of lanterns, lit with burning candles inside. "Try and keep these dry," he said prudently. "But you can use 'em for now."

Bull went back to polishing the counter. "Don't dawdle when you get there. We'll be watching for you two to come back. It's only a couple of blocks to his place in Faralley."

"And keep Vyr away from the bawds'!" Eysman added.

"Aye, Sarge," said Talton wryly.

"Curse this weather!" shouted Vyr as they trudged through more torrential rain. The deteriorating conditions were threatening to soak them through. Drops collected in the grizzled fighter's beard and caused him to complain, "It's no better than the swamps!"

There were even fewer people on the streets now. The trio kept to the open and walked well away from any dark corners where robbers might be hiding.

The dwellings of Westriver boasted many of the peaceful, modest trappings of family life at first, with lights in their windows and smoke from their chimneys, but soon the surrounding buildings became more distressed and divided into ramshackle tenement houses and gated storefronts. The Kierk house was not far from the Black Eel, but it was jammed amongst the clusters of haphazard constructions. In fact, it existed in a space procured within the very middle of four such abodes, reclaimed from what was once an open-air courtyard to a larger villa. When Olen was young, the house had been divided into several dwellings around the sides. Olen's father had roofed off the courtyard in the middle and laid out several rooms. As such, it was narrow and windowless all around, almost like living in a tower. Its door was set where the gate to the yard had been.

Olen turned onto a familiar side street and pointed out the doorway to Vyr and Talton. Someone ran from out of the shadows as they approached, splashing recklessly through the expansive puddles, but they disappeared within an instant and left no sign of damage or vandalism to the premises.

There was precious little light or signs of habitation from the dwellings that encircled—and delineated—the Kierk home. In front of Olen's thick, ramshackle door, someone had positioned a huge barrel which was collecting rainwater. Vyr put his back into it and shoved it out of the way without dumping it out, allowing Olen access. Talton watched from the side, hunched over, and holding both lanterns under his canopied cloak to keep the rain off them as best he could.

Olen produced the iron mortice key that Bull had given him and inserted it into the lock. It fit and it turned. The door creaked and opened. The great portal was bulky and getting waterlogged in the rain. It was already rotten in parts.

With the way now open the three squeezed into the claustrophobic gap between houses that served as an entrance hall. They rushed inside to get out of the downpour but found the interior only slightly drier. Bull was right; parts of the roof had collapsed in at some point. Rain was leaking in, dripping down from fallen rafters and pooling in the joists, making the wood punky and soft. The dirt floor had turned to mud in places. Nothing seemed homey about it, much less at all safe.

"Come back to the Eel with us," Vyr suggested, his voice more audible than when they were out in the rainstorm, though still only slightly louder than the patter of drops impacting above.

Olen shook his head. He accepted one of the lanterns from Talton. "I'm going to bed down here in the entranceway. There's a bit of a dry patch."

"Tomorrow, we'll have the boys scrounge up some supplies to help fix things up," Talton said.

Olen nodded appreciatively.

As his escorts made their way back out the door, Talton scoped out the street for danger. Vyr turned and slapped Olen on the back fondly. He snuck something off his belt, from under his cloak. It was a small flask of drink.

"Here. To keep you warm," Vyr chuckled and handed it over to Olen.

A second later, they had departed out onto the road again, setting out for the Black Eel.

It took effort for the morning light to penetrate the house. Because of its improvised floorplan, there were no windows on the ground storey. Olen sat in slumber on the earthen floor and didn't rise until a sliver of brightness finally filtered through the gaps in the roof. The rain had let up a little, but it was still to be a dreary day.

Thankfully, Olen had managed to get a small fire going in a stone-lined pit to keep him warm overnight. There were enough broken pieces of wood lying around to use as fuel and though damp on the surface, several cleaves of his sword splintered them to reveal drier cores inside.

There used to be several markets nearby. If they were still open, Olen figured he could find some food to allow for a sufficient first meal. But for that, he would need more money.

Now that it was morning, he was better able to take in the view of the home. So much of the house was in disrepair. He began shifting timbers around and clearing a path through the room. He piled several pieces up into a dry area, which would make for a more suitable seat or bed if he had to go through another wet night here.

As he organized, however, he focused on one corner of the room where there remained a raised wooden floor. Several of the floorboards were displaced, which drew Olen's ire right away. He knelt over them to look closely. He pried them further apart, with a fear that he was about to discover yet another setback to his hopes.

This was the spot where his family used to conceal a secret strongbox.

His expectation that it would still be here and safe was almost dashed, but when he thrust his hand under the boards, he surprisingly found that the box was still there. Nonetheless, when he pulled it out, the lock was open, and the box was empty.

First, his stash at Fal Ghreeg was stolen and now he had been raided here too! Olen roared and smashed his fist into the floorboards with anger. Getting onto his knees, he pulled his sword out and began using the pommel to fracture and break apart the old wood until he could get his hand further inside. He swept his fingers through the dust, coming up with a few errant coins, but nothing more remained in the cache.

Someone had taken it, but who?

The house had been sealed up for years. The only access was the key that Bull had kept. The thought knocked the vigour from Olen. He did not want to accuse one of his company comrades of having taken the money.

The warning about the collapsed roof...

The outer houses blocked any view of the roof from the outside. Olen was led to the discomforting conclusion that Bull, who had first told him about the problem, had demonstrated that he knew what state the interior of the house was in.

He must have been inside, Olen admitted reluctantly.

He gathered his things and squared away what he planned to leave behind. He had no idea what time the tavern would be open, but he would confront Bull as soon as it was.

Even this early in the morning, there were people on the street as he approached the tavern in Westriver. Like earthworms, they were crawling out after having sensed the rain abating. Everything was grey and damp. The mud on the streets was rippling with footprints.

Olen turned the handle to the tavern door, and it opened. He strode fiercely inside. There at the counter, Bull was standing, drinking from a steaming mug of what appeared to be tea.

"You're up early," he said as Olen barged in. "Mustn't have drank enough last night."

Olen didn't greet him.

"How did you know the roof was collapsed? When were you inside the house?"

"I wasn't inside," Bull said plainly.

"Then how did you know?"

"I was informed."

Olen gritted his teeth, "By who?"

Bull was becoming more defensive as the exchange persisted. "Neriah told me."

"Who is Neriah? And what was she doing in my house?"

"Apparently, she was checking in on the place."

Gritting his teeth and cracking his knuckles, Olen's anger rose.

"By what right did you give someone else the key?" he demanded.

"I didn't give it to anyone," Bull said dismissively, causing Olen's temper to approach dire levels he might no longer be able to contain.

"Who did then?"

"*She* gave *me* the key," he corrected emphatically.

"Eh?" Olen said, trying to follow.

"I suppose she got it from your brother, Tolen. I presume this would have been at the time—or more likely before—the Karavals sliced his guts open. I didn't ask for too many details."

Olen relentlessly kept on interrogating him. "How? It's the family home. Why did he give the key away? What did she do to convince him to give her the key?"

"Nothing untoward as it sounds like you're suggesting. She's *his* daughter, after all."

Now Olen inhaled deeply in surprise. His anger ebbed to a fizzle, and he was thoroughly confused.

"He had a daughter?" he asked. "Is she..."

"Still alive?" Bull said. "Yes, Olen, you have a niece."

"But where is she?"

"She works at the Half Moon for Dance Karaval. Likely the smartest and safest choice insofar as it kept her from getting murdered herself."

Olen was feeling dizzy and sat down at the counter, resting his head on his hands while his mind swam with the revelation.

"They didn't kill us all then?"

"Of all the Kierks in the world," said Bull, "I still only count two. You and her." He then reached for a pot of simmering water, poured it out into a clay mug and added a handful of herbs to it. He slid the steeping libation over the counter to Olen.

"Congratulations. You're an uncle."

Olen started to stand, shakily. "I've got to go there and find her."

"I'll be damned if you do. I have no intention of losing my new best customer so soon," Bull said in staunch opposition.

"I just want to *see* her," Olen said. "I won't stay long!"

"You will if the Karavals slit your throat and bury you under the floorboards like every other fool with your unfortunate appellation."

Olen grew agitated, his curiosity excited. What did she look like? He wondered how much she might resemble Tolen. How old was she? Did she even know that she had an uncle? Another, more challenging question entered his mind regarding her employment at the Half Moon.

"Why didn't the Karavals just kill her?"

"Good question. I admire your inquisitiveness." Bull said, likely relieved that the threat of having to run out the door to chase his guest down over some wild impulse had finally subsided. He cast a rare, sympathetic look at his hulking friend and warmed up both their steaming mugs with a fresh pour of boiling water. "Drink your tea."

CHAPTER 13

Apart and Away

T he darkness was smothering him. Denn felt something wrapped over his eyes and his breath was short and forced. In his ears resounded the laughter of his captor, Colden, whose face flashed in front of him, menacing in its putrid crookedness.

He could not move. There was a weight on top of him. Colden was in the back of the cart, set to pounce and crush him, seeking to avenge the slaying of his brother Romwin. Nearby, the icy-eyed Balix shouted and played overseer to the abject cruelty.

Someone else pressed down on him as he struggled to get out from underneath. Romwin? No, smaller, like Temis. With a hand free, Denn ripped the blanket from his eyes and pushed against the petite, sable-haired body that was lying upon him. It gasped and cried out, unexpectedly feminine.

Denn caught himself before he tipped over the side of the bed, staring blankly with distress at Livet. She clung to the covers beside him, her leg still entangled in his. Her wide eyes tracked his fit of terror until the panic subsided.

Without a word, he rolled back under the blanket and forced his breathing under control. He strived to recover from the nightmare and to regain some capacity for gentleness. Livet recovered first. Stroking Denn's brow and holding his hand tightly, she tenderly returned him to an awareness that all was alright. They were holed up in the snug, safe nest they had procured for themselves on the upper floor of an unassuming tenement house following the tumultuous council meeting.

Nobody knew where they were hiding. Denn had

recommended that they inform Yael at least, for safety's sake, but Livet recounted the obscure warning she had received. She suggested that they take some time to keep to themselves and cultivate a moment's obscurity while they still could.

Denn was planning to leave on a dangerous task and there was no way that Livet was ignorant of that. It had been evident in his face that he had been lured into serving and accepting his father's and Brevin Farathemun's cause. Since he didn't have to tell her, he began to reassure her instead.

"I'll be back in less than a fortnight," he insisted.

"You don't 'ave to go. We could both leave the city together."

"I've agreed to the job, and I live up to my agreements," Denn protested

"You promise things too quickly sometimes," she said, laying in a pool of her own frustration.

"Well, I promise *you* I'll be back."

"Y'know, we don't need t'go back to the Fals if y'think 'gainst it," she rolled over to look more directly at him. "You know more 'bout the world than I do. You could choose where we go.'"

Her affection for him was so much more than he ever imagined such a tiny frame could even hold. He felt ashamed that within his nightmare he had confused her wispy delicateness with the malign persecutor who circled and swelled in his memories.

"I owe it to my father to repay the debt of my rescue. When it's done, I will be free to grant you the full sum of my remaining attention. Lord Farathemun is raising an army to match those of the Marshal's and the Pillars'. He has the support in place and the troops are ready to march for Caphedra now. What they need is to have a legitimate successor to rally around, which is why he's pledged his niece. She's not been indoctrinated into the Faith as her sister was, nor was she raised like her brother to believe the might of the sword is the only determinant of justice."

"And are *you* going to lead this army?" Livet asked, somewhat mockingly.

Denn had contemplated the asking. When he returned, it would be expected of his father to contribute troops to the cause, especially now that he had assumed the mantle of a lordship. But it was a fleeting whim. The task would likely fall to Yael, even though his skills were better suited for more clandestine collaborations. To

Denn's knowledge, Yael had always worked within the city, strategizing against the machinations of politicians and nobles, combating the unseen. He'd never waged war in mass formations on a battlefield nor rode the lines ahead of a deployed army.

Denn hadn't either, but at least he'd been trained for it.

"Look, I've only been asked to do this one task," he said, putting his imaginings aside. "There were no other requests or expectations. No other hasty agreements."

Livet drew back, sourly. Her sigh suggested acceptance, but her demonstrations of affection had cooled.

"I don't like to be alone," she told him.

"You are smart and quick and sensible. You'll be fine here."

"But I don't like to be alone," she repeated.

"But you lived in Lanstad. You grew up in a city. Caphedra is just a little bigger." Denn sensed there was no mediating her reservations. "I'll hurry back," was the most he could offer.

"Your father's friend will *really* stand 'gainst the Pillars? Lady Ravon is his niece, too, isn't she? I don't *see* any other army."

"Lord Farathemun has a plan, along with the other nobles and merchants. My father has agreed to be a part. Myrhic is set to march Ramid's army south any day now. They'll take on the Pillars of the Faith and undoubtedly subdue each other. We just have to be ready to act for ourselves when we get the opportunity. The citizens will support us."

"And so, you're off now to rescue a princess?" Livet turned away from Denn. She began arranging her clothes on the bed. Denn pulled himself out from under the bedclothes and rose until he was standing tall and could peer out the open slit in the window to where the dampness of the preceding rainfall persisted.

"I'm simply escorting her back. She'll only need rescuing if we fail."

"I don't want to wait here without you for long."

She did not need to reiterate her apprehensions. Denn was worried that she would sneak off before he returned if he abandoned her now. He was not the only one with nightmares. Many nights Livet would wake up with premonitions of being hunted or persecuted again. For all she might love him, she needed the security of familiar people around her, and that might prove difficult in a strange, new city. He'd have suggested she stay with Serenn, but whatever it was that Yael had intimated to her had left her too frightened to remain in his father's house and it left him with no other ideas.

"Stay here. The city is not safe."

"I can go to the Black Eel and find Olen!" she said defiantly.

"With Ravon taking the throne, she's begun confirming the Pillars' rule upon the city. Their thugs are out in legions, and besides them, there are hordes of bloodthirsty bandits and rioters," he warned. "That's just in the city proper. I can only imagine that Westriver is worse!"

Livet slipped her linen dress over herself then approaching Denn, she pulled him into a gentle embrace, tip-toed on one foot to her maximum reach and kissed him resolutely on the lips. "Are you sure you want to do this?" she asked.

"My part in this plan is important," he said, not concealing his pride in the regard shown to him by the city's elite. "They've put a lot of trust in my ability to see the princess here safely, so that they have a figure to rally around."

Against the dim, intrusive light, she eyed his figure and he felt her appraising him. Conscious of the fact that he was quite slim and lanky at the best of times, he hoped the past few days of rest and regular meals had started to make him more solid. Livet's eyes flowed over his shoulders, the muscles in his arms, his strong-set jaw, and even his elevated stature as he stood more nobly and tried to project what might pass as indomitableness. Denn even pumped out his chest a little, to contrast with the cowed, timorous bedmate he had been, when he had woken her moments ago.

"You used to think too little o' yerself," she said accusingly, but he seemed to have passed her inspection. "I'm glad t' see you so brave now, an' I know you will be able t' show them you can be trusted t' do it."

The landlady of the lodging house put together pouches of smoked meats and hard, dry bread for Denn, knowing he was to travel but not being told where. Denn had only implied that he was returning to his field posting. Confidently, she promised Livet would be safe staying in her residence for the time being.

They had chosen to hole up in a multi-storeyed, whitewashed

house that spilled out over a bread bakery in the north-easternmost district of Lords' Lane, close to Castleside, and to Caphedra Castle itself. The district was a home for many magistrates and upper-class servants, and its residents tended to keep to themselves and not provoke much trouble, making it a more secure choice for Livet and Denn to be sheltered in without worry.

Kissing her again on the steps leading up to the door, Denn discouraged Livet from coming out onto the street. The weather looked unsettling and was beset with drizzle and fog, so he bade her to stay in and keep next to the fireside until he returned. Livet clung to the doorway, but paid him no comment save for, "Come back soon."

Denn tugged reassuringly at the baldric which held his sword, Longlimb, tight to his back. He felt under the cloth of his cloak for the horn-handled dagger in his belt. He glanced a few more times at the door, then stretched his leather gloves over his hands and embarked onto the first leg of his travels.

Down the lane and around the bend of a hill, he walked past the protective stone walls along the slope that divided the manors and villas where the affluent and important were housed. Soon, he approached his own former home from behind. He spied where the attackers had positioned their ladder those several nights before and followed a path along the stonework until he came to the gate.

He was about to call out, but the door swung open enough for him to pass. He slipped in without a word and met with the youthful Trin, who had been watching and waiting for him. The young squire was dressed in a deep burgundy riding cloak to keep out the damp and was holding a respectable broadsword by the scabbard.

"Good morning. It's good to see you well, sir."

"And good morning to you," Denn said. "Is everything ready?"

"Aye. Your mount is in good health, sir, and I think she's looking forward to stretching her legs."

Smiling, Denn thanked Trin and moved ahead into the courtyard. Naobe was standing beneath an overhang where a few misshapen pieces of scrap wood had been lashed and nailed together as a makeshift stable roof. Beside her was a smaller, more nimble, dappled palfrey, which tried to nuzzle Trin when he passed by.

Denn started to walk toward the house, but Trin stopped him. "Your father and mother went away with Serenn. The Faith has been visiting the house regularly, seeking payments. I don't think your father is keen to meet with them."

"Any more word from my brother?" Denn asked.

"He dropped by yesterday, sir," Trin said. "I didn't think much of it, but Yael seemed to get an idea that he was unhappy to hear you'd taken up another residence. They didn't speak long."

Denn worked to adjust Naobe's tack then dumped his provisions into some saddlebags slung over her back. He expected more than just Trin to greet him at the house and felt a bit disappointed. Even the cart horses were gone from the stable. It was only the palfrey and Naobe remaining to lend life to the place.

"Is it just us going?"

"When we reach Fallowsea, we'll be joined by the young Lord Farathemun's men," Trin said. He checked that his sword was firmly strapped alongside, then led his horse out by her bridle.

"How many men will return with us?"

"Maybe not too many, sir. The princess's safety has been entrusted to us and the lord personally, but we are to try and travel back swiftly and without notice—so it won't be a large number."

With a nod, Denn slipped a foot into one of Naobe's stirrups and propelled himself into the saddle. Trin stepped back once he knew Denn needed no assistance. It was noticed and Denn felt bothered that he may have to prove his cavalry skills to Trin, but the young man appeared immediately satisfied and even volunteered a bit of praise.

"I'm looking forward to travelling with you, sir. I only ever served here in the capital, and I know you have years of experience in the field."

That brought a smile to Denn as he coaxed Naobe out onto the street.

Trin pulled his horse by its lead and followed. Once they were both out, he secured the gate, then mounted his palfrey, clucking his tongue to get her moving. "C'mon, Blenksy," he said, and the smaller, more vivacious horse immediately rode assertively ahead, clearing the way for Denn and his regal charger.

As much as Denn resented being in the position to owe this

favour to his father, he admitted it was a rare job that would see him interact so vitally with someone of such uncommon esteem as a royal princess. Though he could hardly envision his father advertising his virtues, Lord Farathemun must have gained confidence that Denn was of the calibre to see this mission through.

The bout of rain that started the night of the council meeting persisted for several days. By the time they departed, it had abated though the sky still hung low with bulging, slate-coloured storm clouds, threatening another downpour. Gusts of wind aloft discouraged birds from flight so they congregated along rooftops and or under the bartizans and turrets of the tallest buildings. Prominent among them were mobs of cawing crows whose aggressiveness had chased away the usual doves, starlings, and sparrows.

"The crows are everywhere this morning," Denn commented to Trin.

"They'd be better off in the fields. There's not a lot of food scraps to scavenge here, sir. These are sparse times for the city with the Faith grabbing and stockpiling everything they can."

"I suppose they're expecting a siege."

"The city walls are full of holes. There are a lot of ways into Caphedra for someone who wants in badly enough," Trin said. "And the Marshal's Men are already inside. Who knows how many there are? It would only take a few to sabotage the defences from within. It doesn't lend well to the idea of any lengthy siege. I just don't think they're very keen on people being able to support themselves."

Denn nodded, "You seem to have a good head on you. I see why Yael was so quick to take you on."

"It's my pleasure to serve your family, sir."

"Still, you used to be part of a city brigade. Do you worry about having to fight against people you once served with?"

"I was in the Capital Brigade, sir. Most of my comrades got picked up by the Farathemuns, both younger and elder. Their cavalrymen came from our 13th Mounted–where I squired. Those men are mostly out in Fallowsea now, having been hired by young Lord Kentin. I expect we will see them. Besides that, the father recruited his foot guard from Stonerow Company. The only ones they didn't manage to procure from the brigade were the bowmen. Swift Company has been retained by the Faith and from time to time, you'll see them manning the walls of the Temple. If one of them was fated to slay me, we wouldn't be so close as to blink an eye at each other."

"I expect the archers to be moved to the citadel soon," Denn commented, glancing over his shoulder to where the imposing castle walls jutted up from behind the Castleside mansions. "But it's not just the old city guard they've hired either, it seems. Lord Vlass's men are everywhere."

"Those are the ones with the boar's head on their arms, aren't they, sir?

"Aye," confirmed Denn. "They marched up from Lanstad."

"Can they fight?" Trin asked.

"The old ones can," Denn said. "Vlass was loyal to the king, so they camped with us in the Fals and I know their character. I wouldn't trust the lot of them."

As if invoked by the mention, a number of these imported reinforcements came into view, prowling the approaches to Hamrin Square. Denn watched their movements and made a headcount of their complement. They numbered so many, he could forgive himself for thinking that he was in Lanstad for a moment. He hoped that Livet would heed his advice and stay indoors to wait for him. She was bound to react poorly if she came face to face with the same ilk that had beaten and imprisoned her in her youth.

Denn pulled back on the reins as they approached the statue of Queen Tressa. "Look," he said, pointing to the monument.

"Sir?" Trin queried.

From afar, Denn thought it had been defaced but then realized it was only marred by the addition of blue paint over the gentle curves of the queen's robes. The hue matched that of the robes worn by those of the highest echelon faithful to the Pillars. Denn thought this alteration of such a prominent monument to be incredibly bold.

Affixed to the statue was an engraved plaque; its rapid emplacement suggested it had been re-purposed from somewhere else. It retold the story of the late Queen's tragic mania with a postscript of warning against the dangers to the obedient, posed by those with heretical thoughts. Catching his eye more acutely, however, was the more specific call to action in the text of a crusty, creased scroll beside it. It implored the citizens of Caphedra to hunt down the fugitive enchantress Baressa Hart, and *all those who consort with her.*

This was the woman that Olen and Livet had described encountering. Had their identities also been communicated by the curate whose name was brought up at the council? Were they in danger of arrest? Was this what Yael warned Livet about? The paper christened her 'The Chieftain's Daughter' and went on to list the accused's litany of unnatural transgressions from enchantments and curses–such as those that befell the queen–to the potential for fiendish violence and evil acts–as suffered by the late king.

Again, he prayed that Livet would hearken to his warning to stay hidden and remain clear of this mysterious woman and any of whom she might count amongst her mystic cabal. Baressa had rapidly earned Livet's trust–or so he understood from the retelling of their journey–but just being opposed to the Faith didn't guarantee she would be intent on protecting Livet's interests over her own, whatever they might be. From Olen's and Livet's own testimony, Baressa could warp a man's mind and tangle his thoughts against him. Admittedly, the reappearance of Baressa at such a time, after years in hiding, was a peculiar, if convenient coincidence for increasing the public's appetite to hunt magicians and wizards. Hadn't Lehn implied there were more people who could exercise such powers? That she had remained at large must be of peculiar discomfort for the Faith as they sought to solidify their control.

Denn wondered if he should turn around now, leave with Livet immediately and forget the princess. Several alleged cohorts were detailed on the summons, but none matched with Livet. However, they referenced the Northport seeress as travelling with an armed escort 'of distinct Westriver origin.'

That's Olen, I'd wager, Denn thought. Giving one last look at the noble statue of the late queen, he pulled again on the reins and steered Naobe back to the plaza below.

As he did, a ragged figure strangely appeared at his side, wearing a cowl that obscured his face. At first, Denn thought it was a beggar who had come to seek the queen's posthumous blessing, but the man's voice betrayed him.

"Beautiful lady, our Queen Tressa. So enamoured of by the

people that they said that while the kingdom was her husband's, Caphedra was *her* city. It is a shame what happened to her."

"Yael?" Denn asked, under his breath.

"Aye, lad," said the man. "I couldn't risk being seen at the manor, so I came to see you off from here. You can pick out that massive horse of yours from here to the Folds," he chided.

"Good morning, Mr. Larkin," Trin said politely, and Yael returned the greeting.

"Have you any news?" Denn asked, knowing that anything could have changed since arrangements were made on the night of the council.

Yael, moved between the two horses to be less conspicuous. He reached up and stroked Naobe on the withers. "I just came to see that all is well with you before your departure. I wanted to be sure that you are ready for the job at hand."

"Why wouldn't I be?" Denn defended, a twinge of resentment in his voice.

"This is a grand request you've been granted," Yael said. "I want to be sure you know all you need to know."

"It's a simple ride out and back. We'll be fine," Denn said cavalierly. "After that, the job's done for me."

"And then you'll return to the swamps with your young consort? Or Falbeth, where you can lead a merry life farming peas and tending goats? She's pretty and she loves you, I'll give you that. Many men would be satisfied by that."

"I am not compelled to seek the same rewards as my father. It's up to me to fulfill my life in the way I wish," defended Denn.

"I suppose raising goats would be an even grander life than your father once suspected you might achieve on your own, isn't it?"

Denn steadied himself in his saddle. A suggestion loomed in Yael's discourse that made him uncomfortable, yet Denn swallowed any response of his own and listened. There had to be a point to this.

"When you left, it wasn't because your father placed too high a demand on you," Yael elaborated. "He did that to Hann, and we all saw it—but I think you were angry because he'd *never placed the same expectations on you*. If poor Hann had lived up to your father's ambitions, he'd have been a great man and a proud bearer of the Wellum name into the ages. You could overcome your father's ridicule, but the most you'd ever become would be yourself, the second son."

"Why do you tell me this now?" Denn finally asked.

"Because the tides have changed. Your father has placed a lofty responsibility upon your shoulders for the first time in your life and I don't think you're going to abandon it soon, now that you've got it. No matter how much you hate him, this is what you told yourself you wanted. More than Hann did, maybe?"

"A princess is just a girl. We'll gather her up and bring her back, that's all. She's in Farathemun's charge after that."

Yael nodded. "What of the men your father promised to assign to your command when you return?"

Denn said nothing and Yael let slip a cutting laugh.

"I know you want to be in front of an army. You don't need to give me excuses and stories like you do your woman. If she knows you half a damn, she already knows what's on your mind for when you return."

Instantly, Denn felt he needed to refute Yael's suspicions of his intentions but had no words to counter him. Yael was not wrong. Denn just hadn't allowed himself to thoroughly absorb the implications of the opportunity that awaited him. They were buried under mistrust of his father. Now, he felt shameful and dishonest in his consoling words to Livet.

"Just take my advice, Denn. You've not held any rank before. No one even knows you by anything other than your father's name. You're just the '*living* Wellum boy' amongst higher circles. Fare well at this challenge to bring back Lady Ramisa, and they will take notice. Your father's money can buy companies of men under the Wellum banner, so long as he puts food in their bellies and shoes on their feet. But to fight and maybe die, they'll need iron in their hearts. That comes from confidence in their leader."

"So why pick me to perform this task? Surely other names come to mind," Denn asked.

"Perhaps. But they *have* picked you and that's all the matters. What will you do with this opportunity?"

Denn could not help but think Yael was holding something back. It still sounded highly suspect that his meagre handful of years galloping about a field garrison somehow led to Denn's chief candidacy now. Almost certainly, it came down to being a surety for access to his father's money. Was he an unknowing hostage? Had he traded one captivity for another of his father's devising?

"Let your ambition spur your success," Yael counselled after a short pause. "Let it elevate you and dismiss any concern over your suitability as a warrior and champion. Your father's idle promises of your prowess will not motivate the men under your charge so much as the highly visible gratitude of the Farathemuns and the other merchants and nobles—or the sight of you standing alongside the princess as her chief protector."

He was right again. It was incumbent on Denn to dismiss any doubts that he was fit to lead. He must complete this adventure to inspire, or at least to placate, the concerns of those men who would march behind him, and furthermore, he had to succeed in finally suppressing the same misgivings within himself.

"Why does Farathemun want the princess brought to Caphedra, just as war is about to sweep the city?" Denn asked. "She won't be standing in front of the troops like a general. Can't her authority extend from far away? Rule from where she is safer?"

"It's only a matter of time before someone hunts her down in Fallowsea, for there is only one way in and out of that village. Besides, no one will expect her to be brought here at such a time. It's a decent ruse, though not infallible. Still, when Farathemun's forces arrive at the gates of the capital, he'll want to show her off in person, to cinch the deal with all those men expected to bleed for her."

"It seems a lot to ask of a young girl who's not even seen the capital for a decade. Is she prepared for such danger?"

Yael grew dark but ventured a soft, "One can hope." Looking up at the statue of the girl's mother, the queen, he appeared to reflect. "You may not know, but I was one of the ones who encouraged for Ramisa to be sent away. I was once the Prefect of Stonerow, under Feryl Morea—a favourite of his, all told. Lord Brevin Farathemun approached us when he first had fears that someone was acting against his sister. He couldn't trust the Faith, whom he suspected, nor could he trust the castle guards who reported to the Marshal. Myrhic would have sought to use any discord to his own advantage. Castleside's prefecture was not without suspicion as well, so Morea came to Stonerow and asked me to help investigate instead."

"Why did Farathemun think it was the Faith?" Denn asked.

"Queen Tressa had no physical wounds, but her mind was

turning itself over and over, destroying her, and growing ever more the worse as Precept Golmarra gained access to her. She heard voices and had premonitions. Even more disastrously, whatever might be the cause, it was spreading to the middle child–her daughter, Ramisa. The Precept blamed all manner of foreign curses, rampant spells, and witchcraft across the kingdom, conveniently convicting his own detractors and challengers of the crimes when he could."

"But there are people who *can* do such things," Denn said, his eyes drifting back to the proclamation condemning Baressa and her compatriots.

"Yes, but everything suggested the blight grew worse when Golmarra was around, and he had motive," Yael explained. "The whole event started around the time that Ramisa was to follow her sister and cloister in the temple. But with Ravon already consumed by her studies and Ramid away under the tutelage of the Marshal, Ramisa had become her father's favourite about the castle. The king was reluctant to lose her too."

"What then?" Trin asked solemnly and Yael's craggy face grew deeper in its frown.

"We couldn't convince the queen that she should leave Caphedra. She was an uncompromising populist who insisted that she be allowed to stay no matter how far she deteriorated. So instead, Farathemun used his influence to suggest fostering Ramisa away from Caphedra, for just a short time. His Highness relented under his wife's brother's persuasion, and the girl was whisked away to her cousin for fostering."

"But she evidently remained away much longer." Denn pointed out.

Yael nodded. "We didn't want her to return at all. We felt it was too dangerous. Within a short time, the Precept became furious, and as Golmarra's anger grew, the queen's condition worsened. We were forbidden any further access to her until the day came that they announced her death. She died a martyr, but we do not know for what."

Denn looked up at the statue as if to glean something from Queen Tressa's expression, but the stone was unyielding.

"The shock of her passing, terrible and earthshaking, planted firm the seeds of doubt in the king's mind about the Faith," Yael continued. "But the Pillars were–*are* too entrenched in Caphedra. It would have torn apart the kingdom to act against them on suspicion alone. But it was gratefully enough that he ordered Ramisa to be kept away from Caphedra permanently."

"But now the king is dead," Denn stated. "Could he have learned something to convince himself of the Pillars' guilt?"

Yael didn't answer right away but seemed to weigh the matter.

"Yael, if Golmarra killed the queen, who do you think killed the king?" Trin asked.

Still, Yael frowned. "I am not permitted to say, as it might give credence to unproven speculations." With that, he stepped back from between the horses. "I've delayed you long enough. You should be off. Take good care of Ramisa, for she's a sweet girl and altogether undeserving of this massing of misfortunes that she's now being forced to confront."

Yael drifted behind them and gave Blenksy a light slap on the rump. She took a step forward. As they began to ride away, he added, "One more thing! Though it be obvious enough to avoid mention, be on the lookout for the prince's army. There are reports in the past couple of days of scouts encamped north of the city, just past the Rafters."

Scouting parties were some of Denn's first assignments and he knew that such camps were always positioned only a few days' ride ahead of the main formation. The late king's army formed the core of the Marshal's army, and such tactics were not likely to have changed.

"If that's the case, it could be just a matter of days before war breaks open here. I'd like to be done this deed and back quickly," he said. "You're right. We best be off right away. Thank you, Yael."

"Have a safe journey!" Yael stepped farther back, out of the way to allow them to pass. Adjusting his tattered clothes, he reverted to the role of an innocuous vagrant.

Denn pressed Naobe to continue down the hill, causing Blenksy to also start forward without any goading from Trin. She moved to the flank and jauntily overtook the bigger warhorse.

This morning, the crowds in Hamrin Square were shuffling about their business, avoiding any unsanctioned distractions or dalliances, save for those caused by a cadre of blue-clad officiants who were forcing passage for themselves through the mass of citizens. At multiple street corners, speakers continued to profess their beliefs in the Pillar doctrines, shouting from rostrums and daises, over the heads of grey-faced audiences who maintained proper, submissive attention. There was little hint of disagreement or disruption today.

As Denn and Trin crossed the immense plaza, Naobe reasserted her place and Blenksy followed her obediently, parallel to one of the streams of pedestrians. Sitting high in the saddle, Denn observed Lanstad troops reinforcing a cordon around the public space where the crows from that morning could be seen circling overhead.

They were taking a macabre interest in the dark spectacle of human bodies chained to hoisted pikes, for the Council's decree that had opened the door to Ravon's regency also allowed for the unyielding jealousy of the Faith to now dominate supreme, without any tolerance for derision.

"They've begun purging apostates. Ridding themselves of their opposers," Denn said lamentably.

Trin pulled back the hood of his cloak. He appeared expressionless but was taking careful note of each apprehended transgressor. When his eyes fell upon a face still showing signs of life, he looked away, aghast, before clenching his jaw to steel himself and resume his advance onward.

Denn also felt queasy. He'd seen dead bodies and heard stories of massacres at battlefields like Floral Marsh, Bloody Oaks, or Icemeadows, but it was different when the victims were so helpless. These poor wretches were men and women of every age. They were bound, broken, strung up, and condemned to death out here in the open, without mercy or dignity.

Abruptly as they were passing, a large draft horse cut off their path and forced them to halt while it pulled a wagon in front of them. On the back, freshly hewn and sharpened poles were being transported.

"They must be planning to fill up the whole square," Trin speculated grimly, causing some of the downtrodden beside him to rouse from their torpor, fearful of someone raising their voice dissentingly.

Before continuing much further, Denn scanned the faces of

199 Ian Robert Ross | 199

the victims they were passing. He remembered the detestable Due that the Faith had issued his father and the threats uttered by that woman, Aroon, at the Council. Denn began monitoring the pikes for his father's face. Worse, he feared he might find his mother or Serenn here.

The faces of the persecuted unsettled Denn, as they surrounded him within the square. The cruelty of the Faith of the Pillars, and the throne-seeker Ravon, was incomprehensible.

"Let's not tarry," he said, starting to feel that they might be attracting attention. Though their riding cloaks hid the layers of leather armour that Denn and Trin wore, they possessed tell-tale swords slung alongside their noteworthy mounts. While Blenksy could move through the crowds naturally, the titanic bulk of a warhorse like Naobe drew a lot of stares.

They pushed on anxiously until the plaza was behind them. Though the King's Avenue became narrower past Stonerow, their going was made easier as the street traffic began to thin. Fewer goods in the markets that lined the roadside meant the numbers of shop-goers dwindled. Posted signs were now advising of curfews and closures of the city gates. Most troublingly, rules of conduct were also tacked up on walls and posts, which forbade the carrying of arms by those not under service to the Faith of the Pillars.

Denn pointed the signs out to Trin and chided him for his burgundy cloak. "You're wearing the wrong colour to be carrying a sword. Looks like they're locking down the city now that Ravon is on the throne and Ramid is closing in. We may have a challenge getting out and we will certainly be barred from getting back in."

"As I told you before, sir, there are a lot of ways around the walls for someone who really wants to get in," replied Trin. "I know of a breach running under the city wall near the river that your father employs to bring in goods without being seen. If it pleases you, sir, we can use that."

"Can you fit a horse the size of Naobe through it? Denn asked.

"A princess will fit through," Trin answered pragmatically.

"Maybe we will be able to think of something else by then," Denn said.

As they navigated the avenue west through the city, a pair of armour-clad horsemen began flanking them and following close behind. Denn and Trin nervously hastened the pace of their steeds. The men didn't utter a single word but converged upon them until their horses were almost nudging up against Naobe and Blenksy. Finally, the rider behind Trin, who was following them on the right, called out in a surly voice.

"Yield the road!"

While both men wore all the impressive cerulean trappings of troops employed by the Faith of the Pillars, they nonetheless retained the greasy, hungry look of callous mercenaries. The man who accosted them was wearing ringed mail. His chest was crossed with two green sashes under a blue mantle, and he carried a barbed spear with a worryingly long reach. The unspeaking rider closer to Denn communicated by allowing the edges of his blue cape to slide back, displaying a loaded crossbow resting across his lap. It was pitched upon a groove in the pommel of his saddle to steady its aim should he wish to fire without neglecting his reins.

Their harassers had them severely disadvantaged, so it was up to Denn to quickly make a plan and perhaps avoid trouble through a combination of guise and clout. It was his gamble that being Lehn Wellum's brother would carry more prestige than being Phon Wellum's son would garner condemnation. His coyness took them off guard.

With a hand on Longlimb's hilt, Denn shouted back to them. "I see you are men of the Faith," he paused a heartbeat, then boldly queried, "Are you the men my brother promised me?"

"Are we what?" asked the first, startled.

Denn kept Naobe at a steady, unwavering walk. Her ears were starting to pitch back, and he could tell she disliked the Pillarmen.

"We're the men tellin' you t' move aside, off the road, is whut," said the crossbowman behind Denn.

Trin bolstered Denn's bluff by asking, "Do you know who you're talking to?" This bought another moment of hesitation, long enough for Trin to add, "This is Lehn Wellum's brother. He's a curate. I imagine you know *him,* don't you?"

Denn hoped his brother's name would discourage the men from thinking they had any impunity to act against him. If he made the wrong move, like drawing his sword, the man behind him would instantly let loose his crossbow—and he was lined up for a deadly shot.

"Curate Lehn Wellum is my brother," Denn reiterated. "When he told me that the Faith wanted to recruit me as an officer in its army, I had a different reception in mind."

Keeping fixed on the road ahead, Denn watched out of the corners of his eyes for any opportunity but signalling Trin would be difficult. There were alleyways leading off the avenue where their horses would be forced to ride single file, which offered better positioning to break the stalemate, but one of them would be bound to get that crossbow bolt in the back, should they alter their course.

"Are you on business for the temple now, then? Your brother's business?" asked the surly rider.

"We're going north to check on iron shipments through Bren Hills, for delivery to the temple." Denn lied, but it fit believably within the originally proposed cover of being merchants. His father was the most well-known ironmonger in Caphedra, and the Faith was expecting its donation.

The man with the crossbow interrogated further.

"Ramid's army is up north. You don't plan on going 'round past them, do you? You're awfully well-armed for a merchant."

"I'm a merchant of arms! Of course, I carry a sword," Denn responded contritely.

The riders were starting to fall back and were no longer crowding their horses.

"How many men are in your unit?" Denn asked, turning the conversation on its end by questioning the men instead.

"All of them," the spearman said smartly.

"Not enough for us to waste time in conversations like this," said the caped man, who shifted his crossbow to the side and pulled lightly on the reins of his horse. "Be advised that today is your last chance to leave the city. After today, I highly doubt you'll be let back in until Ramid's been defeated. You are now warned!"

"Thank you," said Denn.

The riders pulled back and the caped man declared "We will inform your brother's office of your departure."

Avoiding any gesture or display to betray his discomfort, Denn fixed his eyes forward. All he could say was, "Tell him I will look forward to seeing him upon my return."

There was a snort as one of the horsemen's mounts began a

circle to reverse.

"I support the Pillars!" the crossbowman said as he departed.

"And I," the surly rider added, then with a spur to his horse's rump, he also disappeared back down the road from whence came.

Trin rolled his eyes. "I support the Pillars? That's what the adepts used to make us recite as children... *I support the Pillars... I support the Pillars...*"

"It's been their mantra for a while. Lehn also used to say it endlessly when he first was inducted," Denn said. "I guess it's making its way into their army now. Although, I don't expect those fellows have been serving the temple for too long, by the looks of them."

Trin shook his head. "Mercenaries. I could tell by the green sashes that the one behind me was from Middlehold Company. They were part of the 8th Brigade, like us, but were disbanded entirely when the army started running out of money."

"So now they're on the hunt for new masters, and the Faith has lots of gold."

"Aye, sir," Trin said. "And Myrhic has promised Ramid's men that very same gold, once they storm the city and take it."

They were almost out of the capital. Ahead was the turn in the road that would lead them east of the elaborate cottages of Highside and past the smithy district of Barforgers. It stretched to the northwest gate of the city, which was now visibly fully manned in anticipation of invasion from the north.

Before long, the rain returned, driving people on the streets to take cover. Denn and Trin raised their hoods higher and pinched them into peaks at the front so the water would run off. Fortunately, there were no other delays in reaching the north wall. Soldiers were too busy rolling barrels of pitch and tar up ramps to the gate towers, while others laboured with sharpening arrow and axe heads against spinning, rumbling grindstones. At the wall, however, a guard called out to them as they rode under the stone archway.

"State your purpose for going through the gate!" the guard demanded. Beads of rain were pooling in the recesses of his helmet and spilling out to drip down his cheeks as he spoke.

"Merchants. Travelling to Bren Hills," Denn said, pulling his hood aside to not appear evasive.

"We support the Pillars!" Trin hastily added.

The guard nodded agreeably and pushed a barricade more widely open for Naobe to fit through. Placated, he offered some advice.

"Bad timing with the rain. Stay to the west of the road if you can. Myrhic's army is assembling, and the bulk of the brutes are bound to break camp at Wodwarden any day."

"We aim to hurry back," Denn said, waving to the guard amiably as they departed out through the barbican gatehouse that led out of the city.

CHAPTER 14

Behind Stone Walls

L ivet fidgeted restlessly in bed, cursing the rooming house with its leak in the roof, the too-narrow window that turned the room into a cell, and the detestable sound of creaking boards as the landlady crept up against the other side of the door to listen and check in on her. She fought the temptation to level curses against Denn, knowing that what he did was for a cause, but she was infuriated that he expected her to remain confined in this cramped bower, alone in a bed that was made for two. It had already been several days since he had left, and she felt antsy.

How close Ramid's army was, she did not know. Neither was she aware of the extent to which the Faith of the Pillars were solidifying their newfound dominance. She remembered how in Lanstad, Lord Vlass had slowly allowed the Faith to encroach on the city's old gods and worshippers. When the arrests started, the reasons were always paired with charges of already illegal crimes, but their real crime was heresy. Her protector, Kell Karr, had been arrested as a common thief, but he was shackled and prosecuted as an apostate and given the sort of punishments reserved for those who were dire threats to the kingdom.

Livet had been captured on the same day but was kept separate from the others. The curate who held her life in his grasp had lost interest in her when she became too broken and stopped screaming. But he told her that he did not desire to kill a child like her so he threw Livet out onto the street, notionally absolving her of culpability in Kell's crimes. She crawled away—a lame, crippled beggar. Even the worst of Lanstad's footpads and alley thugs left her alone out of pity.

No more moping, she decided.

Her memories constricted her far more than this little room did. Livet tightened the strings holding her linen gown together and cinched the thicker bodice around her from hips to chest. She reached for her leather lace-up boots, putting her arm down inside to adjust the padding she kept inserted to balance out the unsteady lameness of her crooked left leg. Slivers of yew were sewn along its length, the wood offering both suppleness and support, to guide her gait as she walked and save her from needing a staff to lean on. For safety, she also tucked away her rondel.

She was ready to leave. Slipping quietly out the door, Livet turned the key in the lock and then stashed it within a fold in the leather brim of her boots.

The landlady was keeping tabs on her boarders, so Livet eschewed the stairway down to the parlour. She walked to the end of the hall instead, where a larger window was cracked open, letting in a damp but welcome breeze. Livet seized upon the fresh air and lifted the bottom pane wider to look out, then crawled through.

The window was set into a protruding bartizan tower that hung out over a narrow alley between houses. The residence next door had been built more recently, however, and it was crowding up against the boarding house, consuming as much space as it could. It also featured a handy, timbered, wattle framework that she scampered down with ease.

Livet dropped the last few feet and, with a celebratory splash, landed in a puddle. Turning, she knelt for a moment and scratched a mouse-like glyph into the side of the rooming house support, near the ground. This place would have been called a '*hool*' back in Lanstad when speaking clandestinely in Scant, the dialect Kell had taught to her and their trusted kin. Scrawl was the secretive means to visually represent the dialect, displayed for allied souls to see as they passed by. The sign didn't mean that the house was guaranteed safe, but that a Kindred member was hiding there, nonetheless. Maybe someday it would be recognized, and Livet wouldn't be left so solitary.

The cobbled streets were cleaner in Lords' Lane, she noticed. The rain had washed away much of the usual accumulation of refuse, and fewer people tarried for any length of time. Everyone Livet passed gave her the impression they were hurrying off to some urgent affair. The street was lined with manors, and no public houses or other dens of recreational temptation broke the pattern.

Yael's earlier warning to remain hidden still occupied Livet's mind, certainly more than Denn's idle demand to stay put. So, avoiding all conspicuity, she grabbed the edges of her hood to keep her face obscured and moved along the gutters and building peripheries, dancing around the downward splashes that poured from the rain troughs that channelled the incessant rain from above.

She'd only travelled a couple of streets over when she came to a towering iron fence. Its bars impeded passersby from entering a vast cultivated green space on the other side. She gripped the metal bars and peeked inside, her expectations rewarded with a delightful breeze that blew through banks of flowers and soaked up the scent of their petals. Beyond was a field of shrubs and lush, dewy gardens, and rising out of them she saw the stone walls of Caphedra Castle. Spires jutted up each side of a wall leading from the gatehouse. They were dwarfed by a trio of more magnificent towers, behind whose adjoining defences demarked the boundaries of the fortress's inner citadel.

When she squinted, she thought she could see the domed panes of purple glass high above that Denn had described to her, and she imagined them providing their violet skylight glow to the regal courtiers below. The view satisfied her for now, and she let discretion take over. Surely, there would be guards patrolling the gardens. Livet backed away from the fence and melted into the alleyways of Lords' Lane again.

But now, the feeling of aimlessness was hard to shake off. If Olen was still in the city, maybe she could find him in Westriver. There was also the letter which could gain her access to the Peahen and Gardia, but that was an expedition she would have rather undertaken with Baressa. Porter's Run was close by, she thought. Maybe Astir could help broker a reunion.

Tracing the slope of the road gave her periodic glimpses of the closest tower of the Northeast gate. The way through Porter's Run led to that gate and using it as a landmark, she plotted her course toward the district. Within a short distance, she spied the bulging wooden constructs of halls and jettied catwalks over the rutted, muddy street that marked the southern start of the famed Greyforest Road.

It was as she had seen it upon first entering Caphedra, except for one alarming detail. The road was now heavily trafficked with armed men dressed in the blues of the Pillars' military. Though they lacked the individual mass and might of most of the Northport men, collectively they were stronger, locked together in prickly walls of halberds and sword points to canalize the foot traffic and contain it within the Porter ghetto. Their attention was on a host of armed Northport men that had begun to gather, and Livet wondered if the Pillar soldiers could be bothered to break ranks to accost a young woman. It would be best to be cautious, however, and a distraction would well be in order.

Livet focused on the group of soldiers beside her who had not yet taken notice of her attempt to penetrate past. They were bearded men with fair hair, though not as light as Denn's. She guessed them to be close to his age, however.

With a little concentration, she was able to send a thought toward them as easily as one would blow a kiss. The first soldier turned his attention to a nearby crowd of men and reached for his sword, partially drawing it from its scabbard. The others closed in and followed suit, searching in anticipation of a danger that they supposed they had heard. Nothing was out of the ordinary after their inspection, so they returned to their vigil, unaware that Livet had adeptly snuck past them and was now out of their view entirely.

The agitation permeating the air made Livet feel pressed and claustrophobic like someone was pulling on the strings of her bodice and making it hard to breathe. As she approached a wall of shops, the crowd thickened, and she was in actual danger of being crushed by the lines of angry men who ringed the edges of the street in their own barricade, their stalwart goal to keep the Pillar soldiers from advancing into their homes.

Suddenly, Livet felt a hand on her shoulder. She turned quickly to break free, but the grasp was not tight. Hunched under a recognizable old cloak was the familiar face of a man who, having caught her, was now showing the way for her to go.

"You'll want to get inside *there*," Kirt said, pointing with his walking stick to an iron-braced, oaken door that rose half again higher than any man in the crowd. It stood beneath an immense, axe-hewn log with chiselled letters declaring it to be the 'Travelling Trapper.'

Livet took the nonchalance in Kirt's face to indicate that it was safe to go in, but she nonetheless hesitated, bit her lip nervously, and looked back at him hoping to elicit more information.

"She's in there," he added.

Livet exhaled, and with a nod, pushed on the heavy door and squeezed inside.

At first, she saw little beyond a vast collection of rain-wet capes and cloaks, hung from pegs, and wrapped over rafters everywhere in a narrow foyer. They filled the air with the pungent smell of sweat, and dank bestial odours as they ostensibly dried out. The floor, the walls, and everything else were constructed of timbers, which were oiled rather than painted. After the austere stone facades of Castleside, and pale daubed walls of Lords' Lane, the interior of the tavern was warm and arboreal like an expertly crafted woodland cabin.

The hanging damp garments attested to the number of people inside and Livet could hear the voices of their owners just beyond the small anteroom. There were sounds of arguing. Shouts of support were answered by choruses of derision, back-and-forth. The woman's voice that caught her ear was Baressa's.

"I implore you, Astir, lead the people north now!"

Cautiously, Livet felt more confident to explore into the great room beyond and she willed the shadows to wrap around her again and suppress any notice of her passage to those that might take exception to a stranger. Her hope was that Baressa's earlier promise of safety in Porter's Run would hold until she could move around the room and get closer to her matronly guardian.

Inside the great room, a score of Northporters convened in a rough circle. Their faces bore expressions of concern and urgency. Livet followed Baressa's attention, which was focused on the young, reluctant chief who had first greeted them when they arrived in Caphedra. He was slumped over and appeared exhausted, planted on a low wooden seat, and flanked by two equally dour attendants. These men had the look of old warriors, scarred but sage.

One other face was known to Livet. Standing close to Baressa was the servant girl from Denn's kitchens. Perhaps dreams were not Baressa's sole source of gathering knowledge.

"None of us wish to leave until we've freed our people," Astir answered and several voices echoed his statement. He wrung his hands as he spoke and scratched at the floorboards with the toe of his boot.

Baressa's face was fierce and unwavering. "If you remain any longer, the Pillars will take more of us, and they won't stop until they've cut down every tree in Greyforest to hoist us up upon."

"Well, if we go, we'll wander straight into Braydun Anders and his soldiers," Astir declared. "They'd love to catch all of us out in the open like that—even the women and children. The Pillars and the Hogheads will be the end of the ones they've already taken, and the Anders brothers will see the rest of us done in before we can even hit the treeline."

Baressa pressed her hand flatly against the table. "No," she said. "He will join his brother. *Pineus* Anders plans to attack Roderin. Now is our chance!"

"Aye, Roddy says that," said a grimy, milky-eyed old man, whom Livet thought she'd seen talking to Kirt on that first night in Hamrin Square. "But the soldiers I spoke with said Braydun Anders and his brother are under hire to the Faith and their men are to attack the prince's army from behind. They aim to cut off supplies to Myrhic and delay the siege of the capital—or at least force him farther west."

Astir shifted his jaw askew and grimaced. "I believe part of that is true. I'm sure the Anders brothers would take the Faith's money and ride out of town with it. I'm not so convinced they'll sacrifice their brigades in a fight against Myrhic and I'm doubly certain that Pineus Anders won't waste a single man on any fight to win Caphedra. He's had eyes on taking Northport for years. Had Roy Pall and Roderin's men not been there to harass him, he'd have already marched north."

One of the battle-scarred veterans on Astir's right murmured in concordance. "With both the brothers' forces together, maybe they will go now to Nor'port, and unseat Dravern."

To Astir's left, the other warrior countered, "They won't go north if they're still under threat at Northwood and Stonebriar by Roderin. In that case, there's weight to the idea that they may go after Roderin's skirmishers first and leave us to pass."

There was a moment of quiet as the group collectively allowed Astir a reprieve to think. Livet knew the decision would be difficult for such a young chief who had lived at least most of his life in the city away from any battlefield. But Baressa, for all her experience, still deferred to him to exercise official authority in line with what the late earl had decreed.

Astir scratched at his beard and brushed his thick fingers through his hair. "Is this what fills your dreams these nights, our dear prophetess?" he asked Baressa.

"In my slumbering eye, I see the brothers mounting their attacks from Stonebriar once they have the advantage, which together they do at this moment. They will cut us down and burn us all out—from Aldertangle to Ashcamp—if we haven't the numbers to stop them. We have very little time."

"What of our people that the Faith has taken? Do you wish me to consign them to death and leave them to the curates and Pillarmen? You've seen the square. They're lifting people on pikes for not following the will of the Folds. We must set them free before we depart."

Baressa rose from her seat. "Leave them to the care of me and of my friends."

"How will your friends get into the temple without the aid of our fighters?"

Baressa's face lit up with a soft smile and without warning, she gestured toward Livet, who'd been listening to everything from a safe, dark corner. "The same way they get in here," she said.

Livet had slipped so quietly through the gaps in people's attentions and gazes. The looks on their faces now suggested that none had even noticed an outsider in the great room. She had kept herself hidden in the recesses, listening to their most critical and confidential plans all this time.

The servant girl from the Wellum house seemed startled and whispered something quickly to Baressa, who clasped her hands over the girl's in sororal communion. A second after they released their grasp, the servant girl squeezed her thin frame through the burly circle of northerners and approached Livet.

The girl's name was Nelissa, Livet now remembered.

"You should have stayed hiding. You're in danger," Nelissa whispered. "You should stay safe with us."

Livet opened her mouth to speak, but Baressa gave her a look that implored her to hold her questions for later.

"Get everyone ready to head north. We'll leave before the gates close for good," Astir proclaimed then rose to his feet. The participants in the discussion followed his lead and started about the business of evacuating the quarter. An impromptu war council, including the pair who had flanked Astir, headed toward kegs of ale along the rear wall of the tavern and poured themselves frothy mugs, then commenced more discussion. As the room began to empty, Astir was temporarily freed from his chiefly duties and came over to welcome Livet back, his plump cheeks inflated with his smile.

"I'm glad you're here with us again. I was a mite surprised to see you," he said.

Livet noted that the confidence he had shown in the meeting was now undermined by sheepishness. Livet grinned. It mollified her own shyness to be addressed so cordially.

"I was without anything t' keep meself busy, so 'ere I am. What do you need o' me?"

"Kirt told us he saw you at the square freeing the ones the Pillarmen nabbed the other night. But now another family of Porters has been arrested. They were accused of hoarding food and not remitting enough money to the Pillars."

Nelissa added, "They were set to celebrate the summer high festival. They'd saved up secretly for a few weeks, but the festival is coming close. One of the curates passed by and smelled bread baking."

"He had a couple of Hogheads break down the door. They said the larder showed they weren't paying their Due to the Pillars and they arrested them," said Astir.

"Eight in the family. Children and an infant too," said Nelissa.

"And now," Livet summated, "You want *me*, t' show *you*, 'ow to get into a place that I ne'er been in—nor seen—and get 'em back out?"

Baressa held onto Livet's hand, with a look of pride that worried Livet. "I know where they're being kept. There are ways in and out, and I am calling on more friends to help us. But you're good with locks and can slip in further and more quietly than the rest of us. We'll need you to do that if we're to get our people out."

"Is it true the other ones they took are up on pikes now—not the gaol?" Livet asked, not really doubting but her imagination conjured a spectacle for her which she hoped her mind was over-embellishing.

"Have you not seen the square?" Astir asked.

She shook her head.

"I guess you should be glad you haven't," he said. "They've already put their boot down on anyone who's challenged them, and then they came after all those who were behind in paying them gold. Everyone's afraid, and if they can't buy their safety then they're running from the city before the prince's army arrives. Once he's here the battle between them and Pillarmen could destroy Caphedra."

He hesitated, then continued with another subject.

"Some people were a bit curious when it was mentioned you'd been seeking the Wellums."

"Oh?" said Livet. "Curious how?"

"That name's not very popular right now. You see, Lehn Wellum is one of the curates who's been directing the armsmen that the Pillars recruited. Even the Hogheads from Lanstad answer to him when he demands it."

"But I came for Denn. I've never even met his brother!"

"No, and that's good," he said. "Besides, Kirt told us how you acted at Hamrin Square and Baressa has guaranteed that you're in no way aligned with his ilk. It's just that coincidence tends to spook a lot of Northporters."

"Miss, I think it's much better if you stay clear of the Wellums," Nelissa said. "I don't know Denn at all, and Serenn is a sweet soul, but the father and the younger brother are locked like a pair of mountain rams set to do each other in—to the harm of everyone around them."

Hearing Nelissa speak like that gave Livet a glimpse into the conflict that ended Denn's older brother's life, but it was still hearsay. She'd yet to meet Lehn and knew just as little of Phon, who barely acknowledged her the two times she'd seen him.

Baressa turned to Nelissa. "Go with the ones travelling north and tell your cousin I love him."

Nelissa nodded and embraced Baressa tightly. Livet caught the glint of a few coins being dropped into the girl's pocket, which elicited a blush and smile before Nelissa sprinted off to retrieve her outerwear from the mass of drying raiment near the door.

"Astir, you should go and prepare the families for the journey. I have to discuss our plans with Livet."

The chief took a polite step back and bowed slightly with his meaty hand over his heart. "I hope I'll see you up north when this is all done."

That brightened Livet's face and she felt a bit disappointed to see him leave so soon. It was clear from Baressa's frown, however, that there was more clarification in order before she was surfeited of talking about Wellum family affairs. As soon as the two were off, she spoke with uncharacteristic bluntness to Livet.

"Livet, do not return to the Wellum house." Livet cocked her head, perplexed. She wondered if Baressa had heard anything more along the lines of what Yael had insinuated.

"What else did Nelissa tell you?" she asked.

"She overheard the master of the house discussing with his men about his plans with Lord Farathemun. He intends to wed Denn off to the Princess Ramisa as a condition of adding his wealth to the Lord's cause."

"Denn said nothing o' that!" Livet said, instantly sounding distressed.

"Nelissa is my cousin through marriage. I trust her to speak the truth. Where is Denn now?"

Livet stalled in answering, which caused Baressa to raise her eyebrow inquisitively. She tut-tutted and surmised, "He's gone after her already, hasn't he? I'd be surprised if he didn't know of the plan."

"He's just escortin' her back to the city. Once here, she's someone else's respons'bility." She felt as if Baressa was purposefully provoking her.

"It's important that you know, Livet," she said. "But more important for you to know that Denn's father intends to have you removed, on account of you being an obstruction to his scheme. There will be no place for a mistress in the royal household."

"Is this what Yael warned me of?"

"His aid? I expect so. I don't know Yael Larkin, save by reputation, but I highly doubt he'd want the blood of an innocent young girl on his hands, no matter what price Phon Wellum is paying him. Easier to just scare you off."

With downcast eyes, Livet tried to recollect everything Denn had told her about the trip and his hopes for their reunion and life thereafter, but it did not soothe her. There was little of consequence she could cling to.

Baressa denied her any time to sink into contemplation and pulled her back. "Stay with me until Denn returns. You'll be safe and I'd welcome the company."

"Very well," Livet consented sullenly.

The back alleys of Porter's Run were far more tangled and disjointed than Livet had imagined. Generations of inhabitation were evidenced through constructions built by those whom Livet thought must have been the most stubborn of carpenters. Newer shacks were built on top of older shacks, and even more shacks were built to span the passageways between. Each domicile could be determined based on the presence of a random, thick, stone chimney, but the exact boundaries of each individual dwelling were hard to decipher.

Baressa could easily have remained hidden in such a place for many years. Her comings and goings, Livet learned, were aided by the fact that her home was part of a loft, erected over a complicated abode located so deeply in the patchwork of timber structures that it abutted the northern city wall on one side. Livet's intuition told her that if she looked hard enough, she would be bound to find a way through or under that wall. That tempted her. If she could find the passageway, it would mean her first glimpse of Northwood and the boreal lands beyond Caphedra.

Baressa's door had no outer lock. It opened easily to reveal a humble space. Her dwelling was lined with furs, tanned skins, and lots of shelves laden with stacks of leather-bound books and an assortment of clay vessels. Livet assumed that these contained spices, judging from the aroma. Glass ornaments hung from several corners of the room and their reflective twinkling enticed Livet to examine them more closely.

"Pretty, yes?" Baressa said.

"Where did you get them?" Livet asked.

"Lots of places, but some were given to me by Kell, actually. I had been looking for more when I met you."

"Do they just sparkle, or are they meant t' be wind chimes or something? They should be outside, if so."

Livet twisted one in her hands and noticed the peculiar shape of it. She had expected it to be flat, or at least symmetrical. Still, they weren't just hunks of glass melted and set. Kell had taught her to appraise and judge craftworks and she knew enough to recognize that they had been ground and worked to precision.

"Think of them like little windows," Baressa said.

"So, you look through them?"

"Yes, but not at what's on the other side of the glass. More at what's on the other side of what's to come and what's been."

"Fortune-telling again then?" Livet asked.

"Of a sort, yes. When I'm not dreaming up visions, these help me see what otherwise cannot be seen when I am awake," Baressa replied.

Livet focused into the glass shapes but, frustratingly, saw nothing that would capture her interest in the way Baressa described. She let them go and they swung back into place with the afternoon sunlight bouncing off them.

"Try this one."

Baressa reached up to where one of the glass prisms hung from a silver chain. It was heart-shaped and appeared dull in comparison. She hung it around Livet's neck and fastened the clasp.

"It might be a bit unsettling, but the purpose is protective—in a fashion."

Livet stared down at the pendant. The chain was pretty enough to command some value and the glass was light and comfortable, but there was something in the near opacity of its translucence that somehow seemed unclean. For a moment, her intuition took over and she felt a growing unease that she was in danger.

In a flash, the room swirled, and she was looking upon somewhere else. Her eyes grew blurry and strained, seeing words on pieces of parchment that, like in a dream, turned to gobbledegook when she tried to read them. She did see a room, however, and then she saw Denn's mother, Esta, standing in front of her. Comprehension flowed into her, and she instinctively knew she was experiencing things through the mind of Phon Wellum. Her heart began aching, feeling sickly and beating in a mortal sense of fear, and she was overcome by a withering sense of loathing for someone—herself... for Livet.

Then it passed. She was back with Baressa, and her heart's thumping began to restore itself to its previous becalmed pace. The amulet felt cold around her neck.

"I had a dream?" Livet uttered, unsure, but then added more assertively, "A daydream. But I was Denn's father!"

"Kell called that little amulet a '*slayer's glass.*' It reflects and magnifies the intentions of those with great malice toward you, enough to seek out your death. After Nelissa's warning, I thought you might test it out, to be sure."

"It felt like I was disgusted with myself—my real self, not him. But it was him feeling it."

"It must be more than anger or hatred. When someone truly wishes you dead and has made the choice to see your killing come to pass—their feelings and thoughts will flow through the amulet, and you will feel it too."

"That's a terrible creation! You're telling me Kell made this?"

"He did," said Baressa. "It helped give him a glimpse into the hearts of his enemies. Hence the shape he crafted the amulet in. Although, after a time he had *so many* people hunting him that he couldn't wear it for fear of losing his sanity."

Livet motioned to remove it, but she was stopped by Baressa.

"Wear it tonight. If you are in true danger of death at another's hand, it may alert you to the culprit before they can realize their goal."

"Why don't you use it?" Livet asked.

"Like Kell, I have too many people wishing me ill. I'm marked. If I were to wear it, I would be locked in a trance for the better part of a week, seeing through the evil eyes of every Pillar curate and armsman that's ever sought my recapture."

Livet's host spread out a patchwork rug of skins and from one of the clay jars emptied some nuts into a bowl. From another, she added dried berries.

"Eat up," she said. "You must be hungry. I don't have much more than this as I don't have a hearth fire here to cook with. You'll need your strength before we go out tonight."

"We'll go at dark then?"

"That was my idea," she said. "I have to prepare, and I expect that you need time to gather yourself too."

Livet nodded and stretched herself out upon a fur rug. It was cozy.

One by one, Baressa began collecting the glass creations and gently packing them into a straw-lined chest. "Astir will be around to pick these up and to keep them safe for me. There is liable to be no one here by the time we get back."

When she was finished with the glass, she retrieved a wooden plank from a corner of the room and used it to bar the door. Satisfied, she pulled at a pile of canvas hanging from the wall, lifting it by the edge where a rope was affixed. She hung the rope on a hook and crawled into it as a hammock. Her eyes stared up to the ceiling above where a few remaining glass artifacts hung and glinted with different hues of light.

Within moments, Baressa's breathing became natural and slow and Livet knew that she alone remained awake.

Curious, she rose quietly and crept up to look out her host's window. The interior of the Run, when looking down on it, appeared more like a courtyard than it did from below. People could be seen working away, many of whom laboured to dismantle portions of the timberwork and reclaim boards and planks. She saw a wall, made from the wood of an old wagon, being lifted down and reunited with its long-neglected wheels. Women carried out bundles from homes and strapped them into place on other carts. The sounds of hammering suggested other abandoned items were also being disturbed from age-old emplacements and forced back into service in preparation to depart.

Livet retreated from the window to lie down again on the soft fur. She had never actually seen the temple, but it was a safe assumption the building would be a challenge and that made her anxious. She downplayed her worries as best she could and when she felt fear, reminded herself that her anger toward the Faith was greater. When she sprung the locks on the cages at Hamrin Square, she had felt a temporary sense of power over the Faith. Striking the temple would embolden her even more—should she be successful.

But as Livet's eyes began to close, she heard a gasp from Baressa.

"Baressa?" she uttered in forceful whisper. "Are you alright? Awake?"

"Uh... strange d- dream, dear," the seeress said stammering a bit.

"You fell asleep and started dreamin' so soon?"

"A strange one," Baressa echoed herself, only half lucid.

"Was it the temple?"

"Yes, but not tonight," she explained. "It was maybe days or weeks from now, and I was inside it."

"What was so strange?" Livet asked.

"I saw myself," Baressa said. "Not through my own eyes as I usually do, but I was looking at myself."

"Like the slayer's glass?"

"No. Different. Maybe they were my own eyes. Oh, I don't know."

Unfamiliar with the intricacies of the prophetic craft, Livet could offer nothing back in comfort or insight. But the unnerving feeling of Baressa's bewilderment gave her concern and it only grew when Baressa had another recollection of her dream.

"I think Kell was there too," she said surprisingly.

"Maybe jus' your imagination," Livet finally suggested. Then pondering, she asked another question. "D'you still dream like normal people? I mean funny dreams—or nightmares? Things that aren't real?"

"Sometimes," Baressa said. "But I know the difference."

Livet listened, both of them were now calm again and eager to return to restful sleep. From the hammock, Baressa shared one happy confession.

"Sometimes I dream of settling down with my husband, in a little cottage in the woods, free from strife and danger. I dream of walking with him safely and happily through the woods, hand in hand, on the way to see our people. Those are pleasant dreams."

CHAPTER 15

Old Enemies and New Wounds

The Half Moon Tavern might as well have been a fortress. The bottom floor seemed welcoming to the public, but the stone façade on the second storey was jetted and lined with narrow windows that angled for use as arrow slits. Hatches and gaps in the overhang suggested the presence of deadly traps for assaulters and the structure had watchtowers that rose above even the prominent city walls. As far as alehouses went, it had no equal.

Several distinguishable pedestrians sauntered past regularly or loitered without seeming to be customers. These were Dance Karaval's sentries, Olen guessed, for he'd spent several days getting to know them by face and manner.

The man whom Bull called Sasser Goll was one of the easiest to pick out. He had a long brown moustache that hung down to his collarbones. He came and went, sporting a big string of knives on his chest and a flare for big metal buckles on belts and straps.

The only person to whom Goll paid heed was an older man who had a foreign look to his features, wavy dark hair, and thick eyebrows, but a nearly white beard. Olen suspected that this would be Goll's minder, the murderous Jensir Udal, as his mind worked through undoing the changes on the man's face that the years must have wrought, comparing it with his memories of the man who'd waged a particularly foul crusade against his brother, Tolen.

On other days, they formed a trio with the addition of a spindly man with a marked or painted face, prickly beard, and sticky, pointed hair. This man had once caught sight of Olen and stared him down for a moment, with a look that hinted he might have some infernal devil harboured inside.

"That man," Bull told him later at the Black Eel, "is Vike Argreff." He stopped polishing a mug and slammed it down on the countertop. "The fact that you're asking about him tells me that you are engaging in some highly precarious foolhardiness!"

"Well, I've kept my distance. But Neriah's never outside! What else is there to do?"

Olen sat on a high stool, absentmindedly spinning his mug around by the handle. He'd been drinking his libations more slowly each day as his money purse got lighter and lighter.

Around the tavern, there was activity and laughter. This was not the place to soak and stew in one's bitterness. The Black Eel was less a refuge for hard-drinking soldiers these days. It had become more of a home for the whole extended family of the Westriver Company.

Shaking off the consternation that left him so self-possessed, Olen surveyed the other, happier, customers at the pub. Both Gastun Holder and Maks Kaler now had come back to wives. In Kaler's case, there was also an unexpected daughter (whose age was a few troubling years shy of the last time Maks had been home for a visit). One of the men who'd escorted Olen home that first night back, Talton Terrod, had returned to Westriver to find that his brother drank himself to death during the score of years in between, leaving behind a family for him to care for too—a wife, Krystlen, and a freckled, red-head girl name Yarma.

There were young men amongst the families too. Nyrim Henser's nephew, who had been named for his uncle but went by the name Kalden, spent hours listening to the old veterans spin tales of their time on disorderly edges of the kingdom. He usually sat together with a slightly older companion named Asher, and their blonde, wavy-haired friend, a thin-boned boy named 'Effie.'

It was mostly Olen that kept a monopoly on surliness, until one particular day, when Effie approached the front of the bar and cautiously propositioned Olen.

"Sir, I could get a message to the lady, if you want," Effie said.

Somehow his offer seemed intrusive, but Olen was forced to admit that he had foregone most reservations of privacy over the past few days. Over his beer, he brooded daily, and most denizens of the Black Eel knew of his earnest, heart-aching desire to recover his niece and have a family of his own again. But Olen was not keen to make this young man party to his problems. In addition to his fair hair, he had very delicate features that made him appear to be from a class far above his actual station in life, and such outward fragility didn't breed confidence that he could pull off a task that Olen otherwise couldn't.

"No. You don't need to involve yourself, son," Olen said.

"Sir...," the young man persisted.

A smirk from Bull compelled Olen to modestly correct the boy.

"My name is Olen and I invite you to call me that... not 'sir'," he said.

Effie stood and absorbed the cordial rebuke, then renewed his offer. "I don't mind helping."

Again, Olen cut short the offer with a straight-up refusal. "No, thank you. The Half Moon is not the place for a young man like yourself."

Effie swivelled around and pretended to speak directly to Bull.

"The Karavals have my sisters working for them," he explained.

Bull nodded and gave a sympathetic grunt, but his eyes were on Olen. It was clear the barkeep had noticed his friend sit up straighter. Producing a jug of ale with which to top up Olen's mug, he accompanied it with a theatrical look as if begging permission, as proffered a second cup and slid it across the counter in front of Effie.

Grabbing the jug, Olen filled both mugs himself and permitted the boy to continue.

"My younger sister, Kelzi, is too young to do the usual work they have for girls, so she cleans pots and stacks firewood in the kitchen, but they hold on to her to keep my older sister, Sandri, in line. Because of that, they trust her enough to let her run errands. That's how I sometimes meet her and find out how she's doing."

"How did they end up mixed in with the Karavals in the first place?" Olen asked.

"No parents. They died of a fever. We grew up on the street," he said. "People always said Sandri was beautiful. She has long blonde hair that got her the nickname 'Flax' since that's what people thought it looked like. When she was old enough, she got a job to look after us all, at a place called the Thimble. The Karavals ended up burning it to the ground in a feud, but one of them took to Sandri right away, and she ended up being asked to work at the Half Moon. She accepted. That way Kelzi would be fed, at least. I kept off on my own and watched over them as best I could."

Olen swirled the ale around in his mug, hummed, and made some hopeful murmurings.

"The boy has a far more sensible plan than you, Olen," Bull opined. "You can't just go peeping through windows until you get yourself caught. Maybe this Sandri girl can find out if and how often, Neriah is ever let out. Then perchance the next time she stretches her legs, you can arrange a meeting too."

Effie's face lit up proudly at Bull's endorsement and the opportunity to help out one of the esteemed tavern elders.

"When do you see her next?" Olen asked him, now plotting.

"Tonight, before the tavern gets too busy. She usually brings flagons of ale and food around to whichever strong houses Dogfish and Udal's men are holed up in for the night."

Olen glanced at the window and noted the setting sun. The long shadows cast through indicated the day was soon drawing to a close.

"We'll go together," Olen instructed Effie, whose face tightened apprehensively for a moment, then eased.

"Sure," Effie answered with a pause, "But we need to be careful to not be seen. I don't want Sandri to get into trouble if she's spotted talking to me or anyone else."

"I'll come too!" announced Nyrim's nephew, Kalden, as he slipped in behind Effie and slapped his hand onto his friend's shoulder. The boy grinned puckishly.

"No!" said Effie in a far less pliant tone. "Just Olen," he said firmly.

"Aw! I bet Sandri would love to see me," Kalden pressed, only to be countered this time by a detractor from behind.

"Flax doesn't even know you!" said Yarma with a derisive smirk that caused her freckles to bunch up. "And aren't you closer to Kelzi's age? Maybe you could ask Dance Karaval if he'd let you meet with her! You could play dollies together."

"That's not true! I am older than that," Kalden answered. "And besides, Kelzi's your age, isn't she? You don't play with dolls!"

"No, because I got you lot to play with!" Yarma replied, sticking out her tongue.

Bull twisted the spigot on one of the barrels, poured a fresh draught of ale into another pitcher, then turned commandingly to the younger partisans to dish out some authority.

"Kalden, you stay here. I can't stop Olen from going, despite all my highly wise and rational nagging, but Effie is wise to want fewer people stumbling around and drawing attention."

Kalden sighed and took his hand off Effie's shoulder. Crossing his arms in front of him, he slouched back against the wall.

"And anyway," Bull added. "If I were to suggest anyone, it'd be Asher. He's arguably of a more manly age—and the girls all love him, so silent and serious as he always is."

Asher harumphed. Despite having been too young to ever have been in the Westriver Company, he'd been adopted by the old veterans of the Black Eel, nonetheless. Before the Lord Chancellor ceased funding recruitment, Asher had done a smattering of training at Keepside Garrison, so he could swing a sword. For Bull to call him serious was an understatement, however. His sparsely bearded face was not enough to stave off the freshness of his youth, but his eyes were always downcast or focused on a point on the wall, away from the gaze of others and engulfed in some inner profundity of his own thoughts. At the sound of his name, however, he involved himself in their conversation.

"You can come with me tonight instead, Kal," Asher said. "The rain's stopped and I want to hang around the Midbridge to see what's up at Dockmarket and see who crosses over."

"Fancy yourself as an armsman?" asked Bull poking at Asher's professed intentions. "Or only looking to keep out the riff-raff from this side of the Darrow?"

"There's a lot of trouble being caused east of the river by the Pillars. If it crosses the river, we might have problems ourselves. I heard they attacked Parachs Ghil at the Council meeting. Hull Homesta had to get him to safety."

"Who attacked? Pillarmen or Lord Vlass's soldiers?" Olen asked with concern, but Asher shook his head, unable to answer for sure.

"Well, isn't Ghil tied into one of those outlawed cults?" Bull asked. "The Faith is going after any totem-worshippers and spirit seekers that they can get their paws on. You can't even wear a good luck charm if you didn't buy it from the Temple, these days." He peered at Olen, "But you won't find too many religious folks in *this* tavern, so I never worry."

"Have you paid your Dues to them?" Asher asked provocatively.

Bull scowled. "They haven't asked me yet."

"Then I'll let you know when they cross the bridge and are on their way," Asher replied. He got up, made his way to the door, and gave a second look to Kalden. His disciple keenly rushed to chase after him, pausing only to give Effie an unexpected kiss on the cheek.

"Give that to Flax for me!" Kalden said and ran out after Asher.

Yarma feigned retching, while Effie glowered and motioned to Bull for a rag with which to rub off any lasting trace, but Bull just shrugged, saying, "Your sister is a pretty young lady. It could have been a worse message."

The smug barkeep disappeared to the kitchen, returning with a sliver of wood, gently aflame, which he used to light some of the oil lamps along the bar. It was getting dark outside now.

With the discourse broken up, Olen, prodded Effie, "What time are you going to meet your sister?"

"We can go now," Effie said, but as he stood from his stool, Olen could not help but notice that the young man lacked a sword.

"Do you have anything on you if we get into trouble?" Olen said as he hoisted his own blade, Coldswept, onto his back.

Effie nodded and displayed a dirk strapped to his thigh. He also thrust his fingers through a pair of gloves that Olen surmised were weighted to help him land a better punch. It wasn't very much. The men patrolling the Half Moon Tavern were all very well-armed. This would have to be a swift, silent, and secretive meeting.

After sundown, all the desperate and danger-courting denizens of the neighbourhood made their way toward the inner concourse of the city's west wall and Bailey Street, which, though cramped and choked by the gradual swelling of houses and flats over many years, was still the main thoroughfare through seedy Faralley.

Bailey Street was its only marked street, having grown up from a footpath along the inside of the city's defensive border. It stretched as far north as the curve in the city wall near the Darrow River inflow and extended all the way south to Keepside. Its buildings were so over-arching and congested in parts that it felt like traversing a tunnel, and if you didn't belong, there were not many safe places along its sidelines to duck into.

Effie explained to Olen that the Karavals had little nests on either end, from which their sentries would watch all those entering and leaving. Dogfish's men watched the north and Jensir Udal's crew the south. He avoided them by taking a tiny, navigable alley that dipped down from between a parchment shop and a cobbler's, and then ascended back up to street level to emerge beside an apothecary on Bailey Street.

They waited there until a striking young woman with long, platinum hair—even fairer than Effie's—stepped lightly along the street holding several cloth-wrapped bundles. Effie motioned for Olen to stand back and then carefully crept alone between recesses along the nearby stone walls. He whistled once to attract his sister's attention and to let her know that he was in place, hiding but ready to meet her.

Olen could view the two of them from a short distance away in the apothecary alley. He saw Effie gesture back toward him and then Sandri looked over, her mesmerizing eyes met Olen's briefly, exchanging fascination.

The rendezvous lasted a moment. Sandri handed Effie one of the bundles, flashed him a surreptitious smile, and flitted away quickly to resume her deliveries.

"She's going to speak to Neriah," Effie said, slinking back into the alleyway. "I told her not to say anything to anyone else at the Half Moon, though, on account of the bad blood. She didn't even know that Neriah's family name was Kierk. It's as good as a passcode for Neriah to know that Sandri is telling the truth."

Taking a heavy breath and sighing with concern, Olen said, "It's not a name she'd want to be attached to around that place. Remember, everyone else she knew that ever shared that name is dead."

"My sister will keep it hushed," Effie said to calm him. "She has no love for that place or her wretched employers."

❖ ❖ ❖

In the message that Sandri was to pass, Olen had invited Neriah to steal away and come see him at the old Kierk house—or to specify a time and place of her own to meet. Since Bull mentioned she had been around the house before, Olen knew she could find it without difficulty, so long as she was permitted the freedom to travel outside the Half Moon.

While he awaited her choice, Olen mostly stayed at home. He'd borrowed some tools from Maks and Gastun and salvaged what boards he could find, adding any scrap wood he could find from around the neighbourhood. He coughed up one of his last old silver civils to pay for a bag of nails. It was a good chance to patch the ceiling and build it up into a proper roof. There was little he could do to alleviate the darkness, though. Enclosed between other houses as his house was, all the windows were small, place high along the walls and mostly ineffective at letting in the sunlight.

As Olen worked, he paused every so often to glance at the door, which he left ajar as a sign of welcome. Once a day, he popped by the Black Eel for a proper meal and to check for any news that Sandri may have passed to Effie. The longer he waited without response, the more worried Olen became that Sandri might have either gotten caught communicating his message or worse, that she may have betrayed them and reported to the Karavals.

It was on the third day that Effie finally brought Olen something noteworthy.

"I saw Sandri last night and she passed along your message," he said.

Olen leaned in toward Effie. "And?"

"I'm sorry, Olen. She said 'no' and asked Sandri not to bring it up again."

Olen looked away. His face went pale, and he began rapping his knuckles on the table while he contemplated his own response.

"Ask her again," he said flatly.

"But she doesn't want..." Effie began.

"Listen to me!" Olen said in a dark tone that caused the young messenger to sweat. "There's no reason that she'd want to work in that damnable pit if she had any way to escape on her own. *I'm* her way out. You tell her that. I'm her *family*."

Unblinking while Olen spoke, Effie chanced a quiet, "Yes, sir."

Olen pushed his chair out and with a heavy head, shuffled out of the bar. His most important business was now concluded, as unfavourably as it turned out.

He did not head back to his house, however. Instead, he found the spot between the stationer and the cobbler, broaching the alleyway to arrive at Bailey Street, then walking along the row of shops until he was closer than ever to the Half Moon.

On a previous expedition, he had noticed that one of the store fronts was vacant and the lock had been broken on the door. With no one looking, he snuck inside. Dust had gathered on the tabletops and thick cobwebs hung like colourless lace drapes, but the window gave him a good view of the Half Moon's main entrance and the comings and goings of its detestable hosts and patrons.

At one point, he saw a girl being dragged out by a customer, only to be rescued at the last minute by one of Karaval's enforcers. The presumptuous admirer ended up with a box to the head from the heavy mitts of Sasser Goll and another long-haired ruffian-for-hire. The girl was blonde but not as brilliantly so as Sandri. He would have expected darker hair, were it Neriah, but Olen tried to avoid spiralling further into any anxious assumptions.

It must be someone else, Olen thought, but his mind kept drifting toward the thought that Neriah must put up with the same vile mishandling by the bar's patrons—and probably had done so most of her pitiable life.

Past midnight, the crowds on the street were thinning. Olen didn't want to risk being the only one on the road when he snuck back out and away from Faralley, as it would have been obvious that he'd been spying. The shop he'd entered was not much more than a stall, with no rear entrance or other means to leave undetected so he played along with the crowds, waited for a pause, and left through the front door.

At once, there were shouts from behind him, but Olen ignored them. He kept walking past the apothecary shop, so as not to reveal the convenient secret passage, just in case he was under watch now. Paranoid, he felt eyes upon his back all the way until he had reached the boundary with Keepside. There, he managed to fit in more with the other pedestrians, many of whom were broad-shouldered military men, like himself. A few even exchanged casual greetings, before Olen changed direction and doubled back through Westriver to his gloomy, lightless home.

❖   ❖   ❖

When Effie confronted Olen the next day at the Black Eel, he did so with Asher and Kalden beside him. Bull monitored them from behind the counter, ready to enforce a truce if need be.

Olen looked at them and, gauging their faces, gave voice to the outcome himself. "She said 'no' again, did she?"

"No more we can do, Olen. If she changes her mind, Sandri will let us know," Effie said, and the others gave corresponding grunts in concordance.

"Very well," Olen said, brooding again.

Bull was chewing on licorice root and busying himself with chores up and down the bar, but he moved more slowly each time he walked past Olen, obviously analyzing and interpreting Olen's expressionless pout as best he could. His masticating of the woody root mirrored his ruminations.

"I find the virtue of dependability to be a close cousin to painful consistency," Bull said finally.

"Eh?" Olen grunted.

"Don't you dare go to that place tonight," he said under his breath. "I know you won't forget about it, but you should heed my advice. Give it time. Give *her* time. Her curiosity will eventually consume her and she'll come find you, just like you want. It's just a matter of patience."

Olen nodded. "You're right," he said softly.

Bull drew two mugs of draught and carried them down to the end of the bar where Effie and Asher were talking. Olen couldn't hear what he told them; he was too preoccupied to care. He was formulating his plans already.

Asher called Kalden over to the private discussion and the three boys gave Bull obedient nods while the bartender slipped something heavy over the counter. Kalden reached for it and quickly stashed it under his tunic.

Clearly the leader of the three, Asher got up from his chair and approached Olen. He rested his hands on the bar peacefully and thoughtfully, clasping them in front of himself when he sat down.

"Olen," he addressed the old sergeant. "When you go, we'll go with you—if we can do it without them suspecting. One more time."

That elicited a protest from Olen, but it was cut short when Asher continued, "Effie's got two sisters in that place. More family to worry about than you."

Olen didn't like the thought of putting these young boys in danger, but Asher spoke like someone with mettle well beyond his actual years and Olen was impressed enough that it lulled him into agreeing.

"Tonight then," Olen relented.

With that, Bull leaned over the counter and stared squarely at him, the scent of licorice on his breath. Whispering for just the two of them to hear, he said, "Olen. I've never known you to waste a young soldier's life. I hope you don't plan anything that would change that."

Olen heeded his friend's words, mulling the whole thing over while focusing on the ale in his mug and drumming his fingers obsessively. In truth, these boys were not trained fighters, and he had little right to expect them to stick their necks out for him, no matter how well up for it they might be.

"If I could send the more experienced fellows with you, I would, but they're not here right now, so I'm left with the new recruits." Bull cocked his head in the boys' direction and sighed.

Calling them recruits, however, had achieved the opposite of his intention. It had a galvanizing effect on the boys instead. They now stood straighter, with chests puffed out and the slack gone from their jaws. Olen could sense the boys' eagerness to prove themselves as worthy of belonging to the defunct, but still honoured company.

"Don't go inside that place, or you might not get out. Just a *scouting mission*, got that?"

"They wouldn't recognize me after all these years, Bull. Don't worry."

"They don't need to know you by name, Olen. They only need to see the same look in your eye that I see now—the look of someone eyeballin' trouble. Keep these boys safe and don't get them wound up in some grand resurrection of an ancient clan war. I told Asher to use that blackjack on you first if it meant preventing a bloodbath. Things are quiet here for us now. We want to keep it like that."

❖ ❖ ❖

It was a beautiful night. The rain had finished its course and having purged the air of its humidity, there was a newness to the evening which drew many people out to the streets, awoke and active. Bailey Street especially teemed with a motley throng of lurkers who ventured back into the open like weeds sprouting amongst the cobblestones.

At times, the quartet of emancipators had difficulty keeping together, at least until they were within sight of the Half Moon. There, a noticeable ebb in the crowd gave way naturally in avoidance of the dangers posed should the wrong person take an unwanted step toward its doorstep or cast a glance in the wrong direction.

Near the tavern, the intake of patrons left Olen wondering. Who would stop a handful more from going inside, just for a drink? Then inside, if the situation favoured them in any regard, a more brazen plan might be effected. The boys were young, but Olen could see they were energetic and quick. He judged that their minds were equally cunning and shrewd.

There would be no rushing this as he had yet to see inside the tavern and didn't know which directions they would need to head if they were to quickly extricate Neriah, Sandri, and Kelzi.

"Here's how we'll do this, boys..." Olen said. The three expectant fighters closed in to listen. "Effie and I will stroll inside like regular customers and look for a table where we can keep an eye on the place without being too much in anyone's way."

"But Bull said—," Kalden sputtered.

Effie tightened up, breathing heavily and a bit unsteady as nervousness seized him.

"It's fine. They have no reason to suspect any of us are out to start trouble, and we've got a bit of coin, the same as the next fellow." Olen placed his hand on Effie's shoulder reassuringly. He could tell by the way the boys looked at him that his experience held a great deal of weight in their estimation. Hopefully, it was enough to counter-balance Bull's mothering apprehensions.

"If we're just going to walk in, why not all of us, then?" Asher asked skeptically.

"Two of us shouldn't appear as much of a threat, and if Effie is with me, Sandri will see him and likely give us a warning before any potential trouble stirs."

Olen turned slightly to gesture at Asher directly, "You will go inside, but stay near the door to make sure we have a path out if a row starts before we get too far in."

"And me?" asked Kalden. "I suppose I'm your lookout?"

"No," Olen said. "I want you to sneak around back and find the kitchen door. Take a look inside to locate the girl, Kelzi. Then, be ready to help us get out. As soon as Effie and I get to the kitchen, Asher will head back to the apothecary alley. If everything goes well, we'll push our way through the kitchen door out back, Effie in front, then the girls, then me holding them off from the rear. Be ready to aid the escape and show us the quickest path back to the alley. If we're chased, Asher will be there to ambush anyone following us."

"We're taking them out tonight?!" Kalden said, shocked.

"I thought we were just going in to talk," said Asher. "There's not enough of us for a rescue."

"You three are the best for the job," Olen said praising them. "You want to see those girls out of that place for good, don't you? Why leave them to rot another day?"

Emboldened faces looked around at each other in the circle, in agreement, and anticipation.

"Questions?" Olen asked for the one-and-only time. He gave a last inspection of his party, then turned around, almost running into someone who came rushing toward them.

"Effrem, what are you doing here?!" A panicked girl with cascading platinum hair appeared from out of nowhere. "Get back! Honestly! Effrem, who are these people?"

"Sandri!" replied Effie while the others instinctively stepped back.

"Effrem, get out of here! I told you to keep your distance. If they see us or if they recognize you, there'll be no more meetings between us. Don't you understand?!"

Looking more like a scolded child than a liberator, Effie began to protest. "We came for you and Kelzi, and Olen's niece. We can help you get out," he began.

"You'll need more men than that," she said. "The Karavals will see you. Run away now!" she ordered him.

Olen moved to protest. "I want to speak with Neriah," he said.

Sandri turned to face him. "She doesn't want to speak with you! Do you even know how dangerous it could be? Her final word is 'no,' and you need to understand that!"

Taken aback by the authoritative strength in her voice, Olen was getting angrier, but the emotion was quickly redirected as two armed men, who had been following Sandri, joined the confrontation. They each had long hair and looked like the pair who were reportedly under the employ of Dogfish Karaval.

"I think it's dangerous for you to go out alone, Flaxy," said one. "This your father?"

"Nah, this one's too ugly to have a daughter like her," said the second. "Don't worry. We'll take you back and keep you nice and safe inside."

Asher tapped Olen on the arm, and they watched as the crowd parted. More Karaval men emerged. They grabbed Sandri and pulled her back toward the Half Moon. Among the men, Olen noticed the presence of one of Karaval's other, more established enforcers. Sasser Gol spread his short topcoat aside to display his array of knives.

"We were just looking for a nice alehouse," said Asher, unconvincingly. "But we'll move along."

Sasser manufactured a mocking grin, which caused the ends of his moustache to spread out like tusks. "I thought you lads already had your own alehouse," he said, with an eye on Olen's twisted eel clasp. "I wouldn't encourage you to rest your fins in our fine establishment." Then addressing Olen directly, he said, "Why don't you take your little elvers and swim off home?"

"We're leaving, boys," Olen said softly and led his team slowly away.

This pragmatic response sat well with Asher, but Effie was unsteady, and it was evident he was overwhelmed with trying to process the threat he'd now put his sisters under.

Kalden was in the middle, taking deep breaths in relief, but also showing signs that the encounter had invigorated him beyond anything he'd been used to. He whistled as they walked farther down the road and even ventured a few inaudible taunts as the Karaval men broke from their pack and went off to see to their other details.

At the rear of their short column, Olen laboured with Neriah's rejection and still refused to dismiss his hope to reclaim her. This was one loose end from the Kierk-Karaval war of which he would not let go. Their conflict would not be over until she had been granted freedom from the misery she was forced to grow up in.

That is what led him to turn back.

He said no words to the boys ahead of him but let them continue their withdrawal. Olen, however, squared his jaw angrily and marched straight toward the impenetrable Half Moon Tavern, as if the last few minutes had been lost to oblivion.

How he had convinced himself that he would not be stopped a second time, he would never be sure of. But he managed to reach within two arms' lengths of the perilous entryway when someone shouted a loud, guttural challenge, and he felt the presence of the tavern's guardians closing back into their earlier ranks.

He looked up at the door and saw the crescent moon cut into its design. He remembered thinking how much it made the building look like a giant outhouse before he was clobbered on his head from behind and the sight of stars overtook the moon for Olen.

He was pummelled and kicked. His senses flitted in and out as more heavy fists—and then clubs—thumped him on his extremities and the bones of his skull. There was laughter and jeers while he was grabbed and pushed.

Pain shot through the sides of his bloody face as his cheeks scraped against cobblestones. His feet were raised up and his bruised body was being dragged away and then hauled around a corner, straining, and crumpling his savaged form further. His body spoke to him of multiple broken ribs. His legs pained where his knees had been kicked out from under him.

But the blows had stopped. Olen blinked his eyes to try and clear the blood.

His eardrums ached to the sound of a woman's voice and her furious command.

"Help me carry him, you idiots!"

Amidst the swelling of his eyes and the congealing redness of blood blocking his sight, there was a fierce, dark-haired woman marshalling Effie and the other boys, and making demands that they transport their fallen leader from the scene of his incomprehensible folly.

Olen gazed up into the woman's face. For a brief instant, he was reminded of the many times when he had looked up at his brother, Tolen, standing above him, and dragging him out of ill-fated scraps with the local kids whenever he'd gotten in over his head as a lad.

There was a resemblance.

"Neriah?" he wondered aloud.

"Don't speak, *dear* Uncle," the woman said, uttering the affectation with such acerbity that it stung him like the bite of a wasp.

A moment later, everything went dark.

CHAPTER 16

The Sandcastle

The landscape outside the northwest gate billowed with rolling foothills and the road beyond stitched together a path through valleys and passes until somewhere, far from Caphedra, it would arrive at the Four Peaks and the mining city of Palinor. On their left, the Darrow River flowed toward and past the pair of riders, its waters, engorged by the increasingly heavy downpour of recent rain, having originated from the alpine streams of those same mountains.

Trin raised his gloved hand and traced the path of the river back to Caphedra. "You see where the river enters the city?"

Denn turned in his saddle. Between two stone guard towers at the city's northeastern corner, a grated portal opened like a wide jaw to gulp down the unending rush of water from the hills.

"If we need back in, take note that the bars do not reach the riverbed on the east side."

"Is that so?" Denn said.

"It's been dug out under there. You can fill a barrel with heavy goods—like iron—and roll or drag it underneath with chains to get it into the city."

"Is that a trick of my father's?" Denn chuckled.

"I wouldn't want to accuse Mister Wel—sorry, *Lord* Wellum, of doing any such thing," Trin said. "But I expect it would be an easy swim for someone needing to get in, secretly, under cover of night."

Denn listened, then gave Naobe a scratch and patted her along the withers. Such a plan did not account for bringing a warhorse back in, he thought discontentedly.

No one was visible as they rode along. Perhaps the locals

were avoiding the weather, Denn surmised. Nonetheless, shacks and shelters speckled the sides of the road and a signpost welcomed travellers to a place called 'the Rafters', so named for those inhabitants whose lives were spent crossing the river on rafts, working its depths as fishermen or its shores as gatherers. It was also a light-hearted reference to being upriver, and therefore *above* Caphedra, like the rafters in the roof of a house.

Denn and Trin planned to venture along the road only so far as to be out of sight of the guard towers. To reach Fallowsea, they needed to cross the Darrow and make their way to a narrow strip of traversable, elevated ridgeline called Bridgecliff.

"I travelled here with my father when I was young," Denn told Trin. "There is a ferry just a short ride upriver that we can take to cross the waters. We'll head there."

Sure enough, as they broached the top of the next rise, they saw a barge moored to a post on the eastern shore of the river, near a small cabin of warped and weathered wood. But beyond that, on the next ridge, something else caught Denn's eye. Through the distance and the rain, above a smattering of other houses popping out of the valleys, a shape stood out against the arc of the hillside. A horseman was looking in their direction, from atop a chestnut horse the size of Blenksy.

Denn pointed the rider out to Trin, who squinted and cocked his head to try and get a better fix on what he was being shown.

"Yes, I see him. He's carrying a spear," Trin said. "But no pennant."

"You've got good eyes," Denn said.

Then, in what must have been a reaction to their scrutiny, the figure hurriedly turned and slipped back behind the rise.

"Do you figure he's from the garrison at Bren Hills?" Trin asked.

"Travelling too lightly and on the wrong horse. They favour black bays at Bren Hills," Denn said.

Taking one last advantage of their elevation, Denn gave the ridge another hard look, peering from one edge of the horizon to the other for good measure.

"It was a scout, likely," said Denn.

"Myrhic's?" Trin asked.

"I'd say. From out of Wodwarden, as Yael predicted."

Scanning the shacks and cottages, Denn failed to detect any other indications the army was approaching. "There is no damage to the houses yet. If the army was closer, we'd see their beaters here pillaging for supplies by now. This fellow is probably riding at least a couple of days ahead of the vanguard, and maybe four or five days ahead of the main body depending on how bunched up they are. That still means we won't have long to reach Fallowsea and get back, before Myrhic's army moves in," he declared. Atop an impatient Naobe, he gloomily pondered, "Do you think that Farathemun will have an army stood up, equipped, and in formation within a week? Will my father, for that matter?"

Trin murmured pessimistically. But seeming less doubtful or deterred, Blenksy began nosing down the hill. Like Naobe, she was eager to move on and Trin obliged her.

Denn remained one fleeting moment longer, pondering whether he had signed up for a lost cause, until he also picked himself up, squared his shoulders, and urged Naobe forward. She let out a fierce snort and a confident whinny, warning the land itself to prepare to receive her indomitable hooves.

Leaving the road behind, Denn could not help but stare ahead one more time. He remembered travelling with his father and Hann on family business. Their suppliers lived higher into the foothills where they brought loads of ore down from the mountains for trade and sale. North of here, folds of earth rose up until you reached the famous Peaks of Palinor, where multitudes of men in deeply descending pits and shafts had scratched out many centuries' worth of the most lucrative metals.

Once this road had been a dangerous trek due to bandits, but King Ramis had heavily garrisoned the route and anchored his holdings by assigning lordships to the most loyal commanders. Lord Tulk Sentor was granted the garrison at Bren Hills, the area closest to them now. Past that, Lord Paxton Remm held Harthal Vale with nearly four times the number of troops that Sentor had. Finally, at the end of the earth was Palinor itself, where Lord Mayor Alin Sunder could reinforce the road from its starting point–that is, if the mountain liege ever broke from his famous reclusiveness and showed any interest in southern politics. If any of these men were supporting Ramid in his march on Caphedra, they would have to come down this road, but for now, the ground was mostly undisturbed, and the trails were silent.

The passing of their horses kicked up rich, red earth. Dragonflies buzzed past as the Darrow River flowed coolly south. Soon, a sign along the roadside pointed to a lazy bend up ahead, as they rode, side-by-side, up the eastern river shore.

"Koster's Ferry," Denn read aloud.

"This is where we cross? Do you think the ferryman's here?"

"I don't know. Never met this Koster fellow. The ferry has been here for ages, but the sign's new to me."

Though its owner was presumably new, the ferry was still the same clumsy, water-logged barge that Denn remembered. Thankfully, it did not need an attendant to be pressed into use. Constructed from thick cedar timbers, it could carry an admirable load across the river, working on a pulley system rigged out with a long metal chain. Examining the links for signs of rust or fatigue, Denn was satisfied that the chain was serviceable, and he gave the order to load the horses.

Together they hauled their way across and unloaded. On the western side of the river, the ground became more elevated. Outcrops of orange and red rock, full of untapped iron, projected from the bluffs and divided the steppes. Ahead, the hills grew steeper, so they let the horses graze wherever grass grew up.

As the night slipped upon them, they pitched camp at the foot of an impressive but impeding ridge that would be tomorrow's first obstacle: Bridgecliff. The formation was like a slice of mountain, jutting sharply from the earth as a barricade against terrestrial life. It resembled the spiny back of some gargantuan sailfish that had washed ashore and perished at the edge of the sands of the Hasen desert—if creatures like that ever existed.

"We could go around it," Trin suggested as he poked their campfire with a stick to stir up the coals.

"To reach Fallowsea? You'd be the first in a hundred years at least," Denn replied, appraising the great height.

It was geographic eccentricities and canalizations like this, that favoured Caphedra's dominance in trade. Nature determined the highways of the land, and therefore its great fortunes and clout.

Bridgecliff bisected the land west of the capitol. Should they venture south, the way quickly became parched and bone-dry. A plain of baked rock and coarse sand leading to the base of the cliff only gave way to rolling dunes and dry plains if you ventured deeper into the Hasen desert. With no known paths up and out, there would be no water and no grass for the horses.

To the north, was the fabled Eldergorge, a broad gully filled with a towering white pine forest. Mist rose around the evergreens and their tops, high above, glistened. Trin stepped off on a few short surveys and initially returned promising reports of each route in terms of forage and concealment. However, Denn knew from his schooling that unseen features ahead provided natural impasses that would prove difficult. Hacking a trail through would be tough and no one had ever charted a path out of the forest valley that Denn heard of. The Palinor mountain range rose at such a precarious incline that the valley was blocked off and rather than providing a low road to Fallowsea, it would only serve to box them in.

Hence, Bridgecliff was the only realistic route and anyone travelling behind them would, unfortunately, conclude as much. It was named so because its long-spanning elevation gave the perception of a bridge across the two unnavigable terrains on either side. It was narrow for a mountain, perhaps the width of a large road at its widest but also had far narrower chokepoints. Two riders would have no problem, though.

"We have to take the rise tomorrow morning," Denn said, encouraging Trin with a pat on the shoulder before getting up to check on the horses. "There is supposed to be a trail near here, which is an easier climb. You'll understand better once we're on the ridge. Just make sure you fill up your water skin first. There are no fresh springs that high up."

With the horses prepared before dawn, Denn and Trin began their ascent. The first light caught the ridge and drifted slowly and steadily down the slope to meet them. The rising sun was on their backs by the time they were halfway up the approach to Bridgecliff, and Denn's promise bore fruit as a navigable way unveiled itself.

Denn's neck was aching from the number of times he looked over his shoulder to scan for pursuers. He noted that Trin kept watching sporadically, but mostly the young squire was glancing in wonder at the expansive vistas stretching to either side. He was more apt to point out a soaring eagle skimming the great pines to the north or call attention to the tumult of a distant dust cloud on the southern desert as it devoured patches of wasteland on its path to the horizon.

They rode for hours, until nearly the close of the day when Denn jerked back on the reins and motioned to Trin. Difficult to see against the late-day rays of setting sunlight, straight lines of cut stone in silhouette could be made out. The signs of human construction were unmistakable where an imposing stone structure blocked the trail.

"Shall I ride up farther and check it out, sir?" Trin asked.

"We'll stay together, Trin. I can't imagine they'll see just the two of us as much of a threat," Denn answered, examining the construction carefully as they drew near.

At the base of the wall, and the blinding sun ceased its harassment and only the brisk wind attempted to deter them. Denn could make out the mortar lines in the rocks and gaps that served as windows. A red and yellow banner flapped overhead–a blood-red holly leaf on a golden backing, flanked by the silhouettes of two arcing fish.

There was no way around the fort, save for descending either cliffside, which would be impossible for a rider on horseback. There were no cracks in the wall or piles of rubble that would suggest disrepair, so ongoing use could be deduced, but no person could be seen readily manning its battlements. Denn managed to identify a gate, but disappointingly–though not unexpectedly–its metal portcullis was down.

"I hope we don't startle them," Denn smiled. "I don't imagine they get many visitors up here. They must be asleep."

"I'll call to them, sir," Trin offered, then followed with a booming, "Oy!" which resonated against the rocks and wall. Denn was startled by the lad's forwardness, but it did the trick and from the docile innards of the fort came an inversely dispassionate response.

"Announce yerselves!"

Denn tried to determine which opening it came from. There were several visible slits cut into the stone wall. He whispered to Trin, "Farathemun *is* expecting us, right?"

Trin nodded.

"Denn Wellum and Trin–" he paused, not remembering

Trin's family name.

"Curraw, sir," Trin whispered.

"Curraw!" Denn shouted.

Dusk was not far off and in the shadow of the wall, with eyes not yet adjusted, it was hard to see, but it appeared as if a head had moved across one of the windows. They were being watched. Judged.

"We are passing through to Fallowsea on matters of business with Lord Farathemun. Are you his men?"

The voice called out again.

"You're a leopard?"

"Say again?" Denn puzzled.

Trin leaned across his saddle, pointing to the image of a pouncing feline on his cloak pin and ventured, "'*Leopard*,' he said, sir." Then, with a slight spark of acknowledgement added, "I think I recognize that man's voice."

Denn gestured permissively and Trin prodded Blenksy to step forward.

"I am Trin Curraw of the 13th Mounted Caphedrans, who is now serving Lord Wellum."

There was a yammering of profanity from within and the portcullis groaned and ascended. A man strolled out, with thin lips and thick, wavy hair upon a high forehead. He was dressed in assorted garments of leather and mail, with his helmet under his arm and a broadsword sheathed across his back. He looked only slightly older than Trin, but his hairline exaggerated his maturity.

"Korbin!" Trin exclaimed and immediately dismounted to greet the man.

"They call me 'Captain' now," the man said. "I thought I recognized this squire. How have you been getting on? We figured you would have ended up here sooner or later with the rest of us."

Trin led Blenksy by the reins and approached the man warmly. He removed his right riding glove and offered his hand, saying, "We are here to see Lord Kentin Farathemun. Will you let us through?"

The captain accepted Trin's handshake and returned it with a friendly clap on the shoulder. Then he turned to Denn and announced, "I am Captain Korbin Saur of the Bridgecliff Tower Guard, serving Lord Farathemun. I welcome you. Think of this hillfort as the gatehouse to Fallowsea. I'll be escorting you to my lord, sir. If you wish to refresh your horses here tonight, we can leave at first light."

Satisfied, Denn climbed down from Naobe and also took her by the reins to lead her inside, but their host paused. He was peering back along the trail from whence Denn and Trin had come.

"Nightfall is approaching. Will the rest of your men be coming soon?" he asked with uncertainty.

"It's just us, Captain," Denn answered.

"I see," Saur said, his eyes squinting a bit as he processed the statement. "The rest are back with your father, I presume."

Denn refrained from pushing the point but glanced at Trin, who tightened his lips and left it to his master to answer.

"I was told that Fallowsea would be providing us with an escort back," Denn finally injected.

"Then you have been informed better than I, sir." His smile drooped and the furrows on his brow contracted. "I've not received such orders to ready my men." Saur called back to the tower, "All clear!" then half under his breath said, "I am sure we will have clearer instruction on the morrow, at the castle."

They advanced through the open entryway and into the cramped, but sturdy stone fortification. Ahead, more stairways led up into the heights of a central tower. Candlelight spilled around corners. It was furnished plainly, but what comforts they saw appeared well-used and inviting. Better still, attendants approached, offering them food and water while grooms led Naobe and Blenksy to a promised meal of hay and fresh, warm bedding.

That night, Denn and Trin savoured mugs of mulled wine taken on battlements where the last of the day's light revealed a pink- and gold-hued panorama stretching across what must be half the world and for the first time for Denn, the storied ocean exposed itself to view. He had never seen the western seacoast and now it spanned across the edges of his view. He wondered how such a vastness of water could coexist with the land yet not devour it.

Below the ridge, dangling into the water at the end of a long, precarious causeway of black earth, he saw Fallowsea's castle, marking the limit of human occupation of the world. Its towers sprouted up like tufts of bone and its pale walls were unartfully strewn into place, like blocks of chalk tossed away by a disimpassioned toddler.

"It's a small castle," Denn commented and at once thought it made him sound jealous.

"A princess lives there, though," Trin reminded him.

"A queen, if some have their way," he corrected.

Denn and Trin woke early and gathered their gear. Captain Saur, seeing them up, roused his men soon after for departure. The Bridgecliff soldiers were a rough lot in the morning as they grumbled and fussed with the trappings of their uniforms. Some passed around a razor and a small glass to trim the edges of their beards.

"To your horses! Two men on me, now! I don't care how cropsick or foggy you are."

"It'll just be a moment," Saur explained to Denn, then shouted again to men out of view, "Get the tack on! It's not like you don't train for this!"

Behind the main wall and tower was a rearward courtyard delineated by more stunted walls, recognizing that any invasion was bound to come from the opposite direction. With the tower built at Bridgecliff's highest point, the trail to Fallowsea now began a lazy descent to sea level. He could see down to the coast ahead, where the rising spires of the young Farathemun's watery stronghold, stood pale as ivory against the backdrop of a surprisingly calm and near-waveless black sea.

It was a tremendous view, but the descent would still take half a day.

Throughout those hours, Denn focused on the ocean, first in awe, then with odd curiosity, for he noticed that the sea, eerily, did not move.

Despite spending all his years living inland, Denn was reasonably certain that there should be waves lapping the shore, but the water was still. Its depths were murky where its atrophied currents were too lazy to push the tide to the beach. The wrack along the strand held only a minimal collection of sun-bleached artifacts, undisturbed across the ages.

As they took in the sight, two more soldiers on horseback rode up alongside them and, following their captain's lead, escorted

Denn and Trin down the grassy slope of scrub brush and bracken toward the sea. The homes of the townspeople sprawled out along a crescent cove. Most dwellings were ramshackle and simply constructed. Dunes of dark black volcanic sand made for a natural border along the civic limits and the small houses rising out of the strand appeared as if they were sitting in ashes, like untouched remnants of a fire and not the vibrant cottages of a fishing village.

People were walking about, repairing traps or sharpening fishing spears. Their faces were cracked and aged artificially by a tame salt breeze that could be heard more than felt. They uttered a few words of laboured greeting as the band of soldiers rode through, though none smiled.

Denn wondered whether these fisher folk ever had the ambition to try and row out beyond the confines of their littoral doldrums to seek larger fish or even just explore. Perhaps, as in the south, they believed the legends that voyaging beyond the sight of land exposed you to the mischief of the ocean undines who would see your ship spun around and lost forever. Maybe they had their own mythologies. In Lanstad they held onto persistent legends that to go too far by ship risked your crew becoming fatally ill. History tomes bulged with tales of daring captains who returned to port on ships infested with plague as a reward for their boldness. Regardless of either fate, Denn was satisfied his destiny remained on land and was content to speculate no further on the ocean's troubles.

Sand kicked up beneath their horses' hooves as they made their way down to where the land shot out across the lethargic saline waters, along a skinny, sandy corridor that led to the castle.

Captain Saur guided them and their horses to a fenced-in run stemming from several stone outbuildings. Other horses were there, parsing the sands to placidly take their midday meal from coastal grasses.

"We will walk out from here," Saur informed them and then pointed to the isthmus. At its end, sat the lusterless fortress of Farathemun. It resembled pale, exposed coral plucked from the water's black depths with its only colours came from the hanging gold pennants with their splashes of red, with which the castle was adorned.

Trin turned to Denn and asked, "Would you like me to remain with the horses, sir? I can help get them ready for tomorrow's ride back."

"No. Let's keep together," Denn directed as grooms took Naobe and Blenksy into the stables and began going over the horses' coats and hooves, satisfying him with their attentiveness.

Crossing the causeway, their breathing felt surprisingly laboured. The air was heavy with moisture, salty and almost motionless with no breeze to give relief. Even when standing at the edge of the vast ocean, waves lapped with such unexpected gentleness that there seemed to be barely any at all. Looking deeper into the water, Denn saw it was choked with kelp and seaweed, giving it the dark, murky hue that he had seen from higher up the hillside.

As they arrived at the castle's immense wooden doors, Saur signalled to pikemen who swung the gates open. They were met inside by stewards to take their cloaks and travelling wear, and by another who offered his hands out to take their weapons.

"I'd like to keep mine if you don't mind. I expect my companion feels the same," Denn said.

He was met with a displeased look from Captain Saur, who explained, "Only lords and those on a lord's business are entitled to keep arms in the castle. I am not aware that you hold rank in the army, and your father's a merchant, isn't he?"

Were he still a simple field cavalryman, he likely wouldn't have been vexed by the challenge in the least. Saur had rightful authority to make the request, but events of late that had tossed Denn into such a conspicuous role, more in line with his distinguished upbringing, which gave him the prerogative to refuse. His father had assigned him this task and there was the vital fact that his father had now reclaimed their family title from disuse.

"My father is Lord Wellum," Denn corrected him. "I am here on a matter of his business—and that of Lord Farathemun, the elder—to be conducted personally with *your* Lord Farathemun, the younger. As such, I will keep my sword with me, and I insist that my attendant—my companion—will do the same."

Trin stood, folded his arms in front of him.

"Very well, sir," Saur said. "The stewards will take you to your room to prepare for dinner. Trin, you're also invited. I will escort you to *your* quarters." He then smiled more amiably. "Besides, there are a few faces around here that would love to see you again, old friend."

The lack of airflow was like a curse upon the castle. The halls were stale, and pennants hung uninspiringly from masts. The smell of brine and seaweed was inescapable and persisted even as one climbed the stairs to the second and third storeys of the fortress, with only a modicum of relief by the time Denn arrived at his assigned chamber.

The steward was a kindly man, dressed in robes with scarlet trim and golden embroidered holly leaves. He replenished a stone bowl with fresh water for Denn to wash the dust from his face. He set down a goblet and clay jug of beer, with which to ease the dry throat caused by the harsh salt air, then pointed out that there were clothes of Denn's size in the armoire to change into before descending to the banquet hall for supper. Excusing himself, he promised to return for Denn's dirty clothing to be laundered later.

Looking out the window, Denn noted how the ocean spread to the horizon without a sail in view. All he could see were small, flat-bottomed skiffs being pulled, with effort, through the inshore kelp forests where working men hauled up their conical fish traps. There were no lines cast in nor any nets. The seaweed must only serve to entangle such things. Still, he saw the flash of silver pour forth from the traps as they were emptied of fish.

After a short respite, Denn selected his dinner attire, and changed into laced shirt and loose trousers. It gave him a bit of renewed strength to be clean and dressed in fresh garments.

Overall, he felt at ease. He appeared to have been granted the run of the castle—or at least provided with no limitations—but his sense of decorum suggested that it was a bit rude of his host to not have greeted him directly. He knew Kentin. They shared the prestige of their lineages as children. They had played together and even received instruction in school side-by-side. Their fathers had always maintained a good relationship and that trickled down to their families—although Kentin Farathemun had no living siblings. One would presume, all this history would have been more than enough reason to personally welcome Denn into his home.

But it was inescapable to conclude that Kentin had risen higher than Denn. While he had no brothers or sisters, he was the sole first cousin to the three heirs of Ramis. His aunt had been Queen. By that virtue, he did not start in the cavalry as a regular horseman but was elevated to leadership in a city brigade early on, which led to the King granting him the title of Commander once he'd proven a basic aptitude for the task.

Then there was his castle. Fallowsea was not an ancestral demesne, but it was titled all the same. At one time, Kentin and his troops had been ordered west to quell a disturbance but managed to convince the people to stand down peacefully. Perhaps moved by his success, he bought land among them and paid them to work it. He gifted the proceeds to King Ramis along with a petition to recognize the ground and make him a lord of it, to which the king agreed.

In that instant, he heard the door latch move and Denn's mind jerked back to the present. The door edged open slightly, then stopped at just a crack.

"So sorry, sir," the old steward said, returning. "I presumed you had gone down for supper by now. Do you need me to fetch you an escort?"

"No," Denn said quickly. "I am leaving now. The castle's not too large. I'll find my way."

"Excellent, sir," he said, as Denn hurriedly brushed past him.

The castle was awash with carvings exhibiting nautical themes. The scrollwork on bannisters and pillars swirled naturally into carved renditions of periwinkles and whelks. Along the walls, however, the mortar was inundated with real seashells which formed white, pink, and black mosaics from clam, scallop, and mussel shells. Their patterns depicted all manner of creatures of the sea, from elaborate schools of fishes to mythic creatures threatening terrible calamity upon the ships of mariners.

Denn found the banquet hall with his nose for it was the only place that did not smell like the ocean. The aroma of food—the scent of fresh bread, particularly—summoned him. In the antechamber leading in, there were fragrant dried flower petals and perfumed oils burning to drive back Fallowsea's natural odours and create solace for the nose. Denn couldn't avoid surrendering a cough, for although the scent was more pleasing, the conflicting airs only made breathing that much harder.

Inside the dining room, Trin was waiting at one of three long tables. The room was prepared for the onset of the day's great meal and other guests had also taken their seats. Oddly, however, Denn noticed servants were removing place settings.

"Did I miss it?" Denn joked, betraying a slight nervousness that such may indeed have been the case.

Trin shook his head. "All's well, sir. Everyone is just sitting in now."

"Is your room alright?" Denn asked.

Trin laughed, "Oh yes, sir! Lots of space to stretch out. I think they were expecting you to bring more people. The quarters I was assigned to could house more than two dozen soldiers. I have quite the surplus of comforts."

"I imagine that's why they're taking up settings. They were overprepared." Denn pulled out an oaken chair and took his place beside Trin.

"I suppose so, sir."

The room began to fill with guests. Castle administrators were identifiable by their red sashes and garment trimmings, or by golden holly leaf brooches. Other attendees also seated themselves and Denn presumed them to be the local elite. But such ranks were relative, for even these people had calloused hands and creviced, weathered faces from years in the sun and the maritime air. From a gallery above, a musician breathed life into a set of reed pipes, which served as their entertainment.

After more time had passed, the guests were still left waiting for two vacant chairs to be filled. Denn could not help but overhear murmurings of impatience that suggested the tardiness of the host was unusual. The undercurrent of commentary had become extremely uncomfortable by the time the senior chamberlain, flanking the doorway to the hall, pronounced in a dull tone, "Good fellows and ladies, your Lord Farathemun."

Chairs scraped and cutlery clanged as those who had been playing with their utensils hastily dropped them back into place and the crowd of expectant diners stood—with Denn and Trin joining them—to greet the host's arrival.

A man and woman entered briskly, with the woman one step

behind. Lord Farathemun kept long dark hair and a coarse beard and moustache that Denn thought unimpressive and hardly worth the effort to grow. His cheeks were angular, and his chin sharply pointed, which made his face appear to grin even though his mouth remained rigid and straight.

Trin nudged Denn timidly. "Is that Princess Ramisa?"

Denn looked and shook his head. "No, I don't think so."

He had never actually seen the princess. Even the Lady Ravon, who was taking on the mantle of queen, was a mystery to Denn. However, while both Farathemuns and Wolstetts—the two lineages of the royal family—had famously dark hair, this woman had hair the colour of honey which was resplendent with finger-width strands in hues of copper and silver, like veins of metal forged into her long locks yet still flowing softly and naturally. There was something different about her round face too. When she scanned the crowd, her gaze momentarily rested on Denn and he saw she had profoundly green eyes, the likes of which he had never seen before. It was as if a jeweller had beset them with shimmering emeralds or crystals of malachite.

The Lord of Fallowsea took his seat while the woman sat down silently beside him. She exuded a warmth and appeared welcoming, but was careful not to overstep Kentin who was otherwise disposed. Was she the lady of the castle? Denn wondered if Kentin had perhaps taken a wife in his time as lord here.

"Bring the food!" the host commanded.

Servants began porting several courses into the dining hall. There were tureens of soups and stews with steamed shellfish served alongside plates of braised and charcoal-fired finfish like those Denn had seen fishermen retrieving from their coastal traps.

An attendant filled Kentin's goblet from a decanter of wine. Without waiting for all the guests to receive theirs, he abruptly stood and made a toast.

"To our guests. Mr. Denn Wellum and his no-doubt courageous, lone armsman."

As Denn stood cautiously to accept the toast out of custom, he stared at Kentin, trying to read his host's face for a clue as to his thoughts. Kentin outpaced him and followed his toast with an immediate interrogation.

"Where are the rest of your men, Denn?"

Denn thought to temper his reply with a plausible excuse.

"We did not wish to attract attention upon leaving Caphedra, for reasons I had assumed you knew," Denn said.

"You realize that having men under your command is part of the bargain?" Kentin asked.

"Bargain?" Denn questioned back. "We're on an escort mission. What is being bargained?"

Kentin rolled his head sarcastically, then when he was again facing Denn said, "More than *just you*. Your father is to finance the raising of at least two hundred men. I expected you would have arrived with at least half of a company of cavalry."

Now Trin seemed to be sweating a little and Denn was getting a feeling that he had not been wholly instructed on the specifics of his father's business with Lord Brevin Farathemun.

"What bargain?" Denn demanded.

Kentin scowled. "Are you playing at being an idiot? If so, you two will make a good match!"

That was too much for the woman beside him, who gave him a cutting look, and he softened his manner.

"The Lady Ramisa has been informed that in exchange for your father's military support of her cause, that you were to be granted this opportunity to establish matrimonial relations between our families," Kentin summarized.

"Serenn," Denn muttered in reply.

"Not your sister," Kentin answered. "Though her reputation for brains might make her a better prize." He sighed. "Your father has promised that *you* will be wedded to my cousin. That's the deal." He swigged a mouthful of wine then added, "Quite the step up, my friend. Congratulations on your betrothal."

Denn processed Kentin's words, momentarily shocked at their implications. That was the unspoken arrangement that was missing from his father's conniving that night in the study. Once this favour was over, his father had never planned for his son to depart Caphedra, much less with someone like Livet. Now to be a royal consort? While Denn could never support the Lady Ravon and her minders in the Faith of the Pillars, he had not consented yet to any participation in ousting her, much less assuming a role as being party in replacing her. He had no idea what would have possessed his father to suggest such a deal.

Furthermore, if Lehn's superiors knew, or even suspected, that the Wellums were moving towards such a public usurpation of the Faith's contender for the crown, it would put all of them into disastrous conflict. There would be no reconciliation with his surviving brother and no chance to ride off with Livet and the life he had promised her.

"Impossible," Denn said. "I hadn't even seen my father in two whole years to agree to such a thing. How could he have even known that I would be in Caphedra at the very time this transaction would be realized?"

Kentin was almost amused; his pointed chin angled down so sharply it could charitably pass for a grin. "He was lucky then," he said. "But that was the deal. He promised you and a host of troops under your command in exchange for our agreement that you would be wedded to the Lady Ramisa, publicly linking you, your men, and your money to our cause."

"Your Lordship, if I might ask," Trin interrupted nervously, "Why not support your other cousins?"

"Because her siblings were moulded into puppets, unlike Ramisa, who has been under my care for the last eight years and was raised to respect the good of the people. Everyone knows Lord Marshal Myrhic controls my cousin Ramid, while the Faith of the Pillars controls Ravon. They would have had Ramisa too, had they not convinced my uncle to foster her with us. My aunt—her mother—ended up paying for that with her life."

"They said it was related to the Queen's sickness that Ramisa was taken out of Caphedra," Denn interjected.

"Sickness, hardly. Madness!" Kentin said bluntly. "They used their spells to drive her insane."

"And you are certain that is what caused it?"

"Aunt Tressa was not the only one affected. I daresay we managed to stave off the worst with Ramisa, but it was too late for the Queen. Without a sound mind to pilot it, her body foundered, and death came to her by her own hand."

Denn now knew for certain, from the way Kentin spoke about the princess that the woman beside him was not Ramisa. He poked further.

"Where is the princess now?"

The woman beside the host bowed her head slightly, looking

somewhat forlorn.

"She eats alone," Kentin said and then took up a small loaf of bread, breaking off parts to sop up his now lukewarm chowder. "We should all get eating too. Morning comes quickly, and now I must ride back with you, along with some of my men to provide a more suitable cadre for protection."

Filling his mouth, Kentin was finished debasing his guest, it seemed. Denn took the cue, raised his cup for a drink of wine and lowered his spoon into a very savoury seafood broth. He managed one mouthful when an attendant stepped sharply into the room with a strange report.

"M'lord," he said. "There is a visitor for Mr. Wellum at the castle gate, begging urgency, sir."

"Doubling your troop count so soon?" Kentin quipped.

"I wasn't expecting anyone," Denn answered humourlessly.

Kentin raised his hand and pointed to the attendant at the door. "See that they are disarmed and then permitted to present themselves."

There was a moment's uneasy quiet as the mysterious interrupter was brought before them. If there was a danger, guards were outside the door and standing at the corners of the banquet hall to handle it. Denn had not brought his sword to supper but did have his dagger concealed on him, and his hand went to its hilt as soon as the visitor was presented.

A clever-looking man with a dark, tufty beard and tightly braided hair was escorted to the doorway and announced.

"Temis Sloke, m'lord. Declared servant to Lord Phon and Denn Wellum."

Denn arose immediately but did not rush the door. His shock paralyzed him. His feet felt stuck to the ground where he stood. One of his two surviving captors had returned and was now standing in front of him, displaying a countenance of the utmost severity and implying a matter of great import.

"My lord, I rode all this way to inform Master Wellum that there are men already in the saddle and riding toward Fallowsea, intent on his demise."

"Surely they seek Ramisa," Kentin said.

"No, m'lord," Temis said. "Though they would be quick to dispatch her also should she be found in Mr. Wellum's company."

Subserviently he turned to address the ashen-faced Denn and expounded.

"I know that I have much to explain, but it was urgent that I warn you, sir," he said. "Furthermore, I must tell you that your sister is also in terrible danger."

CHAPTER 17

Inside the Folds

Wisdom brings us to understand.
Resilience gives heart and guides the hand.
Heritage, the pedestal, on which we stand.
Progeny, our promise to the land.
— Excerpted from *The Path of the Pillars*

In the district known as the Folds, no straight paths ever led directly to the Temple of the Faith of the Pillars or to the majestic campus in which it was nestled. Streets wound around each other in swirling circular layers and merged with alleyways which, like gaps in a robe, allowed a quick glimpse of the next road over as one journeyed closer to the ever-looming edifice erected at its centre.

Throughout the plazas and arboretums, the air hung sweetly laden with the fumes of smouldering incense and late-blooming blossoms. Much higher aloft, in the tame breeze of approaching summer, blue banners slapped at the stonework that surrounded the balustrades along the upper walls.

The temple was the only building in Caphedra that was taller than the castle's citadel. Its lower levels held blocky buildings encased in close-fitting, white-washed brick, punctuated by wrought iron window frames. From immense, impenetrable pedestals rose the temple's four symbolic namesake pillars, together supporting yet another untouchable platform higher up. Towering over the streets from each of the temple's corners, these columns established the boundaries of the Faith's most revered sanctuary and upon each, carvings professed exaltation for the four greater virtues of the

Faith: Progeny, Resiliency, Wisdom, and Heritage.

Yet, somehow, it seemed small to Livet. This singular building was the nexus from which evil entered her life. She had imagined it would have reached even farther into the sky—or down into the earth—without any respect to limit or decency, endlessly mirroring her burden of pain. While she approached it in fear, as something tangible and touchable, somehow the actual sight of it emboldened her in an unfamiliar way. She now saw that it was just stonework with a chipped foundation, bowed rafters, and fragile painted tiles. Even if all she had was a hammer, she could attack this building far more easily than she could wage war against the fear for which it stood.

The ideas, the teachings, and the doctrine of the Faith stemmed from here also. Hordes of adepts came and went from the temple to expand the Faith's reach. Curates and clerics hid behind its walls to birth its edicts and dogma, and to sometimes pronounce decrees of life and death over those whom they would never deign to meet or to condemn face-to-face. The Faith even minted its own coins—now that the king had taken that prized prerogative with him to the grave—although the Faith's collectors, under the command of its pursers, demanded them back from the people faster than they were issued.

And now the Faith was reinforced with armed troops that marched under dark blue banners of privilege and subjugated the citizens with all the authority their captains could derive being custodians of a queen-in-waiting. These Pillarmen, as the Northporters and others had called them, could just as aptly be described as mercenaries, brutes, or wolves. In the evenings, especially, the streets quaked under the resounding footfalls of their relentless boots.

Livet walked through the streets with Baressa, drawing closer to the temple but second-guessing with each step. Were it not so critical to rescue Baressa's people, she'd have turned back at the start. They both knew the danger.

"I wish this place'd just crumble and fall down," Livet said.

The pair tried to avoid any attention as they meandered along the streets looking for a way inside to where the Northporters were said to be held.

As sunset came and they stood together in the long shadow

of the temple, Baressa recollected, "When I was first taken captive from my home and brought to the city, all I could think of was escaping and fleeing back to my father's house in Berryboughs, or to my sisters in Starpond, but when I saw this building here, I was compelled to remain in the city and do what I could to oppose all that it stood for."

Livet craned her neck to take in the entirety of their enemy's bastion. "Me, I always ran from 'em," she said in a low, hushed voice. "Now, here I'm right in front of 'em and tryin' to get even closer."

Martial commands exploded across the cobbled street as a band of Pillarmen formed up. The shouting dragged her back to greater attentiveness. The armsmen's swords remained sheathed, hanging from their belts, but in their hands, they held fearsome truncheons and cudgels. With these, they were empowered to browbeat the evening's resistors and cart more people off to the temple dungeons.

Livet began wondering where they had come from so quickly when she noticed one last soldier exiting oafishly from a doorway wedged incongruously between the genteel shops of a tailor and a jeweller, both shuttered for the night. Before he could take his place in the formation, he ran headlong into a powerful rebuke for his tardiness from the furious curate who was overseeing the commencement of the shift.

Baressa took a step back to conceal herself. Unsatisfied, Livet tugged on the seeress's arms and pulled her even further back behind a column and into the shadow beneath the overhang of a jettied roof. Baressa deferred readily to Livet's expertise.

"This place is familiar. The prison wagons are driven down this road to here," Baressa explained. "There are ways into the temple through many of the buildings throughout the Folds. I am certain one will lead us to where my people are held."

"Tunnels, then," Livet surmised. "No matter how tall they build it, the bottom stays at the bottom."

Livet was more than familiar with underground workings, having navigated Lanstad's subterranean shafts and sewers. Living with Kell and the others, she had been taught to use crypts and catacombs as a private highway. She spent several days at a time hiding or exploring in the below-ground network, away from sunlight. Judging by the distance from the temple proper to where the soldiers had emerged, the architects of the tunnel would not have escaped the necessity for ventilation shafts, even if they sacrificed natural light to navigate the corridors. The dangerous reality was that more soldiers were likely on the other side of that doorway, she thought, but if she could find such a shaft, they could avoid entering by the door and shorten the distance they needed to tread underground.

Livet hoped that the Pillar engineers in Caphedra had been schooled in the same formulas and ratios as those in Lanstad, for she knew her way in and out of the temples there. "Follow me," she said.

Along the streets, Livet leapfrogged between sewer grates. As she closed in on the temple, her eyes caught sight of a part of the building's foundation that was cracked and crumbling. She worked her tiny fingers into the crevices and pulled out a chunk of mortar, crushing it up in her hand into small pieces.

These pieces she dropped slyly and strategically into several of the grates she'd been examining. The first two splashed into water below, and with the unmistakable stench rising up, led her to conclude they were simple sewers. The third stone she dropped, however, was almost inaudible when it struck the floor below the void, and she was encouraged that this indicated the presence of a dry chamber or corridor beneath them. There was another smell she could pick up from that grate. It was familiar and although masked with other odours, the underlying scent reminded her of a crypt.

But there was no way for her to remove the grill. She reached inside, hoping to find a latch or lock, but the bars were set into the stone around the edge of the hole.

"Can we chip away at the mortar? Dislodge it?" Baressa asked.

Livet shrugged and pointed out, "It'd be too noisy. It might call attention."

Baressa frowned and turned to look back over her shoulder.

"Maybe the guards have all left? Could we sneak in the doorway?"

"Too dangerous. Let's try the next shaft," Livet suggested.

She glanced back at the building that housed the exit, then to the last shaft, estimating where the next should be. However, at the expected location, there was nothing like the other grates. To Livet, it was a mystery. They had witnessed a lot of men arriving through the passage and any extended distance between holes would make it difficult for them to breathe comfortably, especially if one were carrying a torch to see their way. Certainly, even if they weren't risking asphyxiating, they would, at the very least, be left in the dark when their torch was snuffed out.

Was there a turn in the tunnel beneath them that they were not anticipating? Livet began scanning the street.

Then she saw it.

There was a small plaza just across from them on the other side of the street. It featured carved stone benches and a podium adorned with a quartet of spiral pillars. On the walls, the tenets symbolized by the pillars were expounded on upon etched plaques. The plaza was empty of people at this hour but must be used as a setting for instruction or direction, Livet thought. There was even water that could be drawn from a stone well for the thirsty speakers and listeners to refresh themselves. This is what she wished to investigate.

When she approached the well, she could see a faint glow of light radiating off the rocks along the interior. Closer, she felt a gentle draft of cool air blow against her cheek, and she could smell the suspicious, musty scent again.

No one was around. The bucket in the well was drawn up and the rope appeared to be strong enough. Livet beckoned Baressa to come closer.

"I don't think I can manage to climb down there, Livet," Baressa said hesitatingly.

Livet pulled Baressa closer to have a look inside.

"It's only finished on the outside," she pointed out. "There's rough stones stickin' out all the way down for you t' step your feet onto. It'll be easy, I promise."

Baressa gulped nervously, but Livet knew the situation was dire enough to compel her to follow down the well.

"It's the only way in," Livet said. "I'll go first."

She lowered the bucket and tied off the rope, then swung her legs over the edge, feeling for the first brick. With a nod to her reluctant partner, she carefully and confidently inched down the interior of the well.

For a short moment, coolness overtook Livet as she descended and helped to relieve her sweaty apprehension. It cleared her head, and she was able to adeptly scale the errant stones and outcrops. Finally, her foot swung, unobstructed, as she reached an opening at the bottom. It was dark and quiet, which she took to mean safe. She swung her body, trying to drop down without plunging through the surface of the water directly beneath.

Her feet landed softly on the muddy periphery of the water. She pressed her hands on the chilly rock wall, circulated around the space, feeling the grooves of mortar to where she discovered a crafted brick archway into another chamber. Judging by her memory of the streets above, it was only a few dozen yards before the passageway would reach the lower levels of the temple.

The memory of Kell's teaching entered her mind as she stood there, adjusting her vision to the lack of light. She remembered how he would always encourage her when she lacked the nerve to press forward into tricky spots like this and urge her to explore bravely with her other senses. She could hear his voice telling her to keep moving ahead and felt a compulsion to reassure Baressa similarly so that they could see this through together.

Her eyes detected again the softly escaping light from further ahead, but for now, she held to shadows and tugged on the rope to indicate to her allied infiltrator that it was safe to come down. The passage was empty. Most of the armsmen and guards must be out scouring the city, she thought.

The rope wagged as it was grabbed from above. Livet could see first one foot and then the other fumbling along the uneven wall.

"Mind the water," Livet coached before the final drop.

With her robe billowing and causing a heavy thud, Baressa arrived at the bottom and Livet quickly nudged her into a corner.

"Give your eyes a moment t' work in the dark."

The older explorer was breathing hard, but steady, showing relief to have made the descent. "We need to hurry," she said between inhales. "Soldiers will be back soon."

Livet nodded. "Once we move up ahead, I'll sneak off and find the prison cells, rush in, and grab who'ever that I can find t' send back t' you," she said. "You stay at the beginning o' the tunnel and guide everyone back t' here."

"Stay safe," Baressa said, as Livet boldly flitted down the

corridor.

The floor of the passageway was of damp, trampled dirt and the walls and ceilings were arched brick. There were no recesses or diversions from the passage, so Livet stayed low and close to the wall, trying to avoid casting a shadow. Livet could hear Kell's voice in her head telling her to *'Wrap the dark around you. Entice it to embrace you.'* With that, she called on the skills that he had gifted to her, as a burgeoning burglar in Lanstad, to repel the light and advance with confidence that she would be unseen.

The sour mustiness pervaded the air now. She knew it as the smell that came from ancient bones and the dust that collected around the remnants of the dead. Kell had introduced her to a life in the solace of the catacombs, but while the tombs of Lanstad granted them safety, she felt the opposite here. This smell had fresher undertones. It was septic and alarming.

As she reached the mouth of the tunnel, the luminance of the chamber grew but did not encroach so closely as to betray her passing. Beyond the opening, she saw a brutally constructed room from which hallways stemmed. A half-full metal trencher of food sat on a scarred wooden table which was mated to a single, straight-backed chair. Casting light along the upper wall, a torch burned in a sconce and illuminated the room with dancing flickers.

No one was here now, but someone must have been eating here recently, so Livet remained wary.

Reaching down, she brushed her fingers through the cool, wet earth beneath her feet, plucking up several small stones. She tossed them back, one at a time, to signal to Baressa to move forward, but was ready to put a finger to her lips to implore her friend to caution.

There was a faint rustling and the brief brush of cloth against brick as Baressa got up and followed Livet's cue. Her pale, contoured face manifested from the shadows and her eyes gazed down on Livet in what felt to her like admiration. It was the same feeling she had gotten from Kell during her days of mentorship.

Without any more words, Livet entered the room, but she took only one step forward before halting and listening to the sounds beyond.

From across the chamber, Livet heard a doleful moan. Weeping carried across the dank air, along with a child's whimpering and the jangling of metal on metal.

"Make space!" an angry voice resounded. "There'll be more of your lousy lot coming in tonight."

Livet pushed Baressa back into the tunnel, then slipped around to get a view. There was only one guard that she saw, but one would be enough to apprehend her if she were sloppy. So, Livet skulked along the floor, keeping out of sight should the guard reappear too early, and crossed the gap to the tiny table.

She wanted a distraction.

Reaching up to snatch the trencher, she flung it across the room. There was a ringing clang as roasted turnips and onions were sent tumbling along the floor.

Fast on her heel, she propelled herself and quickly jetted from under the table to where she could squeeze in behind a tall rack of spears and long-handled axes dominating the far wall. She crouched and stayed still, looking out through the gaps between the shafts of the weapons.

There was a hostile shout and weighty footsteps rapidly grew louder in the nearby hallway. A wide-jawed jailer in a soiled and faded blue tunic stormed into view, cursing into the shadows.

"You!" he shouted. "Stealing my supper?! I'll kill you!"

With impassioned fury, he swung down a truncheon, just missing the whiskered snout of a saucy and galling grey rat the size of a woodchuck. It twitched its nose at the man provocatively, then scampered down one of the other adjoining corridors. Lumbering after it, the aggrieved guard initiated a pursuit and disappeared again.

It was the first animal Livet thought of in a dungeon like this. It was something the guard would have expected, and so she was inspired to employ its image as a scapegoat. The guard was now off chasing the phantom pilferer and she had her chance to creep further in search of the Northporter captives.

At any moment, she knew that more guards could appear. Worse, she could face a whole patrol if any were on their way to assemble for their night's duties. That did not discount those that might already be returning from outside.

Sparing not a moment, she encroached upon an archway

which led to the wailing noises she'd heard. The hall was lined with bars and cages—all empty—but with gratefulness, she spied a dangling ring of mortice keys. She plucked it down with her fingers spacing out the keys so as to disallow them from brushing against each other and betraying her with any incriminating jangling.

Livet pressed forward and carefully entered a slightly wider passage that opened into a room. In neat and orderly rows, methodically organized, the chamber housed a host of diabolical implements. Livet's chest shook as she inhaled. Her hand quivered until she reached down to brace herself against the stone floor, but she still felt weak and challenged to continue.

This was the torturer's workshop. Visible by firelight and arrayed throughout the room were pointed iron spikes, many sizes of terrifying vises, leather straps, and chains, all for employment in eradicating apostasy and giving the cruellest of the Pillar enforcers a wide toolbox from which to exercise their evil. Masonry in the centre of the room had been built up to act as pillories, with iron rings embedded in the stones. One construct was hollowed out to serve as a firepit with grooves where metal brands and pokers could be heated until glowing and red. This hearth is what lit up the room.

Judging from the fire burning in the pit, it had only been lit recently. The coals had yet to begin smouldering, as would be required for proper use once the patrols returned with more victims later tonight.

The guard had yet to return, so Livet willed herself to move onward to where the dungeon cells would be located close by. It was just a few strides to cross the room, but as she stood up to move, her perspective of the room changed, and she recoiled at the sight of a large, wooden frame. Chains dangled from its head and base, and spokes radiated from its heinous mechanisms. It was on such a device that Livet first learned what it sounded like to hear the joints in your legs pop.

Muddled memories swam about her now. In Lanstad, Livet had been squeezed in the vises, crushed under mallets, and her skin bubbled under red hot pressing irons. They fed her noxious elixirs until her stomach twisted and she vomited. Her ears rang with the preachers edifying the names and virtues of the Paragons. It was on a rack like this that she was pulled and stretched so that one of her legs surrendered and splintered. It remained so, maimed until, by some miraculous mercy, she was permitted to finally crawl away. And while *she* had escaped death, the Faith appeared to have only moved on to their next victims.

Onward, Livet forced herself down to the next corridor, trying to keep to the shadows. Both sides of the hallway here were spaced with barred doors, and the interiors were dark, musty, and fetid. That smell of suffering persisted here also. Livet hated herself for thinking that she was getting used to the horrible stench. It only meant death, if not today, then inescapably soon for those locked inside.

Livet barely heard the chain rattle, but by then it was too late.

A fist full of bony, scabby fingers seized her by the neck. Livet desperately shot her legs out across the corridor to lock her feet around bars on the other side. She tried pulling away, but the thing pulled more strongly, grunting, and moaning feverishly as the beast of a man aimed to haul his catch into the lair of his cell.

Her feet could not produce the strength to anchor her. He was too powerful. With his other hand, he was reaching through the bars to find another grappling point. His hungry fingertips strained toward her, trying to grab her by her long, black hair.

Then suddenly, another pair of hands clamped down upon her ankles and she felt a force dragging her toward the adjacent cell on the other side of the hallway. With a jerk, the grip of the feral prisoner was broken, and Livet tumbled across the floor.

"Leave her alone, Mouldy-Oh," said a more human voice.

The hands that were wrapped around her legs released her. From the darkness, she saw a sturdy, bearded man shifting his gaze, between appraising her and eying the ring of keys she had dropped on the ground.

In the cell opposite, the fiend slunk back into a corner to slobber and seethe.

"He wouldn't eat you, as he doesn't have any teeth," said the bearded man. "But he'd do other things."

Trying to stop shaking, Livet kept herself as equidistant between the two cell doors as she could.

The man who spoke to her maintained a gentle tone as he explained. "The Pillarmen broke him a long time ago, I'd say. They keep him here, feed him some scraps and slop, then bring other prisoners to him for a few hours at a time as punishment. Poor bastard seems happy."

Livet shuddered, having seen such results before as prisoners went crazed from their ordeals. But that was no acquittal, for she knew that there had always been a seed of evil in them that the curates found, coaxed, and nurtured. It was usually a prisoner they found who had already shown the desire to turn on his fellow inmates, or someone naturally criminal-minded who had demonstrated the capacity to hurt others insatiably before they were apprehended.

"Well, you're safe now, my sweets. How about you return the favour and let me out?" He prodded, "I can help you find a way out if you just give me those keys."

Seizing the ring of mortice keys in her hands, she held onto them tightly to her chest.

"Or just unlock the gate yourself, miss," he persevered.

The man was clever enough to not be irreparably mad, at least not yet—and he *had* saved her.

"Why are you 'ere and not with any others?" Livet asked him.

"Oh," the man said sheepishly. He paused. "They have me here to get extra punishment." He pointed to the room Livet had just crossed. "Lots of terrible things they do to me."

"Why are you different? What is it you did t' cause that?" Livet interrogated him further.

"They were angry with me, see," he said. "I was trying to stop them from hurting some others—women and little children. Babies. They wanted to kill babies." He smiled. "I stopped them! I'm a hero! Save me, please."

"I think you're a liar," Livet said.

"No," he said. "You should let me out. Don't let them turn me into some animal, like old Mouldy-Oh over there!" The man grasped onto the bars. Livet could smell the rot on his breath as he panted. "If you don't, I'll call the guards." His eyes grew wide. "They'll either lock you up in here with me or over there with *him*!"

Livet took the man's threat seriously, but she didn't dare risk letting him loose for fear he'd turn on her anyway. Delicately, she worked her fingers over the key ring.

"You don't need to threaten me. You need only ask," she said. "Which key is yours?"

The man smiled. "The big brass one," he salivated.

Livet worked through the mortice keys until she came to the key that he had identified. With a slight tug, she slipped it off the ring.

"May I have that key?" the man asked politely.

"Don't ask me," she said, with a glance at the cell behind her. "Ask him!" Livet tossed the brass key toward the shambling creature across the hall. The deranged beast heard the ringing as the key struck the stone floor and reacted, grabbing, and securing its new toy.

Livet pulled back farther from both of them.

"If you make a single sound to the guards, they'll know that you 'ave the key an' they'll beat it out of the both of ya," Livet said.

The bearded man froze. "You damnable wench!" he said savagely.

As Livet retreated down the hallway, she heard his desperate begging.

"C'mon, Mouldy-Oh. Just give it here. You don't know how to work it, do you? Just give it here," he cajoled, only to be met by defiant grunts.

Livet knew that she was pressing her luck, but she heard the sad sounds of more captives ahead. Wary of being detected, she edged cautiously around a corner in the hallway and saw that it led to more and more cells. Many of the doors were open and swinging freely. Livet suspected they were emptied daily to feed the need for spectacles in Hamrin Square by day and resupplied by arrests at night, though tonight's unfortunate cohort appeared yet-to-be apprehended.

But the persistent, pitiful sounds informed her that not all were bare. Livet advanced on one whose door was fixed firmly shut and from whence cries were drifting out into the dank dungeon passage.

This time, she focused on renewing her shadowy enchantment. Amid a delicate whitish glow seen only to her, she crept up to where she could see past the bars.

Inside, there were more than a dozen men, women, and children clustered unenviably together in the cramped darkness.

Livet could tell by the weave of their clothing, the stockiness of the women, and the voluminous, bestial beards on the men, that they must be Baressa's entrapped kinsfolk.

Permitting the shadows to recede from her body, she scrounged up enough courage to unveil her presence to the poor captives inside.

"Who's there?" asked one.

They reacted to the sound of metal scraping metal, as Livet began working away on the lock. She tried each of the keys, praying no guards would yet arrive. If these keys did not work, she would have to employ some other magic trick to pick the lock.

Finally, there was a click and the mechanism yielded to her tugging on the latch.

"Quietly," she instructed now. "Turn 'round the corner. There are tools and weapons on racks at end of the 'allway. Go there now—then 'urry where you're told, so you can get out," Livet commanded. Weak as the prisoners were, Livet breathed deeper with relief that they had better numbers now and could overtake at least a few guards, should they appear.

Sprung from the prison, the rescued Northporters hurriedly consolidated to help each other move as quickly as they could. Livet followed, pointing out the path back as she went.

Two burly men took off and swiftly moved ahead of the group. They reached the cells of the condemned mad men first. When they saw the man Livet had spoken with, their anger bubbled up and spilled over into curses. As Livet got closer, she could see the man was in tears.

"Please," he begged.

One of the big Northporters shook his head obstinately, but after a few whisperings, he turned toward the wild man across the hall. With a pitying look, he approached the cell. As Mouldy-Oh's hands shot out to reach for him, the Northporter grabbed first and pulled the fiend tight against the door to the cage. There was a racket of maniacal gurgling and a hissing sound from behind the bars. The women in the party, especially, grew noticeably tense, staring sharply at the beast behind bars.

"Not this one," the Northporter at the cage said, and with giant hands, he held on to the unsalvageable wretch. "No saving him. Nothing's left of him to forgive, and no desire to be forgiven."

Livet heard the crack of the creature's vertebrae and the clang of the dropped key upon the floor.

"Let the other one out," he ordained mirthlessly. Another Northporter scooped up the key then passed it off to the man nearest to the other cell. He shoved it inside the keyhole, turned it with a jerk, and the lock yielded. Roughly, they yanked out the prisoner who emerged in tears.

Quickly now, the escape resumed with a dash into the original chamber where Livet pointed to the weapons rack and the Northporters, men and women together, liberated a collection of imposing implements with which to defend their flight.

Thankfully, the guard had not yet returned. Somewhere, Livet imagined he was still wondering where the giant, thieving rat could have run off to. The thought amused her. In fact, as she oversaw the last of the escapees to reach the chamber, Livet even became energized. She felt pride in her act of defying the Faith. It would have pleased Kell, very much, she thought. Even now, she could hear his praise in her ear, with a clarity of recollection that she had never before experienced.

'You've done well, dear Livet,' said the voice in her head. 'But you've not freed all. Just a little farther.'

She stopped, uncertain of what she sensed. "Who? What? Kell?" she inadvertently questioned aloud. It was her mentor's voice, but were they also his words?

In the dimness around the last corner, Baressa was ready to greet her countrymen and lead them out of their imprisonment. But Livet hesitated. She was still listening for Kell's voice. It was faint, but it was enticing her to revisit the other hallway leading out of the chamber.

"Where... are... you?" she stammered.

CHAPTER 18

Heirs

What manner of guile brought this villain here with such presumption? Denn wished to respond to Temis carefully, feeling he must evade talk of the kidnapping for fear that Kentin would further condemn him for weakness on its account. He laboured to control an urge to fly into a dizzying rage, but with such capriciousness on Temis's part, it moved him to figure out what role this scoundrel was now playing.

Certainly, he could straightaway ask Kentin to order his men to seize him, but then he would have to explain Temis's crime, causing unacceptable embarrassment during this delicate time. Perhaps Kentin would oblige but later would use it to erode Denn's worth even further in this concocted powerplay.

Denn looked the intruder over. Temis was submissive and almost cowed but could not help but appear poised like a coiled snake. His eyes exuded a heightened awareness and seemed continually looking for some advantage.

Though, in retrospect, Temis had never raised his hand against Denn in the way that Colden and Romwin had. He was the one who had seen that Denn was fed, his thirst quenched, and his restraints loosened when opportunities allowed. But it was not enough to pardon one who was still party to the crime, however.

Denn considered all these things against the magnitude of Temis's dire warnings. In either case, there was no way he wished to interrogate this man in front of his host.

"I beg your forgiveness, Kentin," Denn said. "I wish to excuse myself to speak with this man further."

Kentin, amused by the abrupt severity of the situation,

chuckled, "I bid you your leave to settle this matter, dear friend." Raising a goblet to his lips, his failure to stifle his mirth as he sipped sent droplets of wine to spew forth.

Denn faked a smile and left the table. His petition ostensibly accepted, Temis lightened perceptibly and accompanied Denn into the outer corridor. There they were alone, save for the sculpted faces on the walls and the characters on the hanging tapestries of the outer hall.

"Now you understand why you were brought back to Caphedra, yes?" Temis began.

"So, this was all engineered by my father before you and I ever met," Denn said. His fingers hovered over the hilt of his weapon. "Tell me what inspired him to conceive of such an act. What was your part? Tell me all of it."

"Yael enlisted me to watch over you when he found out what your father had planned," Temis said.

"He planned this behind Yael's back?" Denn asked incredulously.

"It was a negotiation he made in private with Farathemun. Yael didn't know about it until it was already transpiring. If he did, there would have been no Marshal's Men involved. Your father arranged it himself to get you back to Caphedra. He didn't figure you'd return on your own."

Denn was quiet, so Temis filled the gap with further confessions.

"As soon as we reached Caphedra, I took your horse to your father's stable and informed Yael that Balix would be coming to demand ransom. He did, and we took care of him. Then I led Yael back to the carriage house where they had you stashed and I opened the door for him, Trin, and Brae to enter."

"My father needed me because he had arranged for me to be married off to the princess, to seal his deal with Farathemun and the other merchants and nobles. They didn't suspect my father was overstepping my wishes?"

"Family quarrels aside, a marriage to the princess would be a desirable prize. They'd be suspicious of anyone who refused it over some filial grudge."

Denn still wanted to kill Temis, but it would have to wait until they were outside of the confines of Kentin's palace. He placed a hand on the brick wall next to him, leaned into it, and contemplated. Like stoked coals in a furnace, his hatred for his father emerged anew.

"I'm leaving tonight," Denn declared angrily. "No princess."

Temis hesitated, then chanced to speak. "Fair plan. But we have a problem that you really need to be worried about."

"This is the part where someone wants me dead? Who now? Did my father have a change of mind?"

"Your brother," Temis said seriously.

"I just saw him back in Caphedra. What do you mean?"

"When you left, your brother assumed that you would be disowned and that he would become the heir apparent to your father. Your father is old, and Lehn did not expect the two of you to reconcile before the family wealth passed to him."

"His needs are provided by the Faith. Why covet father's gold?"

"Gold is a useful tool. Such a donation would elevate your brother's prestige amongst the curates. However, when your father assumed the title of lord, that enticed him to act more recklessly. He seeks that mantle of nobility to legitimize a courtship."

"Princess Ravon," Denn said flatly.

"Yes," Temis said and mused, "He's always plotting. More than you, I think."

"So how did you come to learn all of this? From Yael, I presume."

Temis was more talkative now that he was confident in having his audience's attention, but his expression soured.

"I am afraid that I heard it from your brother."

The statement took Denn aback. Instantly, he suspected this was an elaborate, rhetorical setup for Temis to reveal himself as the instrument of his brother's intent. He took a step back, as his hand stretched toward the hilt of his concealed dagger, but the messenger continued his confession.

"I regret my part now, but please, hear me," Temis asked.

Denn was ready to lunge but listened. He was hungry to hear the whole story.

"After you last spoke to him, your father had the idea to increase his odds. The raid on your family manor by the Marshal's Men troubled him and encouraged him to negotiate a peace, of sorts, to ease his fears."

"Don't tell me," Denn scowled. "He's trying to play both sides."

"I was assigned to protect Serenn while Yael was ordered to offer her as a bride to Prince Ramid. Should the Marshal accept the offer, your father would support the prince's march on the city instead."

"And if I married the princess like he'd planned? What then? Two weddings?"

"No. Princess Ramisa has not formally declared her intent to take the throne so if she were married to you, she could be encouraged to abandon any such fancies. The nobles of Caphedra would not be brave enough to support her as a pretender if your father's wealth wasn't backing them, Farathemun be damned. Perhaps she would even be moved to endorse her brother and cement his rule."

This forced Denn to ask a troubling question. "Where is Serenn now?"

For once, Temis's eyes drifted, and he ashamedly turned away from Denn. He took in a deep breath and began, "I must preface this to say that I had the best intentions."

Denn narrowed his eyes, threateningly.

"She confided in me, as her protector, that she did not wish to marry the prince. So, I took her to the only person that could offer her true safety. At least, I had assumed at the time. I didn't anticipate how your brother would respond until we came face-to-face."

"And that's why you are here," Denn observed. "You didn't come to save me. You came to me to help you save her."

Temis continued to look away, but he winced when Denn made the accompanying assumption.

"And Yael doesn't know."

If he could have shuffled off his skin, Temis looked like he would have.

"Time was precious," he answered. "In that regard, I elected to prioritize your safety by bringing the warning to you as soon as I learned of your brother's intent. Regrettably, he now knows about your business with the lady Ramisa."

"My brother, Lehn..." Denn began, then postulated. "Serenn

is knowledgeable about all my father's business holdings, so he needs her once he's gotten rid of my father and me. How many men has he sent?"

"More horsemen than Trin and I can help you defeat alone, I am afraid."

Denn pondered over the extent of his little brother's clout within the Pillars that he could employ their soldiers to make good on all these threats. The promise of the wealth of the Wellums must have already been a powerful lure that facilitated his quick ascension.

"In that case," Denn reluctantly decided, "we must escort the princess as planned because that is the only way Kentin will send enough troops with us to counter the enemy. But I will inform him of the danger."

Temis's smile rebounded. "Good plan, sir."

That night, Denn pulled Trin aside to relate what he had learned from Temis and to pass along instructions for the following morning. He was carrying his sword on him now and was diverting his attentions to planning how to counteract the danger they faced.

"Have Captain Saur fetch us lances or long arms from their armouries and to equip his men likewise. Then prepare to leave early and inform Bridgecliff Tower that there are hostile riders believed to be bound for Fallowsea."

Trin eagerly accepted the orders and pledged to act on them immediately, but he was obviously distracted, and his countenance faded as he spoke to Denn.

"I am sorry, sir," he said. "I didn't know Temis had been involved in your ordeal. He served with us in your father's house, at Mr. Larkin's bidding, for quite some time. I just thought he'd moved on to find other employment. I had no idea he was sent to steal you away like that."

Denn worked past Trin's explanation. "Temis will ride with the main body tomorrow. I can keep an eye on him better that way. Now go off and do as I ask. We'll need as many of Saur's men as we can get to help us break through and ensure our return."

Trin nodded and took a step backward, saying, "Goodnight, sir."

Denn turned and plodded up the stairs, exhausted and still blistering with outrage. He was forced to react to Temis's warning, but also to prepare for the possibility that the devious hireling might be engaging in another act of deception, to perhaps sabotage their journey at a critical time. Maybe he had even developed a taste for ransom money and was harbouring a scheme to go after the Lady Ramisa.

As he continued up the stairs, he heard movement above. It was soft and gentle. He saw a swish of cloth as a woman's dress flashed across his view, higher up on the staircase.

Taking a final step to the top of a landing, he encountered a woman waiting at his door. It was Kentin's dinner companion for the evening and her appearance here was completely unexpected.

"May I help you?" Denn asked innocently.

The woman did a slight curtsey, holding the hem of her long, flowing skirt as she bowed. The metallic streams flowing through her hair were more visible now. Denn was convinced her locks were surprisingly natural, though he still felt amazed and curious as to the richness of her deep emerald eyes.

"I am Avenda, attendant to Princess Ramisa. Lord Farathemun neglected to introduce us at dinner after you understandably left your place early. I wanted to discuss our travel tomorrow."

"I wasn't expecting to be leading a royal procession. Can you ride?"

"It matters not. The Princess cannot ride, so we will be travelling by carriage, with either my sister or me in accompaniment."

"I have little confidence that a carriage will survive the descent downslope to Caphedra once we've crossed Bridgecliff."

"And yet it must," Avenda said matter-of-factly.

A royal carriage was another complication for Denn to consider, but it did not entirely spell an end to his strategy. He nodded to the woman to signal his compliance with her request.

Avenda started back down the staircase past Denn, then slowed. She revolved on her heel and faced him again.

"You'll meet the princess tomorrow, but be prepared to make certain allowances, as she demands."

Denn smirked. "Extravagant requests from a princess?

Special considerations for Her Highness above and beyond keeping her alive until we reach the capital, you mean?"

"No!" Avenda shot back incensed and it startled Denn, who realized his jibe angered her. She evidently considered her information as essential.

"The princess has been here for eight years. She was brought here after suffering many horrible symptoms that my sister and I have sought to help her overcome."

Denn felt the colour drain from his face, so poorly administered had been his attempt at humour. He stared into Avenda's green eyes to signal that she now had his full attention.

"She had to be brought here for her safety, away from Caphedra and the central temple. We have continually done as much as we can to allow her to get through each day, but the small challenges of a tranquil village like Fallowsea are incomparable to what she will face in the chaos of the capital. Furthermore, we do not know what will happen once the Faith finds out that she has returned."

She reached out and clasped her hand on Denn's arm for emphasis.

"It is imperative that one of us is with her when she travels tomorrow."

"Very well," Denn agreed, now even more alarmed that the ride back promised yet greater potential for hardship.

Denn awoke the next morning wearier than he had been when he fell asleep. The reappearance of Temis triggered his restlessness and the resumption of nightmares full of kidnappers and their dead brothers. In his nocturnal imaginings, this time, all those who surrounded him were Colden's targets—even Trin and Avenda. Denn was awoken in a sweat when Colden sought to bury a dagger into Livet's back as she drifted before his mind's eye, pleading for her lover's return. Fitfully, he tried to at least rest his body before daylight's first rays roused him from his bed.

Again today, there was a negligible breeze and the smell of decaying seaweed on the shore permeated throughout it. Cicadas and other insects buzzed and click-clacked noisily from out of the ocean's detritus, while gulls conversed above, loudly transmitting the location of potential meals to their fellows.

On his way through the castle, Denn stopped to procure a bowl of pottage from the kitchens and pocket a couple of yellow apples, then joined the assembly on the causeway.

Grooms had brought the horses around and two of Kentin's were already hitched to a small carriage. Naobe looked well-cared for, which comforted him. He fed her one of the apples, then hoisted himself up onto her back, before letting her stretch her legs in a sauntering review of the yard.

Kentin and Captain Saur were looking over the men who were selected to accompany them on horseback. As Denn had requested, they had been outfitted with polearms but seemed to have lost any familiarity with their use. With a long glaive, the captain was demonstrating the proper balance and grips, angles for carrying, and where on the body their impact would serve the most considerable damage or be most likely to knock a man from his horse. Those under his tutelage were sporting a mix of light lances and fauchards, while a trio of long-shafted partisans were reserved for Denn and his men.

"You look energetic," announced someone behind him.

Denn paid the comment no heed as Temis rode up beside him and Naobe. He was on the back of a youthful black rouncey.

"Good morning, Naobe," he said, addressing Denn's horse with a grand articulation that was far beyond his station. "This is Coalsmoke," he said, pulling back on the reins of his horse. "Please don't step on her, you lovely girl."

Denn was convinced he detected a hint of covetousness, which made it hard, still, to not think of Temis as anything but an aspiring horse thief. Maybe it was wise, Denn thought, to have ensured his charger's loyalty with one of the apples he had palmed.

Just then, from out of the castle proper, two servants emerged and descended a flight of stairs. Each was carrying chests and they loaded them onto the carriage which was just large enough to accommodate two passengers and their luggage. Cargo secured, they sprinted back to stand motionless beside the staircase.

Next, two more figures came into view between the servants. Avenda was slowly and carefully leading the other by the arm and, with apparent effort, guiding her toward the carriage. The other woman was thin and frail but elegantly dressed and possessed of natural dignity, despite whatever condition marred her movement and debilitated her. Her face was that of her mother's and Denn recognized the Lady Ramisa instantly.

As the princess moved in the direction of the carriage, she was stiff-necked and kept her head rigidly forward to match her trajectory, but he caught her staring at him out of the corner of her eye. If she were evaluating him, Denn sensed, she seemed satisfied.

Then, before entering the carriage, she resisted her helper's goading and addressed Denn. Her words were polite but stilted. She spoke awkwardly as if such parlance was a rarity, and she was woefully unfamiliar with her own voice. "Thank you," she said, then demurely added, "I look forward to our journey."

Having allowed this little extravagance of expression, Avenda now silently insisted that the princess enter the carriage. It was low to the ground, but a wooden block was placed under the lady's foot, nonetheless, to aid her in climbing up. Her body moved as rigidly as her speech.

As the carriage door closed, Denn could hear her confiding inside. "Soon we will be home. My father must miss me terribly."

There was a shushing from inside, but Denn instantly absorbed the weight of what she said. Beside him, Trin remained stoic, but it was clear that he was also having reservations about how truly fit the princess was to contend for the throne.

Kentin was already mounted on his steed and with barely contained impatience cantered over to Denn, only to find himself interrogated about the matter.

"She doesn't realize that her father is dead? How does she not know?" Denn asked in disbelief.

Temis also trotted closer on Coalsmoke and eyed Kentin with extreme curiosity as the lord responded.

"She doesn't even understand that her mother is dead. She still talks to her like they were in the same room," Kentin answered reactively. "The whole mess with those priests and her mother left her addle-brained since she was a girl." Then peering at Denn he added, "That's why it's so important that we find her the *right* husband, as I am sure you understand. Though I'll be happy to be rid of her."

Kentin did not wait for Denn to comment on the matter. He spurred his horse and rode away from the carriage, calling out to his men. "Let them catch up," he said dismissively, then gave the command to Captain Saur to commence the journey east.

At the top of the ridge, fresh air washed over them. Denn felt more awake, but it took an effort to remain vigilant and watch the path ahead for danger—while keeping one eye on Temis for any signs of duplicity.

The riders proceeded with the carriage following slowing them down considerably. When they reached Bridgecliff Tower, the better part of a day had passed, and they found the fortifications bathed in the setting sun reflected off the billowing clouds behind them. Denn feared a storm might be brewing.

Trin and Captain Saur had left them hours before to ride ahead and ensure the garrison was prepared to receive visitors, as well as to check for any signs that Temis's pronouncement carried a spark of truth. When the caravan caught up, Trin was elated to see Denn arrive. He proudly confirmed that he had passed along his master's instructions to the letter.

"They've sent out scouts, and there's a work party ready to go, as you requested. There's no sign of the Pillarmen, though."

Denn, pleased, gave Trin a pat on the back then sat down with him so they could share a stew of wild mountain goat, such quarry being not uncommon along the ridge. In turn, the young squire presented Denn with baked buns, explaining that they were a gift from the princess, which she had shared from her personal stash of victuals. He accepted only when satisfied that there were enough for both of them—as well as one more for Temis, who gladly mopped up his bowl of stew with the welcome bread.

"When do you think the Pillarmen will get here?" Trin asked.

"Anytime, now that we're passing beyond Bridgecliff. They could be out there as we speak. They wouldn't get through the garrison unnoticed, so they'll be waiting for us somewhere on the other side. Beyond that, it's a gamble."

"How so?" asked Trin.

Denn explained, "If they wait until we're almost to the Rafters, then they catch us when we're far from any reinforcements or any fall-back positions. However, if they know Temis escaped and suspect that he has warned us, they may push and attack us sooner."

"But you're counting on them being further out?" observed Trin.

Captain Saur joined their discussion but did not disagree with anything Denn was saying. He listened.

"We have the advantage tomorrow," Denn began. "We choose our place."

He sketched two narrow lines in the dust before him.

"First, consider that the enemy is on horseback but not likely skilled cavaliers. Even if the Faith had them in their ranks, not many respectable cavalrymen would be eager to take on the dishonour of acting like a mob of assassins hired in secret."

"Even good men need to work. What if they *are* cavalrymen?" Temis asked.

"Then they know, as you and I do, that their horses will rear before they ever impact upon each other and Bridgecliff is too narrow for either of us to veer off. It will be resolved with the sword, not lances."

Denn scratched more lines into the dirt to illustrate their advance.

"There is only one route in and out. They can't flank us on horseback because the horses can't navigate along the sides of the ridge. They're also constrained in that they can only attack where I am because I am the *alleged* target." Denn glanced furtively at Temis but received no reaction.

Trin and Saur were well up for the clash, but now Saur challenged Denn. "By fighting them where you choose and knowing that they must come to you to fulfill their mission, you say you control the ground. But what if they refuse, knowing that you eventually have to pass by them regardless?"

"Then they risk us gaining reinforcements or possibly even fear that we could find an alternate route down the ridge, on the presumption that Lord Farathemun knows this terrain better than they do. At the very least, once their position is exposed, we have the option to choose the timing of when to approach it, and that also gives us an advantage."

"So, we encounter them and then what?" Trin asked.

"We fall back behind the spot I selected for the work party to prepare. If they've done their job, we can ambush them there. If they still hold back, we know they can't leave the ridge on horseback to flank us, and your infantrymen are much better suited to exploit the sides of the ridge and attack their sides. At any time, the princess's carriage must remain *behind* our line of defence."

"Of course, they could dismount and sneak up on foot, at night," Temis suggested.

"We're safe inside. The walls are sentried, and there's no other way around without scaling the cliff," Denn said. "I wouldn't fear tonight."

Captain Saur nodded and got up from his seat. "My men will be heading out under darkness now, to begin manning their positions. I'll leave enough here at the garrison to watch the walls."

He paused a short distance away, where the young Lord Farathemun was reclining, armour doffed and sword leaning beside him, next to the steady blaze of an open-hearth fire. Denn watched them in discussion for a moment, then Saur continued with his duties, his lord seemingly likewise assured.

In Caphedra, Kentin had commanded the 8th Capital Brigade, with hundreds of men from heavy cavalry to archers to engineers, but it wasn't a field unit, and it was doubtful that the lord had ever been involved in more complicated actions than the suppressing of riots and uprisings in Caphedra's crowded streets. When he was sent out to put down troublemakers in Fallowsea, he solved the insurrection by purchasing the land they worked and investing in it himself. However, Denn conceded that skirmishes in tight city streets shared many qualities with fighting on a stretch of terrain like Bridgecliff. Kentin should understand the plan and be happy to stand back and let Denn oversee it.

Denn walked over to the hearth fire, only so close as to be visible in the glow but not yet in the heat. He called out to the figure draped over the chair, warming his feet.

"If there are no other matters, Kentin, I would like to bid you good night."

Kentin grumbled and shifted to lean upon his other elbow. He did not turn to look at Denn, but managed a slovenly, "Good night," in response.

Step by step, Denn began the climb up the ancient, cracked staircase that twisted up through the tower. Along the ascent, each landing housed personal chambers for the lord, when in residence, and his staff. The ordinary soldiers were quartered in a blockhouse at the tower base, but this time, Trin had been treated as a personal attendant and offered a room in the tower next to Denn's.

Before Denn reached his room, however, he was met again on the stairs by Avenda. She was wrapped in a thick, green dressing gown and carrying an empty clay water jug in one hand. Again, the metallic strands woven through her hair glistened as they reflected the light from candles burning in nearby wall sconces.

"The princess has turned in for the night," she announced to Denn. "We hope that you sleep well also."

"Thank you," Denn said gently. "Would you like me to help you fetch that water? It would be no trouble."

Avenda smiled gratefully but declined. "No, I am fine. I must also go down and instruct Lord Farathemun's staff regarding preparations for the princess's travel tomorrow."

"Of course," Denn conceded. "In that case, good night."

Avenda said nothing further but silently slipped out of view down the stairs. Turning to his own door, he yawned and rested his hand on the latch. The day had been exhausting. Denn thought it must be doubly so for the princess, who never left the castle at Fallowsea.

But as he was about to press down to open his chamber door, something invaded the quietness of the tower. He heard words upstairs, coming from the princess's room directly above.

Knowing that Avenda could not have returned without passing him again, Denn froze in place and listened carefully. Whoever it was up there with her, they must be just listening, for if it were a conversation, he only heard Ramisa speaking.

Her voice was getting louder.

"Leave me alone!" she suddenly exclaimed. Then in wrenching sobs, her voice cried out, "I do not wish to die!"

His sword, Longlimb, was in his hand. Without any further thought, Denn drew it from its sheath and bolted up the stairs to the princess's aid.

"Open the door!" he half pleaded, half commanded.

But grasping onto the handle and squeezing the latch, Avenda had left it unsecured. Quickly, he flung open the door with one hand and advanced with his blade held in his other, ready to strike forward and slash at whatever danger awaited inside.

CHAPTER 19

Voices in the Dark

Livet's divergence failed to attract Baressa's notice. The seeress was too busy leading the escaped Northporters out through the tunnel, toward the doorway they'd seen earlier. Without pause, Livet pressed on. Her instinct beckoned her to delve more deeply into the lower depths of the temple. She was acclimatizing to the fear generated by the dungeon and her curiosity was tugging at her. She could sense something vital waiting just beyond the next doorway and a presence that was just as intrigued by her as she was with it.

There was light glowing from across the room, yet it still felt cold, and the air was heavy with the grim, necrotic stench. Through this, Kell's voice guided and reassured her with the sense of his presence. At least, it sounded like him.

Ahead, she smelled the woody musk and dull mouldiness of old parchment. Some kind of library or repository, housing a store of scrolls and records, was in the next room. Everything there appeared ancient, and the heavy odour of the texts exuded a palpable demand for reverence.

But someone was there. Edging forward, Livet saw a pair of smooth, pupil-less eyes staring in her direction. She gasped and for a split second froze still like a rabbit, conserving what concealment she could yet wrest from the cloak of darkness beneath the entrance arch. Her vision brightened in contrast to the true light around her she cajoled into retreating from her umbrage.

Livet squinted.

It was only the bust of a man carved in marble and, behind him, she saw he was joined by a stony cohort. A multitude of statues stood in an assemblage, evenly spaced around the room. Each was mounted upon a base pedestal, decorated with the ubiquitous four pillars, and bearing names like Malthus, Dagremahr, and Parscia—a baker's dozen in all. Each was matched with a single word extolling a greater or lesser virtue that Livet recognized from the Faith's alliterative indoctrinations: Peacefulness, Primacy, Prophecy. The others all branded similarly.

Conspicuous gaps at the bottoms of each pedestal along the edges jutted out and looked like they were separate and movable. Livet wondered if sliding open the slabs beneath the effigies might reveal treasures. Perhaps there was something she could pocket or profit from as a modest installment against the price of her revenge for past pains.

She tried to slip her fingers under one of the stone slabs. When that failed, she pulled out her rondel and used it to wedge open a crack, just enough to get at the contents. With effort, the slab slid open. There was dust and the acrid exhalation of decay wafted out.

She pulled back her knife, and the heavy lid dropped down again, resealing the contents. Livet exhaled with disappointment; she should have known. It was a bone box—an ossuary. The Faith was keeping their most venerated forebears entombed in their basement.

Livet recoiled from the stench and surprise but was neither unsettled nor moved to lose her silent composure. Most of the human remains that she grew accustomed to encountering in the catacombs of Lanstad were kept in far less orderly care than these.

For a moment, she considered lifting the slab again and sifting through the remains in the hopes that there might still be a ring on a finger, or a necklace strung loosely around one of their disjointed neckbones. After all, these remnants were nothing but the vestigial vessels of evil souls and Livet felt no compulsion to afford them respect. For all the suffering that their followers had inflicted on her, she deserved something back.

With the blade of the rondel poised along the gap in the stone, she set upon a second attempt to exhume whatever valuables she could. But suddenly, there was a rattling from one of the boxes and the slab on top appeared to lift on its own before settling again.

It was subtle, and Livet wanted to doubt she had even

perceived it, but a cloud of dust assaulted her, and she coughed. She was gripped with panic and wished Baressa was here for company.

'The Paragons know you are here and will warn the others,' she thought to herself, but it wasn't her own voice that Livet heard. Again, it sounded like Kell's and this time she knew that it was not the recollection of some childhood lesson nor any forgotten moment together. It was his voice that was speaking now, cognizant and aware.

"Kell?" she asked.

Then in her mind, she heard her mentor answer, 'I am here, Livet. Seek me.'

Livet trembled slightly. "Where are you?" she whispered imperceptibly.

'Just one more door,' the voice guided her, and Livet turned to the light emanating from another chamber ahead. Despite the shakiness in her step and trepidation that caused her lungs to rattle and tremble as she breathed, she felt the urge to approach.

Strange new aromas drifted from the next room. Ordinary earthy scents were overcome by exotic, unfamiliar perfumes, and other untraceable stenches. It was smoky, too, and the air hung encumbered, though the pungency helped to cover up the pervasive scent of death that clung to everything else.

As Livet crept low to the floor, her eyes stretched wide as she looked upon a cornucopia of corpses arranged around her. Bodies, in whole or in part, hung from the walls and were displayed on pedestals next to vials and jars of ointments, herbs, and oils. A large brazier was burning in the centre of the chamber, throwing off a deceptive heat and casting shadows. This was not a simple embalmer's workshop but rather a dark atelier that housed the evidence of a vast, macabre undertaking.

One poor soul, strung up across the way, appealed to Livet inconsolably. Its empty eye sockets managed to gaze mournfully at her, and she recognized some of Kell's clothing, ripped and rotting off the body. In places, meat still clung to the bones, tanned and dried through clumsy preservation, blackening in the smoky fumes.

But just when she thought fear might overwhelm her, Livet was overcome with reminiscence of her mentor's love, which brought her to her senses, before a doleful, belaboured confession spoke inwardly to her.

'I begged them to let you go, my young one. But, myself, I was unable to escape. I am sorry.'

Wondering how this was all possible, Livet only allowed a few words past her lips. "What can I do?" she said.

Kell's spirit continued, *'I regret I could not save more of our kindred.'*

"How? How can I save you?" she asked again.

'I cannot be saved. Only released.'

Livet placed her hand over her heart and began to cry, struggling through the grievous thought of her long-time protector so tormented. Most terribly, she realized he must have been suffering all those years since their captivity together—all those years when she had been so alone.

'You are not yet friendless, my child.'

Stepping forward, she rushed to undo the pins in the chains that held his body aloft. He was mostly just bones. She could carry him if he did not fall apart the instant that his leathery ligaments were wrenched or contorted.

"I'll get you down from—" Livet stopped amidst a flash of awareness—she could see herself through her own eyes.

There she was, standing in the room next to Kell's desiccated form and all she could think of was how she wanted to kill that dark-haired intruder who had violated her sacred lair. Where had the girl had come from? How had she so arrogantly trespassed into the Faith's deepest sanctum?

"Livet!" came a cry from behind her, and she was wrenched out of the vision in time to deflect and dodge the slash of a blade as it cut through the air around her. The slayer's glass hanging around her neck felt icy cold.

Baressa charged into the chamber and plowed into a furious woman with curled, auburn hair, clad in blue. Livet instantly recognized the woman as the orchestrator from the night the council declared Ravon as queen.

"You!" Postella Aroon shouted, throwing Baressa off and into the chamber wall, scattering skeletons and knocking red dust from rusty chains.

More danger. Another woman rushed in, whom Livet recognized as the other councillor, Kabra Zimmin. Her streaming hair was floating off her shoulders as if suspended in a gyre of air.

She did not touch Baressa, yet somehow delivered a tremendous force that swelled in front of her and impacted like a gust from monstrous, unseen bellows.

Livet scrambled to get around the workroom table to help, but Postella cut her off, wielding a dangerous dagger.

Knocked backward to the floor, Baressa tried to rally herself. Her face went pale as her eyes darted around the room and she took in the macabre sight of the chamber, but seeing Kabra, she unblinkingly clambered to her feet and stepped forward. "*Wither*," she commanded.

Kabra did not retaliate but faltered, stricken with confusion. An instant later, her hand shot out to frantically grab onto a table to prevent herself from falling over. In an apparent daze, she dropped to her knees.

Baressa continued toward her, kicking her solidly in the head, then shouting, "Run, Livet!"

But Livet was blocked from escaping through the arch by Postella, who was brandishing the dagger and slashing feverishly. Livet had to try something else. The brazier caught her eye, and with uncanny inspiration, she willed the flame to rise—which it did. The fire blossomed and expanded causing Postella to retreat from the threat of the imminent inferno.

The lack of commensurate heat betrayed the surging fire as an illusion, but its job had been accomplished. Livet had her opening. She rushed beyond Postella's reach, to the arch with Baressa on her heels. Together, they ran into the outer hall and raced to the tunnel.

It was harder to see where they were going; their eyes had lost sensitivity in the brighter light of the workroom. They fled through the darkness—then calamity occurred.

Baressa cried out. She had fallen.

Livet turned to help her friend back to her feet, but she had dashed too far ahead before reacting. She heard Baressa call out in the dark and the sound of her body scraping along the floor, being pulled back from where she had first faltered. Kabra's silhouette crossed the light spilling into the tunnel, her arms held out expectantly.

"Get out of here, Livet! Get help!" Baressa screamed as another figure appeared behind her.

But this one was not Postella. It was a man who was wide-chested and tall. His face was bathed in shadows, but within the din, his eyes glowed and scanned the darkness. They settled momentarily on Livet's face, and she felt his presence accost her mind. It clawed through the flurry of emotions swirling through her thoughts–until she felt pure terror only, as if it were slithering through her head.

Livet fell over herself as she reversed down the corridor. Her eyes were transfixed as the man turned and reached down toward Kabra's helpless prisoner, who was struggling on the ground before him. He lifted Baressa up and the prophetess screamed and choked.

Livet heard the twisting and futile flailing of Baressa's limbs before a stomach-churning cry filled the passage. The Chieftain's Daughter was released to fall lifeless onto the cold floor.

In a panic, Livet scuttled like a crab into a corner, then demanding a burst of energy from her drained body, got up, and bolted through the dark into the hallway that housed the jail cells. Her survival instinct blocked out the pain of shock.

On cue, as it had when Postella first arrived, the slayer's glass alerted her to the man's deadly intent. Livet's head swam and she was now standing still in the hallway with the statues. He did not see her.

Livet sighed in relief and removed the amulet so that she could see again with her own eyes. She could not hide here without the risk of getting trapped, and although the sensation was not as pervasive now, she still felt the evil man's thoughts reaching out to corrupt her own.

Livet was terrified. She had to force herself to keep running but knew that she could not outpace her captors if she had to go far. Her lameness prevented her from taking swift strides or powerful steps, and she was already overtaxed.

With all her concentration, she knew that she must conjure an umbrage and cloak herself in shadow to remain unseen. The guard's room was the last open space she had to traverse and as she did, she used her miraculous talent to cloud the guard's eyes as she ran–almost hobbled–past him and into the tunnel.

By the time her feet hit the damp dirt, voices were resounding from the chamber behind her. Livet had to hurry to reach the well's dangling rope. With a crucial, successful leap, she caught hold, then swung forward to find a footfall and handhold against the protruding stones and outcrops of the rocky wall, before beginning her ascent back up to the street.

As she climbed, her body grew heavy, and she feared the swaying rope and bucket would betray her escape route. But she had just about reached the top when she heard splashing down below.

"There she is!" a woman called out, sounding like Postella.

Flinging one leg over the brim of the well, Livet had begun rolling herself across the top when everything started to shudder and shake. The walls around the well were ripped apart and debris fell down below, where it plunged into the water. The sides of the well crumbled beneath Livet and she was left clambering to grip the edge as a chasm opened around her. Suddenly there was nothing beneath her and she was hanging by her fingertips.

Livet screamed as she felt a gust of wind swirling around her feet, then wrapping itself around her. A ribbon of air moved higher up her body until it encircled her torso, then it plucked her up into the air with all the strength of a giant corporeal hand, snatching her from the well's edge and suspending her above both the hole and the street, helplessly.

Below her, Kabra Zimmin stood, arms outstretched, pale dress fluttering at the terminus of the wind current that was trying to draw Livet closer. Livet reached out to grab something to hold on to, but nothing was within her grasp save for a gloved hand. It grabbed her.

The owner's grip was warm and tight, and it pulled her from the reach of the deadly zealots just as she felt a gust blowing above her. This one cleansed the air of Kabra's devouring wind and answered with its own tempest–a cyclone that funnelled down the shaft like a spiralling shockwave.

Her pursuers were repulsed from the bottom of the opening. The gloved stranger lifted Livet to safety on the street and she saw that her rescuer was a gaunt man in an embroidered brocade vest and dark blue topcoat. He had a sharp moustache, and his sideburns were neatly trimmed in straight angles. The hair on his head was grown out, however, lacking any such sophistication.

At his side was the man who had answered Kabra's windstorm with his own. He was dressed in leathers and of less descript appearance, save for deep blue eyes that were set upon a scruffily-goateed face that–despite the fantastical force he had just projected–remained expressionless.

The man in the vest relaxed his grasp on Livet's arm but did not let go entirely, for at the base of the well, Baressa's murderers were rousing. "We have to run now," he ordered her, as she tried to catch her breath. Her lungs were burning and strained from being caught in the competing storms.

"They're coming..." she said hoarsely.

"Where is Baressa?! Why isn't she with you?"

"She's supposed to be here," added the blank-faced man.

"Dead! They killed her!" Livet spat out.

"Unlikely," said the first man. "Don't fear. You are with us now. Follow closely and we'll get out of here."

Livet complied. For an instant, her mind slipped back to Kell and his abominable circumstances, but she got no further than sputtering, "And... my friend..." before her tongue was drowned in confusion about how she could ever explain, or even if she should.

The destruction of the well in the plaza was doubtlessly heard throughout the district, and in response, heavy boots were rushing toward them. Pillarmen, like those Livet had seen heading out on patrol, had returned, and were hastily responding to the disruption that occurred within their home turf.

Livet and the pair of men receded into an alley and watched the troops pass. Notwithstanding her fears of being intercepted, Livet's heart sank, for encircled by the soldiers were more captives being herded through the secluded building entrance. The dejected prisoners showed bruises and bloody cuts that evidenced the severity with which the Pillarmen conducted their duties. She had helped to save Baressa's people, but by the end of the night, the cells would be overflowing once more.

"Harbud! Look there!" said the leather-clad man. He gestured to the Pillarmen's quarry and his partner's response was one of amazement.

"Is that who I think it is? Whoa, they caught a big fish tonight!" Harbud finally let go of Livet and strained his eyes for a closer look at the nearest group of paraded prisoners. "I know that face. It's Phon Wellum!"

Livet followed his gaze. It was indeed Denn's father, and he was being treated like all the other victims of the Faith's fanatical mob.

Something must have led Phon to feel the notion that he was being watched. As beaten and bedraggled as the faded merchant appeared, he raised his head and shot a look in Livet's direction. He saw her. He recognized her. Voicelessly, she knew he was imploring her to help him.

But she was not inclined to spring him from captivity. She remembered looking through his eyes with the slayer's glass and though he had been the cause of Denn's providential rescue, his intentions toward Livet were unmistakable and she could not feel any anguish at seeing him prevented from threatening her further. For that reason, she looked away as a cuff from a Pillar soldier sent Phon's head back down into a defeated stoop.

There was no more time to dawdle. Soldiers were fanning out and would be upon them at any moment.

"Where are we going?" Livet questioned the man called Harbud.

"For a drink, I hope," was Harbud's answer, and he indicated a path down a secluded alley while calling out to his companion. "Stop dallying and let's go."

Harbud walked up to a recessed doorway that was set into the side of a regal-looking tenement. Like so many throughout Stonerow and the Folds, the door's casing was marble, and its sturdy, reinforced planking was fixed and unyielding. Oddly, there was no keyhole, Livet noted.

"How do you unlock it?" Livet asked, her hands already reaching past him to trace the edges for a crack or seam.

"It takes a particular knack. Stand aside!"

Harbud looked mildly perturbed. Brushing her away, he reached into his vest to produce a small stick of what appeared to be chalk. Though challenging to spot at a distance against the marble, Livet could now see that someone had scratched out intricate symbols in white around the doorframe. Most strangely, some resembled characters of the roguish Scrawl that Livet was proficient in, but she was unable to glean the full meaning of the glyphs, save for one that was the marking for a 'shutt,' which Kell had taught her was an indication of hidden doors.

Harbud ran his finger down the left side of the door casing to where there was a gap in the glyphs, then with one last careful look over his shoulder, he jotted in another with the chalk. As he did, the writing began to sizzle and burn with a yellow glow that made Livet step back. Then the door itself began to glow around its edges and appeared to float in the place where it was once was fixed.

The other man stooped slightly to whisper into Livet's ear and put her at ease. "It's a quicker way, the way that Harbud does it," he explained. Then turning to the recessed entrance, he walked through without opening the door, and faded from sight.

"Next," Harbud said curtly to Livet, who stalled nervously.

"I've never seen..." she began.

Harbud rolled his eyes and abruptly pushed her through. Joltingly, she was bathed in a sudden luminescence, and the feeling of being tugged away from the street, the Pillarmen, and far from the Folds.

Livet stepped out of what appeared to be a cellar storeroom. Large casks were stacked from one end of a long wall to the other. Noise from ambient conversations drifted through nearby hallways, visiting her ears, and stoking her curiosity about where she was—where she'd been brought. The voices sounded haughty and happy.

She only had a glimpse, however, for she was ushered toward a side room that appeared to serve as an office. Parchment and ledgers were bursting from the shelves of a towering bureau, but so were myriad trinkets and ephemera. To one side, there were chairs and an old wooden table, heavily scratched up and looking worse for wear.

Having already arrived ahead of her, the man in leathers reached for her arm and pulled, conducting her a few paces further into the room before she thought to resist. But it was only to make room as Harbud entered through the portal. There was a glow behind him that subsided as he took a step forward and Livet saw etchings that mirrored those on the other side illuminated faintly, then began to fade.

The calm-faced man let go of her arm and began removing his gloves but continued to monitor Livet intensely. "My name is Taringer. Please tell me yours."

Harbud acted a bit impatient but held his tongue for Livet to answer properly.

Livet looked up, not knowing if she should lie–or even what lie she would be able to get away with if she chose to try. Instead, she settled on honesty.

"My name is Livet."

"Of course, it is," Harbud said abruptly and with a raised eyebrow toward Taringer.

"Baressa's not here to confirm," Taringer said. "It's appropriate to ask."

"If not a little late," Harbud mused. He reached into a pocket of his vest and pulled a comb with which he feebly tried to give order to his wild coif.

"Welcome to the Peahen Tavern, Livet. I will advise Gardia that we have returned," he said. "Wait here."

Livet perked up right away at the name of the establishment and its owner. This is where Baressa had told her to come if she needed help. She dropped her hand down and felt for a pocket along a seam in her clothes. It crinkled where she had stashed the old letter from Kell that Baressa gave her. Thankfully, she still had it.

Harbud had not gone far. From behind the bureau, a mature woman, high-cheeked and delicate-featured with piercing eyes and bright red hair, stood up. Her skin was colourless, almost translucent. She wore a gown made from a near-weightless fabric that floated softly when she moved. Livet could only guess as to its luxuriousness and cost.

"This is the girl from Lanstad?" asked Gardia.

The men both nodded.

"She was with Baressa?"

Harbud and Taringer glanced at each other apprehensively, appearing collectively challenged to answer the question.

"We were late arriving to the meeting spot..." Taringer began, but Harbud interrupted him.

"We went to the dungeon entrance next to the jewelry seller, where we planned, but it seems Baressa was already inside. She and the girl ran into some trouble and only the girl escaped."

"Captured?" Gardia asked.

Harbud shrugged noncommittally.

Livet broke the moment's silence to continue the explanation. "The two councilwomen attacked us, but another man came and 'e killed Baressa." She wanted to say more about the man, for he had terrified her so much. She wondered if Gardia knew something about him that would quell her fears.

The proprietress' face lost its glow, becoming stony and grey.

"I'll want to hear everything about what happened to you inside the temple," Gardia said. Then she collected herself and took a step back. She analyzed Livet suspiciously, from head to toe, while the others remained expectantly silent. Reaching for Livet's hands, she took them and examined them with care. They were bleeding after having been fumbling for handholds amid the crumbling rock of the well. Livet had not stopped to realize it during the chase, nor did she notice in the weak light of the alley as they departed the Folds.

With some semblance of sympathy, Gardia guided Livet's hands back to her side. "I'll have someone take care of these cuts," she said, then called out to one of the rooms branching off the outer storeroom, "Please see to this young woman's wounds."

"Taringer, can you bring her here, please?" responded a woman's voice from without.

Heeding the request, Taringer directed Livet to a small room near where they'd arrived. Sitting next to a low bed was a tall, pretty woman whose long dark bangs arced in a widow's peak in the centre of her forehead. Her lips were bright red like cut rubies. Livet noticed that the woman already had another patient, for a large burly man was resting quietly in the bed.

"I'll have a look at you," she said. "My name is Neriah. Who are you?"

"I'm Livet," she murmured with temerity.

"Livet, is it?" she confirmed.

The man beside her stirred, causing Neriah to mutter a brief and profane curse before roughly pushing her other patient back into the bed with authority.

The injured man appeared to be in a great deal of pain, but with a renewed effort he rolled over again, against Neriah's protest, and Livet was able to see him much more clearly. His face and head were bandaged, and his eye sockets were tender and blackened as if they were behind a blotchy purple mask. But when he looked at Livet, she recognized him immediately.

"Olen!" Livet shouted.

"You know this oaf?" Neriah asked, surprised. She curled her lip in an exasperated display of ire.

From the doorway, Gardia stood watching over the impromptu infirmary. The imposing matron frowned as she, too, groaned with disgust.

CHAPTER 20

The Charge

W ith commanding urgency, Denn forced the door open and barged into the room as he heard Ramisa cry out again.

"No! Go away! Leave me!" She flopped and flung her arms about herself, and her thrashing threatened to spill her off the bed.

Hastily taking in all the corners of the room, Denn searched for whomever—or whatever—was terrorizing her. The chamber was dimly lit but not altogether dark. Avenda had left a few candles burning while she went on her errand. But Denn saw nothing except for the princess, who pulled herself up in bed, hands clasped over her ears, her head and neck compressing toward the tops of her knees, squeezing herself into a tight ball.

"Stay away! Stay away!" she pleaded in a tearful petition, but there was no one there save for the princess in her madness.

The thought landed frighteningly on Denn that she was screaming at *him*—that she was crying out for *him* to leave. But every few moments, she would lift her head and glance to the corner of the room as if scared of her own shadow. Something imperceptible or illusory had overtaken her senses.

"My lady, you are safe! There is nothing here to harm you," Denn said to her as he drew close to the bed and tried to attract her attention. He hesitated to touch her, fearing the impropriety, but she was in distress. He took her firmly by the upper arms and held her up, preventing her from slouching back into her position of instinctual protection.

"I can fight you," she said to the air in an exhausted whisper that left her quivering, her words carrying questionable authenticity.

Denn kept her as still as he could until he could examine her. She was transfixed in some kind of nightmare. It was a waking dream, he concluded; that was all. But he felt his skin tingle, and a chill went down his back. It was unnerving the way that the princess focused so clearly on repeated points about the room.

It was then that he saw her oppressors.

Swimming in the milky whiteness of her wide eyes, reflections of faces and forms danced. There they held dominion over her, unsensible to anyone else.

Yael's warning did not prepare him for this.

Suddenly, he turned and saw Avenda streak into the room.

"You need to get out, now!" she directed to Denn.

"I can help!" Denn offered weakly.

She looked hurried and anxious. Denn retreated at once and Avenda took up the spot next to Ramisa. She stroked the princess' forehead and clasped her hand.

"Bar the door," she said to Denn. "Kentin mustn't know."

And thus, Denn fell into their conspiracy. He stationed himself at the doorway, with the portal closed and secured, listening for anyone else who might come up the stairs. He watched Avenda as she administered care to the princess.

"Can you wake her?" Denn asked.

Avenda shot a condescending look toward him. "She *is* awake. Too much awake."

Resuming her focus on the addled princess, she breathed deeply and regularly, her calmness contrasting with the agitation of her tormented mistress. Slowly, however, a placidness was restored. The princess was becalmed and Avenda's presence could be felt encircling the room as if it were a ward. It was an odd sensation, Denn thought.

When everything had ceased, Avenda smiled at Ramisa and whispered, "I've scared them off."

"Is she alright?" Denn asked, uncertain as to what he had just witnessed.

"Yes. Thank you for your concern. I'm not sure that there was much more you could have done but thank you for standing on guard."

So, this was the princess's insanity, he thought to himself. Now he had seen it, but Avenda's role in the matter was a new mystery. A hundred thoughts swam in his brain, including an awareness that he should probably leave the princess' chamber and get to his room, quickly.

"If you need me, I am downstairs," Denn said, excusing himself.

He exited the room and clandestinely stepped back down the staircase, hoping no one else had been awoken or made aware of the incident higher in the tower. Outside the windows, rain was beginning to fall heavily and Denn hoped its forceful tapping may have dulled the sounds from upstairs, if only fractionally.

It was best, he thought, not to mention anything in the morning, or ever. But now he was consumed with questions. Now that he had seen the magnitude of Ramisa's malady, he was afraid. What sort of evil was at its root? Did they really try to hide this from Kentin? How could they? But even if Kentin knew, it was doubtful he would be happy with Denn being also aware of the princess's state. That left silence as the best course to take.

Nonetheless, Denn kept cycling through what he'd seen in his mind all night. And seeing the princess in that bed, crumpled, her dark hair mussed and wrapped around her, it was not a stretch for his mind to wander toward Livet. His first order of business when he was back in Caphedra, would be to make it clear to Livet that there was a danger in such mystical perversions. He did not wish to see her risk a descent into the same dangerous mania—or be the cause of it in others.

It rained fiercely overnight and although the downpour subsided within a couple of hours, it remained drizzly the next morning. The cloud line that perennially sat just atop the northern slope was swollen and encroached upon the ridge, making it difficult to see.

"Keep riding," Denn encouraged the cavalcade of horsemen. "It's a straight line between us and them."

From atop his imposing charger, Denn led the way while Temis and Trin followed closely. Behind them, Captain Saur was able to muster only five more horsemen, since that was all the fresh steeds they had at the tower.

As they rode, Denn spurred Naobe further ahead, hoping to

trigger the expected attack himself, to give those men following him more time to react and facilitate the schemed fallback. With the Eldergorge to their left and cliffs overlooking the Hasen desert to their right, the enemy must be straight in front of them.

He wanted his plan to work, but Denn was nervous and haunted by doubts now. His mind recycled every complaint and criticism he had ever received from his old constable, that bastard Hannellin. But he knew that Saur's men were professionals. They would not let him down.

The more nagging question was whether he had Kentin's confidence. The Lord of Fallowsea was likely the one person here who discounted Denn's fighting prowess more than Denn did himself. The lord's disrespect and petty disparagements, Denn thought, might prove to be the greatest motivation he had to overcome his misgivings that day.

They rode toward the sun. At first, Kentin remained further back, escorting the carriage, and giving all indications that this was Denn's fight to win or lose. But after a short while, he noticed that Kentin had ridden up toward Captain Saur. The lord uttered some commands to his captain and instantly the formation changed. Three of the garrison riders dropped back to provide closer protection to the carriage.

That angered Denn. This battle was not Kentin's undertaking to command. Denn had more training to orchestrate this mounted skirmish than did the lord of a fishing village. He considered bringing the precession to a halt and having it out with his competitor before it was too late.

As Denn had instructed, the carriage was maintaining its distance, but now those three horsemen were farther away and not immediately able to lend support if needed. That left only a three-man wedge of Saur and his two soldiers to reinforce Denn, Trin, and Temis. It was soon too late to make changes, however.

At that moment, the first signs of their interceptors appeared through the cloud. Trin, whose eyes could cut through the fog better than any, was first to announce the warning.

"Rider!" he called out.

Denn slowed to get a better look and the other horsemen followed suit.

"I think he turned around," Trin said.

"Do you think he saw us?" Denn asked.

"Hard to tell," Trin said. "But likely."

"Maybe he's going back to set up an ambush," Temis interjected smartly.

"Then we must advance and draw them out," Denn said, guiding Naobe only a few more steps forward before he pulled on her reins to stop and listen.

It was quiet.

Denn tried to strain his eyesight as best he could, scanning between wisps of clouds as they rolled over the ridge, producing only thin gaps between them to expose the path in front of them.

"Do you want me to go ahead, sir? Trin offered.

"Stay together, but be ready to turn tail when I–" Denn stopped when he heard something. It was like a magnification of the patter of the rain, an unambiguous rumbling from the front.

"Riders! Withdraw now!" Denn shouted as the pounding of horses drew nearer.

Blenksy and Coalsmoke twisted across each other and began galloping back towards the tower. Naobe reared up so monumentally high that she almost broke through the cloud as she stood and pivoted. Then with a smash of the earth, she landed and dug in her tremendous hooves to push off into a hard flight back along the ridge.

He could sense them close behind. There must be at least a dozen in pursuit. He kicked his spurs into Naobe to send her barreling down the ridge toward the spot he had chosen for Saur's men to install their barriers. Horses could not leave the trail, but soldiers could still be sentried on either side and hidden in pockets along the steep downward slopes. Once surrounded on both sides, the enemy riders were to suffer an onslaught of arrowheads and spear points until Denn's party converged upon them to ultimately make the capture or kill.

This finely crafted sequence of events repeated through Denn's mind as he hurried along the clifftop, and he caught up with Temis and Trin just in time to see his plan go wrong.

Kentin, and the three riders he had poached from Saur, had bunched up around the princess' carriage–but at the first hint of action, they'd made the decision to close. Though they were now several lengths ahead, the carriage had advanced much too near to the fight where it had overtaken Denn's ambush site.

Knowing that the enemy riders would now attack the princess' carriage before they were weakened by the concealed garrison troops farther back, Denn was forced to issue a change of orders.

"Protect the carriage!" he shouted.

Turning to face the attackers anew, Trin and Temis followed the order with their partisans levelled and aimed toward the aggressors. Saur and his flankers speedily rose to join them in a charge. They only had a moment to get up to speed.

The horses might buck and bolt at the last moment, but at least it would disperse their adversaries' oncoming assault. Taking up the centre, Denn motioned for his line to sweep into a wedge. The mist was torn open by a line of cobalt-clad Pillarmen five-abreast and two- or three-deep, atop a vaguely controlled stampede of horses.

Denn's line exploded toward their challengers. Heavy dust and curls of mist swirled about their hooves.

Denn sized them up, seeing them outfitted erratically, in a fashion that revealed the motley providence of the Pillar force. They were mercenaries alright. If they could fight, it was doubtful they could do so very well together, much less ride with cohesion.

And none of them sat atop such an unrivalled weapon as he did. Beneath him, the awesome Naobe led the other horses, fervid and energized with unchallengeable power of purpose. All her breeding and rearing set her toward this moment.

And as she consumed the distance between combatants, the rest of her determined brood coursed behind her unfailingly. The other steeds were followed her lead, galloping at a pace that outran any hint of their own fear. Behind Naobe, they too were invincible.

The mounts of the opposing force approached like a thunder squall over the narrow ridge, outnumbering the defenders by at least half. But they did not have the benefit of an unyielding and undefeatable titaness to lead them. As they raced forward, they shifted and twisted against their masters' reins, seeking a way to avoid the imminent destruction of impact.

The Bridgecliff line rolled ahead, decisively quickened as they neared the adversary. Denn leaned forward, his partisan in position to strike the chosen point of impact that would unseat his chosen foe.

Then in the last moment, the enemy wavered.

Two of their horses brushed into each other. Another horse in the back reared up in an abrupt halt and sought to reverse away from the mayhem.

With Naobe leading the charge, Denn's line split through them like an axe head. The enemy's horses panicked and were driven aside, but Denn's Bridgecliff cavalry held fast, their steeds confidently keeping pace behind their matriarch.

The dispersal extinguished much of the fury in the enemy centre. Horses veered to the sides in fearful self-preservation. The width of their formation, no doubt chosen to block anyone from going around them, was a detriment. The Pillarmen on either flank were much too close to the edge. As their steeds attempted to bypass along the extremity, the rain-moistened soil of the northern ridge gave way. It sent them careening off the top into the Eldergorge.

Two horsemen broke through the middle, managing to squeeze past Naobe, but found themselves blocked by the carriage and its circle of protectors led by Kentin. He and another Bridgecliff rider, swords drawn, closed, and launched into them with relentless ferocity, while another continued forth ahead of the carriage, which was rattling onward at an unbroken pace.

Saur, Trin, and Temis, together with the two other Bridgecliff horsemen, each squared off against separate adversaries, slashing and cutting, but they were unable to counter pairs of horsemen on either side who skirted the growing fray and bore down on the carriage and its lone defending rider.

Denn was battling from within the enemy formation, having plunged so effectively into the heart of it. The riders bore down on him immediately. A Pillar horseman rode up along his right, cleaving the air with a long-handled axe.

Then, the formation leader appeared before Denn. This man engaged with a more modestly-sized blade less fit for horseback—a black falchion. The weapon flowed through the space between them as he swung it, more like a shadow of a blade than actual steel. Denn unsheathed his own sword—his uncle Phar's—and he raised it to counter and block. But when the two blades encountered each other, he felt an eerie reverberation run down its length and into his hand.

Denn had seen this man before. He was Wex Sulford, who

had stood for the Faith at the council. Denn had not taken him for a warrior then, but nonetheless, the onyx-coloured weapon would be a devastating tool in anyone's hands. The air shook and shivered for an arm's length around it when he swung.

Denn tried to widen the distance between them. Longlimb gave him a better reach than Sulford had with the falchion. The second horseman, however, moved to block him from his egress. Forced to parry both Sulford and the other attacker, Denn was stymied and endangered when through the corner of his eye, he saw something which would lift the stalemate—but replace it with a terrible new problem.

A wild horse, still hitched to its fearful companion, galloped into their confrontation, dragging the Princess' carriage along behind it.

Denn gasped while Naobe instinctively ambled aside and ploughed the other rider's smaller horse out of the way. But as the carriage went past, Sulford's horse reared. The carriage smashed into the horse, sending the councillor soaring from his saddle.

With his adversaries distracted and off-balance, Denn tugged on Naobe's reins to turn her around and spurred her on after the carriage. With a burst of speed, she galloped up aside the runaway conveyance. Summoning as much strength as he could—and risking a dangerous spill—he swung Longlimb down upon the heel chain and managed to partly separate the terrified carthorses whose continuing pull wrenched the carriage, which twisted and caused its wheel to dig in. The transport lifted off the ground and then crashed, its axles shattering into splinters.

Denn pulled the reins and directed Naobe back to the overturned carriage. He dismounted quickly and raced to pry open its door. Avenda's moon-shaped face appeared in the hole and Denn could see that she was cradling Ramisa against her body. Putting Longlimb into the sheath on his back, he reached in with both hands and lifted the injured princess. She moaned, exhibiting a hint of wakefulness, and Denn hoisted her onto his shoulder.

"Follow the edge of the ridge and keep out of sight," he commanded Avenda. "I'll take the princess to safety."

Atop Naobe, their unmatched stature put them easily in sight of everyone on the battlefield. As three of the Pillar riders broke free of the fight and regrouped, he heard Sulford rally them and shout,

"Wellum! Get Wellum!"

The princess was slumped across Naobe's withers, but he could not hold her and the reins and fight back all at once. So instead, he leaned forward, his body covering the princess's, and put his faith in his steed to carry them through the gauntlet. Unstoppably, Naobe coursed straight toward the blockade.

Clashing steel rang about Denn's ears as they penetrated and pushed forward. Temis and Kentin moved to his defence, hindering the enemy horsemen long enough to force a wider, safer gap through which Denn fled with the endangered heir.

By the time that the remaining Pillar riders caught up with them along the ridge, they were in position for the original ambush to be sprung. Saur's infantry pulled on ropes to tauten nets that rose up and entangled trampling hooves. Once their quarry had been caught and immobilized, a flurry of javelins and crossbow bolts struck. Red blood soiled blue tunics and the riders and horses collapsed in a confusion of carnage. Denn's immediate pursuers were all but massacred.

Denn witnessed the resolution of the attack only briefly. He pressed on until he reached Bridgecliff Tower with Ramisa. Lauded by the garrison soldiers who received them, he dismounted and carried the waking maid aloft into the tower.

Once they were safe inside her chamber, Denn laid the princess down on a mattress of straw and linens, but she squeezed him tightly, refusing to release him. She pulled him closer until he was lying beside her.

He had entered the day full of doubts over his prowess to fight the battle. But it was here, in this moment, that Denn realized how his apprehensions had vanished with faced with the duty of protecting this supposed future queen. He had stepped up to the task, despite any worries of falling short once the engagement began, and now felt an unfamiliar strength in being retained for the lady's purpose.

It was not a clean victory, for it was likely they had lost men. But though Denn was the original target, the outcome served the more essential purpose of safeguarding the princess. Perhaps the Faith did not realize how close they'd come to uncovering and ending Farathemun's rebellion in one simple engagement. Denn only hoped that none of the Pillarmen survived to betray the princess' movements. If his brother had cause to want him dead before, it would be doubly so now.

Next to him, Ramisa jerked and inhaled sharply.

Denn rolled over, pressing her against his chest. He stroked her forehead as Avenda had done. It worked. She fell back to sleep, this time without demons, and shortly after, Denn did likewise.

It was peaceful for only a brief time. Denn awoke to Ramisa fidgeting and distressed again. He pried himself from her grip, got up, and prepared to attend to her. Crossing the floor, he cracked open the door.

"Water," Denn demanded to a guard outside. "And coals to start a fire."

The soldier acknowledged the task crisply and trotted down the stairs to fill the order.

Denn closed the door and gauged how long it would be before Kentin showed up to check on the welfare of his cousin. He had passed out with Ramisa following the scare and upheaval of her rescue from the shattered carriage. Now the princess lay on the bed breathing in fits and seeming to be caught up in the persistent memory of the day's events. If it was something more, he did not want to know. He did not want her to open her eyes in case he might see the tormenting shadows again. Better it was a nightmare, he thought.

Feeling awkward at providing comfort, he held her hand as she tossed, and he whispered more comforting words until her breath regulated and calm settled again upon her slumber. He thought she might be uncomfortable, still wrapped in her riding clothes, but again fearful of the impropriety, he lacked the courage to free her from the garments and chose to prop her up on pillows instead. He wished Avenda would hurry back.

There was a knock at the door; the soldier had returned with a jug of water, a metal washbasin, and a small iron box that housed the embers that Denn had requested.

"Thank you," Denn said.

"If there is anything else, sir, just ask. The men are coming back now, and Lord Farathemun has requested to know the disposition of the Lady Ramisa. What may I tell him, m'lord?"

"Tell him she's alive and resting," Denn said, then added, "You're alright to say 'sir.' I'm not a lord."

"Pardon, sir," the man said while departing and leaving Denn to begin the job of building up a fire.

He blew on the coals until there was crackling from the wood. There was a cough behind him and when he turned, he saw Ramisa's unassuming grey eyes softly observing him.

"A drink? Water?" he asked her.

"You saved me," she said. "I should thank you."

"It is my duty," he said, then added, "and my wish to protect you."

Denn felt it sounded like he was already pledging himself to the bride his father had selected for him. He wondered what it would mean to be a husband to this woman, but such conjecture taxed him. Far from clear was the image of Denn at the head of Ramisa's army of men, marching toward a seat in the royal court of the land. And there was still the question of Livet and what life would he share with her, should they strike out together upon his return to Caphedra?

It occurred to him that if this girl did become queen, Denn would be vindicated for his complicity and absolved. But if he refused the betrothal, parted from her now and was not instrumental in her ascension, what would he become instead? A mercenary? A merchant, like his father? Or worse, if Farathemun failed in placing Ramisa on the throne, Denn would be faced with spending the rest of his life as an outlaw.

"Where is Avenda?" the princess asked.

"She'll be here soon," Denn said, agnostic of the truth to his claim. "I brought you here as quickly as I could."

"You saved me," she repeated, then shook as some tremor briefly seized her. She looked as though a chill ran down her spine, but when it passed, her gentle smile returned.

Denn realized she had caught him staring into her eyes. In the back of his mind, he was still searching them for the vague faces and forms he had seen the previous night, but Ramisa's eyes were empty of anything but admiration and unmistakable fondness. He blushed and she seemed to notice that too.

"Do they talk to you?" she asked, somewhat hazily. "They called to me. They know I am returning. They say I should go to be with my parents."

Denn was pulled back to the awareness that she was still suffering from the dissonance with reality he had seen at their departure from Fallowsea. He tried to restrain his cynical imaginings.

"Once you're rested, we'll resume our journey," Denn told her. Then, careful to not express any signs of tension or pity on his face, he forced a milder tone and tried to better gauge her sanity. "Do you know where we're going and why?"

"My mother's city. Caphedra," she said. "But I don't want to be queen."

Denn detected a hope of lucidity in her statement and was eager for some other glimmering spark of something that would unveil an intact mind buried under her mental infirmity. Instead, Ramisa only offered a laugh that was short, sad, and self-mocking.

Denn reached out again and took her by the hand. This time, she returned his grasp, squeezing tightly and familiarly. "Do you remember Caphedra?" he asked her.

"Yes," she answered. "I remember the castle, the square they named for my uncle, and I remember saying goodbye to my sister and brother. And soldiers. My father had a lot of soldiers. He loved soldiers."

"There are still lots of soldiers there, m'lady," Denn lamented. "They're dressed up a bit differently, but still a great many of them."

"Do the people know I am coming?" Ramisa asked.

"They will."

Then with a doleful tone, she added, "The Paragons know."

"What?" Again, she confused him.

"They were the ones that came to me last night, still angry that I left Caphedra. Now they've gone on to inform the curates."

Denn was under the assumption that once she was removed to Fallowsea, the princess had grown up shielded from the teachings and influence of the Faith. The Paragons were leaders of the Faith who had died long ago but came to be held up as exemplars for their adherence to the principles of the Pillars. Each had come to hold lofty positions in the hierarchy of their philosophy and were invoked by the creed's followers as pseudo gods. But they had all died long before Ramisa was even born, so her reference confounded him as to why she would name them as her ghostly harassers. Perhaps, it was just the legacy of her childhood indoctrination.

"It was just a dream," Denn consoled her. "I am here with you now. There are no demons, m'lady."

She nodded, nestled her head on his shoulder, and closed her eyes.

"I know," she said. "I told you, they've gone and are waiting for me in Caphedra."

She rested, but the eeriness of her words about the Faith removed all remaining drowsiness from Denn. He watched her until he was sure she was comfortably composed and asleep.

Just then, there was a knock on the door. Without waiting for Denn's response, one of the tower guards called out, "Your men are back, sir. One of them is hurt quite badly."

Denn quietly berated himself for the brief indulgence of hoping it was Temis. He urged himself to remember that it was Temis' information and efforts to warn him that saved him from being murdered by Wex Sulford and his men today. Temis fought well beside him also. In fact, he and Trin had comported themselves quite excellently in the fight.

Getting quietly to his feet, Denn dared to leave the princess' side long enough to answer the soldier's call and prepare for the worst. He opened the door a crack and slipped through.

"Take me to him."

The soldier led Denn to a room several floors below in the tower. Captain Saur stood in one corner while Temis was sitting sentry over a bed soaked in blood. Trin was lying upon the sheets, his face pale and body convulsing. He was saying words, but they were unintelligible.

"Did you see that sword that Wex Sulford was swinging around?" Temis asked.

"The black blade?" Denn asked and Temis nodded.

"These wounds," Temis pointed to Trin's injuries then finished in a whisper, "they won't heal up."

"Cursed?" Denn said, his heart sinking from an immediate feeling of helplessness.

Temis gave another nod.

Both knew that Trin would be dead within the night if something was not done. The gory, defiled bedsheets attested to it.

"Where is the blade now?" Denn asked.

Captain Saur produced an old, beaten wooden case and opened it carefully at the hinges to reveal the shining black falchion that Wex Sulford had wielded in the fight.

"We were scared to touch it," he said.

Trin moaned and the bleeding persisted despite the rings of tourniquets administered to stop the flow. A discolouration was setting in around his wounds, bearing varying shades of hues from sickly yellow to an already gangrenous violet.

Denn placed his fingers on the sword's hilt. He could sense the blade disliked his touch, but nothing terrible happened. Bravely, he lifted it, this time flipping it over to see engravings that ran along the edge of the blade. An inscribed incantation read, '*That the Faithless be emptied of hope, heart, and vein.*'

"Do we need to call a curate?" Temis asked. "I think the last one is lying dead several lengths to the east of here."

CHAPTER 21
Legacy of Lanstad

A t first, Olen's countenance soared at the sound of Livet's voice. There was warmth, affection, and a grateful recognition in the way she called his name. But he was surrounded by people who thought far less of his misplaced bravado and incurable bullheadedness. He feared their condemnations would spread to the young girl that he had befriended in the Fals, and who cherished him. Embarrassment consumed Olen, and he did not welcome Livet seeing him in this manner.

His foolish run at the Half Moon left him broken and badly beaten. He had squandered the admiration of Effie, too, and who was now nowhere to be seen. The other boys still checked in on him at the Peahen—Asher and Kalden—but they had told Olen that Effie was overcome with worry that his sisters would receive a vengeful backlash over the poorly planned raid, and he refused to come by.

Worse still, Neriah—against her wishes—had been compelled to risk her own life and security to drag him to the safety of her friends who were profoundly unimpressed with this turn of events. Now, she was forced into nursing his wounds while berating him for the whole idiotic escapade which had cost her, and everyone who relied on her.

Neriah had worked as a hostess at the Karaval's tavern since she was young, and rose in stature there on account of her natural good looks and charm. She had not told anyone there that she was a member of the same Kierk family that the crime lords of the Half Moon had driven into assumed extinction.

She had voluntarily left her background behind her at the Black Eel when she surrendered the key to the family house, not wanting to be ever caught with it. She had never really expected her mythical uncle would ever return from the army, but to continue working at the Half Moon, the Karavals demanded that she live inside their sordid den, under their constant watch, and she accepted. It would keep her safe, and it fitted with the needs of her only other protector, Gardia. Neriah had been Gardia's most important mole. She was a pipeline of information that enabled a safe gap to be maintained between the two Faralley drinking establishments, and their respective stables of streetfighters and champions.

"How many days did it take for you... once you returned to Caphedra?" Neriah asked Olen while she was cleaning blood from Livet's fingers and smoothing out the girl's nails where they had been torn and cut.

"Eh?" responded Olen.

"I asked you how many days it took for you to march into this city and try to rekindle a war!"

With shame, Olen blushed beneath his bruised cheeks. His niece then began directing her tirade toward Livet, ignoring her first patient's stammering and mumbling.

"Gone for more than a decade, and despite all of the old troubles we had, the first thing he does when he comes home is to offer himself up to getting slaughtered–just like my father, and my grandfather, and everyone else!"

Reflections from lamplight betrayed the tears welling up in Neriah's eyes, but none fell.

"I'm sorry," Olen said for the hundredth time. Even his eyes were dampened, but ultimately, any display of remorse was backstopped by the joy of knowing his niece was alive. Not all his family was dead. He desperately wished that Neriah would give a hint that somewhere, deep down, she felt the same.

"Well, they know she's one of you damned Kierks now," seethed a voice from the doorway. "No good to send her back there again."

Gardia entered the room and settled down to review her guests like a lioness sizing up prey. She lifted some of Olen's bandages and poked fingers into his side, which made him recoil in pain, such that he was not sure if she was assessing him–or taking revenge.

Olen swallowed nervously.

"Are you not using the ointment as I instructed?" she asked Neriah.

The aspiring healer produced a small tub of beige-coloured paste. "I made it last night—like you showed me."

"Give us a sniff," she said. Taking the container, she waved it around under her nose. "Not enough roseroot."

She took a pinch and checked the consistency by running small circles between her thumb and first two fingers. "More black dendril."

Neriah frowned and offered to make another batch, but Gardia stopped her.

"I have something else, she said, pulling out a flask that had been tucked into a fold in her blouse. She passed it to Neriah, who removed the stopper and examined it. A waft of assaulting aromatics expanded toward Olen's nostrils immediately.

Appearing satisfied, and vouching for its efficacity, Neriah handed him the vial. "Drink up, Uncle," she said.

Olen trusted her, so he did. The mixture was thick, almost congealed, and slipped out of the vial to slither down his throat, tasting powerfully of woody, bitter botanical tones.

Gardia now moved along to sizing up the quiet, dark-haired lurker beside him. Livet was hunched on a wooden armchair, clasping her hands together and observing everything.

"Does your family have a name? Another history to worry about?" Gardia asked her.

"Karr," she said.

Gardia raised an eyebrow and suppressed a narrow glimmer of amusement. "You took on his name? Baressa never mentioned that."

"Baressa didn't ask me. She seemed t'know I'd been with Kell all along," Livet said. "What other name could I take?"

"It's her natural talent. Baressa has prophetic dreams and meeting you was one of them. I'd asked her to go to Lanstad on an errand, then she told me about a vision of a girl that she had." Gardia appeared to pause with sombre sentiment at the recollection. "She insisted you were connected somehow."

Gently with her fingers, Livet reached into her bodice and retrieved an old scrap of parchment. She held it between herself and

Gardia. "Did this have somethin' t' do with your errand? What were you looking for?"

"You have the letter I gave to Baressa," Gardia acknowledged.

"She gave this to me to show you, if we ever met," Livet explained. "Proof should I come here without her."

"So she did." Gardia plucked the letter from Livet's fingers. "I am satisfied." For a moment it looked as if she might crumple the letter, but she paused and slipped it soundly into a fold in her dress. "I regret that Harbud and Taringer were supposed to meet you earlier. Baressa had already informed us of what the two of you would be undertaking, so I sent them to your aid."

"They were not there in time," Livet replied, indicting them over their failure.

"You weren't at the entrance that Baressa told us about. They did not expect you would be able to gain entry to the temple so quickly. They had no idea that you found another way inside—until they heard the commotion. But as a student of Kell's, I should have anticipated it."

Livet's head slumped, and her cheeks were ringed with trails of falling tears. "They killed Baressa," Livet said.

Olen was overcome with confusion. Who killed Baressa? He had been so preoccupied with his own failings that he had not properly addressed the terrible ordeal that brought Livet here.

"Are you sure?" Gardia asked.

"The man and the council ladies—I'd seen the two women at the council meeting. When we ran, they just pulled 'er back through the air, and the man killed 'er."

Olen tried to sit up and reach out for Livet's hand to calm his friend, but she failed to notice and continued wringing her hands as she sat.

"Who was the man?" Gardia pressed.

"It was very dark. I just saw 'is eyes glowin' and the shape of 'im. He picked 'er up and dropped 'er down again, dead. She'd screamed, then nothing."

The door creaked. Someone was standing behind it, listening, but gave themselves away with discontented muttering at Livet's retelling of the attack on Baressa. Gardia acknowledged the eavesdropper with a clearing of her throat, then invited Harbud into the room. "Did you see any of this?" she asked him.

"No," Harbud said. "But we saw the big hole that they made, trying to suck them back into the temple. It was highly fateful that I had Taringer there with me, to at least pull this poor maid out to safety."

"Fortune favoured us," came the voice of Taringer from the hall where he, too, was listening.

"Not so much that we could arrive in time to retrieve Baressa. She was relying on our assistance, but we did not find her in time." Harbud dropped down tiredly onto a chair with his arms draped over it, as if someone had hung a wet jacket there.

Turning to Livet again, Gardia softened. "I'd like to learn more about the people in the temple," she said. "Apparently, Taringer's not alone in controlling such powers as his, if it's true that he was in a tug-of-war with another so-learned soul, on your way out of the dungeon."

"It is rather unnerving to hear of someone else with that particular talent," Harbud added.

Gardia nodded gravely. "Such disciplines are highly unlikely to be stumbled upon separately. Discovering new realms is not a simple task and not one that many dedicants have cause or opportunity to pursue. Knowledge of the realms is more likely to be passed on. Either they are taught willingly, or their secrets are stolen."

"It was the long-haired woman from the council, Kabra," Livet told them.

"So, the Faith is teaching councillors to conjure now?" Harbud mused. "The ability to cast spells is quite the reward for casting a few favourable votes."

"In the end, it only took one vote to put Ravon on the throne, and I doubt we'll see many more votes held hereafter," said Neriah.

"I'll ask my brother Hull about her. He attends council regularly and will know what her background is." Gardia stood and walked toward the doorway as if to leave. Then she stopped and gently, through the open crack of the door, called out, "Taringer. Please come here."

The young, serious-faced sorcerer who had saved Livet stepped into the room.

"Your teacher died a long time ago, yes?" Gardia asked.

"He did," Taringer answered.

"And you've never taken on an apprentice, have you?"

"Correct," Taringer said.

"Never taught anyone how to draw so much as a breeze from the Sylphan Realm?" Gardia interrogated further.

"Just Kell," he said. "I helped him so that he could operate a forge without a bellows. I thought it useful after he and Edrum had parted ways. No *formal* apprentices, though, if that's what you wish to know."

"I can't imagine Kell sharing such things with the Faith. Pray they have not found his refuge before us," Gardia said. "If so, I hope they haven't found his grimoire amongst his trove of treasures."

"We lived in the catacombs beneath the city. That was all. No lair full of treasures. Is that what you were lookin' for in Lanstad? Some kind of lair?" Livet referenced the mysterious letter once again.

"No," Harbud said. "Well... yes."

Livet looked at him.

"Yes, we were looking for his lair... his *workshop*." He wrinkled his face, making his sideburns twitch as he corrected himself. "But that was not supposed to be among the crypts of Lanstad. Kell was foremost an artisan, not a gravedigger—at least not at first. He had a Fal forge where he worked alongside a blacksmith, and together they performed their craft. They made lots of very curious trinkets for some very exceptional people. Edrum, the partner, worked the furnace while Kell etched in the designs, cut the gems, and shaped the glass. They used the Fal forge to achieve absolute precision and perfect their craft."

"But he and his partner had a disagreement," Taringer said. "It was such that Kell left Lanstad and came here, which is when we met him and shared a few... ideas."

Harbud gathered himself up and straightened the creases in his vest. "Eventually, we suggested that he consider returning to work on his own. Through various enchantments, the forge could be run single-handedly and with Taringer's ability to enchant the airflow, the flames would probably run hotter than ever before—to forge items of even greater accuracy and application, otherwise un-manufacturable by mortals."

"He also confided that he left behind a huge cache of

previously-forged masterpieces," Taringer added.

"Not to mention the financial proceeds of his craft from over the years." Harbud sighed wistfully.

"What sort of items?" Livet asked. "Glassworks, like Baressa showed me?"

"Yes, and metalcraft," Taringer said.

"But such items require exceptional materials and demand exceptional secrecy, said Harbud.

"This is why Kell relied on thievery," Gardia explained somewhat resentfully.

"He stole to survive," Livet defended. "We all did."

Harbud grunted disparagingly. "He stole to feed his craft with a supply of gems, gold and silver. He distrusted moneychangers and merchants, so no one knew how much work he and his partner were producing."

"Livet, you must understand how special Kell's creations were. I don't know how much you learned from him, but a lot of the talents he taught to you—and us—were mirrored in his creations," Gardia said. "He instilled them with qualities that went beyond the simple, into the magical."

"Were he and Edrum both enchanters?" asked Livet.

"No, just Kell," said Taringer. "He would put the finishing touches on the items to endow them with their qualities... at least at first."

Olen caught Gardia level a warning look at Taringer, who continued but bowed his head slightly, and stared off into the wall as he spoke.

"He eventually did take on an apprentice, but it didn't go well. It caused him to leave the forge and come to Caphedra, where he met all of us," Taringer recounted.

"And then left us," Gardia said. "It's true that we suggested he return to reclaim his work, but he found his own reason to remain afterward. He had promised to come back."

"Was that the last time you saw 'im?" Livet asked.

"Yes." Her face was expressionless but said everything. "I imagine by then he'd taken you on as his ward and was content to remain in Lanstad with his little pack of swindlers and thieves."

"Holed up in the tombs and crypts," Harbud said, shaking his head. "Why? He had money stashed away and could have fled

Lanstad. He could have come back here. Why didn't he?"

Taringer spoke up. "The Faith of the Pillars had already started rooting out dissenters and apostates here in Caphedra, and Kell likely ran into them in Lanstad too. Martan Vlass was made Lord Mayor of Lanstad around that time and he welcomed the Faith into the city, hoping they'd build a temple to rival the one in Caphedra."

As if tiptoeing around Gardia, Harbud continued. "With so many curates in the city, it was only a matter of time before they started purging Lanstad as they did here—and they were quite thorough. Caphedra would have been safer, ironically."

"What happened to his apprentice?" Livet asked.

"If you did not know of her," Gardia said, "then perhaps they never met again."

Livet also seemed desirous to treat the matron's mood delicately, so she spoke to Harbud. "Why did you say Caphedra would have been safer?"

"King Ramis allowed the Faith to conduct its business here, but he kept them mostly in line. Queen Tressa had once been very devout, but Ramis distrusted priests. During the years he was alive, he never permitted such widespread hunting of apostates by the Faith as is happening now," explained Harbud. "But without the king to keep them restrained, their perniciousness flourishes."

"What you experienced in Lanstad is beginning here. Perhaps far worse," Gardia warned. "They will locate and dislodge the disloyal. Every peasant will be squeezed dry of all they own until they have only blood and flesh to give. All enchanters will find themselves hunted, like the Jerozi of old, throughout this world and all others, wherever they seek to hide."

Olen groaned and reached for a damp cloth to put over his eyes and hide the sights of the crowded room. Then he lamented to Neriah with a hint of incredulity, "You've brought me to a den of sorcerers? Traded one mark on my head for another?"

Neriah poked him. "You're no sorcerer—though you're a blundering liability in your own right."

Gardia appeared not unaware that she was the object of attention so she summed up, "I heard of Kell's arrest and death, and I was seeking his old workshop—not for what others have accused me of—but so that his tools and creations would not fall into the

Faith's hands. We simply had no idea where it was. Baressa was helping to narrow down the place through her dreams, but even she could not locate it. We presumed Kell had told no one until we learned of your survival. We hoped he might have shown you where it was."

"There were others," Livet said, "but they're gone too. As I was the youngest, the Precept said he'd give me mercy and let me go when he was done with me... but that... wasn't right away."

Livet sat back in her seat with her arms crossed. Olen could tell she was on the verge of disappearing again into the darkness of her recollections. To relieve the pressures of attention that weighed upon her, he chose this moment to contribute to the discussion.

"I've seen the remnants of some of those forges in the swamps of Fal Ghreeg and Fal Margoon, Olen said. "I was told my sword came from one of them."

Taringer reached out. "May I see the sword?"

Olen's pain was now lessening after the draught from Gardia's flask. He sat up in bed and reached down to where his scabbard was lying. Neriah had threatened to move it further away from him when he first arrived but upon figuring Olen was a far greater danger to himself than any of them, she relented and left it handy. Drawing the blade from its housing, he passed Coldswept over to Taringer, who studied it, twisting the sword in the light and causing its jewelled hilt to twinkle.

"The iron in the steel seems like it's from the Drott mine on the road to Palinor. Other metals in the inlay and decoration are likely from Northport's Old Bear mine, or Hepashim near Hasen. Not sure where these sapphires are from, but likely the hills around Wodwarden. To be truthful, it's in a style that I've seen before in Edrum's work."

"Metals. Gems. Are you a smith? A jeweller?" Olen asked.

Taringer nodded. "Smith. My father, Whitinger Surt, was the former Lord of Harthal Vale until King Ramis ordered our lands dispersed and sent troops in with an army to take it from us. He granted our ancestral land to Paxton Remm. Before then, we had come from a long line of miners and metal crafters known throughout the mountains and valleys around Palinor. As a boy, while my brother learned swordplay, I squired for him. I learned a lot about weapon craft, embraced it and pushed farther, petitioning our father to have me trained as a smith."

"But with your power, why couldn't you just fight with magic an' take back your home?" asked Livet.

Taringer, whose face never changed expression, blandly responded, "I was young, and my powers still required a lot of practice to perfect. That came later, here, under the guidance and aid of my friends. But now, my brother Winager is the Lord now that my father's dead, and when he's ready to move against Remm, you are correct that I will be there to aid him. Though I am afraid that will be some more distant day."

Taringer handed Coldswept to Harbud, who almost dropped it.

"Heavy, isn't it," Harbud observed, and with exaggerated effort, brought it up with both hands to examine the weapon before finally admitting, "I can't tell if it's Kell's work or not. The engravings seem to point to someone else. A competitor, perhaps?" suggested Harbud.

"Another student?" Taringer postulated.

Olen could have sworn he saw Gardia grit her teeth and heard her whisper, "A lover."

"Who told you it came from a Fal forge?" Harbud asked.

It was all that Olen could do to not sound boastful. "Lord Vlass," he answered.

Harbud arched an eyebrow.

"Well, one of his men did." Olen retrieved his blade and held it up to reflect the candlelight. "Spoils from the night we took Fal Ghreeg... I thought it the most beautiful sword I'd ever seen, and it seems that it caught the lord's interest, too. I overheard his men discussing. I've always felt there was something strange in the blade. I feel it sing and dance a bit, whenever it takes a life."

"At the moment of death, then?" Harbud iterated as if postulating the weapon's intent, but his speculation was cut short.

"The work is too similar." Gardia's scorn for the sword's anonymous creator did not fade from her face quickly as she readied another barrage of questions for Livet. "Are you sure he had no other apprentices? Can you think of nowhere that Kell might have kept his notes or housed his projects? He must have safeguarded his grimoire and even likely added to it. Where is it hidden?"

Gardia squeezed her fingers together and clenched her fists.

Her words issued forth faster than Livet could keep up, leaving the poor girl to stutter and choke.

She continued, "As the Faith grows stronger, we will need all the advantages we can get to remain outside their grasp. I worry how long we can even remain in Caphedra now that they've plopped their little plaything onto the throne."

Harbud interrupted. "With Ravon, the best we can hope for is that her brother and his army can knock the crown off her head and cleanse the city of those blue-backed tyrants for good."

"The Marshal doesn't have enough soldiers," Olen said. "Lord Vlass's troops have come to reinforce those of the Faith. Lord Drohen has stood up all the armsmen of the Caphedran prefectures and they have control over the citadel. Now I learn they have curates who can even cast spells to destroy the streets under our feet!"

"We don't know the extent of enchantments they've amassed or how many of their number are proficient in casting or conjuring them," Gardia said.

Taringer added his voice. "It's still going to be a fair wager on which side wins. The Lord Marshal has help from Lord Kullan of Wodwarden. Quite likely, he can draw from Sentor in Bren Hills, Sunder in Palinor, or any of the lords and chiefs in Greyforest. Remm will likely send soldiers from Harthal Vale, too. I heard that even men in the southern brigades were breaking ranks to march north on the mere whisper that Myrhic was recruiting."

"Once the Marshal's army is assembled, he still has to breach the city walls and make his way to the castle, all while coming under attack from the battlements," Olen reminded him. "They'll be made to struggle for every step forward."

"Maybe it's not so difficult to get in if you have people on the inside. What about the Marshal's Men?" commented Livet, subterfuge being the one matter that suited her mastery.

"It doesn't matter. The citadel is secure. It always has been. Rebellion was never possible," Olen said, refusing to acquiesce to her point of dissent. "Never you mind the citadel, I've witnessed hundreds of foolish men pit themselves against Ramis's garrisons, only to learn that lesson at the cost of their lives. I've dragged a good many off to a funeral pyre myself!"

"But isn't Myrhic's army made up of the same men that fought beside you–not against you?" Taringer asked.

"His army is made up of mercenaries fighting for plunder. My brothers fought for king and kingdom. We fought against anarchy, not to cause it," Olen.

Harbud ventured to disagree. "The cities you conquered were not uncivilized wastelands, you know. To say that you fought anarchy is to suggest something completely different from the truth."

Olen started to stand up, but Neriah stopped him. "Olen, rest."

Struggling to choke down more words in response, Olen nonetheless accepted his niece's guidance. She was right. There was no need to let his temper get the better of him. These men were not entirely wrong. He slid again into bed, quieted and seeking comfort over confrontation.

Livet brushed her fingers through his hair and smiled. Olen was thankful to have her near him again. Neriah was his long-lost niece, but Livet felt just as much or more like family. Still, he could tell that she remained unsettled. She was sweating and looked nervous. Something was on her mind. She took a few deep breaths then cleared her throat.

"Gardia," Livet said. "When I was in the temple, Kell spoke to me, and I think I saw him."

"What do you mean?" Harbud twisted around in his chair more directly to speak to her. "He's dead. We were told that died in the Pillar dungeon at Lanstad."

It took a moment, but Gardia responded thoughtfully. "Sometimes we carry our ghosts with us. Was it in your mind, perhaps? What did you see or hear him say, Livet?"

"Not just a ghost," Livet said. "I think they kept his body. Well, it's jus' bones now—but somehow, 'e's alive. There were bones in boxes and corpses hanging from chains in the dungeon, rattling and shaking. Then I heard Kell. I heard 'im speaking to me when I was there... asking that I find a way to free 'im somehow."

"Grotesque," Harbud said, with a revolted look on his face. "Why are they keeping the bodies? Necromancy? The dead don't belong here, whether they wish to return or not."

"Just a ghost, I'm sure," Gardia said, but her words lacked enough sincerity to provide any ease.

"What if you ask his ghost where he kept his workshop

hidden?" Livet suggested, shivering a little.

"You said it was inside the dungeon here in Caphedra. Are you willing to speak to it again?" Gardia asked Livet. "If we can get you in there, that is?"

Eyes widening in panic, Livet answered, "No! That's not what I meant. One of you, I thought—"

"Maybe she doesn't have to go all the way in," said Taringer. "How far in were you when you first heard his voice?"

"Before the chamber, but not until I was under the temple," Livet said. "I shouldn't 'ave said anythin'. I don't want t' go back in there. That's where Baressa died! And I spent enough time in their dungeons in Lanstad. One of you could try t' help Kell. You were his friends, too, right?"

Gardia nodded. "Yes. But perhaps you knew him better."

Sitting up again in the bed, Olen braced himself and tried to rise to her defence. "If she doesn't want to go, then she doesn't have to," he said protectively. It seemed to ease the concern on Livet's face to have an ally.

"That's true. She doesn't have to," said Gardia, betraying her dissatisfaction with a curl of her lip. "We won't force you, but this is something that begs investigation."

Harbud and Taringer nodded in agreement.

CHAPTER 22

Squire's Rest

Hope dissolved. As surely as the blade's inscription had pronounced, Trin was dying. The once victorious day was ending in miserable defeat and imminent loss.

When Denn excused himself and departed Trin's chamber, the boy was perishing in his own, drained, fluids. Seepage stained the bedclothes and formed congealed puddles on the floor. His coughing and gasping had slowed, his lungs lacking the strength to pump with any degree of vigour.

Taking his leave, Denn left the vigil. He sought to address another matter—another presumed death—the outcome from which, likewise, weighed heavily upon him.

Avenda had still not returned.

Horsemen had reported that they had seen no sign of her and feared she had ended up over the side of the cliff.

As Ramisa laboured under the pains of this recent trauma, Denn worried that the demons which encircled her before may revisit at any time and overwhelm the princess entirely without her dedicated attendant to stand in their way. So far, all was quiet.

The tower was dismal and uninviting as Denn perambulated its spirals, winding his way first to Kentin's study. As he approached, he could see the firelight spreading around the corner, filling the crevices of the stone walls, growing then shrinking in shimmering, golden respirations. From the comfort of a spongy wing-backed chair, the lord's two stockinged feet protruded and pointed toward the warmth-giving flames.

Denn announced himself with a cough.

"Wellum," acknowledged the lord. "How's your man?"

Denn answered glumly. "He's not moving. Asleep maybe. He is beyond the point where he seems to feel any suffering. I expect his passing within the hour."

"That's a shame," Kentin said, his tone unaltered.

"It's a shame that things did not go according to plan," Denn said. "You moved the men around and went against what we discussed. It set things out of place."

"We can't always expect everything to turn out as we anticipate, Denn," responded Kentin. "But *you're* still standing, and that accounts for most of your plan, yes?"

"I gave direction for the carriage to stay back and armed riders to be at the front. Why did you dare to change that? It risked catastrophe. The princess could have been killed!"

He saw Kentin's fingers tighten as he gripped the arms of the chair. "I corrected your oversight," Kentin said.

"There was no oversight. Had the carriage stayed back, we could have dispatched the attackers before the princess even got in sight of them."

Kentin withdrew his feet from the fire and planted them on the floor. He leaned forward in his chair and levelled a disapproving stare at Denn.

"Am I to heed the wisdom of a man who lost half his army in one day? Somehow, I do not share your confidence. Had you brought more men to deal with your own problems, from the onset, you would not have had to gamble the princess's life to preserve your own. It's a shame about the boy, but I am thankful that today's losses were so minimal."

"You call my strategy a gamble? All battle is a gamble, but my plan would have kept the princess's carriage safely to the rear. Now we've lost the carriage and I believe, sadly, that we've lost Avenda too. Doesn't that bother you?"

"Such misfortunate rests entirely on your head," accused Kentin.

Denn clenched his teeth and took a step closer. The fire lit his face and highlighted the outrage that was swelling up inside him. He wanted to face Kentin squarely while they were speaking and drew closer. He reached out, pressing against one of the winged sides of the chair which was as close to levelling a push against Kentin's shoulder as he could get away with. Kentin leaned forward, refusing to shrink back, and spoke directly into Denn's face with mutual animosity.

"You explained with certainty that those men came to kill *you*."

From the corner of his eye, Denn saw a spark of orange hovering beside the chair. Looking down, Denn realized that Kentin held an iron poker in his hand. The tip wavered in the air as he went on.

"You wanted to station my men at the front of the charge, for *your* protection!" Kentin bristled. "You didn't give a damn about the safety of the carriage or the ladies inside!"

"I came to Fallowsea to escort her safely back to your father. I have no intention to fail at that task."

"Yes, of course, you'll take her back. You're promised to marry—and you covet a lordship. You seek fame. My father always said that about you... *Your father* always said that about you! When he wouldn't give you the satisfaction, you ran off from home and thought you'd be made a high constable on your own merits—yet you barely ascended above the rank of stable boy, didn't you?"

Denn pulled back, smarting over the insult. He released the wing of the chair and balled his fingers into a fist. He would not be made to feel shame from these insinuations.

"At least when faced with a fight, I didn't buy my way to victory," Denn said. "You should have paid more for your land. Maybe then the locals would smile more often whenever you ride past!"

Kentin waved the poker in the air, then plunged it into the fire and took out his temper on a helpless log. Sparks flew back and like the hapless coals, he smouldered in his chair as he replied.

"You're an expert on wealth and conduct now? You fancy yourself to be quite a sage today, it seems. Let me give you some wisdom in kind, Wellum." Kentin stabbed again at the log. "Heed my words. Don't be too quick to spend the dowry."

Awash with loathing, Denn reeled his anger back and overcame the desire to avenge his pride. He still had a purpose in coming here, after all, and it required Kentin's consent and cooperation. Despite Kentin's verbal scourging, Denn softened his voice, and rather than risking the semblance of begging for himself, he hid behind the princess's name as he maneuvered their conversation.

"The Lady Ramisa's attendant," he said. "Am I to understand that she has not returned?"

Kentin grunted.

"I am taken to understand that the princess can not continue without her attendant." Denn wished to lodge the request while honouring his promise to keep Ramisa's recent episode in confidence. Denn did not know the degree to which Kentin was aware of the current state of the princess's condition, but the way Avenda urged secrecy suggested that it garnered no sympathy.

"Her return at this late juncture holds little promise. The loss of her handmaiden may be something my cousin may be forced to accept," said Kentin.

"Avenda had a sister who also aided Ramisa. We should send for her right away."

"Jokira? That humourless hag?!" Kentin said bluntly. "No. I wouldn't waste a rider to go back for her and let her drain the last measly bits of pleasure from our party. Absolutely not."

"The princess must have someone to travel beside her," Denn ordered. "Avenda is not here, and I understand the sister to be the only replacement."

"Understand that *you* will have to look after the princess. It might make for good practice before the marriage, should your father make good on his promise to contribute to our army—and lest my father hears any worrying accounts that might make him disapprove of you in the meantime." The latter came across as if Kentin was threatening to malign Denn himself. The Lord of Fallowsea stirred the coals and stoked the fire, then made his decree. "From here onward, you can ride in the rear file with her on your horse."

"My horse?" Denn asked.

"As you pointed out, her carriage is smashed beyond repair," Kentin said. "Your warhorse is the largest beast in our stable. It is only natural that you'll have to give up part of your saddle. Besides, your mount looks brave enough to carry her."

"She could ride on Blenksy. Trin won't be going back with us—not as he is."

"That horse of Trin's is hurt, too," said Kentin. "She won't be leaving the stable for a while."

Denn frowned. He hadn't thought that Trin's mount might have also gotten injured along with her rider. "Is there not another horse for Ramisa to ride?"

"Besides our mounts? As it is, I can only spare two fresh horses and my men will be riding them. The princess is unable to take the reins, anyway."

"Perhaps she could learn?" Denn said, pushing the point with final futility.

"It's not that simple. You know that horses are sensitive creatures, and they sense when something's wrong. Whatever afflicts my cousin spooks them terribly. She can't ride because of it. They would always buck and throw her from the saddle whenever she tried."

"Yet you think that Naobe will be fine with her?"

"Your horse doesn't seem to fear anything," the lord praised. "As long as you share the saddle, I expect you can keep both of them quiet, at least until we get to Caphedra. It is mostly downhill now. I'd say it will take us a day and a half since we don't have to slow down for the carriage."

Just then, a shadow interrupted the flickering light. Captain Saur entered the room and with a quick, respectful nod to Kentin and the uttering of "m'lord," in greeting, he gave his report to Denn.

"Mr. Wellum, I came to tell you that Trin is near death. We've not been able to stop the bleeding, and I thought you'd like to be with him when he passed."

With this, Kentin's face drew long and genuinely remorseful. "Go see your man off," he directed. "You should be there for him."

With reluctance, Denn pardoned himself from the room and ascended to Trin's chamber. Saur followed somberly.

Everything in the room was quiet save for the sounds that escaped the body on the bed. Trin's lungs gurgled as the last wisps of air breezed through them. His body was white as chalk, for it barely held more than a few spoonfuls of blood which coursed thin and languidly in his veins then escaped through his wound. His final moments were short and wordless. When his breathing ceased, Denn reached over and folded Trin's hands over his bestilled chest.

That action invoked some disturbance from the deathbed. Denn stepped back. From the corner of his eye, a shape like a hoary shadow appeared to manifest and circle the room. Briefly, it drifted near the motionless corpse. It circled Denn once before following the ascending smoke trails of burning candles and dissipating beneath the sooty ceiling.

One of the guards swallowed hard, with his voice pronouncedly elevated. "Did I just see a..." but failed to finish his thought. The others glanced at each other speechlessly.

After a suitable time had passed, the hush was broken by a heartfelt request by Captain Saur. "Sir, the men of the old Thirteenth have a small stand of trees picked out on the hillside here. It serves as a burial plot for our brothers. With your consent, we'd be pleased to have him interred there."

Denn nodded. "Find him a nice spot with his fellows."

"We will, sir," the captain answered, then stepped back out of the room, sortieing off to inform the rest of his company. A moment later, two more Bridgecliff guards took up positions next to the corpse.

Realizing he was feeling exhausted, Denn climbed the staircase and retreated secretly to his chamber before sorrow overcame him.

Trin had died to save Denn. It was no more complicated than that. Kentin's words condemned Denn to a burden of guilt that weighed like a millstone. He felt like collapsing. His stomach churned with the inescapable feeling of failure and the shame that arose from the accusation that he had sought only to reward himself with laurels of fame and accomplishment. It wrenched him inside, as the thoughts welled up within. His innards twisted upon themselves.

He was going to throw up.

Desperately, he stumbled backwards on his heels, trying to close the door while his hand reached out for a basin or a bucket—whatever he could find.

Then, instantly, a new shock struck upon him. The lump of bile that had sought to eject itself through his throat plummeted back down into the pit of his gut and lodged itself securely in place.

He was not alone in his chamber. Staring at him from across the room, sitting upon his bed, was the face of the Lady Ramisa appearing before a halo of diffused candlelight. She watched him in silence.

"M'lady," he said, swallowing with difficulty.

She pressed her finger to her lips to communicate that they should be quiet, and Denn nodded, aware that this time they were much closer to where Kentin could overhear them. He had already likely indited himself by making such a racket in clamouring to shut the door.

Lowering her eyes, Ramisa offered her condolences for Trin. "I'm sorry that the boy died," she said. "I came to see if you were alright."

"Just now, yes. You heard the news already? From Saur?" Denn asked.

"No. I just knew," Ramisa said, reaching out for him, and taking a bold step to invite him down beside her on the bed. Denn was uncertain but he was driven by both curiosity and the revelation that he found her voice soothing right now. He asked, "How did you learn that he died?"

"His passing awoke me," she said. "At first, I thought it was the Paragons returning. I felt something wash over the room. It was unsettling."

"What of Avenda?" Denn asked, instantly worried that he sounded too direct, but wanted to know if a similar omen had presented itself concerning her attendant. "Is she...? I'm sorry that we still haven't found her."

"She has died too," Ramisa said. "She has gone to join the same world that the Paragons inhabit. But I hear her voice still—if only a little. I keep a braid of her hair that helps keep us connected. She is very much afraid for my safety."

Just glimpsing those visions in her eyes the past evening gave Denn a seed from which to germinate some form of comprehension, but now she claimed a special power from a knot of hair that she clutched like a holy relic. "How is it that you can hear her voice, or see the Paragons when they come to you?"

"The Faith forced it upon me when I was first old enough to be considered for cloistering. They were courting people of influence and it was expected for the women of the royal household. But they had exceptional plans for me, as I learned they had for my sister and mother. They wanted us to bear the spirits of the Paragons. Then they taught me to know when they were speaking—but had hoped to demand more of me before I was taken away. The Faith taught me to listen, but Avenda taught me to speak back to them. She... *her people* have such a talent."

"Including her sister, you mean?"

"Jokira, yes—and her cousin, Caliana. There are others." She leaned forward and whispered, "This is how I was able to survive in Fallowsea, but it is not something to trust to my cousin. My cousin looks strangely upon people of Avenda's heritage, of whom there are few in Fallowsea. But he would often take it out on me for insisting on their companionship. Avenda was my key to tolerating the suffering I felt every day."

"That is terrible," Denn said. His fury toward Kentin began to reassert itself, but also did his hatred of the Faith. "I hope something can be done once we reach Caphedra, to undo all this pain you endure."

"It will be over soon," Ramisa said gloomily. "The Paragons tease me about death all the time."

"Don't say that!" said Denn.

"It is as it is," she said acceptingly. "If I do not supplicate myself to the Paragons, I have little to stand between me and them now that I've lost Avenda. Now I am also to understand that the Faith is sending soldiers to kill me."

"Your uncle is raising an army which will prevent them from harming you—though I admit that these ghosts of the Paragons are another matter. Tell me, what of your mother and father?" Denn inquired. He was uncertain if Ramisa was as ignorant to their deaths, as he had assumed, or if some other connection existed. "Can you hear *them*?"

She lowered her head, and her mouth quivered with sadness. "They were far away from me when they died. I do not hear them so clearly, but they have also remained with me in part. They loved me. They want to see me again."

"Do you have a lock of their hair or something? Like you do Avenda?"

Ramisa shook her head, but then a tiny chuckle arose from her. "I have me," she said. "My whole body and being comes from them, does it not? That is the way of making children, isn't it?"

As soon as she said it, Denn felt his face redden with the very thought of the act she mentioned. She smiled, having struck her point. Denn could tell that Ramisa savoured his embarrassment and bore a playful desire to explore his reaction further. Whatever inner voice or guidance granted her the strength to fight off her ticks and peculiarities, she sat there in the candlelight, beautiful and still in the moment. Denn felt her warm caress on his cheek and returned it. As she stayed with him in his chamber, she expressed to him that it brought peace to her thoughts. Denn's, on the other hand, were consumed by the echo of her words, and the way of making children.

❖   ❖   ❖

It was the middle of the night when Denn opened his eyes, alert and clear-headed.

A cold draft invaded the chamber through an open window. As the uninvited wind grew more frigid, his body kept warm under the bedclothes, clutched tightly by Ramisa, but outside the covers, the air felt like he'd been slapped in the face and his cheeks left numbed.

She was sleeping beside him, the reason for which he found himself galloping between coast and capital. Had he accepted the task to show off? Was he only seeking glory, as Kentin accused? Denn refused to chastise himself for ambition. A man of good character should always strive toward betterment. Settling for less than one was capable of was not virtuous modesty nor polite humility. It was the shameful habit of laggards, which only served to tempt good people to waste themselves wallowing alongside them— or opening a path for the conniving to rise without challenge.

Despite the storms that swirled around her, Ramisa preserved a gentility of character. He felt more noble with her as his cause and wanted to see her ascend as well. He had accepted the duty to escort her because it was an honourable task.

His father's complicity in his kidnapping expunged his obligation to perform the job out of a personal debt. Denn was his own man and would conduct himself in the manner that stemmed from his own choice of actions. Guardianship over the delicate and deserving lady lying in contentment next to him was his duty now. Denn would not allow his reputation to be tarnished by Kentin—or anyone—who would challenge his authenticity while cravenly eschewing the privilege of stewardship themselves.

How this translated into sharing a bed with her, would be a matter saved for another night's deliberations, he thought. It was cold. Perhaps he should end his ruminations and get up to somehow block the chill from the window. He listened to the howling of the currents of wind rising off the ridge. It had not been half as blustery on the previous nights he had spent here.

Something about the frigid disquiet called out to him and Denn remembered one last chore he had forgotten.

The black blade remained cached within the tower.

Denn gently lifted Ramisa's fingers from under the folds of his shirt. He slid sideways, dropping one leg to the floor and then the other, searching for his boots. When he was reasonably confident that the princess had not been irredeemably disturbed, he grabbed his cloak and slipped into the outer corridor. Then, to keep the chamber's occupancy a secret, he noiselessly pressed against the door to close it, hooking a finger around the latch to soften the din of its fall.

There was a candle solemnly burning where the two members of the Bridgecliff Guard stood watch in the charnel cell bearing Trin's corpse. Both the soldiers had swords drawn with their tips pointed downward and pressing into the wooden planks of the floor. Their mailed gloves rested on the ornamented hilts, as they stoically and silently flanked the entrance.

Denn approached softly, for he did not wish to breach the sanctity of the men's mourning. They, too, had known Trin as a squire during the more exalted days of the army's peak. Despite their new allegiance to the Farathemuns' money and clout, both still were marked with the leopard sigils of the Thirteenth etched into their shoulder pauldrons.

Closer to them now, one of the men acknowledged Denn. "The boys, and us, are looking after him for you, sir."

"I don't doubt that you are," Denn said. "I regret this result has followed your reunion. Trin was..." Denn paused, stumbling for words.

The soldiers held their tongues for him to continue.

"He was an excellent soldier," Denn finally concluded.

"He was," they said together, and returned to their despondent trances.

Denn added nothing further but entered the room. Trin's body somehow seemed tinier than in life. His cheeks were sunken in. They gave his face an inverted appearance when set against the bones of his jaw and its uncompromising chin. In death, he looked much older than just twenty-one years.

All final farewells that he wished to communicate, he kept private. Denn turned from the corpse and located the wooden box within which the murderer's tool—the jet-black falchion—had been enshrined. Picking it up in both hands, he tucked it under his cloak. He carried the box past the soldiers, aloft in the tower to the battlements—into darkness, and into the blowing gusts that threatened to lift one right off their feet and toss them into the wooded Eldergorge far below.

Even in its containment, the wicked weapon seemed to sense his antagonism to its very existence. It unnerved Denn that the Faith could craft something of such irremediable ruthlessness and that he could have come across such a thing so randomly. Inside its casing, he could feel it humming and knew that the blade hated him for what he planned to do.

The wind felt oppressively cold. Were it not almost midsummer, Denn would not have been surprised to see a flurry of snow swirling about. He wanted to be rid of this thing quickly so he could retreat to somewhere—and someone—warmer.

He flipped open the latches of the box, one at a time, when a voice called out from behind him, barely cutting through the moaning blasts of wind.

"That would be a very valuable weapon in the right hands."

Denn turned to see Temis had followed him up the stairs to the top of the tower. Like Denn, he was keeping warm under a dark wrap. His usual smirk was tempered, and a slash of red traced his jawline showing where some Pillarman's blade had come too close during the battle. Did Temis crave the box and its contents? Denn was convinced the hireling was eyeing it with an envious stare reminiscent of how Denn caught him looking at Naobe.

"It doesn't belong in the hands of anyone I would ride with," Denn said. "I don't know what its power is, but I assure you that it is fueled by something wicked, and I mean us to be good and rid of it."

Inside the box, he could feel the black blade shift and scrape against its wooden confines.

"How do you know someone wouldn't just recover it from the bottom of the gorge? There's a forge in the fort below. You could melt it down. It's the only way to be certain of its destruction."

"Too much commotion and I don't want the garrison to get

curious. Best that I just fling it off the tower. No one will ever find it so far down below. There it can remain lost forever."

Denn opened the box to find the sharp edge of the blade right up against the cracked lid. Denn's heart jumped, and he drew his fingers back, wary of getting cut. This was delicate work. One mistake and he could be pricked and cursed to bleed out without mercy.

"What's wrong?" asked Temis.

Denn turned the box over, thinking to dump the falchion onto the stones of the tower landing to get a better look at it. "Do you have gauntlets or gloves?" he finally asked.

The question took Temis off guard and must have unsettled him. He kept his hands out in front defensively as he came closer, eying the box that enclosed the sword.

It quivered, and the falchion's steel began to ring on its own with a doleful vibration as if calling out to Temis to give it one final reprieve.

"Get rid of it!" Temis said. "Throw the whole thing over the side with the sword in it."

Denn clamped down on the top of the box, closing it with great effort, as the blade could be felt spinning around inside, to use its own broadness to wedge the crack open as much as it could. Before he could thumb closed the latches, the sword lurched inside, and he heard a growl.

The look that Temis shot toward Denn proved he had heard it also, but it was not coming from the sword. The growl thundered at the two of them from overtop of the screaming wind. It was sinister and fierce.

Denn snatched the box back and quickly did the latches. Then, fighting against the imprisoned sword as it jumped and jerked inside the box, he held the case up and courted the wrath of the unseen spectre that had come to the blade's defence. He could not waste another moment. Heaving the wicked package into the air, he sent it over the battlements, beyond the crest of the ridge to tumble into the silvan darkness of the bottomless Eldergorge.

As he did, the wind picked up and swirled around them, but the snarling of the mysterious force faded.

Temis grabbed Denn by the arm and led him quickly inside to the safety of the tower.

"Well done, I think," he congratulated uncertainly.

Denn turned and pressed himself flat, with his back against the wall. He sighed in relief that the task was completed but uttered a defining proclamation to Temis.

"Now you know what I've seen. You understand that the Faith is enlisting more to their cause than men like us are fit to comprehend. This kind of sorcery must be ended."

Thick lines and creases of concern marred Temis's face. With a heaviness in his voice, he reminded Denn, "More reason that we must get Serenn out of the temple. Your brother holds her in the temple priory. I can lead you to her if you help me find a way back in."

Once they returned to Caphedra, things would move quickly. They needed to rescue Serenn, but war was almost upon the city. If the conflict began before they could free his sister, Denn might be thrust into commanding his father's hired soldiers before he could render her any aid. Worse, he still did not have a solid plan on how to get her out, with the temple already so high on alert for the arrival of the prince's army. Truthfully, he had no plan to get into Caphedra, either.

"We'll reach the city the day after tomorrow. We'll take Ramisa to Farathemun, and then we will find a way to help Serenn," Denn said.

"Delay the nuptials?" Temis asked.

"Let's save them for a happy day," Denn said.

Temis nodded. "I'll see that everything is in order, for an early departure in the morn. Sleep well, sir."

"Aye," Denn concurred then proceeded down the stairs. As he reached the door to his chamber, he waited for Temis to pass lest he chance a glimpse of Denn's illicit guest. But once free and alone, he slipped inside, hoping to find the princess still asleep.

She was lying on her side, her face toward the door, and spreading the blankets to invite him back into the bed. Denn threw off his cloak, tossed it over the back of an old wooden chair, and settled in next to her, aware that his body must be freezing cold.

Ramisa wrapped her arm around him tightly and warmly, pulling herself into him even more closely than before, seeming only half-asleep

"You made him angry," she said groggily.

"Who?" Denn said, suppressing panic.

"Dagremahr," Ramisa mumbled. "Of all the Paragons, *he's the worst.*" With that, she drifted off back to sleep.

CHAPTER 23

The Trail Home

Before daybreak, their procession started east again, greeting the dawn with fewer travellers. The party was halved. Kentin could now only field two horsemen to ride alongside them and that had left six riders to share five mounts.

Temis proved a much more sober companion this day. Either it was the thought of Serenn's rescue drawing nearer or the unsettling encounter during last night's errand with Denn, but his mood had become one of heightened wariness. When he began exploring farther afield, closer to the edge of the cliff, Denn finally had more freedom to converse quietly with Ramisa.

The princess shared a saddle with Denn, as Kentin had ordained. She was incapable and unfit to ride by herself and her carriage unusable so Denn agreed that there were no other options. Naobe was the largest of the horses departing Bridgecliff, and with her being Denn's steed, it was sensible to take the princess with him.

Besides, after their night together she insisted. The princess no longer had Avenda to rely on for support.

Sitting together on Naobe's back, Denn could feel the princess tremble beneath her cloak whenever something frightened or disturbed her. She was particularly shaken when they passed by the corpses of Pillar horses and their riders, which were still lying jumbled and lifeless along the trail where they fell. When the wreckage of the demolished carriage came into view, Ramisa crammed her head tightly into his shoulder and sealed her face behind the edges of her hood. He held her and steadied her, then spurred Naobe to a canter so they could hasten past it.

Denn hadn't even noticed that Temis had fallen behind until

Coalsmoke came galloping up behind them. She whinnied amicably to Naobe as Temis brought her aside the regal charger.

Temis had been collecting and made a point of presenting his plunder to Denn—an assortment of blue tunics peeled off the bodies of the Faith's failed assassins. He also intimated another reason for skirting Bridgecliff's edge. With cryptic nods and cocked heads, he and Denn engaged in a wordless exchange in which Temis indicated that he'd uncovered Avenda. With her face still buried deeply, Ramisa was unable to see the unfortunate reporter point and grimly identified the location along the ridge where her aid and confidant's body had tumbled over.

Further on, the trail began to slope downward, and they marked their gains by observing the grand vista ahead. To their left, the uplands of Bren Hills rose to their crescendo; while on the right, the dry wastelands of Hasen were becoming tamed by the fertile valley of the Darrow.

"We're making good time," observed Kentin with unusual optimism. Denn felt Ramisa's fingers clench his waist more securely as her cousin dropped back to ride beside them. His voice appeared to agitate her.

"I expect you'll be happy to see your father," Denn said. "His men will have assembled in the city by now, I expect?"

Kentin rolled his eyes and scowled. "I thought you were more astute. We need to be opportunists here and seek surprise, Denn."

Ramisa nudged Denn beneath overlapping cloaks. He wrapped his arm more securely and comfortingly around her, letting Kentin's disrespect flow over them.

"Look at what we face," Kentin continued. "The Faith has the money to put a lot of food inside the bellies of hungry mercenaries— if the bread and wine are there to be bought. They sit on centuries of Dues, and now have their claws on all the gold in Stonerow. But on the other hand, the Marshal is a proven victor. Harsh as he is, his reputation will attract fighting men like maggots to a mausoleum."

Again, Kentin's derisive pedagoguery fell flat. Denn remained straight-faced and unperturbed. "How many men are you expecting your father will muster to fight these hordes you speak of?"

"Loads," said Kentin. "But they are not to be spent until *after* the other two armies have a go at each other first. Then, we can match and overpower whoever remains standing."

"And who do you think will be standing for your father's troops to meet with? It sounds like you've studied strategy." Denn risked mocking but savoured the chance to reflect the lord's manners. Kentin shared Denn's upbringing. They both dedicated hours to being mentored by expensive tutors, although Denn knew by reputation that learning did not always come so easy to his lordly competitor. Kentin's attitude as a student was famously repellant to the memorization of historical precedents and theoretical teachings. Still, between the two of them, Kentin was one who was granted a command upon coming of age, so forcing humility upon himself, Denn scaled back his half-concealed contempt.

"I don't know," Kentin surprised Denn with an honest admission. "The whole point is for the two armies to be as evenly matched as possible. If something happens to tip the balance in favour of one, then they might achieve victory without sufficient attrition. In such a case, we could face a challenge."

"Do you know who is commanding the Faith's soldiers? Anybody of note?" Denn asked.

"The only man who could rival Myrhic would be Kier Durrow," said Kentin.

"Not likely. Durrow was the High Constable—a cavalryman. He wouldn't gamble his reputation fighting a war on foot, in the city streets. He can't abide infantry tactics." Denn considered another possibility. "At council, they asked about Lord Anders, what about him?"

"Pineus or Braydun? They are both in league with the Pillars, I hear. Pineus commands Northwood Garrison, although the rumour is that Braydun was sent up by the Faith to join him in case his brother strayed over to the Marshal's side. It's possible that one, or both, have been recalled to mount a defence of the capital, that's true—but unlikely."

"Havel then?" Denn asked.

Kentin grunted. "Influential, but not a fighter. He was nothing but a house servant and coin counter for the Wolstetts."

Ramisa shifted in the saddle, reacting to Kentin's reference to her family name.

"Merix Drohen?" suggested Denn, with another proposal from Caphedra's catalogue of lords.

Kentin raised an eyebrow and considered it. "He'd have a vast number of men to call on, but they're armsmen—not infantry. They're fine policing the streets against curfew-breakers and pilferers, but not likely to effect a victory in the first place. Though by sheer headcount, he may have the largest share, you're right."

Denn struggled to think of any remaining lords who might be called upon by the High Precept, other than Lord Vlass of Lanstad, whose troops were in the capital now. But there was no indication their lord was with them.

"There must be someone else," Denn said, his passion for speculating was stoked, but no clear answer was forthcoming. "I can't imagine someone untested at the head of so many soldiers."

"Damn it, Denn! We'll find out when we get there, I am sure. You've been in Caphedra more recently than I have! You should have a better insight into its workings."

"Until three weeks ago, I was a simple cavalryman stationed in a swamp, seven days' ride from the capital. I'm afraid I fell far afield of any of Caphedra's politics over the past couple of years."

Denn's excuse caused Kentin to shake his head and sigh, but it was enough to get him to pardon the lack of insight. Denn appreciated learning as much as he could about how the coming battle might shake out and what Farathemun's plans fully entailed in response.

"Myrhic has to get through the gates and storm the citadel. It won't be easy. Perhaps the Faith can better afford someone untested," said Kentin. "And if they promote someone, they can choose a commander without any intrinsic loyalties beyond the Pillars. Most of the veteran army commanders, still respect and revere the Marshal, if they're not outright cordial with him."

"He has his men on the inside too—the Marshal's Men. They will find a way to get him through the gates and sabotage the defences of the citadel if they can. I only wish we had someone to do the same for us. The gates are likely to be closed up tight by now."

Just then, he remembered Temis's garment collection, scavenged back by the carriage. He called to get the horseman's attention.

"Temis!"

"My lord," he answered and Denn beckoned him to approach. He directed Coalsmoke closer, and the dark horse pulled up alongside Naobe again.

"How many tunics did you find back there?"

"Four," he said. "I didn't want to presume we'd get the princess to suit up in one, but I snatched enough to clothe the rest of us. I wish I'd thought of it before we had ridden past the ambush site. I might have gotten more, but we'd have an awful time explaining away the arrow holes on those ones."

Denn was not disappointed. He would rather have the tunics tattered and bloody as they were than to have had the Pillarmen finish the fight unscathed and successful in achieving their aim. He acknowledged Temis's point, but a plan was now forming, thanks to his companion's foresight.

"The ones you showed me are bloody enough. I guess we'd better come up with some heroic tale of a grand fight if we're going to use them to gain entrance from the gate guards."

Kentin interrupted with a grunt and pointed beyond the ridge. "You can tell them we ran into Myrhic's army!"

Temis and Denn both inhaled sharply. One of Kentin's men gasped while the other moaned forebodingly.

A sight of inauspicious grandeur caused them to both marvel and quake. The land below Bridgecliff was now pockmarked with defensive mounds and ditches and blistering with pavilions. Prince Ramid's army was on the approach to the capital, and his mass of soldiers would undoubtedly rival the ranks stood up by the Faith. Like a plague of insects, they were spreading over the fields, cutting down every useable tree for their fires and shelters. Everything they touched was cut, stripped, and burnt, to fulfill the needs of their numbers.

Evidently, Lord Marshal Myrhic had pulled troops from across the lands of the north to join in his march. Denn spied the intimidating battle axe standard of Lord Paxton Remm and the sharp-taloned saker of Lord Veleeren Kullan. Farther down the line, the battle flag of the 7th Bren Hills Brigade, Lord Tulk Sentor's men, flew above the diverse unit insignias of its constituents; the three horseshoes, black on white, for the cavalry; a cauldron which denoted the old North Caphedran infantry; and a large-eyed owl denoting his notable archers.

The greatest surprise came from seeing the ursine crest of Lord Kolis Grandt. This sizeable and unexpected contingent under the fearsome bear's head pennant were Northporter warriors from Stonebriar and Greyforest. They would undoubtedly be forming the vanguard when the prince advanced.

"There is your brother's army," Denn said to Ramisa, who pulled back her hood and observed in silence.

Temis rode along and commented, "Once we don the tunics, I recommend not riding too close. It'll be hard enough to convince the guards at the northwest gate, but the prince's soldiers will kill us on sight if we're dressed in blue."

"It's possible that they won't even open the north gate, regardless of our dress. Why would they risk lowering their defences even for a moment? Myrhic is in front of them, as we speak," Kentin said to Temis.

"If they put up a fuss, it's worth remembering that those Pillar guards are there because they *can be bought*," Temis said.

Denn nodded. The men were mercenaries. They had a price.

Temis looked toward Kentin and added, "Check your pockets, m'lord. If there's a jingle, I suggest we let commerce turn the key."

Kentin scowled and Denn found himself preventively redirecting the lord's attention before the rudeness was addressed. "It's getting close to the end of the day. Let us travel a little farther, then camp. I'm sure we're all hungry," he said.

"Very well! I'll be happy to be finished this trip and be back to Fallowsea." Kentin continued gawking at Myrhic's encampment. Even he looked humbled by the teeming legions and brigades before them.

Denn, too, shuddered at the intimidating sight but clucked his tongue and sent Naobe forward.

The downward slope twisted back upon itself several times, but the shallower gradient led to less wear on the horses. The wind tapered off so that the heat of the late-spring day met them on the descent. They were far enough below Bridgecliff's crest that clustered stands of hardy pine and spruce reappeared, splitting the rocks and shooting skyward. Further down, the sweet-smelling firs surrendered to groves of leafier poplar and birch, and bushy thickets that were full of fat, frolicking hares, and easily startled woodcocks.

As nightfall came, Denn selected a secluded pass in which to set up camp. The horses were pastured in a small patch of grass a little higher on the hillside. Kentin was determined to light a fire, attributing its necessity to the princess's condition, so his men fetched whatever downed logs and suitable brush that they could collect. Denn chose not to protest. Firelight could normally be seen for quite a distance at night, but here it was obscured within the depression where they camped, and nobody would likely be close enough to see or smell the smoke against the night sky.

For Ramisa, Denn scavenged what extra comforts he could. The day's saddle blankets were wet with horse sweat and needed to dry out, so he hung them up, but did so in such a way that they afforded the lady privacy—at least, as much as possible. It was appreciated with a private tenderness. She did not chance to show any further affection this close to the others, but her smile was enough for Denn to feel her contentment.

"If you see, or hear, or sense *anything* tonight, know that I am close. Just call to me," Denn said.

"I will," she said calmly, then bundled her cloak about herself and rested against a lichen-covered pine stump.

A watch schedule was arranged by Kentin, who assigned himself the first shift. Denn suspected he had organized it so as to personally prolong the campfire and enjoy it as long as possible. Afterward, he would hand off to Denn who could decide if he wanted to keep the flames burning or not. Temis would follow, with Kentin's two soldiers taking the final posts before dawn.

Supper was a meal of chewy, dried fish in a briny broth that one of Kentin's men steeped over the fire then served in small wooden cups. Denn's hunger overpowered his lack of enthusiasm for the dish. He knew he would need to replenish his strength before tomorrow took them into the perils of the city, but he would have preferred a nice roast partridge or grouse. It got him hoping that perhaps there might be a chicken left somewhere in Caphedra, by the time everything was over.

The thought of dining back home, in peace and luxury, gave him a warm memory with which to settle in for a nap before the watch but it dissipated when his mind turned to the problem of Koster's Ferry. He was relying on the crossing being functional—not overrun by the prince's army. If the troops were foraging, it could bring them to the banks of the Darrow for fish and freshwater. They might even turn to scrounging for building supplies and if they found the barge, they might put its lumber to alternate uses.

Denn was mulling over this potential dilemma when Kentin trudged toward him and churlishly kicked the bottom of his foot.

"Nap's over. You're up," said Kentin in a harsh whisper. "Nothing to report, save that the fire's dying out." He coughed and huffed, sounding more bored than exhausted. "I'll check on the princess so that you don't have to."

"Thank you, and good night, Kentin," Denn said, overlooking the lord's dearth of manners. Kentin's attention to Ramisa was a valuable reminder that she was still, in all reality, the Farathemuns' ward. He could not allow himself to feel possessive over her despite the marriage arrangement.

Denn got to his feet, his boot slipping on the dewy grass, which was already collecting moisture from the cool night. It was seeming a better idea by the moment, keeping the fire going to provide a more pleasant spot to stave off the onset of the chilly dampness.

Higher on the hill, Denn heard one of the horses whinnying. Checking on their animals would be his first order of business, so he set about scouting for any dangers along the edges of their grazing spot.

To be safe, he carried Longlimb with him as he trekked up the hill. In these woods, it would not be out of line to come across a pack of dogs or wolves. Their party had put enough distance between them and the Eldergorge, but who knew how far the beasts in there would roam if one got the notion that it was hungry for a horse. Denn had read about one sizeable breed of ravenous leopard, with a coat of inky blue, that was relentless when seeking prey. If such a beast had picked up the scent of their ponies coming down from the ridge it could certainly be out there now, stalking its supper.

Certainly, Naobe would be a match for such a creature. The undisputed alpha mare of the tiny herd, she would ensure the smaller horses were protected. She gave Denn more confidence as well, and as he climbed the hill. He relaxed at the sight of her crest and withers against the luminous backdrop of starlight, however, as he approached, he noticed she was quiet. Her ears were pinned back. He could hear her tail swishing. Something had her attention, and she was not happy.

Denn drew Longlimb from its sheathe quietly. He crouched low to reduce his silhouette and strained his eyes to peer into the bushes around the grazing ground. He saw nothing. Scanning higher, he examined the tree limbs for the shape of a big cat–or anything that might be awry–but again, he saw nothing.

Ramisa? He wondered now if something other than an animal had followed them. Was he about to provoke that demon laughter again? *What did she call him? Dagremahr?*

Then there was a whisper.

A voice in the bushes was trying to calm Naobe. "Easy now. Easy does it," the voice repeated as a placating mantra. Denn's eyes looked left and right, then settled on an unobstructed path behind the bushes that would let him sneak up. He had to remain silent.

Denn moved so slowly, that the other moved first. He saw the man's form extricate itself from the bush, slip out the back, and carefully begin a retreat. He only saw one man, but that man was about to escape.

What information the watcher would carry back—and to whom—was unknown to Denn, however, the spy needed to be intercepted. He could not be allowed to report back anything of their passage through these woods.

Denn planted a foot securely into the soil under him, scanning for low branches that might trip him up, then abruptly burst forth into a sprint that sent him solidly into the surprised intruder.

They collided with great force and the man gasped and struggled for air. Denn had knocked the wind out of him, but for good measure, cuffed him hard, twice about the head. He sprung back to stand over his prone captive, with Longlimb pressed into the man's chest at the spot where his captive's heart was beating. Denn could tell that the man had been intending to travel lightly and quietly, dressed in leathers without a pack or any other encumbrances. He gave the man a quick inspection and saw there was a knife in a sheathe on his belt.

"Mercy," the man uttered. "I'm a trapper! I work these woods. An honest living, sir!"

"Where are your traps?" Denn queried sharply.

"All laid!" the man said cagily.

Unconvinced, Denn retorted, "I didn't see traps around here."

"They're all hidden, aren't they?" the man answered. "That's how traps work... so I guess that I did a pretty good job!"

Denn leaned into Longlimb, causing the tip to at least pierce a few layers of skin on the man's chest. "Put one hand behind your head and keep it there. Unloose your belt with the other one."

"My word, what are you going to do with me?" the man said, afeared.

Denn pressed again, incensed by the man who was now gasping and whimpering from the pain. "You're going to keep that knife in its sheathe and toss it to the side before we finish our chat about your *honest* livelihood."

The man's hands trembled, but he obeyed. With one hand tucked under his head, he fumbled with the fastening and tried to loosen it before apologizing, "I'm having some trouble, given the situation, sir."

Denn looked closely at the buckle that was causing the difficulty, and when it caught a moonbeam in the dark, he instantly recognized the symbol of the tower.

"Hands to the side!" Denn commanded. The man drew back his hand back rapidly from the belt. As he did, he forcefully slapped the flat of Denn's blade and knocked it aside. Desperately, he turned over on the ground and tried to launch himself into a run for his life, but Denn set upon him, with a knee driven into the man's back to force him back down.

"Oy! To me!" Denn shouted down the slope to the campsite. The man squirmed beneath him but finally surrendered.

In an instant, Denn heard twigs snapping and branches breaking behind him. Temis and Kentin were running together, weapons drawn, responding to his call for aid. The trapper stopped struggling.

With his supporters taking up positions to block the man's escape, Denn eased up and rose to his feet to look down on the intruder. "What is your name?"

"It's not my job to tell you anything!" he said, rolling over onto his side and into a crouch, preparing to stand if Denn allowed it. "What business had *you* on Bridgecliff?"

His audacity was answered by a painful kick at the man's backside from Kentin, which toppled him. When he picked himself back up, he was more attentive to Denn's companions, cocking his head back and forth like a cornered viper. His stare lingered on Temis, however, and his face changed from discontent to fury. "I know you!" he said through gritted teeth.

Denn looked questioningly toward Temis, who had been standing a step back, but now advanced toward the prone prisoner.

"You're a Marshal's Man," Temis said, confirming what Denn had already discovered."

"And you're the wretch that sold out Colden's brother! Temis Sloke, isn't it? We figured out who you were, and how you double-crossed them." He spat but it lacked the power to travel far. "Was Balix in on it too? Or did you sell him out too? Colden wants you dead—you and that whole Wellum family you work for!"

Temis twisted his mouth as he recollected, "Halbrun, isn't it? You've seen better days. Look at you!"

"Hal-*VUN*," came the staunch correction.

"Halvun Sibbar? The old captain of Middlehold Company?" interjected Kentin. "What brings you out here? You never seemed like a rugged, exploring sort. Rather soft was my impression. That's why my father never hired you."

Halvun shifted on the ground and responded to the new voice. "Commander Farathemun?"

Denn cringed at the sound of Kentin's identity being uncovered, too, but the lord himself failed to care. Moreso, he took the moment to correct the finest point of the misnomer.

"*Lord*," Kentin educated him, then leaned in to take over the interrogation. "Working for the Marshal's Men, eh? What about my old replacement, Trowel? Is he one of you now, too?"

"Saw you coming down Bridgecliff," Halvun acknowledged, "and I see you *survived*, too. How is the princess? Would I be right to presume this tall fellow to be Denn Wellum, then?"

Denn cursed as he leaned forward, trying to reach for Halvun's neck, but Temis, who had been standing with his two short swords at the ready, moved first. He had placed one back into its sheathe on his belt and now closed on Halvun with the other. Slipping in behind, he pressed the blade to the kneeling man's throat and Denn heard him whisper, "*Poison.*"

Halvun's eyes widened, and his head retracted into his neck as if he were trying to use his jaw to shield his throat while the blade hovered over his vulnerable windpipe.

"You didn't come all this way to ask questions," Temis sneered. "What brings you here? Scouting? Spying?" With his left hand, Temis adeptly searched the man's pockets and the creases in his clothes. He withdrew Halvun's knife from its sheath on his belt and tossed it away, then with a boyish squeal of success he resumed the search. When he found a folded slip of parchment, he proclaimed his deduction. "I see. You're a messenger."

Kentin reached for the note but was circumvented as Temis promptly handed it over to Denn first.

The letter was a palm-sized piece of parchment, and Halvun's sweat had made it dirty and damp. It was folded and held closed by a wax seal displaying the ever-identifiable tower. Denn noticed there was no other writing or marks on the outside, so he broke the seal to unfurl the letter and look at its text. The dark made it impossible to decipher in full, however, a few elaborated letters stood out—such as the highly undulating 'M's of the words, "Marshal" and "Myrhic." It was unsigned, but the official seal was plenty to its veracity and importance.

"What's it say?" Denn demanded of Halvun.

"It's an invitation to the Lord Marshal," snickered Halvun, causing Denn to growl with impatience.

Temis stood back and motioned for the letter. Denn passed it back to him, and he had a try at reading it.

"It says that Lanstad is withdrawing. They're leaving the city and travelling south."

"That's wonderful if true, but why would they go now?" Kentin wondered. "Did they get scared off?"

"Lord Vlass is no coward," Denn said. "And he's loyal to the Faith. I can't see him abandoning the city unless he had a good reason."

Temis shrugged, "What reason would be more important to him than displaying his value to the Pillars just as Caphedra comes under attack?"

Kentin hemmed and postulated aloud, "It's a long way around, but they could be moving to join with the Anders brothers via the east, to outflank the Marshal."

"Or coming our way to squeeze the Marshal from the west," Temis added concernedly.

"It makes no sense," Denn said. "To leave safety and give up ground before the fight? They would have to cross the Darrow to attack from this side, yet they would lose valuable time and risk their plan being uncovered if they went east. Why give up the protection provided by the citadel and the city walls?"

"I'll tell you why," said Halvun. "They're going to lose. They've seen the Marshal's army on the doorstep, and they want to get out with their hides intact."

Kentin looked toward Denn to validate the man's assertion. Halvun's claim was not inconceivable. Nonetheless, the revelation frustrated them and while infected by that inconclusiveness Halvun became energized.

"Let me go, and I can plead with the Marshal to forgive you and remove the mark on your heads!" he said greasily. "You're smart. You know that once he's taken Caphedra, he'll be less inclined to entertain mercy for those that plotted against him or his men—even wretches like Colden."

Indeed, if the Marshal's victory was so pre-ordained, it would lead to a dangerous world for Denn. He knew he had to refuse, but hesitated. Buried under layers of military command, the Marshal had been his ultimate authority figure for years. He felt unable to close the door to a pardon entirely. After all, the feud had been with his father.

"We don't like Colden. His brother was the only reason we let Colden in, but we owe it to our man to see him avenged. It doesn't have to be your neck that gets chopped, Wellum. Just give us Temis. He was the one that worked against us. Set us up. He's to blame for Romwin," said Halvun.

Temis looked uneasy with the time it took for Denn to answer. "The Marshal's not a forgiving man. You know that Halvun—and I don't think you hold much sway with him."

"Then throw in the princess, wherever you've got her stashed," Halvun added. Denn felt his pulse quicken at the mention of Ramisa. The Marshal's Men, somehow, must have had heard about everything that transpired on Bridgecliff. His instinct was to blame Wex Sulford as the culprit since he was the only one they knew of who had made it off the ridge faster than they had.

Kentin was disturbingly silent. His eyes tracked Denn's face, no doubt scrutinizing him for a hint at his thoughts. Even though Denn resented the lord, he pronounced his answer by addressing his peer as equally as he did the man kneeling at his feet.

"We are committed to the good of the princess and your confidence is misplaced. The Marshal does not know what awaits him in Caphedra."

Uncomfortably, Denn prosecuted the captive's fate. The man was unarmed. Neither was this a field of battle. He was a captive and should accordingly be spared death. Nonetheless, they could not risk the Marshal learning any more about their plans. If Sulford was indeed the source, then perhaps the information had only reached Caphedra and not the Marshal's camp. Perhaps the letter Halvun held was meant to be the conduit. They could stop it here.

"Let me take your answer to the Marshal," Halvun begged to offer again. "Tell him you'll not stand in his way, and he will appreciate that."

"You will tell the Marshal *nothing*," said Denn. Then, as he stood between a grateful Temis and an intrigued Kentin Farathemun, Denn readjusted his grip upon Longlimb to place both hands on the sword's pommel, and he swiftly thrust the weapon forward. The point pierced Halvun in the heart, and blood burst from the sides of the blade, evacuating in a singular gush, ejected with the force of the man's last heartbeat.

Kentin had a satisfied smile at the execution. "Shall we bury him?"

"Get some sleep," Denn said. "I'll cover him for now, but I don't care if the wolves find him, to be honest."

"He must have had a horse close by," Temis said.

Denn nodded in agreement. "In the morning, we'll find it and let it loose. We can't take it, and there's no reason to leave it tied here."

Taking one more look at the body, Denn added. "We have to leave early. If Vlass's men are on the march southward, Southgate must still be open. We'll enter through there, which means we must press onward to Darrow Bridge."

CHAPTER 24

Unravelling at the Edges

"**G**et back to your bed!" Neriah commanded as Olen begrudgingly obeyed.

Whether it meant sweeping floors or washing dishes, the truth was that Olen just wanted to find some way to keep busy and help out. His latest run-in with trouble was in trying to reorganize a pile of unmatching vials and flasks to take up less space on the shelf, and Neriah had to rush in and scold him for touching things to which he was not a party to.

"Gardia has very particular classification methods," Neriah educated him. "You're not doing me any favours by mixing these bottles up. Do you understand?"

Olen took her rebuke on the chin and made it a point not to cross his niece again—at least not so far as medicine bottles were concerned. She was barely twenty years old but could scold like a schoolmarm. Perhaps she had learned that from Gardia, but whereas the proprietress of the Peahen was always icy and would freeze you with a paralysis-inducing gaze when displeased, Neriah would burn hot and find ways to scorch you with uncomfortable admonishment.

"You need to be careful around these medicines. They're not safe if you don't know how to use them," Neriah explained. "Spill a drop of one, and you'll burn your hands off. Simply pop the cork on another and inhale a draught, and you might collapse into slumber for a year."

"I wouldn't want for us to miss any more time than we already have," Olen lamented. Shamelessly, he would catch himself dropping the odd comment to fish for her affections or show some sign that she was also willing to nurture their family bond. He had found some success. More and more gradually, she came to smile. In time, harumphs of amusement would sometimes even replace her deeply disapproving sighs.

Olen wished he remembered her better, but she must have been just an infant when he left, and he did not know his brother to have taken a wife. Tolen had been a rake with lots of girls on his arm back in those days. He was a strong man and an intelligent fighter who had no hesitation in putting another man into the ground if they were a danger to him—or anyone for whom he cared. Under the ceiling of his protection, he picked an entourage of those who needed security and could not achieve it themselves. That included a lot of the neighbourhood girls.

Such were Olen's good memories of his brother. Tolen also had a reputation of bullying to get what he wanted whenever it suited him, and he would single-mindedly pursue the objectives he sought, applying force if persuasion was impractical. Neriah had that stubborn determination, too, Olen could tell.

"Do you remember Evelyne Groll?" Neriah asked him one day while seeing to Olen's dressings.

"Evelyne Groll?" he repeated and winced while recollecting. "I do. Maybe. Her father worked at a brickworks in Potshollow. But there was a fire, wasn't there?"

Neriah nodded. "So my mother told me."

"Halrin Groll," Olen said. "He was a big man. A hard worker. Westriver would have been a better place if we had more men like him to look up to and keep things right."

Neriah stared down at her hands as she stripped wax from the neck of a green glass flacon. Her hands were tiny and nothing like those of a brickmaker or builder.

Now untapped, Olen's memory began to flow openly, though sadly.

"His wife, I remember, drowned herself in the Darrow when she heard Halrin had burned to death," he said. "Tragedy for their girl to grow up like that, without them. Poor Evelyne."

"My mother," Neriah bluntly acknowledged.

"Really?" Olen asked, then wistfully added, "Tolen was crazed with love for her, I remember."

That coaxed a wee smile from Neriah. "She said that your

father—my grandfather—didn't approve of my father courting her."

"What? No!" contradicted Olen. "We all thought she was sweet as spring rain—just too gentle a girl to get caught up with our clan. What a shame." Olen reached out to hold Neriah's hand. For a moment, it seemed like she may have resented the pause in her work, but she acquiesced.

"I guess I was told differently," Neriah said.

"Tolen loved her very much, but our father feared for her getting too involved in our business. Guilt sat heavy enough on his brow already. We were at war with the Karavals, and she would have gotten hurt."

"That's why you never knew about me. She raised me apart from the Kierks, because of his objections. I suppose that I was born just a short while before you left Westriver, during some of the worst of it."

"What happened to your mother? The Karavals didn't find her, did they?" Olen wondered how the story continued, but the apparent absence of Neriah's mother from her life made him regret asking as soon as the questions spilled from his mouth.

"No," Neriah said, and removed her hand from Olen's. She went back to work, this time dusting shelves. "She died of a fever. With my grandparents gone—and her very young to be having me—there wasn't a lot of food. I remember her getting sick often. One winter, when I was only seven or eight, it ended up being her last. Then Gardia took me in. She and my mother had been friends."

"You grew up healthy and smart. Your mother would be pleased," said Olen. "I wish Tolen lived to see you grow up. Damn the Karavals."

"Well, it's only partly the fault of the Karavals," Neriah said. "You have to know which battles are worth fighting."

"I'd like to stop fighting," Olen said. "I'm not sure what else I'm good at doing, but there must be something."

Neriah moved closer to Olen and took his hand in hers. "Stop the feud. Do not let it start again. Promise me."

He could not refuse. He knew that Neriah's acceptance of him was contingent on being free from that ageless familial curse. He had certainly sought the same once, which was why he had left Westriver in the first place, and so long as his niece was safe now, he had no reason to go back and rekindle the blood war.

"If I promise," Olen began, "will you let me out of this room to enjoy a decent mug of ale?"

Neriah scoffed at him. "Drunkard," she called him, but with a hint of teasing. "Only if you take Livet with you, to watch over you when I can't. She has more sense than you do. She knows when to run away from a fight."

Olen started to roll his eyes, but it hurt. He was left rubbing his temples to ease the persistent pain.

"No more than a couple of hours at a time until you're fully healed," Neriah directed, then reached up to a shelf above to pull down a clay jar. She opened it to remove a pinch of dried, green leaves. "And put one of these in your mug before you drink. It'll mix with the ale like a tonic."

Olen chuckled and pledged to heed her prescriptive advice. "I will," he said, "...and *I promise*."

The Peahen was vast but vague and ripe with peculiarities. It was constructed with sweet-smelling cedarwood, and the aroma was enhanced by a melange of exotic incense and clouds of lingering spices. Mosaics and patterns flowed upon the walls, assembled from colourful, painted porcelain tiles.

Olen was heartened to see Livet embrace it as a happy playground, for Gardia had granted her full exploration of all but the most private sanctums. Though she cautioned her to be careful mentioning anything to do with magical charms or enchantments on the public floor. That was a matter for the backrooms only.

As Neriah began returning to her other responsibilities, more and more, Livet took over the role of being Olen's guide to enjoying the lively and eccentric establishment. Diagnosing him to be in peculiarly good health for someone who had just been injured so severely, Livet coaxed the old warrior out more often, inviting him to convalesce at a tiny table set off in an alcove overlooking the bar. Eager for a belly-quenching mug of ale, he protested very little. Neriah, who had originally given him her blessing, let on that she was displeased by his racking up of so many hours swilling and swallowing. But as she had presciently expected, it had a positive constitutional effect on Olen—and since Livet kept him out of trouble, it was permitted.

As Livet and Olen sat, she filled him in on the events that led Denn to accept his father's errand and to return with Farathemun's niece–the princess.

"So, he's chosen a side?" asked Olen. "He's braver than I."

"It's one last task he says he owes his father," Livet said. "And as soon as he's back, I'll run 'round and fetch him to bring 'im here. Then, we can get away from Caphedra and stay clear of the Faith an' all the troubles."

"He'll hate it—this place, I mean. Everyone here looks shifty and sneaky," Olen said to Livet. "Except you. He *loves* you."

She grinned. "And *I* like it."

Eyes sweeping the gallery, Olen took in the clientele. They were a mix of conniving merchants on the prowl for gold, local dandies in imported fineries, and drunkards sloppily carousing and crooning out all manner of songs, from Midsummer folk carols to solemn and foreboding cantillations best reserved for funerary rites. The tavern bore several wide-open spaces with long tables cut from pine and spruce, but everywhere there were recesses and private nooks where people could meet and secretly confab or conspire. Livet liked these spots most of all and would tuck herself inside, hidden behind Olen's bulk, ever enthralled to peek out and observe the Peahen's regulars.

Gambling went on throughout the nights with some folks playing dice and other contenders competing in memory games. One salon was boisterous with people racing brightly coloured lizards around a tiny makeshift track. It was a cause for a lot of fights that would spark tempers at a moment's notice until some biological function of the creatures would actually ignite the track and send the spectators scurrying for a bucket of water to quench the fires. Olen was surprised that Gardia would allow it, but many of the matches were overseen directly by her brother, Hull, who was enamoured with wagering and risk-taking in all its forms.

After spending a lot of time with Gardia and getting to know the way of things here, Livet had been the one to identify Hull to Olen, from amongst the menagerie of personalities.

"That's Gardia's brother over there," she had said, pointing quickly to the dour-faced man playing dice with four others. "I saw him at the Council, too. The bearded man behind him is a councillor named Ghil, but he doesn't gamble like Hull does."

Livet looked as if she were rummaging through her head for a moment then said, "I know the other one with the shorter beard, too. He was in the crowd when we first arrived in Caphedra. That man spoke for the poor people that the Hogheads had locked up."

"Hogheads? Where did you learn that word?"

"Porter's Run," Livet said proudly, causing Olen to frown. She truly had been making the most of her past few days in the capital. He could foresee Gardia finding a real use for her. With her ability to slip out of sight so thoroughly, and talent for information, she would make a good spy. Maybe, better than Neriah.

Less than a moment later, Olen could feel the men's attention shift toward their table. They were pointing at Livet and talking. Without warning, Hull rose and walked over to the bar counter. Taringer was there, and it appeared as if he was relaying a message because he promptly disappeared through an unassuming doorway into the backrooms of the tavern. Hull then strode across the floor and approached their table, his attention on Livet particularly.

"You were the girl with Yael Larkin at the Council," he said bluntly. "What dealings do you have with the Wellums?"

Hull's approach had surprised Livet and left her temporarily rattled, so Olen fielded the answer for her.

"We are friends of Denn Wellum. We came to the city to find him after he was kidnapped." Surely, Gardia must have already told her brother most of the tale of Livet's arrival—and Olen's too. Hull was the bar mistress's most trusted agent.

Hull's grimace became more animated but no less surly.

"Well, he's not kidnapped now. He's been seen travelling with King Ramis's younger daughter. What's he up to?"

"Seen travelling? You've seen him?" Livet gasped.

"Not me," said Hull. "Seen by men belonging to that big, stupid fool over there." He pointed to a bulky man with a sloped forehead and dull eyes, who was lost in conversation with a ravishingly beautiful barmaid. Although the man wore light, fancy clothing, it was a poor attempt at masking a soldier's physique. Olen surmised from the man's easy manners that he was some kind of commander. He was all dressed up as if it was his first night back in garrison and he was after the ladies. The man was familiar, however, and in a moment of recollection, Olen remembered the man was from Keepside Garrison.

"That's Nile Alamm," said Olen. "From Keepside. He must be a captain by now, judging by what he must have paid for that shirt."

"Is that his...," Livet hesitated, "wife?"

The unnaturally scarlet-haired woman, on the other hand, was gorgeous. For a member of the staff, she looked like she'd never served a drink throughout her entire employment at the Peahen. She was far more capable of exercising the soft skills of caresses and compliments to those who thirsted for her doting attention as much as they craved endless flagons of strong ale. Her neck was long, and her shoulders delicately slim, and Olen thought it quite a journey downward before one's eyes reached the top hem of her clinging blouse.

"That incredible creature is Gardia's girl, Celebra," Hull said of the hostess. "The giant goon, Alamm, is enamoured with her and he likes to talk."

"Forgive me," Olen said, "You're not jealous, are you?"

"What?!" sputtered Hull, bringing a speck of colour to his stony face momentarily. "I was the one who sent her over there! Alamm is still working for the Lord Marshal, and I aim to find out what he plans to have his men do when the war starts. Celebra is quite talented at getting secrets out of fellows like him."

"He's a Marshal's Man?" Livet asked.

"He's one of their leaders," Hull answered. "He has men outside the city, who saw a Pillarman on his way back through the Rafters from Bridgecliff. The man looked like he had been in a fight, so they captured him to find out what he'd been up to. That's where your friend's name came up, in league with the princess."

"What happened to Denn? Where is he now?" Olen asked with concern.

"The Pillarman said he had been sent out under orders from Lehn Wellum, but that they ran into about fifty men riding east out of Fallowsea, under your man Wellum, and travelling with the Lady Ramisa in her carriage. All this was around the same time that Taringer and Harbud say they saw the father being arrested. Whatever they are planning with the princess, your friend's brother seems to be taking a personal stake in addressing it."

"Please! Did he say what happened to Denn?!" Livet

repeated.

"Only one of the dozen came back, that they know of. So, your friend's chances are pretty good, I'd say. But I'd welcome knowing what's drawing the Marshal's Men out of the city to observe the Bridgecliff approach."

"They likely have eyes on all the approaches to the city, spying for the Marshal. Where is the Pillarman now?" Olen asked.

"Swimming face down in the Darrow River with a stone on his head, likely, although Alamm didn't say," Hull replied.

"If Denn survived and he's fit to travel, I'd expect him not more than a day or so behind this Pillarmen," Olen said to Livet. "You might want to keep an eye out for his return."

The thought lit up Livet's cheeks and gave her eyes a renewed sparkle. Her head immediately turned to the door as if preparing to leave that very moment.

Olen, too, looked to the door, but his attention was on the three men entering. Asher and Kalden had just arrived at the Peahen. Olen assumed this was one of their check-in calls, to see how he was recovering, but Eysman was with them this time and Olen felt instinctively that this was an unwelcome omen.

He raised his hand to catch their attention and invite them over to where he was sitting in the central parlour. Asher saw him and responded with a nod, leading the other two over to the table. His fellow sergeant cocked his head and gave Olen a once-over, examining his friend's wounds.

"Come to check on my dented head, Eysman?" Olen asked his old company counterpart.

"Not today, Olen," he said and took a deep breath. "Bull sent me to bring you news of what happened last night at the Black Eel."

"What do you mean?"

"Karavals barged their way inside on account of you being too brave the other night. They wanted to try their hand with the rest of us, they said."

"You must have given them a good thrashing, those arrogant bastards," Olen said.

"They had swords and axes. We had fists and beer mugs to fling at them, Olen. We weren't expecting trouble like this. They showed up around the time that most of the families were there for sup."

Olen went grey. He put down his ale. "What happened?" he asked.

Asher continued. "Udal brought his strong men—Sasser, Vike, and some fellow named Jemm. A few of Dogfish's boys came out, too. They all had their swords drawn when they entered and came in so fast that they took the old guard by surprise. Vyr, Tomton, Maks, and Gastun all got knocked about... or cut up."

"Maks stood up to them when they grabbed Larke and Preycee and ended up getting a nasty gash," Eysman said.

"Gastun's wife, Malee, got taken too after they clobbered Gastun. He was blacked out on the floor when they left with her," added Kalden.

"Effie says they took the women to the Half Moon, so we need to go there and rescue them. We can't afford a ransom," Asher said. "It looks like you'll get your raid, after all."

"But they'll be expecting us," growled Eysman. "And we've only got a couple of axes and clubs to split between us."

"Bull's got 'em sharpening the table legs!" Kalden added.

Hull listened then chose to speak carefully.

"The Karavals have dominated Faralley and Westriver for over twenty years. You all had better make sure that you have the numbers to settle the score for good, or you will just be getting into another endless series of scraps. Just ask Mr. Kierk here, about how well that worked out for his family."

Olen clenched his fist. "We barely got enough men, and we're scraping for weapons. That's not very promising."

"Between you and me, Bull is pretty angry that you dragged this blood feud to our door," Eysman whispered to Olen. "He's counting on you to find a way to fix this."

Olen's skull throbbed. He reached up to rub his temple again, not knowing if the dampness he felt was sweat or if one of his wounds had reopened. The report from the other Eels sent his brain into protest but through the throbbing, he began trying to formulate a plan.

"It's my fault," he said, putting down his ale so that he could reach over and latch onto Eysman's shoulder and offer a couple of reassuring pats. "We'll get them back. I will make sure of it... *I promise.*"

CHAPTER 25

Highwaymen

Throughout the Darrow Valley, spring's blossoms had run their course and their fragile, fragrant petals piled like snowdrifts around the trunks of fruit trees, as vernal orchards drew their essences into a new season of budding fruit. Frogs splashed along the riverbanks at lazy intervals, and honeybees buzzed casually about the wildflowers, provisioning their pollen for honey-making.

Nowhere did nature match the pace at which Denn urged his people to ride now.

The decision to travel south increased the distance of their journey, but if there was a chance to slip into Caphedra without having to storm the gates, he wanted to take it.

Temis had the stolen tunics and Denn prepared Naobe as well as he could. Little could be done to prevent the charger from gaining attention due to her sheer size, but Denn had unfolded her saddle blanket so that it hung over her flanks like a caparison and hid her characteristic diamond markings.

As they got underway, Denn's concerns extended beyond subterfuge, however. He rode upright and tall in the saddle, but he was less alert and even neglectful of his passenger. Ramisa had pulled back the hood of her cloak to ride bareheaded, so as to take in the sweetness of the Darrow breeze. Ahead of him, riding side-saddle, she would sometimes glance back and study his expression.

"You're bothered. Troubled," Ramisa said.

"Mmm," Denn murmured.

"I shouldn't distract you. I'm sorry," she said.

"Eh? No," Denn replied contritely. "Please do."

He marvelled at her now that her face was unobscured and stunningly lit upon by the vibrant daylight. Her outward beauty did not match any of the inner turmoil he knew she endured. Ramisa appeared splendid in every regard, from the flow of her long, midnight-black hair to her elegantly sculpted and flawless face. The damage was only underneath.

She must have had other suitors, Denn thought, although he was unsure where she would find them in Fallowsea. He did not want to ask or appear jealous, but he wondered if she knew why *he* had been the one selected to carry her home to Caphedra. They had never discussed the particulars of their betrothal. The Farathemuns controlled her and kept her from knowing such essential matters, even concerning her own well-being. He wanted to ask her what she wished for and hear her answer in her own words but posed his question vaguely.

"Are you content with me?" was his simple query.

It was a question with broad intent and Ramisa appeared to appreciate its import. The twist of her former guardian's hair was tied around her wrist and it slipped along her arm as she clamped onto Denn and pressed her forehead against his chest.

"Yes. But I am not so content to condemn you to share my troubles," she said.

"Do you feel someone else might serve you better?" he asked.

"I already know you have a better heart than my cousin," she answered. "You are the one who honours my trust and my confidence, but I've put you in danger. Though it is at the insistence of my uncle, I regret I ask so much of you."

"I was in danger before I left Caphedra. It seems that you and I both attract the sort who only wish to impose upon us for their own gain." Denn felt the resentment welling up inside him. His eyes drifted first to Kentin, and then to Temis who reminded him of his father's destructive schemes. He began to squeeze the reins in his fist, but the princess wordlessly consoled him by placing her smooth fingers around his taut hands until he relaxed them again.

This calmed his anger, but Ramisa's temporary silence gave his brain all the slack on the leash that it needed for him to lose himself again in worry and regret. The mire of doubt in his own ability haunted him, as did the feeling that he suffered from incurable foolhardiness for being recruited into this fantasy of a conspiracy in the first place. He had been played as easily as one exhaled breath across a reed pipe.

Denn summoned the rider behind him. "Temis!"

"Sir?" replied the horseman on the black steed.

"What was that man's name again? From last night." Denn asked.

Temis hesitated. "I'm sorry. I don't recall well," he said, excusing his lack of an answer. "It's not important."

But it *was* important to Denn. Killing in battle was one thing, but this had been the first time Denn had slain a captive man. It was an execution. He felt sullied—more like a murderer than a just and honourable protector. The man served a lord. Convention would have dictated they take the man hostage and ransom him.

"It bothers me, taking the life of an unarmed man," Denn said, choosing to confide in Temis.

"He was armed up until a moment before. That should count for something," Temis said. "And you can't deny that man would do more harm with his mouth than he would ever do with a blade. You made the necessary... proper decision."

Denn's lament was that he found himself lured into the position of having to make that decision in the first place.

"I should still know his name," Denn said. "He died at my hand, after all."

"I might remember it if it ever becomes vital," Temis said, in what Denn perceived as a haughty refusal. "For now, sir, you don't need something like that to bounce about inside your skull. Aren't you preoccupied with enough things already?"

Temis was right. The boredom of riding for three days straight was bound to make him cling to minor considerations, and there was no other more expedient way to dispatch the Marshal's spy. Furthermore, another name hung more menacingly over him. He lowered his voice and spoke again to the princess, riding tightly pressed against his chest and lap.

"Ramisa, I'm not an adept or a scholar. Before we reach Caphedra, I wish you to explain to me," he hesitated, "who is Dagremahr?"

The name made her convulse as if she were turned inside-out. It was as if he had plunged a knife into her, and he became instantly fearful. Perhaps he should not even say the name aloud.

But Ramisa recovered. She leaned into him again while Denn turned an ear toward her, allowing him to hear her without straining or confusing anything she might tell him.

"He is one of the Faith's progenitors, the Paragon of Primacy, who would submit to no one and suffer no opposers. In life, he was a feared warlord, employed at the behest of the Faith to conduct the merciless killing of a people who challenged their power—people of a different sort from us—and he remains just as wicked in death, only with more fervour... and immortal."

The memory of Dagremahr's laughter remained unsettling, but so did the memory of the other spectres that had circled and swam in Ramisa's wide, teary eyes. "How many are there, like him?" he asked.

"There are thirteen named Paragons if you look at the months of the year. I believe that we were in communion with at least half of them."

"You speak to them?!" Denn repeated, stunned.

"Avenda could. And there is a part of me that does, too."

"My childhood schooling on the matter does not seem to be sufficient. From what you have told me, the Paragons are not just fables for the chroniclers. What makes a Paragon? Why are they not dead like they should be?"

"When a person dies, it is in this world—the world that we touch. Like an image in a mirror, they can continue in other worlds, where death is unknown and ignored."

"The otherworld? Ghosts?"

"Yes. Those are words to describe it. But ghosts are more like memories. The Paragons persist as they were—philosophers and prophets. They reached an extraordinary level of understanding and interaction with this world and eventually learned how to apply their reach across many other worlds. This learning sustained and informed a canon of philosophies around which the Faith of the Pillars was built. But while attaining a form of godhood, the Paragons were still mortal in this world, and so, they all died, one by one."

"If they're dead, why do you hear them now?" Denn asked.

"As I said, they died here but continue elsewhere. However, out of obligation and duty, the Faith has long sought to restore them, and for this, my sister, my mother, and I were offered as vessels. Golmarra had an unbelievable influence over my mother once and convinced her we were of a suitable pedigree to contain the spirits of the Paragons in our own bodies."

"This is the cause of your affliction?" Denn asked. "This is why they removed you from his reach?"

"Also, it is what precipitated my mother's death," Ramisa added, "and why they have elevated my sister. She had studied in the temple longer and had fallen more assuredly under their sway. She met our ordeal with acceptance, while I–and eventually my mother–*resisted*."

Denn turned to stare, mouth agape as he asked, "What do you mean that she accepted? She hears these voices also? But she doesn't appear to suffer for it, as you do. At least, no one has said as much."

"She's no longer attached to this world for the suffering to be apparent. In the husk that is my sister's body, resides only Centurra, the Paragon of Possibility. I don't believe anything of my sister remains–although Centurra no longer communicates with me either."

"Then what about Dagremahr? Is he your Paragon?"

"No. Lyseia is the Paragon that was paired with me. She is known as the Paragon of Purpose. I continue to hear her screaming and shouting and trying to convince me to receive her willfully. The whole ordeal has driven her mad, and me almost likewise. Whatever the Faith did to bind us, she cannot escape me, nor can I her."

"How can a spirit go mad?"

"She is obsessed with fulfilling her role, yet I have the power to deny her that. I refuse to surrender to her or permit her to command my own flesh and blood. Thus, she has been trapped between worlds and will remain so until I either give in completely, or I die. Then we would go together to the otherworld, where she would be free to have her revenge on me for the torment that I have caused her in this one."

"Lyseia is unable to leave you willingly? Surely, there must be a way."

Ramisa appeared somewhat defeated. Her eyes darted to the sides and sullenly she said, "Lyseia knows when I am contemplating how to rid myself of her–and it draws her out. Makes her angrier."

"What was it like for your mother, Queen Tressa? You said

she came to resist, too."

"I loved her so much," she began. "The Faith selected, Parscia, Paragon of Prophecy, for my mother. As the spirit moved into her, it gave her the power to see that resurrecting the Paragons would lead to catastrophe and my mother immediately began to fight back."

Ramisa was gently weeping now but continued.

"The High Precept had prepared the spirit of an ancient sovereign, a dead king named Dagremahr, to inhabit my father or brother. Golmarra conducted the rituals and brought him back, but Dagremahr turned out to be quite different than the other Paragons."

Denn was now stone silent, listening eagerly and fearfully at the same time.

"Dagremahr did not wish to be brought back and became angry and troublesome. In life, he had been harsh and cruel with a famous appetite for dominance. When he died, he learned there were more realms to conquer than this one. Whereas the other Paragons have placed value on life and sometimes sought a return to this world, he only seeks to rule here that he may shepherd the dead to fill his ranks in the otherworld. Some also call him the Paragon of the Perished for vanquished soldiers look to him to lead them in the afterlife, to restore their honour or satisfy them when their lust for fighting cannot be sated."

"And your mother, she died all because of this?"

"Yes, and I fear for her. Sometimes I hear her trying to speak to me, but I can't understand. She is too far away."

Denn realized they were lagging behind the other horses but wanted to do his best to remain out of earshot of the others. He wanted to learn more, though he feared that he was dangerously close to upsetting her. The princess's eyes were becoming red and puffy. It would do no good to have her descend into a frenzy of tears here on the ride.

"Lyseia told me that my mother knew the dangers of bringing Dagremahr back into this world. There were already disagreements amongst the Paragons and inviting them here would draw their conflict into the world of the living. But these could all be Lyseia's lies. I don't know because it happened after I was taken to Fallowsea. She said that my mother had asked Parscia to bargain with Dagremahr and he withdrew without demanding a host for himself, but as her part of the bargain, my mother poisoned herself."

"But why has he returned now. Has he come back for you, too?"

"Maybe. Somehow, he has been reawakened and is seeking lives again. Perhaps, it is he who is responsible for my father's murder." Ramisa had to swallow back tears but continued. "I don't think he would hurt my sister since she has welcomed Centurra within her. But, my brother, whose ambition draws him to the crown—Dagremahr may have plans for him."

"Why doesn't he just fade away, back to the world of the dead, content to fight his battles in the afterlife?"

"Because a soul can live many lives across many worlds, but it is only here in this one that is created, and its purpose determined. It is only in this world that one can enslave the dead. Golmarra knows this too, which is why he has kept Dagremahr's mortal remains within a venerated sepulchre deep in the temple where he has him bound.

"So Golmarra commands the Paragons?" Denn asked.

"Golmarra has been fooled," Ramisa said. "He believes he can control the Paragons because he controls the tomb that houses their remains. But the more power and influence they gain, the less bound to their bodies they become. By his doing, they will be free to return and enact a campaign of great evil among, and against, the living. Dagremahr does not yet protest because he takes joy in causing more death—in hopes of gaining more followers, more power, more realms to control."

"More death," Denn shuddered.

Ramisa nodded. Her tears were beginning to ebb, and it was a surprise to hear her become this talkative. He wondered how long it had been since someone listened to her. Still, the depth of her knowledge posed a question.

"You couldn't have learned this all from Kentin. Who told you? Does your Paragon whisper these things in your ear?"

"I don't believe much of what Lyseia tells me. It was Avenda who taught me most of what I know about the different worlds. Her people are different. They understand. She could reach out and push back against the Paragons where they existed, and she did it quite naturally. You see, Avenda is the one that taught me how our world was unique—that each person's birth in this world is an act of primordial creation that sends ripples across worlds. Some may return to be reborn, but all life begins here."

Her statements struck Denn with reverent wonder. But as incomprehensible as it sounded, he was reminded that Dagremahr was real. That was enough for him to see the necessity of action. "If we can send him back, we will. But at the very least, we must refuse him what he seeks."

"And Golmarra... and all his followers with him," Ramisa added.

"I find it incredible to believe someone could be so bold as seek to enslave the dead and act without any fear."

"Golmarra is careful. He knows that he can be consumed by his enchantments and that he risks losing his bond to this world— over time. A waking death while his essence is trapped elsewhere. That is one cost of such endeavours. The other is that in the end, he may win nothing save for a legacy of vengeful souls waiting for him once he succumbs to death, himself."

Denn's expression went grim. "Destroying oneself, then? For power? Magic?" The possible repercussion of her words sent a chill down his spine. Livet was playing with such things. Denn had more questions he wished to ask, but he did not wish to betray Livet's existence to Ramisa. Livet's encounters with charms and little tricks may be minuscule in comparison with the Faith's ability to claw back spirits from death, but he knew he had to find her. Above all, she needed to be informed of this dangerous outcome and not be allowed to follow any new friends into such damnation.

Ramisa's answers started to come out as mumbles. She was tiring now. Her life of interplay between these worlds must be enough to physically drag her into a morass of exhaustion.

Denn had resolved to allow her some rest when, without warning, the other riders raised their voices in a merry commotion. The western wall of Caphedra had appeared off their left flank. They were almost to the Darrow. Soon they would see the borough's watchful garrison and the worn and welcomed arched bridge, over which the road to Caphedra would be near completion.

"When we enter the city, I am sorry," Ramisa said, "I don't think we will have much chance to speak further for a while. The Paragons have granted me respite so far, but once we arrive at the walls, they are bound to assail my thoughts anew. I wish I could be hidden from them."

The anticipation of her coming ordeal brought renewed tears to her eyes, and her breathing was interspersed with sniffling and running tears, as the apprehension welled up in her throat.

By midmorning, they had reached the banks of the Darrow and followed along to its namesake crossing. Darrow Bridge spanned the river with seven, pointed ogival arches. Centuries ago, its construction had once been a cause for jubilation by the landowners to the river's west. It allowed their heavy-laden carts to bypass barges and deliver their produce and wares to Caphedra unimpeded. It was built as a gift from the city to the collective lords of the Darrow, so long ago that Caphedra was not even thought of as a capital at that time. But while this development ensured the vast multiplication of the lords' wealth, it also eroded Darrow's political clout—to their detriment. The more roads that pointed toward Caphedra, the stronger that city became as a trade centre and local gentry were inspired to pack up their new riches and left to take up residences in Castleside and Highside. Even nowadays, some of Caphedra's wealthiest noble families still traced their lineages back to this migration of the Darrow Lords.

The high absenteeism soon gave Darrow a reputation of being a paradise for those who sought the opposite: opportunity without wealth, out-of-sight of—or even free from—the yoke of noble masters. The character of the people took on a stubborn independence which caused Denn's uncle, Phar, always to report favourably on the place, almost romanticizing it.

King Ramis had been less impressed with what he deemed as a predilection toward lawlessness. He answered by funding a garrison to house the 4th Brigade, under Lord Mirsey Don. A triangular fort of block-cut sandstone, with three spiralling towers, housed the king's troops and policed the roadway and river. It made sure that any passing wagons—or barges sailing to Hasen—had paid their taxes and were not transporting contraband or criminals. However, Lord Don had grown lax and lazy since Ramis's passing, and if he did halt a merchant or pilgrim, he kept the money for himself.

"Do you see any soldiers on the road?" Denn asked as they approached.

"There," said Kentin, pointing. "There's a shelter on the other side of the bridge."

"Likely not very profitable to collect tolls on this side," surmised Temis.

"Saves them having to cross back over the bridge for a mug of ale at the garrison," said Kentin. He began pulling his gauntlets more tightly and checking his fastenings and straps. "We are crossing this bridge today. There is no time for any further delay. The sun is getting high, and I wish to be in the city soon."

Kentin pointed and sent his men to reconnoitre the roadblock and report back. With eagerness they stormed ahead, riding over the hump of the bridge toward the pavilion.

"Perhaps it's a good time to hear that jingle, m' lord," advised Temis smartly.

"Boy, if you knew what money was, you'd be less quick to spend it," answered Kentin without turning toward the source of the audaciousness, though sounding just as cocksure in response. "These men will be paying taxes *to us* someday."

"Whose side has Lord Don taken in this war? Has he come out in support of any of the heirs?" asked Denn.

"I don't think he's spoken of it with any clear determination," said Kentin. "He's quite slippery at the best of times, and he has yet to have his hand forced. Myrhic has recruited mostly in the north, bypassing Darrow. The Faith have drawn support from Vlass in Lanstad, and from some of the old home guard in the city. Being as it is, I don't think either side has had the surfeit of patience that it would take to get him to come off the fence."

Denn began to strategize. The prospect of a well-positioned lord, with military assets, close to the capital, would be a boon if they enticed him to their cause.

"Perhaps Temis has struck out on the right path, if only short-sightedly. Maybe Don's support could be bought. What do you think?" Denn said.

"Maybe. I don't know," said Kentin. "These lords know that if the Faith wins, they'll be bled dry of money. But on the other hand, if Myrhic wins, he'll rob them of men. The Lord Marshal does not make a habit of keeping valuable troops in garrison under indecisive or impotent masters. That's why Don was stripped from command of the Thirteenth after they were ordered out of Hasen."

The 13th Brigade had been Denn's uncle's. Denn slipped his hand down and ran a thumb over the engraved Jasmine inlay on the crossguard of his sword. Though it was his weapon now, it felt odd to think that Longlimb had once been sworn to serve the lord whose keep dominated the road ahead of them, and perhaps an unfortunate omen if he were forced to draw it.

At that moment, Kentin's two riders returned over the bridge, crossing the span at a brisk trot. They sat high in the saddle, optimistic and undeterred.

"Two men on guard, m' lord," said the first. "Swords. No horse."

The other added, "Seems light for a garrison. The men have either probably gone off for better pay or sloughed off their posts and gone back to their farmsteads. I don't think this pair will trouble us if we look like we'll put up a fight."

"Very well," said Kentin. "We will proceed."

Riding over Darrow Bridge, the expected reception awaited them as soon as they began the downgrade. The pair of Darrow guards wore breastplates, and on their heads were bascinets with mail skirts in back, draped over the nape of their necks. They stepped onto the road but did not draw their weapons when faced with five armed riders. Instead, the two sentries partook in offering uncommon politeness with their demand.

"Sirs, this bridge belongs to Lord Mirsey Don. It is customary to pay to cross it."

Kentin edged his steed closer to the men so that they had to step back or risk getting a foot crushed under one of its hooves. "This bridge was built by Caphedrans. To whom has Mirsey been remitting these fares? Since it is, most certainly, *not his bridge.*"

The man stammered out, "It's c-cus-customary—just *customary*, m' lord."

"I'll spare a silver civil for each of you if you can tell me whose troops have been crossing this bridge in the last seven days."

The guards looked back and forth at each other. The more senior-looking of the two answered, "None, sir. The Pillarmen ordered the farmers to supply the city, but they left them to protect themselves in getting there. They won't spare the troops so long as the Marshal threatens to attack. That's why the roads aren't safe these days."

The other nodded. "There are a lot of violent, unpaid men on the highways, ever since the king died. They make a living off the backs of honest travellers and merchants."

Temis rolled his eyes. "You must do well with your little venture, here," he said snidely.

Kentin made good on his offer but tossed the coins to the side of the road, forcing the men to bend down humbly to retrieve them. As they did, he bid them," Good day," and spurred his horse to resume travelling.

The soldiers muttered something that Kentin did not seem to hear. Then as Denn passed, one soldier strained his neck to get a look at the cloaked and concealed woman who was riding in front of Denn. The eyes of the other landed on Longlimb's hilt, and he nudged his companion. Both became serious and stone-faced then stepped back entirely off the road as he made his passage on the back of Naobe. Whatever had caught their eye, at least it led to no fuss, Denn thought.

The relief was short-lived. As soon as he had ridden on, another concern erupted right in his lap. Ramisa twisted with a tremendous, painful convulsion. He was sure the other riders must have noticed, and he clumsily attempted to cover it up by saying, "Adjust yourself in the saddle, m' lady. Be comfortable."

Kentin dropped back to scrutinize them. "If you feel anything other than a pommel horn, dear cousin, report to me," he said.

Ramisa ignored him and pulled Denn closer once more. "Oh, Denn! Something felt like it seized my insides the moment that we crossed the river. They know I'm coming and are trying to divine where I am," she said meekly.

"How can we deliver you safely? What will they do if they learn you are coming?"

"I am sure they will send agents to collect me," she said. "I fear that Lyseia can use my own ears to listen, and the closer we get to Caphedra, the more she will hear and spread the word to the others." She pressed upon the strands of Avenda's gold and copper hair around her wrist as if drawing strength.

"Somehow, we must keep you hidden from their sight," Denn said worriedly. "At least until we get you to the safety of your uncle's house."

Compliant, she let go of the comforting braid and replaced the hood of her cloak over her head. The fair and sublime face of Denn's travelling companion became hidden from him, once more.

Between the Darrow and the highway leading to Caphedra's south gate, the road was stony and dusty. Any puddles from the previous week's rain had long since dried up, with channels of deep ruts, remaining to show where wagons had been traversing the route on those wetter days. Wherever the dirt was not solidly patted down, their horses' hooves scattered pebbles and flattened it.

Vlass's men notwithstanding, Denn suspected the Faith was keeping the Southgate open to furnish the city with fresh crops and summer wheat, as much as possible, in preparation to withstand a siege. The increase they began to see in traffic attested to it but nowhere more so than when they reached the crossroads where the southern highway split, running west to Darrow or east to Falbeth.

Then, nearer the city as predicted, he saw the squads of troops sporting wooden shields, all painted with the Lanstad boar's head. Denn noticed that they were only carrying supplies for two or three days at most—not enough to reach Lanstad without reprovisioning. Was Vlass sending a caravan of stores to meet them? If instead, they planned to strike out to the east and north to circle the city, they would have enough food to make it to Northwood, and that supported the idea of a plan to outflank Myrhic's army in the field—as foolish as that might be. Perhaps, stockpiles of provisions in Caphedra were simply too low to spare. Maybe the Faith could pay *but not feed* an army of this size. They could be leaving out of sheer hunger. Whatever the destination, they were marching quickly and in a steady flow along the highway.

Just then, Temis and Kentin fell back alongside Denn. They had been eyeing the road ahead where a scuffle had appeared to have broken out, centred around a merchant and his wagon.

"That fellow has got himself into a spot of trouble, I believe," Temis said and pointed out the halted wagon in the middle of the road. Pulled by a herculean brick-coloured ox, it was heavy-laden with wooden casks and barrels of various sizes. Several men blocked the driver's path. It had the appearance of a confrontation—but one with woefully uneven sides.

"Let's see what this is about," said Denn.

Ramisa grasped his arm and softly warned him, "Be careful."

Atop the wagon, the old, wiry driver was doing his best to threaten the men on the road by standing up on his bench and savagely swinging a long-handled axe, back and forth through the air. His ally was an equally thin, but younger defender who stood his ground in front of the wagon with another axe that was more fit for chopping wood than hacking up men. Standing against them were four blockaders, with spears and swords, who were jeering and menacing them as they cut off the wagon's route to the city.

With unconvincing authority, the boy before the wagon declared, "We are commanded by the Faith to deliver to Caphedra. Move out of the way!"

"I know some people that would rather enjoy that cider themselves," answered the leader of the would-be robbers. "Step down! You and your father can carry on by foot. We'll take the wagon!"

One of the robbers feigned a punch at the boy who flinched and drew back before promptly reasserting himself as a buffer between the thieves and his family's valuable transport. The older man, whom they presumed to be his father, shouted furiously at the highwaymen to step back.

"Brave fellow," admitted Kentin, gesturing toward the boy. "If he were a few years older, we could use someone like that."

"Someone without the good sense to run when you're outnumbered four-to-one?" asked Temis. "Yes, I could see how you would view that as a virtue. Must be damned good cider he's protecting."

Independent of the others, Denn urged Naobe to ride up alongside the wagon, and as he reached it, he lifted Ramisa out of the seat and onto one of the barrels to keep her safe. The old man looked back with surprise but seeing her slight feminine form clamouring over the casks and realizing that he was being boarded by something other than a brigand, his anxious expression eased.

Suddenly the boy up front cried out. Denn could not see the damage, but one of the robbers had struck for real this time—and used a blade. Blood spewed from the boy; he stumbled and fell.

"You were told to step back!" Denn shouted to the attacker,

announcing his entrance into the fray. Atop Naobe, he towered above both the highwaymen and the injured youth who now lay in a heap on the road.

Two of the spearmen quickly planted the butt of their weapons into the ground, meaning to deny him the chance to charge. Denn had to pull back on the reins and Naobe reared up on her hind legs, increasing her form to a formidable and awe-inspiring height. The spearmen trembled with panic. Even the massive ox could be seen to cower.

As Naobe's front hooves hovered frightfully at head height, mesmerizing the terrified highwaymen, it was easy for Temis and Kentin to ride up from the other side of the wagon and blindside hapless robbers. Bearing down from horseback, Kentin slashed at one spearman who crumpled and rolled to the edge of the road.

Beside him, still wielding the partisan he had brought from Fallowsea, Temis whipped the polearm in an arc where it sliced across the other man's shoulder and neck. The victim dropped his spear in surrender and wrapped his good arm about himself as if trying to hold his torso together.

The soldiers from Fallowsea soon secured the capitulation of the remaining highwaymen and cleared the path between the merchant and his son.

"Rodin!" shouted the old father, who clumsily leapt from the wagon to tend to the boy. Weeping, he repeated his son's name as he fell to his knees and clasped the pale figure in his arms.

Denn dismounted and rushed past the ox and wagon, to the boy, but Ramisa was already ahead of him. She knelt beside the father, and joined in cradling the boy who coughed, sputtered, then managed a weakly responsive, "Father..."

"Praise the Pillars! Thank the Paragons," exclaimed the father.

Ramisa was shaken—still shaking—but her fingers were busy. She had produced a piece of material, either a scarf or a sash, and tied it tightly around the boy's wound. It was a violent, near-fatal gash, but he was conscious and alive. She began soothing him with reassuring words.

Kentin motioned to his soldiers, and in unison, they plunged their swords into the men that they had apprehended. The dead bodies fell to the road and were dragged off behind a nearby bush while the patient ox, hitched to the cart, lowed, snorted, and watched.

Gently, the merchant carried his son to the wagon where he hunted about for a cup. From a tap on one of the casks, he poured out a draught of golden apple cider and helped the boy to drink. "You'll feel better," he said, then expressed gratitude to the saviours around him.

"Haven't you heard? The roads are dangerous these days," Temis said. "Why were you travelling without more men?"

"I am travelling under the Faith's authority. I have a letter! They ordered me to bring cider to Caphedra. I've come all the way from Calkairn!"

"Maybe the fellows couldn't read," Kentin suggested with disparaging sarcasm.

Denn was greatly interested. "May I see the letter?" he asked.

"Here," said the man, pulling a piece of parchment from under the driver's bench. "'Authority granted to Rendrin Stramm. Purchase for six puncheons of strong cider and an open request for additional approved wares.'"

"You've got eight," Kentin counted suspiciously, "and then some."

"The other two are for sale in Caphedra. The Faith only pays the bare minimum and I need some profit."

Denn handed the letter back to the merchant. "As my companion said, it's dangerous on this road, but you're a businessman and I have a proposal."

The old man peered at Denn and nodded that he was listening.

"We are travelling to the city. You can hire us as your security for the price of one puncheon," Denn said. "That leaves six for the Faith and one more for you to sell to the taverns."

There was a clopping of hooves as Kentin maneuvered his steed closer to Denn. "Don't be distracted from our task, Wellum. You're not that hard up for money, I hope, nor do I think we will have time to celebrate with a barrel that size at any time so soon. We've done enough for this man and should be on our way."

"I propose that we accompany Mr. Stramm into the city on his very official business." He smiled and Kentin caught on to Denn's plan.

Stramm, without such knowledge, was deflated but resigned to the idea of armed accompaniment. He looked to his son who was weak and had only narrowly avoided death on this very spot.

"I accept," the old man said.

"Excellent," Denn said. "Temis, help me overturn one of the barrels!"

"I'm not that thirsty, right now, sir."

Denn gave Temis a stern look that indisputably conveyed this as an order. Temis dismounted and wrapped his arms around one of the massive puncheons. "Help?" he asked Kentin's men, who looked back and forth at each other, before volunteering to get off their horses and lend a hand.

The barrel sloshed and tipped onto its side with a great force, causing the wagon to rock and the oxen to protest.

"Do you need a tap?" Stramm asked Denn.

"No, but I'll borrow your axe," he said, and taking the heavy lumberman's axe, he brought it down hard against the flat end of the barrel and hacked at it until he revealed a wide, splintery opening. The cider poured forth in a tide of amber, and the strong stench of alcohol wafted around them. The river of drink spread out and seeped into the muddied road intoxicating the dandelions and drowning crickets.

Everyone looked shocked and stood speechless.

Turning to Ramisa, he apologized. "I don't think we can do much about the cider smell, but we can put some saddle blankets inside, so you don't rock around too much. As we enter Caphedra, you should remain hidden within. No one will see you."

Ramisa stood listening to the plan, dumbstruck, but Kentin found his tongue and whispered to Denn, "You're putting a lot of trust in this old man. Do you think he'll be so eagerly transformed into a *smuggler*?"

Denn responded with uncharacteristic ruthlessness. "Why don't you ride next to his son and encourage the man's complicity?" He tapped lightly with his finger on the horn-handled dagger at his belt.

Kentin shrugged, nodded, and grinned with cold-blooded approval.

"I don't want anything to happen to us," Denn said, "and I am sure he does not want anything to happen to his boy, so I'll entrust the fate of young Rodin to you. Leave the princess to me."

CHAPTER 26

Southgate

"**Y**ou would have me enter my mother's city smelling like a drunkard?" the princess moaned. "That cider barrel is disgusting!"

"It's the best way to keep you out of sight," Denn pleaded. "Please understand. If you are recognized before we reach your uncle's manor, the Faith will be alerted, and they will hunt you down."

"It reeks!" Ramisa said emphatically.

"Until you reach your uncle's house, you're not safe. Make it there and you will have hundreds of defenders to keep you from harm. But for now, your security is up to us."

Hoisting the empty puncheon to the top of the barrels, Denn cleared a space in the middle of the wagon for Ramisa. In his estimation, the barrels closer to the back, on their sides, would be the easiest to tap and sample, should a thirsty gate guard choose to inspect their goods. He avoided those.

Kentin handed his reins to one of his men and rested his foot on the wagon's wooden step.

"Change of plan? Not using those filthy tunics?" he asked.

"One half-believable story is sufficient," Denn said. "Today, we will be escorts for Mr. Stramm."

The cider merchant descended from his bench at the sound of his name. With a bent back, and taking short steps, he looked weighted with apprehension. "I hope you aren't planning trouble in the city." Wrinkly furrows on his forehead deepened as he muttered, "I can't afford trouble."

Kentin dismissed the concern. "Not much trouble, old man.

The city is about to turn topsy-turvy and there's little that we could do to ever rival what's to come." He grabbed a piece of rope, tied it to the bridle of his horse and tossed an end to one of his men.

"Even so, I wouldn't dally," Temis advised. "Make your delivery then get back on the road before they seal up the Southgate too. Go back to your cidery. Watch your apples grow."

With the mention of home, Stramm glanced at his ailing son and nodded his begrudging compliance.

Ramisa pulled herself up onto the wagon and stepped over a stack of casks to find her spot, then settled in like a nesting swan.

Denn directed her. "If you need me, I'll be riding beside the wagon. Don't call out. Just knock thrice on the wood and wait for me to instruct you or find a way to check on you." Together, Temis and Denn lifted the emptied, bottomless cider puncheon over her head and brought it down to conceal her, like a wooden cloche covering the main course of a banquet. Denn whispered, "Stay quiet and stay safe. They won't know that we've got you tucked away under here."

Inside the barrel, Ramisa's voice sounded muffled and enfeebled as she answered, "I understand."

From atop the wagon, it was an easy leap to Naobe's saddle. Denn signalled for the procession to recommence. Each horseman took up positions to encircle the wagon, while the ox reluctantly resumed its plodding path. The wagon's great wheels creaked and rolled forward with its valuable cargo.

The well-travelled bridge to Southgate spanned the slowly churning waters of Caphedra's begirding moat, which channelled its flow from the Darrow. Denn did not know how deep it was. The source waters passed through the city wall below the Rafters, coursed through the city between Westriver and Dockmarket, then flowed out through the arch at the base of the wall beneath Keepside's fortified tower. But here, below the humped Southgate bridge, the current was less vigorous. Who knew what manner of refuse and filth had gathered at the bottom? Any unsuccessful invader that escaped drowning would undoubtedly die of disease if they fell in.

Traversing the bridge, Denn tried to signal to the other riders to stay close as they passed through the oaken-timbered and rust-flecked iron gate, but they were too busy watching to make sure they did not inadvertently trample anyone. While the way was broad, it was choked with citizens in flight, as well as departing troops who mostly sported Lanstad regalia.

The soldiers boorishly pushed their way through the peasants and smashed their shields against the parapets of the bridge to generate an unnerving clatter with which to announce their passage. It made them seem more like they had just sacked the city rather than being the ones pledged to defend it. A few of the soldiers noticed Denn's disparaging stare and increased the racket as they brushed past him, but none were brave enough to come anywhere close to a warhorse like Naobe, so they kept at least a few arms' lengths away when projecting their bravado.

What concerned Denn was how the noise and the ruckus made it difficult to hear if Ramisa was knocking to signal him. He did his best to be attentive but knew the decisive moment would soon be upon them.

"Keep moving, Stramm," said Kentin to their driver as the merchant steered his ox through the arch of the gate. Passing into the cool shade of the entrance, Denn's eyes began to adjust to the darkness, and he saw that the Faith had multiple officiants stationed on duty, monitoring the traffic, checking manifests and recording.

A hard-faced Pillarman, dressed in a brocade vest of cobalt and silver over sky-coloured robes, scratched away on a piece of parchment. He was the master inspector. Around him, a cadre of strong-handed and relentless armsmen served as assisting examiners. These armsmen were dressed in mail coifs and habergeon shirts with a collection of blue capes and sashes testifying to their allegiance. Short swords were sheathed on their belts. In their hands, they carried long axes and hooked gaffs, which they used to pull and pry at the belongings being transported in the carts of the departing peasants. When they found something of value, they confiscated it with a smug acknowledgement and a showy appreciation for that person's faithful donation to the Pillars.

One ragged man was caught carrying a basket of bread and meats, which roused a haughty chortle from the armsmen who had sniffed it out like fox hunting mice.

"No food is to leave the city!" one said, robbing the man of the victuals he had prepared for his journey. Behind him, a woman who must have been his wife, along with their children, tried to plead for at least a portion to be returned, but the armsman was devoid of mercy. "How do I know you haven't stolen this? It will go to the men on the walls. They're *earning it*."

"But—" the frantic wife began to protest. The armsman reached out and seized her by the chin, pressing in with his fingers and tilting her head upward to cause her discomfort. He looked her up and down while her husband was powerless to step in. For a moment, the examiner appeared captivated by the woman's struggle for breath and the wet tracks of tears down her cheeks. Then, just as quickly, he released her and returned to her a single loaf of bread from the basket.

"You may thank the Pillars," he said, smiling dangerously.

The master inspector, who had watched all of this, commented, "That will come out of your pay, Toblin."

The burly armsman grunted loudly. He snatched back the bread and bellowed, "Move!" The fearful family, awash in tears, complied.

Free to move on to their next inspection, the examiners fell upon Stramm's wagon. They eyed the accompanying riders—Denn and Naobe especially—but called out to Kentin, who sat upon the driver's bench with Stramm and his son.

"Your business?" asked the master inspector.

Kentin leaned forward. "Delivery for the Faith."

"What's in the barrels? Ale? Cider?"

"Vinegar, at this rate," Kentin snapped at the man.

"We have a letter of request for provisions," Stramm informed the inspector as he handed over the parchment from before. His fingers trembled slightly.

The master inspector skimmed it, doubtlessly having seen many similar notes over the past days. He stepped forward and began personally navigating his way around the wagon. He ran his free hand over the wooden casks then halted with an observation. "You have a lot of protection for one load of cider."

Denn tried to think of something he could say to answer the query. All he could say was, "The roads are dangerous."

The head guard and examiner, Toblin, tapped his fingers on the shaft of his poleaxe, which rested on his shoulder. The longer the inspection took, the more attention they drew. Several other armsmen forewent harassing other peasants and began to assemble around Toblin, gathering like a pack of dogs. Every moment that passed, another would station themselves closer to the wagon, vigilant and mindful of the interchange at hand. One moved casually to the back of the cart and traced the barrels with his gloved hand longingly, probably checking for a tap or a spout.

Each of the armsmen was built with heft and stacked with muscle; there was not a scrawny one among them. *Here is not the place to start a fight*, Denn thought.

At the midpoint of the wagon's payload, the inspector came worryingly close to Ramisa's hiding spot. Denn's heart beat faster. If a fight started and they had to force their way out, he could not draw his sword quickly enough, nor could he be sure that he could maneuver Naobe around within the congested gatehouse. He tried to calmly cross his arms in front but pressed his forearm to his belt to reassure himself that he could at least reach his dagger in any event.

"Four riders," counted the master inspector, "and one of them of some means, it would appear." He was referring to Denn, atop Naobe.

The interest shown did not sit well with Denn, but he was keen to absorb the attention if it meant drawing it away from where the princess was secreted away.

"Mr. Stramm has hired us to protect his wares. For that purpose, we are obliged to carry arms and be outfitted as best we may be," Denn said.

"Perhaps," the master inspector said. He began to withdraw with measured steps, edging closer to the armsmen, but with a slight swish of his robes, he turned abruptly and asked, "But can you explain why there are five horses?"

"A spare," Denn said hastily, causing the inspector's eyebrows to arch sinisterly.

"I think the spare nag might belong to you. Where *did* you come by this magnificent charger? On the road? Who was its previous owner, and where are they now?"

Naobe snorted annoyedly as the inspector levelled his insinuation. Denn, on the other hand, felt like boiling over in rage at the suggestion he might have stolen his cherished steed. He was about to answer when he heard a sound from Ramisa's barrel.

She was not tapping or knocking on the walls of the emptied puncheon, as they had prescribed. Rather, it was a soft thumping of the wooden cask across the deck of the wagon. The container scraped and shifted perhaps a finger's width one way, then another. Perhaps her muscles were aching from being cooped up, Denn thought, wishing she would settle herself immediately. Now was not the time to make herself noticed.

The master inspector waved his hand about airily, with undisguised contempt. "Are you the leader of this lot?" he asked Denn.

From the driver's bench, Kentin coughed rudely.

"Mr. Stramm has hired us," Denn said, "But yes, I am responsible for our safety. You can speak with me."

Kentin gave up a discordant grumble. Perhaps it was inadvertent, but this second reaction caused nervous stirrings to bounce about the gatehouse. Kentin's horsemen, who seemed to have fallen complacent, were prompted to alertness by their lord's audible objection and looked like they were poised to escalate the confrontation.

Such an altercation would spell disaster. It was dark within the sunless entranceway, with only torchlight to illuminate the shady corners where more armsmen might be yet unseen. With the wide wagon taking up so much room, and so many horses jockeyed together, they were already choked and squeezed within the confines of Southgate's passage. With escape blocked off and no place to maneuver their mounts, they would be slaughtered at the first hint of a challenge.

Denn tried to think of anything that would ease the peril. A bribe, perhaps? He still did not know what was causing Ramisa to fidget so. He had to think fast.

"It belongs to the boy on the wagon," Temis said and pointed to young Rodin Stramm. Rodin was sitting behind the driver's bench, wrapped in a blanket but still shivering and pale.

The inspector turned his attention to the young man. "Sick? Disease?"

"No," answered Temis. "He was injured. Can't ride."

"How?" asked the inspector.

"Robbers! The poor young fellow was ambushed by faithless criminals on the Ki—Queen's Highway, sir."

Coalsmoke bore her rider a step forward out of the shady periphery, to be illuminated by the gatehouse's torchlight. On the wagon, the wounded boy did nothing to betray how far Temis was stretching the tale. He barely reacted at all, possibly already too far gone to pay notice.

Temis explained further. "We told you how dangerous it is out there, sir—especially for faithful pilgrims and those seeking to lend a hand in such times, like this dedicated young fellow. It is a good thing we were there to be called upon, to ride to his salvation. Otherwise, he would have been mortally struck down, and his horse stolen, sir."

The explanation appeared to go a long way toward satisfying the inspector, but Temis would not relinquish his spokesmanship right away. He masterfully guided the Pillarmen away from the suspicion in their guts to the greed of their belly.

"Everyone has been eying our rather enjoyable cider since we left Calkairn," Temis said, impressing Denn again with his attentive recollection to the details of Stramm's origin. "It seems everyone has heard of Stramm's Cidery! The finest, crisp Darrow apples, pressed and casked with the savvy of generations, leading to only the strongest, sweetest draughts!"

Several of the armsmen took steps forward at this point, but their hands were looser on the hilts and shafts of their weapons. Their lips glistened where their lolling tongues had wettened them.

"The temple has requested his cider to go directly to the curates and adepts. Read the letter! I was here a couple of weeks past when Precept Golmarra ordered a wagon load for himself!"

The only wagon Temis had steered through these gates a couple of weeks ago was the one in which Denn had been gagged and tied up. However, there were no guards, no inspectors then, and Temis knew it. It would be hard to disprove that facet of his story.

"I am sure this cider will be well regarded by the faithful," the master inspector said. "If you will allow me, I just need to update the numbers on your manifest. Six puncheons? The rest to be donated, yes?"

"I am sure we would be pleased to donate a cask *here*, to reward your hard-working examiners," Temis said, pointing out one of the casks that were already tapped. He smiled invitingly and dug out a large cup for them to pass around and share.

With indecipherable mumbling, the master inspector resumed his tour around the wagon, counting and recording. From a wall sconce, he procured a torch to light up the cracks between the barrels. The lead armsman, Toblin, gestured to two others in his cadre to retrieve the barrel of cider Temis offered—a surplus kilderkin which they rolled off the back, lifted and carried out of sight.

The master inspector was again drawing closer to the surreptitiously repurposed cask. Denn held his breath unconsciously and observed him make what he hoped were his final rounds. He trusted Ramisa could sense that now was a time to be absolutely silent.

Denn calculated. How many men? Ten? Eleven? More upstairs in the gatehouse tower? They had answered all the questions. If only the master inspector would sign off on the tally and let them pass.

Kentin also turned around in his seat impatiently, but Denn could tell that even the arrogant lord was uneasy. His eyes drifted up to Denn, then darted side-to-side to indicate his awareness of how narrow the gatehouse was. If something happened, they would need to get out fast. That would have been possible with a horse-drawn cart, but there was no way they could rely on Stramm's slow, lumbering bovine for a speedy escape.

"How soon are you to leave Caphedra?" the inspector asked.

Kentin huffed, "We'd probably be gone by now if you'd just hurry up!"

That forced Temis to rush again to deflect. "Ah, ah! What he means is that we are aware of the complications with Lord Ramid's army and will be happy to be out of the way at the earliest. Does the Faith need us, brother? Are you still recruiting? We are all hireable fighting men, of course—as we said. It would be an honour."

His tone was bordering on smarmy now, but it was working. The inspector stepped back from the wagon. From a small recess, he dipped his quill into an ink jar and scratched his endorsement upon the letter of trade. Denn finally allowed himself to breathe again. As soon as they were out of earshot, he desperately wanted to check on Ramisa and find out what caused her commotion.

"Silver, bread and work enough to be had here in the city, for any healthy seeker," advised the inspector. "See the master of arms at the temple. He's raising a militia out of any who present with experience and who are not otherwise already employed in a company of arms. His numbers grow by the day. At least four hundred, by the last count."

"We shall go see him right away," Temis said hurryingly.

"You'll want to, soon," said the inspector more affably. "His sergeants will be eager to put you to work."

"That's a lot of men," Denn said. "All drawn from the common folk of the town?"

"He feeds them, and they come," the inspector exposited. He made his way closer toward his own band of armsman, who also eased up with their rigidness and harsh stares. They moved to clear the way for the wagon to depart, dragging a wooden sawhorse out of the path and standing to the sides of the gatehouse. More travellers were waiting outside.

"You'll need to bring your cider to the temple stores," the inspector instructed. "Turn right and head for Stonerow. Ask the curates along the way which routes are open. Many of the roads are blocked off. They may have you go straight to the citadel."

"Whatever. Let's go, Stramm!" Kentin ordered the cider-man, who used an ox goad to send the bull surging onward again. The wooden wagon strained, and the heavy wheels resumed their motion.

Denn offered the inspector his gratitude then tapped his spurs on Naobe's side, encouraging her to take up a slow pace with the sluggish wagon.

"Hold on!" exclaimed Toblin, out of the blue.

"Eh?" Denn uttered.

"Your load is teetering. You've got a loose barrel! Wouldn't want the weight to shift on the road." The brawny, well-intentioned armsman sprung toward the cart and with two muscular arms prepared to push hard and set the errant barrel further back toward the centre of the wagon deck. But the instant he applied force, it tipped over altogether.

Out spilled Ramisa.

Toblin shouted in surprise but was momentarily stupefied.

Before the armsman could react and seize her, Denn sent Naobe ploughing into him. She knocked the big man off his feet. Denn had no time to think, only time to instinctively draw his weapon. He pulled and Longlimb emerged from its scabbard.

The remaining armsmen moved to sidestep the other horses which became excited and panicky as their riders clumsily tried to arrange to protect the wagon, but there was no room to reposition. Temis backed Coalsmoke up with one hand on his steed's reins and the other poking with his partisan, trying to keep the armsmen at a distance. Kentin's riders also drew close. One defended with a longsword. The second tried managing the reins of both his horse and Kentin's.

"Get this beast moving!" Kentin shouted to Stramm.

Armsmen rushed toward the open gates at either end, while others engaged Kentin's men. A rough-looking, deeply scarred man charged at Temis and tried to parry partisan strokes with a long-handled axe. Coalsmoke backed up as far as she could, but she was already pressing against the stone of the gatehouse wall.

The wagon might as well have been standing still until Kentin took charge. He lunged from the driver's bench toward a sconce on the wall, ripping down one of the torches. Then, like a providential storm cloud issuing a bolt of lightning, he thrust the burning flame into the hairy backside of Stramm's ox.

Feeling the fire scorch its buttocks like a brand, the ox bawled loudly. With a ripple through its colossal muscles, it thundered forward in a burst of unrestrainable power. The sawhorse splintered and the armsmen blocking the door were crushed as the ox and wagon launched out of the gatehouse and into the street.

It was a short-lived spectacle. After overcoming the immediate shock from Kentin's fiery prod, the ox swerved and pulled angrily, then stubbornly planted its forehooves into the ground. The wagon behind could not take the shifting strain while still burdened by the weight of its load. An axle snapped, sending a wheel careening, and the whole platform tipped. Its front corner wedged into the ground.

Stramm held on with one hand. Kentin swung himself around to land where he could avoid the vengeance of the furious steer. The boy, Rodin, screamed in pain as a cask rolled against his back and sent his already injured body sprawling. His wound reopened, and blood was again drenching his shirt.

Ramisa shrieked. She had been tossed the farthest from the wreck and was flailing on the ground. It was as if she were unable to regain control of herself or get back to her feet. Kentin sprinted toward her, snatched her by the arm and brutally dragged her away from the dangerous debacle—and out of Denn's sight. Toblin and some of his men darted after them, and also disappeared as they gave chase.

Denn tried to use the void left by the doomed wagon to better his position, but Kentin's riders were quicker to spur their mounts through the sudden gap. Their horses were sleeker and faster than Naobe. In their flight, they unavoidably blocked Denn's escape, leaving the bulk of the armsmen to turn on him. Slashing through the air with Longlimb, Denn made several critical cuts against his adversaries, but could not stop from being swarmed.

Below him, Naobe huffed and exhaled breath like fire. She whinnied as the other horses bolted off. In the frenzy that ensued, Denn felt the hook from a gaff snag the back of his neck, and when its employer pulled, Denn was wrenched from Naobe's saddle. He crashed to the stone floor where fists and boots rained down upon him.

At least three armsmen converged on Denn. Two grabbed his arms and painfully pinned them back while the third smashed a fist into his face as destructively as if he were swinging a bag of horseshoes. Sharp, unbearable pain shot across Denn's cheeks, eyes, and jaw. Blood poured from his nose. He lost balance and dropped to his knees.

One of the soldiers let go, let him slump, then made for Naobe's reins to pull the big horse into submission. She resisted, nickering and bucking violently, and shaking the whole tower. Her thick, muscled neck curved around so she could chomp at the offending armsman. Feeling her hot breath and nearly having his nose amputated by the charger's powerful teeth, the man retreated.

Denn couldn't see through the mist of blood clouding his vision. Where was Temis?

"Demis, go! Fin' the princess. Save Serenn. Leave ne!" he spat blood, and it felt like he had teeth that were knocked loose. He received a gut punch for his entreaty. Denn winced and lost his voice. He didn't know if his ribs would collapse, or if his thumping heart would burst inside his ribcage first. He was almost to the ground. His head hovered above the one knee that jutted up from the floor to brace his body. The blood dripped down, and he tried blinking his eyes to clear his sight as best he could.

In one corner, he saw Coalsmoke bolting toward the city-side opening. At a near gallop, the jet black rouncey ran so swiftly that she appeared to drag the shadows with her in passing. But she was riderless.

Denn despaired, but at least Kentin might have managed to get away with the princess, and the Fallowsea riders fled in time to provide them with a buffer of protection. He hoped this to be the case. If he were defeated here in the gatehouse, Denn wanted his last thought to be that the princess was safe.

The men that had held him were no longer on his arms. Denn did not know what was happening. He fumbled for his sword and tried to stand, only to be horrified. Naobe was exploding with rage in the tiny space, bucking and striking everywhere. She emitted a horrendous equine scream that echoed against the walls of the narrow stone corridor. Her rear hooves danced high in the air, and with a mighty thrust, she snapped a man's head from his spine.

As soon as her hind legs returned to the ground she reared up, with her height reaching the second storey of the inner tower. Around her, men with spears and pikes braced to pierce her heart and sides as she descended. Her chestnut coat became saturated with crimson, and her titanic heart gushed out a deluge of blood.

As the behemoth of a horse collapsed, her head fell toward Denn. He looked into her enormous brown eyes and saw the flicker of life extinguish itself with dreadful mortal dullness.

Denn's sword fell from his hand. An armsman spun him around and seized him. With ropes around his wrists, he was bound again—just as he had been the last time he passed through this same gate.

Toblin returned, looking grim and out of breath. "This one," he said and gestured toward Denn. "He is in league with the Farathemuns." His mail coif draped over his shoulders and jingled as his chest, rose and fell with wheezing inhales and exhales.

Appearing out of a small, safe recess in the gatehouse wall, the master inspector re-emerged. "Good work. You support the Pillars well. This man, Wellum, has been declared to be an apostate."

"Shall we take him to Councillor Sulford?" asked the armsman who was holding onto Denn from behind and confirming what had been heard and suspected. Indeed, Sulford must have survived. Thankfully, Denn reassured himself, the councillor's black blade was far away, somewhere within the dense woodlands of the Eldergorge.

"Sulford is recovering from his last expedition. Let him rest for the coming battle. We will take this man to Curate Wellum, instead."

"Wellum? Off to the priory, then? Is this man a relation?" asked Toblin.

"Yes," confirmed the inspector. "The curate's brother."

"But what will Wellum do to his own flesh and blood?" Toblin asked.

The master inspector was unconcerned. A slight look of contentment even settled across his face as he handed Toblin a laudatory mug of drink with which to help him revive his strengths. Denn couldn't smell it through his bloody nose, but he suspected by its colour that it was the cup of cider from the cask they'd given up earlier.

"Lehn Wellum is the adept who signed the apostasy charge," said the inspector. "His heart is with the Faith and beyond reproach. He will know how to dispose of this renegade."

Taking a deep swig from the mug, Toblin refilled it, then passed it around to the other armsmen to toast their victory and Denn's arrest.

"So, his other brother's a curate? I guess it doesn't run in the family. Who knew such good cider could come from a rotten apple? This drink's got a nice bite, though," Toblin mused. He retrieved the mug from its rounds and splashed the final dregs into Denn's face. "C'mon then. Let's go see your brother."

Denn stumbled as he was pushed into motion. As he took his first steps, he felt the stickiness of Naobe's blood underfoot. It had pooled over much of the floor. The soles of his boots were stained by it.

Free from dealing with Denn, the master inspector turned to address the matter of the dead warhorse blocking passage through his gatehouse.

"Summon a butcher to cut that up. The meat should not go to waste at a time like this," he ordered. Then taking up his quill, he dipped it in ink and began scribbling his notes.

❖　❖　❖

Toblin and a pimply, foul-faced helper tugged and dragged Denn artlessly through the streets of Kroftstalls, on the way to the Folds. Denn was having trouble seeing out of one eye, which had swollen nearly shut. He also worried that along the side of his face, he could feel numbness. It made the pain bearable but was not an encouraging turn for his injuries to take.

One foot at a time, he lurched along and tried to keep up with the brutes that hauled him by a tether. He was not embarrassed. No one would recognize him with his face swollen as it was. Besides, the sight of ruffed-up apostates being led to their demise was now commonplace. He was more concerned that his brother was liable to have him on a pole in Hamrin Square before the Marshal even reached the walls.

Toblin had ceased speaking more than a few grunts and growls. The chase after Kentin and Ramisa had worn him out substantially, it seemed. He was more fatigued now than when he had first returned to the gatehouse. At least, the pace with which they were pulling him was slowing to a more manageable crawl. The poxy man also looked to be dithering. It was this man who had Denn's sword slung over his back.

A suspicion crossed Denn's mind that something was amiss. They certainly would not be slowing down for his benefit. He ventured a plan to engage them on the matter to glean some clue as to why. Maybe he could yet find some advantage.

"Whe' a' you takin' ne?" His mouth pained to say the words, and it hurt when he tried to move his lips to speak.

Toblin stopped, causing Denn to brush past him, and as he did so, the armsman pushed him again. It was a solid, full-body push that felt more like the oaf was falling into him.

"Shuddup," Toblin answered, also with some apparent difficulty. "Keep t' yerself," he slurred. Foamy spittle projected from his mouth.

Surely, he couldn't be so drunk from that slight measure of cider they'd had. But Denn heard the laboured footfalls of the other guard behind, and the memories of that night at Ayren's cottage rushed back to him—and of the soporific in the wine.

Poison? In the cider?

In an instant, the hand pressing against his back had disappeared. Before Denn could understand what was happening, the rope lead fell slack, then tightened again and suddenly jolted Denn forward as Toblin dropped to all fours ahead of him.

No words came, only the sound of a raspy, panicky gurgling from a slit in his throat. Like a snake at the side of the road, Temis had been coiled and ready to strike. First, he slashed the throat of the man in the back, then he set upon Toblin.

People on either side of them rushed away from the terrifying scene. Two men—Pillarmen—lay murdered on the street, and the wrath of the Faith would invariably descend once the crime was spotted.

Temis sliced the rope that bound Denn's hands together and its bristly strands came undone.

"Can you see well enough to walk?" asked Temis.

"I—I...," Denn stammered. "Yeah."

Temis grabbed Denn's arm and inserted Longlimb into his hand. "You'll want this back before we go see Farathemun," he said.

Denn grunted out a thank you and, with effort, strapped the sword to his back by its baldrick. Temis helped with the buckles.

"I know a quiet well nearby where we can get some cool water and try to bring that swelling down. I saw the Pillarmen splash the cider on you. You'll want to wash your face before you feel the effects of the Pashter oil. It will make you numb and sap your energy."

"You poisoned the cider?"

"I didn't. I hadn't the time to spike the keg," said Temis. "So, I coated the mug with the oil instead."

The toxin helped numb Denn's facial pain, but seeing the pair of bodies they left behind, it would be prudent to have the residue removed if there was the chance it might knock him out. He was going to need his wits, and to be alert.

Everything was unbearable, right now. One foot in front of the other, ploddingly, Denn started after Temis.

"Naobe?" he asked with pathetic futility.

"We're walking. I'm sorry," Temis replied.

CHAPTER 27

The Helpless and the Hopeful

Far from the uproarious clamour and noise of the Peahen's raucous tavern floor, Livet crept, stalking her objective. Down a narrow, artfully panelled corridor of sliding screens and beaded tapestries, her eyes traced the sought-after siren's silhouette illuminated by candlelight behind a thin, draped linen. An ancient musk drifted suggestively on the air, consorting with delicate florals and hints of fruit. A brush could be heard, pulling and stroking someone's long, indulgent hair.

Celebra called to her. "I know you're there. Don't be timid." The hostess continued her grooming. "Come closer."

Livet gently drew the partition aside and entered the candlelit boudoir. Celebra was sitting on a high-legged, plush-cushioned chair, before a vanity of carved rosewood. Even seated, the woman was taller than Livet. In the vanity's centre was a mirror of the purest, clearest glass that Livet had ever seen. In its perfect reflection, Celebra gazed back and continued her brush strokes, applying a bright scarlet preparation of carmine into her already cherry-red hair.

"You're Gardia's new girl?" she asked.

Livet was momentarily taken aback by the assumption that she was already a part of Gardia's cabal—or was even sure she wanted to be—but if such an intimation allowed her to interrogate Celebra with more weight, she would allow it.

"Harbud and Taringer brought me 'ere," Livet said. "I came to Caphedra with Baressa."

Should she have said Baressa's name? In strange company, perhaps she should have reverted to calling her Portia. Livet mulled it over briefly before returning to her actual reason for the visit. What she wished to know was what, exactly, Captain Alamm had said about Denn. Hull had skimped on details. Perhaps Celebra had more information and Livet felt encouraged to press her further.

The room felt very relaxing and Celebra was uncommonly welcoming. Livet could not help but feel drawn to her, somehow. The nervousness she felt in deciding to approach the hostess had dissipated and her gut feeling compelled her to see Celebra as a safe confidant.

"Your drinkin' companion tonight–the soldier–what'd 'e say about Denn Wellum?"

"Oh," Celebra said, pursing her lips playfully. "Just what you've heard from Hull. Nile confides in me, but most of the things we speak about are intimately private matters. Denn Wellum–he is of interest to you, is he?"

Placing her brush onto the vanity, she unscrewed a small sapphire-coloured ampoule and dipped her long, slender finger into the concoction that it held. She dabbed a spot of it behind each ear. It smelled appetizingly of cherries mixed with spicy peppermint. Livet inhaled deeply.

"Denn, is he your friend? I'd wager he might have been a lover, except that he's travelling with another woman—and one of some notoriety, I gather. The Lady Ramisa, yes?"

Livet swallowed, taken aback.

Savouring the reaction, Celebra twisted in her seat and offered Livet her full attention. "It bothers you? What is the truth, dear Livet? *Tell me.*"

"I love him," Livet said without evasion. "I'm to meet 'im when 'e comes back."

This mention of the princess irritated Livet. For the first time, she felt jealous. What did Celebra hear about Denn and this woman? Was there more to their pairing that she was not saying?

"I'm sorry if I suggested anything otherwise. I'm sure he holds a place for you in his heart," the hostess offered in reassurance. Despite their softening tone, Celebra's words scraped and dug into Livet. She felt an urge to divulge the vast trove of her thoughts, but such contemplations included a host of poisonous misgivings best kept locked in tight. She worried whether it was wise to let Denn slip off on his mission with the princess. Maybe she should not have let him go.

"He should arrive in Caphedra with this other woman soon," Celebra said. "Gardia is usually very protective over our storeroom, but there might be a little something I could slip to you that would... *enchant* him and bind his desires in your favour."

Like in a blast of cold air, Livet was abruptly returned to her senses. Undeniably, Celebra could draw on more than just her unparalleled physical beauty when seducing her prey. Something more powerful complemented her charms, and realizing this, Livet did her best to close her mind and her mouth to any more unfettered disclosures.

But before such prudence became necessary, she was interrupted.

"Livet!" Neriah's voice carried down the hallway.

Reaching to open the linen drape a crack, she replied, "Over here."

Appearing at the doorway, Neriah looked displeased and glowered at the woman seated at the vanity.

"Gardia wishes to speak with you, Livet. Now!" The last word punctuated her message with an implied warning toward Celebra, who casually floated a farewell to Livet, smirked, and went back to primping.

Gardia was neither toying nor trifling.

"What are the Eels' plans for the Half Moon?" Gardia asked. She sat in an office, upon an elevated chair, across from Livet behind a messy, scratched table. Its surface was ancient, discoloured, and pitted with knife marks. Neriah stood to the side, uncomfortably between them.

"I dunno, as it's not my business," said Livet.

"It's *all of our business!*" contradicted Gardia. "Any threat of upsetting the order of Westriver or Faralley is a concern for everyone living here."

Livet remained tight-lipped and unforthcoming. She had first hoped that Gardia would offer some help, but now she feared that saying too much might lead the powerful proprietress to issue some injunction or decree against retaliation.

"Now, Neriah has been marked by the Karavals and the

imbecile who beat down their door has fled here, instead of to the Black Eel where he belongs!"

"But they took two of the men's wives and a daughter!" Livet pleaded.

"And so, they *are* your business now?" Gardia snapped.

"Maybe there's a way to sneak three people out without causing a ruckus?" Neriah offered before dismay descended upon her and betrayed her skepticism. "Or five people," she reminded herself. "We'd need to include Flax and Kelzi, too. It's no longer safe for them there."

"You don't think they'd notice the loss of their hostages—and their most popular hostess? How soon before they counted the two empty washbasins and three empty bed chambers. Right now, the Karavals are just playing games. They're trying to goad the Westriver boys into doing something foolish so that they can embarrass them and knock the pride out of some returning soldiers."

"The Black Eel was already being watched," Neriah said. "It's like you have said, Gardia. They noticed all the soldiers returning and have been waiting for the time when they would reassert themselves. It was inevitable. The Karavals are afraid the men of the Westriver Company will upset the way they run things here. Knowing that one of the soldiers is a Kierk can only convince them of the need to act sooner, rather than later. They waited years to see if he'd ever come back."

"You're right," Gardia said. "Dance and his brother grew up picking fights with a lot of them that went off to Ramis's army. Faralley and Westriver were left to them to be boss over. They don't want anyone coming home and proving how unworthy they are of their pathetic throne."

"You think they are afraid that Olen's friends will take over? But they're old. They've laid down their swords—most of 'em."

"Not quite, but if the Karavals were ever weakened, they know that it could leave opportunity for someone else. If I were to order it, they know Hull and his gang could seize the chance to clean them out. And the line's been drawn between there and here, so they know I've been watching."

Livet couldn't get a read on Gardia's mind, but she swore she saw Neriah's face brighten.

"What *does* Hull think about this Gardia?" Neriah asked.

Gardia shot a look at Neriah, and her response was unexpectedly waspish. "He thinks as I do. Always."

Neriah nodded as if reprimanded, while Livet cast her eyes downward defensively. The momentary silence gave her a chance to take in the table in more detail. Avoiding any stares, she set her attention to examining the gouges. They weren't just from wear and tear. There was something purposeful and peculiar in them.

"Tell Olen and his friends that the Black Eel is on its own," Gardia said, pronouncing her non-negotiable edict.

"You won't help them?" Neriah snapped briskly, and unwisely bold.

"I told you what I have decided," Gardia said, her words crystalizing like frost in the air.

Granted permission to depart from Gardia's presence, Livet weaved through the gaggle of gamblers and relentless hustlers to hunt down Olen. The worn-out warrior had camped out in a screened-off booth where a crack in the panelling allowed him to watch the tavern door.

He was holding court, of sorts. But his retinue pressed against the walls and filled the cramped space. Each of them gave off the saturated smell of sweat and the sourness of ale seeped through the men's pores as they sobered up. She recognized the younger men—Kalden and Effie—as well as Eysman, the other Westriver sergeant who had been first to relate the news of the raid on the Black Eel.

Livet was unfamiliar with two new faces that joined them, but from their close comradery, she was safe to assume they had served under the same banner. Sitting next to Kalden, and bearing a slight resemblance, Nyrim Henser was introduced to her first. This man seemed peaceable and relaxed, almost aloof at first, but as they plotted, his mind worked steadily to sort out complications or suggest contingencies. His restless eyes darted as thoughts bounced about inside his head and were randomly ejected for consideration.

In contrast, the other man with the thick, dense beard, carried himself more jovially. Olen presented him as Vyr Ockslo. He clasped Livet's hand fondly when introduced, smiling, and retaining his grip just a little too long—enough for Olen to roll his eyes and proffer a mindful, corrective slap on the back of the man's hand.

Spread out across the table, numerous pieces of flatware had been re-arranged at angles to each other or laid out in precessions to form lines. Little pulled tufts of bread were corralled inside or spaced without. Together it all resembled a map.

"We have to presume they're watchin' for us," Olen said and pointed to some of the breadcrumbs on the periphery. "Udal's men. Dogfish's men. Dance's sentries. Here, here, and here."

"He can't have all of his men on sentry constantly," said Nyrim. "He'd have no one to collect his taxes from the neighbourhood."

"And his men have to sleep sometime," Vyr added.

Olen studied the arrangement.

"The longer we wait, the more over-stretched they might become. Time doesn't give them an advantage so far as bringing in more fighters or being any better holed up and protected than they are now. But then there are the hostages..." Olen chewed on his lip as he pondered.

Eysman's brow rippled as a thought moved from his brain to his mouth. "I still don't know where I'm going to get enough swords and axes for the men. I'd welcome a bit more time, but we don't have it. A couple of thousand troops are staring at the city from up in the Rafters already. They will be through those gates before the sun sets tomorrow. Mark my words."

"We need weapons? Maybe we wait for the fight to start then pick from the corpses," suggested Vyr, his cheeks pink and blustering while his tongue protruded at the distaste of his own suggestion.

"We can't wait for that!" Effie interjected. "We have to help them before then."

"No one wants to wait," agreed Nyrim, sympathetically. "I don't expect that Maks or Gastun would agree to draw this out either. It's their wives and daughter that got taken."

Olen tapped with his fingers on the table and mumbled as he thought through the conundrum. "Do you think Hull has any weapons he could give us? What has Gardia said about this?" he asked Livet.

"She's not promising any 'elp from Hull," Livet said. "She

doesn't want to bring a war with the Karavals to the Peahen."

"Says the woman who had a spy watching them from the inside all the time!" Kalden pointed out, and it was clear from the turn of her head, that Neriah was listening from a few seats over.

"I think she was just bein' safe," Livet said.

"Why don't we ask Hull?" Vyr suggested.

"You do not want to go around behind Gardia's back," Neriah warned from across the distance.

"Lord's Oath! Faralley's split between the two of them—Peahen and Half Moon—both too firm-rooted in their own little kingdoms to trouble the other, or tip the balance," Olen said.

"There's not enough of us, Olen," Effie lamented. "You saw the place is jammed tight with Karavals. How are we going to get our people out?"

"Swords. Axes. We need arms, Olen! We can't go in with clubs and broken bottles," pleaded Eysman.

"We only need to get past the first guards, then pick up what they put down." Vyr shrugged and tried to give the impression his revelation was indeed viable, but around the table swirled a round of unappreciative groans. He answered their derision with a belch.

"Too risky. Things will happen far too quickly once we lose the shock of surprise," said Nyrim.

Olen's finger rapped upon the tabletop again, before seizing his mug of ale for a big gulp. The members of his war council eyed him expectantly. Finally, he offered one single word. "Keepside."

"No!" several of the men shouted in unison.

"Not a chance!" bellowed Vyr. "You want more cracks in the bones of your head?"

Olen grumbled at the lack of a welcome reception to his suggestion. He slammed his mug onto the table and reasoned with them. "It's the only place west of the Darrow that has an armoury."

"Keepside Garrison has walls two arm's-lengths thick and ten men high... and it's full of Marshal's Men," said Eysman.

"I thought you wouldn't want to have any more dealings with them after your little night together in Fal Ghreeg," added Vyr.

"Well, if Hull's men won't help us, maybe he could arrange some kind of deal. Are they looking to hire men? Maybe they would let us in if we signed up," Olen proposed.

"Only former royal guards," said Nyrim. "They don't want

any of us field soldiers coming in with muck on our boots to dirty the place."

One of the Peahen's serving hostesses, a dark-eyed maid, named Ilyea, slid through the crack in the partition and brought them a tray with freshly topped off mugs. The frothy drinks were immediately dispatched around the table to the thirsty plotters. The men took deep, mollifying slugs of the ale, and silence encroached as their ideas waned.

Everyone drank except for Effie. He stood up from the table and excused himself to venture off and think, alone. The strain of having his two sisters chained to the Half Moon must tear at him continually, Livet thought. When he left, she slipped out after him.

She noticed Effie stand still for a moment, then push through a small crowd into a less-trafficked part of the tavern. There he lingered quietly, staring absently toward the wall, not seeming to notice its gaudy tile mural but remaining vigilant enough to edge away self-consciously whenever a cluster of bar patrons nudged him to one side or the other.

He was startled when Livet materialized behind him, wrapped her arm through his and held his hand in solidarity, hoping to assuage his worries.

"I know it's a curse to have someone you care for locked away and trapped, like your sisters," Livet consoled.

"If ever I could do something for them..." Effie began. "When I met Olen, I had heard a lot about him already. The old men said he was a good fighter and dependable. I thought he might turn out to be the answer, but our going to the Half Moon has only made the situation worse."

Fair-haired, with a pale complexion at the best of times, Effie looked entirely colourless tonight. He was exhausted and weary with fret and fears for his sisters which had only grown after the Karaval's retaliation.

"Olen never refuses to lend 'elp," Livet said. "That's what's good about 'im. It's not in 'is heart to abandon anyone, ever. He just needs a plan." Then she rolled her eyes, "But t' be honest, if 'e doesn't have one, he'll 'elp anyway. Maybe that's what's bad about 'im."

Effie smiled lightly, and she detected a faint flickering of hope in the corner of his eyes.

"Listen. Olen and I 'ave a friend. His name is Denn, and I am going to find him. The army captain said 'e's got fifty men with 'im now. "

"That's almost a full company of soldiers!" Effie said energetically.

"Denn won't turn 'is back on Olen and neither will Olen turn 'is back on you or your sisters."

"I trust what you say," Effie said. He gently turned toward her and hugged her politely and purely. Livet was moved by his genuineness and squeezed him back, in return. Their shared touch reminded her of the way Denn would embrace her after a long day riding. Effie and Denn shared some resemblance, but more so in comparison with how Denn was when Livet first met him—when he was the young cavalryman who would ride up to visit her at Ayren's cottage. His muscles had rounded out, and he cut a more mature figure, but Livet remembered how Denn had once been just as lanky and fair-haired and presented himself as uncertain as Effie appeared now.

Her reminiscing was interrupted when, at that moment, she felt like they were being watched. It was a sensation all too expected in the Peahen, but was she mistaken? She always felt the irrational anxiety that someone far away was probing and seeking her out, but this was somehow more tangible and immediate. To be cautious, she thought to engage her special talent and paint a shadow around them, to better enshroud her private audience with Effie.

Effie did not appear to have ever experienced such an effect before. Livet watched a pang of confusion wash over him, to be replaced by an intense curiosity. He could not know what she had done, but he acted warily and asked, "Did the room just brighten? Or is it me?"

Livet stifled a grin, so as not to appear to make light of his confusion. For the first time, his cheeks took on a livelier hue as he blushed rosily.

"No one should be trapped or in a prison where they don't belong," Livet said. "We must save yer sisters an' the others."

"Perhaps, you've just given me a bit of hope, Livet. Thank you." Effie let go of her with reluctance. "We are returning to the Black Eel soon to plan further with the rest of the company. How soon do you think you can come back with your friend and his soldiers?"

"I'm goin' to go find 'im right away," Livet said reassuringly.

Effie nodded and said, "Then return safely."

"I will," she answered, and adding one final urging, she said simply, "Trust Olen."

"I will," Effie promised.

The colours of the Peahen took on their normal tint, as Livet dispelled her charm. Effie stepped out of Livet's umbrage and back to where he would be more visible. With one last bashful smile, he reversed into a crowd of revellers and left her sight.

To Livet, this seemed like a good time to also depart and begin the long trek across the city to the lodging house at Lords' Lane, and her expected rendezvous with Denn. But then she froze. A tingling down the back of her neck gave substance to her earlier hunch that someone had been observing.

"Trapped, or in a prison, you said?" Harbud repeated her self-stated axiom. "No one should be '*trapped or in prison.*'"

Livet glared at him admonishingly for his nosiness. Gardia had too many spies here, and they were far too bold! Harbud was leaning haughtily against the wall, carefully keeping out of the earshot of the other patrons. He looked noticeably incensed.

"What are you getting at?" Livet challenged him.

"What about Kell, then? How would you describe the awful predicament he's in?" asked Harbud. "Isn't he worth a share of your concerns?"

Who was he to accuse her of hypocrisy? Truthfully, in speaking about Effie's sisters, Kell had also entered Livet's mind. She kept trying to convince herself that the voice in the temple basement was all in her imagination, but Gardia and the others did not dismiss it so readily. Their unexpected acceptance nagged at Livet and clawed at her until doubts made way for possibility, which eventually morphed into a crushing sense of dread. She feared returning to the diabolical prison beneath the temple but now suffered from the inescapable unease that Kell's spirit had reached out to her, and she had ignored and abandoned him.

"Taringer and I are going into the temple dungeon to find him. Your aid would be welcome. You know where he is and can hear him. From there, he can guide us on what to do."

With a slight tremble, Livet shook her head. "I can't do it."

"You've already been inside. This time, whatever danger lurks, you will have the two of us to defend you and keep you safe. Why do you still fear?"

"I spent too long in the dungeon at Lanstad to risk gettin' trapped in one 'ere in Caphedra," Livet said defiantly.

"Yet you wish this on Kell? A poor spirit who can't even escape by dying?"

Shuddering, Livet grew increasingly uncomfortable. Her eyes were moist.

"Anyone that can fix a spirit to its corpse must also have countless means to punish them—to manipulate their very spirit. What else would compel it to be so? How else would one bend the dead toward one's own will and keep them bound to this realm?"

"You best stay away from the temple!" Livet advised. "There's only evilness down there in the dark and the people there 'ave powers beyond staves and swords."

Harbud's arrogance retreated for a moment, and Livet saw a very human glimmer of apprehension, but he answered. "We have to go. Please. Kell was our friend too, and we need to know he is free and at peace. He should not be shackled to this world any longer."

Livet locked her lips stubbornly. She said nothing but remained teary and disturbed.

Softened into rapprochement, Harbud discontinued further talk of the dangerous foray. He addressed his earlier affront instead.

"You should know that I wasn't spying on you and that boy. It's none of my concern," he said. "I came to you with more information that Celebra has procured from Captain Alamm. It seems that open-mouthed ponce of a captain has eyes from here to Castleside."

"What has he said now?" Livet asked sharply.

"Your man, Denn, was arrested upon trying to enter the city."

"No! Where did they take him?"

"Not far, it seems. The rumour is that the guards were later found overpowered, and the conclusion was that Mr. Wellum is free again on the streets. I tell you this as I expect you will need to move quickly if you are to retrieve him. Gardia suggests you bring him here for safety. She'd like to meet him."

"So Denn's alright?" Livet asked.

"That is unknown," said Harbud. "But if you tell me where

you need to go, I can try and help you cover the distance. He is probably being hunted, so you should not waste time. Come with me."

Plucking a candle and holder from one of the tables, he urged her to follow him. They wound through a labyrinth of portieres and glass-beaded chain curtains that divided the Peahen's secret backrooms, then down crumbling stone steps to the cellar. Here, rounded archways were spaced along the rock-hewn walls, and Harbud's glyphs decorated each. Some were in chalk, but others were in paint to give them permanence. In the brisk moment of rescue from her dungeon pursuers, she had not noticed so many other doors existed in the same room.

If they were all for travelling, Livet imagined this room to be like a private nexus from which Harbud's portals emanated. She scanned them, trying to decipher the glyphs and determine which one would take her closer to Denn, or at least to somewhere familiar from whence she could navigate.

Her intuition served her well.

"This one," she said and pointed to one of the archways to the right of the centre, beside a worn wooden support beam that was sagging and compressed with age.

Harbud peered at her incredulously. "Do you know where this goes?"

Livet reached her hand up and pointed at the symbols which she knew represented the words for "plaza," "square," and the longhand forms that spelled the name of "Hamrin" across the top of the arch. They were written in Scrawl, identical to the script which Kell had taught her to decipher, many years before. Encountering the symbols, Livet suddenly solved the mystery of the scratches and carvings on Gardia's office table, too. It finally struck her that those markings had also been characters written in the same clandestine script. She had just been viewing them upside down from across the table.

"So, writing in Scrawl lets you do magic?" Livet asked for confirmation.

"Scrawl?" Harbud asked, then muttered, "Oh yes. That's right. That's what Kell called it, isn't it?"

Livet looked around the room at the other arches. She thought that she could decipher at least a few others, including the one which had carried her to the salvation of the Peahen.

"They're words. An old language. Your mind gives them meaning, and it's from your mind that we can pursue magical arts." Facing the archway, he waved his hands about the inscriptions and said, "Most of it is from Jerozi with a few other ancient symbols that I can read but couldn't tell you where they came from. I just know what they mean, and now I know that you do too."

His last statement was devoid of his natural smugness. It almost hinted at pride or welcome solidarity.

"What opens the doors?" asked Livet.

"Once the right symbols have been refreshed..." he produced his shard of chalk and traced some of the symbols, "...then it just becomes a matter of making your way through. It's all about intent."

"If so, why not just have one door? Why so many?" Livet asked.

"The true corridors through the realms were laid down long ago. These are additional paths that I crafted, with great effort, as my shortcuts. You can't just go to any point you wish, from anywhere you happen to be standing. The Passage Realm has its own natural design. It has its own structure that must be learned and studied. Maps are rare, believe me."

Reaching out to touch the wall beneath the arch, it felt rather solid. Livet ran her hand along the cracks and ridges in the mortar between bricks. There was nothing out of sorts.

Harbud gave her a moment, then coached, "When you slip through the shadows, you see the effect, don't you? You see *something* that changes around you.'

"I don't see shadows. I see the opposite. Everything brightens for me."

Harbud stared placidly at the stonework. If there was something there to look at, Livet had not observed it yet.

"What am I supposed to see?" Livet tried to match his gaze. Still, nothing appeared beyond the brick and stone.

"There are realms between us and our destinations—or between the visible and invisible. That which I use, I call the Passage Realm," Harbud explained. "I don't know how much Kell taught you, but you're dipping your foot into a similar realm when you cast your spell to hide from sight."

"Half there, he used to say," Livet recalled.

"Which implies that your other half is elsewhere," Harbud said.

"I suppose so."

Her eyes remained on Harbud. Livet could think of nothing save for more questions. Her face must have been alive with bewilderment for he paused, sighed, and continued.

"I see Kell taught you application, but not theory. He always did approach things presumptuously backward."

Harbud leaned closer to Livet so that she could pay better attention. His vest and jacket smelled intriguingly of smoke and spice, and his moustache and close-cropped, sculpted beard now appeared less uniformly black but was flecked with points of grey.

"When you look at something, you believe in it based on how you see it," he began, and Livet nodded weakly but receptively. Harbud then placed one of his hands over her right eye.

"But it changes depending on how you look at it."

Moving his hand from her right to her left eye, he demonstrated, "It's all perspective."

"It's just where your eyes sit in your head," Livet commented.

"But each is a perfectly valid way to see the world. It is just more common that we combine them." He removed his hand and sat back. "It all comes together in your head, and that informs your awareness. It's the same with your other senses. Peel away some layers, however, and we see things in a different manner."

"What's the true way t' see things?"

"There's no single *true way*. What Kell taught you was the power to see from the other side—the other realms—then *choose* which one becomes real to yourself and those around you."

"But we moved from the temple to 'ere. It wasn't an illusion. We really moved!" Livet said.

"The realms affect each other," Harbud said. "A quick, subtle change in one, can make a huge result in others if you can see and influence the right realm in the right fashion. And we are not always fixed to any one, especially. I can take a few steps in the Passage Realm, and it's the same as an hour's walk in this one."

Livet gasped in appreciation for what she was beginning to understand. Harbud grew more intense and built upon his example with another. "Imagine, Livet! There is a realm known as the Sylphan. With a wave of his hand, Taringer can pierce it from almost anywhere, fan a puff of air, and grow it into a tempest in this world!"

"Is there any danger in this?"

"Only if you want there to be," Harbud drew back his dramatics and resumed a look of tedium. "This is our native realm, and we always want to keep some connection to it. One could get lost traversing the others—so to speak—but even the best sorcerers would tire themselves out first. Exhaust yourself, and you end up where you started. In most normal cases."

"But what is *normal*?" Livet asked, aware again of how fanciful her surroundings were. Harbud ran his thumb along the line of whiskers leading down his chin.

"Look, what you do is difficult. You remain where you are, looking through both eyes, but forcing others to adopt only the view you wish for them. You straddle the realms, whereas I tend to just jump headlong through them."

Livet grew perplexed, "Into where? Where d'you jump?"

"Here and there. It's all the same. But when I land, I do so where I want to. The doorway is mostly for show," he smirked. "But it helps me concentrate and remember my starting points."

"Coming from the temple was so quick, so instant," Livet said. "And it was so real—real enough for us t' go through."

"It's real because I willed it to be, and somewhere there exists the realm which agrees with me."

Livet could not yet understand the full breadth of the art that Harbud was attempting to bestow. Kell had already implanted some skills in her. Perhaps she understood those a little better. The umbrage—an Umbrage Realm? A refuge in the pockets and gaps of the visible, the umbrage must exist along the dark edges of its own realm.

Standing straight and adjusting his vest, Livet got the impression from Harbud that her lesson was over.

Again, Livet peered hopelessly at the archway and felt its solidness beneath her hand. It was cold and stubbornly unchanging. Seeing a piece of chalk nearby, she picked it up and could not deduce anything special about it, but she inconspicuously tucked it into her cloak, nonetheless. She placed her hand in the centre of the Scrawl arch. Under her fingers, the sandy, granulated mortar became smooth. Reflections of torchlight bounced off the stones set in the door, but in her mind, the light came from beyond.

When Livet entered the umbrage, it was like she was using shadow as a cloak. She could spread it over herself like a bedsheet and disappear beneath the covers. Entering the same well-practiced state of mind, this rocky, arched doorway was more like a curtain, Livet realized. The more she shifted her focus, the more it billowed in the breeze from beyond. She smelled wood smoke, felt the warm afternoon air enter her lungs, and heard the commotion caused by voices loudly speaking over and above each other.

There was no arch. There was no curtain.

Her foot settled upon dry, dusty dirt, as she stepped forward. Ahead of her, Hamrin Square opened up with the beatified statue of Queen Tressa across from her. The road through Porter's Run branched off to her left, cluttered with more discarded refuse that the Northporters had left behind in their haste to flee. Soldiers draped in blue vestments and military adornments were assembling into ad hoc formations. Bodies of the tormented apostates, once atrociously hoisted here, were pulled down and scattered about in heaps. For now, there was more value in reusing every sharpened stake to construct defences across the open space.

Livet turned to the gateway. At her back was a wall of solid brick at the base of one of Stonerow's imposing edifices. From her pocket, Livet pulled out the small piece of chalk that she'd palmed a moment ago, and marked the stones of the wall in Scrawl, then set the location to memory.

The scene before her grew more pitiable and abhorrent. Not all the bodies were cold and still. Some of the dying captives wailed and called for mercy. They writhed in agony in the dirt. Heavy-hearted, Livet forced herself to ignore their cries this time. She had to hurry. Denn might already have reached the lodging house, and it was not just for her own sake that she was rushing. Olen, and those depending on him, would be doomed if she were not able to return with Denn and his company of soldiers.

CHAPTER 28

Farathemun's Reward

A splash of frigid, bracing water sloshed over Denn's throbbing brow. It helped alleviate the uncomfortable warmth from the swelling and rolled down his tender jawline to drip off his chin. He opened his eyes.

From beside the well, Temis yanked on a rope and pulled up another bucket, into which Denn reached in and cupped his hands. Bringing them gently to his lips, Denn took in a gulp of water, swished it around to cool his mouth, then spit it out onto the ground, defiled with redness from his bleeding maw.

"I think I have all my teeth," he said but noted that a few were certainly feeling loose.

"You'll be the handsomest man at your wedding," Temis encouraged and sat down with him. The well sprung up like an oasis in a tiny pedestrian alley, shaded from the midday sun and out of view of the Stonerow thoroughfare. At some point, Temis must have rejoined with his mount, Coalsmoke, for she was tethered nearby. Her muzzle was deep in a stone trough of water, and she slopped noisily as she drank.

Denn groaned and refreshed his face again with the water. The numbness from the Pashter oil was fading the more he washed it off and he was again feeling the pain from the damage wrought upon his bashed-in face. With that pain came awareness. As his head began to clear, he remembered a litany of ever-increasing and urgent crises.

First, he had to confirm that Kentin had borne Ramisa safely to her uncle's strong house. He wanted to inquire about the fate of Stramm the cider man, and his son, too. Anything further to do with weddings and armies would have to wait, however. Now that they were in the city, he also needed to scheme with Temis on how to retrieve Serenn from the temple.

Knowing that the armsmen were watching for him, he could not escape consideration that the Pillarmen might be in pursuit of his father, and even his mother, too. Undoubtedly, the Wellum manor was under watch, but with luck, the lodging house in Lords' Lane remained undiscovered. But would Livet even be at the lodging house when he returned? It was not in her habit to remain on her own for long. Maybe she had thought to seek out Olen, but more likely her curiosity would lead her off in search of those conjurers she had threatened to take up with. If so, he needed to warn her. After seeing Ramisa's condition first-hand, and feeling the ire of Dagremahr himself, Denn needed to forbid her pursuit of any such waywardness.

"Wake up," Temis urged, shaking him. "Get your senses about you. We need to move on."

Dull, heavy voices were close by. The well would not remain private and unshared for long on a hot day like this.

"I'm awake," Denn acknowledged. "We need to reach Farathemun's, then work out a plan to get into the temple priory."

"Why not the priory first?" Temis asked and Denn shook his head.

"I don't believe Lehn will place Serenn in imminent danger. However, we must satisfy ourselves that the lady Ramisa is in safe hands. Anything could have happened to her."

"Very well," Temis said and looked to Coalsmoke. With an affectionate scratch across her throat latch, Temis got the animal to raise her head and part from the trough. He grabbed her reins and led her back along the alley, using the horse to shield his reconnaissance as he peered out from behind. Then, looking back with a tilt and jerk of his head, Temis summoned Denn to follow.

More evidence of a pervasive dread was increasing in the capital. Windows were boarded up and the sellers had fled from their berths beside the roadways. The same troops that were once harassing the insolent and disobedient were now busying themselves with forming blockades in strategic alleyways and thoroughfares. They knew their enemy had as much knowledge of the city streets as they did, and in preparation for the coming assault, they were trying to sculpt the available routes to their advantage. The invaders would be channelled into alleyways and blocked with surprise dead ends, all in attempts to limit their ingress toward the citadel.

From across the distance came yelling and shouting as the heavy weapons masters and engineers along the city walls, and high up on the parapets of the citadel readied their mighty range weapons in defiance of Lord Marshal Myrhic's oncoming army. Urns and wide vases placed as cisterns along balconies and second-storey walls were also noticeable. The call must have gone out to preserve rainwater for the inevitable siege.

Denn and Temis edged along the side streets until they reached sight of Castleside. As worried as he was, he could permit himself no time to check on the family home. The grander estate of Lord Brevin Farathemun lay just ahead, closer to the citadel. His father's men would likely be rallying there.

The armsmen patrolling Castleside were conspicuously absent of the blue ornamentation of the Faith in their dress. These hired men sported an abundance of different emblems and shields belonging to the nobles and the wealthy. Denn slowly eased the tense grip he had instinctively placed on his sword hilt.

Having grown up in Castleside, Denn knew what to watch for amongst the banners. The elder Farathemun's arms depicted a sable holly leaf on white or silver. Manning a wrought-iron gate head of them, several men had just such an emblem painted upon heavy, teardrop-shaped, reinforced metal shields. Denn picked up his pace and led Temis toward where they patrolled.

Behind a high wall, the tops of bone-coloured towers rose up, with each boasting a Farathemun pennant. Holly-bearing shields occupied the gaps between the wall's crenellations, where a legion of soldiers must be keeping watch.

"We're here," Denn said.

The guards at the entranceway took notice of them immediately. They halted Denn and Temis, and looked unimpressed when petitioned for admittance.

"By what right do you seek entrance to our lord's home, sir?" asked a grey-haired gatekeeper, his face dominated by leathery jowls and bulging eyes.

"Lord Farathemun is expecting us." Denn was too sore and

aching to suffer long explanations.

"Aye. Is he? And whom do you serve?"

"I am Denn Wellum. I arrived with the young Lord Farathemun and a companion," Denn declared, certain that he must look more exhausted and ill-tempered than the guard. "Let us in. These streets are not safe."

"Horse crap," the guard shot back. "The lord's son came here almost an hour ago. You weren't with him."

"You dolt! How dare you accuse me of deception. My father is Lord Phon Wellum!"

Denn saw Temis suppressing a chortle over the outburst. The guard mumbled something to another man who, successively, called out to others for the gate to be unlocked. It swung open with an ominous creak, and the second man hurried inside.

The gatekeeper motioned for Denn to go through, but warned, "Keep under the archway until you're requested." Then he spat and waved his calloused hand. Two more men took up the task of escorting Denn, Temis, and a whinnying Coalsmoke.

Beyond the arch, Denn saw that the Lord Brevin Farathemun's estate was as grandiose as would expectedly befit the brother-in-law of a king. Its grounds were diligently groomed yet vibrant. Cultivated gardens grew up around artfully rendered statues and mosaics. Water from artesian wells in the Caphedran hillside flowed from slotted spillways through the walls to nourish the tangles of ivy and other flowering vines that spread over the stone-like veins. Most impressive of all was the white stone manor house, which ascended several storeys into the sky and pierced the clouds with its spired towers. Angular-cut tiles formed pathways that radiated colourfully outward from its main entrance.

The grounds bestowed tranquillity, but Denn did not like waiting. Were the guards not told he would be arriving? Or were Farathemuns, as a clan, just habitually amiss in welcoming their guests?

Finally, a tall man strode toward them, his ring mail jerkin jingling. He was rugged and hook-faced with an air of authority. He carried no shield but was armed with an axe-bladed bardiche, the shaft of which he planted solidly into the ground in front of Denn.

"I am Captain Tirall of Lord Farathemun's Guard," he introduced himself. "Your audience is requested. You may find food and wine to replenish yourself in the great hall. Lord Farathemun is eager to see you."

"Thank you, Captain," Denn replied and took a step forward into the gardens. Temis attempted to follow but was blocked by the outstretching of the other guards' arms.

"Only Mr. Wellum is privy to the Lord's business," said Captain Tirall dismissively to Temis. "If you want, you can stay out in the stable with the grooms and see to Mr. Wellum's horse while my lord entertains your master's visit."

"*His* horse?" Temis started.

Denn motioned to ignore the slight and maintain whatever particulars of decorum were requested. "They don't want to disrespect us. I am sure it is just a matter of keeping their inner circle tight. Remember, they are allies. They want my father's money and men."

Temis nodded, spurned but compliant.

Turning his thoughts to it, Denn wondered what his father *had* provided? Where were the soldiers? Obviously, the two hundred men promised by his father were not here. Even Farathemun's guards were sparse compared to what Denn had expected would greet them once inside. He could see only a scant few perched along the walls above; many of the shields visible from the street were unattended. It was as if they were set in place to beguile challengers into thinking the defences were substantially better-manned. Where was Farathemun's army?

Denn climbed the flagstone steps to the manor-house door. The heavy oak, expertly crafted and balanced, moved surprisingly well on its hinges; Farathemun's affluence showed in everything. The entranceway opened to reveal a parlour so cluttered with displays of wealth and elegance that even cut-glass vases had to be stacked upon each other. They towered so high as to obstruct viewing the wall-to-wall masterpieces of painted canvas and tile. Stretched across the floor, and into the room ahead, a lavishly embroidered rug chronicled Farathemun history spanning back to King Arrim, the last so-named Farathemun to sit on the Caphedran throne.

Following the ancestral carpet, Denn found himself in an immaculate sitting room just ahead of the reception hall. A silver serving tray of fresh fruit sat to one side, from which he plucked and pocketed a couple of apples. Denn wavered a moment, remembering poor Naobe, but his stomach was growling. He opened, stretched, and aligned his jaw to take a bite, only to be stymied by tender gums that made him think better. He vowed to save the crisp fruit for later.

At the far side of this room, his host awaited. The next doorway led into the truly audacious spectacle that was Brevin Farathemun's improvised court. Here, the old lord and close friend of Denn's father sat central, as if he were a monarch in his own right, like his forebears.

Farathemun pulled himself up from a lethargic slouch as Denn entered. His jewels of status dangled from golden chains and caught the light like sudden sparks. His face was puffier than it had been in the council chambers, either from lack of sleep or, as the splotchy rosiness suggested, he may have been turning to drink.

Dispersed throughout the room were about a dozen soldiers. Beside them, were men in colourful, well-tailored robes whom Denn took for strategists, advisors, or just plain sycophantic lesser nobles. He scrutinized the faces, peering and probing. His father was not among them. But there, at Farathemun's side, with her hair freshly tinted to a sunset red by the application of carmine and punctuated by topaz jewels in a familiar circlet, Denn's mother, Esta Wellum, stood straight and elegant.

Denn approached stone-faced.

Esta reached over and laid a gentle hand on Farathemun's shoulder as he greeted his guest.

"Welcome, Denn," Farathemun said. "I am pleased to see you have evaded lasting harm. I was informed by my son of the events you shared this past morning." There was an unsteady twitch in his cheek as he conjured a smile for his guest.

"It is merciful that you are safe," his mother said. Her mouth curled up slightly, with affection that stemmed from politeness. She did not rush toward him to embrace him and nurse his wounds with motherly care. Her hands remained distant, with one on Farathemun and the other grasping the stem of a wine goblet.

"Where is Lady Ramisa?" Denn asked.

Farathemun's smile unexpectedly crumbled. "She is resting. The hardship of her journey has caused her to suffer from fatigue and she needs to collect herself before seeing any visitors."

With a semblance of compassion, Esta said, "She will be fine, dear. When you next see her, I am sure that the lady will have recovered tremendously."

A sharp, corrective glance from Farathemun halted her tongue from saying much more, but if Esta was implying that it would be a while before he saw Ramisa again, Denn was not going to have it. He wanted to see her now. He could not rely on anyone else to calm her. Avenda was gone. Perhaps Kentin remained with her, but his presence would only exacerbate her discomfort.

"Is she still with Lord Kentin? I demand to see her now!" Denn said in a manner so forthcoming that the periphery of highborn aristocrats snorted and gasped.

Farathemun responded rigidly. "My son is readying for departure back to Fallowsea and the princess is resting. You will make no such demand to see her."

"You have already done so much, Denn," Esta said diplomatically, setting her cup down and leaning forward. "Certainly, you will also welcome a rest from your labours. You will be pleased, I am sure, to know that Brevin plans to reward you well for your efforts."

"I have become aware of my intended reward, mother. I presume you also know of Father's intentions to arrange my betrothal to the lady." He turned, "Lord Farathemun, by that right alone, I appeal to you to let me see the princess. The journey was taxing and dangerous for her. Now, her well-being is at risk in this city. We should never have brought her here."

Farathemun reverted to a slouch, and Esta peered at him with a frown. "I've been forced to reconsider my bargain with your father," the lord said.

"What do you mean? What remains of your agreement? Have you no intention to honour it?" Denn accused.

All of a sudden, a commotion in an adjoining corridor interrupted them. Two soldiers nervously and clumsily shuffled aside, and a woman staggered through a doorway. "Denn!" Ramisa called out to him.

Denn broke past where Farathemun and his mother sat, ignoring their abrupt protests, and bolting for the princess before the soldiers could move between them. With what strength he had in his hands, he steadied her.

"Are you alright? I lost you at the gate. What happened?"

She reached out to him also and through the slips of her sleeves, he saw scratches and scrapes. She drew him closer, oblivious to the gawking courtiers and her uncle's disapproving grimace.

"They know I have come here," Ramisa whispered. "The Paragons set upon me as soon as I reached Caphedra, howling at me with their threats and taunts. I still hear Lyseia in my head complaining about my ignorance of my purpose—always, *my purpose*. Their voices have all become stronger now that I am within the city walls."

She gasped and seemingly lost her breath. She gripped Denn's fingers tight with one hand and clutched onto his shoulder with her other, as if afraid of collapsing or being ripped away.

"You're hurt," Denn said, pushing back her sleeves with his free hand and acknowledging the wounds on her arm.

"Kentin's horse refused to carry me. So, my cousin ended up dragging me here... *to safety*," she said.

Lord Farathemun began shouting angry orders to his guards.

"If I could only find a way to make the voices you hear stop," Denn began. "I am sorry to have brought you to Caphedra. I thought you'd be safest with your uncle."

"I was safe with you," she said. "Lyseia, in her rants, admitted as much. My cousin, my uncle—the others do not care. Everyone refuses to even acknowledge my suffering for they cannot see nor comprehend the true cause. Then they ignore the tragedy of my mother, just as they refuse to consider that I may be fated the same one day."

Denn's eyes locked with hers, and he raised his voice, "Because they only care for what you can achieve for them." From deep inside his heart, he began to quietly mouth his words and spoke below a whisper. "Your uncle has promised to protect you, but I won't let harm come to you, either. If I can, I'll find a way to free you of the Paragons. I am going to go to the temple, and I will confront my brother. He will tell me how to help you—even if I have to cut it out of him."

"No!" Ramisa cried.

Guards yanked her from him at that moment. Ramisa flailed as her uncle's soldiers dragged her backward, and Lord Farathemun ordered them to take her to her chamber. But as firm as they were in forcing her uncooperative body through the door and back up the stairs, the guards didn't dare rise above their station to press their hands to her lips and quiet her.

"Denn, there is danger in the temple. Don't go!" she called out. "The Paragons and Dagremahr–"

With a slam, a guard closed a door between them, leaving the rest of her words too muffled and diminished to be made out.

"Release her!" Denn called out to no avail.

"No. You have disturbed my ward, Denn Wellum," Farathemun said sternly. "Return to me now and hear all of what I have to say to you!"

Around the room, listeners hushed themselves and froze, cravenly consuming the impromptu drama.

"Bringing her to Caphedra was a mistake!" Denn declared. "I regret helping you."

"Help? You would not even be here were it not for the protection of my son and his soldiers. You are nothing on your own, young man. Certainly not a match for Ramisa! I would like this matter resolved, and then you will be on your way."

Denn's mouth was going dry with anger as he realized how wretchedly perfidious this man truly was. "I see why you and my father got along so well," Denn said. "Did he teach you—or you him—how to slither around your promises so? How presumptuous I was, to think that any of you were capable of holding to any pact in which you did not enrich yourselves first–and how easily you could disavow your bond when another opportunity arose."

His words were meant for Farathemun, but Denn could not help but glare at his mother as he said them. Timidly, she shuffled backward, placing the seated lord more directly between them.

Looking up at Esta, Farathemun patted her hand on his shoulder before resuming.

"Before that distraction, you asked me about the arrangement I made with your father, and I will tell you," Farathemun said. "Nothing remains of it because your father was unable to live up to *his* promises. Look around. Not even one Wellum shield stands to defend this palace!" Farathemun scoffed.

What *did* happen to his father's troops? The last Denn had heard of his father's plotting came from Temis, who told him about the desire to strike a bargain to exonerate himself with Lord Marshal Myrhic. Had it worked? Were the hired men, absent here, now hoisting a Wellum banner among the ranks of the prince's army?

"Why is my father not beside you?" Denn asked, knowing that it would sound naïve, but he was helpless without the answer.

Esta uncomfortably answered, "Your father has been ordered taken to the temple dungeons by adepts of the Faith. I regret, it is likely that he will die there—if he has not succumbed to death already."

Denn reeled in shock. After his kidnapping and all the accompanying manipulations that sat upon years of hatred and mistrust, his father's misfortune evoked little sympathy, but it reinforced his understanding that those circles in which his father moved and conspired were just as disingenuous and untrustworthy as those they protested.

That included his mother.

"So, you've chosen to await his death here?" he asked. "Or *have* you waited?"

Denn's spiteful indictment infuriated Farathemun, who brushed off Esta's grip and stood up as if to square off. His hand went to his belt, where a glint of gold revealed the hilt of a short sword, menacingly close to his quivering fingertips.

Esta maneuvered close to her new protector, seeking to restrain him against the blood rush swelling from Denn's accusation. Though Denn sensed she cared well enough for both of them to want to halt any violence, her position next to Farathemun revealed the camp she had ultimately joined.

"Where is your army? Where are all the little stingers of the Wellum honeybee?!" Farathemun frothed. "You and your father are both declared to be in apostasy. The Faith will seize every coin, in every coffer, that your family has hidden away in Stonerow because your father could not—would not—raise enough men to stop them in time. Now, if he is even still alive, he will be ready to give up everything down to his last bronze Squire, for a crust of bread and mug of water that doesn't have piss in it."

The mocking glances of the court riled Denn. These motley conspirators took so much pleasure in the collapse of his family's fortune that they were blind to the mortal danger of trusting in Farathemun and his imperial promises. Unless they found another army, soon, it would spell the end to their vision of gaining dominion over Caphedra.

These useless men, Denn thought, will be impaled on pikes within a week, no matter who wins the city. He had listened enough.

"Where is *your* army? Where are the armies of all these *powerful* nobles that you surround yourself with?!" Denn retorted, his hand gesturing to the tiny garrison surrounding them. "This little cottage is pretty, *Brevin*, but it's not the fortress that the citadel is. Why are your battlements empty of men? Maybe you should fear sharing a cell with my father soon!"

Dropping the formality of title left the lord disappointingly unfazed. But that was irrelevant. Now that the deal had eroded, and his host's feigned magnanimity was at an end, Denn was loath to afford the lord any further respect.

"I was informed that you lacked understanding and cunning," Farathemun said insultingly. "You would have me betray my intentions to the enemy so soon? I assure you that my army is marching into place as we speak, and they will reap our harvest from the field of battle once our adversaries have graciously dispatched each other."

"And then, what of the princess? You know she suffers. What will happen if your intentions overwhelm her? You will force her to take the crown, regardless of any price her health might pay," Denn said.

"I told you she is exhausted, but it is no more than simple fatigue," Farathemun answered. "She is perfectly fit to sit on the throne and like a reflection in a mirror, she will resemble her mother—my poor sister. The people will heap their love upon her at first sight and she will shine in time."

"At the very least, allow me to protect Ramisa until this battle is over." Denn tried to subdue his fury enough to reach his own agreement.

"*Lady* Ramisa," Farathemun said, "will be attended by my guard until her betrothed arrives. Then he will be granted the role of Lord Protector."

And who is that?" asked Denn jealously, not surprised Farathemun had already negotiated another bargain.

"Manyx Larsen, noble son of Lord Derid Larsen, Master of Kramwen. He comes from an ancient royal line, and he commands many men."

Denn understood it all now.

"So, you've aligned with the Larsens. That's your army?"

"The Larsens have five times the men your father promised before the embarrassment of his capture. They will provide far more security for the princess than you and your vast ranks of *Wellum* men can!"

The insult passed by him for Denn had expended his anger. A ready-made army, well-trained and experienced, was at Farathemun's beck and call. With Incis Myrhic's men occupying the north, the army of Kramwen could traverse the southern highlands to Greenplain, then emerge upon Caphedra's south whenever the opportunity birthed itself. Following the mutual slaughter of Ramid's and Ravon's armies, once they clashed in the city, the balance of power would favour these fresh newcomers.

The two hundred promised soldiers were a fantasy. They were another lie of his father's engineered to appeal to his son's longing for importance. Kramwen's entrance into the fight would consign the last of the good, unspoken-for fighters under a banner and it was too late to strike up another mass of men. He would command no Wellum troops in the coming fray, nor play a role in crafting the future of the kingdom. Denn stood there and accepted this, instantly feeling very solitary and alone in the lord's court.

"Leave the city, my son," Esta said. "I would not want any more tragedy to befall you. Your father's lies have caused you to sacrifice too much, already." She stepped forward and reached out toward him but fell short of touching his skin. Her eyes drifted to Farathemun as if waiting for permission, or a response.

The lord's hand moved suspiciously along his belt again, but instead of the sword, he pulled out a fist-sized velvet pouch. "I am sorry," he said. "Onto you, I have transferred my displeasure with your father. That is inexcusable."

The pouch rang noisily with the jingling of coins as he held it out toward Denn. Looking at it, suspended in the air, Denn remained motionless.

"Your mother fears for your safety, so I have promised not to let you risk greater injury by taking up arms under my banner. Instead, to reconcile my debt to you for your efforts, I offer you my gratitude in gold, under the provision that you leave Caphedra. In the years ahead, should you return, I assure you that you will have the favour of Queen Ramisa."

Incensed, Denn fumed at the offer. "I am not a mercenary, nor did I perform this task out of avarice. I will not take your gold. Granting me my leave from your company—from *all of you*—is reward enough!"

Farathemun lowered the pouch and said nothing, allowing Denn to continue.

"I am rewarded with the understanding that there is no one who seeks to rule this city through virtue or deservedness—not the Faith, nor the Lord Marshal, and neither my father nor you. All of you seek to step upon the backs of others to achieve your ambitions. Your solidarity is riddled with contempt for each other. It is pitifully compromised by knowing that every one of you is just as rotten as the next. Caphedra will be destroyed by ambition, deceit, and greed, long before peace settles on this land. I will happily leave this horrible city again, now that I am no longer beholden to any of your schemes—and when I leave, it will not be with your gold in your pocket to remind me of this whole affair."

A muffled tap on the rug behind Denn signalled to him that Captain Tirall was standing there. Raising and lowering his bardiche, he repeated the tap. Farathemun gave a nod.

"Mr. Wellum," the captain addressed him.

"Goodbye, Mother," Denn said softly, then acceded to the enforced departure. He looked back one last time at the doorway from where Ramisa had emerged. Alone as he was, he accepted that he could not keep her safe, so he consigned his last embers of hope to the promise that if her uncle fell short, the capable Larsens would be waiting to protect her.

At the opening of the stable door, knee-high eddies of wind scattered sawdust about the wood-planked floor of the manor's carriage house. Stable hands ignored Denn's entrance. They were too busy scraping muck out of stalls and laying fresh straw beddings. The horses also neighed unconcernedly.

Stall by stall, Denn searched for Temis, until the sound of his voice drew the mindful retainer out.

"Come to invite me in for supper?" he asked snidely, upon

seeing Denn out of the blue.

"I know she won't welcome it so soon, but you'll need to saddle Coalsmoke. We are leaving. Bring a bag of oats with you." Denn said.

Temis scratched at his braided locks disbelievingly. "We just got here!"

"We're not welcome anymore."

"What did you do? No, wait, we're innocent!" he raved. "What did your father do? Did His Highness hear about the deal for Serenn?" Temis's eyes started about nervously, but still, no one cared or appeared to be listening in.

Denn produced one of the apples, placed it in his palm, and held it up to Coalsmoke's snout for her to sniff as a peace offering. With an excited chomp, she snatched it between her teeth and hungrily swallowed.

"Fate has exhausted its patience with my father, it seems. He is chained up in a prison cell in the temple," Denn said, explaining. "He never raised an army, nor did he manage to provide any of the support to the Farathemuns that he promised, which means all deals are off. The Larsens of Kramwen will be taking on Ramisa's cause in our place."

"So that's who he has sided with now!" Temis said. "And now we have two to rescue from the temple."

Denn turned to frighten off a stable hand who was sweeping too close to their conversation. The boy quickly turned tail toward another corner of the sizeable carriage house.

"No. Just one. I'm done being a fool for my father," Denn said.

"Very well, but once we've rescued Serenn, you'll still return to fight for the princess, won't you?" Temis asked, seeming to test the waters.

"My mother has asked that I not be involved in the fighting," Denn said with mocking disdain. "We will retrieve Serenn. Then we shall see. I may not have troops, but I will aid the princess however I can, before leaving the city. The cure for her illness must lie in destroying the Paragons or loosening their grip somehow—and they too are in the temple."

"Being a fool for a woman is far more preferable, you're right," said Temis. "And you were wise to only promise to kill people who are already dead—but I gather it's not that simple."

"Do you remember throwing the black blade off the tower at Bridgecliff?"

"Yes," Temis answered, looking a tad more wan than usual. "If that thing wants its sword back..."

"As you say, it may not be that simple," Denn said.

Temis pulled on Coalsmoke's reins, and the horse reluctantly gave up the rest of her well-earned meal. She swished her tail at some bothersome flies and, led by Temis, she stepped out again into the stifling midday sun.

"Let's start by finding Yael. He might be of help to us," Denn suggested.

"You're right," Temis said solemnly. "He told us when we were leaving that he had been involved in studying the queen's troubles. Perhaps he knows what must be done."

"Go back to our manor, and if it's safe, get some things ready so that we can leave Caphedra quickly," Denn said.

"What about you? Where are you going?" Temis asked.

"Lords' Lane," Denn said. "I have another promise to fulfill."

Denn knew Livet would not have been content to sit still and silent all these many days, but he would not go back on his word to attempt to reunite with her as soon as he returned. Success would rely on whether she had kept her part of the bargain and stayed nestled in the safety of the lodging house.

All the homes in Lords' Lane were either empty or nailed tight. Many residents held offices and positions in the castle, so were likely sequestering themselves there for safety. The remainder knew to stay indoors and burrow in until the coming troubles had resolved themselves—that is if they hadn't been displaced by the new regime, and either chased out of town or strung up.

When Denn reached the lodging house door, it was locked solidly. He raised his fist and pounded, calling out to the landlady to open up. "It's me. Wellum. I'm a tenant! Open the door!"

He heard the bar scrape as it was lifted from the inside. The door parted with a raspy and timid, "Come in, quickly."

The white-haired landlady's hands looked frail, but they were capable enough to drag him through the portal with a good yank. As

Denn replaced the bar on the door, she inspected him. "Are you hungry?" she asked as she roughly slapped the day's build-up of dust from his clothes.

"The girl that was lodging here in the room I spoke for. Have you seen her?"

The woman shook her head with a discouraging, "No."

Denn was prepared for a wave of guilt to wash over him, but it was assuaged with unexpected relief. Her answer gave him hope that Livet had fled the city and escaped in time, but he had to see the empty room for himself, nonetheless. Perhaps she had left a note.

"The key," he demanded. The old lady reached into a green-tinged copper pot on a bookshelf and fished out a mortice key. Denn nodded his thanks and ascended the creaky stairs to the room. He twisted the key in the lock, and the door opened.

No one was there.

The bed was unslept in; its blankets and covers were pulled up and tucked in neat and flat. The tables and shelves were devoid of any personal possessions save for a small box of candles that Denn had procured for Livet, but which looked largely unconsumed. Other than that box, the room appeared as they had first found it.

A crude mirror sat on a narrow, lacquered table in one corner of the room. Denn picked it up and reluctantly took a survey of the cuts and bruises to his face he had endured that morning. It was less terrible than he had imagined, but he still looked like he had been dragged through the gate upside down.

He set the mirror down and turned desirously to the bed, allowing himself a moment of indulgence to imagine how nice it would feel to just lie down and fall asleep. But that was impossible. Serenn needed him now. The prince's army was bound to breach the walls soon, and he wanted to be gone before the inevitable clash filled the streets and imperilled everyone left inside.

Denn gave the room one last look, but he already had his answer; the room was abandoned. There was nothing left to do now but turn and leave, but the instant his hand touched the door latch, he heard a voice.

"Are ya goin' without me?"

Denn spun around. Livet was right there, behind him.

"You mustn't have expected t'see me 'ere," she said. A frivolous smile lighted on her lips. "Goin' back t' yer princess?"

"Livet!" Denn said, and with an inestimable longing, he rushed to embrace her. She squeezed him back, but he inhaled sharply, his injuries betraying themselves.

"You're hurt all over!" she fretted.

Denn took her by the hand and related most of the violent events of his journey, from facing his brother's murderous riders on Bridgecliff–and Trin's death–to the sudden melee at Southgate and Naobe's brutal slaughtering. He told her of the kidnapping plot, and, with effort, he even managed to explain how Temis had reappeared, and why.

"Livet," Denn said darkly, "When Trin died, there were things I saw and heard. His wound was cursed–" He stopped, unsure of his words. "The princess's affliction, just the same, is not a sickness. Both are fruits of the wicked magic of which I must warn you. Adepts and curates of the Pillars are summoning terrible spirits back from the dead."

"I know," Livet said simply.

"No, you couldn't possibly know!" Denn replied, bothered that she minimized his warning with empty rhetoric. "The dead seek to aid the Pillarmen in doing ill to the living. They are the Paragons, as recounted in lore, but I have heard them, and seen them."

"Me too," said Livet, annoying Denn further by her seeming lack of seriousness. Then, stuttering and stammering, she continued, "I've seen... where they... sleep... and they're not alone in bein' raised from death."

"What do you mean? Not alone? More than the thirteen? Who–*what* else?" Denn asked, alarmed. Admittedly uncertain even how many Paragons they faced; he was relying on the canon taught in his school days.

"The temple dungeon 'as a room full of corpses and bones, only *half-dead,* you could say." Livet paused and breathed, "I saw Kell. They have him, and I should help him. *I need to help him.* My friends will know how to break the spell and set him free."

Grasping her firmly, Denn commanded, "No."

Livet recoiled slightly, pulling away from his solid hold and staring back questioningly.

"Now that I have seen what has happened to the princess, I want you to swear off any fascination you have with these unnatural arts."

"Why d'you ask this?"

"No matter who performs the deed, it is fraught with danger. The Paragons are watching."

Denn knew he was beginning to sound frantic, so he let go of Livet and held his tongue until he could speak less rashly. He took deep breaths to calm himself.

"I am going into the temple," he said after a moment. "My brother has Serenn held in the temple priory. I can try to help you too. Tell me what I need to know to release your friend from his prison, and I will spare you from the danger."

"You can't do it alone," Livet said. "Besides, I 'ave to repay Kell for all 'e did for me."

"I have Temis, and he will get Yael," Denn said. "I am not alone."

"That's not enough!" Livet rebutted. "You need more than a couple of hired swordfighters."

"Olen... Perhaps, Olen will help me."

Livet shrunk back slightly, seeming to recollect something. "Of course, he would," she said. "But you'll need to go 'elp 'im first. He has 'is own problem. I came to find you to help."

As desperate as he was to free his sister, Denn preserved his belief that Lehn needed to keep her alive. She held the secrets of their family's countless stashes of wealth and treasure. He also knew that should Lehn not otherwise be convinced through compassion or be able to be dispatched by force, he would likely not survive to aid his friends after, and ultimately Olen could not be abandoned.

"Let us go to Westriver," Denn said. "Show me where Olen is and how I can help him."

CHAPTER 29

To the Moon and Back

"**F**or a man that brought down such a ruckus of pure malevolence upon yourself, you don't look half bad."

Back at the Black Eel, Bull Draemun pulled the licorice root from his mouth with one hand and reached over the counter to grab Olen's jaw with his other. He swivelled Olen's head around to marvel at how completely mended were the wounds on the big man's face and skull. Even Eysman Rowl, who did not typically make such a fuss, studied the returning sergeant and gave an unexpected poke into Olen's ribs to check if they were still fractured.

"Something in the ale at the Peahen, I guess," said Olen, avoiding the admission that Gardia's mysterious potions were behind his recovery.

But while Gardia had treated the damage levelled upon his manhandled and contused body, Olen's guilt remained unassuaged over its fallout. His ill-considered march into the Half Moon Tavern had resulted in a vengeful counterstrike by Karaval men upon the Black Eel, and he had no scars to show that he had shared in any of the repercussions. He appeared unscathed while Maks Kaler and Gastun Holder were hurt badly. Worse, their wives—and Maks's daughter—were taken as hostages by Karaval thugs who were using them to taunt the men of the Black Eel into ill-advised reprisal.

Neriah had followed Olen back from the Peahen and was tending to the two wounded soldiers now. For the benefit of encouragement, and despite what Gardia had proclaimed, she promised that there would be help once the retaliation took shape.

"We need to find some weapons—or scrape up enough coin to buy back our old ones," said Gastun, mulling over their quandary as he drank from a mug of barley beer.

"Why did you sell them in the first place? Isn't fighting your only trade?" Neriah asked, unaware of how dismissive she sounded.

"It wasn't supposed to be," said Maks, "Not anymore, for what that's worth."

"We have families now, but no other money to live off," said Gastun. "We're all owed months' worth of pay, not to mention our company purse got emptied. We had no choice but to sell what we could to get by."

"Besides, if someone did hire us again, we'd wear their colours and they'd pay to kit us up all properly, wouldn't they?" said Vyr Ockslo, who was warming his bones by the fire. A spark landed on his heavy knit sweater, and he brushed it off.

The other regulars sat beside Vyr, sharing the comfort of the crackling blaze. Nyrim, his nephew Kalden, Asher, Effie, and the rather sizeable Tomton clustered about the hearth. The wire-haired dog snoozed on its side. Only Talton Terrod was missing from their group, for he had been at home seeing to his niece, Yarma, and his brother's widow, Krystlen, when the Eel was besieged. He promised he would be back when they were ready to march.

"Ludicrous as it sounds, we may have to consider Olen's suggestion. Keepside has a big armoury that's only half-spoken for, and *we are desperate*," Eysman pointed out.

"I can't think of anywhere else," said Olen dismayed.

Bull cocked his head and stared strangely at Olen. "Tell me why Red made you a sergeant again? You seriously want to bring the garrison down on us, too?"

Effie, who had already suffered from Olen's overconfidence, returned a frustrated and disparaging look from the other side of the room, where he was eavesdropping.

"Here's a plan," said Eysman. He held up his hands and brought them together with a slap of palms. "We could have them and the Karavals knock heads with each other over who gets to fight us first."

"Funny," said Bull. "I'm not used to you making jokes, especially when any moment now, this city is going to bust open. Captain Alamm will have his men on the ready to link up with the Marshal as soon as he's through the gates." Bull's nervous shake flared up again. He clenched both his fists and pressed them into the counter to brace them and stop the tremble. "So, what I'm saying is that now is hardly the time that we'd catch them asleep with their door unlocked."

"We'll fight Dance Karaval with our damnable bare hands, then!" cursed Olen in exasperation, but his mood lightened immediately when the tavern door opened, and a wisp of a girl trotted in. By the hand, she led a blonde-haired and lanky man in a brigandine vest, with a long sword on his back.

"You lost?" Bull asked the girl.

But Livet stayed on course toward Olen, greeting with a joyful smile. Olen stood and squeezed her in a tight hug, then clasped Denn's hand in his, and elatedly slapped the errant cavalryman on the shoulder. "I heard you were away," he said. "Travelling with royalty!"

"Yes. That part was supposed to be kept quiet, yet I'm learning that everyone seems to have heard." Denn complained. "Nevertheless, I'm back now–for a short while, at least." He approached closer and more privately voiced his intention. "Livet explained what happened here. I want to help you."

"So, you've heard it all, then," Olen said, again feeling sheepish from shouldering the blame. "When we heard you were at the head of a company of men..."

"Not my men, I am sorry to say," Denn said. "You heard wrong."

Olen's face flushed. He knew the rumour was too good to be true. Nonetheless, he was undeniably eager to have even one amiable supporter. The weight of this whole ordeal, and his need to indemnify himself against his past failings, had left him feeling very alone.

Leading him around the Black Eel, Olen introduced Denn to his fellows. He explained what they had been discussing, and the dearth of arms was something Denn seized upon immediately.

"Who's your quartermaster?" Denn asked.

"Eysman used to be," said Bull, as the dour, balding sergeant in front of the counter, nodded in concordance.

"Then Eysman and Olen will come with me. We're going to Barforgers," Denn said.

"We don't have enough money to pay their prices," said Eysman.

"We won't need money," said Denn. Turning back to Livet, he asked, "Please stay here. I need to talk to Olen."

"Why don't I go and ask my friends t' help?" she offered, but Olen noticed that Denn immediately stopped her.

"No. I'd rather we not speak to too many people about our intentions," he said, then without giving her a chance to respond, he strode out the door. Olen and Eysman downed their mugs of barley beer quickly and hopped up from their seats in pursuit.

Out on the street, Olen was quizzing Denn about his journey when his friend unexpectedly halted. With a discontented huff, Denn switched subjects.

"You need to be careful of those whom Livet would so quickly join. The mind-bending and charms that you described seeing on your way here are all tied to a path that can lead her toward worse. I have seen what the outcome can be, and I do not think either of you should be around the likes of this Baressa or her friends. You have heard the stories of what befell Queen Tressa." He leaned in conspiratorially and lowered his voice. "The Princess has been damaged by the same reckless evils you describe coming from that Northport woman. The Faith has people just like Baressa, who are playing with the powers over life and death. You should know this."

"Baressa is dead. She died when she snuck into the temple with Livet," Olen said.

"What?! The temple?" Denn's jaw dropped. "Olen, I don't want to see Livet come to any harm. I need to go to the temple to confront my brother, but Livet should not be anywhere near there. It's for her own good. And if she's taken up with others like Baressa, I won't abide by it."

Olen allowed Denn's warning to soak in and did not argue. He also chose to hide that he was the beneficiary of Gardia's powers, seemingly begotten from the same school of skills. But that craft was helpful—and even Denn had once thought Livet's trickery was humorous and harmless. His journey must have given him a reason to reconsider. Olen did not know what Denn thought of Livet's abilities now—not that Olen truly understood them himself—but if Denn suspected it was anything more than playing hide-and-seek for her, or that they could lead to something terrible, what then?

"The Pillars openly speak against spells and curses, but they are using them all-in-the-same. I lost a man to unhealable wounds, caused by a cursed, black-bladed sword that came from them and their demons, the Paragons."

"I thought the Paragons were made up to give guidance... myths to make the Faith's rules carry more authority. Demons now? If you say so, I will not doubt you," Olen said, mulling it over.

"They are more than myths," Denn informed him.

Eysman, who had been walking a few arms' lengths quietly behind, interjected. "A black sword, eh? I've heard of such things, but never seen one," the quartermaster said. "Folk always said that Lord Vlass had a rack full of them in Lanstad."

"It all sounds hard to believe, but I do believe you," Olen repeated. "Leave the dead in the ground, they say—and don't be in a hurry to join them. This I understand. I'll be on my guard."

"There is much that is hard to believe," Denn said. "I haven't told you what I learned of my kidnapping." Relaxing, he allowed a gentle, cynical laugh, then recounted the particulars of his father's scheme, Temis's acts of redemption, and the attempts by the Pillarmen to hunt him down—all while Serenn was kept captive by his brother, Lehn.

Denn had become more than the naïve little pup he had once come across as when they first met at Fal Ghreeg. He felt sorry Denn had to undergo such ordeals, but there was pride in seeing Denn overcome them. Olen sensed a renewed, even novel, sense of determination in Denn's speech and bearing.

In contrast, just hearing about these trials made Olen's head swim by the time they had crossed the Midbridge and started north toward Barforgers's protracted row of blazing smithies. Once they reached the district, the dizzying temperatures only made his head worse. Waves of heat were rippling through the air of an already sweltering afternoon. All around, quenching buckets sent forth clouds of billowing steam when red-hot iron was plunged inside with a rush and a roar. Every forge was occupied with last-minute repairs and the mending of armour while rumbling grindstones whet the edges of swords and axes, atrophied with rust. Upon each shield, adolescent apprentices painted a unified, predominant pattern of four white stripes.

"My father was the largest provider of ore and ingots to the weaponsmiths here. They owe him money, so I'm hoping one of them might cut us a favour," Denn said, explaining the trip.

Proceeding down a short alley, Denn introduced them to a man named Fernwood Drosst, explaining that he was the Head Guildsman of the Unified Trade Guilds. Sweat rolled down the man's long nose and drenched his beard and dark hair. A red, blistery heat rash crept out from under the crook of his jaw where perspiration pooled.

Even upon entering the guild master's tiny, closed office, it was hard to hold a conversation over the din. They were subjected continuously to the pinging and clanging of hammers on anvils and the whoosh of bellows feeding the oppressive infernos next door. Along the walls, metal stamps for pressing the coats of arms and martial sigils of honoured clients were hung.

If Drosst was only slightly familiar with Denn, he certainly knew Phon.

"Give your father my warmest regards! I haven't seen him since the last council meeting. What brings you here in his stead?"

"I need enough of your wares for at least a dozen fighting men to be outfitted with weapons, mail, greaves, shield and helm," said Denn.

Drosst frowned and mumbled discouragingly at the request.

"The Pillars have spoken for all that we have in our stores, Denn. I don't know how many we could spare," said Drosst.

"How much are they paying?" asked Eysman, joining the discussion. The question gave Drosst a momentary halt, and the answer was obvious.

"They don't pay for anything, do they?" Olen said, reading the man's face. "They demand and take."

"That's how it goes now," Drosst said, acknowledging Olen's truth. "At the risk of being declared an apostate, I oblige. But when the Lord Marshal returns, they'll be cowed and forced to settle the debts they've racked up!"

"And your debts will likewise come due, won't they? I understand you owe my father a large sum of gold."

"Nonsense! He'll get what he paid for. But I just can't promise you any more product than what you've already bought." He leaned over toward a dog-eared register and started thumbing through the pages.

"What product?" Denn asked.

"I have it all recorded," he answered and showed Denn the

register. "His signature," he pointed to the bottom of the page. "This shows that we are square."

"So... my father collected on your debt to him already," Denn said. "Goods instead of gold."

"After the council meeting, he became obligated. It's expected of a lord to have more men than just his household guard. Our stores held a leftover lot–swords... axe heads... arrow tips and bolt tips... crossbow mechanisms–Your father spoke for them immediately. He had Yael sort out the finer items, then when a load was ready, we packed everything onto a skiff bound for downriver. One of his men was to meet the delivery a little further down, outside the city. A fellow named Stamish."

Olen saw Denn look both a bit flushed and enlivened. He couldn't read every line on the page, but Olen noted it was quite a long list of goods

"Yael organized this?" Denn asked.

"It was your father who signed for them. He came to us and offered to let us square up with him this way," Drosst answered.

Eysman was looking over Denn's shoulder and spotted something. His voice sounded a bit higher-pitched than usual. "You've ticked off a bunch of things and dated them, but not all. Is there more to be had?" he asked.

"The smaller pieces, spear points and arrowheads are all accounted for and shipped since we had lots on hand. Phon asked for some of the more intricate pieces to go through additional finishing, honing, and sharpening. A bit of extra ornamentation. You'll have them soon, I promise."

Anxiously, Denn laid the open register on Drosst's desk. "I'll sign for them if you can get them to me now–whatever state they are in."

"Really? Excellent! I'll have them fetched," said Drosst with pleasure, calling out to a handful of boys within earshot and harrying them to lend a hand.

"My quartermaster will oversee," Denn said. "Load them onto a skiff like the others, and we'll float them down the Darrow ourselves." Turning to Eysman he asked, "You're capable of handling a boat?"

The wrinkled storesman nodded. "Aye. I grew up on the river, the same as the rest."

"Good," Denn said, then under his breath, he completed his instructions. "Olen and I will meet you under the Midbridge with the others."

"Aye, sir," said Eysman.

The sun had barely moved in the sky by the time they stood on the bridge to greet Eysman. The skiff was lying low in the water, laden with weapons wrapped up and concealed under an oiled, canvas tarp. Sometimes rowing, sometimes dragging his oars to steer, the quartermaster guided it effortlessly down the stream, ready to re-outfit the soldiers of the Westriver Company.

Nyrim was already there to receive the line when it was tossed to him, and he pulled the skiff alongside the bridge's abutment. Asher and Vyr quickly unloaded the cargo, pulled the oars from their locks, and stashed the boat under the bridge, next to an old hawthorn tree that Olen remembered from in his younger days. The thorns made for good fishhooks.

"Your tavern is probably under watch by the Karavals," Denn said. "Go round up the rest of the men and have them leave discreetly, in pairs. When they find us here, they can take from the pile, then we will form up to move against the Half Moon right away. We're running out of time, and I have to attend to other matters tonight."

Two at a time, men snuck underneath the stone arch of the bridge and grinned as they picked from the pile. Maks was looking better after a few doses of Neriah's medicine; he hoisted a fearsome axe and grunted his satisfaction. Talton and Vyr reached for swords while Nyrim and Gastun—still looking drained but defiant—drew out spears and dirks. The newly recruited members of the warriors' trusted circle, Asher, Effie, and Kalden—the "elvers" as Sasser Goll had called them—each procured their arms as well. They had never imagined the chance to pick from the rack of the Barforgers smithies.

Counting the men as they arrived, Olen conferred with Bull, who showed up last. He reported that the Black Eel was locked up, but he pointed out that if any Karavals were close enough to try the door handle, it would alert them to the ale hall's conspicuous emptiness all the same.

"That's all of us," said Olen.

"The arms are yours to keep," Denn announced to the men magnanimously. "My friendship with Olen obliges me to help, and I won't be the one that forsakes him."

"Then we owe you," said Maks.

"When the big row comes and the Marshal is fighting the Faith for the city, my name's not well-liked by either side. I don't plan on sticking around Caphedra any longer than I must, just to collect on debts. I'll be happy to unshackle myself from this rotten capital for good."

"Howsoever this day turns out. Thank you for helping us, sir," Nyrim said.

Bull stood against the hawthorn. Eyeing the men standing together, he declared, "Looks like Mr. Wellum's generosity has restored our infantry company—either what's left of it, or the start of a new one, I'm not too sure."

"Let's just get the work done," Eysman prodded.

Olen growled with eagerness. "Aye. We'll square up with these hoods and whoremongers." He led the way, as he did in his days as the company's first sergeant. The newly replenished Westriver Company and its new recruits paraded through their namesake quarter until they were in sight of Faralley's Bailey Street. There they drew weapons and drew their line in the cobblestone landscape.

"Livet!" Denn called out.

Olen did not see the girl but knew she would be somewhere nearby, in the shadows behind them.

"Keep away from our main attack up front. It's too dangerous."

"I'm helping," she answered, putting her foot down.

Denn thought it over and relented.

"Then go with Effrem, please. Sneak in and help him find his sisters and the others, while we keep the Karavals busy out here," Denn directed. "If we make enough noise, there should be very few fighters left out back. We want to bottleneck them at the door."

"The kitchen entrance is out back, next to the city wall," said Neriah. "They'll probably have been put to work there, and hopefully not upstairs. Though if any of the girls are missing, there's a servant's staircase to the second floor that you can use. Search behind any door that has brass locks and bar on the outside."

Olen called attention to the empty apothecary near where he had once sat vigil for his niece. "See that old shop?" he said to Neriah, "You can act as surgeon, there. Maybe it's still got some medicines and supplies that aren't too old. We'll send the wounded to you."

"I'll be with her," said Bull. His condition made his sword arm too unsteady for the assault, but he had anticipated his shortcoming and brought a crossbow, which he could rest on a window ledge and aim one-handedly, "When fates aligned," he told them.

Down Bailey Street, some of the guards at the Half Moon door were beginning to notice the armed men congregating on the cobbles.

Denn took one last look over the company. "Let's get our people to disperse before the Karavals get a clear count." Turning to Olen, he signalled for the next step. "When you're ready, choose your ground, and we'll advance."

Olen heeded the command and took to the open street on a path toward the Half Moon, tracing, in reverse, the same route along which he had been dragged on the night of his botched raid. Seizing Coldswept by the hilt, he drew his sword on the first of two Karaval sentries in front of the tavern door and took a primal pleasure in the look of terror on their faces. The first man tried to parry, but Olen's strike was merciless. It sliced through the sentry's shoulder and split him open, painting the tavern's breached entrance in a splattering of red. The man's death sent a vibration through Olen's blade, the same familiar hum that happened each time it helped him take a life.

At the same time, Nyrim sped to Olen's side and plunged his spear through the second guard—entering at the man's collar bone and sending the guard's head jerking upward.

The rest of the Westriver men moved forward as the Half Moon became frenzied like a hornet's nest ripped asunder and Karavals beginning to swarm about.

Over his shoulder, Olen caught sight of Kalden. The boy was tracing his uncle's path and ended up well ahead of where a novice should be, but keeping devotedly close, Asher matched his pace and defended the boy with a shield in one hand and a bastard sword in the other, deflecting attackers like an ox plough. Whenever a chance opened up, the tip of Kalden's spear would emerge from behind Asher's shield, lashing out like the tongue of a viper. Together, they won Effie an opportunity to sprint to the rear of the tavern before the Karavals could discover him and chase him down. Olen knew Livet would be moving with him, infiltrating the Half Moon's kitchen, unseen.

Just then, three men rushed out of the bar to counter Olen's assault—and behind them were the two long-haired lieutenants who ran with Dogfish. Maks and Tomton moved up on Olen's right. With two hands on the haft of his war axe, Maks thrust the weapon's sharp dague upward into the chin of a guard, pushing him back inside, then hoisted and smashed him against the door jamb before withdrawing the weapon. With the artfulness of a butcher preparing a swine, he drew his axe back and cleaved him in two with a savage swing. Beside him, Tomton kept one hand on his hammer and used his other massive mitt to pull the dead man's halves apart with a congratulatory grunt.

That gained them entrance to the main room: a sombre ale hall with walls dressed by stretched black fabric under cornice-capped valances. A tile floor was cluttered with broken ceramics and glass, recently ejected from a spate of overturned tables now acting as defensive breaks.

Nyrim stood to Olen's left, and together, they clashed with the other two challengers. Nyrim ran his spear through the side of one while Olen maneuvered Coldswept for another gruesome victory. Blood drained from his victim's side, and their body crumpled. Olen felt his blade quiver appreciatively.

This exposed Dogfish's men. Olen overestimated how averse they might be to getting their hands dirty. Each moved forward unabashedly for retaliation, and when a flash of steel narrowly missed Olen's head, Nyrim caught the blow and was left cut and bleeding.

One of Dogfish's long-haired fighters named Castler wielded a curved sword like a sickle in a storm. Tomton took a frightening slash to the leg, being too large and too crammed against the doorway even to attempt dodging the strike.

"Forward, You Eels! Forward!" Unhesitatingly, Olen stormed

through the door into the main parlour. Though his forceful entry split apart Dogfish's men, a new wave of Karavals closed upon him. They clamoured to get at the brazen invader at their entrance. Olen looked back but the others were already engaged in a fight that was underway out on the street. Adding to the enemy's numbers, Jensir Udal's men had returned early from their rounds, and they dived straight into the assemblage of Westrivermen outside.

In the pit of his stomach, Olen felt the void that comes from the first intimation of doubt. He looked on the ground at Tomton, whose lungs were creaking cavernously with each breath. Locked in a corner beside him was Kalden. The boy was too young to begin a life of chasing vindictive conflicts and running from endless reprisals. Nyrim had raised his shield in front of both of them but was also starting to show signs of faltering from the constant blows he was forced to absorb.

Olen cursed himself. They were there, again, because of his impetuousness and the back-alley war that he had inherited and been too stupid to abandon. He risked losing his brothers-in-arms just as he had his brother by blood.

Moving in front of Nyrim, Olen protected him the way that he was shielding his nephew. He blocked, parried and—when he could—kicked and punched to repulse the pile of determined brutes, crushing them against tables and retaking space to alleviate the pressure on the confined corner. He was losing his breath, and cuts on his arms and legs were soaking his sweaty clothes in blood. The shoulder of his sword arm was burning with fatigue from the exertion.

Finally, just as he plunged Coldswept deep into an adversary's bowels, two Westriver men burst through the door and created a second front that drew away some of the defenders. Denn and Asher, fighting side by side, as if in a predestined pairing, moved swiftly into the crowd, slicing with steel, and terrifying the Karaval horde with their ferocious intensity.

More of their side entered—Talton and Vyr—establishing a new line of defence across the centre of the tavern, ready to thwart other counterattacks.

Through strength of arm and determination, they had captured ground in the heart of the Half Moon. Dispatching the few remaining hold-outs, the Westriver fighters positioned themselves to block the staircase and doorways leading into the parlour, but they could not hold it forever. Sounds above told them that another retinue of Karavals was forming up to assail their position.

"The kitchen!" Denn called out and pointed to a swing door along the tavern's back wall. "Give us time to go through and collect the ones we came for—then get yourselves out of here and back to the Eel!"

Olen thundered into the kitchen door, nearly knocking it off its hinges. He entered in a hurry with Asher and Denn and found Effie squaring off precariously against an axeman twice his size. Effie stood his ground while behind him, his sister and the other captives huddled together in fear. Olen noticed that a dead man already lay on the floor as an expressionless witness to Effie's now-proven swordsmanship. Still, the young fighter looked outmatched.

Racing to Effie's aid, Olen expertly swung and sent the startled foe falling backward into the side of a bubbling pot of stew. It sloshed and toppled, forcing Asher to jump forward to save a petite, platinum-haired girl that Olen assumed to be Effie's younger sister, Kelzi. Quick-to-act, Asher flung her away from the blistering flood of broth. Her sister, Sandri, pulled the child in close, with a grateful look toward Asher.

In the fleeting calm, Livet emerged into sight, with her rondel drawn. She was protecting the three others—the wives of Gastun and Maks, as well as Maks's daughter.

"Everyone's 'ere," she confirmed.

"Out then! Move!" Denn shouted, and with Livet leading, and the warriors formed a ring around the rescued captives, and all exited out the back door, except for Olen.

He cursed his nature but could not abandon the opportunity he had right now. Beyond the kitchen were the Half Moon's storerooms and offices. A burning lantern hung from a hook and lit up the area. He could easily smash it and start a fire. With the turmoil out front, it might go undetected until it was too late. After all, the Westrivermen should all be safely out of the Half Moon by now.

Suddenly, a voice around a corner alerted him. It shouted and growled to anyone in earshot, and it was coming toward him.

The corridor was too narrow to swing a blade as lengthy as Coldswept, so Olen pounced forward with his sword arm pulled back, ready to thrust. Unintentionally, however, his shoulder jolted the lantern and it swung, disturbing the circle of light in the room, and sending it oscillating against the walls, down the tight passage, and illuminating the face of the high-ranked confidant of the Karavals, Jensir Udal. The old racketeer jumped back in surprise.

"You're a brave one to sneak back here!" he said to Olen then yelled, "Men! On me!"

"Seems it paid off," sneered Olen. "You're the one I want!"

To his credit, Udal recovered before Olen could set upon him. He planted himself and drew his sword, but his weapon was like a kitchen knife compared to the sizeable sapphire-hilted blade of hardened steel Olen wielded. He had watched Udal fight his brother over and over in his memories. He knew Udal's style, but it seemed to have grown slower than he recalled. His brother's murderer was older and lazier now.

"Is this how you fought my brother? My father? My cousins?" Olen taunted his foe.

The crime boss slashed at him. While Olen found it hard to go on the offensive in the narrowness of the corridor, it was easy to block. Coldswept's broad command of the space in the passageway denied Udal any chance to return attacks with his shorter weapon.

"You look familiar," said Udal, between breaths. "You have the look of a gambler. Do you owe me money?"

"I'm no gambler," answered Olen.

"There's ten men, or more, following behind me who'll say you are if you stay here," Udal quipped as he reversed around a corner.

It did not deter Olen. He was intent to stoke Udal's fledgling spark of recognition. "The only debt I have to repay to you is a gutful of steel from Tolen Kierk!"

"Kierk? I thought you were here to avenge the reputation of the Eel!" Udal said, narrowing his eyes into an appraising squint. "*Leave the dead in the ground* if you know what's wise. They care little for us."

"The Eel's score is settled. I'm here to finish Tolen's fight."

"That's an old name. It died with 'Duke' Domin and the rest. Why bring him up now? No breathing soul here gives a lick o' thought to any of that sewer-spawned tribe. Faralley is better with them all dead."

"They're not all gone." Olen punched with his sword arm so that the pommel struck into his adversary's brow. The wound squirted blood, and Udal was dazed briefly.

"Ah... yes," Udal muttered while stumbling. "Ha! The 'soldier' son. You should have kept marching away, as far as you could keep step."

Olen bristled at the implication he had been a coward. Since he'd left, he'd killed at least a hundred men like Jensir Udal, for far less personal a motive. "No. I am back, and I owe you this," Olen said. He drew back Coldswept for one conclusive, final strike. There was a futile attempt by Udal to parry with the short sword, but he was stuck through. No more words. No remorse. All that remained to be communicated was stored in Olen's heart and said silently in benediction for his brother.

The dying racketeer spat and gurgled, then slumped and slid from Olen's sword. His years of lethality had ended in this single act of revenge, for which Coldswept resonated jubilantly in Olen's hand.

Olen tugged and withdrew his weapon and reversed back around the corner, listening. There was one more man he needed to kill, but if Dirlen Karaval was as secure behind fresh guards as Udal promised, Olen's attempt would be risky.

That was when he became aware of an inner voice that sounded a lot like Neriah's. Second thoughts came as a novelty to him, but this one spoke and made sense: Udal hadn't known there were any Kierks left, which meant he hadn't identified Olen. Nor did he seem to know of Neriah's blighted ancestry. Tolen was murdered while she was still a young child, and it was not until she had grown into a woman before their paths crossed again. Udal was likely being honest when he said the blood feud had ended years ago. Its orchestrators, Udal and Domin, were both dead, and the only one who could keep the war alive now was Olen.

No more.

So long as Neriah was alive, he had a family to protect, and that would be impossible if he were foolhardy enough to walk into the Karaval's most inner sanctum to challenge a man he had never met. Even more senseless would it be to try and cut down a room full of bodyguards to realize such an absurd misadventure.

"Curse the Lord's Oath," Olen muttered, then in an unpracticed and unexpected move, he withdrew and softly slipped back the way he came. There was still a rising commotion of footsteps in adjacent hallways–and in the contested ale hall–but he was too far removed from the middle of the fray to be at risk of being accosted now.

Olen made it back to the empty kitchen. The unattended cooking fires had burned down to coals, and the spilled stew was cold and congealing with hairy black forms swarming over it. A mischief of rats was gathered around the sloppy puddles of broth, and the pint-sized scavengers postured aggressively as Olen entered. They communicated with vulgar squeals and hisses, telling him he was not welcome to share their bounty.

"It's all yours," Olen whispered to the wretched beasts. "Have the whole tavern. I'm done with this place."

The outcome of the fray was still being assessed at the Black Eel when Olen returned, but the first sounds he heard were far from celebratory. A woman's wailing and the sobbing fits of a child overpowered the alehouse's boisterous din. Larke Kaler and her daughter Preycee, learned that their rescue came at the cost of their husband and father. Maks Kaler's body was lying drained of life, while his liberated family grieved around him.

Also on a table was their quartermaster, Eysman Rowl. Olen choked on his own breath when he saw the old sergeant's unmoving form. Bull kept the watch closest to their aged comrade. Both his hands were shaking as they clutched a mug of strong ale. He was mumbling a few words from an old martial ode.

> When duty's demanding,
>   A Westriverman knows,
> He who dies standing,
>   Lives on in repose.

Wistfully, the barkeep glancing upward. "The old man's with Karla now. Husband and wife reunited, I'd wager."

"I didn't think you believed in a life after death, Bull," marvelled Tomton as he limped along, supporting himself with one arm on the Eel's countertop, on his way to the fireside.

"I believe in saying the right thing at the right time," Bull said as he looked at the wounded giant derisively. "It's a skill that I am, quite apparently, *alone* in possessing."

Olen leaned in and rested a hand on Eysman's stiffening arm, giving it a futile squeeze while peering into his friend's gaunt face. He observed and absorbed the peacefulness over its closed eyes and relaxed wrinkles. "Remember how young he looked when we signed up together?" he commented.

"Yeah, I do," Bull answered. He turned his face for a moment, then reached to offer Olen a mug of barley beer. "Have a seat. You look pretty worn out, too."

Olen dragged a stool backwards to give more room against the serving counter. "I'm still sorry to have gotten you all caught up in my mess."

"It wasn't just you," Bull consoled. "The Karavals got their mitts on everything once we were gone. They infested the whole borough. It kept the Faith out, sure, but things will change once one of the king's brood is wearing the crown. Even with tonight's victory, the men are talking about folding their tents and marching out of here for good."

"Leave Westriver? After we just came back?" Olen asked with his eyebrow raised disbelievingly.

"This is a place for dirty hoods and thugs—not families." Reaching under the counter, Bull pulled up a flask which he uncorked and surreptitiously poured into Olen's mug. It burned Olen's nose when he first leaned in to examine it.

"You have a tavern here—a good business. Why leave it?" Olen asked.

"Not a day goes by that some local loon doesn't try to force his way in to levy a 'tax' or push their weight around. I knock a lot of them senseless for the asking, sure, but there will be more once things are settled over at the castle. Armies rack up huge tabs. If you thought the Karavals were bad, wait until the Marshal's Men have their hands out—or the Pillarmen start flooding the streets with summoners and taxmen demanding Dues here like in the east of the city. I figure it's getting near time to uproot."

"But where would you go, Bull? Where would the men go?" Olen asked. "Back to the swamps?"

"Some nice plot of land they can plough and sow and reap

from," he suggested.

"All the good land's spoken for," Olen said pessimistically.

"Spoken for by absent noblemen, and the man who granted most of the land titles is mouldering in a mausoleum. Without him, the landed lords can wave around parchment all they like. What they need now are men like us to work the soil and keep their holdings in hand, under arms if need be."

"If need be," Olen repeated and took a swig from the mug. It tore down his throat and made him cough out loud, but he felt a hand slap him on the back and steady his spasm. It was Talton.

"Glad to see you well, sergeant," Talton said.

"Talton here is a family man, Olen. Why don't you ask him," Bull said, but then undertook the task himself. "Talton, if you could provide anything for Krystlen and Yarma, what would it be?" Bull was eager to make a point.

Talton shook off the question with a huff, but then opined, "Whatever it is, it's not here. There's not much on these streets that one can give to a woman—or a child."

Olen rolled his eyes. "Bull's eyeing you all up to be farmers and he's already spreading the manure. Fancy yourself as a crofter, or a shepherd, then?"

Talton laughed and his stern face softened. "A cottage and some sheep would be nice," he said. "And a great big hound to herd them. Woolen coats for the wintertime. A mess of mutton to fill my belly."

Giving up, Olen sighed hopelessly. They had just spilled blood together, all to establish that Westriver was their home. Why? What had they won? On the morrow, or soon after, they would be putting two more of their number into the ground as a further consecration to that territorial bond. But like his blood feud with the Karavals, maybe an end was coming. Maybe they could find more, somewhere else, and fight for that, someday.

Olen offered Talton a drink from his mug, which the warfighter wisely refused. With a shrug and a raised glass for Maks and Eysman, Olen downed a gulp himself. "Tell me how they died," he said, clearing his throat from the liquid fire. "I was with Maks, holding the door. I could barely see what happened outside. What do you remember?"

"We were about to follow you in," Talton recounted, his brow stretching again with its trademark severity. "But Udal's gang showed up. We killed that fella Jemm right away, but Vike and Sasser were there too. They fought like a pair of wolves. Bull put a crossbow bolt through Vike, but the bastard kept coming. That's when he killed the sergeant. The bunch of us just jumped on him then, so he's dead now. It wasn't easy. Sasser got cut up trying to save him and is likely dead in his own blood and piss in some alley."

"Tomton and I pulled Maks out of the Half Moon and tried to drag him to Neriah, but it was too late." Nyrim filled in the remaining part of the story from a couple of seats away. "He had been on my right when another troop of Karaval goons came down from the upstairs and got to him first."

Next to Nyrim, Kalden was sitting with Tomton, and they both nodded in synch with Nyrim's account. There were bandages sopped with blood around Tomton's leg, and someone had propped a heavy walking stick next to him. It looked like the big man might be barely able to stand on his own.

Five innocents saved, but at the cost of two dead Westriver fighters, Olen tallied. At least Gastun was back with his wife, Malee. The pair had withdrawn to the back of the alehouse, holding each other silently. Their hands were clenched and locked together to stop each other from trembling any further.

Effie was also at the back of the bar. He sat guard between his platinum-haired sisters and the rest of the tavern patrons as if still making up for his past failure to emancipate them before. But the boy's vigilance was marred by his drifting attention, which fell upon the rear-most table of the alehouse.

Together at the very back of the tavern, Livet and Denn were rejoined. But while Olen expected a display of celebratory affection, there was a distinct distance between them. Livet had a pleading, almost wounded look. Denn appeared unrecognizably harsh and held something aloft in his hand. He stood and loomed over Livet angrily.

"It belonged to Kell," Livet said. "I thought you could—"

"I already warned you about these things!" Denn shouted at her and sent the item colliding into the floor with a sound like the cracking of an egg.

"No!" Livet screamed a curse at Denn and lashed out at him, knocking him off balance.

Olen was stunned. He approached his friends but stopped just short of the quarrelling pair. Instead, he held back, closer to Effie and his sisters, and placed his arm out in front of the boy who was getting ready to rush to Livet's side. Whatever had just happened, Livet and Denn needed to sort it out by themselves. Olen just stared helplessly at his friends and the damaged necklace on the ground.

CHAPTER 30

Promises

Denn instantly regretted his intemperate outburst. However, destroying Livet's heirloom was the product of an abrupt, intense fear. He closed his eyes, waiting for her to pummel him further while challenging his mind to absorb all that he had seen in the vision.

After returning to the Black Eel, Denn had been singularly consumed with planning the infiltration of the temple. He spoke carefully of his intention to reason with his brother, Lehn, but Livet's fears were not easily placated. She knew Denn too well. She detected his inadvertent and thinly veiled tones of cynicism. He spoke as if he expected a finality to the foray, and she chastised him for it.

But when she suggested seeking help from her newfound circle of wizards and witches, he became riled at the notion. Then she produced a charm she called a 'Slayer's Glass.' She explained that it had the magical ability to show a person the mind and perceptions of any potential transgressors who held the wearer in fatal contempt.

Truthfully, he had only planned to confiscate it and counsel her on its dangers. "Why would I wish to see inside the head of my own killer?" he asked, aghast.

He was even more surprised that the pendant seemed to work. Once his fingers wrapped around it, the charm's clairvoyant effects began dominating his awareness. His vision clouded until finally resolving upon the sight of an unfamiliar chamber. The room was wood-panelled, to just above waist height. It was opulent in decor, replete with plush, pillowy chairs and detailed oil-painted portraits of lofty elders dressed in Pillar-blue. Not all its furnishings spoke strictly of splendour and comfort, however. Shelves full of lavishly bound manuscripts and weighty tomes of literature implied a hefty onus on academic labours. They spanned the room, only outnumbered by the racks of parchment and scrolls lining the walls. Denn realized this must be the temple priory where his brother kept his office, for once he had adjusted to the vision, Lehn was suddenly standing there, gesturing in a fit of displeasure as if Denn, himself, were standing in the room to receive a dressing down or to receive orders. Looking down he saw dressings on his arms and a falchion hanging from his belt.

Denn did not speak. He kept as silent as everything else within the purview of his mind's eye. His brother's lips moved, but they were soundless too. It was only a vision, but it disturbed him. Behind Lehn, he suddenly saw his father's chained body dangling from an upright rack positioned to one side of the room. Phon looked pale and close to death but jerked his arms and raised his head weakly. Dark, shadowy forms swirled in the old man's eyes.

The terrifying recognition brought him back. He lobbed Livet's priceless, personal artifact onto the Black Eel's stone floor as hard as he could. It took him a moment to completely break from the trance, so he barely noticed Livet screaming at him. Her furious punch, however, brought him quickly back to his senses. He braced for another, but when he opened his eyes, he saw she had already turned around, bolted for the door, and raced out of the tavern.

Every eye in the alehouse was watching him. Across the room, Olen stood still, his mouth open but wordlessly having witnessed what had happened. Some of the Black Eel patrons stood dumbfounded. Others began to coalesce and whisper like an ad hoc jury. In a split second, he had gone from wearing the laurels of a triumphant saviour to bearing the black mark of a villain.

Livet's admiration and devotion had always sustained him during their time in Fal Ghreeg and afterward, helping him to brace against the weight of his most unconquerable doubts. But now she did not understand, and his vision only further vindicated his fears. If she did not how grave the danger was, he had to make her realize.

Denn rose from the table, seized Longlimb out of prudence, and sprinted after her.

Outside the Black Eel, he searched up and down the street.

He had no idea which way Livet may have run. He did not know where Gardia's tavern was, and the few people who were milling about ignored him when he inquired. Worse, the sun was getting low, and the shadows were fanning out. The dark was consuming the streets and giving her ample space to conceal her flight.

"Livet!" Denn called out into the evening, stepping forward, then back-tracking and reversing again. He was careful not to stray too far beyond the firelight from the Black Eel's windows, yet he was desperate to pursue her.

"Livet!" he shouted her name again.

Perhaps it was for the best. It was nearly sundown; he would have to depart Westriver soon to face Lehn. Now that Livet had run off, he could find his way to the temple priory alone and spare her from stubbornly joining and endangering herself.

Just as he turned, he was addressed.

"*She* turned you against me? And my friends?" an irate voice accused from the crook of a wooden truss projecting out above him. Livet had wedged herself under a building overhang that he had passed under several times.

"It's because I don't want to see you hurt—I already said so," Denn said. "The tricks that your friends indulge in sound pale compared to what I've learned of, yet you don't know the danger at the end of the path. The Paragons are waiting to harm anyone who willingly wanders into their reach."

Livet scoffed at him. "*You* don't understand, which is why you should stay away from the temple. You promised we'd leave once y' got back, anyway. Why not now?"

"We can still do that once I've rescued Serenn and dealt with Lehn."

"You know that's not true. You felt it in the glass," Livet said. "They'll kill you b'fore you can leave the temple. That's the purpose of showin' you, is n' it?"

"If they do...," Denn began, but her words had their intended effect. He fumbled for words. His absolute dread of this mission weighed too heavily upon him.

Livet slipped around the truss and dropped, dangling by one arm. With her other, she reached out and pulled Denn close. She kissed him softly, with tenderness reminiscent of the times she had soothed and quieted him in Ayren's cottage. Back then, he was untried and desperate to prove himself. Now fate had finally afforded him a succession of challenges for him to overcome, and as he feared, his nerve was lacking.

"No more promises," she said, releasing her grip on the truss and returning her feet to the ground. "I know this won't be the last thing that you get called t' do. The Faith will keep hunting you, and you'll fight back—maybe because you 'ave to, and maybe because you want to, or sometimes because y' think you are the only one that *will* fight back." She paused. "I like that about you."

"Whichever side wins, I'll be an outlaw, and you with me if we're together. Perhaps the Marshal's enforcers would give you a miss, but if the Faith defeats them tonight, expect no quarter. For all the Pillarmen that hunted you as a girl in Lanstad, the Faith would come out hundred-fold stronger to chase you again—as the mistress of a condemned apostate." Denn refused to consider such a punishing sentence. "If I die tonight, it will spare you from that life. You have no good reason to be burdened with the same misfortunes as me. I won't allow it."

"I have my own reasons to go. I have Baressa... and Kell," Livet replied. "Even if you and I had never met again in this life, they would be reason enough for me to renew my own fight."

"They wouldn't want to see you die for their sake, either. It's already too late for them."

"Then maybe I should do it for your sister," she countered. "She was nice to me."

Denn brushed Livet's hair back. He could tell by the furrow creasing her brow that she was about to protest again.

Perhaps he should let her come. Even though he wanted to keep his plan to enter the temple a secret from strangers, he could conceivably petition for aid from her friends if they knew of some spell or charm to get rid of Paragons. Denn certainly had no idea. Maybe Lehn was not the only hope to dispel Ramisa's curse.

"I will do this alone. I do not want anyone to risk themselves needlessly. Let the Lord Marshal's army fight the Pillarmen," Denn said. "And in the end, this is only a family matter, between Lehn and me."

Livet shook her head, exasperated.

Denn's last excuse was his weakest, but it served its purpose. He squeezed her in a close embrace and said, "Please keep yourself safe, Livet."

"Just go," she answered poisonously. Then with her head low, cresting and drooping, she ambled off down the alley in her half-hobbled way, until she was enveloped by darkness.

If death was assured, there was no reason to risk any of his friends. Unencumbered by allies, Denn could set off for the Temple of the Faith now and move quicker. It was better to avoid an unseemly round of goodbyes. Guaranteed, Olen would offer to come and join his expedition, but Denn could not abide the thought of his friend also perishing. As he had told Livet, this was firstly a family tragedy and scandal. There was an unavoidable tinge of embarrassment implicit in this shameful confrontation. In honesty, he did not care what fate befell his scheming father, but the only person he planned to risk for Serenn's release was himself.

Setting out for Midbridge, a knot of trepidation plagued his stomach, and the descending dusk brought a heavy, humid drabness to the air that caused Denn to sweat vigorously. The Lord Marshal's army could be upon the city at any time, yet in Westriver in contrast, there persisted lazy pillars of smoke from the chimneys and the aroma of meat cooking on wood fires. A nightsoil man caused a loud clang as he tossed a shovel into the back of his cart and started on his rounds. A dog barked. Stubborn signs of life continued, unconcerned by the descending danger.

Denn was lying. He could not do it alone. He needed Temis to show him where to find Lehn's cell in the priory, and he needed someone—anyone—to tell him what must be done to rid this world of the Paragons.

He had not travelled far when a figure standing alongside a tenement house caught his attention. The person wore a short cape and cowl, which hid most of their face, save for deep lines around their mouth, and their square shaved chin. They wore studded leather, and a sword hung from their belt and turned their head to follow Denn as he passed.

"I am assuming you have some sort of plan?" said the watcher in a recognizable voice.

"Yael!" Denn answered. "How did you know I was here?"

"Fern Drosst," he said. "As soon as you left, he sent a runner to advise me of your visit. Perhaps he was scared that in settling your father's accounts, you overstepped your authority—but you haven't. Still, you made off with enough of his inventory that my curiosity was stoked. Drosst was observant enough to spy the eel pins your friends were wearing. He mentioned them."

"I arrived in the city with Temis, who confessed his part in bringing me to Caphedra. Do you know where he is? Have you spoken to him?" Denn asked.

"I am here," Temis replied, stepping out of the shadows to stand beside Yael. "We rode together, across town to find you. Brae warned it wasn't safe to leave the horses at the manor, so we've stabled them nearby."

Yael's expression soured quickly. "Temis told me about how he has put your sister in jeopardy." He gave the humbled hireling a scornful look that blurred between that of a displeased taskmaster and a disappointed father.

Suitably cowed, Temis pledged, "I assure you that I will die before I allow your brother to harm you or your sister over my mistake."

"Is that so?" Denn asked.

Temis nodded his affirmation, but with a half-hearted smirk qualified the vow to say, "That doesn't mean I am convinced you'll live, so much as I think we'll both die... and me first."

Yael shook his head and groaned.

"But what is important is that there is a chance for Serenn, and for us to aid the princess while we're at it."

He was hushed by a raised hand from Yael.

"I know Temis front and back. I was the one who entrusted your sister to him without sage reservation. That binds me to seeing this misfortune resolved, also. The princess is another matter but one that I am inclined to pursue if it helps me understand the mystery of her mother's death."

A third voice chimed in, "Whatever the plan, you'll need someone tougher than these two!"

Olen emerged from around a corner with an offer that was not unexpected and his strength and fighting prowess would be vital.

Yael was recruited to the cause through the pride of duty. Temis had a heartfelt obligation to Serenn, which while Denn was unsure he approved of the bond, he at least respected it. Olen's offer came as the mark of an unconditionally loyal friend. Denn did not mean to drag him into this, but his support helped dispel the stubborn knot in his stomach. He welcomed Olen, gratefully.

Olen's arrival also brought news of what had transpired in the meanwhile at the Half Moon. After Denn's hasty departure from the Black Eel, Neriah and Asher returned to report that Hull's gang, with Gardia's consent, had shown up in sizeable numbers. They had been late, which Olen surmised was intentional. Nonetheless, they had scattered the remaining Karavals.

They also presented a request for the Westriver Company. The prince's army was at the gates and the Marshal's Men were poised to see their compatriots through, undermining the city's defences from the inside. But from the onset of the battle, Gardia wanted to consign any potential pillagers and raiders to the eastern shore of the Darrow, force them to keep to the city proper and out of Westriver. To that end, Hull had ordered his men to defend the Highbridge, which crossed just below the city's northern spillway, across from the Blocks. Word was passed along from Captain Alamm, through Celebra, that the soldiers of Keepside would protect the bridge there. Though many, if not most, were aligned with the Lord Marshal, they had no desire to let anyone run havoc in their own backyard, should either army descend into a mob and become unruly or greedy.

That left Midbridge to the guardianship of the Westriver Company.

"Olen, do you not wish to be a part of the defence of your home?" Denn asked.

"Nyrim and Asher have called the men to arms, and Bull is overseeing them," Olen explained. "You'll need me at your side. Besides, I'm certain we'll be back in time if we stick together." Olen offered further. "But just say the word and you can have more men. I assure you. The Eels would be happy to stand at your side."

Yael stepped in. "If Olen's company is in possession of Midbridge, I recommend we return there for safety once we complete our business. It will be good to have a secure path out." Looking eastward, he frowned.

"Sounds like a great idea for afterwards," Temis praised but urged, "We still need an *actual* plan on how to rescue Serenn."

Olen cast a disparaging look at Temis, bristling at the very sound of his voice. Turning and staring him down, Olen confronted him. "You're a crafty fellow, from what I've learned. Why don't *you* suggest something?"

Temis backed up cautiously and stepped away from the more substantial veteran, and Denn noticed the more alarming, subtle and savvy slipping of Temis's hand into his leather jerkin.

Temis's myriad roles had already been explained to Olen when they went to the smithies, but it was naïve to think he and Temis would grow into compatriots on Denn's simple say so. It had been a difficult feat for Denn to levy even a fraction of trust upon the man who was once party to the villainy of his kidnapping.

"He's my man, Olen," Yael said, shielding Temis. "If he must prove his worth to you, I'm sure he will. He's already proved it to me. So long as the young Mr. Wellum has no objections..."

"None," said Denn, smoothing the situation enough that Temis withdrew his poised hand. "He will help us get into the temple and find the priory because he knows that Serenn is in danger until we do."

Olen shrugged, but presumptuously pushed a little further. "Temis works for you, Larkin, I got it. But to be clear, who do you work for?"

"I work for the Wellums—but that is a fair question," Yael said and turned to Denn. "I will offer my advice and I will follow your lead. But please understand that if your father is found and turns out to be still alive, I owe him my first sworn loyalty. Even if you order me to abandon him, I will not."

"Even though I do not think I can be so dedicated, I understand, Yael. Thank you for being honest."

"Well, whatever we aim to do, we must hurry," Olen reminded. "The Marshal's army is on the doorstep. We have information that his men are in place to crack the gate for him once he signals that he is ready. It won't be long now."

Denn considered the situation. With four swordsmen, they stood a better chance of forcing their way into the temple, and harder to sneak in should they opt for a clandestine route. His mind fired with random thoughts of approaches and tactics.

"Temis, do you still have those Pillarmen tunics from Bridgecliff?"

"They're with Brae back at your family manor house, either being laundered or burned," he answered. "After three days in a saddlebag, they were positively rancid. I had no idea blood could ferment so horribly."

Yael cast him a sideways glance and quipped blackly, "If you want to keep working for the Wellums, you had better learn how to get blood stains out of clothes."

Crossing Midbridge into the city, they struck southward, skirting the worst parts of Dockside, along a road that would take them to the Old Caphedran Commons. There they could continue directly along the King's Avenue.

On the way, Denn recounted the more recent revelations about the tragedy inflicted by the Faith upon Ramisa, her sister, and mother. Though its obscure process remained incomprehensible to him, he had seen the effects of grafting the spirit of a Paragon with the soul of a host. Ramisa was enfeebled and left conflicted with Lyseia inside her, but Ravon's embrace of Centurra was an altogether unpredicted escalation of the mystery. What did it mean to unite fully with the soul of one already dead? Was it true that in doing so, the sister, Ravon, had ceased to be?

Yael was especially attentive. He voiced his satisfaction at having the gaps in his knowledge patched and filled by what Denn had learned, no matter how fanciful. But upon reaching the Commons, it was still a speculation game.

"Entwining two souls, one dead and the other alive," Yael muttered. "I wouldn't begin to know how to treat such a thing much less imagine it done in the first place."

That was discouraging. Yael had vast knowledge over every mundane happening in this city and was looked up to as an expert in the ways of the world. Denn had hoped he would have been able to provide some solution.

"Ramisa has said that death is the only end to it. The souls only uncouple when the body they share dies, and their essences pass from this world into the next."

"If the Paragons spoke more loudly to her when she approached the city," Temis postulated, "then it's sensible to assume their power is tied to here, likely to the temple."

"That temple took years to build," Yael said. "You won't destroy it in a night."

"Worth a try," suggested Olen, shrugging.

Again, Yael dismissed the suggestion with a tired huff.

"Maybe if she travelled far enough away–farther than Fallowsea–it might release their grip, and the spell might break?" Temis said.

"If so, I am guilty of doing the exact opposite," lamented Denn. "Besides, Fallowsea is at the end of the land. There is nothing farther."

As they travelled, they kept to the sidelines, and to their relief, they passed unmolested by the legion of defenders who were busy taking up their posts. The Pillarmen were expecting an army– not four rough stragglers who could be mistaken for just another handful of mercenaries. The uneven, disparate assembly of the Faith's army meant that Denn's crew did not seem out of the ordinary in the least.

But as they crossed the Commons, something changed around them. Forced to traverse the open space, they detected that the sultry, static air, was now bubbling with a sudden frenzy. The Pillarmen were becoming uneasy and desperately watchful.

"Hold up. Be steady." Denn slowed the pace. "Listen."

At the Commons, the King's Avenue swung around into the Blocks, then Barforgers and up to the northwestern gate of Caphedra. It was in that direction that attention was focused. All eyes were looking north, further up the avenue to where the Market Round broadened out. Up and down the street, formations of Pillarmen were maintaining a defensive stance. Hundreds of blue and grey mismatched soldiers crouched behind overturned wagons, stacked timbers and piles of loose stone and brick. Far away, shouts and screams were flooding the air.

An orchestra of battle trumpets resounded, and Yael made the expected pronouncement. "They're through the gate!"

The Pillarmen took to their feet and braced for the coming rush. The clashing of countless steel swords and axes grew, then reached a crescendo as the vanguard of the Lord Marshal's army– the prince's army–crashed into the successive ranks of steadfast but hapless defenders.

Drawing back to the edge of the Commons with the others,

Denn leapt up onto a cistern and lifted himself onto a terrace that projected from the daubed side of a public house. From there, his keen eyes could better scope out the coming onslaught.

These first invaders were the men Denn like what he had seen in the field at Bren Hills—men drawn from the unstoppable hordes of Kolis Grandt, Chieftain of Stonebriar. Their hefty battleaxes chipped away at all manufactured and living impediments to the Marshal's advance, and their crushing war hammers swung down to shatter shields and widen the gap through which their oncoming army could march unopposed.

"The prince's army is through and gaining ground!" Denn called down to the others. "We have little time until the battle line reaches where we're going. We must make haste!" He motioned toward a path along an empty back street, dropped to his feet, and led the way further eastward with renewed urgency.

Before they could approach the central temple, they needed Temis's blue tunics, but Denn did not feel comfortable travelling the whole distance out in the open. Lehn likely had agents keeping watch on the house, waiting for Denn to make a mistake and return for one last armload of gold from the family coffers, or to snatch up other belongings. They might even expect him to return out of stubborn sentimentality.

Instead, Denn guided them to an unnoteworthy easement used by delivery carts and used it to cut between some of the larger Castleside estates. In addition to being less conspicuous, the sun had dropped below the taller buildings, making the route cooler and they only had to deal with the humidity.

After a brief stretch, they came to an intersection. Denn motioned them to follow him into an obscure alleyway where he paused and knelt, surveying the ground. Olen, who was less familiar with Castleside, looked tense.

"Where do we go from here? Someone is bound to notice us skulking about." Olen said, swivelling his head left and right to watch either end of the alley.

Yael touched his finger to his lips to hush the wary soldier and carefully pushed past to speak to Denn. "You've got it. That one will do," he said confidently. Together, they crouched near an iron grate protruding from the cobbles of the dark, dusty lane.

Denn put his hands on the grate. "Help me lift it off."

With combined efforts, the grating came loose with a single swift tug. The scraping of iron against stone was loud, however, and caused Denn to freeze, listening as to whether it attracted any attention. When he was satisfied that it hadn't, he relaxed and continued.

"Temis, you must go get the tunics. I'll come with you and show you the way through the catacombs to reach the manor."

Yael held up a gloved hand. "With your permission, I'd like to accompany you. I have not risked entering the house since your father's abduction and there are some matters of business that I was unable to administer."

"Now?" Denn asked.

"This may be the only opportunity, and I believe it to be vital to your family's preservation," Yael said.

"So long as it stops the Pillarmen from gaining any further advantage over my family, I give you full permission," Denn said.

"Thank you, sir," said Yael. Slipping into the gap left by the opened grate, he plunged through, downward into the depths. A crunching marred his landing—a sound like twigs breaking his fall. Denn knew it to be the sound of brittle bones.

Peering after him, Olen grunted disapprovingly. "Looks tight," he said.

"Perhaps you can stay here and guard the entrance. Pay heed to anything that passes on the street that might pose a danger."

"I will," Olen answered, drawing Coldswept from its scabbard and stepping out with the sword held ready.

"After me," Denn told Temis, then they followed Yael into the dark hole. More bones broke under their feet, causing Denn to wince. For peace of mind, he reasoned to himself that these were not his ancestors who they were clumsily desecrating.

"That wasn't your great grandfather I stepped on, was it?" Temis questioned, almost reading Denn's mind.

There was a clacking sound from his direction, then a flash of light flickered and expanded to reveal Yael's face, as he held a newly lit torch. Its oily, resin tip was soon burning nicely, and through its sooty haze, they could look more easily upon the crypt's grim tenants.

"These crypts belong to either the Triynes or the Awlors—I expect the latter," Yael explained. "Mostly, it's the less monied families that live here, along the edges of Castleside's hill, who hold positions more on formality than wealth."

As Yael had indicated, many of the elite families of Caphedra shared these catacombs, and the permutations of well-known emblems guided Denn in charting his progress. Directly under ancestral homes, the most antiquated symbols predominated in the burial chambers. The further out each passage branched, they came upon more recent and contemporary crests.

The quality of the mortar and masonry changed too, with the worst areas being midsection in the tunnels. The stone supports and arches were usually well-maintained directly below family dwellings where altars were crafted to pay respectful remembrance to ancestors without having to wander too far down the dimly lit tunnels. But the condition of the bricks and cut stones deteriorated as one continued past these family chapels, until entering newer sections with more recent excavations and construction. In older tunnels, space eventually ran out, however, and the burial chambers of two or more families would inevitably intersect. These inauspicious connections provided an effective and unobservable system of transportation around—or rather under—the most affluent part of the city.

The cool tunnel offered a rewarding respite from the persistent and wilting temperatures above. It invigorated them and they moved quickly underground to outpace the accumulation of fumes from the torch.

The Wellum family represented a long-established lineage in Caphedra and Denn knew that they would soon reach the family vaults. But it was the slowing of Yael's pace that alerted him that they had arrived. Ahead, desiccated, calcified skeletons were laid out beneath rotting and tattered palls, and upon which rested shields that depicted the unmistakeable Wellum bee.

All but for two.

Beside Denn was the body of a fighting man, under a shield that bore a fiery salamander. This had been the older emblem of the family for generations, chosen when the Wellums lit their own forge fires and ran their own smithies. Trade of metal ore still made up the bulk of their revenues, but now they were just middlemen. When the family expanded into other commodities, they adopted the honeybee as a symbol of industriousness.

The body was not so old as that. This salamander sigil belonged to his uncle, Phar Wellum, whom Denn had always admired and respected beyond measure. His uncle had re-adopted the fiery creature—proclaiming the bee to be too weak an emblem to go to war under—but mostly to set himself apart from his firstborn brother, Phon, the family heir.

Less descript, lying next to Phar, the other decaying corpse had no shield at all. It lay wrapped tight under a plain dusty cloth, absent of iconography and resting on a simple limestone slab that bore nothing more than the chiselled-out name of '*Hann*'. These were the remains of his brother, for whom he loved without limit.

"Temis," Denn said. "The tunics. Please go and get them."

"Right away," he answered and ventured off, immediately swallowed by the dark.

"There is a cord that he can pull to signal Brae to let him in," said Yael, who seemed to be delaying. "I doubt he will have any trouble in finding it."

Denn did not acknowledge him. He wanted to be alone with his brother, at least for this moment. He had never seen where his father had interred Hann after they expressed their final farewells. Now he saw there were only four chiselled letters to distinguish his brother's interment. Even the family name was omitted.

"Did father do nothing to mark him as one of us?" Denn questioned aloud. His voice sounded scratchy from breathing the torch's acrid smoke.

"We can find something suitable from the armoury," Yael said consolingly. "He was a fine young man. Worthy of the name."

Denn kept a distance, daring not to disturb his brother's repose. It overwhelmed him to be next to his unhappy sibling. "I'm sorry," were the first words he could manage, until his eyes grew damp, and he confessed, "I should have stayed home and helped you with your duties, like a good little brother. I failed you. And Lehn, too... and our sister—but I will do my best now."

"Denn," Yael said. "I will leave you alone, should you wish. You can take the torch as I know the way from here, but first, I needed to confide in you, privately. Now may be the best time."

"What is it you must tell me?" Denn asked.

"It was around the time you were brought to Caphedra. A man—an adept—visited the house and had words with your father. He had come to demand a payment in exchange for secrecy, to protect the Wellum name."

"Protect from what? What did he blame us for doing? I can imagine quite a few things. My father did not easily get along with the Faith."

"He claimed knowledge of the circumstances of the king's death."

"Whom was he accusing? Me?" Denn asked, rolling his eyes.

"No," Yael said. "He bragged of having regular dealings with Wex Sulford, and it was while in that capacity he became privy to the information. He claimed to have overheard something for which your father might be willing to part with a great amount of gold to keep silent."

"A Pillar adept? So, Lehn was involved?"

"He told your father that Sulford had arranged for your brother to meet up with the king, who was relaxing at the Azure bathhouse. It was an unknown subject of business, but whatever your brother sought to discuss was not favourably received. Whatever the matter, the outcome was said to have precipitated your brother's furious indignation, and subsequently, he displayed a 'perverse power', the man said, adding it was 'beyond the capability of any normal curate'."

Denn's eyes were stinging from the torch fumes. He swallowed back a lump in his throat. "They say the king was boiled alive."

"They do," Yael said, "and it seems he was."

"You've verified that the story is true?"

"My sources saw the body, although I cannot prove or disprove the means by which the death was achieved," he admitted. "Your father asked me to follow up on the matter before making his decision, but it was too late. The very adept who had attempted to pedal the accusation was already dead and hoisted upon a spike in Hamrin Square with his tongue cut out."

Denn leaned up against a carved archway and braced himself, bowing his head in regret.

"I know I failed my brother by leaving, but now I am uncertain I can ever repair the cracks I must have caused in his heart and character. What has he done? What has he become?"

"I predict we will soon find out," Yael said. "But it's not your doing. Your father planted the seeds of your brother's transgressions, not you. I only wished for you to be forewarned."

The sound of footsteps on dirt could be heard approaching.

"That'll be Temis back. Did you say you had other business?"

Shuffling over to a rough-plastered section of the wall, Yael reached into a recess and pulled out a leather satchel.

"This," he said. "I gathered a few things some time ago, prepared for a time like this. They will serve you in the future."

"What's inside?" Denn asked.

"I'll explain later, but I promise that you will find them of immense usefulness once you leave Caphedra. For now, you should keep the satchel here, safely out of sight."

"Very well," Denn agreed.

As expected, Temis re-emerged. He was out of breath but held the promised Pillar garments, bundled in his arms. Gesturing to the bone boxes and crypts surrounding them. "I think we've disturbed these fair people enough," he said and tossed clothes both to Denn and Yael. "Here, put these on and let's get on with it."

The tunics were a bit damp from Brae's attempts to launder them, Temis explained. The fabric remained stiffened in many places where blood had saturated through, but the wash had significantly remedied the odour. Brae must have employed some manner of scented oils when cleansing them, so now, instead of smelling like they were dragged through the decomposing meat scraps of an abattoir floor, the scent was overpowered by a sickening floral odour. Rather than soiled battlefield pickings, one might easily confuse them for having been stolen off embalmed corpses in a funerary chapel. It was a marginal improvement, granted, but the tunics were otherwise thankfully intact and, importantly, blue—to facilitate their planned ruse.

Denn took his and slipped it on over his leather vest. Once Yael and Temis were likewise attired, they returned through the dim passageway until they arrived again under the grate. Olen was waiting with an outstretched hand to help them back up into the feverish evening heat, one-by-one. Then he, too, shimmied into the last of the tunics that Temis provided. It was a tight fit for his broad build, but owing to the poor condition, the odd slash and tear gave him the grace he needed to accommodate his physique.

"The battle is approaching," Olen said, then he curiously queried Temis. "That man... the Marshal's Man who was with you that night at the cottage–and who broke into Denn's house. What was his name?"

"Colden Wess was the one that got away," Temis said. "Why?"

"Just before you returned, I am pretty sure that I saw him and a dozen others, making their way on foot toward Castleside."

"They're working to advance the Marshal's cause from behind the Pillar lines," said Yael. "I expect they are on their way to the citadel with some plan in mind."

Gritting his teeth, Denn fumed, "If we catch him on the way back, he's a dead man. But, for now, there is no time to spare. Serenn needs us, and I won't be distracted for the sake of revenge. Are we ready?"

Marshalling his men into one short line, Denn met the gaze of each of his companions and conducted his inspection. The foursome was passably dressed in the guise of four pious warriors of the Faith of the Pillars. After imparting individual nods of encouragement, he led them south to forge their way into the Folds.

CHAPTER 31

Revisitations

Forsaking her usually reserved and unpronounced manners, Livet grabbed onto the brass handles of the Peahen's front doors and pulled as if she meant to bring the whole building down. Still foaming with anger, she crossed the sawdust-plastered floor to Taringer. The mild-tempered mountain man was parked in his usual seat, in a raised and balustraded booth that provided him with a lookout over the tavern.

Between them, some bar patrons had pushed away and stacked tables and chairs to form a lane wherein they could engage in a game of knife throwing at each other. Livet ignored the flying blades and floated through and over their heads by scaling the furniture piles, finally vaulting over the railing. She landed beside Taringer and a pair of surprised ladies who were joining him for a meal of ale and crusty bread.

"Where's Harbud? How soon 'til we can go?" Livet demanded.

Taringer stammered and stuttered but failed to answer quickly enough.

"Another girl, Tarry?" cooed a pouty-lipped hostess with tressed hair. "You *are* in demand!" She traced her index finger along her exposed collar bone. Taringer, even more speechless, became scarlet-cheeked with an overabundance of bashfulness.

"Enough Cayla!" said the other girl, whom Livet knew to be Ilyea Moor, the server she had met the previous night. "Do we need to throw you in the Darrow and cool you down? These two need a turn to talk. Leave them." She spoke strictly to Cayla but softened her tone with Livet. "I can fetch Harbud for you if you wish."

"Thank you. Yes," Livet said. "Now, if you would."

Cayla offered Taringer one last theatrical sigh of adoration then yelped, "You're bruising me! Ouch!" as Ilyea dragged her away.

Now only the two of them, Taringer more readily found his voice and made meek excuses. "The way she goes on, I'm sorry. She acts like I'm the only man between here and Harthal Vale."

"She's pretty. Not s' much as Celebra, but I imagine she gets by fine 'round 'ere," Livet commented cattily. Her pulse was still racing but sitting and musing upon Taringer's embarrassment helped abate her temper.

"It's not my mind to pay heed to her or any of the other girls," he said flatly, then swung the focus around to the matter for which Livet had alluded. "Are you going to come with us? Really? Did you change your mind? But you seem upset."

"We 'ave to go tonight," Livet said firmly.

"I agree. There are already skirmishes breaking out across the city. After tonight, we might lose our chance. Once we are in, you must lead us to Kell right away, wasting no time."

"But 'ow do you plan t' get in? Can Harbud use the Passage Realm?" she asked.

A weighty thump behind Livet prefaced the answer. Harbud stood, carrying a gnarled wooden staff which he brought down upon the floor. "No, I can't."

Inwardly, Livet cringed. The long walk to the temple would undoubtedly leave her in a bad state. Her leg and back already ached with exhaustion from journeying to-and-fro across the city earlier.

"I can't just send us someplace I've never been before. You're the only one of us who has been inside the temple. Besides, the Faith seems to have some sort of ward upon their walls. I can't pass through with my magic, even blindly," Harbud explained. He smacked his staff on the bench to force Livet to move over and give him a space to sit down. "However, I can get us close to where the old well fell in," he suggested.

"But the well's collapsed!" Livet bemoaned.

"Only the mouth of the tunnel. We'll sort something out to remove the blockage," Harbud promised, with an expression indicating it was a trivial matter.

"And what do we do when we find Kell? How can we free 'im from where 'e is?"

With a frown, Harbud admitted, "I've looked into it, and I don't have a good answer for you. I know little of the more macabre arts. When Kell came to Caphedra, many years ago, he taught a great many things, but nothing of that sort. He was quite against it, in all actuality. I understood it to be one of the causes of discord which had led to him leaving Lanstad."

"But I've seen you digging into it since Livet told you what she saw in the temple," Taringer said. "You have nothing?"

"The prevailing convention usually involves deeply dug graves or high-piled pyres of flame to send the dead off to their peaceful slumber. Though it is hardly prescriptive, I can recall an old verse I was forced to memorize once:

> If the dead persist upon the surface,
>   And jealously our world bespoil,
> Bake them into ashes in the furnace,
>   Or bury them beneath the sea or soil.

Livet puffed up her cheeks and huffed with frustration. "What's it mean?"

"It means unless we can divine a better idea from Kell, I say we plunder his bones and bring them somewhere that we can sprinkle some soil on him," Harbud said.

"Or send him off in a big bonfire," Taringer added.

"Or off the side of a boat," Livet said to finalize the poetic triumvirate.

"Whatever be the custom our dear, late colleague prefers," Harbud replied accommodatingly.

There was one more question that Livet wanted to ask. The importance of returning to Kell had been upheld as sacrosanct and critical, but the disagreements and delays over the Half Moon raid left her skeptical of one thing.

"Is Gardia coming t'elp?"

Harbud hunched over next to his staff and looked squarely at Taringer, who shrugged.

"They didn't part on good terms," Taringer said. "And I think that meeting you brought back ill memories." His voice drifted off and he neglected to elaborate further. Livet was left to her imagination but was assured that the answer to her query would not be positive. Now, Livet regretted not taking the time to decipher the rest of the letter Baressa had entrusted to her.

"This tavern is not the place to discuss it," Harbud stated. "And, quite honestly, we need to get moving. It's just about dark, and this could be a long night. Eat something to gather your strength, then let's be off."

❖   ❖   ❖

With a smacking of her lips, Livet dabbed the last scrap of a loaf of bread through a sloppy bowl of lentil pottage, provided by Ilyea. She hadn't had much chance to fill her stomach at the Black Eel, but the food at the Peahen was much more savoury, always with a hint of far-away flavours enhancing the recipes. Gardia's cook boasted culinary concoctions to match the complexity of the proprietress's many potions. This simple meal was enough to satisfy her hunger and make her feel strong enough to confront the Faith again.

Livet pushed the bowl away but before she had a chance to rise from the table, a gloved hand tapped her gently on the shoulder. Livet spun around on the bench to meet a narrow, angular face and a flop of golden hair.

"I figured you'd be here. I came looking for you," said Effie.

"You startled me," said Livet. She motioned him to sit at the table across from her, in the spot Taringer had vacated a short while before. "I was just getting ready to leave."

"I thought you might want some company. I overheard you and that Wellum fellow back at the Eel. Truthfully, I guess *a few of us* heard. That's why I came... here to the Peahen... to find you."

She could tell he was in danger of rambling, so she responded to save him from sounding awkward or unpractised.

"You needn't 'ave worried. There's nothing amiss. All's well," she falsely reassured.

Effie pulled off his gauntlets, extracting long, thin fingers that matched his physique, then he folded the gloves into his belt.

"I see," he said. "I was just worried you might still be a trifle upset. It seemed Denn wronged you somehow."

"Oh? I s'ppose it did look like 'e did." Livet took a sip from a clay mug of water.

"Perhaps I was too forward in my concern. I'm sure you're smart enough to stay rid of him now." He nodded as if to affirm his point.

"We'll see. I still plan to go to the Temple of the Faith," said Livet, eying Effie incitingly. "Denn doesn't want me to go, but I know 'e'll take Olen. But never mind them. His reasons are 'is own, and mine are for me."

"What reasons could you possibly have?!" Effie questioned.

"A long time ago, they threw me into the Pillar dungeon in Lanstad," she explained. "I wouldn't want it for anyone. You understand? When I went into the temple, here in Caphedra, it was to help some people who were locked away as I had been. But I failed and left someone there. Now I must go back and get them out."

"I'll come with you." Overtaken with a ripening cocksureness, he pumped up his chest with a deep breath and professed, "I am a good fighter—as good as Asher—and on my way to being as good as some of the Eels! You helped me get my sisters away from the Karavals, so I owe you this much."

Livet wanted nothing more than to refuse him, as Denn had done to her. However, something inside caused her to entertain his notions more credibly.

"You ever seen a ghost?" she asked, expanding the scope of their conversation. It caused Effie to deflate, somewhat, and his eyebrows knit together as he pondered why she would ask such a question.

"When I was young, I thought I saw fairy lights among the rushes on the banks of the Darrow. Now, I suppose they were only fireflies, but I wasn't afraid at the time. I expect I'd be even braver now."

Leaning in closely and narrowing her eyes, she delved again. "You ever looked some musty ol' corpse in the sockets where its eyes used to be—with their jawbone wagglin'—'ave a talk with 'em?"

"No," he said, then gulped. A worried wrinkle began spreading across his forehead.

"Alright, you can come, but you better let me do the speaking, then."

Effie's face drained completely of colour. Without a hint of disagreement, he conceded, "If you say so."

❖ ❖ ❖

The four departing rescuers gathered at the top of a staircase leading down to the storerooms. Harbud looked unimpressed. He turned to Livet and said, "I think we're being followed."

"Eh?" she mumbled, confused.

Harbud pointed his staff at Effie, anticipating an introduction.

"This is Effie," she said. "He's offered to come with us."

"You've warned him about what he's going to see?"

"Of a sort, yes," she replied.

"And to not talk about it to anyone afterward?" Harbud added.

Livet shrugged and shot Effie a mildly intimidating look.

"I don't know how you could prepare someone for such things," said Taringer, mulling it over and appearing sympathetic toward their newly enlisted swordsman.

Setting his jaw square and straightening his posture, Effie again extolled his value. "I'm capable. You can trust me."

"I've seen 'im fight at the Half Moon. He'll be a help," Livet said, reinforcing Effie's cause.

"Very well," Harbud said. He lifted the dusty lid off a crate, from which he procured a large bundle of burlap. "Our new warrior can carry this sack. We'll need it to bring Kell out of there."

"You're going to put someone in this?" Effie asked, holding the bag with uncertainty.

"As much of him as we can," came Harbud's cold reply. Livet could see Effie beginning to sweat.

Harbud lifted a lantern and felt for a footfall upon the stairs leading down to the Peahen's cellar. With his other hand, he waved his staff in the air. Livet expected it to burst into a light of its own through some enchantment, but it didn't. Harbud's application of the rod was simply to knock down the accumulation of cobwebs.

The thought inspired her, however. Tapping into her own skills, Livet conjured and drew out rays of light like pulling the threads from an old garment. To her, they were wisps of darkness, seen in reverse. To the others, however, they lit up the room with a spectral glow. That must have met Harbud's approval because she caught the wizard smiling as he ushered them onward. Through a narrow passage, he turned and walked sideways like a gangly crab and led them into the room with the portals.

"I'll go first," said Taringer. He was also equipped with a staff. It was heavier and straighter than Harbud's. Parts of the shaft were iron-jacketed, and at its tip, the metal bore glyphs that were either reflective or composed of some unknown, lustrous medium. As the staff moved, the strange symbols gave off luminance, glowing with a violet colouration, not unlike that of the gloaming sky outside.

The staff fascinated Livet, and Harbud caught her staring.

"You should get one," he said. "Helps extend the reach of the mind—and in your case, it might straighten your walk, too. We can't always take shortcuts."

His forwardness to comment on her limp left Livet without words, so she raised her nose and strutted past Harbud, in her own fashion. As she went past, she kicked at the bottom of his staff, knocking it out from under him and forcing him to catch himself before he stumbled.

Taringer was already a step ahead and standing at the inscribed archway leading to their destination. As he moved forward, he faded through its stone façade without a sound. A breeze rushed in to take his place.

Livet turned back to Effie. "It's easy. Pretend it's not there." She took his arm and guided him forward through the portal, adding, "But don't stop walking until you see Taringer. That's when you know you're in the Folds."

"The Folds?" he began, but Livet pushed him through. Like Taringer, Effie dematerialized through the archway.

Next up was Livet, but as she took a step forward, Harbud reached out to her. He did not grab her but placed his hand upon her shoulder tenderly and bade her wait a moment.

"Think about what you want to say to Kell when we find him," he advised her gently. "It will be your last chance. This must be your farewell."

His words sent sadness washing over her, but Livet nodded demurely, then continued through the arch.

❖   ❖   ❖

This time, there was less of an adjustment for her eyes. The sky had grown dark. The glint from flickering torches helped Livet trace the path back to the collapsed well. As soon as Harbud emerged from the receiving arch, Livet surveyed the streets for a route that would let them skirt the jumble of Pillarmen roadblocks and sidestep the rows of impenetrable abatis which fanned out like porcupine quills.

With Harbud and Taringer keeping pace beside her, and Effie behind and tracing her footsteps obediently, Livet strode through the torn-up streets with vigour.

Most of the storefronts and houses were sealed shut, while Caphedra's hapless citizens awaited the arrival of Myrhic's vengeful horde. Ahead, orders were being shouted out as a squad of undisciplined Pillar troops were frustratingly marched into position. They moved like a mob, and only half-obeyed the directions coming from the man trying to command them. The soldiers might look robust and confident, but they were being shepherded by a blue-frocked Pillar adept who was painfully scrawny and short in comparison. He was no field marshal. He had the languid pallor of a cloistered scholar, the ways of war as uncommon to him as daylight must be.

Thankfully, the soldiers were too busy with their own shenanigans to notice their tiny incursion. With Livet's blade hidden and Taringer and Harbud only carrying walking staves, they did not look like troublemakers—only oddities for having the foolhardiness to be out in the open on the cusp of battle.

Only Effie carried a sword openly and for that alone, Livet suspected, he was singled out as they skirted the soldiers' line. From the top of an overturned wagon, which he'd fashioned as a command post, the adept accosted him.

"You there! Why aren't you on the lines to protect the city? Will you not defend your queen, boy? The Pillars richly reward their heroes, you know!" His eyes darted from one side of his troops to the other with a smug smile. It wasn't his personal wealth he was promising, after all.

"Tell him there's food," catcalled one of the unruly men. "Looks like he hasn't eaten in a while!"

Another ribbed, "Not much of a sword. Think it's even sharp?"

Effie gripped his rapier to respond. His voice wavered slightly. "You can be sure that I've whet my blade for what's coming tonight!"

"Wet his pants, more likely!" mocked another faceless fighter from the back.

"Just make sure you serve your queen and soak that sword in blood—not piss," the little commander carried on. "In the morning, malingerers will be up on stakes!"

"We'll keep that in mind," interrupted Harbud.

The adept then relented from the hazing and appealed to Harbud instead. "If you are heading to the temple, tell them to send more men forward to cover the side alleys... and more archers! Send archers to take up places in the upper storeys, street-side on the square."

"Men... archers... square. All understood," Harbud repeated in a monotone while pressing the head of his staff on Effie's back to hurry the boy onward and away. Once they had made some distance, however, he celebrated with another smile to Livet. She flashed back a grin, but Effie, who was right behind her, only frowned and blushed from the encounter.

All the armsmen and available soldiers of the temple must have been mustered to preserve the Faith's grip on Caphedra, for each intersection and chokepoint was manned by groups of Pillar guards, staring out hypnotized in anticipation of the moment they would clash with the enemy.

"Listen," Taringer said. Livet detected the noises of fighting from the north, perhaps just a block away. Then suddenly, from behind, she heard louder sounds of metal clanging and imperilled shouts.

"The prince's men—skirmishers," Taringer declared and pointed back at the line of men they had just passed.

Fast-moving figures were harassing the defenders, sowing havoc amongst the freshly assembled line, and testing to see if it would break.

"Let's get away from here quickly!" Harbud recommended.

"How much farther?" Effie asked as they hastened their stride.

Praying that they were almost there, Livet placed one foot upon a pile of rubble and spritely scaled it, finding footholds wherever she could. Arriving at the top, she relayed details of the vista ahead.

"The temple is just over there, so the entrance to the well must be close!"

Through breaks in towering stone buildings, her vantage allowed her to see Prince Ramid's forces wheeling away from the central King's Avenue. Many of the prince's soldiers had broken through to the south. However, they were not attacking the heavily armed and reinforced citadel. They were stomping toward the temple, and she feared that Denn and his men were likely already in the attackers' path.

"Which way?" Taringer asked.

"The well is there!" Livet found her orientation and steered the others toward the little plaza where Harbud and Taringer first found her, only to learn the well had already been purposefully blocked off, doubtlessly in response to Livet's earlier trespassing.

"I don't think we can go through the old way," Taringer said.

"They wouldn't expect us to go through it twice," Harbud said. "Do you think we could clear the debris?"

Taringer examined the collapsed stone, which was now overlaid with thick sawn logs and iron bars. "Where to begin?" he pondered forlornly to himself, but aloud.

"The tunnel runs under my feet, this way." Livet hopped down off the rubble and began walking with calculated steps. Tackling the debris pile, she worked away at the rock and shattered bricks and when a small gap became exposed, she ducked her head in to examine the state of the murky, black drop she knew existed below.

It was dark, but there had been no cave-in. She could still see a glow escaping from the connecting—and *undamaged*—subterranean corridor. It was sufficient for her needs. The light flowed over the rocks and found its way into the black expanse of her widened pupils. She let it pool and cast it back outward, letting her make out the state of the debris pile and tunnel.

"We can climb down the ol' bricks on the inside. We jus' need to widen the hole up 'ere and squeeze through!"

"There's four of us. It shouldn't take long," Effie said and promptly straddled a wooden beam lying on the pile and tugged fervently to unloose it.

Taringer looked at Harbud and motioned toward the chaotic congestion like a silent taskmaster. He received a profoundly discouraging sigh in reply.

"I was saving my energy," Harbud said as he started to unbutton his vest.

Together, they managed to pry off some of the top strata of clutter. Livet could not help but urge them to clear faster. Thoughts of Denn drove her to near desperation. She wondered if he was safe. Finally, when a gap appeared she blurted out, "I can fit through now!"

"What about us?" Effie asked. "We need to keep working."

"Slow down, Livet. It's not safe to go in alone!" Taringer warned.

"I'll find Kell and tell 'im you're comin'," Livet said. "But I hafta find Denn, too. He'll be inside by now."

"We need to go together!" Harbud proclaimed firmly.

Taringer flung another reminder at her. "Think of the sorcerer with the glowing eyes—the man that killed Baressa. It's safer for us all if we venture in as a group!"

He was right. That man might still be in there somewhere. She felt for the handle of the rondel tucked into her belt but was undaunted. With no second thoughts, Livet promised her cautioners, "If I see 'im, I'll kill 'im!"

"Livet..." Effie pleaded one last time, but in the blink of an eye, Livet arched her back, limbered up, then slithered headfirst into the narrow crevice.

Down she flowed over the cascade of debris sloping from the mouth of the old well. The lower rocks were the most dangerous. Many of them had sharp corners sticking out and were wet and glistening. Livet almost slipped as she tried to get back up to her feet. But once she was inside the tunnel, she could stand up straight again, and nothing remained to hamper her.

Quickly she conjured a shadowy umbrage to drag the darkness of the tunnel with her, as she darted down the passageway to the chambers ahead.

However, the rooms she entered offered countless places to hide, with or without using her special gift. Unlike before, the space below the temple was brimming with sundry items and artifacts all packed tightly together. Expensive furnishings were stacked and piled like an ornate labyrinth of carved woodwork. Rolled tapestries stood in rows, dividing up the room like gaudy palisades. The odour of acrid lacquer upon ancient luxury hung throughout the dusty temple basement, and almost overpowered the older, necrotic stench she had been so averse to.

Further along, great wooden chests caught her eye. She was sure she could hear gold and silver crying out to her from within them. The locks would be simple enough to pick, but there was no time. She cursed and relegated herself to snatching only a few glittering chains and bobbles that hung more conspicuously off the arms of a nearby candelabra.

Even that small act of thievery, however, exposed her to an overwhelming feeling of indignation and offence. Again, something sensed her presence, and she was unwanted here. The sensation came upon her suddenly and could only have been generated in the crypt that she remembered as the Hall of the Paragons.

Livet crept forward and stood at the archway leading to the reliquary, but then she saw that even here had been desecrated and converted into a storehouse for the temple's treasures. Oil paintings populated the room with dramatic and historic scenes. Their intricate frames were arranged such that the canvases lay atop each other like pages in a gigantic tome.

Underneath it all, a hiss escaped from a rattling bone box and several other ossuaries appeared to quiver as Livet snuck closer.

A deep-rooted feeling of loathing welled up in her.

"If you can 'ear me," she said to the room's unearthly denizens. "Know that I *hate* you!" Unafraid, she inserted herself deeper into the warehoused menagerie. Stooping to crawl under a heavy hardwood table, then climbing up and over the back of a velvety settee, Livet wormed her way to the next archway–the one leading to that horrible workshop where Kell would be inside. But would he speak to her again, as he did before?

"Kell?" she called out, her hand squeezing the hilt of her drawn rondel.

Instantly, the awareness of the Paragons' displeasure sank away, and a levity settled over her. A voice called out to her from the workshop, as before, but markedly different. It was one she could hear with her ears, for it spoke aloud to her, unexpectedly feminine. The words were welcoming, but strangely sad and hollow.

"My dear Livet," said the woman. "We knew you would come. Don't be scared."

Livet feared a trap and clung to the corner of the room. She did not recognize the voice—or did she?

As before, the air was thick with the morbid scent of decay barely suppressed under layer upon layer of mystical, exotic aromas. The brazier burned, giving off erratic light. It cast silhouettes around the room that swayed and flitted upon the dungeon's limestone walls.

Livet carefully entered the unnerving workshop.

Suddenly, and reassuringly, she sensed her old mentor communicate to her. *'You are needed, Livet. Her chains. Please undo them.'*

Kell's tangled corpse remained suspended from the wall, but beside him hung a newly imprisoned form, dressed in tattered clothes. Its figure was still meaty and thick, especially around the hips and bosom. The body had not stiffened as Livet knew corpses did but had remained supple enough to be seen moving weakly. The curly coif of hair on its head had retained its brown hue, save for intermittent locks of silver-grey, and though sagging and wan, the captive's skin showed the faint rosiness of life when Livet approached and peered into the brown eyes of the woman's familiarly contoured face.

"We waited for you," Baressa said and painfully raised her arms until the chains tightened and held her back.

"Are you...? Can you...?" Livet stammered in awe and shock.

'Free her, Livet,' instructed Kell. *'She is not so far gone as I.'*

Livet reached into her boot cuff and found a suitably sized hook pick. She inserted it into the little iron lock that kept the chains bound together and sprung it, freeing Baressa from the wall. Helplessly, the seeress crumpled and fell into Livet, collapsing into an embrace upon the chamber's hard stone floor.

"You're so cold!" Livet exclaimed. Baressa's spruce-green cloak was draped over a chair nearby. Retrieving it with one hand, Livet used it to swaddle the poor woman. Something still did not seem right, but she nonetheless tried to speak soothingly. "You're safe. Gardia can make you all better. Taringer and Harbud are comin'. They're right behind me!"

Baressa seemed to struggle with her expressions but

manifested a faint smile. "Good," she said. "We will need them."

"Kell, we are here to save you too!" Livet said to her former guardian. "Just tell me what to do. How can I free you?"

'You will need Harbud and Taringer to help you,' Kell told her. *'When they come, I will explain. For now, you must pay heed to Baressa. She will instruct you.'*

Livet supported Baressa with one arm but reached over with her free hand and drew the hood of the cloak back, away from her friend's face.

"What is it? What d'you need t' say?"

"You must find your companion now," she said. Then taking a breath and running her tongue across her lips to wet them, she continued. "He is about to face an evil that transcends this world."

"He seeks his brother. Do you mean him? The curate? Lehn?" Livet asked.

"The man that killed me?" Baressa added. "No. Far worse than him."

Livet shuddered at Baressa's strange confession. If it was Lehn that tried to murder Baressa that night they met in the dungeons then he had failed, as evidenced by the woman surviving right now in Livet's arms.

"But you're not dead!"

Baressa moaned. "Not entirely—but I'm not alive either, my dear."

"So... what? You're *half-dead,* then? I don't understand," Livet queried.

"Not now," Baressa answered. "Your friend, Denn... you have to keep him safe."

Her charge was reinforced by Kell's ethereal instruction. *'Denn is in danger. Go to him while he is still among the living.'*

Not far from where they lay, there was an opening in the cut-stone walls which revealed a staircase leading upward. Baressa gestured toward it, saying, "That is the quickest way. By the time you return, I will have collected Taringer and Harbud and brought them here."

Livet had intended to protect Denn, but now that she was commanded to, she felt a reluctance to leave the sufferers in the dungeon. Yet Baressa seemed to be strengthening, and their friends must be nearby, by now.

"Very well. I'll come back as soon as I find Denn," Livet said. Then, as soon as she had helped the seeress to her feet, she dashed up the staircase, cloaked once more in arcane shadow.

CHAPTER 32

The Aspirant

High sandstone and chalk brick walls draped in languid blue banners obscured the evening sky and herded Denn and his band through the spiralling streets of the Folds. The day's mugginess was devolving into a sticky, summer evening. Between the valleys of building rows, strained noises of the besieged city became muffled. The only clear sounds came from the cooing of pigeons taking refuge for the night on ledges and in crevices where the birds stared blankly, unimpressed by the quartet of rescuers.

The buildings soon gave way to a courtyard housing several stratified plazas.

"Over there." Temis pointed to the city block that housed Caphedra's Temple of the Faith. Four impossibly tall marble columns shot up from each corner like alabaster geysers, encircling a lofty, white-walled enclave where, in more peaceful times, initiates and adepts would assemble.

Together, the columns supported an immense square platform presiding high above all else. Whatever was constructed upon the platform was a mystery, for it could not be viewed from the ground, nor were there any surrounding hilltops or towers high enough to afford a good view. Every Caphedran knew that this was the exclusive, private abode of Averin Golmarra, the preeminent Precept of the Faith of the Pillars. Only his select cadre of most-trusted adepts was ever invited to view the temple summit, to preserve its secrets.

Drawing everyone's attention to the base of the temple, Temis offered it up as a possible point of entry. "There is a storm cellar door where the stewards receive food for the temple larder.

That's how I escaped before. It was unlocked then, but even if the door is secured now, it's likely that we could still force our entrance."

Denn scanned the grounds. There was a modest assembly of Pillarmen milling about, but not as many as he had initially feared. Still, they would all come running if they sensed anything to be out of the ordinary.

"We're dressed up like Pillarmen, so we should think as Pillar soldiers would," Yael told him. "Why would we break into our own temple—especially through a cellar, as the edge of war approaches?"

Denn considered for a moment. "They'd think we're either stealing food or worse, that we were a pack of cowards, skulking off and hunkering down before the big fight descended. They'd run us through with their swords if that's what they suspected."

"Well, if we look like we belong among them, I guess we should just walk straight in," Olen concluded with an innocent shrug.

"That's right. We march right up the steps and through the main door," said Denn. "Walk tall and push back on anyone that questions us."

The temple entrance was on the north face of the building, between the Pillars of Progeny and Resilience. Tugging on his blue tunic to straighten it one final time, Denn climbed the stairs confidently. He passed a pair of dozing armsmen posted to the door and even chanced to issue a polite, "Good evening."

"An' t' you," one of them mumbled, proving their disguises believable.

The companions were met inside with an anteroom that led to a spacious hall of marked splendour. It had a vaulted ceiling with clerestory windows in the upper extremes. A hardwood table ran down the entire room like a spine, branching off into smaller tables where handfuls of adepts and acolytes were engaged in animated discussions. Candelabras were mounted in the nooks along the walls, between towering buttresses, where they presided over wooden desks and scroll racks.

Most of the chamber's robed inhabitants were still labouring away. Working in teams or alone, a cohort of exhausted and perspiring novices were diligently packing and porting away some of the most exquisite artifacts that Denn had ever seen. He watched them transporting paintings, wood carvings, and ornate chests upon wheeled carts and dollies that strained under their weight.

"Must be stashing them deeper in the dungeons for safe-keeping," said Yael. "They wouldn't want to risk them getting damaged or stolen should the Marshal's army ransack the temple."

"They'll need more soldiers to prevent that," said Olen. "I wonder where they've positioned all their forces. Perhaps the men on the street are meant to fall back to here if need-be."

"There were many more men here a week ago," Temis said. "Perhaps they've been called to man the walls and approaches. Maybe they didn't expect that the Marshal would breach the gates so quickly, nor advance this deep into the city."

"Where is the queen?" Denn asked.

"The citadel, most likely," Yael said.

"Then that's where the soldiers are, too, I wager. The castle and citadel are far more defensible than the temple grounds." Denn felt his heart skip. He hoped his brother was still here, and not also removed to the safety of the city's inner fortress. If Serenn's hunch had been right, Lehn would want to stay close to Ravon during all of this. That is if the Faith's elders permitted him to. But if he did leave, what would he have done with Serenn?

Denn was about to ask Temis to guide them toward Lehn's chambers when a diminutive, grey-haired adept in equally fading robes strode across the room to take up a defiant position that blocked their ingress.

"Ahem," the officiant coughed.

Denn stared at him, puzzled, and waited for the man to elaborate upon his challenge.

"Shouldn't you soldiers be elsewhere? The arrival of the queen's brother and his army is imminent!"

"We were told to come to the temple," Denn lied.

"What for?" the man probed. "You're needed to defend the city!"

Denn was suddenly jostled to the side by two labourers carrying a long, furled-up tapestry, which gave him an idea.

"We're here to secure some artifacts for Curate Wellum. Can you direct us to his office in the priory?"

"Curate Wellum?" the man's hostility melted instantly and was replaced by an almost simpering sympathetic mumbling. "Oh, I suppose, yes. He has been tremendously busy of late. I imagine he might not yet have everything in order. You must go to him if he requires help. Four of you are enough? Should I send others?" Then with his eyes darting from side-to-side to check for listeners, he whispered, "You're not transporting anything unseemly, are you? Should I fetch a blanket or a covering, maybe? I could clear a path down the back steps for you to transfer his belongings privately."

"Not necessary," Denn said. "Please, where can we find his quarters?"

The man shot forth his finger so quickly that the sleeve of his robe flapped. "Through there! Just beyond the statue of Elsius... upstairs in the outer east corridor."

"Elsius," Denn repeated the name.

"Thank you. That will be fine," interrupted Yael before ushering Denn and the others along. "We can find it from here."

"Do you know the statue?" Olen asked Yael quietly.

"Yes, the Paragon of Patience," Yael said. "Just look for a statue of a starving prisoner in chains, covered in bugs and vermin. That is how he is usually depicted."

Olen's face crinkled up with distaste.

"Don't worry," Temis reassured. "His copious agonies should be portrayed rather tastefully. His sect celebrates that sort of thing."

Racing up a rounded staircase, they found the prescribed hallway leading away from the next landing. Unusually tall doorframes were staggered along the corridor's length. Interspersed between the doors was a pantheon of painted sculptures. The figures appeared too large and heavy to be easily moved into the protective passages beneath the temple.

"Who are they all?" Denn asked, impressed by their detail but unnerved by their eerie stillness.

"The Paragons," Yael answered. "Some of them at least. I expect there are more statues throughout the temple the farther you go. Over there, I see Elsius. Are you ready?"

Compulsive curiosity drove Denn to examine the nameplates on each one. He approached the first statue, a beautiful woman holding out her palms to present a broken sceptre. The text etched upon her pedestal identified the woman as Perspica, the Paragon of Persuasion. This was the mythical lady for whom the current month was named, Denn noted.

Moving to the next, Denn scanned for another name. This

sculpture showed a woman who might have been fair, were her face not obscured by a blindfold. She was barefoot and captured in mid-stride, upon a pedestal that erupted into a mess of delicate and painstakingly carved thorny tendrils curling beneath her feet. '*Lyseia, Paragon of Purpose*', her nameplate read. Denn gazed at her. This was the demon that haunted Ramisa from the inside out.

Shuddering, he turned to Yael. "Where can I find Dagremahr?"

"Almost certainly, it's that brute across the hall," Yael said. He pointed to a hulking beast of a man in scale armour and wearing an ancient crown of spikes.

Approaching the lifeless effigy, Denn peered into its defiant face. He examined the coat of armour and centuries-old manner of dress. The sculptor had recreated dazzling patterns in the stone's faux textiles. Upon the cold skin of his creation were even marks depicting pores on the arms. Strangely, however, the rock around one of its legs was still rough-hewn and incomplete. It was not just the failing of an over-ambitious sculptor running out of time, Denn presumed. The malevolent monarch's statue was unfinished, and it appeared an intentional shortcoming.

"What is the meaning of the uncompleted portion, Yael?" he asked, desiring to be educated on his foe.

"That the life of a warlord like him never ceases. He is the Paragon of Primacy—employed by the Faith centuries ago, to eradicate their opposers. Yet even when you dominate your enemies, you can never rest. Challengers arise. Wars begin and end, only to start anew once the balance shifts. A warrior's role never ends. The job is never completed."

From behind them, Olen sputtered with a mirthless grunt.

"So, after a lifetime of war in this world, he now seeks it in the next," Denn said.

"As you say," Yael said solemnly.

"Sir," Temis broke into their conversation, pleadingly. "Before we lose our nerve, let us go through that door. We have dallied here long enough at Serenn's expense."

Temis took up position beside the sought-after statue of the prisoner, Elsius. The frail Paragon stood vigil next to an overly tall wooden door framed with carved mouldings and topped with a transom set with frosted glass panels. With a finger to his lips,

Temis warned that the panels were cracked open and might allow sounds of their activity to creep into the next room.

Denn gave a confirmatory look to Yael and a nod to Olen, who stood at the ready. Each man quietly drew their weapon: Denn unsheathed Longlimb, his uncle's sword; Temis, drew his venomous short swords, one in each hand; Olen, wielded the hefty broadsword, Coldswept; and Yael, produced his flamberge—a sword he named "Crucible" for its curving, wavy likeness to the lick of a flame.

"You're not going to knock, are you?" Temis asked worriedly.

Denn answered with a disapproving growl. His hand hovered above the latch, and he breathed carefully to steady himself. Everyone waited for his signal, but instead, he motioned to them to step back.

In the vision that had proceeded from Livet's pendant, there were no signs of guards in Lehn's chamber. In what Denn had seen, only a handful of conspirators accompanied his brother. The most dangerous among them was Wex Sulford, who had already been beaten once, and whose diabolical sword had been already lobbed a thousand feet or more down the side of the Eldergorge. If they had to fight through, Denn and his three companions could manage it. However, the chance of a trap awaiting them could not be discounted and it would be wise to keep some or all of those accompanying him hidden as a reserve. They could rush in and counterbalance any fast-deteriorating situation, once Denn had flushed out the dangers ahead.

Or fighting may be unnecessary. The whole confrontation could resolve itself with a dialogue between brothers, he thought. Wasn't that the original plan? Renounce his inheritance in exchange for the liberation of his sister? There remained a chance that his brother might be open to reconciliation, but even Denn could not deny how foolish it would be to hope.

Directing the others to hide behind the statues, Denn grabbed his soiled, saggy Pillar tunic and pulled it over his head. There would be no further need for the disguise.

"If my brother is not up to bargaining, and I run into trouble, then you enter without delay," Denn said in a low voice, "but *save Serenn first*." He directed the order to Temis, especially. While the others might stubbornly risk rescuing Denn, he knew Temis would abide by his command to focus on Serenn. Her freedom was the only measurement by which to claim success in the night's endeavour.

Denn returned to the door alone. Sword ready in one hand, he reached out with the other to depress the latch. It clunked under his thumb and sent the door swinging wide open.

Someone called out as Denn entered.

"Who enters? What is it? Do you have news?" It was his brother's voice that carried across the chamber then dropped its tone to convey his sinister disappointment. "Oh. It's you."

This was the same room imagined from the pendant except now it was full of sound. Denn heard the creaking of the floor, the crackling of a smoky orange fire burning in the recessed brick-walled hearth–and finally, Lehn's voice. It was assertive and unafraid. Here, was a cogent and capable man. He was not the boy Denn had grown up shielding and protecting but ultimately forsaking.

Just as he envisioned, his brother was not alone. Serenn was there but more incredibly, so was his father. Denn's heart skipped. Phon's drooping body hung in chains from a wooden frame that had been wheeled into the room. Farathemun's story was true. His diabolical father had been imprisoned by his vindictive brother. A shiver went down Denn's spine.

Besides the prisoners, Lehn was attended by the Faith's political minions. Wild-maned and ragged, Kabra Zimmin stood several paces back, restraining and menacing Serenn into obedient submission. Near the erected wooden frame, Postella Aroon–the loud-spoken matriarch of the gang who had flung insults at their father in council–was again tormenting the aged Wellum chief.

Another lady, in painted visage, also presided over Denn's entrance. Above the smouldering, ashy fireplace in the far wall was an immense portrait of Queen Ravon. His brother's muse, she appeared dignified, almost sacred, in the robes of a Pillar Adept, clutching the sceptre of the land which had once symbolized her father's unchallenged domination. Lehn must feel all the more empowered under her commanding image, Denn thought.

"You've saved me the hassle of sending more men to find you," Lehn said. "I am surprised you are not with Farathemun. I find it quite upsetting to know my father and brother have allied themselves with the queen's treacherous uncle–but we've dispatched summoners for him, too. In the meantime, brother, I welcome you to my office and accept your submission."

Closest to Denn was the most immediate threat: the man who had escaped death on Bridgecliff. Wex Sulford's face bore the odd bruise, but he looked fit to fight again. As Lehn spoke, Sulford advanced carefully and held open his palm, expecting to receive Denn's weapon in forfeit. But his hopes were premature. Denn chose to meet the hand with the point of his sword.

"I am here to negotiate," Denn proclaimed.

"Are you? Then lay down your arms and let me hear your offer," said Lehn.

"He wants to kill you, Denn!" Serenn called out warningly. "There is no reasoning with him!"

Denn moved forward and could see that Serenn looked worn and exhausted. No wounds were apparent, but blood on her dress suggested she had experienced violence of some fashion.

From this vantage, Denn was also better able to observe the predicament of his father's captivity. Near to Lehn, the wooden construction was like a gantry and looked out-of-place in the office of an adept. Its beams were rife with notches and peg holes which showed it to be an invention with countless configurations. Phon's body was suspended by chains from the top beam, easily mistakable for the hide of an old goat being hung to cure in a tannery. His limbs dangled like broken twigs, held together in a casing of bark-like skin. Phon's last remaining vitality was reserved for his piercing eyes. They stared obsessively in Denn's direction, casting an intensity that carried across the whole of the vast distance of the room.

"Do you honestly want the blood of your family on your hands?" Denn asked. "Or is there already enough from others that it'd be just a drop in a stream?" Ushering past Sulford, he moved closer to his sibling. "I left once. I can leave again. I don't want to fight you, Lehn. If you let Serenn go, I will relinquish all my claims to the family wealth and our father's title... publicly, if you wish. I can announce to the world that my brother is the first and last in the line of Wellum men. Unless you suffer some crazed compulsion to see it done, why must we spill blood?"

He studied his brother for a reaction. Lehn's nostrils flared in contempt.

"You went off to be the soldier. You're all about spilling blood," Lehn answered. "Why should I be bothered by it if you aren't? After all, I am doing it with the grander purpose of supporting my queen and all that she will become with me at her side."

"I didn't leave because I thirsted for blood. You know that."

"Nor did I, though such circumstances have come to prevail of late, it seems," said Lehn. "Tell me, why *did* you come back? Has Lyseia not found some purpose for you yet? Or is this part of her designs?"

"I don't pray to Paragons," Denn muttered then shifted attention toward Phon. "It was our father who arranged my return. I did not come willingly."

"He had ambitions for you. An afterthought to mitigate his failure with our sad brother, the true scion. You are blind *and* seditious. You're a plaything in a traitor's conspiracy."

Denn weathered the accusation, determined to remain civil. There was no shred of love or loyalty to his father remaining. "I am not his agent!"

Lehn snickered, "I didn't call you an agent. That would suggest you were possessed of less ignorance than you let on. You lack the propriety to be an agent."

Beside him, Sulford was snickering and the women councillors, closer to Lehn, cast mocking looks, but Denn resolved to ignore his brother's emasculating remarks.

"I wanted this to be an apology, Lehn. It was my mistake to leave you and Serenn to carry the family burden in my stead. I should have stepped up and filled Hann's place, I know. Perhaps, had I not been so eager to separate myself from the cause of our troubles... maybe things would have been different."

"I didn't mope about the house missing you, brother. That was Serenn whom you confuse me for."

"Had I stayed—"

"Ha!" Lehn waved his hand like a cat swishing its tail at the impotence of its owner trying to beg its affection. "We were both barely out of our childhood. You ran off soldiering, but I had the Faith of the Pillars to guide me. While you were overcome with whinging tantrums and the infantile avoidance of your duties, I had already begun to walk a luminous path that transcended them. I supported the tenets of the Pillars with all my heart and being, and they have supported me in kind."

Looking around the room, Denn found it hard to argue that the Faith had not provided. Lehn's office was many times the size of their father's and standing within was an entourage of sycophants that powerfully represented a full quarter of the Caphedran Council, just waiting for their master's word to pounce.

"You understand that the Marshal is going to destroy your order once he arrives. I have seen his army. They're already within Caphedra's walls. You don't have enough soldiers to defeat him now that Vlass's army has abandoned you."

"Vlass has done no such thing," Lehn said. "His men have only returned to deal with an uprising against Lanstad."

"Don't be foolish," said Denn. "There are no uprisings in that part of the land that can threaten Lanstad—nor require that many troops to put down. I know. I patrolled those lands."

"It appears you know even less than I had thought," Lehn answered. "The Larsens have brought the Army of Kramwen down from their southern highlands, thinking they might use this opportunity to breach the gates of their old enemy. They have coveted Lanstad since the day Ramis forced them to pull back from Hasen—part of their dream for a kingdom of their own. Old one foot they call Derid Larsen. One foot on each side of the highlands, with his toes dipping into each city. That's what they say. But now the arrogant Larsens are going to lose their army, for I've already received the news that Vlass has them in a vise. Kramwen will be added to our spoils by autumn."

Denn stood rigid and outwardly dispassionate but inside his heart pounded at the grave news that his brother delighted in. He hoped someone had gotten word to Farathemun that his promised soldiers had unexpectedly detoured—and possibly been annihilated. There would be no merchant army to exploit Caphedra's carnage. No last-minute counterattack would seize victory for his hungry circle of nobles and self-aggrandizing elite.

Poor Ramisa. Denn's head pained, unable to shake the sense that he had abandoned her too. Just walking into the Farathemun manor, things did not seem right. Denn cursed his naïvete, and his heart anguished over thoughts that he had left her in danger of capture or worse. Of all the crimes he had to rectify, it was his complicity in bringing the princess to Caphedra that was paramount.

He resolved to save her. But first, he had to surmount his present situation.

"Lehn, don't sully yourself," Denn pleaded. "I know what acts you have committed, but do not be known as the curate who murdered his own family. I have already told you that when Father dies, you may take over our family affairs. I only wish to be away from this horrible city and everyone in it–and I have not wavered from that desire since we buried Hann."

"Our father did not suffer from the king's indecision. His succession was made clear. I cannot have you outlive him. That is why your survival in Fallowsea complicated my plan and forced me to rely on more drastic measures to sustain him longer than I had wished."

Walking over to where Phon hung, Lehn examined the emaciated patriarch but dodged his father's vigilant gaze. Serenn gasped and fearfully drew back, but Kabra Zimmin tyrannically pushed her to keep watching.

"What measures?" Denn sought his brother's explanation.

"I've had to keep him alive in the best way I knew how," Lehn said. "And it worked out."

Denn clenched his teeth. In professing power to command life itself, he knew what his brother was insinuating.

"You're in league with Golmarra and Dagremahr! What have you done to our father? By what privilege do you seek to lord over life and to command death?"

"Command?" Lehn said. "Preposterous. That's where Golmarra's arrogance has undone him." He reached out and cruelly twisted his father's head by the chin, finally making eye contact. Tiny muscles in Phon's cavernous cheeks jumped and twitched. At that moment, Denn despised both of them with unprecedented severity but was fascinated, however, at knowing whether his brother's hatred truly surpassed his own.

"I told you that the Faith presented me with more than could ever have asked for when Hann died," Lehn explained. "The scholars teach that the end of life is not the end of being, but Precept Golmarra elevated those teachings. When I was chosen as his student, he offered me a glimpse of what could be achieved, and I sought only to replicate the success of my teacher. I had come to the Faith with a problem, and here was a solution."

"You wanted to bring Hann back," Denn said.

"At first, yes," Lehn admitted. "Then I received wiser counsel." He lifted his head toward where the queen's portrait presided over the room and exposed his undeniable adoration with a fawning sigh. "I went to Ravon, for she was the one I trusted the most. I told her of my desire and my need for her help in learning more of Golmarra's secrets. Her talent abounds and her abilities were growing endlessly, but more importantly, she had our master's confidence. He trusted her, but I knew she would not betray me—even though she did manage to dissuade me. She understood my feelings over Hann's death for she bore the same sadness over her mother's death, and over the theft of her sister. We consoled each other, which is how we became even more profoundly entwined. Then, she told me of Golmarra's plan for the Paragons—and how it had involved her."

Lehn's breathing quivered as he spoke, but he pressed on. "Since then, I preoccupied myself with not just emulating him, but learning how to *undo* what he had done."

"Have you discovered the answer?" Denn asked, anxiously.

"Golmarra travelled between Caphedra and Lanstad often, so I exploited his absence. I could not enter his sanctum above the temple, but I found what I needed hidden deep below. Golmarra was averse to keeping such things so close to where he took personal refuge. That was his first mistake."

Lehn smirked at his own cunning.

"Golmarra's other, *greater* mistake was to seek to control and cage the spirits of our forebears to advance his own desires. This only angered them. I opted to bargain with the spirits instead. I sought out the benefit of partnership with those from the realm beyond. Negotiating anything that might free my queen of her burden."

Denn comprehended what must have happened. "Golmarra bound the Paragons to the queen and her daughters, but you..." his spine tingled, "You have made your pact with Dagremahr."

"A pact sealed in flesh, yes," Lehn said.

"No!" Frantically, Denn scanned around the room, and his eyes fell to Wex Sulford. With contempt, he yelled, "Tell me you have not bound him to this wretch!"

"Hardly," Lehn laughed. "Dagremahr requires a host of more

stature. He must be matched with someone who can receive more respect... *fear*, even."

If the slight affected Sulford, the councillor hid it.

"Then is this why you approached the king?" Denn asked. "You wanted him to carry Dagremahr?"

"No. My intentions for him were unrelated. Our conversation touched on something more personal... more *familial*."

With this Denn noticed Wex Sulford swallow uncomfortably. Lehn shot him a dark look and the councillor timidly took a step back.

Denn's brother now approached the gantry and looked into their father's eyes with paper-thin devotion. "Regrettably, I needed someone else. There was only one person who could manipulate and terrorize those around him enough to be paired with a great lord the likes of Dagremahr. So, I chose—"

"Father," Denn expelled the word as if he were coughing up a noxious vapour.

"A more vivacious, living host would have been better, but I was forced to improvise out of necessity, you see," Lehn continued. "Had you died before our father did, then I would be heir by default, and this mess would not have unfurled as it did. I could have left him to die alone in a cell and Dagremahr could continue to counsel me immaterially." Lehn gave the wooden frame a flippant rap with his knuckles then turned his attention back to Denn. "However, predictably, Father turned out to be susceptible to the chill of our dungeons, while you proved to be a better fighter than I had anticipated. Thus, I had to maintain the charade that our father still lived for as long as I could—or at least, until you were out of the way."

"I find it hard to imagine our father accepting Dagremahr willfully. That is essential to complete the transition, isn't it? Are you sure you haven't only succeeded in ensnaring Dagremahr, the same way Lyseia is trapped?" He repeated lessons from Ramisa's understanding now, testing Lehn.

"Our father's spirit is stubborn. The same magic that tied him to his body in the first place still allows him to cling to it. But I have found a means to make him more malleable."

Phon's corpse shuddered in what Denn imagined was a rising rage.

"Besides, he remains of some use. I have been occupied with learning the whereabouts of all the family wealth that he has been hiding. I've had to pry it out of him rather unorthodoxly."

Lehn left the dangling body and returned to his desk, where he picked up a vicious leather flail. Denn felt revulsion. It was not a warrior's weapon, but something more suited for a slave master or a wrathful teacher.

"You see, he cares for Serenn. He hates it when I threaten to demonstrate my frustrations on her."

"No! Leave me alone!" Serenn cried, pulled away from Kabra and tried to retreat into a corner of the chamber. Postella moved toward her with demented glee. Seizing Serenn by the arms, she spun her around to face the room. Denn saw that a tear was already trailing down his sister's cheek when Kabra reached out with the palm of her and gave the air a little push. Serenn choked and gasped. Her chest appeared to compress and crumple as if under the pressure of a crushing weight. When the air returned to her lungs, she pleaded, "Please!"

"There remain a few things that can coerce someone already dead," Lehn explained. "Sometimes duty, compassion—and love, of course—can survive the passing of the spirit into the next realm. Golmarra found a way to make the dead more compliant by use of the bonds they retained to this realm." He flicked the leather flail with a snap. Serenn closed her eyes in terrified anticipation of the blow. Across the room, Phon's body became more animated. The iron chain links that held him scraped together, betraying his discomfort.

"Don't touch her," Denn demanded as Postella cackled. In a sudden frenzy, she spun the captive around and tore at the fabric along the neckline of Serenn's dress. The garment ripped. Serenn's back became exposed.

"Horrible monster! Your depravity is boundless and still, you boast of it to your family!" Serenn sobbed. "Let me go!" Serenn pleaded but another of Kabra's movements caused her to gag and choke on the rest of her words.

Sounds of scuffling were heard from the hallway behind Denn. The others must be watching or listening, alerted by Serenn's screams, Denn thought. Now was the moment. He should call them in now. But as he was about to shout out, his brother circumvented him.

"See to our privacy, Kabra," Lehn said. "This is a family matter."

The ratty-haired witch used her other hand to make a fist, then gestured toward the entrance. Denn felt a gust of air, and the door slammed shut, cutting him off from his companions.

Beside him, Wex Sulford smiled and feinted with a lunge, only to return to his spot beyond Denn's sword reach. It was not an attack so much as a reminder that Denn was a near powerless observer.

"See how the weakness of affection can transcend the grave— even if such tenderness was withheld in life," Lehn reflected, but despite the calmness in his speech, Lehn's irreconcilable resentment toward his birth family was undeniable.

Suddenly, the arms of the leather flail cracked and Lehn brought the fistful of whips down upon the desk with a hideous slap.

Phon's lips moved weakly. "Don't," he uttered in a dry, panting voice.

"Don't what? Don't use it as you did on your sons? The way you used it on us when we failed to satisfy your wishes? The way you had your men use it on Hann the day he... the day *you* damned him." Lehn's voice trailed off until he bitterly added, "You only ever spared Serenn."

"Don't blame Serenn for that," Denn said, but Lehn laughed it off.

"It is an efficient stratagem that Golmarra has used often and that I have adopted on a few occasions such as this. Our father's love for his daughter was his undoing. The threat of harm to Serenn was enough to loosen his lips enough to tell me about the Farathemun plot. It helped me condemn you. Perhaps, I don't even need to hide your murder anymore now that you've returned to Caphedra and incriminated yourself!"

He raised the flail again, but Denn shouted to him, "You threaten her... and me... but have you never struck our father?"

"The detestable old buzzard is too stubborn. He would never let on that he felt a thing," Lehn said.

"You believe. Have you looked into his eyes when you strike Serenn? Do you see any discontent? Or do they remain as icy and cunning as when we were growing up? He only spared punishing her

because he couldn't marry her off as easily as us if she were scarred."
Denn had to say something to draw this out. He was listening for his
men, hoping they could find a way to break down the door or
uncover another way to enter the room.

Lehn stroked the handle of the flail in his hands and turned
to study Phon.

"Everything is a game for him—a balance of advantages and
disadvantages. How do you know that all he's told you is even true?"
Denn wanted to sow doubt in his brother but was unsure if what he
was saying was even a lie. His father was crafty and untrustworthy,
and Denn no longer believed there was any vestige of paternal
compassion in his moribund heart. What else would his father do,
but deflect pain away from himself—even if that meant casting it
onto Serenn?

"He's lost this game," Lehn said. "Only Dagremahr himself
can free him now. Only he knows the way."

"Our father's not completely dead, so he hasn't lost. His mind
is still alive, probably planning his escape. He senses the world. He
sees you. He feels and suffers, yet you spare him while taking out
your wrath on your poor sister who loved you."

Lehn scoffed. "You were gone too long. Your memory is
weak. Our sister's love didn't extend to me."

"She trusted you enough to come here when father decided
to barter her off in marriage. She was to be a commodity for
exchange, but he discarded her like the tailings from a copper mine.
He cares for her less than you do."

Denn's doubts began to take root. With a horrendous cry of
rage, Lehn screamed at the insinuation that he was being treated as
a fool by his contemptuous sire. "I'll give you one last gift, brother,"
he seethed. "I'll let you see a glimpse of justice before you depart this
life. You can die knowing that I'll be avenging us all."

Phon pulled and stamped against his chains, his body moved
with restored energy brought on by imminent danger. The flail
snaked and loudly snapped. Each time it came down upon him,
Phon shrieked like the screeching of an eagle. Over and over, Lehn
struck, with no abatement to his anger.

Sulford still had Denn at the point of his sword. Why couldn't
Olen and the others burst in and storm the room? Where were they?
What were they doing?

Lehn cursed his father loudly and drew back, fumbling around the top of his desk, angrily. Then spying a more suitable implement near the fireplace, he grabbed an iron poker with which to replace the flail and better beat his father. With every vicious, pulpy thud, Phon's swaying body convulsed in pain. His wheezing screech became deeper and more guttural, then grew to an ominous bellow.

Denn never thought to see the unrepentant master of their household give up or surrender to anyone, much less to his own child whom he had a part in bringing into the world. Their father had always acted as though their very life was an unpaid debt that they owed to him. Children were an investment for which he expected a profitable return.

Too late, Denn realized that he had backed his father into a corner. "Stop!" he called to his brother.

Lehn ignored his brother and lashed out harder. The calmly composed cleric had completely disappeared and now Lehn's face shone red with an exploding vengeance. He was raining down blows upon his father, remorselessly, like threshing grain or a launderer beating a soiled coat.

"Stop!" repeated Denn fearfully.

There was a loud clang as Lehn threw the iron poker to the floor and stepped back, but his anger persisted; he raised his hands, and a haze overtook him.

Denn blinked and squinted, for it appeared as if the air around his brother was rising in waves of heat. Soon he could feel it. Whatever power his brother was conjuring, it felt like he was about to incinerate the room. Was this the last thing King Ramis had experienced before he was boiled alive?

With his arms bent inward and palms up, cupping the air in front of him, Lehn unleashed a surge of crackling fire into Phon's trapped body, causing their father to writhe, then tighten up with pain. Again, Lehn summoned the fire, and as it built up in his hands, he menaced his victim anew.

Out of Phon's lips emanated a tiny, helpless, and fragile moan of surrender.

The chains jangled as what should have been their father's corpse raised a halting hand. Lehn complied, remaining motionless with fascination. There was a metallic popping as links of chain burst open. The form of their father straightened its stooped back and stood tall before them.

"Wine!" it commanded in a quaking voice.

There was a decanter nearby, and Postella rushed to retrieve it. She handed over the whole vessel, which the figure raised and poured across his lips and into his greedy, expanding gullet.

"M'lord," Lehn addressed the resurgent being before them.

"This is a poor host to contain my essence, Wellum," said the creature's voice which Denn immediately knew to be Dagremahr's.

"The key is in the visage, m'lord. People will see my father, know him, and afford you powerful credentials because of it," Lehn promised.

"My name alone does not carry such weight?"

Denn was unsure if the infernal regent was testing or teasing.

"The citizens have not been prepared to welcome the Paragons to this world again and there is no time to do so tonight," Lehn excused, sounding impatient. "We have a deal. I trust you to honour it."

"It robs me of my full energy to have to keep this fragile heart beating, but no matter. I care little for this world," Dagremahr said, shrugging off the affront. "Have the armies assembled as planned?"

"They are in the city, engaged in battle. Your army is almost to the citadel."

"Very well. Then I shall make good on our arrangement. I shall visit the prince's army and reap from its dead, that I may fill my legions. Our business will be concluded tonight, and this body will have served its purpose."

"Then Ravon?"

"Your love will be parted from Centurra," Dagremahr said. "I shall uncouple them as we agreed."

Phon's weakness was fading. Dagremahr was more physically capable now that the chains were off, and his body freed. The monstrosity took a few steps and approached Denn who felt the hairs on his neck stand up. Longlimb was still in his hand, and Denn considered striking out, but despite the sword's empowering reach, it was doubtful he could cross the room's distance before one of the sorcerers stopped him. Both his brother and Kabra had already demonstrated their abilities. Perhaps Postella also harboured similar talents to call upon.

Denn was able to muster enough courage to address the reawakened warlord. "Why will you not leave Ramisa in peace? Why torment her?"

"The one bonded to Lyseia," Dagremahr acknowledged plainly.

"Tell me how to separate them," Denn asked. "Or do it yourself and leave her be."

"Perhaps you could offer a bargain of your own," Dagremahr's words sounded eerily natural when spoken by the body he possessed.

Denn pressed, "You are said to be powerful. Disentangle them. Free Ramisa too."

"You are too bold!" Lehn interrupted his brother. "Do not make demands of your better!"

But Denn's petition did not anger Dagremahr. Instead, the warlord peered at Lehn and sneered. "I do what pleases me."

"Can you? Can you honour your bargain with Lehn and separate the princess from the Paragon?" Denn probed again. "How?"

"It will be done," Lehn interjected. "But you do not need to worry about Ramisa. The need for your request will have expired soon for Lyseia will be freed once Ramisa is dead. There are armsmen already on the way to Farathemun's house to see to it."

Denn was overcome with anger. "You're a murderer! First the king. Now Ramisa?"

"What were you told about the king?" Lehn shot back. "You know nothing, I guarantee."

Denn stepped back and tightened his hold on Longlimb. The agitated tone edging into Lehn's voice suggested they had spoken long enough.

Dagremahr's shambling movements were becoming sturdy strides, and he walked toward Wex Sulford, who received him eagerly.

"I have come to forge an army and I think you can agree, Sulford, that Denn is a capable warrior. I empower you to recruit him for me. Let him await me in my realm." Then he ordered, "Kill him, Sulford"

"Yes, I will, my lord. Thank you!" Sulford accepted the opportunity with a child-like zeal and devoured the implied forgiveness for his past failure.

Making good on his decree, Dagremahr reached out with Phon's bony hand and caressed the blade of Sulford's sword. There was a sound like cracking ice. From tip to guard, the weapon's lustre burnt off and the sword changed colour from silvery iron into a charred black. An instant later, its sheen returned, and it took on the gleam of polished obsidian.

"Wounds from this blade are incurable. Every drop of blood spilled, pools and collects in the beyond, and there are oceans of it in my world," said Dagremahr. "You will learn, as your hireling did. You will reawaken in servitude to me, and like him, you will take up your post in my army and wage infinite war on battlefields without end, until all my enemies are gone, and all the realms are mine."

Trin! Denn immediately recalled the boy he had left on Bridgecliff, but there was no time to mourn anew. Sulford stabbed at the air and Denn was forced to jump back to avoid the deadly touch of the weapon. He planted his feet and raised Longlimb to parry the next blow.

From the back of the room, Serenn protested again, while the two council hags observed the standoff like crows anticipating a fresh carcass. At any moment, Denn knew they could step in and overpower him. Yet for now, they appeared content to watch the sport.

Denn dodged another jab before Lehn broke up the audience. "Escort our lord to the citadel, Postella. Let him walk in the paths of the fallen and consume his fill of the dying."

Postella nodded, and her lips curled. Like a practiced courtesan, she approached the gruesome double-souled entity and lithely wrapped her arm around his with a saucy, triumphant smirk. Appealing to her less sophisticated counterpart, she made a request.

"Kabra, please open the door for us."

CHAPTER 33
Daggers

L ivet vaulted up the staircase, two steps at a time, ignoring the pains in her leg. Echoes of the dire clash of armies outside reverberated off the temple's stone walls and grew louder as she ascended. The prince's soldiers had broken through. She was sure of it.

Temis had said Lehn was in the priory, but she had no map or knowledge of the temple layout beyond the dungeon. Worse, she feared that if she began her hunt on the ground floor, she could get swept away by the imminent fighting.

The choice was made for her. The staircase did not even open out to the ground floor but led straight up into the personal offices and residences of the Pillar adepts and curates. Along the doorways, small plaques of cast bronze bore their names and titles. She scanned them for one that displayed the name of Denn's brother.

It would be harder to hide up here, Livet thought, as she sprinted the length of the corridor from door to door. Lines of dust and candle soot showed where tapestries and curtains had been removed, leaving the walls bare. But thankfully, it was night. While the battle swirled about, the area both around and below the temple was largely unlit, evacuated, and disused. The only glow of life came from further down the hallway, around a corner.

Peering around the corner, she discovered a host of heavy and immobile sculptures that remained planted in place when more portable treasures had been stripped clean. Candelabras along the length of the hallway cast enough light that she could identify the shapes and figures of the statues. She did not know them all by name but recognized what they represented. These were the

Pillarmen's forbears and gods—the Paragons.

All of a sudden, there was movement. A stone's throw away, a trio of statues appeared shifting and scuffling.

Livet stopped in her tracks. They were not statues, she realized; they were guards. In the dimness, she could make out the blue of their tunics, and when she listened, she heard one of them speak in a deep, brutishly coarse voice that harped on with urgency.

She crouched behind the sculpture of a faceless, cloaked woman, held her breath, and listened. Her fingers touched tiny grooves carved in the woman's cloak, where the artist had fashioned the stone to look textured and corrugated. It reminded Livet of the Rham River weave worn by the nobles back in Lanstad.

"We could use this statue as a battering ram," said the voice, closer and more audible to Livet, until overcome by the rough sound of stone scraping on stone.

"Stop! The hallway's too narrow to get a good run at it. Besides, the statue's too heavy to pick up—even for the three of us!" said another.

"Why don't we use *him* as a battering ram?" said the third.

"Lord's Oath, I should box you in the jaw to shut you up," the brutish sounding one muttered. Instantly, Livet's ears pricked up.

"Psst... Olen!" she projected a powerful whisper.

The big man paused his fruitless strategizing and looked over to her. He craned his neck and peered behind the statue as Livet popped out of hiding. His jaw dropped, then his cheeks stretched into a gargantuan grin.

"Livet!" Olen called in response. Then grin faded and he gestured wildly at the monumentally tall door beside them. "Denn's inside. We can't get in. The door's locked!"

Rushing up to them, Livet spied Yael's sharp, pensive face right away. Then she recognized Temis. His presence took her aback, despite Denn having explained the twists that had now come to align them.

Livet maintained her distance as she approached but did not question or object. She even ignored that the three men were all dressed in shabby, matching blue tunics of the Faith, and single-mindedly slipped past Yael to concentrate on the door. The latch depressed when she tried it, but the door could not be pushed open. She pulled, also to no avail. The door would not budge.

"It's stuck or somethin'. But it's not locked," she said. Cupping her ear to the door, she heard loud thuds and the frightening clash of metal. "We need t' get in!"

"Hack it down, then!" Olen exclaimed, readying Coldswept for a strike.

Livet looked around, then glanced at the top of the door. "Keep trying," she said as she leapt up and got hold of the doorframe. She shimmied upward naturally, propelling herself with one foot upon the nearest statue and the other finding foothold on the irregular, carved mouldings that lined the door jamb. Reaching the top, she pulled herself up like a leopard commandeering a favourite tree and perched upon the door's lintel.

Squinting, she looked through the breach in the glasswork of the transom and was about to ease open the panes of glass when through the warped translucence, the forms of two approaching figures startled her. Quickly, she pulled her legs up just as the door was flung open.

Beneath her, emerged one of the two councilwomen who had chased her and Baressa from the dungeons. Postella appeared now, strolling defiantly on the arm of Denn's father. Livet was initially taken aback by the unexpected pairing but soon seized the opportunity. She used the opening of the door below to help distract from her widening the gap in the transom at the top. She pushed, and the metal arms that held the panes of glass in place popped open.

Inside, could see Denn engaged in combat with another councillor, Sulford. Denn jumped back defensively. His eyes were wide, and he was maintaining what distance he could, but each time he dodged, he was invariably sent spinning or tumbling by the tempestuous conjurings of the habitually dishevelled councilwoman, the witch Kabra Zimmin, laughing from the rear of the room. Looming at her side, was the fearsome curate who had sought to murder Baressa. He lorded, in turn, over Denn's distressed sister, pushing her helplessly back, and forcing her to witness her brother's precarious duel.

Livet was confused and overwhelmed. She looked back to the hallway and could not shake the sense that there was something more dreadfully dangerous in the situation. Why had Phon just walked out? Had he double-crossed his son again? Denn was fighting for his life, blade-against-blade, while his father nonchalantly sauntered out the door.

Phon had halted at the urging of Postella, and no sooner than he had exited, he came face-to-face with his devoted right-hand man.

"Sir, you've been freed," Yael said. Lines swelled on his brow, betraying extreme calculations that he, too, must be engaged in as he deciphered this new event.

Postella interrupted. "This one's a smart one, m'lord. Yael is truly your best servant."

Phon grunted once, then again, then more, until his utterings turned into a deep guttural laugh.

"I remain at your service, m' lord. Are you in danger? Have they released you?" Yael asked, manifesting a disturbing obeisance.

There was the slow sound of metal being drawn from a leather scabbard. Temis craned his neck upwards to where Livet straddled the transom and, observing both sides of the doorway. She heard him quietly say, "Go."

"Removed to another, temporary prison, you might say. But I am very well, thank you."

Yael stared at Postella, teeth clenched while he held his tongue. Livet could see he was desperately seeking something to alleviate this obliviousness they all felt.

Temis cleared his throat. "Go," he said more loudly to Livet, who remained frozen.

"As my servant, Yael, it is my wish that you let me examine your sword," Phon said plainly.

Yael hesitated, then relented and offered up the hilt of his flamberge to his employer and master. Phon took the sword and instantly, the blade was consumed with a mystical blackness that flowed in spirals over the curves of the rippled blade, like smoke belching from a quenched fire.

"Move back! He's cursed it!" Temis cried out in warning, but no one reacted quickly enough.

Phon thrust forward, one-handedly–slicing through Yael's outstretched hand and piercing the duty-bound lieutenant through the navel. Then, with remarkable strength for such a feeble frame, the perceived patriarch drew the blade upward into Yael's chest. It hit his ribcage made staccato sucking sounds as each curve of the flamberge struck bone when it was withdrawn. Laughter erupted from Phon as Yael's organs spilled out and the eviscerated body dropped to the floor. "I reward your servitude," he enthused.

Yael's death seemed to corrupt the air around them. A wispy, streaming cloud of greyness spewed from the chasm in his chest and swirled about the corridor. It elicited more laughter from Postella, and gasps from the others.

"Serenn and Denn are inside! Go to them! Now!" Temis wasted no more breath. His pair of short swords were out, and Olen was already beside him, shoulder-to-shoulder and battle-ready. The all-encompassing fear that Temis expressed in his eyes drove Livet over the lintel, through the transom and into the priory chamber.

As quickly as she entered the room, Livet immersed herself within the occlusive wrap of the umbrage. Yet even in this state, Livet could feel a pair of eyes looking and searching for her. They were the same eyes that had sought her out in the dungeon—that threatened to see through her tricks then. Now she knew that they belonged to Denn's brother. Lehn shared the family's fair hair, but his complexion was devoid of the gentleness and grace of his siblings. It was him who orchestrated the crimes she had witnessed in that cold, secret lair, deep below this treacherous temple. Now, he had trapped Denn and Serenn, as well.

Even after conjuring an umbrage, Livet knew that Lehn might be able to see her silhouette against the light spilling from the transom. She had to move. Higher on the wall, above the alcoves and arched recesses, she squeezed into gaps along the triforium that ringed the chamber. She was sure that Lehn was tracking her movement. His eyes burned and glowed, sweeping over the whole of the scene in the room. To evade, Livet scaled and traversed along the upper regions of the wall, only to work herself into a corner, and inevitably nearer to his predatorial gaze.

The pace of Denn and Sulford's fight quickened, as Denn lunged into an offensive. His blade streaked in an arc through the air and blooded his foe. However, as soon as Sulford was able to lift his ebony blade in response, Denn gave up his advance, parrying on the defensive, instead.

Unmoved by the display, Lehn remained transfixed as if he could still sense Livet maneuvering in the shadows at the top of the room. With all the concentration she could manage, Livet entreated the darkness pooled within all the room's crooks and crannies to thicken the masking of her presence.

How long could the umbrage keep her hidden from Lehn's magical talents? She scrambled along the reliefs at the top of the room. The curate's unsated eyes moved back and forth. In trying to move away from his focus, unavoidably, she was now almost on top of him and the closer she came, the more likely he would detect her.

If Livet could not obscure herself, perhaps she could chance to conjure confusion. She did not dare try to fool her foe with phantom rats or rabbits. It was not a matter of making him see the unexpected. Maybe she could make him see what he wanted to see and mollify or dull his higher reason with succour for his basic, emotional senses.

Livet edged along the upper boundaries of the chamber until she maneuvered herself next to the vast, magisterial portrait of Lady Ravon. When Lehn inevitably set his eyes upon Livet, hiding in the shadows, his own affinity for the queen regnant caused him to only see his beloved's painted likeness, in the place she was meant to be. Livet's round face and petite form morphed into a blurry mirage–a kind of double vision crafted by her mystical manipulation. In effect, when Lehn looked toward the painting, he was blinded by love.

THWUMP! Something walloped into the wall, and it shook from the impact. For a moment, Livet thought she might lose her grip on the mouldings of the triforium. Below her, Denn had crashed into the wall, nursing his elbow as he stood back up. The bruising and tiredness she had seen on his face, earlier, was returning. He was running out of fight. His sunken cheeks were pale, and his lungs strained to draw each laboured breath.

Livet, however, was energized by her enmity for Lehn and all the others. Sulford may be wielding the sword, but Lehn held the whip and presided as master over this detestable display of cruelty.

Kabra's laughter swelled out of her like a rhythmic moan, as Denn's gasping grew louder. Finally, the witch invoked her powers to rob the last of the air from Denn's lungs and choked him from the inside. Denn's sword arm flopped wildly in a pathetic refusal to surrender. Furiously, Lehn then muttered an incantation and reached out his hand until Denn cried out in pain and dropped his sword. The blade and handle were turning orange-red, and Livet smelled the sick sweetness of burnt flesh.

"End it!" Lehn called out. "The queen needs us. Our *lord* needs us. The real battle is without. Sulford, do your duty and execute the apostate now, in the queen's name!"

As he said the words, his eyes rose to the portrait of the woman whose office he had just invoked. But if he sought reassurance or praise, he saw neither—only the tip of Livet's approaching rondel. She launched herself upon him from above and propelled the dagger which bypassed the shoulder blade and plunged deep into Lehn's chest cavity. With great agility, Livet landed upon him to arrest her fall. With her free hand, she grabbed onto him by his medallion then secured herself by wrapping her legs about Lehn's torso. She stabbed again, and again, side-to-side, before dropping the remaining distance and rolling away.

The perforated curate collapsed to the floor. His eyes remained open and static, but no words escaped him. There was only the moist, frantic suction from his horrendously compromised lungs.

Kabra shrieked. She fell onto Lehn, shielding him protectively as Livet scrambled away. "You horrible rat!" she screamed apocalyptically.

Wex Sulford, spying the aftermath of the newcomer's pouncing assault, sidestepped Denn and bolted toward the nimble assassin.

"No!" Denn screamed as Sulford's black blade hummed. It cut through the air and made contact. Livet heard the savage sound of the slice cut the air as she was pushed out of the way by Denn's sister. Serenn reeled around on one foot from the blow, then dropped to her knees, clutching her head. A tide of red spilled out from between her fingers.

Sulford had no time to curse his misdirected blow. Serenn's sacrifice gave Denn the moment he needed. Enraged with righteous wrath, he charged the cruel councillor and bowled him over. Sulford crumpled. The black blade coasted across the stone floor, before ominously coming to rest beside Kabra, who snatched it up.

Denn jabbed his fist violently and vindictively into Sulford's face. He unleashed blow upon blow until Serenn's attacker was limp and bloody.

Kabra raised Sulford's sword, and though she did not appear to have the skill to use it, the dark enchantment of the blade made her a deadly adversary regardless. Worse yet, Denn was unarmed. Even if he could rally to pick up his sword, there was no way to quench the heat and it looked like the blade had already liquefied and warped.

The only advantage they had was that Kabra's magical powers were temporarily occupied. While she held off attackers with the black blade, her free hand was shielding Lehn's wound. Her palm hovered over his chest, rising and lowering in sympathy with his beleaguered breaths.

Livet felt herself being tugged backward. Denn grabbed both her and Serenn and was pulling them toward the doorway. At some moment proceeding Livet's fateful leap, the door must have opened and now stood ajar. Livet's heart was thumping. She could see bodies lying prone and stretched across the hallway. "Olen!" she cried and wrenched free from Denn.

Temis intercepted her at the doorway. "Watch out!"

Held back by Temis's arms, Livet struggled to tear into the corridor. In panic, she saw Olen writhing on the ground, clutching his head and eyes. Temis was shaking with a cold sweat, but he was still on his feet. Phon and Postella were gone, leaving only the shattered remains of the blackened sword spread out across the floor. Yael lay a few feet farther away, dead.

"Don't touch the shards!" Temis spoke with such fear that Livet was compelled to obey, but her biggest concern was for Olen.

"What 'appened to him?!"

The brawny Westriverman clenched his teeth and gritted against the pain in his eyes but seemed otherwise unhurt. He stomped his foot on the ground angrily and clumsily, almost stepping on Yael's unmoving corpse.

"Gods' greed! That woman can fling poison like a viper. It got in his eyes." Temis released Livet and she ran to her injured friend. Meanwhile, Temis began calling out desperately. "Serenn! Where are you?" He wheeled around and dashed toward where Denn was supporting his ailing sister. Serenn tried to take a shaky step forward to meet him but teetered.

"Easy," Denn said, keeping her upright and balanced. Then to Temis, he explained, "It was Sulford's blade that struck her—the mate of his old one."

"No! Black? Not another, surely!" Temis cried, and Denn's

grim face affirmed it.

Rushing to Serenn's side, Temis took up her weight and murmured meek reassurances that contrasted with the anguish displayed across his face. He cut a strip from her clothes to quickly dress the wound and staunch the blood flowing from the side of her head. He wrapped his arms around her and pulled her into an embrace.

"What happened?" Denn asked him.

"Your father turned Yael's sword into the same. Pitch black and deadly. We fought him and it splintered when it struck against Olen's! Scared him off, I think. But be careful and mind the shards for I think they're still dangerous."

After mentioning Olen, Temis appeared reminded of the big man's plight. With one hand supporting Serenn, he reached into a pouch on his belt and tossed a small vial to Livet. "It's a salve. It might help dispel the poison's effects. Put it on his eyes."

Together, Denn and Livet took charge of Olen. The sidelined champion was clenching his jaw and frothing from pain. "It's us, friend. Hold still." Livet tried to sound calming. Denn gave her the vial. She uncorked it and poured out some of its milky contents. "Move your hands away," she instructed.

Olen grimaced. Once he pulled back his hands, Livet could see a glob of foul yellow-green ooze covered his eyes. There was a discarded Pillarman tunic on the ground, like the ones she had seen them wearing before. She used it to carefully wipe away as much of the ooze as she could, then splashed the contents of the vial into his face and massaged it around his eyes. The surrounding residue became watery and dripped down his cheek in tracks of sage green, like the runoff stains from old copper. He blinked several times.

"Can you see?" Livet asked.

Olen shook his head. His panic was beginning to diffuse, however. "It's blurry. The pain's gone, though."

There was a gust of air from the office, and the door beside them slammed shut again. Kabra, it appeared, had regained enough concentration to resecure the entrance. It was safer with her on the other side of it. Livet sighed in relief

"Where is Dagremahr?" Denn asked to the bewilderment of Temis.

"What do you mean?"

"My father's body contains the soul of Dagremahr."

Temis moaned concernedly. "That explains the blade—and Yael," he said, still gripping onto Serenn steadfastly. "He gave me an awful knock about the head. It was more than I'd expect from an old buzzard like that. He took Yael's sword and cursed it, then killed Yael. But Olen charged him and shattered the black blade with his broadsword. He would have killed him, too, but then that woman pelted him with poison, and they took off!"

"I'm not so sure." Denn frowned. "I think Dagremahr can do worse. Maybe you are lucky."

The time was hurtling along. From the temple floors below them, they could hear the conflict metastasizing. The attacking soldiers were filing into the temple without nearly enough Pillar armsmen to slow their assault. Livet could only imagine their ire at seeing the temple treasures already removed, making the place unsackable, despite the easy ingress.

"The Pillarmen will be on us soon—that is if the prince's soldiers don't arrive first. We are going to need another way out," Denn said.

"Ask Livet. She came in from the other direction," said Temis.

Livet was holding Olen by the arm, helping him to stand. Her abject tininess when standing against his lumbering bulk made her seem like no more than a walking cane. She guided him along while recounting the route she'd taken.

"Back staircase. It's empty, and my friends are waiting down below. There's a tunnel which takes ya out through an ol' well."

"Denn, what about Lehn? Your brother... did you...?" Temis cautiously started to ask.

"We have Serenn. We're finished here," Denn said, showing no appetite for further discussion. Livet could see that Denn's injured sister was only marginally more transportable than Olen. One of her eyes was still closed, and the vicious gash next to it was weeping fluids. It seemed she had to fight to open the other, too, so as to be mindful not to trip or falter.

"Yael? Do we just leave 'im?" Livet asked sadly, her stomach knotting at the sight of the dead man with the unenviable reward for blind loyalty. The body was disturbingly unhinged along the middle, already drained out. Highwater lines marked where the blood had pooled around him and ended at the cracks between the stones of the hallway floor.

"I don't think his joints would keep in one piece if we picked him up," Denn said grimly. "Let my brother see him—if he survives. Yael's death is on his head," he added in spite. Then finding his tenderness again, he offered to carry Serenn. Temis clung to her protectively, but Denn pushed him gently away. "You're the only one with a sword to swing." Hoisting his sister's arm across his shoulders, Denn nodded at Temis and gestured toward the head of the small troupe.

In the flickering candlelight, Livet examined the man she had come to aid. Denn appeared vacant and near defeated. He was slumped over with the burden of his wounded sister. In his hand, he held a dagger that was not much longer than the knife Livet carried. It would not be enough to keep him safe. She knowledgeably offered the same suggestion she had once given to the caged Northporters. "I saw a guard's station down b'low. You can find yerself somethin' to fight with there," she urged. "It's near the tunnel that leads out."

Between shallow, winded breaths, Denn nodded appreciatively. Tugging and propping up Serenn's wilting body, he trudged along behind the others.

CHAPTER 34

All That Remains

They moved in a haphazard gaggle. Temis led but followed directions from Livet. Olen came next in line, his hands upon her shoulders and still blind, helplessly carried along by the current of their precession. Assisting Serenn with each of her steps, Denn took up the role of a weary and spent rear guard.

With each step she took down the secluded staircase, Livet listened for Kell to call to her. Just a little farther she kept insisting to herself, but all she heard was clomping as Olen's heavy boots made their uncertain footfalls behind her.

"I see a light ahead," Temis finally whispered.

"That's where we're going," Livet said, encouraged when the distant candlelight became visible.

At the bottom of the staircase, she could make out the landing that curved toward the temple's charnel laboratory. The pulsing orangeness of flickering flames drew her until she caught something unexpected, reflecting the light from the doorway of Kell's chamber.

Livet lunged forward and grabbed onto Temis's belt to pull him back. "Quiet," she whispered. Delicately, she pried Olen's fingers from her shoulders, brushed past Temis, and crept down the next few steps, disappearing into the darkness as she went.

A man was waiting there.

A swordsman stood at the doorway, preparing an ambush. His arm was coiled back at the elbow, and he clutched a rapier in hand, ready to thrust. The illumination behind him cast a halo about his already golden head. Livet could see the man was lightly tottering from holding himself so rigidly.

If he had seen her sneak around behind him, he reacted too slowly. Livet moved beyond the reach of his sword and called to him. "Effie!"

The lad spun around on his heels. "Livet! You've returned!" He leaned toward her and unspun his arm to cup her in a tight embrace. Livet returned it uncomfortably. "We were just waiting for you to find your way back!"

Calling to the others, Livet summoned everyone into the chamber. As Temis strode in, his eyes widened at the plethora of fluted flasks, cauldrons, and stacks of alchemical tomes. He ran his fingers down the spines of catalogues labelled with potions and preparations, scanning them with immodest envy. "Incredible. This workshop has everything. Oh, what concoctions they must know how to make!"

Olen felt his way along the wall next. Effie moved aside for him, speechless when he realized Olen's condition. It was only Denn's passing that snapped him out of his trance-like concern for the veteran. He watched ruefully as the cavalryman entered, only softening with sympathy when Serenn, still bleeding, arrived close behind.

Across the room, Taringer rose and approached them. Harbud was moving amongst the workshop's cabinets and shelves, rummaging as he went, in an even more systematic manner than Temis. Baressa sat next to the remains of Kell, which had been delicately retrieved and laid out upon a scarred and scorched wooden workbench.

"Is this where it was done?" Denn asked Livet.

She shrugged.

"This is where they restore the dead to this world?" Denn continued. "Corrupt the flesh of the living with the souls of their gods."

"Yes," Livet said when she was surer of his meaning. "Prob'ly."

"Then how do we destroy this place? How do we stop them?" Denn was choking on an angry lump in his throat. "How do we undo what they've done?"

Livet looked around without any simple answer, but the beginning of a solution entered her mind. She could feel it coming to her from some profound and providential thought spring.

'*With my help,*' she heard Kell say, enunciating and giving substance to her inspiration. His disembodied voice crept into her head, and answers flowed into her.

"How do we stop them, Kell?" Livet asked.

'*I must make amends. Without me, the art would have remained hidden,*' he said. '*But once I confess, you must promise to do as I direct—to ensure the Pillars may never employ me again.*'

Livet was sobbing gently. She slid over to where Kell lay and cradled his pitted, yellowing skull in her hands. She felt a trembling in his bones, but his words drifted surreally as if carried upon the burning incense that surrounded them.

'*Love was always my weakness, dearest one,*' Kell told her.

"No. Your love kept me alive when I was abandoned," Livet coughed. "You didn't need t' love me, but you did. I was just some trouble for you."

'*You were never willfully abandoned,*' Kell intimated to her. '*Even when your mother was dead and gone from this realm, she found a way to reach out to me. She asked me to look after you, and I did.*'

"My mother? You knew who she was. From the beginning?"

'*Her name was Vaeya, and she was betrayed, as I would be.*'

Kell's words resounded with sadness. Livet was unsure who else in the room could hear them, but everyone was staring at her as she mouthed her responses. They were intrigued and not daring to interrupt.

"What 'appened to her?" Livet prodded.

'*She came to me already proficient in her own craft, so we taught each other and shared our arts. I showed her enchantments, and she instructed me on how to unravel the threads of life and weave them back again. But her obsession grew, and I withdrew from her. It was for this knowledge that she died, and I cried without end when I heard.*'

"Who killed her?" Livet asked, but Kell continued his narrative, unswervingly.

'*She died by the same hand that tortured you—in the same dungeon. You know his name.*'

Livet riled at the memory of Averin Golmarra's crimes against her. She wrapped her arms around herself tightly, but it did nothing to alleviate the chill she felt.

'To my astonishment, however, your mother transcended her death to speak to me again from her grave—and she spoke of you. I heeded her commission to be your guardian. Then devoted myself to understanding the realms of life and death that she had once been a mistress of. I had hoped to bring her back.'

"So devoted that you lived in the crypts," Livet surmised. All around her, the assemblage of eavesdroppers shifted on their feet and cocked their heads to listen more intently. If they could not hear Kell, they could certainly hear Livet's side of the conversation.

'It was out of convenience and necessity,' Kell said. *'You well know that we were hunted.'*

"By Golmarra... in Lanstad, and by Lord Vlass," Livet said.

'Golmarra sought parlance with his own ghosts, the Paragons,' Kell explained. *'And even when they had slain me—and one would think me untouchable—I returned from beyond to negotiate for your deliverance, much as your mother did when she sought out my promise to her. That was my bargain in Lanstad, and the deal was lamentably repeated here in this chamber, with Golmarra's devotee, when I tried to save Baressa.'*

"You helped the Faith... helped Lehn to bring back—," she stopped, conscious that her words would incriminate Kell if spoken aloud. No matter what he had done, his faithfulness—his dedication to Livet's protection—moved her toward ensuring his absolution.

'Livet, help free me so that they may never use me again,' Kell pleaded.

"Tell me what I must do," Livet said.

"You must hurry!" interrupted Harbud from across the chamber. He was agitated and periodically glanced over his shoulder to the staircase from where Live's party had arrived. "We all must hurry. There will be soldiers flooding these halls. Besides hunting us down, these corridors are filled with priceless relics they will wish to defend."

"I know," Livet said. She noticed that he held several of the Faith's antiquated grimoires in his hands. At Harbud's feet, Livet saw that the burlap sack he had brought was already ballooning with items.

"We need that bag t' carry Kell out o' here!" Livet said scoldingly. "What's inside? Loot? Treasure?"

"Kell doesn't want to leave," Harbud told her. He continued plucking books from the shelves and tossing them into the sack. Taringer shuffled over and stood next to her. He stopped short of placing his hand on her shoulder or saying any soothing words, but his ever-doleful eyes looked toward her with a hint of pity. "Livet..." he started to say.

"He just asked me to free 'im! To get 'im out of here!" she argued.

"Baressa is walking out with us, but Kell is staying," Harbud said.

"I have to free him!" Livet shouted angrily. Her legs tensed underneath her in a combative stance while her hands were bundled into fists and turning white from being pressed so tightly.

"We *are* freeing him where he is. He wants to stay and make sure the temple vaults are purged of their records so that the Faith can not abuse his art and knowledge again." Maybe Harbud was not being purposefully obstinate, Livet thought. She sensed he regarded her with genuine empathy.

Taringer, too, gently repeated the plan to her.

"He wants us to burn everything, with him inside the blaze to stoke the flames, Livet." Taringer indicated with his staff toward the room's contents. "The Faith has filled their dungeons with parchment and wooden furnishings, all slick with oil and lacquer. They will burn fiercely. Once the fire is set, I will command a powerful draft to blow down the hallways and passages of their vaults like a bellows. It will turn this place into a furnace with a heat so great that it will incinerate everything."

"It will be as hot as a Fal forge in here," Harbud said. "Hot enough, Kell tells us, to turn his remains to ash, along with any other relics and bones that the Faith has in their collection. Kell is bound to his earthly body—or what is left of it—so this is the best way to sever that bond and allow his spirit to exit into the next realm."

"How will you prevent the rest of us from burning in the fire?" Livet asked skeptically.

Taringer looked to where Kell lay, then carefully turned back to apprise Livet. "*You will.* You can shield us from the heat just as you do the light."

"Wha—? How? A fire doesn't cast a shade," she said.

"Kell says that if you try, you can bend heat in the same

manner that you bend light," Taringer coached. "He is here to help you. Let his magic increase the scope of yours."

"He can magnify your powers, just as he has promised to help us to open a pathway through the Passage Realm, out of the temple, and back to safety–something I could not do without him," Harbud added.

Whatever power Kell had left in his bones was being gifted to them to provide a chance at success and escape. Livet's throat was rough, and her eyes stung. She was still moved to weep, but there were not many tears left in her reservoir.

You should know that you can do much more with the knowledge and powers that I introduced to you. You have it in you to surpass me. Such is the benefit of outliving your teacher,' Kell said.

"How much more could you have taught me?" she queried the corpse. "What else should you have told me before I lost you?"

'Vaeya,' Kell repeated Livet's mother's name like the whistling of a gale. *'Find Vaeya's resting place in the crypts of Lanstad where we once dwelt. Find the heart of seven points. Hidden at her graveside is my grimoire, preserved for you. You will find answers.'*

It was difficult to look at her mentor for the last time. Livet averted her face and as she did, she found Denn had approached beside her. But after their falling out, it was too soon to have any new words of affection to share. True, she had saved him from death up above, but it was his brother she had to murder to do so. Kell was right; love was a weakness.

"I heard your plan," Denn said. "It is good. Necessary."

Livet did not need his approval.

"Thank you for finding me and saving me," he added.

He was foolish, Livet thought, to have ever thought she wouldn't. But while she scoffed at his acceptance of their plan, she welcomed his words. Appreciation was something she took to heart eagerly.

"Temis wishes to take Serenn, to travel with you and seek care from your friends. She is dying," Denn said, his words drenched in despair. "But I must go and find my father, and Dagremahr, and hope that I can find a means to have him reverse the curse."

"I understand. We must do everything t' save your sister,"

Livet said. "I will take 'er to Gardia. She may be able t' elp."

"Thank you," he said, then continued, "And the princess..."

For an instant, their future had brightened again, until, like a cloud passing in front of sunbeams, he eclipsed her happiness with a pronouncement she should have foreseen. Livet's drawn-down face stretched longer, but she did her best to steady her voice. "What of 'er?"

"I have also promised to seek out a cure for her, and I am honour-bound to right my error, and ferry her away from the peril she faces in this city. My brother reported that the men of Kramwen were marching on Lanstad instead of Caphedra. That means that the army which was hired to secure her safety has disappeared. But whether they win or lose, Ramisa is in jeopardy. Both the Lord Marshal and Golmarra must know that she is in the city, and they will easily step over her uncle to get to her. Neither will let her live to challenge her siblings for the crown, and if they succeed in murdering her, I will be as complicit as Farathemun if I don't try to stop it."

"Well, good luck t' you. You've probably already dawdled too long," Livet said, casting her gaze to the wall and swinging her short leg to scratch at the floor. "You should be off."

Denn stepped back, his eyes taking her in sadly, before dipping his tall frame in a hesitant bow.

Livet feigned a smile through her taut lips, but then curiosity overtook her. She was mindful that now was a good time to part ways, but she found herself wondering.

"Dagremahr," she said. "How will you find 'im? What will you *do* when you find 'im? You don't even 'ave a sword."

Denn stopped. "Finding him should be easy. He'll be where the dead are piled up."

"And your plan then?" she quizzed.

"I don't know. On my honour, I've sworn my help to Ramisa, but I know of only death as the means to split apart the soul of a host from that of the Paragon that inhabits them. This same condition that afflicts both Ramis's daughters now condemns my father."

"You should ask the man that did it," Livet said. "Or ask me to ask 'im."

This confused Denn, who appeared shocked when Livet

addressed the corpse beside her.

"How d'we break them apart, Kell?"

The dried-out bones quaked perceptibly, startling Denn, who twitched in corresponding surprise. Livet, on the other hand, pulled herself closer to the remains on the table, preparing to listen to their grisly guidance.

However, Kell came up short.

'I was only a novice,' she heard his voice say. *'Would that you were able to ask your mother. Her knowledge of the mystic mechanism that effected the pairing was greater for she had experienced it herself.'*

"She performed it? Brought back a Paragon?"

These newfound revelations that Kell and her mother were so entwined with these dark experiments continued to gnaw at her, but she would not permit her resentment to build. If love was a weakness, it was an excusable one and perhaps she could forgive herself for failing to hold those she loved to account.

"Is that 'ow my mother died?" Livet asked.

'The ritual that fell upon his father was performed crudely, by an inexperienced mage upon a corpse that was almost nearly dead. Their union is irredeemable without the death of the host. But tell your friend to take heart, Livet. More skill and care were afforded to the princesses and their mother. There may be hope for them. Find my grimoire, it may lead you to discover more. It rests with your mother, and she lies in Lanstad.'

With sullen gratitude, Livet gave a gentle brush of her fingers over the brow and orbits of Kell's pitiable eye sockets. The smoothness of the bone, worn away of flesh, framed the emptiness from where her protector's eyes had once looked sweetly upon her.

"Who died, Livet? What did he say?" Denn asked.

It was all too unsettling and overwhelming. Livet backed away from the corpse on the workbench and turned toward Denn. "Your father's lost," she summated, refusing further elaboration.

Denn's face remained stoic and accepting. "Then I must go and do what needs to be done." He grabbed her by both arms. "We'll see each other again," he said.

Livet did not dodge nor flinch from his kiss. She allowed him to lean in and convey his true farewell with his lips. It was the only way she could feel his sincerity.

"We'll see each other again," Livet repeated.

He circled the room and give a cautioning nudge to Temis, who had taken stewardship of Serenn. Denn kissed his sister on the cheek, away from the injured side of her face. Then he spoke for a moment with Olen. "Have your men hold then line at the bridge," she heard him say. "When I return, I'll need to know that I'll have safe egress from both the Marshal and the Faith."

Olen nodded obediently. At the end of their short exchange, to Livet's amazement, he handed over the scabbard that housed Coldswept. The two warriors embraced before Denn sprinted off through the underground to find his way out the tunnel and to the surface.

Unsteadily, Olen rose to help push and pull furnishings and bundles of paper into the middle of the room. His eyes were still failing him, but his back was strong.

"It's a lonely life you'll have," she heard a bitter voice say behind her. The prophecy came from Effie who asked, "Do you always fall in love with men who leave you?"

Livet looked at Kell's bones before her and rebutted the jealous suitor. "They don't really leave. Not all of them, and not forever."

At that moment, a breeze blew through the dungeon labyrinth. It lifted wisps of Livet's dark hair. She turned to gauge where it was coming from and saw glowing glyphs of Scrawl etched upon a bare patch of wall in the workshop. Harbud had opened the portal to Westriver.

"Perhaps I'll leave, too," Effie said.

"Yes, you should," Livet told him. She did not mean it to sound harsh. Livet just wished for one last moment to say goodbye to the spirit of the man who raised her, who would finally commit himself to one last endeavour then be at peace.

"Thank you, Kell," she said. "I'll honour you, somehow."

Those most wounded in the temple were helped to march through the portal. Harbud saw to aiding Baressa, and Temis guided Olen while simultaneously supporting Serenn, who staggered forward weakly. Next was Effie. The last to leave before Livet would be Taringer, who patted her on the back to signal he was ready. He raised his arm with a torch in hand.

In front of Taringer was a stack of paintings, leaning against a heap of piled furnishings in the middle of the workshop. The image at their forefront was of the Paragons, thirteen motley-but-monumental, venerable figures. The Four Pillars were in the background. Levelling the hungry flame at waist height, he used the torch to light up the canvas. The oils in the paint ignited nearly effortlessly, and the bonfire began.

Livet listened for Kell's instruction, which she sensed more than heard. She could do this. Livet conjured a safe pocket within the umbrage, but this time, kept them apart from the heat as well as the light.

It is cool in the shade, Livet repeated to herself as if it were a mantra she had divined. The waves of warmth and wafting smoke skirted around them. Kell's power was tangible. She could feel his magic bolstering her own.

Livet tapped Taringer on the back, signalling to him, as he had to her. The fire was already blazing—blisteringly so—but he commanded the flames and engorged them until everything in the temple dungeon was turning to cinders and ash.

A draft rushed in, drawn along by the deft movements of his hands. The whole chamber became a tunnel breathing rhythmically like air through the mouth of a giant. The reddish glow grew orange around them and finally took on a dazzling whiteness as all the manifested evil in the room fed the flames and was purged. Painted images crinkled, blackened, and vanished. Rivulets of molten metal dripped from the chamber's more lustrous contents. First flowed soft, pliable gold and then came scarlet trails of molten iron.

Against the flow of the air, Livet gestured to Taringer to move in tandem toward the portal. Her protection did not extend far but it was sufficient, so far, to protect them against the inferno. She saw that the table upon which Kell lay had become engulfed and was burning furiously. The last vestiges of his body were being cremated. Livet knew that once Kell's spirit was released, she would lose his unearthly help in shielding them from the flames. Left unaided, she could not guarantee they would not be incinerated along with everything else. They must go now.

Taringer nodded at Livet and together, they retreated in unison. The mountain mage passed through the white-hot rock and disappeared. Livet followed his footsteps up to the brick. She stood in front of the source of the air that was invading the dungeon and fueling the monstrous destruction. It smelled summery, like the night, but also bore the fetid stench of Faralley gutters and the distinctive muddy, fishiness of the Darrow. It was the surest and quickest way out and back to safety.

If Livet felt any sense that her labours were finished, she would have walked through the portal toward its comforting pungency. Instead, however, she gambled to enjoy her imperviousness for a little bit more.

The cyclonic fire looped around her, but she concentrated on the enchantment that kept her safe within the eye of the storm. Her mentor's influence had already faded. This was an enchantment solely of her own crafting, and in the tepid doldrum of her own manufacture, the fury stayed diminished.

Livet made up her mind. She navigated the scorching passages of the dungeon's oven and ran off, fleet-footed, in the same direction that Denn had journeyed scant heartbeats before.

Kell was right. She could do more with her powers.

CHAPTER 35

The Princess in the Keep

A promise of fresh air tugged at Denn's nostrils and drew him down the underground passage to the base of the collapsed well. He scrambled up the rubble and emerged out of the debris, aware that he was only barely evading the tumult of the temple grounds. Clashes between the rival troops were close. Screams and cries echoed within earshot. Cautiously, he refused the main streets and chose a more clandestine route to Farathemun's strong house.

But despite taking the backstreets and alleyways, he was still forced to step over the bodies of struck-down soldiers. Fallen fighters from both armies were piled upon each other in mounds where they had died, clamouring upon comrades, or remorselessly trodden upon where they perished.

When he signed up to the king's cavalry, Denn had been too late to partake in any legendary conquests by Ramis's army. In his days at the academies, he only studied historic contests–like the cruel siege of Northport, the alpine ambushes of Palinor, or the seizing of the Highgrounds of Hasen. Denn was more used to riding through rebellious villages to intimidate agitators and instigators from the saddle of his warhorse. It involved a great deal of menacing theatrics and pageantry and usually cleared the way for the king's officials to do their work. If the inhabitants still insisted on carrying out their revolts, it would be the infantry or armsmen who did the actual work of quelling disorder.

And that was the only brutality he knew of. Denn remembered their work vividly. He had seen the corpses and smelled the dead on the breeze, their stench carried aloft on the smoke of communal pyres. These corpses surrounding him now had barely begun to decay, but that same septic odour was escaping from them and saturating the sultry, oppressive night.

Denn kept moving steadily leaving behind the sacked temple and seeking out the looters' lure that was Castleside. There too, Marshal's forces appeared to have recently rampaged through the district. Damage was everywhere. Along the walls of buildings, Denn saw gashes where steel struck against stone or timber. Pits and craters were left by errant bludgeons to coexist with traces of bloody handprints where people had struggled to pull themselves up and continue their stand. Here in Castleside, the dead were not all soldiers. Many were once-prosperous citizens trying to protect themselves and the last of their centuries-old fortunes.

Spying this bloodbath, Denn already had expectations of what he would find at Farathemun's. The carnage was arrayed all the way up the hill that led to the lord's flung-open gate. Inside, he saw the trampled yard and the smashed and splintered door. Its thick reinforced panels were chipped and dimpled from axe blows. It looked like a ram had been employed.

Denn's heart was beating rapidly. He was wary but suppressed his misgivings. Whatever terror took place appeared to be already finished. The merchants' rebellion was put down before it started.

The unsettling feeling soon grew to a foreboding anxiousness. Thankfully, Olen had entrusted him with Coldswept. It was a heavy blade but when Denn tried swinging it the steel electrified the air. It was a masterpiece of metal—unquenchable with its own peculiar energy—and among whatever other secrets were imbued into it when it was forged, it left Denn flushed with confidence to know Coldswept could shatter a black blade.

Nervously, Denn entered the manor. The door sentries had died at their post, where the invaders had breached the cordon at the main entranceway. The vases and statuettes were tossed about and shattered, and the welcoming bowl of fruit had been flipped. Apples and grapes were strewn across the floor where heavy boots smushed them into Lord Brevin's exquisite carpet. Denn summoned his courage and pressed further but as he explored the inside the scene grew more disastrous.

He arrived at the threshold of the grand court chamber

where Lord Brevin had once greeted, then discarded him. Here was also where he had last seen his disingenuous mother, lulled by the falsehood of security, and clinging to another scheming nobleman to replace her husband. Was she gone too?

Deny as he might, he felt a modicum of guilt. He did not condone his mother's choices, nor dare to contradict them, but neither should he have left her here. There were never enough troops to provide safety and Denn knew it. It was naïve to think Farathemun was holding any more cards than the short-sighted usurper had already presented. Nonetheless, Denn had been kicked out by Farathemun, under escort, he reminded himself, and had been in no position to refuse or remain.

Denn entered the ruins of the court where more slaughtered men lay sprawled out in puddles of their own vital liquids. Everything appeared lifeless and still. Before he could manage a survey, however, something rattled across the room. It quickly snapped him to heightened awareness.

Peering about, he explored for a source. A couple of torches were burning but they were dying down and provided very little luminance into the room's dim corners. Denn seized one from the wall and arced it around in a circle. Unable to determine the origin of the noise, he moved to the centre of the room with his sword firmly in hand. If anything were to leap out at him, he would be ready.

Then he saw the insignia.

From what Lehn had said, he had expected to find no one save for the Pillarmen sent to facilitate Lord Farathemun's arrest. One of the bodies, however, displayed a belt buckle plate embossed with a golden castle tower. Had the Marshal's Men had gotten here first? If so, they did not escape without cost. Olen was right when he reported seeing them scurrying toward Castleside. Was he right that he had also seen Colden among them?

Denn continued eying the room for the source of sound when the light from his spluttering torch ultimately revealed the inevitable. His stomach lurched inside him when confronted with the horror that the Marshal's Men's mission had wrought. He saw the pair of bodies still sitting upon the chaises where they died. A blade had been thrust into Lord Farathemun's throat, piercing his vein and windpipe and the resulting gush of fluids was congealing down the man's unstirring breast. Perhaps thinking herself safe, Denn's mother had remained beside him when the Marshal's Men came. Her head was slumped over her lord's shoulder. Her stark red hair was entwined indistinguishably with streaks of her own blood. It streamed down and fanned out beneath her, along the folds of her soiled gown. Her golden circlet was missing.

This time, Denn could not bear to touch her. It would only confirm the irrevocable tragedy that was her demise. He stared at the grisly sight before him. Choking, he swallowed his tears then removed his cloak and laid it over her lifeless body.

It was imperative that Denn search the rest of the house. One more victim tugged at his conscience, and this one was an innocent. He avoided the sprawled-out forms of the slain and explored further, looking for a staircase that would lead to the upper floor. Perhaps they caught the princess there, hiding in fear, resisting the fateful spectres she believed already imperilled her return.

Shreech. This time louder, another sound disrupted the quiet.

Denn braced and listened. It was metal scraping on the floor.

This time Denn was determined. He walked across the room and probed into a mass of bloodied arms and legs that lay mangled and grotesquely stacked. With Olen's sword, he poked with quick, piercing thrusts into all the possible fleshy sources. He tried this over and again, attempting to elicit a reaction from anything that might yet survive in there, until a sudden apprehension stopped him with the fearful realization that the princess's body could just as easily be concealed in the pile.

Changing strategies, he opted to search the hard way—the dangerous way. With methodical jolts of exertion, he strained to pull body from body, springing back each time to survey the results.

Some of the dead men, Denn noted, wore blue tunics as expected. Farathemun must have played host to the competing, murderous intentions of both the Faith and the Marshal's Men. It was no wonder that the massacre was so thorough. Farathemun had his wish, but the timing was off. His men were in position when the two competing sides met, but they came up short of seizing the promised advantage.

Suddenly a body moved by itself. One of the fallen soldiers rolled out from the pile and over. The man's face was sliced, contused, and freshly painted in its own red juices. He ejected a mass of spittle from its mouth and followed up with a horrible boast.

He coughed, then his eyes rolled back into their sockets as he smirked and said, "We got the little bitch."

The dying man expelled air from his lungs in excruciatingly slow and wavering measures. Denn stood poised to clamp a foot down upon man's chest but restrained himself. The brutish braggart wore a belt buckle that matched those of the golden-towered Marshal's Men like that Denn had discovered on the body in the middle of the room. Mercy was a distant thought, but maybe the man held the critical information Denn needed.

"Where is she?" Denn said.

The man sneered, "The boys are keepin' her for the night."

She was alive. Perhaps Denn could extract her location, but the man was so close to death that any threats held little weight.

So, Denn tried a different tract.

"The prince doesn't want any harm to come to his sister," Denn proclaimed. The ruse was a risk since that the prince was believed to want nothing more than to see both of his siblings committed to their tombs.

The man coughed but was unmoved.

"I was sent to fetch her," Denn lied again.

The man remained quiet but was listening. He blinked his eyes to free them from the crust that had formed about their edges. Only the Pillarmen wore a uniform these days. Aside from lacking a King's Guard belt buckle, Denn's appearance was not unlike any of ex-soldiers that the Marshal had mustered. Judging by the bodies in the streets, with war imminent, Myrhic had not been very concerned with setting any standard of dress, as the Faith had.

Frustrated, Denn grabbed the man by the shoulder and wrenched him. "The Lord Marshal has demanded the princess be brought to him immediately! It's a direct order!" Denn stated boldly, then added, "Where's Colden?"

"Colden?" the man asked. The lie finally took hold. Too dazed and drained to think clearly, it succeeded in shaking the man from the edge of expiration into one last urgent attempt to show loyalty to his lord and master.

"At the baths," he said. "He took her... he took her down into the bathhouse." Then laying at Denn's feet, he closed his eyes and went limp.

Concern flooded over Denn. They had carried the princess to their place of pilgrimage, that ill-fated sanctum they venerated where Lehn had infamously murdered Ramisa's father.

Denn knew the way and bolted back out of the court chamber and out the door. Only haste could permit Denn to redeem this tragedy. The Azure Bathhouse was not far from the Farathemun house. He prayed to all the nameless gods of fortune that he could reach her in time.

Returning into the night, Denn bolted down the alleys and laneways carelessly. Every wasted moment further endangered Ramisa. The girl was already frail, and her unsteady mind must certainly be on the verge of collapse.

Inescapable sympathy drove Denn. Like him, the princess had grown up in the shadow of an older sibling for whom such nobility was better suited and more expected, and when that failed, each of them had been forced back to Caphedra against their will, as sacrifices for the same cause. But Denn was as guilty of playing the same untoward role with Ramisa as the men who had kidnapped and transported him. Those villains still dwelt in his nightmares and lurking out there now was the last survivor.

Denn quickened his pace. The battle could be heard to the south, creeping this way as the Lord Marshal's army marched from the crumbling central temple to the heavily guarded citadel. By tomorrow, the sun would be shining on the bloody victors. If Denn could save Ramisa tonight, they could spare themselves of the consequences, and both be out of this terrible city before dawn.

The door of the Azure Bath House was soon in sight but as Denn arrived, the hairs on the back of his neck stood up. He spied a movement by the bathhouse door and heard a faint voice say, "Go and fetch them."

Denn ducked out of sight as two dark forms stepped out of the shadow of the entranceway.

The same man spoke again. "I'll guard the door while you summon the Marshal."

"The girl?" queried the other. "Should we leave her with Colden?"

"It can't be helped. We're all that's left," the first replied. "Go and find the Marshal. Bring him here with enough men to ensure her captivity–and do it before that louse defiles her. She's still the king's daughter... and the Marshal may have plans for her."

"Aye. I'll hurry back."

Footsteps pounded upon the ground then faded, as the man departed at a weighty trot.

So, Colden is inside. The thought made Denn queasy, made his mouth go dry.

Coldswept vibrated in his hand. It seemed to sense Denn's intent. But no such cue benefited the hapless sentry. The man left at the door began to cry out in surprise, but the sound became buried under convulsions welling up in his throat, as Denn brought his sword down.

It was too dark to gauge exactly where he hit, but Coldswept's blade was long enough to leave a long trail of contact. A warm spray erupted, and the sword hummed encouragingly.

The sword craves blood, Denn thought, wiping the blood of the blade with a shred cut from the man's blouse. He dragged the body a short distance to conceal it under a bushy hedgerow then turned again to face the Azure's entrance.

A hefty cedar doorway stood between two alabaster pillars, each carved with bacchanal images of people on the backs of marine beasts. A small banner depicting a castle tower was affixed and hanging above the door. High up to one side, water poured from a duct into a fountain that provided for passersby, with a run-off trough for horses and a lower tier for dogs. The remaining overflow splashed into a stonework gutter along the edge of the street.

There was no time to find another way into the bathhouse. Denn entered through the main door and carefully went down the stone staircase, step-by-step until he reached the cavernous chamber that held the underground baths.

The walls of the bathhouse were smooth, and the floor was marble, interspersed with ornately tiled mosaics. Golden fixtures along their edges spoke to the establishment's former elegance. Within its irregular-shaped boundaries, separate pools descended beneath floor-level to serve as private basins for the enjoyment of its former customers. Now the water was cold. Frigid damp air clung to Denn as he proceeded inside. The pools were developing a layer of scum, making it feel like he was descending into a primitive cave. No fires were burning to heat the water, so everything took on a cold, clammy feeling, and the moisture made walking on the tiles precarious. The bathhouse was quiet and empty, but Denn remained vigilant; Colden was here, somewhere.

Though cloaked in algae and scale now, the Azure was designed to be a place of relaxation where well-off citizens and nobles could be coddled and cleansed. It was difficult to imagine this as the scene of the violent act precipitated by his brother's volatile rage.

But this was where King Ramis died in a standing pool. His attendants said the water was only lukewarm when it suddenly took to boiling. Several of them, Denn recalled hearing, were scalded trying to get him out, but it was too late to save the king.

He believed the story now. The way Lehn's magic had made Longlimb scorch Denn's hand was still fresh. His palm held blisters, and his uncle's sword was now lying in a pile of slag—as a testament to Lehn's supernatural power. Denn could pair the legend with what he saw and experienced for himself.

Droplets of water splashed into the various pools around him, and the sounds of their dewy descents bounced off the walls. Denn's steps across the firm floor were quiet in comparison. The dripping grew louder the longer he focused on it. He stepped over a stone half-wall and avoided the patches around the room where rays of moonlight entered from narrow windows above.

The dripping reached its crescendo as a sudden splashing erupted from a pool around a corner. Denn tried to leap out of sight and flatten himself against one of the walls. He heard sobbing, and a muffled wail like the bleating of a distressed lamb. There was a series of slaps in the water, and the splashing became more violent.

"You pipe up any louder, and I'll slit your throat!" threatened a man's voice.

Denn recalled receiving the same threat once and immediately knew the identity of the Marshal's Man who remained as watchman. The greasy, crooked face of Colden Wess, which haunted him from the back of his mind, came to the forefront of his thoughts just as its flesh and blood manifestation appeared around the corner, only a few steps away.

He had the benefit of surprise. As with the guard at the door,

Denn decided to rush Colden and commit to the monster's slaying. Light shimmered against the water in the bathhouse pools and danced upon his steel blade. He raised the sword, ready to deal a savage blow the moment he turned the corner.

But Colden heard him. There was a gritty, accidental scraping sound as Denn drew back too far and brushed Coldswept against an unseen, low-hanging pipe.

He had given himself away, and his quarry leapt up, flopping through puddles of water, and flailing like a fish freshly flung onto a ship's deck, before twisting around at the ready. In the blink of an eye, Colden was poised before him, dripping from the wetness of the floor tiles, with one hand on a long-handled knife and the other clutching at the waist of his water-logged breaches.

It took a moment in the dim light before Colden recognized Denn, but when he did, his grin was less pronounced than in the past. His face contorted with the displeasure that Denn had caught him at a disadvantage.

Behind him, Ramisa shrieked. Her feet pattered against the wet floor, propelling her rearward slightly amid slipping and futile splashing. Her dress was sopping wet, and her chemise showed rough handling; its drawstrings appeared either cut or pulled from the eyelets. The sleeve of her cote was torn, too, and the bracelet made from Avenda's hair was missing.

Colden took a lunge forward and swiped at Denn with the knife but did not dare get close enough to risk contact. It was evident he was trying to force a standoff to buy time. The wretch might be alone now, but he wouldn't be for long.

"Did you miss me, Wellum? I've got someone else now... A princess!" Colden licked his lips.

"How dare you bring her here!" Denn answered hatefully. "You know what this place is."

Colden cut through the air with another feeble swipe and snarled. "You shouldn't have followed us. Are you hoping to die where the king died, you pompous pup?" He stepped back, yielding ground unnecessarily and Denn seized upon it and pressed further forward.

"Are you afraid?" Denn taunted.

"My grudge was with your father, but if I have to take it out on you to make up for Romwin, then I will... *gladly*."

"You won't get the chance against my father, because I'm here to square up with you now!" Squeezing the hilt of Coldswept, Denn was more mindful of the space around him after his last mistake. He was desperate for a good strike that would end this. Such a blade did not require finesse to be effective. "Ramisa!" he called out to the shivering girl, "Is there anyone else with him?"

"They're coming!" Colden shouted, pre-empting her.

"He sent them away," Ramisa said. "They went for the Marshal."

Denn's heart pounded. He had precious little time.

No more posturing, he thought. For the moment, Colden was his only obstacle.

"Tell me, Wellum, what was your mum doing at Farathemun's? I should've asked before I cut her throat."

Denn swung. Coldswept streaked in a great circle and came down upon Colden, who tried to leap back. The sword was still unfamiliar to Denn. At the last second, he overextended, and it threw off his balance. He slipped in a wet puddle beneath his feet and windmilled. The sword connected with Colden's knife instead, detaching the smaller blade from its handle.

But while Denn remained off-kilter, Colden recovered and sprang upon him. The two splashed together onto the floor, sliding toward one of the pools. Colden seized Denn's wrist and smashed the back of his hand against the tiles and forcing him to drop Coldswept so that both the knife parts and sword were lying on the ground. With his other hand, he reached for Denn's neck and tried to push him closer to the edge of one of the baths, where he could plunge him under the frothy waters of the pool. Furiously, Denn responded by squeezing Colden's head anywhere he could get his fingers in, trying to twist and force him off.

It brought back the vile memory of those horrible times in the back of the cart, with Colden's full weight on him, crushing him— the episodes that populated his nightmares. But this time Denn was not tied up. He was not helpless or incapable. With a hunger for vengeance, he concentrated his strength into yanking Colden off and launched the transgressor headlong into the shallow water of the bath.

The impact made a tremendous splash. As Colden plunged in, he flailed uncontrollably in all directions. His violent immersion had been aggravated by the collision of his head against the opposite side of the pool. Blood seeped out and filled the bath while water frothed and escaped over the edges, flooding the tiles even more. A moment later, his seizures diminished as his last twitches rippled across the water, accompanied by a pathetic gurgling.

Denn wanted to roll over and get away from the blood-tinged tide that was spreading from the bath when he saw something glimmer in Colden's pocket. It was his mother's golden and topaz circlet. He freed one hand, reached over, and retrieved the jewelry from the thief's pocket—the most unfortunate of trophy to mark his victory.

Ramisa was already fumbling along the tiles to get close to him. She grabbed him tightly, and in the joy of temporary relief, they held each other. Both drenched and soaked, they kept each other warm despite knowing their safety was fleeting.

"We need to go," Denn urged.

"Hush," Ramisa told him, then ducking under the half wall, she pulled herself toward a tiny hiding spot around the corner, to a recess. Denn hurriedly crouched down and followed her lead.

Lifting his head above hers, he listened. The bathhouse had gone silent once more. Colden was not moving. A mess of greasy hair floated around his shattered head where it protruded above the water of the pool. Even the constant dripping seemed to stop.

Then they heard a dominating voice issuing direction.

"Where is she? Take me to her immediately. I cannot leave Prince Ramid unattended for long!"

Armed men were filing into the bathhouse. Denn could not count how many soldiers there were, but there were enough that they did not fear generating noise or clatter.

Still holding Ramisa, Denn edged along the tiles behind the partition for a better view. Again, he found himself disarmed. Coldswept lay a few feet away and any attempt to retrieve it would alert the enemy to their whereabouts.

"Sir, Piers was found already slain outside, m' lord," said one of the commander's attendants. "We may be too late."

Lord Marshal Incis Myrhic presided over a retinue of armoured guardsmen from the centre of the bathhouse. His armour was burnished with elaborate mouldings of contrasting gold on the breastplate. A medallion of his former office hung around his high-collared neck. The Lord Marshal was tall, but his advanced years had thinned his frame so that he appeared more wiry and rigid than Denn recalled. He wore no helm, and his dark grey hair was brushed back in waves above sharp eyebrows that peaked over shrewd, cunning eyes and a close-cropped moustache paired with an angular tuft of hair to frame his serpentine mouth.

"You must have been followed, coming out of Farathemun's house. There may still be sympathizers in the service of the nobles. Find out where the killer is, and what has happened to the other man you left with the princess. Search this bathhouse," Myrhic said.

Denn's eyes flitted from one corner of the room to the other. There was no way out. Somehow, they would have to hide and wait for the Lord Marshal to depart.

Suddenly, one of his men shouted and pointed in their direction. "Captain Alamm! Look in the water, there."

A large man with the trappings of an officer walked forward and stopped next to where Colden lay dead in a bath. The officer appeared almost primitive in his looks, with a sloped forehead and a dull stare that suggested a belittling disinterest in the body of the floating ruffian. He lifted the soggy corpse with one hand. A cascade of water poured down.

"One of your men?" Myrhic inquired with impatience.

"A brother by blood to one," Alamm said. "His name was Colden Wess, sir. His brother was Romwin, who served under you in the Lord's Guard. This one wasn't much of a man, but we took him on as a favour to his brother." Turning to berate the soldier, he angrily asked, "Why did you leave him to guard the princess?"

"Colden, Piers and I were the only ones who made it out of the manor, sir, after we were ambushed by Pillarmen," the soldier explained.

"Fortunate that you're still with us to take responsibility for losing the princess," Myrhic said to the survivor. Then as he peered down at Colden's water-logged body, he scolded the captain. "You should have been more selective when you recruited your men."

Alamm took the dressing down squarely on his shoulders. "I'll assign more capable men to hunt for her. If she's this close, she will turn up in the end, m' lord."

"Find her, or I will see that end comes swiftly to you," Myrhic warned. "We need to find the Lady Ramisa. Her presence in

Caphedra risks detracting from our honourable prince's authority."

"Yes, sir," chorused the soldiers, but echo from the bathhouse tiles cast back their reply and morphed it into a disconcerted muffle that exaggerated their nervousness.

Myrhic nudged the corpse with his boot. "Get this out of here," he commanded. "It reminds me too much of the last body I pulled out of these abominable baths–a far better man than this sodden refuse was. You have no idea how much I detest this bathhouse!"

"Sir," said Alamm. "The men honour this place. Each of us took an oath of remembrance and fealty in these waters–in the king's name and yours. These bath chambers are a shrine."

"I suppose the sentiment serves the cause," said Myrhic. "To this day, I cannot eat pork stew. This whole place should be torn down, brick-by-brick, filled in with earth, and the waters allowed to run back to the river and out to sea."

The Lord Marshal came dangerously close as he maneuvered around Colden's body. So far, he remained oblivious to Denn and Ramisa, who had only the corner and a tight alcove in which to hide, but the moment the Marshal or his men walked one step farther, Denn and Ramisa would be seen.

There was nowhere to run. The Marshal's soldiers were blocking the exits, and the windows were exposed, and unreachable. The drains carrying water out of the bathhouse were too small to squeeze through. Even if they tried to flee, Denn was reminded of the princess's condition which might jeopardize the success of even a short dash, should her legs give out or her balance fail. Denn, too, was cramping up now from crouching so long in the cold wetness.

Beside him, Ramisa had stopped shivering–a bad sign that her body was succumbing to the chill. She was freezing wet, but Denn had no cloak to offer for warmth. His was in the ruins of the Farathemun manor, covering up his mother. Ramisa's only relief would come once she was away from these damp, cursed baths–and that needed to be soon.

The Lord Marshal took another step and erupted. "We are wasting time! Search this place! It is crucial that I return to the battle. Our army holds its position at the temple, on my orders to taunt and entice the Faith until they expose their men. However..." He huffed and snarled. "Our short-sighted prince threatens to act *boldly*. He desires to advance upon the citadel tonight."

"Sir? Why not press for the victory?" Alamm queried.

"Victory requires timing. The boy is adamant about striking the citadel while they are still shut in tight, whereas I rather we wait until their troops are drawn out and compelled into a counter-attack, in the streets where I favour our odds."

"How long do you think they will avoid the fight, sir?" another man asked.

"They will lose patience soon. Our possession of their cherished sanctuary lends to a most conspicuous insult. Their strategic advantage is erased by their spiritual loss."

"Sir, we have heard that the temple is on fire."

"Perhaps that will hurry the process along, then," Myrhic sneered.

Searchers were beating about the room now. Denn tried to move his leg slowly and quietly, to get his blood flowing again and ease the cramp in his thigh.

Encircling the Marshal in an entourage, the soldiers listened to their leader. Many faced Myrhic obediently, their backs remained toward Denn so that their bodies helped obstruct the Marshal's view of the hiding place.

"Our dear prince doesn't see the temple's value," Myrhic continued, lecturing his men as the investigation of the baths progressed. "The citadel is at the heart of their defence, but the heart of their commitment is the temple. Yet the prince is determined to reach the castle where the crown lies in the citadel, for his ambition so equally distracts him. It comes down to which side can suppress its innermost urges the longest." Anger and frustration began to infect the Lord Marshal's voice. "Unfortunately, patience is not the prince's strength. The boy insists on pressing his luck. He won't do so while I am over his shoulder—but alone and given a chance, I fear he may conjure enough nerve to defy me." Myrhic paused and added, icily, "So you understand, Captain, I can not afford the luxury of patience here."

"Sir, my men can stay and hunt for the girl," Captain Alamm offered. "If you wish to go back to the line and *advise* the prince."

"How many men do you even have left?" Myrhic scoffed. "I want her found! Search outside if you must but retrieve Ramisa and immediately report back to me. I will entertain no other challengers to the prince. Is that clear?"

Several men acknowledged him with a brisk, "Yes, sir!" and ran off.

This improved the odds for Denn, but only minimally. The Lord Marshal had drifted even closer now and Coldswept was too far from Denn's grasp. Instead, he pulled out the horn-hilted dagger from his family armouries and set his goal on reaching Incis Myrhic's valuable neck.

Denn's eyes had adjusted to the lack of light. He squeezed Ramisa's arm gently to get her attention and silently pointed to where she needed to go once his grand distraction was enacted. A staircase lay behind a narrow opening, close by. He hadn't noticed it before; it was likely for the use of servants and meant to be obscure.

He nudged Ramisa again.

She did not respond. The cold was getting to her. Her eyes were fixed in a rigid stare, and her breathing was shallow, across her pale, wan lips. Again, he squeezed her arm harder. This third try worked, but she gasped loudly at the shock of being brought back to sudden awareness.

The Lord Marshal's soldiers rushed over and levelled their sword tips toward where the pair kneeled helplessly on the floor. Captain Alamm separated Denn and Ramisa, roughly picking up the princess by her arms and shoving her in the Marshal's direction, then returned to stand watch. Perceptively, he followed Denn's gaze to where Coldswept rested on the tiles, out of reach. He looked down at Denn and smirked.

The princess was presented, face-to-face with the Lord Marshal.

"Lady Ramisa," Myrhic acknowledged. "You've grown up—like your brother and sister." He sounded almost paternal. "The last time we met, you were ten years old... just before your uncle absconded with you." He smiled thinly. "Welcome home."

Ramisa squirmed, but Myrhic took her by the arms and stared into her face nostalgically.

"You were away when the Faith sent their killer to murder your father. Horrible people, they are. You see why we can't let them win." He turned his head, cocked it, and gestured toward a bathing pool only a short distance away. "Right there," he said.

The bath he pointed to did not appear different from the

others, but as Denn stood up, he saw that, at the bottom of its waters, was a collection of items tossed in like offerings to a wishing well. This was the heart of the Marshal's Men's religion, where a new faith had been born out of the tragedy that occurred in that stagnant pool of water.

"The attendants said that a curate—a presumptuous fellow named Wellum—accosted your father and was not well received. The Faith has tried denying it, but they could not silence every mouth."

Denn shuddered at the sound of his family name. Until now, he feared her finding out that it was his brother who had murdered her father. What was she thinking? Denn tried to focus solely on his pledge to protect her. A full accounting of Lehn's crimes must wait until after they made it out alive.

"Whatever his request, the curate was refused. Angry at the rebuke, he summoned some diabolical enchantment. They said the water went from warm as piss to bubbling hot like in a giant cauldron. Your father was boiled to the bone by the time we were able to pull him out."

Upset, Ramisa's voice quivered from both the cold and from her emotion, but she composed herself enough to ask, "Do you seek to honour him by killing me in the same place?"

"I swore to rid your brother of any challengers to the crown. Were you to gain an army, you could be a threat against his claim."

Denn feared for the princess but swore he could sense uncertainty in the Lord Marshal. As Myrhic looked Ramisa in the face, the venerable general relaxed slightly. Although his grip remained firm, his scrutiny grew gentler, and his expression was almost tender.

"All grown up," he repeated. "You might even give off the appearance of a true queen."

"She is no threat to you, Myrhic. Let her live!" Denn surprised the assembly of soldiers by addressing the Lord Marshal so directly.

"You interrupted me. Who are you?" Myrhic demanded.

"Only her servant," Denn answered, but Myrhic was not dissuaded. Seeing Coldswept lying on the ground, he released one hand from Ramisa and bent down. The sound of metal scraping against tile screeched as he drew the weapon closer and lifted it up.

"My lord, I believe the man to be Lord Wellum's son,"

Alamm exposed him. "We had reports that he escorted the princess from Fallowsea."

Myrhic gave a choppy, belly laugh. "A-ha! So that is your name... Wellum. Quite brazen for another of your clan to come back here! You're not a curate, though... curiously."

"I am Denn Wellum. I am the princess's protector."

"You Wellums have a penchant for playing a lot of different sides. You must all take after your father in the worst ways." Myrhic lowered Coldswept, rested its point upon the tiles and leaned on it like a cane as he glowered pensively. "I suppose you seek to be her consort. From there, is a short path to the authority of a king. Rumour has it, that was the same path your brother chose, so angering the king, right here in this very establishment." The Marshal glowered at Denn, then gazing up and down at Ramisa's wet clothes, clinging to her expressive form, he lecherously added, "I hear he has already taken liberties with his beloved. I hope you have been more honourable."

"Let us go," Denn offered, "I will ensure the princess leaves the city... I'll take an oath to it, and you will never see us again!"

"Maybe I let you go, and *I keep her*," the Marshal said, dropping his smile. "Or maybe we cut off your head to bait a trap to flush out your murdering brother. That would see justice levied, and for the same sake, I'd just as soon put all you Wellums to the sword."

Lifting his foot, Alamm brought it down upon Denn's back, compressing him helplessly against the cold floor. The commotion drew laughter from the other soldiers, but it fell short as a peculiar disturbance curtailed their derision.

Myrhic turned to the brackish bath where his one-time liege had perished. Bubbles were beginning to rise and pop along the surface. The rest of the pack of soldiers also sensed something, and they stepped closer to watch too.

It had the appearance of returning to a boil, just like in the account of that night six months previous. The number of bubbles increased. No warmth could be felt, but where they broke across the top, the remnant droplets began combining into a foggy mist that floated above the water's surface like steam. All heads turned toward the eerie apparition.

A chill worked its way down Denn's neck as he gawked incredulously. Was this another otherworldly summoning perpetrated by the Faith? Did another spectre dwell in the pools of the bathhouse?

Before the Marshal, the mist rose equal to him in stature, then higher. Its form began to take on a distinct shape of a man, topped by the points of a crown. Its face floated, twisting, and straining into a profoundly dolorous countenance which resolved itself into an expression of anger as it mouthed the words, *'Release them.'*

The Lord Marshal's soldiers stepped back, disbelieving of what they saw, unable to explain the vision of their late king before them, nor deny they understood the command.

"Sir," Captain Alamm inquired to his earthly master. "What would you have us do?"

"It is not real. It can't be! I order you to..." the Lord Marshal shouted, then suddenly cried out in pain. Doubling over, he dropped Coldswept, and the sapphire-bedecked sword clanged loudly to the floor. He released Ramisa as well. As she scrambled to get away, the blade from Colden's knife dropped from her hand and a flood of ruby-red emerged from a gash under the Lord Marshal's breastplate. His blood fell in globs upon the floor.

Denn seized the moment and in the blink of an eye sunk his own concealed dagger into Alamm. The massive man lurched backward then dropped to his knees, gasping.

Soldiers rushed in disarray to the Lord Marshal's side where they tried to administer aid to their leader. Others stormed toward Ramisa and Denn, who were already rushing toward the narrow passage Denn had spotted. The princess faltered but Denn pulled her along and kept her moving forward, snatching up Coldswept as they passed.

The mist began to move. The wrathful wraith was not yet placated. It rippled across the air of the bathhouse and filled the void between the escapees and the hapless soldiers, stopping them in their tracks and sending them skating across the slippery tiles. Its spectral arms arched outward, and its tendril-like fingers extended to ward them off from their pursuit. Overcome with terror, the soldiers splashed water around the room, some walking backwards on their hands in flight from the phantom fog.

Higher up above the tiny staircase, Denn could see an elevated window that opened to the street outside. He lifted Ramisa through it, but she was panicking.

"Help! I must find help! I must—" she repeated unthinkingly. "I must go to the castle!"

"What? No!" shouted Denn as he tried to lift himself through the window to chase after her.

"We'll be safe in the castle!" she promised, stricken by a daze of fear and mania.

"We will not!" Denn countered futilely.

It was too late. Ramisa was already stumbling toward the citadel and the cataclysmic convergence point where the battle for Caphedra was reaching its portentous pinnacle.

Struggling to pull himself up and over the window ledge, Denn could have sworn something—or someone—gave him a helpful boost. Once he squirmed through the opening, he glanced back but saw no one there. The ghost of King Ramis—or whatever it was—had not followed.

CHAPTER 36

Witnesses

D enn emerged through the window and sprang to his feet quickly. He was reminded right away how insufferably hot the day had been. The humidity did little to alleviate the weight of his dripping wet clothes, but his cramping muscles began to relax now that he was out of the cold baths. He scanned for the princess to no avail. Ramisa had vanished.

Cursing, he broke into a clumsy sprint and headed in the direction of the castle. The Marshal's invaders were choking the streets. Their determined ingress caused a commotion that roiled and surged around him. They littered the night with trumpet blasts and deafening roars as they jeered and taunted the Pillarmen on the parapets.

Denn could smell the acrid sweat of a thousand men upon the languid air. It rolled in like a fog, between buildings and enveloped the hustling troops but felt unnatural. Torch and firelight became diffused, making the shapes of the besiegers seem distant and phantasmic so that when oppressed by the overwhelming loudness, it was like being submerged within a rip current in a swirling sea.

The haze hid much of the carnage which accumulated most thickly over those places where the bulk of the dead had piled up. If Denn could not see, how could he find the princess?

He stepped forward and tried fanning away the murkiness, but the banks of fog resisted his attempts. He was walking into the field of battle, blindly.

But the mist also served to mask Denn, and alongside the prince's troops, he emulated their dress and habits well enough that no one took notice or barred his approach to the heart of the contest. That was until, morbidly, he tripped over a body that lay prone in the dirt. The fallen soldier appeared to have died quickly, and his corpse made only a passive protest, but as Denn picked himself up, he realized that the eerie fog was emanating from out of the corpse. All around him, it seeped from the dead and coalesced above them like a pall.

He shuddered, unable to withdraw from it. Cringing, he felt the mist floating across every inch of his face and body. A pair of mournful eyes floated in the thickness in front of him. Denn reeled back and fell over as the spectre passed him by and faded into the ashen breeze.

It reminded him of the ghostly cloud he had seen rising from Trin's body at Bridgecliff. The fog was forming above the ground where the dead lay because *they* were its source—and Dagremahr must be the cause. The dead would gain no rest. The soldiers who fell here were cursed to serve again in Dagremahr's otherworldly legions. Isn't that what the evil warlord threatened?

Walking through the densest parts of the hoary mist should produce a path straight to his father's stolen body and the Paragon that inhabited it—but first, Denn needed to find the princess. He got back to his feet to resume the hunt.

Ahead, a column of men had skirted a logjam of barriers and formed up on the march. They boldly advanced under a bone-white banner sporting seven bloody red circles, while on their shields were painted black shapes that resembled cauldrons or braziers. Unlike the disorganized Pillarmen that Denn had spied before, these troops displayed staunch discipline. They marched rapidly, locked in formation, shoulder-to-shoulder. Along the edges, spearmen bristled, but running through their centre, two files of men transported a makeshift ladder which had been knit together from scraps of debris.

Not wishing to lose sight of them, Denn decided to follow from a few paces back. He would go where they were going, he thought. But their cadence picked up, and Denn could soon feel the terrible rumbling around him of more than just this singular company. Horns blew. The prince's army was commencing a full assault against the citadel.

Startled, Denn had to deftly dodge an excited captain who

rode up from behind, atop a galloping steed. As the officer coursed past, he shouted out, "To the wall! Onward!"

The fog broke slightly and Denn saw the fortifications of Caphedra's ancient keep take shape before him, intact and unyielding. Their crenellated battlements teemed with the Faith's defenders who were adorned in blue mantles, tunics, and sashes, and poised to repel the charge. Pike blades and spearpoints angled downward toward any who might endeavour to scale the wall. Lined up behind them, archers readied their bows and crossbows in menacing preparation.

"Heave! Up!" cried the captain, hacking at the air with his sword and trying to lead his company via a frantic lexicon of blade-waving and thrusts. His men hoisted their rickety ladder in response, and the first assailers took to the rungs.

But rather than meet the tops of the wall, the ladder came up short. The only things the brave climbers encountered were sharpened steel and showers of scalding oil as it was poured down upon them. Perforated and scalded bodies dropped from the top, knocking off those below. Bubbling oil streamed down on one of the men anchoring the ladder at its base. As he screamed and recoiled from the source of the searing pain, the ladder jerked. Its shoddy rungs popped out, and it began to split, ending hopes of any further ascension. The scalded man was dragged backward by other retreating besiegers. Denn revulsed when he caught sight of the man's blistered and melted face.

Helpless, Denn withdrew as well as a symphony of whistling projectiles whizzed past. The archers were loosing their arrows against the fleeing men who desperately scrounged up whatever protection they could find–from abandoned shields to lifeless comrades. They bounded between each volley, then took up their shelters anew as the next storm of arrows landed.

Taking his chances, Denn ran too. Leaping over debris and injured men, he sought the cover of the fog which both protected him and mocked him, for the faces of the dead swirled within it. They harassed his senses, and the coldness of their ill-fated breath gave him a chill.

At that moment, Denn heard a pair of voices nearby–first was a demure, soft, and unsteady voice, then a second that was confident and commanding.

"Have them re-form again!" directed the first cracking voice. "Make them go again!"

"Form up! Wait for the order!" boomed the dutiful second.

Just then, the cloud swirling around Denn parted and he nearly collided with a burly, exhausted porter. Behind the man spanned a long, wooden pole and more carriers who were transporting an armoured palanquin that could only belong to Prince Ramid.

It was the realization of the Lord Marshal's fears. The boy, freed of his dominating but rational general, had pressed the attack under dangerous circumstances, to contest for an unconquerable objective. Denn knew that the Marshal could not be here. The old man was bleeding out in the bathhouse far behind them, after the knife wound received from the princess.

The mass of dead and dying bore witness to the prince's folly. Rather than coax the enemy out of their stronghold and into a counterattack, Ramid had run his men headlong into slaughter against the citadel's defences. Worse, his failure was unknowingly feeding and bolstering the ranks of Dagremahr's army of the dead.

Denn looked back upon the mist rising from the freshly slain. Somewhere cloaked within, Dagremahr was harvesting and consuming the fruit of his bloodlust. The battle-hungry Paragon would be revelling in tonight's massacre.

By engineering such a confrontation, Denn's brother had delivered on his promise, and somehow, Lehn would win Ravon through this. Only Dagremahr knew how to separate the conjoined souls that Golmarra melded together.

"You're taking too long!" Prince Ramid shouted from his steel-clad cell. Denn could sense the young leader was struggling to sound regal and bold, but it was a difficult feat from inside the conspicuous security of his box.

A troop of men in ruby-red plate armour surrounded the prince's privileged conveyance, awaiting a more specific order. Their commander was a longish-haired soldier who would be handsome were it not for silvery scars that marred his cheeks and temple. He relayed Ramid's demands with added heft and authority.

"Perhaps..." said another man beside the fortified sedan, struggling to be heard. Denn knew the man to be Lord Khaem Wryn, having seen him at the council and having recognized him as

Ramid's boyhood tutor. In contrast to his appearance then, he now looked rather shabby and worn, and was dressed in an oversized vest of hardened leather to conceal his vitals.

"We are already committed to the attack, m' lord!" yelled the scarry-faced troop commander, shutting Wryn down abruptly.

"I said go!" shouted the prince from within his cage. His cadre of soldiers continued to mill about. Perhaps they took it as simple arbitration to end the nascent squabble between the two officers. They remained still and seemed surprised when the prince began reiterating the words, "Go! Go now! Go, go, go!" and they were jolted by the realization they finally had been given direction.

"Go!" repeated the troop commander superfluously.

A banner was hoisted to signify the next push, fluttering ineffectively against the grey cloud that hung about them. It was doubtful that anyone besides the prince's retinue would even see it. But the commander's word carried, and the order to charge percolated through the mist on powerful voices. The human war machine geared up to test fate again.

Where was Ramisa in all of this? Was she watching? Was she safe somewhere? Denn slinked further back, trying to remain unnoticed, but a guard in red pointed a metal-gauntleted hand at him. The easily deduced meaning sent a shudder rippling through Denn's anxiety-stricken innards. Toward the citadel, Denn ran fiercely, joining in the charge as indicated, but once out of sight, he dropped to a cautious creep. He had to find the princess.

Screams pierced the air ahead, signifying another futile escapade for the prince's army. More soldiers were dying. This time, the glow from behind the billowing banks of fog led Denn to conclude that the boiling oil had been set alight.

From shoulder height above the victim-strewn ground, the prince could be heard swearing and cursing. Denn looked over and saw the palanquin rocking. Ramid was evidently in the middle of a raging tantrum inside. The bars on its windows shielded their liege from onlookers, but the pole-bearers had to struggle to keep it aloft.

Denn squinted, realizing he could see the sedan more clearly now. The fog was lifting. Had Dagremahr feasted enough? What cause had he to dispel the spectral haze now? Denn used the abrupt clarity to survey the scene.

The Pillarmen had done their job against all the odds. The

citadel remained unbreached, and the prince's army looked as if it was all but shattered. Ramisa was still nowhere to be seen.

The prince's army was pulling back from their latest assault, but Denn paused to observe one small section of men. Around these soldiers was a peculiar air of assuredness and fearlessness. They marched across the field defiantly, clad in blue and holding glistening swords in their hands that reflected the black of the night sky above. At their centre, Denn recognized the face of his father; Dagremahr was leading his pack of scavengers across the field of battle and as they went, they pierced the wounded with their dark blades, one-by-one, poisoning their passage to the afterlife. Each corpse released its former host as if exhaling a final, sighing breath. The wraith-like remnants, now conscripted into the Paragon's army, ascended to circle above their new master in a lazy cyclone which followed him as he sauntered along.

Even though Phon's soul was already evicted from its body, Denn could not help but see his father's face upon the venerable old form that stood out among the others so imperiously. It was the same judging eyes, in their merciless severity, that had looked down on him with patronizing conceit throughout his whole life.

But the reaper's corps did not pass unnoticed. Ramid called out for his men to chase the brazen interlopers from the field, not knowing that time had run out.

Beside Dagremahr, a lone crossbowman raised his weapon under a silent order. Before the bolt left the weapon, the wicked warlord reached out, and with Phon Wellum's slender finger, he gave the projectile his blackened blessing. The shaft of the bolt became like polished ebony as it absorbed the enchantment that Denn recognized right away.

As the crossbowman squeezed the release, the bolt cut through the air toward the prince's palanquin. Against the inky backdrop of night, it appeared to be sheathed in a glow. It arced astoundingly as it flew, as if knowing its course. It passed untouched by the audience of soldiers, evading head and helm, until it disappeared through the barred slits of the prince's tiny, impregnable encasement. The prince's barking ceased, and everyone knew instantly that young Ramid had been pierced by the mortal missile.

Everywhere, soldiers were standing with mouths agape and

eyes stretched wide. All were shocked and wordless. Lord Wryn demanded the sedan be lowered. With effort, the red guards broke open its locks, and threw wide the doors, confirming the decisive damage.

The only sound that resonated was a woman's shrill scream.

Ramisa, too, had viewed the crossbow bolt find its mark and dispatch her only brother. She stumbled over herself at the sidelines, appearing small and alone, a hundred strides away from Denn across the battlefield.

Denn raced toward her, conscious that her wail had irredeemably drawn danger toward her. He fought to reach Ramisa before anyone else, pushing through the ranks of soldiers as they collapsed and crumbled in disarray, and more importantly before Dagremahr could get to her—or ready another crossbow bolt.

"Run!" he called out to Ramisa when it looked like he might not close the distance in time. Startled, she turned toward him in apparent recognition. She heeded his warning and ducked quickly out of sight behind a stone wall.

Denn knocked aside the dead prince's aimless and demoralized troops, clearing a path and hastened his stride until his lungs burned, and he was beside her.

"My brother," she stammered. "And my father... *Your brother... he killed...*"

"The same brother who sought to kill *me* on Bridgecliff," Denn said, searching for breath, "because I chose to serve you."

They embraced tightly for just one brief instant. There was no time for long consoling. They needed to find a way out. Denn hunted, but instead of an escape route, he discovered only his father emerging from behind them.

Or at least, it was the ill-begotten visage of his father that stood gloating and brandishing a corrupted, black cutlass.

"I can't tell which of you is staring at me," Denn said acerbically. "If it's you, Dagremahr, then you do great justice in mimicking my father's scowl."

Against the backdrop of mayhem that was unfolding, Denn positioned himself against the monstrous merging. Here were the two most cunning and cruellest men he had ever known—neither truly living nor dead. His father's gaunt and strained physique was visible, but its new host appeared to have animated it with an unreal vitality, such that its limp muscles were now taut and sinewy over his long, curved bones. Most fearsome, however, was the aura of unnaturalness around him, unseen yet perceptible.

"I've collected many soldiers for my army tonight," the warlord bragged morbidly.

"Then you've won," Denn said. "Take them. Honour your deal with my brother if you choose but leave Ramisa and me alone. Two more souls will mean nothing to you."

"Not all souls hold the same value," he corrected. "Though I am happy to replenish my ranks, my sisters remain trapped in corporeal bondage. How dare your low-born priests defile a Paragon's essence in such a way or try to impede our rightful place and power."

"Then extend your bargain to uncouple Lyseia from Ramisa as you would Centurra from Ravon. I would not deny you that. Let them both return with you," Denn pleaded but felt the request to be unaccountably hopeless. Perhaps irrationally, he could not shake the impression that he was asking his father for a favour, and he had learned since boyhood that Phon Wellum refused to grant charity to anyone, even his own offspring.

"Gladly. I will grant equal fates upon their hosts. You can be assured," Dagremahr answered.

Denn's mind instinctively was roiled with suspicions.

"How?" he demanded.

"You know the answer," replied the warlord. "Step aside and you won't have to die, Denn."

"You lied to my brother. There's no other way!" Denn choked, now that the truth of Dagremahr's intentions was displayed.

Dagremahr shook his head, and a rough cackle slipped out. Its pitch and cadence were no different than Phon's when boasting of an impending triumph. "The sword provides way enough."

"You'll not slay Ramisa so long as I stand between you," Denn replied. "Nor will you harvest any more souls in Caphedra tonight. There too, I will stop you."

"A hollow pledge," Dagremahr declared. "Centurra and Lyseia are my sisters. They suffer, but I will restore them and free them from their bindings of flesh."

"Not if I put you to the sword first!" Denn took a step forward with Olen's sword raised, keeping himself positioned between the princess and the Paragon. Coldswept hummed eagerly.

More laughter erupted as Dagremahr stretched out his arms and flexed. He swirled his cutlass in a lazy fashion, as if working out the stiffness in Phon's joints. His adopted muscles were small, but they were tight and rippled now, like chain links across his stark chest and arms.

"Why would you kill your father, Denn? Weren't the two of you in league together?"

"I have chosen my path. He knows it—and he will be no part of it," Denn said, Coldswept at the ready. He realized that their standoff was beginning to draw stares from a handful of sharp-eyed onlookers distributed in pockets across the approaches to the citadel.

"Do you know that your father still speaks to me? He says you were the honourable son." Then Dagremahr's voice morphed and creaked. "Don't kill me, my son. I love you!"

What might have elicited a pang of mercy in others only served to empower Denn. Even an entity like Dagremahr could not have known that his foe held a lifetime's worth of resentment for the man whose shell he had hijacked, and by the warlord's admission, there was no remedy. Dagremahr had condemned Phon to death, and it was offered to Denn to play executioner.

"You mock him!" He stomped toward Dagremahr and clenched his teeth. "If those are his real words, then he takes you for as much of a fool as he did me! My father is the source of our family's demise. My mother. My brothers. My sister dying now. I renounce him, and I will gladly cut you down and prove it!"

Denn was ready. With a tight grip on Coldswept, he widened his stance to wield the heavy blade better. As an adversary, Dagremahr would be at a disadvantage to manipulate Phon's weak and unfamiliar body, but that did not discount the otherworldly warrior's prowess and battle sense, honed over the centuries since he had taken his first mortal steps on this earth—nor did it prepare Denn for the unknown powers with which such a deified immortal could avail himself.

Behind him, Denn could hear Ramisa muttering with an inner conflict. Perhaps she was confronting her Paragon, but the sudden commotion distracted him and allowed Dagremahr to slash first.

Sidestepping the cutlass swing quickly, Denn felt it cleave the air around him. One touch of that blade, if it cut the skin, would be fatal. He knew this because of Trin. Even a small wound would not heal until Denn was purged of blood and woke up in his next life as a slave to this same beast who was coming at him now.

"Denn!" Ramisa called to him. "Let me help you!"

Angling sideways, Denn made probing jabs to enforce the distance been him and Dagremahr.

"Stand back!" he ordered. "Don't get near him! You can't help."

"Lyseia can help," she replied.

The princess could not control the entity within her, and why would her Paragon levy aid now? Lyseia had spent years trying to drive Ramisa either to accept her or to take her own life and free her. Why wouldn't the Paragon of Purpose invite Dagremahr to strike a killing blow? Could she even provide help without Ramisa first giving in and surrendering to her?

"Do not!" Denn yelled at her. "Do not give yourself over to Lyseia. There is no way to reverse it!"

"She promises to help!" Ramisa replied.

"She lies!" Denn yelled at her.

Should Lyseia align with Dagremahr that would seal Ramisa's outcome and Denn would be forced to turn his blade against her too.

Laughter overtook Dagremahr, who expelled a deafening wheeze of air that streamed from him like the buzzing cacophony of swarming cicadas. "If you fear death, dear girl, give up yourself to Lyseia—then I will not have to pierce your soft chest!"

"Never!" Denn shouted at him, understanding now. From the start, his foe had planned to kill Ramisa to release her Paragon. But why Ravon? Hadn't she embraced Centurra?

Denn advanced with a vicious swing toward Dagremahr, sending the fiend backward. Coldswept was the only advantage he could think of. *He must recognize this sword*, Denn thought. Temis had said that Olen's sword had shattered Yael's flamberge when the latter was cursed in the temple corridor. Denn swung again, hoping to connect with the black cutlass.

"You won't defeat me," Dagremahr chided.

"If you were invincible, you would never have died in the first place!" Denn shot back.

Whirling his blade furiously, Denn tried to goad Dagremahr into parrying, to force him into offering up the black blade.

But as he closed toward his adversary, he heard Ramisa's voice become muffled. He turned to look, but his eyes were met by the thick, creeping mist. The swirling clouds had descended around the confrontation, and the rest of the battlefield was also again becoming vague. Was Dagremahr hiding? Everything became lost in indistinguishable oblivion, save for his father's voice in the fog.

"You will enjoy my realm, Denn. Whatever Lyseia has told you of your purpose, know that you will serve alongside the hundreds... the *thousands* whom I already command."

It would be easy to get turned around without the benefit of sight. If he moved aside, or changed his stance or facing even slightly, he risked losing track of his enemy altogether. Worse, should he get completely disoriented, he might strike out and inadvertently hit Ramisa.

But what Denn could not see, *Coldswept sensed.* Like a huge needle on a compass, its hilt quivered when held out in what could only be Dagremahr's direction. Summoning his determination, Denn chanced one desperate strike through the fog.

"I will never answer to you!" Denn cried out. Coldswept whirled around him, from right to left, in a dangerous radius. Denn felt the two swords connect as the shockwave vibrated down Coldswept's hilt. There was a splintering of metal as Dagremahr's blade fractured and shards jetted out in all directions. Denn felt a stab of pain as one of the pieces lodged into his shoulder.

Denn was barely able to see more than a few hand widths around him, but he felt his arm grow slick and wet. He wanted to hide the wound, to ignore it, or discount it. For all he knew, Dagremahr could detect his injury like a predator smelled blood.

But maybe, perhaps, the black blade needed to be whole for the curse to work. If only he could hide in the mist long enough to hatch some scheme that would turn the tables and not pass out from the blood loss.

Denn's hopes were soon dashed when he looked out into the fog. Within it, he could see the perplexed and helpless faces of a legion of souls being dragged into the spiralling storm of aether. No longer did they appear as vacant-eyed phantoms, but he saw them rise out of the corpses and stand bewildered on the field where they died. And seeing them as flesh and bone instead of the doleful wisps that floated there before, Denn knew that he was about to join them. He was only grazed by the toxic shard, but the black blade's appetite for death was absolute and unnegotiable. The ranks of the fallen soldiers stood to receive him.

"Do you see?" Dagremahr asked. "I see *you* without any trouble, afraid. You try to withdraw, yet do not understand that, veritably, you *approach* me nonetheless. Your wound..."

Denn was dying. It was a slow bleed, but definitive in its outcome. As the realm of the living slipped away, he could make out Dagremahr's spectral form in front of him, much like he must be materializing now before his foe. The warlord stood with the jagged remnants of his sword in hand. He had changed. Somehow, his enemy had grown bigger and more menacing. The true apparition of the Paragon had appeared, obscuring the body of his frail father.

"It is decided," he said coldly to Denn. "You have lost. Step aside and take pleasure that the princess shall be yours in death, if not in life. I have the power to grant that."

"No," answered Denn. Painfully, he kept Coldswept raised and at-the-ready, noticing that in this realm of half-death, the blade felt less heavy and the sapphires on its hilt sparkled with unexpected brilliance.

He also became aware of cries and curses rising behind him. He looked back to check on the princess, to see two people return his gaze—two people, sharing one space. Ramisa was there, shivering, and so was Lyseia. Denn recognized her from the statue that he had seen in the temple. It hadn't been a perfect likeness. She was not blindfolded, but she stood barefoot, just as the stone effigy had captured her. She also seemed more cogent than Ramisa had described until Denn detected a hint of delirium in her eyes.

"All curses to this woman!" Lyseia screamed. "Oh, how this one can be so weak in body but stubborn in mind! My lord, release me. I have been caged, but you can free me. Drain my spirit from this vessel that we may pass to our realm, and I may teach this one what it means to be so entrapped."

"Rest easy, my cherished sister. Together, I will restore you and Centurra to our realm," the warlord answered. Dagremahr stepped forward. He towered over Denn. His scaled armour was coal-black but tinged with a strange iridescence. A halo of thorns and spikes jutted out from the crown he wore, now truer in semblance to the great king of old.

"Hurry. Centurra has grown quiet!" Lyseia urged. "I am afraid for her. That sorcerer has killed our kind before, and I fear he has done so again!"

Denn was struck by the contrast between the two female forms behind him. Lyseia teetered maniacally as she coveted death, while Ramisa's face displayed abject terror and helplessness in silencing her inner demon.

What sorcerer? he wondered, perplexed.

Around the mayhem-strewn battlefield, those still alive spread out in terror, while the dead, began to form up. The swirling mass of souls was even more perceptible now. Denn could distinguish the forms and faces of individual men. Under the command of their demonic new lord, they were signalling their readiness for battle. Within their ranks stood the late fallen prince.

Denn could see the boy's unfortunate spectre in step with the others, leaving behind the sedan and the pale body still held in his former teacher's arms. Lord Wryn had remained with the dying prince long after the Marshal's loyalists dispersed. Now the prince was dead. At that moment, the pitiable pedagogue looked toward the scene of Denn's duel, but he gazed obliviously through the creature that had engineered the prince's murder, to look at Ramisa with fascination.

Suddenly, out of the dissipating mist, a voice rang out from across a vast distance. "You are unwanted in this world, Dagremahr. Be done with your shell and leave it now."

Denn strained to see who was speaking. The words carried on the wind but seemed to come from atop the citadel battlements. It was a man's voice, elderly but defiant and unafraid. He was soon joined by the words of an equally stern and threatening woman.

"Centurra is alive, but she is not yours to take, Dagremahr. She is mine, and neither will we bow to you."

Dagremahr craned his neck, cocked his head, and listened. "Centurra?" he whispered with uncertainty. "Where is she? Are you there?"

"I am Ravon, and in my body lies Centurra, but know that if you kill me, you will lose her. She will never be able to return to your realm. It is not as before."

Across two realms, the warlord frothed with anger. He clenched Phon's knobbly fists in one world while squeezing his own massive hands in the other, as if they were a pair of boulders.

"You impudent witch! Your death will release her back to me, and you will learn obedience at the same time. For your part in this desecration, I will make you and your sister beg for mercy for eternity."

Denn's fingers tensed as he lifted Coldswept. He could end this now if he could only get one clean swing.

"You will not dare harm me," declared the far-off voice of the woman. "I promise you, kill me now and you lose Centurra forever."

"Sister?" uttered Ramisa, timidly joining the discourse. "My sister." Her eyes opened wide as she searched for the source of the voice that she, too, could apparently hear.

"Return to us, Ramisa," the man interrupted. "Rejoin your sister in love and fealty, and let me show you the purpose of your twin selves."

"No!" Ramisa yelled then broke into sobs. "Denn, take me from here!"

"Dagremahr, you may have slain our brother, but you will not wipe out the Wolstett line," declared Ravon.

As she spoke, the air around Dagremahr began to sizzle and flicker with sparks of blue light. The warlord's body trembled, then became grotesquely rigid. An instant later, he dropped to his knees. The aura that Denn had once felt encircling Dagremahr began to waver, assailed now by another force. A powerful force.

Denn's heart was beating faster and faster. If the woman speaking was the Lady Ravon, then the man must invariably be her guardian: the storied and invincible Precept of the Faith of the Pillars, Averin Golmarra. He was the 'sorcerer' who desired to control the Paragons. Was it true that some had died at his hands? Had this man really killed his own gods?"

"Ravon will not surrender easily. She is a prodigy who has studied the artistry and manipulations of magic for her entire life," said Golmarra. "So have I... and I promise my lifetime has been much, much longer."

"And you forget that I have lived more than a lifetime!" responded the warlord.

"Yet you were never more than a mercenary, overpaid with glory and a misplaced promise of permanence. Worse, you were a dog, uncaged, only when needed."

"Insult me? I will show you my teeth... *my bite!*" Dagremahr planted his feet. From the pores of his body, he exuded fumes like black smoke which encircled him in a gyre before solidifying into a hailstorm of obsidian-like crystals.

But suddenly, Denn heard something snapping and popping. There was a crunch, and then another, and Denn realized that beneath the veneer of what he now saw as Dagremahr, his father's brittle, earthly bones were breaking.

"Your mortal body is weak. Vulnerable," Golmarra said.

Dagremahr, as if to disprove the Precept, stiffened his frame and, in fact, responded to the sorcerous attack by standing even taller. Then with a flick of his hand, he sent the black shards in unison, coursing toward the citadel wall like a thousand tiny knives. Denn could not see the result, but Dagremahr shouted jubilantly– until halted again by the voice of Golmarra.

"I warned you before that I hold sway over all migrations between life and death. I denied you from coming here, yet it seems you have found another way. It is of no consequence. We will return you to your realm and let you pillage the souls of the living no more."

Unhappy at being stymied, Dagremahr turned to where Ramisa and Lyseia coexisted. "Something is wrong. Where is Centurra?"

Denn too pondered why there was no voice calling out from the third Paragon, but his mind was too cloudy. He was growing faint from the loss of blood.

"She awaits the freedom of death, as I do!" Lyseia called out. "Dagremahr! Do not abandon me to be enslaved in this realm of dirt and mud. Will you not take this one's life?" she squealed and pounded with futility at the ground with fists that made no impact on the earth, before beginning to fade and blur. The two female figures appeared to consume each other and Ramisa cried out, writhing in apparent pain, her body twisting.

Lyseia's apparition coiled itself around its host, fighting for dominance. Ramisa convulsed and whimpered. Meekly she called out Avenda's name, but to no avail. Her whimpers became screams.

"Fight her, Ramisa!" Denn yelled, just as he saw another cloud of black smoke pouring forth from the air around Dagremahr, and reaching out, tendril-like, toward the warring souls of the women.

At least it seemed that way. Around the edges of Denn's vision, all was going black while his blood continued to drain unstaunched.

"Denn..." Ramisa prompted. "You must... I cannot..."

Despite how weak he had become, he heeded her command and sprung up like a wolf, lunging to attack before his foe could manifest a strike in response. Coldswept vibrated in his hand, anticipating the blow. For a fraction of a heartbeat, he saw his father before him, yet he did not hold back. The slice cut through Phon's body—through Dagremahr—just above the waist. It went so cleanly through that it took a full moment before the waxy entrails slipped completely from his gut. The blood pulsed out and pooled around him—thin, watery, and sick-looking.

The steel blade rang out in triumph; its sapphire-encrusted hilt lit up with an even brighter glow of celestial blue the likes that planets would envy. The warlord was gone. In his place were left the remains of just one man: an ill-fated merchant and cruel progenitor. The half-fragmented sword that had fallen to the ground beside him returned to an unremarkable grey din, as if forged from lead.

Behind Denn, Lyseia's last forlorn cries sounded like echoes around the castle walls. The two forms began merging, their struggle ended with one, teary-eyed but victorious, and buoyant with exhilaration; the other wailed in despair as she was subsumed back into her mortal prison.

The grim mist that had marked the ghostly legion dissipated. While it may be too late for those already dead, Denn was convinced there was some form of salvation at hand for the wounded and infirmed—including himself. He gripped his shoulder and saw the blood from his wound was beginning to clot. Earnestly, he prayed that the same respite might be granted to Serenn, now that Dagremahr's influence was gone from this world.

But that did not mean they were safe. Already, the Pillars were sending soldiers to collect Ramisa, and another frighteningly familiar voice bellowed out.

"Any man that can walk is a man who can carry a torch!"

Lord Marshal Incis Myrhic reappeared. Though the general was staggering, he refused the support of others to help him stand or navigate the battlefield. Briefly, he looked over the prone body on the palanquin before disparagingly ordering his men to ignore it and withdraw.

"We are regrouping!" he explained, choosing to avoid the word retreat. "Bring the princess. Do not let the enemy capture her first."

Hearing this, Denn turned and grabbed Ramisa by the arm. "We have to run! They're coming for us!"

Pandemonium was erupting with the Lord Marshal's return. Commanders began shouting to their captains, who then called to their sergeants. They, in turn, harangued what remained of their sparse formations, grabbing onto any threadbare and battle-oppressed survivors, and establishing an order of march. Trumpets sounded from atop the intact citadel wall as fresh contingents of Pillarmen likewise assembled to march out and hurry the Marshal's withdrawal.

Holding Ramisa by the hand, Denn tried leading her away from the plaza, but there was no route open. The Marshal had sent men to surround them and block their escape. Should they somehow slip past, a column of Pillarmen was also stepping off to intercept them, and their captain was eying Denn and Ramisa threateningly.

There was no choice. Denn raised his sword and bellowed, "Get out of the way or be cut down! Who dares to challenge the man who killed a god?!"

His bravado failed. The living appeared to have less regard for Dagremahr's menace. They had only seen Phon Wellum, after all. To them, he had not killed a god. He had only renounced–then killed–an old man, who happened to be his father. Despite having observed Phon Wellum walking in step with the Pillarmen, in many minds, Denn feared that the crime of patricide would transcend any allegiances.

Already exhausted, Denn was left with no other option. He swung his sword as intimidatingly as he could. "Run!" he pleaded to Ramisa. "I'll hold them off as best I can."

But before they could move, miraculously, Denn's fight was taken up by a squad of burly, red-shouldered protectors who flooded his flanks. The prince's men positioned themselves in an unyielding perimeter, promising violence against the Marshal's forces if they approached. Those who attempted to seize the princess were violently set upon and expertly driven back.

Denn fell back and came face-to-face with the captain of the scarlet line, who announced himself.

"Jeddin Sadirus. Captain of the Prince's Guard by way of the Queen's Guard. I served her mother."

"Denn Wellum," Denn answered back almost speechlessly. He needed a moment to catch his breath. "I serve the princess... that's all."

Captain Sadirus nodded and flashed a smile. His men encircled them like the walls of an ironstone tower, but a narrow pathway opened that led away from the fray and out of the plaza.

"Lord Wryn has asked that we pass along his endless affection for the princess—and to request that you bear her far away from here!" He finished by saying, "He asks that you keep her safe, sir."

More soldiers were mustering on all sides, seeking Denn and Ramisa's capture, but the Prince's Guard persisted in holding them at bay. The stalemate would not last forever, however.

Denn looked toward where Lord Wryn kept a vigil over the dead prince and gave a nod of thanks. Another squad of crimson soldiers, which included the battle-scarred commander, were making ready to carry the boy's body from the field.

Turning to the princess, Denn was relieved to see her inner demon had subsided and Ramisa looked unharmed.

"Hurry, Denn," she implored, then grabbed his hand and together they briskly sped off through the protected gap.

Behind them, great fires were burning, and smoke was creeping into the sky.

❖   ❖   ❖

As soon as they had evaded the dangerous eyes of their would-be captors, Denn pointed at the ground where an iron grating rested atop an opening.

"Down here. We'll be safe," he told the princess, then pried open the barrier to reveal access to the city's underground architecture. As soon as they were through, he set the bars back in place across the entrance hole and began feeling his way in the darkness to where Caphedra's catacombs began.

Much of his navigation was guesswork. He and the princess held on to each other tightly and closely, so as not to lose each other in the pitch-black passages. Every time he came across an accommodating crack or another unattended grating, he would lift himself up and gain his bearings from the starlit street above. Though the tunnels were unfamiliar, he knew the manors and villas of Castleside well enough, and after a long trek through musty crypts and cobwebbed corridors, he finally spied his own former home and crept along a tunnel toward it.

Denn did not dare knock at the trapdoor to summon Brae. He knew his family kept a small oil lamp by the entrance, and thankfully its reservoir was full. He had a small piece of flint in his pocket. With his knife, he scraped and produced a smattering of sparks which were caught by the oily wick. It ignited and gave off a comforting light that reflected in Ramisa's doting eyes. She smiled. She was no longer shivering, though her newfound warmth was more from the exertion of their flight than from the heat of the lamp.

"We're going to leave this city," he promised. "Finally."

She nodded placidly, but the corners of her lips fell to a frown. "I can smell smoke drifting through," Ramisa said.

"The Marshal threatened to burn the city, and I think he's making good on it," Denn said.

He leaned tiredly against an earthwork wall beneath his family manor house. All around him lay the remains of generations of Wellums, yet he felt oddly out of place now. He tried to ignore that his victory had come at the expense of killing the reigning head of the family—the man that sired him—no matter how justified it was. His brother, too, was left dying with an open lung. His mother was dead. His sister was quite possibly dead.

Denn sat down next to his dead brother, who had preceded all the others. In a way, that death precipitated all others, though Denn was unwaveringly in fixing the blame for his family's fall upon the schemes and ambitions of his father.

Denn placed his hand on a stone relief of the family crest. His shadow in the lamplight ebbed and flowed over it as he swayed with fatigue. He could feel the honeybee beneath his fingers and traced its outline.

"How is your shoulder?" Ramisa asked, but Denn ignored her inquiry.

He was an outlaw now, disowned, and diminished, but he had made good on his pledge to the princess.

"Sit down and rest for a moment," he said. Then ducking down, he stooped and crept to where his uncle Phar was interred. Reaching into the promised hiding spot, he retrieved Yael's satchel and used the lamplight to look inside.

"What is it," Ramisa asked, but again Denn kept tight-lipped.

In the dim illumination, he made out some marginally legible papers, bundled together along with a jingling of coin and jewelry. He scanned the parchment papers.

Years ago, Yael had procured land and title for his uncle, Phar, in the lower reaches of Darrow. Denn's uncle had never lived long enough to lay claim to the land in person, but the document was signed and sealed. It was legally purchased. Furthermore, Yael had seen fit to bundle it with Phar's will and that held a further boon. His uncle, being the second son himself, had seen fit to bequeath his possessions to Denn rather than Hann.

Phar could not have foreseen Hann's death, or the passing of the Wellum heirship to Denn—no matter how temporary. If Denn's apostasy did not prevent him from being declared heir to his family's fortune, surely the public renunciation and killing of his father would irredeemably disentitle him. The Faith of the Pillars now ruled Caphedra and whether Lehn survived or not, they would recognize their curate, Denn's little brother, as holding title to the Wellum wealth, and would seize every golden sire or dame in the family's name, held in any vault from Stonerow to Highside.

Yael knew how fortuitous these documents would be for Denn. Phar's inheritance fell outside Caphedra's purview. It was quite likely that the Faith did not know of Phar's clandestine holdings so far afield from the city. Other papers showed that the inventory of arms, which Denn's father had paid for, had been secreted there under Yael's direction—to be received by one Hendrik

Stamish. This provided the most proof that Yael was convinced of the seclusion of the place. Here was a hidden retreat that would provide refuge to him and Ramisa–a place called *Endgreen*.

This posthumous instance of unexpected generosity made Denn more deeply regret the loss of Longlimb, his uncle's sword. So, he thought, maybe, that he could adopt something else in remembrance of his uncle. Let Lehn keep the Wellum honeybee. Denn unhooked Phar's shield from its place of rest. Satisfied that it was sturdy enough to be of use, he strapped it to his arm.

In that moment, he adopted the more ancient Wellum sigil of the salamander, in both gratitude and solidarity with his late uncle, who had fought across Hasen with the mythic beast painted on this very shield, and who was somehow watching out for him.

"Are you fit to travel again?" Denn called to Ramisa.

She remained silent for a moment, appearing surprised to hear his voice finally, but eventually nodded. "We should try to find our way soon. I feel something has happened."

"The battle's lost to the Faith and the city's aflame," Denn replied.

"No. There is more. Lyseia still haunts me," she began, then furrowed her eyebrows in concern. "But all the other Paragons have gone quiet."

"More than just Centurra?" Denn asked.

"All of them," Ramisa said.

"Then maybe we have achieved something," Denn suggested with a weak smile. He laid his hand gently on her shoulder. "Get up," he encouraged her. "The streets are dangerous, but we must make our way to Westriver. I have friends there who are loyal and trustworthy. They will help us escape Caphedra."

CHAPTER 37

The Blackened Night

O len and the half-dozen other harried returnees from the temple were ejected from the dusty granite wall, each with a thud and a puff of grainy dust as if the stone exhaled or coughed them out. The dank, wet algal odour of the Darrow River hung on the warm breeze where they landed, and Olen could hear the unconcerned current as it rushed along the riverbank nearby.

It was dark. He knew that much.

But suddenly, a radiant brightness in front of his face expanded to fill the limited scope of his damaged eyes. It smelled like a torch burning, and he felt its dry warmth reflecting off his cheeks.

"Good. You're back." Bull greeted them. The barkeep's brash and irreverent voice was unmistakable.

Olen started to take a step forward but thought better of it. "Livet!" he called out instead, looking for a shoulder to lean on, or a hand to guide him.

"It doesn't look like she's with you," Bull said. "She's run off, maybe?" Where's that other fella? She with him? And what's the crud on your face? Why do you look so dazed?"

Helpless to look for her, Olen could only call again. "Livet! Livet?"

Someone grabbed his arm with a firm grip. "I've got you, Olen. It's me, Effie." At first, Olen felt tense, but soon relaxed and swallowed his regrets, resigning himself to being led by the boy.

Bull could be heard muttering a curse. Then Olen smelled the licorice as two hands seized him by the cheeks and swivelled his head for examination. He grumbled and slapped the hands away, promising "It's just temporary."

"You hope," said Bull. "Is that how you lost your sword, too? Leave it sitting around somewhere? Not much of a squire, this lad you came back with is." Effie lurched to the side, tugging at Olen's arm. Bull must have given him a swat.

"I lent my sword out to someone with better eyes and more use for it," Olen said. "It's with Denn. He'll make good of it, then I'll have it back in my hands tonight." He huffed and pondered aloud, "Where, by the Oath, is Livet?"

Effie let out a dismal grunt beside him. "She didn't come through the... wall... with the rest of us. Gone after Wellum, I expect."

"Mister Wellum, to you," Bull corrected. "That man was the providential benefactor who helped us get your sisters out of that predicament with Dance's boys. Heck, the man's in league with a royal princess. You will show him some respect."

If the dressing down made any impression, it went unanswered, but Olen felt Effie's hand slip from his arm, and he knew the boy had walked away.

Olen was not abandoned for long, however. A smaller, softer hand soon latched onto his arm, replacing Effie's.

"Uncle," Neriah said, announcing herself to him. "Gardia is looking after Baressa and the Wellum girl. Temis told me you were blinded. I came right away." She called for someone to bring water and a moment later was delicately dabbing around his eyes with a wet cloth. "Can you see *anything*?" she asked.

"Darkness. Some shapes perhaps," Olen said uncomfortably.

"Give it time." Neriah stopped fussing with the goopy residue on Olen's face but remained steadfast in holding onto him. The big man rested one of his huge-knuckled mitts upon hers to show her his appreciation, but he sighed in frustration, nonetheless.

"Bull! Are you still here?" Olen asked. He listened to the voices of more of his comrades milling about. In the distance, Nyrim was issuing a litany of orders, as if he were a seasoned sergeant.

"Still here, old friend," came the answer from an arm's length away.

"Get me a sword and lead me to the Midbridge. Even if I can't see, it might do a speck of good if anyone trying to cross sees me beside you all. One more soldier in a show of strength—pardon my present uselessness—might help dissuade a few otherwise braver men." He leaned in toward Neriah and asked in a low voice, "Can you tell me if you see Denn? I've got to watch out for him. He'll be coming this way, looking for a place to hide out."

"I don't see him yet," she said sympathetically.

Despite Neriah guiding him, the path through the streets to Midbridge was tedious, and in Olen's mind, shameful. On the arm of his niece, he was a poor image for a warrior. His job now, if he could manage to look fitting of the ploy, would be to act as a scarecrow. Nothing more.

Someone—Kalden, he believed—ran up to him and offered him a broadsword. Olen could not see to appraise it, but he could feel it. Mindful to not swing it anywhere that might accidentally cut through a man—or Neriah, for that matter—he held it up and paid heed to its balance. He ran his finger down the blade to confirm its length and gently, with his thumb, he tested its edge.

"It's sharp," Olen pronounced.

"Why wouldn't it be?" Neriah asked as she guided him along.

"Given the circumstances, it'd be the sort of thing Bull would do, to give me a dull blade in case I accidentally got carried away and hurt someone with it," he said, adding, "He's a bit of a worrier."

She laughed, "Smart man. There would be fewer people for me to mend afterward."

Under his feet, the course of the cobblestones sloped upward, and Olen could smell a fresher, cooler breeze overtaking the sultry doldrums that hung between the crowded old buildings. It came from the north and cleansed the scent of effluents from the river air. It worked to strip away some of the lingering sweat from his neck and forehead, leaving him reinvigorated. He remembered how even as summer dawned on Caphedra, the nights would often bring a chill to Westriver while sparing many other neighbourhoods and he looked forward to it.

"Your post," Neriah said as she halted him. Then with both hands, she forced him to pivot slightly and straighten up. "The enemy is this way. Good luck!"

"Wait... what?" Olen sputtered.

Neriah reassured him, "I'm not leaving you. It was just in jest. I'm sorry."

Olen relaxed.

Lights from across the river seeped through the sightless void. Everything remained blotchy and undefined, but he did his best to identify the brightest spots and take his bearings off them. Somewhere to the east, the Temple of the Faith of the Pillars was burning, and two armies were clashing.

"Any sign of Livet?" Olen asked.

"If she doesn't return, Gardia said she'd send Harbud out to look for her," Neriah said.

"Good... and Bull?" he called.

"Yup," came the surly response as the barkeep hacked and spat phlegm. "On your right."

"How do the men look?"

"Lonely would be the word I'd use," he answered. "Including us, we're only ten in number."

Olen took a breath and sighed. "That's it then. They're all on the bridge?"

"Yep. Two ranks of four each," Bull said. "I took the liberty of making Nyrim an acting sergeant to step in where Eysman was. He's holding the line with his nephew, Talton, and Gastun. The reserve rank has the other two elvers, Asher and Effrem, with Tomton and Vyr in the centre to keep them in line. Each can switch out with the one behind if they get tired, or if they... well, you know."

Olen muttered his approval then waited. With his boot, he kicked at the crumbling pave stones on the bridge floor. When he grew tired of that, he scratched at the bridge's parapet wall, dislodging other rocks, which he tossed into the stream below.

Far away, the nightly noises of the city were lost. They were drowned in the sea of shouts and cries as the Marshal's army pressed toward the citadel. By now, the battle might even be decided. Soon they would encounter the survivors in retreat. Olen anxiously asked again, "Do you see Denn yet?"

Neriah sighed.

"Anything? Has Livet come back?"

"I'll tell you what I see," said Neriah. She drew closer to him and wrapped an arm casually about his waist, her words cast directly into his ear. "I see the big storehouses and granaries of the Blocks, just beyond the bridge–they're quiet. The piers at Dockside are bare, save for the odd net left out to dry. The boats have been pulled up and, I think, taken inside. The river flows but the water's low for this time of year. Looks like someone's lost a barrel. You can see it floating downstream past the Potshollow docks."

"What of the soldiers? Any men approaching? Whose are they?" Olen asked.

"None that have paid us any mind yet. There are a few arriving now but they are busy rummaging the stores across the river. Looting and stealing what they can, I suppose. A heap of them didn't come here to fight, I expect. They probably just wanted to fill their bellies and pockets one last time before the whole city crumbles."

This time, Olen reserved his judgement. Hundreds of those men were likely in the same predicament as him. Had it not been for the generosity of Bull and Gardia with their liberal stew pots, Olen would have gone hungry. He never did recoup much of his own cache of coin.

"Wait," Neriah said. "That looks bad..."

"What is it?"

"The sky was full of stars when we came out here, but it's hazing over. It's all smoky, though I see a bit of light behind the buildings. They've set fires!"

"That's an ill omen," said Olen. "Stonerow and the Folds mightn't fare too bad if they get it under control early, but it's bound to catch the wooden homes in Porter's Run and spread quickly there. The city's too busy fighting itself to put down the flames. If it gets to Middlehold, everything east of the river could go up."

"I don't think anyone is in a position to put out the flames with the fighting that's going on," his niece commented.

Olen now was sure that he smelled smoke on the breeze.

"If it comes this way, we should all consider taking up some hasty religion so we can pray the sparks don't jump the river," Bull interjected.

Neriah murmured in agreement then squeezed Olen's wrist to get his attention. "A man's trying to cross the bridge." She hesitated, then added, "Your men don't seem too concerned."

"Eh?" Olen prompted. "What sort of man?"

"It looks like Red!" Bull said, then for Neriah's benefit added, "He's our old captain."

The man hollered, "Bull! Olen! Is that the pair of you back there? Where's Eysman?" Olen heard the sound of a few friendly pats and shoulder slaps which became scuffs and shuffling as their old leader, Captain Redwyn Ersmine, wormed his way through the thin Westriver line. Olen tried to avoid making eye contact and giving away his weakness. So, he listened for the sound of Bull's voice and turned his head in that direction instead, as if his fellow sergeant had his full attention.

It took no time at all for Red to dredge up his earlier appeal, just as he had presented to Olen in Falbeth.

"Come with me!" he said. "This city is going to be flat by morning. Me and some others are falling back to Wodwarden to start a new company. I'd be overjoyed to have you all back!"

"Why are you leaving in your moment of victory?" asked Bull. "What of the prince? Is he not to be king by the 'morrow?"

"The prince's war is over. He took an arrow to the chest," Red said darkly. "Incredibly poor luck. I'm surprised that I am the first to tell you."

"What of the Marshal, then?" Bull continued. "Is he not pushing the attack anyway? I didn't think this had much to do with the prince, to begin with."

"Maybe he had a change of heart. There is a rumour that reached the line saying old Myrhic ran afoul of the king's ghost, and it gave him a warning—or maybe he only wanted to destroy the city, out of spite, in the first place. Who knows the truth? The fact is the men are dispersing. They are heading back to our stronghold in the north, but I expect we'll be back in Caphedra by harvest. You still have an opportunity to earn your place in our ranks."

"Your offer's appreciated," said Bull. "It's not in the stars for me, but you've said your piece and none of the men are obliged to stay. Ask them."

The answer was immediate. Red's offer was uniformly declined by all his old company—though awkwardly, Olen thought. The men had once been willing to follow their captain across the whole of the southeastern swamps but now they would go no further together.

All save for one lone voice which diverged from the consensus. "I'll go," said Effie. "It's time I venture out and make my name."

A whisper from Bull was laden with concern. "Damn him. If he's serious, someone should go with the welp. Those savages will grind him right up," he said.

"Effie, what about your sisters?" Olen questioned, hoping to discourage the rash adventure.

"My sisters are safe now. I can do no better for them as simple as I am," he answered.

Talton was next heard by Olen, commenting privately. "I've got to look after Krystlen and Yarma. I can't run off and play nursemaid. He knows what he's getting into, Sergeant."

"No, you're right," said Olen in agreement. "And now that Gastun's back with Malee, they deserve a life together, too. Everyone's got a family to keep, or at least a woman at their side."

"Some of us have quite a few women," interjected Vyr.

"Is there any man among us who wishes to be a soldier anymore?" Olen asked loudly. He could not read their faces, but he could tell by their silence.

"Me," said a curt voice at the front that could only have come from Asher. "I'll go with you, Effie."

Right away, however, Effie shut him down. "This is my road, Asher. You go your own way."

Not one to fan the rivalry, Asher conceded. "Then let us meet again as friends. I wish you safe travels, Effie. I'll miss you."

Those last words were levied with sincerity and took the edge off Effie's bile. The wounded pride that usually marred his speech was temporarily patched enough to allow him to answer meekly and heartfully, "I'll be as good as you someday, and then we will meet as *true friends*."

"Well, if there's no one else coming..." Red prodded.

"Listen to your captain," Tomton advised. "And good fortune to you, lad."

"Give all my love to Sandri and Kelzi," replied Effie at last. Ahead on the bridge, boots scraped the dust and mail jingled as the men shuffled and spread to fill the gap.

Olen wanted to call out his own farewell, but he sensed that Effie had already left them. Instead, he stood stoically and paid heed to the change in the wind. "The draft is from the west now. The wind's changing direction."

"You're right. The blaze is growing and getting brighter," said Neriah. "I hadn't been watching. The fire's drawing the air toward itself. I can see the flames towering over the midtown of the city. It looks terrible."

"As I said, pray it doesn't cross the river," Bull added.

"It'll drive people our way. All the more important to guard the bridges. What are we down to? Seven fit men?" Olen sighed.

Bull grumbled. "Depends on what you deem fit. Little Nyrim—er, Kalden—is still too young to be here, and Tomton's only got one good leg, in case you hadn't kept track. Though, each one of his legs is as thick as the pair on any other man, quite honestly."

Olen sniffed at the air. The breeze was being drawn eastward, but he definitely smelled more smoke. It was inescapable. He could hear people milling about on the opposite shore now. Panic was evident in their shouts and cries.

"Keep together!" he called out of habit, having no actual confirmation that they were anything but assembled into a tight, orderly formation.

"Yes, Sergeant!" someone replied, in a voice so gruff as to be indistinguishable.

"Tell them to keep moving!" Bull shouted past Olen, who had no idea whom his friend referred to. He could only assume that the people gathering on the far shore were showing their intent to cross the river to safety from the coming inferno.

"What about the women? The children?" called out one of the Westrivermen. It was Gastun, probably.

"I don't see any women and children," Bull yelled back. "I see a bunch of bloodthirsty axemen and leatherchests that want to burn down your home and drink your ale! Half of them look like murderin' mead-swillers from Northport! Do you want to share your roof with them? How about your bed?!"

Ayren would have to forgive Olen for laughing at that.

Again, Neriah squeezed her uncle by the wrist and alerted him. "Here comes the Queen of Westriver," she said.

"Gardia?" Olen asked.

"Her too!" Neriah joked. "She's here with Taringer and Her Ethereal Majesty, Celebra who is as shining and sparkling as ever." Then she poked him rudely. "You're blind. Stop smiling."

"Madame," Bull greeted the arrivals smartly.

"Where's the sightless oaf?" Gardia asked.

Olen wanted to reply, but something about her commanding presence choked the air and made him tense up and struggle for words. "Me?" he stuttered stupidly. He could feel her evaluating him before she even let on that she was looking. He could detect her sizing up the seriousness of his malady with her own eyes, levelling a glare that stabbed at him like the poke of a two-pronged fork. He did not need to see it to feel it.

"You can open your eyes, so I presume the pain is gone," she said, placing her fingers along the ridges of his eye sockets. He did not slap her hands away, as he had done to Bull's. As coarse as Gardia could be with him, her hands were soft and she smelled delicate, with a cross between jasmine petals and minty spruce that captivated his nose.

"The salve your friend used helped to weaken the toxin. It saved your eyes," she said.

"I'll see again, then? My sight will get better?" Olen asked.

Gardia's silence was unnerving, especially since he could not read the look on her face. "It will take time," she said. "The poison you encountered is rare. I am surprised that Temis was able to identify it, much less be the sort that would see fit to travel with a treatment for it. I must search out a remedy before I can promise you a cure." Olen was becoming agitated, but her reassuring grip—firmer than Neriah's—calmed him. "Be still," Gardia soothed. "There are other ways if we must."

"Where is Temis? I suppose I should thank him," Olen said.

"He's with the girl, Serenn," Gardia said.

"How is she? Denn will want to know as soon as he gets here."

He heard Gardia inhale a deep breath before answering. "It was a terrible wound. It was beyond my talents to help but somehow it finally stopped bleeding on its own. Although, I am afraid the injury will remain for the rest of her life. Whatever caused the wound infested the flesh rather unnaturally. It frightens me that the Faith could create a weapon that would leave such horrible injury."

"Denn said that the sword was cursed," Olen explained.

"Oh, very much so!" she said. "Poor girl. I may have Celebra work with her to ease her troubles as best we can. Maybe, we can find a way to hide the damage." Letting go of Olen, she passed direction. "Celebra, you should go back to the Peahen now."

A velvety voice replied, "I want to stay here. Nile will be returning, and I will need to tend to him. He may have information to pass along."

It was audible in her tone that Gardia did not like her orders countered, but surprisingly, she relented and coldly replied, "Very well. You may wait."

That left only one more of their party for whom Olen sought to inquire. "Baressa is well, I hope?"

"Her state is complex, but at least she's back with us," Gardia said. "I'll say no more for now. Besides, we have more immediate problems."

Behind him, he could hear Bull shouting again. Olen turned, still without any clarity of sight, but listening to pick up on what was happening. He could feel the evening air getting warmer when he turned back to the east. There, the glow repelled the darkness in Olen's eyes and left a murky brown, with streaks and splotches flaring across his vision when he tried to focus. "The fire is growing?" he inquired, safe to assume.

"If you could only see it," Neriah lamented. "It's gargantuan."

"Do you think it has reached Middlehold? Highside?" Olen asked.

She gasped. "I think some of the storehouses in Dockmarket have caught fire. If they go, the city will be without food."

A more powerful gust of wind hit Olen from behind. The fire was sucking air unto itself.

Beside him, Bull gruffly narrated the scene across the river. "The people are starting to flee the flames. They're huddling like rats on a log over there, pressing up against the Darrow to get away from the heat."

"The Faith is likely blocking the gates again," murmured Talton. "Forcing people to stay and fight the fire, rather than allowing them to flee, and letting it destroy the city."

"It's not working," Bull said.

Nyrim called back. "Sergeant, we can't force them all away. They'll be burned to cinders if Dockmarket and the Blocks catch!"

Olen cursed again that he was unable to see for himself. Livet and Denn were both still unaccounted for in the disaster that was unfolding. He could not abide by standing and waiting. Hope was a commodity that did not come easy to Olen.

Olen could feel the infernal hotness on his cheeks, and the air that had been so humid earlier in the evening was becoming parched. Behind him, the wind was howling as it dashed toward the river and fed the rising currents of air generated by the fire.

"No torches. No arms. But let them cross," Olen commanded.

Bull swore a litany of promised regrets but did not counter the order. He only added, "If you catch anyone looting, especially at the Eel, take an axe to them. No mercy to thieves or grifters!"

"We have to keep watching the bridge," Olen reminded. "Denn and Livet will know to find us here." He turned his head left and right out of habit, attempting to look, then asked, "Is Taringer still here?"

"I am," sounded a plain, steady voice from behind, near the Midbridge's northern wing wall.

"The wind listens to you. If you can manage, see that it doesn't change and start sending sparks to drift over here."

"I don't know that I have the reach, but I'll try," he pledged.

At once, he felt Neriah pull on him while Bull gripped him tightly and ushered Olen back. The barkeep smelled of spilled beer and, again, the spicy scent of licorice root clung to his breath. "Here they come. Don't get too close," he advised.

There was a vociferous uproar and the clamouring of the crowd as it rolled over the bridge. Olen raised his head to the sky and kept back as best he could. He was mistrustful and wary but helpless to spy anything that might be amiss with the Caphedran refugees now storming into Westriver. His company mates yelled and shouted, doing their best to herd the masses with calls of "Keep moving!" and "Watch yerself!"

He had expected to be fighting off infiltrators and scavengers, not obliged to orchestrate the desperate salvation of all the deprived and displaced of the city. What would happen next? How would the city rebuild? How would these people be fed? Such goodwill could be Westriver's undoing but there was no conscionable alternative.

Then there was a rumble.

The ground trembled with a massive boom from the east. It reverberated across the city. The crowds stopped their shouting and grew quiet, save for frightful gasps. No one knew what had caused the thunderous noise.

"What... was... that?!" Bull asked.

"Sounds like it came from the citadel!" said Gastun.

"Nah. It came from further south. It came from the temple!" argued Talton.

They wrestled with theorizing, perplexed and woefully agnostic of the cause of the apocalyptic intonation. Even the crowd's migration paused until Bull raised his voice and shouted, "Quit gawking and keep moving!" In short order, it was back to the rush of clamouring and shoving.

"Where's Livet?"

An arm seized Olen's shoulder, causing the warrior to go rigid and bristle at the impropriety until Neriah whispered to him, "Your friend. He's alive!"

"Denn?" Olen chanced to hope.

"Olen!" came the response. "Can you still not see? Yes, it's me, my friend—and I am not alone."

"Livet's with you?!"

"No," Denn said. He ushered Olen to the side, away from the passing multitude. "Someone else is with me. You must help us escape the city. The Pillarmen are barricading the gates again. We won't be able to pass through without being caught."

"You're safe to stay here as long as you need to," Olen offered.

"I don't know how long any of us will be safe here," Denn answered. "Where is Temis? He knows of some secret passages through the city wall, ones that my father used for smuggling. I am trusting he might know how to get us out."

"Who is it that's with you?" Curiosity overtook him and Olen swung his arm abruptly—and somewhat unmannerly—for it impacted on a thick woollen cloak that concealed Denn's companion. The form underneath was slender and emitted a feminine protest.

"The princess?!" Olen's impotent eyes widened.

"Shush," implored Denn. "She must not be recognized. They are looking for her. I must get her out of the city."

Olen's mind raced. "Where will you go?"

"I have refuge in the south," Denn said.

"Back in the bog?"

"No. I've a place in Darrow where we can find safety. But I would rather not say anymore until we are underway, and I'd appreciate if you kept even that morsel of knowledge from passing back through your lips."

Nodding with comprehension, Olen called over to where he surmised Bull would still be standing. "We need Temis! Now!"

"That shifty fellow with the twisty hair?" Bull asked, then immediately was heard enlisting Nyrim's nephew for help. "Fetch him, son. Tell him it's urgent."

CHAPTER 38

A Dangerous Dawn

O len had never known Denn to be so jittery or nervous. The fated protector of the last remaining challenger to the throne paced back-and-forth over the creaky floorboards of the Black Eel. Still unable to see more than a pale glimmer against the black backdrop of his enfeebled sight, he could trace the young cavalryman's movements by the sound of his restless footfalls and the number of times Bull told Denn just to sit down and stop wearing out the floor.

The young woman Denn had brought—the princess—seemed quiet and placid in comparison. He wished he could see what she looked like. It was hard to get much of a sense for her since she only spoke to Denn and whispered when she did. As soon as they had arrived, Denn requested the girl be given the chance to rest.

And there was still no sign of Livet.

"Listen," Temis began. "Maybe, I might know of a few cracks in the city walls. Trin was right that there are ways in and out of Caphedra. I just don't know if we can slip through any on horseback."

"I don't have a horse," Denn reminded him bitterly.

"Yael had a stallion named Astral. He's a beautiful dappled blue roan. He's rested and ready in the stable next to Coalsmoke, waiting for you."

Denn's footsteps slowed noticeably. "I don't know if the princess can ride with me. She still suffers from her affliction. It was fine with Naobe but on an unfamiliar mount..."

"Something I can help with," Neriah asked. "Or Gardia?"

"No," Denn refused bluntly before mustering enough

politeness to add, "I'm already in her debt for her care of my sister while I was away. I don't want to involve her any further unless need be."

"There might be a cure to be had," Neriah pushed further.

"There is. At least I think so. Her sister seems to have uncovered some means that may have permitted a remission. But for now, I have to keep the Lady Ramisa safe and get her out of Caphedra."

"Denn has been my only saviour, but I appreciate your desire to help," declared a feathery feminine voice which Olen assumed to be that of the princess.

"If there is something to be done, m'lady, we'll do our best to cure you. I couldn't imagine living as you have done," Neriah said sadly, silencing the room with a shared, contemplative sense of pity that passed through the close pack of conspirators. Once they had returned to the sanctuary of the Black Eel, they pared their numbers down to only the most essential planners who could devise a means of escape for Denn and his ward.

Temis quickly tired of the pointless compassion and drew them back to the immediate issue. "So, you want to get up and walk out of here? Just find some hacked-out hole in the wall, pull yourself through, then hike down to Darrow on foot." He sounded unenthused.

"Trin told me that the cage that guards the river channel where the Darrow enters Caphedra from the north has bars that do not touch the bottom of the river," Denn said. "Maybe the southern opening at Keepside is the same."

"If you're going south, why not take the river all the way?" Bull suggested. "You have a boat. The skiff from the smiths in Barforgers is tucked away under the Midbridge. Our boys could have it pulled out, readied, and in the water faster than cats have kittens."

"How do I get it under the bars, though? Even if there is a space beneath? We'd still have to leave it to swim under," Denn said.

"Raise the bars," Temis said. "Forget about gaps and cracks. Get inside Keepside and raise the bars to the spillway, then you can row your boat on through."

"I'd wager that Keepside's pretty much empty right now," Olen pointed out. "They sent men to their bridge just as we did, and that's after a whole lot of them were marched up to commandeer the northwest gate and do whatever deeds they got up to in Castleside."

"They were sent to murder," Denn said sharply. "Murder and die. You're right, though. There can't be many of them left to spare."

"Those men were among those who came to my uncle's home... seeking me," said the sniffling princess. "But thankfully, Denn found me."

Olen could detect his friend was upset but did not know why, nor did he have any useful words that might diffuse such a foul and sudden change in temper.

As it was, Denn shook it off himself. "Dozens of them died at Farathemun's estate before I arrived, but they had already murdered my mother and the princess's uncle. Most of them were killed, save for a few," he said. "Then I slew three at the bathhouse, including the one that dragged me back here to this cursed city in the first place. They all deserved it! I drowned that swine Colden after I took care of one of his men—and then I stuck through a captain named Alamm."

Neriah sounded like she had begun to choke on the name. "Alamm? Nile Alamm?"

"The same one Celebra was courting?" Olen asked with seriousness.

"Not courting. He was just a simple toy with connections and information," Neriah said. "She spun that man like a ball of yarn and played with him like the cat she is. I do not think she had any true feelings for him. She might miss the perfumes and presents, but there's bound to be a new suitor who will step up to spoil her."

"Not to be impudent or ill-mannered," Bull began, "but I presume the captain slept in the garrison. Perchance does this girl have the means to slip inside in secret, if indeed she is so familiar with his bedchamber, as you imply?"

Olen could not see Neriah light up, but he heard the smugness of her answer. "She has a key!"

"She prob'ly keeps it in 'er fancy vanity," came a sudden and unexpected interjection. Judging from the surprised intakes of breath around the room, Olen was not the only one shocked to hear Livet's voice. "I can find it, but this'll be my last favour t'you tonight, Denn Wellum." She sounded unhappy, almost melancholy.

"Livet!" Denn called out.

"After this, yer lady here can take care of doin' you favours."

Olen guessed Livet was standing in the centre of the room now, but she moved so stealthily that he could hear nothing save for the source of her voice that tipped him off.

"The king's ghost. *That was you in the baths, wasn't it?*" Denn quizzed her, leaving Olen puzzled as to the implication of the question. What was he asking? Where had Livet gone when she did not return from the temple?

"Not sayin'," she deflected curtly.

Olen heard a woman gasp. It was the princess, he assumed. She whispered something to Denn, but Olen could not make it out. In the same moment, Neriah cleared her throat noisily, calling the room to order and returning to the matter at hand.

"About the key, you're right. It is in the top drawer of Celebra's wooden vanity. Do you think you can get it?" Neriah asked.

Livet grunted.

"Go with her, Neriah," Temis said and gained an icy rebuke from Livet.

"I can do it m'self!" Her quick burst of temper sent out a shockwave. Perhaps it was a coincidence, but something fell off a shelf across the room and Olen heard it break.

"I don't doubt that," Temis said. "It's not about the key. Neriah needs to bring *Serenn* here. She must also be ready to travel downriver with us tonight when we push off."

"Alright then," Livet obliged. "We won't be long. Go get yerself ready."

Denn was dedicated to escorting Ramisa, so it fell on Bull to lead Olen down to the riverside. Over and over, he cursed. Each time Olen asked why Bull expanded upon the same answer. More and more buildings were collapsing as he viewed the destruction of Caphedra.

"Even if you could see it, old friend, you wouldn't believe it. The whole city seems flat and smouldering. It is as if the place was buried under lava from a volcano. Just burnt sticks and old bricks left stuck in the ground in most places, and those are all scorched and charred. The temple's still standing, but I swear it looks peculiar, like one of its legs is gone. Hobbled, you might say. Listing to one side and crooked."

"I didn't know you could see the temple from Westriver," Olen said.

"You can now," answered Bull ominously. Then he groaned and declared, "Maybe it's better that you can't see it. Maybe it is better to remember things the way they were. It's going to take a lot of work to rebuild, even to half what the city used to be."

They reached Midbridge and Olen could hear his comrades deliberating below. They were deciding who among them would sneak into Keepside and open the spillway. Bull set Olen up against the old hawthorn tree's trunk and joined the discussion, leaving Olen to brood. He felt disrespected and cast out. Gardia had said his sight should return in time, but why couldn't it be fixed tonight? Why could she not mend his eyes like she did his cuts and bruises before?

In the end, most of the final details were decided by Denn. In the short time since they had hatched the plan, he had made a thorough study of its strengths and failings. His scheme made pragmatic use of each of the men, and he outlined their roles commandingly, with authority and competence on par with any seasoned tactician.

Olen, however, had never felt so useless as he did now, forced to step back and do nothing but say farewell to his friend. By plan or by happenstance, Denn had taken on task after monumental task and came up a better man for it. Against his will, he had been thrust hotly back into Caphedra where the turmoil of the city, tempered and hardened him. He had made an impression on the Westriver Company men, for sure. Whatever Denn was growing into as a soldier—and as a leader—the men had embraced with zealous admiration and curiosity. There would be stories told around the Black Eel for years to come.

"Denn Wellum, the man who brought a real princess to the sorriest alehouse in Westriver!" Olen joked aloud.

Bull overheard him and replied with a chuckle, "I'll commission a plaque and charge extra."

Topside on the bridge, the sound of approaching clip-clopping meant that Temis must have arrived with the horses. They snorted and whinnied, shifting from hoof to hoof with thumps on the bridge's wooden deck, until Temis led them down to the shoreline and Olen could sense the big beasts nearby. Their powerful nostrils exhaled hot air, and he caught a breath of it.

"Here comes Serenn," Temis said nervously. "Asher, can you hold the reins?"

"Aye," the young fighter responded.

It must be close to dawn, yet it was still so dark, Olen thought. Maybe daylight would help improve his vision. Promptly, there was a splash, and he heard water flowing against the boat's wooden hull. Someone mentioned affixing a mooring rope to the dinghy to keep it tied up under the bridge as they readied it.

"Uncle," came the reassuring greeting from his niece.

"I'm here," he said dolefully.

"I am going too. I will help Serenn, and I am told that the princess is a concern for which I may be of use."

"But I don't want to lose you!" Olen said, embarrassed by the desperation overtaking his voice. He squeezed his eyelids and swallowed, willing his sight to restore itself. His eyes were watering again, he realized.

"You won't lose me," she said. "I want you to come with us so that I can take care of you, too. Away from here. We'll find a place for you to rest and get better."

"That's a mountain of a burden on you. I'm not really fit for travelling. Gardia says I will heal. Can't we wait it out here?"

"No. You just need time and medicine but it's not safe here. She showed me how to make it. Besides, now that we're together, I want to keep to you, also."

He was about to protest again but a realization struck him. "Gardia knows we're leaving? You told her? Denn said not to say anything!"

"You can trust Gardia, but what you can't do is keep anything from her." Neriah picked up his hand and led his fingers toward a small pouch. There were small stones inside. No, he felt again; they were seeds.

"I eat these? Crush them up and rub them in my eyes? What do I do?" he asked.

"Seeds? You *plant* them." She gently pried his fingers open and took the pouch back. "Once we find a place to settle in, I can grow a flower with them. The medicine must be made from its nectar–but only when it is fresh and harvested on a full moon. Those were her instructions, or part of them, anyway."

"And then? What else did she tell you?" Olen asked.

"It's a rare plant. When it turns to seed, we must replace what we have borrowed," explained Neriah.

"So, you'll refill the pouch and bring it back in the fall?" He was forced to admit that was a fair request.

"You will," she said. "Gardia wants you to bring the seeds back to her personally. That was one of her conditions."

Olen raised an eyebrow and felt a lump of trepidation invade his stomach. He had figured Gardia would be quick to see the end of him. "She's summoning me back, then?"

"Something like that," Neriah said and laughed.

The time to leave would soon be upon them. Olen called for Bull, hearing him answer from only an arm's reach away. Then, after taking a deep breath, he soberly charged his fellow sergeant with the most important task. "Take care of our men."

"I will," Bull agreed. "Neriah is right to take you away from here. She's a smart one. If you find a nice patch of ground, send for us, too. We'll come."

"I didn't think you'd ever want to leave the Eel."

"We'll see what the morning brings," he said. "Speaking of which, you all need to be away before first light! Get moving."

Olen nodded while Vyr called out to him.

"Olen, get in first! You're the biggest, and you shouldn't rock the boat with the ladies aboard."

"I'm coming," he replied and after embracing Bull like a brother, he shuffled off under his niece's guidance to the water's edge. The men gathered and helped him place his foot in the little dory, holding the boat so it would not float away. "I can row if someone takes the tiller," Olen offered. He felt around for the oarlocks and lifted the long wooden oars into place. The boat dipped and bobbed back up, as ahead of him the princess was placed politely upon one of the cross thwarts. Serenn was guided to her seat next, with Neriah in the middle. Carefully, Olen angled Coldswept so its scabbard would not get in the way, having now exchanged swords again with Denn who received the broadsword that Bull had given Olen, after vouching for its sharpness and suitability. After all, it was purchased by the cavalryman already, as part of Denn's original haul from Barforgers.

Denn grunted as one of his feet splashed in the bilgewater

collecting at the bottom of the little boat's hull, as he stretched to straddle the shore and boat. Again, he thanked the Westriver men for everything then took his seat and leaned toward Olen. "I'm glad you're coming, but you understand that to travel with us means you risk branding yourself an enemy to the Pillars should the Faith find out."

"I worry more for the men and their families that we are leaving behind. Though maybe the Pillarmen will leave them alone. They always have. Westriver is too unruly, and the Dues too hard to collect. The Faith has never so much as threatened to cross the river, at least until now."

Denn murmured his acknowledgement but added, "If they can't squeeze money from Westriver, then they'll come looking for men to fill their ranks which would be worse. Your boys may be called upon yet."

"They'll say no," said Olen.

"Then tell them they are welcome to join us," Denn gave a short chuckle but then sighed. There was something else he regretted. "I am sorry to have to part with Livet," he said.

"Are you?" Olen prodded him.

"I am," he affirmed in a creaky voice that betrayed his sentiment.

"Is she here?" Olen asked. Livet was so quiet out of habit that there was no way to be sure but at that instant, cold water droplets splashed over his face, causing him to let out a perturbed, "Hey!"

"I can't reach t'kiss you goodbye properly, Olen," Livet said. "That's the best I can do for you."

"Will you do the same for Denn?" Olen asked jokingly.

"T'do 'im right, I'd 'ave to drown him," she half-teased.

He never knew how Denn took her meaning. Urgings from the shore told him that everything was down to final preparations. Dawn would be here soon, and if they were not free of the city by then, they risked not getting out at all.

Temis had Asher working with him to handle the horses. The beasts were rearing and stomping energetically, unhindered by their hitchings. Denn, likewise, was fussing with impatience. When the boat passed through the spillway, he wanted the two horsemen to be in position to ride as escorts and follow them down the Darrow from ashore. There would be no slowing the boat for them to catch up, and the horses would not be able to pass through Keepside. That meant leaving now then not stopping until they could charge through the gate at a gallop and sweep back west.

"Don't try to talk your way through—just ride. When you get to the Darrow River Garrison, cross the bridge and ride along the western shore," Denn coached. "Watch for us, but if we are separated, keep riding for Calkairn. We can outfit ourselves there with provisions and arms—and maybe pay back an old cidermaker who's short a wagon."

"If all goes well, we may pass through the Southgate easier than you pass through Keepside," Temis said.

"The boys have a key," Bull reminded. "Nyrim and Talton are going in, and they know their way around. We all trained there once, and I don't expect those big stone walls have moved much since we left. I would worry more about them still having men on the bridge. You folks need to pass under it before you get to the wall."

Temis exchanged words with Asher to make sure he was adjusting to Yael's mount and vice versa, then Olen heard him shout, "Heeyaw!" There was a spattering of mud in Olen's direction and the dull scent of clay was in the air as he heard the two steeds turn over the dirt of the slope under their hooves. The horses whinnied as they scrambled up and away into the night, their clomping hoofbeats quickly disappearing out of earshot.

"Let's push off!" Denn said. Olen grabbed the oars but before he made a single stroke, Denn asked him, "Can you at least see the edges of the river?"

"Maybe a bit," said Olen. "But the current runs dead centre from here to Keepside. Don't worry. I grew up on this river and I can navigate it by feel."

"Liar!" Denn spat, jovially. "You were never a fisherman."

"I was! Caught eels and sold them until I was fourteen." Olen defended.

"I thought you caught eels in traps," Denn shot back.

"A line works too if you know where to drop it. There're so many thick weeds and old, discarded junk on the bottom that anywhere is a good enough spot, pretty much."

Denn allowed a slightly diminished chortle. "Keep your good memories. I'll be happy to be free of this city, Olen." Deeply he drew a breath as if savouring its mundane odours. "I never meant to come back. I kept away by choice. Now, I'm cast out for good."

They spoke around Ramisa, neglecting that she was there. It was easy to do, considering how quiet and unintrusive was her manner, but now she responded. "There's a reason that things turned out as they did," she said. "Lyseia is very quick to remind that I was not meant to live in Fallowsea forever, and you were not meant to be ignored by fate either, Denn. She has implied so much since we left the citadel."

"I'm just a cavalryman. Not even. I've lost my post, and my horse was taken from me and slaughtered while I was helpless to save her."

"But you saved me, and spared the souls of many who would otherwise be bound to endless suffering in the next life, their ghosts waging war in battles that last eternally, serving Dagremahr in his realm—the realm of the Paragons."

"We are not immortal. We will all end up there someday. Perhaps I will have time to be a hero in the next world," Denn said.

"Don't fear what is to come. Many people search for a purpose. That is why that, for centuries, seekers have meditated upon the teachings of Lyseia and the stories of her wanderings, praying to, and deifying her. Tonight, to her dismay, she says you've been granted a gift."

"I am interested in what *you* have to say. Your voice will need to grow louder to be heard, m'lady—and I have great suspicion that it will. I admit that the first time I saw you in Fallowsea, I did not have confidence you would make it this far, with or without me. You have done well to weather the fight you wage inside. You are so silent that I forget how hard you must secretly labour. Now, I know how much of your strength does not come from the Paragon that you keep, but from some well of deep determination that is all your own."

"Perhaps that is something I will boast of to Lyseia," said Ramisa.

The declaration was accompanied by the escape of a soft, bashful laugh that filled the air like the tufts of dandelion seeds taking to the wind. If, as Denn said, the lady possessed a demon inside, then no hint of the creature seemed to pass through her lips in that moment, Olen thought.

He was brought back by the sound of splashes close to the boat. Someone was racing along the riverside, light-footed and spry.

It was Kalden and the boy called out, "Get moving! Talton and my uncle just gave the signal. They're opening the spillway—but watch out for the bridge! The whole garrison is lined up along it. A brigade of Pillarmen is on the march and heading this way!"

"Good. That means the bridge sentries will be distracted," said Denn. He placed a hand on Olen's shoulder. "Keep us moving."

"I won't stop until we reach Hasen," Olen promised. "Just watch the battlements for archers, and the murder holes in the keep, too!"

He could no longer see it, but the details of Caphedra's western fortifications had been engraved in Olen's mind for twenty years. He remembered its impenetrable grey stone walls, choked with climbing vines and crusty lichens; the pointed windows overlooking the district, out of which discouraged recruits would pine; and the echoes that followed you everywhere you went when you were shut away inside. It rose above the city walls to defend against all attackers within and without. Above, banners flapped from flagstaffs to advertise the units that needed new bodies for reinforcements. At the summit of its grandeur, straddling the Darrow, twin, tented towers housed the officers in seclusion. There they learned the art of tactics, the science of strategy, or how to navigate the intricate expectations of their elevated stations.

Denn acknowledged Olen's warning then called out instructions to the passengers. "Neriah, you need to steer from the back if Olen goes off course. There is an old broken oar I found that you can use as a rudder—or to paddle us in another direction if need be. I'll stay on the prow to cut down anyone who tries to stop us getting through." Then to the princess, he entreated, "Please see that my sister doesn't fall overboard?"

"I will hold onto her tightly," the princess replied.

The boat lurched as Denn shifted further up to the bow. "Ready m'lady?" he asked.

"Ready to leave my mother's city? Yes. For now, I am. It is no longer hers, and nor is it mine," said the soft-spoken regent.

"Sir! Please hurry!" shouted Kalden, sounding more and more worried with every moment his uncle spent skulking around inside the keep.

"If you're waiting for the tide, Olen, the ocean's downriver," Bull cajoled. "Do you need me to sing a shanty to see you off?"

Denn gave his final coaxing to Olen. "Do not slow down. Do not stop. The current's in our favour to carry us downstream. We sail under the bridge and through the spillway. Temis and Asher should be on the other side, waiting."

"Yes, sir," said Olen. There was a noticeable thump as Vyr threw the ends of the mooring rope into the boat. Olen stretched out his arms and rotated his shoulders, cracking the joints. He seized the ends of the oar handles in his huge hands, submerged the blades, and pulled. Water sloshed ahead of them as the boat cut through the rippling river and glided forward.

The breeze tussled Olen's hair. They were moving quickly, yet he pulled harder. "What do you see?" he called out.

"Keep rowing!" Denn answered.

The rushing of the river surrounded him, and his ears took in its bubbly roar. Ahead of them, Olen could hear the sound becoming baffled. That would be where they would pass under the Keepside bridge. They were upon it already, he marvelled. The spillway through the city wall was only a couple of boat lengths past that. On purpose, the two landmarks were laid out near enough to each other that archers could line the city wall and loose volleys on any attackers who sought to cross the bridge, or reverse themselves and rain their arrows upon anyone exiting the spillway.

They had hoped for darkness, but the night's labours had persisted too long. Olen could deduce the luminous hue of the dawn beginning to invade the dark blurriness. Twilight was upon them. He imagined how to the others it must be pink and orange, full of vibrant promise, but to him, it was just a muddy, copper brown that obscured the dangerous scene shaping up around them.

"Stay down!" Denn called out.

They were moving fast upon the bridge now, Olen could sense. Bootsteps thundered overhead as the shouts of soldiers taunted their battle prowess to the ears of an unseen enemy, and sergeants compelled their men to hold their position, open their eyes and shut their mouths. But they were not shouting to the boat.

The Pillarmen must have arrived, Olen thought.

The blessing was short-lived. A boyish-sounding soldier called out excitedly. "Boat! Approaching from upstream!"

Olen pulled harder on the oars and prepared for the worst.

He heard Denn scrape up against the dinghy's hull and plant

his feet firmly against the foremost gunnels and felt him as he pressed against Olen's labouring back.

Then, just as he expected to be feeling the jabs of spearpoints, a harsher voice growled to the bridge defenders, "They're overtaking us on the wall! Shields up! Take cover!"

The Faith must have split their force, with some of their number bypassing the street for the wall. Olen clenched his teeth and concentrated to power the boat forward and under the bridge.

Everything darkened. The Darrow's heady rush echoed against the cutwater and off the underside of the bridge's spandrels above them. On the deck, the sounds of *thup, thup, thup* heralded a hail of arrows lodging in the planks. Fearful shrieks erupted from the dinghy.

The noise of the water quickly dissipated to relative quiet as they burst out the other side of the bridge into the open air. Above and behind, in seeming disarray, the Marshal's Men of Keepside hollered curses while the Pillarmen above were certain to be busy notching a new volley of arrows, Olen thought.

Olen bore down on the oars brusquely, hoping that in the coming moment, they might yet reach the spillway and make it out of Caphedra alive.

It was then that he heard a voice coming from out of nowhere. "Journey well, sergeant!" Talton or Nyrim, at least one or both of them, were still inside and ensuring the spillway gate was kept open.

Again, the resounding loudness of the river's current engulfed them with its dull rumble as the boat slipped into the gloomy enclosure that housed the spillway gate. Despite the rapid pace at which they plied the tunnel, their transit seemed unending, so thick were the city walls.

Finally, they were overwhelmed by a gushing of water. The darkness disappeared and light was restored. The Darrow's thunderous gurgling subsided as the sound of its swirling waters radiated unimpeded into the limitless sky.

Olen's sense of smell was soon overtaken by the pastoral fragrances of clover and cowberry, and the sweetness of meadow grasses in abundance. The air was fresh and the dampness he felt was from dew—not the lamentable dank patina that fouled the air of the city.

They were out, but not yet safe.

"Watch yourselves! Stay down!" Denn called to the others to the aft of the dinghy. Olen dared not let up on the rowing. Above them, he heard the slapping of bowstrings being released and the whizzing of more arrows.

But there were no impacts on the boat. There was no sloshing of arrows, entering and cavitating in the water. Instead, Olen heard the whinnying of horses and taunts and jeers from riders on the shoreline.

"Temis and Asher!" Denn announced. "They're distracting the Pillarmen."

Olen admittedly enjoyed the catcalling he heard from the riverbank. Asher was fond to mock the Pillarmen's lack of skill, but he lacked the imagination of his associate. The sheer vitriol and barbarity of insults that Temis produced from his mouthy arsenal tainted the eardrums enough to elicit dizziness.

"Are we good now? Safely away?" Olen asked.

"We're good," Denn proclaimed. "Caphedra's behind us."

"We made it?" the princess inquired once more, sounding disbelieving.

Denn gave a deep laugh that expressed his gratefulness, then answered, "M'lady, we're free. We are men and women of Darrow now. Would that we never see that city again. How is my sister?"

"Serenn is well, and I believe I can say the same for all of us." Neriah replied, then calling out to Olen, "Us too. Let us leave it all behind and make peace, Uncle. Let us be free."

"Aye," Olen said. "And if these stricken eyes are ever restored and made well, I would still be happy if it were another twenty years before I saw Caphedra's walls again."

CHAPTER 39

Last Surveil

The departure of Denn and Olen from Caphedra gave Livet a sense of relief. Her friends would be out of harm's way, at least for now. It would be a while before the Faith could dedicate the vast cadre of summoners needed to seek them out for there was too much work to be done in the capitol. The city had been razed to the ground and their monument to prestige and dominance, the Temple of the Faith of the Pillars, was on the very real verge of physical collapse.

Livet had just returned to the Peahen that night when the ground-quaking boom had shaken the city. Vials had jiggled, and glass jars of oils and unguents had slid from the shelves around her. The sound rumbled and rolled over the room quickly, and although Livet had a knack for determining the source of such things, at the time, she could only deduce it was significant and far away.

"D'you know what that noise was last night?" Livet asked Baressa after returning at dawn.

The seeress sat upon the edge of a small bed, sequestered in a closet-sized suite that granted privacy away from the tavern traffic. She glanced around, dodging eye contact, and furrowed her brow in a way that intimated the strain upon her wandering mind. "No," she said.

Livet had not expected much of an answer but she hoped that the question might get her friend to converse more naturally. Since coming back from the temple dungeon, Baressa had begun moving, sitting up, and muttering the occasional word or short sentence. Gardia had visited several times, administering care and medicine, but her examinations only confirmed that the injured seeress would require a long recuperation.

Baressa looked up at Livet with fixed-open, glassy eyes, with a spider's web of blood vessels that emanated from pupils as wide and black as iron skillets. When she chanced to blink, it seemed like she was unfamiliar with her own mannerisms and performed actions consciously and peculiarly.

"Thank you for finding me, Livet," Baressa whispered dispassionately.

"I was afraid t' go back sooner, an' I thought you dead. I am sorry," Livet said.

"There was nothing you could have done. But Kell…" Her breathing was imperceptible, but still, she was talking.

Livet listened carefully, desperately hoping for a restoration of her friend's former gregarious warmth. "We could've 'elped you to not get so hurt. If we'd gone back–*if I'd gone back*–maybe you'd be better now."

"You saw the fatal instance, my dear. You couldn't have stopped it."

The words hung frigidly in the air until Baressa provided the grim confirmation. Livet could feel a tingle down the back of her neck.

"That Aroon woman tried to bind my spirit to my broken body and trap me." Baressa's eyes trailed off, but she continued speaking. "Perhaps it was just my gift of sight, but I saw so many exquisite visions swirling around me, the faces of those that passed before and the multitude of realms converged around me like the spokes of a wheel–all at the very time they were being denied to me," she reflected.

The last words she spoke betrayed her sadness. Wasn't Baressa happy that, in the end, she was recovered and pulled back from the edge of death? Livet was overcome by what Baressa must have experienced, but she could not deny feeling optimism that the friend she knew was awake and might yet be made well again.

"Your husband. You'll see 'im again! That must give you joy, doesn't it?" Livet asked.

"I must go to him," she said, "soon. And my sisters, too."

"Just not *too* soon. You're not too fit for travellin', yet." Livet said. "Look, you almost died. You should take time to rest."

"I was dead," Baressa said, "I know because I saw Kell

standing beside my body. His ghost came to me, and he touched me, and we spoke while the Pillar witch plied her wicked craft to my corpse. Kell calmed me and said he would protect me. He asked that I find someone to watch after you, as your mother had once asked him, so that you wouldn't have to be alone again."

"He spoke to me when I saw him, too," Livet said, immediately sounding to herself as if she were jealous.

"And he hears you now," Baressa said.

"Then he should know I don't need anyone t' take care o' me," Livet said. "I know I can do things for myself now, and I don't always have t' hide. I'm not a burden t' look after."

It seemed like Baressa smiled. "No. You are not."

Sitting together, Livet reached out and held onto her friend's hand. The fingers were chilly, and the joints felt swollen and knobbly. The seeress was too feeble to return any more than a negligible grip.

"Here. Wrap the bedclothes about ya!" Livet said, pulling up neglected blankets from where they had collected around Baressa's lap.

"Your appearance in the temple emboldened him, Livet. It allowed him the strength and hope to reach out." Turning on the tiny cot where she sat, Baressa made an effort to look squarely upon Livet. "He told me all about you."

Fear conflicted with curiosity in her, but she wanted to hear. "What did he say?"

Gradually, Baressa's face lost its flicker of emotion and grew paler as if all her energy were now being directed toward recollection. She looked two-dimensional, like an old worn-out book reading from its own pages to relate a story.

"When your people—the Kindred—were made prisoner by Lord Vlass, you were taken immediately to Precept Golmarra. He was visiting Lanstad at the time. He sought to secure a greater place for the Pillars there. The Precept suspected Kell harboured much of the knowledge your mother once maintained and ordered that all those shared secrets be extracted and recorded to be part of the Pillar's private teachings. Golmarra himself authored some of the books that Harbud brought back."

"My mother... Her name was Vaeya." Livet repeated the name Kell had finally granted her but then became defensive and a bit defiant. "Kell would never have taught anything to outsiders," she said. Livet could attest to her mentor's avowed adherence to secrecy. He had drilled it into her and the others unendingly to preserve what they knew, did, or said–to be shared among the Kindred only. She rejected Baressa's accusation and said, "Kell would have fought them."

"But they held his people, so he could not refuse. Your freedom was a part of the bargain," Baressa explained.

Livet sat in shock. She believed it. Kell had insinuated as much. Guilt latched onto her. It was not just that her teacher sacrificed and compromised a handful of spells and cantrips to free her, but that the deal ended with only her being released. The Pillars had spared no others that she knew of.

"But why'd they 'ave to kill him then just to bring him back?" she asked.

"In death, Kell could report back knowledge of the other realms with greater clarity. But the Faith could also rely on the inescapable and indomitable sense of despair brought on by his passing, interrupted as it was. That, together with the threat to the lives of his cherished but imprisoned Kindred, moved him to surrender." Baressa rested her other hand on the wall and tried to pull herself up to sit straighter. "In life, Kell resisted and gave up nothing, but his passing was so corrupted and impure..." She looked away from Livet now. "You would not want such a violation committed against anyone for whom you loved."

Taking a moment to digest the story she swallowed and tried with futility to wipe away the flow of tears. "But you're alive now? Could Gardia have healed Kell or brought 'im back to us, like you?"

"My young dear, all I can say is that I am not *dead* so far as my essence has passed on. However, I'm not convinced that I have rejoined the living, either."

"Half-dead," Livet murmured. An unease gripped her as she speculated about Kell's present state. Was he still bound to his earthly remains? What had happened when the fire overtook the dungeon and incinerated everything? She wanted to confirm, "Is Kell gone?"

"Kell has been freed from his temple prison," Baressa said, "There are only ashes left of his bones and from what I recall his spirit saying to me was that such utter destruction of his body was what was needed for him to overcome the evil bonds that shackled him to this world."

Livet nodded and accepted the answer, entertaining no further appetite for curiosity. With her actions throughout the past day and the heavy burden of sorrow now upon her, Livet was exhausted. She motioned toward the cot, and Baressa made room for her.

"Sleep," the prophetess said and with colourless lips, she levied a kiss gently on Livet's head. Baressa was still devotedly watching over her when Livet awoke hours later.

At noon, Gardia returned to administer more treatments to Baressa. To Livet, the mistress of the Peahen felt distant and seemed resentful for Livet's delay in returning. Or perhaps, it was something else.

The lack of being paid any heed by the matron did not bother her, however. As Gardia muddled and mixed an elixir of nettle and chamomile for her patient, Livet used the time to slip out and learn what she could of the previous night's outcomes.

The Peahen was nearly empty as Livet walked into the main room. Gardia had closed it off to the public to temporarily deny Caphedra's refugees from storming in and overtaking them. However, the aroma from the kitchen suggested that the hungry hopefuls outside would be permitted to enter soon. Celebra was ushering around a couple of the other girls, trying to take advantage of the imposed lull to direct them into cleaning the place up to her standards. Taringer was standing near her, as reserved and expressionless as usual, calling out inventory items from a tally sheet he held in his hand.

A voice shouted, "If you're looking for the rest of them, they're at the Black Eel, swigging ale and passing out!"

Harbud sat reclusively at a table, stockaded behind a confusion of books and parchments, making notes, and diligently cross-referencing his precious tomes.

Once again, Livet eyed the writing on the books with flashes of familiarity, and her attention elicited a comment from Harbud.

"You've seen these before? You recognize Kell's script, yes?"

Edging closer, she scanned the open pages with her eyes,

hesitant to reach out and touch the genuine artifacts. While they had a clear connection to her cherished mentor, they were nonetheless commissioned under vile means concocted by horrible people. The books were tainted, and it repelled her at first, but then she noticed something awry that sparked her interest. As her eyes squinted and her brow narrowed in shrewd examination, Harbud glared at her expectantly.

"This one," Livet said and pointed to a symbol.

"Yes?" Harbud replied.

She sighed and bit her lip in contemplation. Her tiny finger drifted in line with her scrutinizing. "This one, too."

"Yes?" Harbud said, less patiently.

"You know, there are errors here."

That made Harbud look slightly anxious. His jaw hung down as his mouth drooped and his eyes stuck into her like needles. "What do you mean? How do you know? This is rather advanced. Did Kell teach this to you?"

"No," Livet admitted. "But I know his script. These markings are jumbled. Whoever wrote 'em down did a terrible job."

"Are these Kell's books or not?" Harbud asked her.

"No, they're copies," Livet said.

"So, you're saying the scribe made errors? I'm surprised they didn't compare them more closely when copying." Harbud sighed. It was clear that Livet had just added even greater complexity to the task before him.

Or they were given bad information on purpose, Livet thought.

"I think they're something else. I think it's Jerozi—or a kind of shorthand based on it. I have seen it used in the areas around the old ruins south of the Glass Plateau. If you know the rest of these symbols so well..." Harbud began but Livet cut him off.

"I'm going to explore the city. I want to find out what happened after last night." She pushed herself away from the table and the stack of books.

"The city's still dangerous, Livet. Why don't you swing by the Eel and take someone with you?" Harbud suggested.

"I'll be fine," she said and skittered out the door, leaving him to his studies.

❖   ❖   ❖

Alone and unencumbered, Livet moved faster. She was learning the quickest laneways and alleys that could get her across town the fastest, with no need for Harbud's Passage Realm. The thought of travelling alone always had filled her with worries and fears, but now she had proven that she was capable enough and maybe better for it.

She crossed freely at Midbridge, scurried through the Caphedran Commons, and clung close to the King's Avenue, travelling east through a landscape of destruction. Many of Caphedra's grandest buildings, Icarian edifices that once stretched the sun, had collapsed in the fire. The appalling lack of shade made the day feel warmer than before but the sun's rays on her face felt energizing despite the bleak vista before her. Their brightness reminded her that the month of Perspica had passed. It was now Midsummer and the first day of Obreyn, which was said to bring wisdom.

She had a few coins in her pockets but the shops were either destroyed or rendered inaccessible throughout the city. No streamers of flowers strung from rafters of houses, nor any other festive paraphernalia plastered to the sides of merchant boutiques to mark the holiday. Where the carts of street sellers had been, all were overturned, smashed, and charred. An antithetical blackness coated everything—the legacy of the failed invaders' fiery retribution.

Livet's progress met far worse calamities as she approached the citadel where things grew more gruesome. Many citizens had forgone exodus, seeming to have hoped to wait out the tumult, only for the rush of flames to lap them up. Their charred bones cluttered the street. Everywhere there were dead, skeletal forms clinging to each other in last, desperate embraces of consolation, or reaching impotently to scratch at the earth as they crawled forward, propelled by faint vestigial hope.

Where the two militaries had clashed, the bodies of soldiers were piled up and burned together. Livet could only imagine these macabre bonfires lighting up the surrounding houses and cottages. They were cadaverous monuments to defeat, feeding the fire with their very bodies. She trod with caution below them, for the ground was made slippery by all the ghastly, congealed renderings that seeped out.

But survivors were returning to the streets. Livet was not the only wanderer out this morning. Some had returned to shovel the shattered tiles and debris or to begin breaking apart the cluttered, tangled timbers that collapsed where rooves once rose. Birds had flown back into the city–crows especially–and flies buzzed arrogantly. In the alleys and creases, dogs and cats prowled for their breakfast.

As Livet made her way through Stonerow her curiosity swelled. She coursed between building rows and edged along the brickwork of the temple outbuildings that ringed the Folds. Despite the awfulness of the surrounding stench, she wished to see the site where the final battle had determined the fate of Caphedra's crown.

Since she was young, Livet's eyes were gifted at determining perspective and judging relative positions, but anyone could realize the source of last night's ominous rumble once they saw it. Caphedra's Temple of the Faith of the Pillars had been damaged at its core. Between its four great pillars, the walls sloped inward, and cracks ran from the limestone foundation up its sides like beanstalks. With the temple's base displaced, one of the pillars had begun to slant and the Precept's Sanctum high above was tilted and in danger of crashing down entirely.

A group of acolytes and adepts were walking along the street ahead of her. Livet listened to them as the lead adept passed along his instructions to the blue-clad and bedraggled cadre.

"Avoid the temple and make your way to the castle. Today is Midsummer. The Precept has decreed it to be the Queen Ascendant's coronation day–to celebrate our victory. Ignore the work ahead. This day is an auspicious one!"

Studying the scarred and broken monolith, Livet's mind raced back to when they had made their escape. Yes, the city had been burned to the ground in places, but she thought of the fire in the dungeon. Deep in the building's hideous core, it had been hot enough to melt iron and incinerate everything it touched. Had they caused this? She circled the structure admiring the damage and knowing the temple would have to come down.

Already, while the Pillar adepts passed by, crews of labourers were being organized to enter the temple–risking their safety in doing so–that the Faith's most precious artifacts could be saved. The workers formed chains and ushered cart after cart of gold and silver, now reduced to misshapen ingots and melted lumps of metal.

Livet smiled roguishly at the feast of portentous prizes. Most of the enlisted Pillarmen were heartily engaged in reclaiming the Faith's wealth and preserving its heritage, but only a handful of witless sentries patrolled the precious piles of sacred salvage once extracted. They must not think anyone would be so daring, she surmised.

Irresistibly drawn to the sparkle of jewels and treasures peeking out of carts and chests, she slinked quietly and slyly past the guards. By purpose, her old cloak was prolific with pockets. She collected as much as she could manage before slipping away and promising to herself that she would make a return trip after the coronation if there was anything left. Having gotten close to the hoard, she noticed that the Faith's mercenaries were equally as interested in their own surreptitious pilfering. They were unlikely to have halted Livet while they were too busy doing the same.

At the citadel and Caphedra Castle, the lofty fortress's wall still stood proudly, though now marred with a layer of soot. Livet did not want to risk befouling her cloak or leaving traceable marks on the side of the wall when she clambered up, so she pressed a little farther to a slightly sheltered recess and scaled there, more safely out of sight.

At the top, she noted that the outer wall marked the extent of the great fire's reach. Inside, the castle grounds remained verdant, their luxury unscarred. The palace itself appeared white and immaculate, contrasting against the black wasteland outside.

She scaled down the interior face of the wall, then hopped the hedges to where she could find a way up the side of the castle, higher still. Few soldiers remained on the battlements or in the towers. More of a threat came from the disgruntled, besieging sufferers at the gates who sought entry to the grounds for relief and charity.

Finally, Livet lighted upon the rooftop and spied where she wished to perch. The great glass skylight that Denn had described as symbolizing the illuminant beauty of the Wolstett monarchy, lay splendidly before her.

She was awed by the size of the panes of glass as she crept close, but the fabled purple hue—said to be like gazing through the petals of an enormous violet—was blue now, matching the colour of the Faith of the Pillars. She remembered Denn once saying that two panes of glass, like ruby and sapphire, had combined to make it a deep amethyst shade. Now, where the edges were fixed in their framework, Livet could see there had been room for a thicker assembly. The red panels must have been removed with small shims installed to remedy the resulting gap, and leaving only its companion layer to remain, to transmit and exaggerate the bright blue of the sky.

It made the identification of Faith leaders much harder. Looking through its tint, the frocks upon all the officiants appeared only in shades. Those in grey were indistinguishable from those who had been more lavishly garbed in soft cyan or deeper cerulean.

Some faces were recognizable, however, clustered upon a dais in the centre of a royal atrium. As she expected, High Precept Averin Golmarra was orchestrating the coronation spectacle. As such, he held the reins of the queen herself. But as frightened by Golmarra as Livet was, her fear was nothing compared to the pure hatred she felt when looking upon the evil, arrogant visage of the man distantly across from him. Denn's brother, Lehn, was stooped and leaning heavily upon a staff. Armsmen hovered nearby, and Kabra Zimmin stood behind him so closely that he could have been wearing the witch like a cape.

Lehn's presence meant Livet had to stay alert. Even wounded and preoccupied, he might detect her surveilling the ceremony. Surely the blue prism would help obscure her.

The ceremony was commencing, and for the first time since the portrait, Livet saw the revered Lady Ravon. The imminent monarch was far below, beneath the sky-coloured glass. She possessed a strong resemblance to her sister, Ramisa, especially when most finer details were difficult to make out at first, but around her eyes, the edges were dark, and the corners of her mouth were curved downward in a perpetual frown. Around her neck hung an array of medallions, while her hair was hidden, tucked under a silvery hood of mail. But the most sizeable difference Livet could see was in her body and it was remarkable. The queen-apparent, or Ascendant as the adept had called her, wore an expansive and billowing gown that protruded conspicuously from above her waist. Underneath the dress, Livet was certain the Lady Ravon was expecting a child.

Triumphant shouting shook the skylight as Ravon took each of her oaths and assumed her titles of regency. Anyone who remained to contest this moment had lost their chance to keep her from wearing the crown. Caphedra—east of the Darrow, at least—belonged to her and in her name, the Faith also staked claim to all the inherited land of her father's decades of conquest—'from here, to where the water becomes salt, in all directions' as was espoused to Council, the night she was first proclaimed.

Not unexpectedly, the moment the crown was slipped over her head, she was ushered to the side by Golmarra. He centred himself on the dais and began an impassioned speech to the audience of the atrium. The span of his arms extended greedily. His vile gesticulations intimated a threat to all who would dare oppose his plans, imagined and real. Livet could hear no words, but she sensed his meaning. In market squares and within tavern walls, many had speculated upon his ultimate goals. It was proclaimed that Golmarra would rebuild Caphedra and then retake the four great cities, making the whole of the country into one vast temple to the Pillars.

The venerable Precept's ambition was never so rewarded as at this moment, but neither had he been so close to such a rival. Though it obviously pained him, Lehn Wellum observed the ancient pontiff with the intensity of a deeply avowed competitor, unwavering, save for one flash of an instance when he looked up and stared directly at Livet.

She gasped and drew back from the edge of the skylight.

Each of the surviving Wellums had taken up the banners of a different princess. But Livet could tell that Lehn had taken a further challenge upon himself—that of usurping and unseating his divine mentor. Perhaps he even desired Golmarra dead. Maybe he wished it even more than she did.

Livet shuddered.

Hull Homesta had been spending most of his days at the Half Moon, solidifying his hold on his new conquest, but he still kept daily check-ins with Gardia. It was on one of these visits, Livet found him and Harbud fussing over a pair of dray horses in a small livery stable behind the Peahen.

"What's the matter with her?" Hull was asking.

"I've been watching her. She's not been eating for a little while. She has a touch of colic, I expect," Harbud said. "I've floated her teeth and kept changing her water. I think getting out of the city will be the cure."

"She'll be happy to get her belly full of fresh green grass," Hull added.

"I didn't know your knowledge stretched t' horses," Livet commented to Harbud as she approached.

"You're joking," he replied, clearly irked. "I'm just not used to carthorses. I've ridden on the backs of Halbernans since I was four years old."

"'Albernans?"

"Yes. The Steeds of the Brokenlands, as they say. Spirited and quick. Fearless and fast. Terrible at pulling wagons."

"Harbud is a Hepashim if you didn't already know," Hull said. "His brother Selud still rides at the head of their clan."

"More of a mob, really," Harbud corrected, then reverted to the business at hand. He pulled on a leather strap until taut then fastened the buckle that was latched onto it. "Look, are you going to help me with the tack or not? Taringer will be here in a moment and Livet is ready now."

Hull let out a short chuckle and went back to adjusting the harness on the two horses.

"I know these horses," Livet said. "This is Baressa's wagon!"

"Gardia's wagon, to be correct," Harbud said. "But yes, it is the one that brought you here." He disappeared behind one of the horses but continued to opine, "You know, it wouldn't hurt you to learn how to ride."

"No, I suppose not," said Livet. "I think I would like to."

"It's better than walking," said Taringer as he entered. He was carrying several packs in his hands, and he hoisted them up onto the wagon before hopping on, himself. "We need to stash these and make it look as close to empty as possible if we're going to get out of the city easily. The Faith is confiscating all the food they can. There are restrictions on taking any goods or supplies out of the city."

"Pillarmen are already spreading out across the countryside like locusts, demanding every scrap they can find in the fields or stables," Hull said. "That way, they can dole out food to the poor citizens who they force to clear the rubble and rebuild."

"I saw the lean o' the temple and the cracks in the walls," Livet said. "D'you think it was us that caused it t' teeter so?"

"The whole city east of the Darrow is destroyed and we didn't cause that. That was the Marshal," said Harbud.

Taringer sat up straighter in the cart. "The temple's foundation was made of limestone blocks. When we incinerated all those things in the dungeon, the heat almost certainly affected the stone. I think the supporting understructure must have given in to make the place fall inward. It reminds me a bit of a collapsed mine now."

Harbud recited, *"Baked into ashes or buried beneath sea or soil,* as the old verse said. If the bodies of the Faith's old masters were not burnt to ash, then perhaps the piles of rock that fell upon their crypt were enough to bury them."

Taringer shrugged then went back to sorting and secreting away their supplies. "I still think it would be good if you came with us, Harbud. Once you've visited Lanstad, you could find a path between there and here in the Passage Realm to make things easier next time."

Harbud let out a dismissive hiss. "Someday, perhaps. My studies are consuming my time now. It's of greater importance for me to work my way through the scrolls we rescued from the temple and to do so quickly," he said. "That, and I despise people from Lanstad... except for Livet, of course, I find the whole raft of them to be routinely fickle and ridiculous."

"It's a centre of culture for the most accomplished craftsmen and artists," argued Taringer.

"Only for *their* culture and at any given moment their tastes and fashions change with the tide," Harbud said. "Let me know when you find Kell's forge and get it working. Then bring Livet back as soon as you can so she can help me with translations."

"What if Taringer likes it there and decides to stay?" Livet chirped.

"I seem to recall that *you* had little love for the place,"

Harbud said. "Lanstad, now Caphedra. Next, you could try Hasen."

"Is it beautiful there?" Livet asked.

Harbud twisted his mouth as if exasperated. "It's a mud puddle at the edge of a desert."

Taringer laughed and motioned to Livet to leave it be. Everything was finally in place for their departure. As Hull helped Livet to climb on board the wagon, Taringer held up the reins.

"See that Baressa gets well?" Livet entreated Harbud.

"And say goodbye to Gardia for us," Taringer added.

The wooden boards of the stable doors creaked as Hull opened them, one at a time. Age and use had warped them, but they kept the horses in and some of the sunlight out.

Once the day's journey was done, and they had gotten at least as far as the treeline at Greenplain, Livet promised she would treat the carthorses with a couple of apples she had lifted from a barrel in the Peahen's larder that morning.

As they ventured out, Livet asked Taringer to steer the horses toward the Black Eel. She gave herself one last look of the weathered old tavern then pulled out her rondel from where she wore it. She used the blade to score the wood along the tavern's timber framing, two arrows overtop combined circles, the Scrawl symbol for *friends*. Work done, she hopped back up onto the wagon and signalled to carry on.

Taringer adeptly guided the wagon through Caphedra's streets. He told her that the tight lanes were nothing compared to the narrow trails that spiralled up Palinor's four great peaks, and Livet learned he had ridden supply caravans up and down at least two of them.

Livet wondered about their earlier conversation. The theory that Taringer professed about faults in the limestone, convinced Livet that it was *by their hand* that the temple had fallen. It kindled a notion that, in the end, she had realized a real act of vengeance against those that had hurt her years before, and if she could send the great central Temple of the Faith of the Pillars in Caphedra tumbling down, then perhaps she could do so even more destruction against Vlass's accursed replica in Lanstad.

But first, she must keep her hatred restrained long enough to seek out a more important prize. In the coastal city's great necropolis—the domain where Kell and his ilk once lorded over centuries' worth of sunken sepulchres and charnel caverns, her mother was entombed with her secrets. In one of those dark holes, where the generations of Lanstad's forebears resided for eternity, Vaeya awaited her, as did Kell's original grimoire.

As they passed the Southgate, the price of leaving Caphedra turned out to be quite cheap. Two jugs of Hasen wine were enough to bribe the guards to let them quit the city and join the streams of the departing. These people had lost everything, but Livet realized how much more she had gained. She was not as weak as she once felt, nor was she condemned to powerlessly endure the fetters of past pains. Dwelling in the shadows gave her refuge, but she was a potent force in the light of day as well. And like Denn and Olen, she may be an outlaw, but not an outcast.

She would return to Lanstad, reforged and ready to dismantle the heinous dominance of Lord Vlass and the Pillars. She was finally without fear or apprehension. Her home awaited at the end of this road.

"Would you like to take the reins for a while? Taringer asked.

"Yes, I would," Livet answered, then gripping the leather straps, firmly in hand, she clucked and called to the two dray horses to speed up.

THE END

About the Author

Ian Robert Ross is a fantasy and science fiction author living in Ottawa, Canada. Growing up in New Brunswick, he honed his imagination on roleplaying games, reading, and illustrating. His career took him to the publishing industry where he spent twenty years in newspapers, community magazines, and trade publications.

Crown of Caphedra is his first novel-length work of fiction and marks his debut into the world of epic fantasy. It was written to serve as a foundation for his upcoming works to expand upon the kingdom of Caphedra, and the Path of the Four Pillars.